C000252646

THE
HOLLYWOOD OMNIBUS

Books by P. G. Wodehouse

Fiction

Aunts Aren't Gentlemen
The Adventures of Sally
Bachelors Anonymous
Barmy in Wonderland
Big Money
Bill the Conqueror
Blandings Castle and Elsewhere
Carry On, Jeeves
The Clicking of Cuthbert
Cocktail Time
The Code of the Woosters
The Coming of Bill
Company for Henry
A Damsel in Distress
Do Butlers Burgle Banks
Doctor Sally
Eggs, Beans and Crumpets
A Few Quick Ones
French Leave
Frozen Assets
Full Moon
Galahad at Blandings
A Gentleman of Leisure
The Girl in Blue
The Girl on the Boat
The Gold Bat
The Head of Kay's
The Heart of a Goof
Heavy Weather
Hot Water
Ice in the Bedroom
If I Were You
Indiscretions of Archie
The Inimitable Jeeves
Jeeves and the Feudal Spirit
Jeeves in the Offing
Jill the Reckless
Joy in the Morning
Laughing Gas
Leave it to Psmith
The Little Nugget
Lord Emsworth and Others
Louder and Funnier
Love Among the Chickens
The Luck of Bodkins
The Man Upstairs
The Man with Two Left Feet
The Mating Season
Meet Mr Mulliner
Mike and Psmith
Mike at Wrykyn
Money for Nothing
Money in the Bank
Mr Mulliner Speaking
Much Obliged, Jeeves
Mulliner Nights
Not George Washington
Nothing Serious
The Old Reliable
Pearls, Girls and Monty Bodkin
A Pelican at Blandings
Piccadilly Jim
Pigs Have Wings
Plum Pie

The Pothunters
A Prefect's Uncle
The Prince and Betty
Psmith, Journalist
Psmith in the City
Quick Service
Right Ho, Jeeves
Ring for Jeeves
Sam the Sudden
Service with a Smile
The Small Bachelor
Something Fishy
Something Fresh
Spring Fever
Stiff Upper Lip, Jeeves
Summer Lightning
Summer Moonshine
Sunset at Blandings
The Swoop
Tales of St Austin's
Thank You, Jeeves
Ukridge
Uncle Dynamite
Uncle Fred in the Springtime
Uneasy Money
Very Good, Jeeves
The White Feather
William Tell Told Again
Young Men in Spats

Omnibuses

The World of Blandings
The World of Jeeves
The World of Mr Mulliner
The World of Psmith
The World of Ukridge
The World of Uncle Fred
Wodehouse Nuggets
  (edited by Richard Usborne)
The World of Wodehouse Clergy
The Hollywood Omnibus
Weekend Wodehouse

Paperback Omnibuses

The Golf Omnibus
The Aunts Omnibus
The Drones Omnibus
The Clergy Omnibus
The Jeeves Omnibus 1
The Jeeves Omnibus 2
The Jeeves Omnibus 3
The Jeeves Omnibus 4
The Jeeves Omnibus 5

Poems

The Parrot and Other Poems

Autobiographical

Wodehouse on Wodehouse
  (comprising Bring on the Girls,
  Over Seventy, Performing Flea)

Letters

Yours, Plum

THE HOLLYWOOD OMNIBUS

P. G. Wodehouse

Hutchinson

London

First published 1985
Expanded trade paperback edition (including *The Old Reliable*) published 1993
© in this collection the Trustees of the Wodehouse Estate 1985, 1993

All rights reserved

Random House UK Limited
20 Vauxhall Bridge Road, London SW1V 2SA

Random House Australia (Pty) Ltd
20 Alfred Street, Milsons Point, Sydney, NSW 2061, Australia

Random House New Zealand Ltd
18 Poland Road, Glenfield, Auckland, New Zealand

Random House South Africa (Pty) Ltd
PO Box 337, Bergvlei, 2012, South Africa

A CIP catalogue record for this book is available from the British Library

ISBN 0 09 177984 7

Set in Erhardt by Pure Tech Corporation, Pondicherry, India
Printed and bound in Great Britain by Mackays of Chatham PLC, Chatham, Kent

Laughing Gas, first published by Herbert Jenkins Ltd, 1936; *The Old Reliable*, first published by Herbert Jenkins Ltd, 1951. 'Monkey Business', 'The Nodder', 'The Juice of an Orange', 'The Rise of Minna Nordstrom' and 'The Castaways' appeared in *Blandings Castle and Elsewhere*, first published by Herbert Jenkins Ltd, 1935. 'George and Alfred' appeared in *Plum Pie*, first published by Herbert Jenkins Ltd, 1966. *Bring on the Girls*, first published 1954, *Performing Flea*, first published 1953, and *Over Seventy*, first published 1957, are reprinted in their entirety in *Wodehouse on Wodehouse* (Hutchinson, 1980).

Contents

'THE GIRL IN THE PINK BATHING SUIT'

As a matter of fact, I have been to Hollywood, though not recently. I went there in 1930. I had a year's contract, and was required to do so little work in return for the money I received that I was able in the twelve months before I became a fugitive from the chain-gang to write a novel and nine short stories, besides brushing up my golf, getting an attractive sun-tan and perfecting my Australian crawl in the swimming-pool.

It is all sadly changed now, they tell me. Once a combination of Santa Claus and Good-Time Charlie, Hollywood has become a Scrooge. The dear old days are dead and the spirit of cheerful giving a thing of the past. But in 1930 the talkies had just started, and the slogan was Come one, come all, and the more the merrier. It was an era when only a man of exceptional ability and determination could keep from getting signed up by a studio in some capacity or other. I happened to be engaged as a writer, but I might quite as easily have been scooped in as a technical adviser or a vocal instructor. (At least I had a roof to my mouth, which many vocal instructors in Hollywood at that time had not.) The heartiness and hospitality reminded one of the Jolly Innkeeper (with entrance number in Act One) of the old-style comic opera.

One can understand it, of course. The advent of sound had made the manufacture of motion pictures an infinitely more complex affair than it had been up till then. In the silent days everything had been informal and casual, just a lot of great big happy schoolboys getting together for a bit of fun. Ike would have a strip of celluloid, Spike a camera his uncle had given him for Christmas, Mike would know a friend or two who liked dressing up and having their photographs taken, and with these modest assets they would club together their pocket money and start the Finer and Supremer Films Corporation. And as for bothering about getting anyone to write them a story, it never occurred to them. They made it up themselves as they went along.

The talkies changed all that. It was no longer possible just to put on a toga, have someone press a button and call the result *The Grandeur that was Rome* or *In the Days of Nero*. A whole elaborate new organization was required. You had to have a studio Boss to boss the Producer, a Producer to produce the Supervisor, a Supervisor to supervise the sub-Supervisor, a sub-Supervisor to sub-supervise the Director, a Director to direct the Cameraman and an Assistant Director to assist the Director. And, above all, you had to get hold of someone to supply the words.

The result was a terrible shortage of authors in all the world's literary centres. New York till then had been full of them. You would see them frisking in perfect masses in any editorial office you happened to enter. Their sharp, excited yapping was one of the features of the first- or second-act interval of every new play that was produced. And in places like Greenwich Village you had to watch your step very carefully to avoid treading on them.

And then all of a sudden all you saw was an occasional isolated one being shooed out of a publisher's sanctum or sitting in a speak-easy sniffing at his press clippings. Time after time fanciers would come up to you with hard-luck stories.

'You know that novelist of mine with the flapping ears and the spots on his coat? Well, he's gone.'

'Gone?'

'Absolutely vanished. I left him on the steps of the club, and when I came out there were no signs of him.'

'Same here,' says another fancier. 'I had a brace of playwrights to whom I was greatly attached, and they've disappeared without a word.'

Well, of course, people took it for granted that the little fellows had strayed and had got run over, for authors are notoriously dreamy in traffic and, however carefully you train them, will persist in stopping in the middle of the street to jot down strong bits of dialogue. It was only gradually that the truth came out. They had all been decoyed away to Hollywood.

What generally happened was this. A couple of the big film executives – say Mr Louis B. Mayer and Mr Adolf Zukor – would sight their quarry in the street and track him down to some bohemian eating resort. Having watched him settle, they seat themselves at a table immediately behind him, and for a few moments there is silence, broken only by the sound of the author eating corned beef hash. Then Mr Mayer addresses Mr Zukor, raising his voice slightly.

'Whatever was the name of that girl?' he says.

'What girl?' asks Mr Zukor, cleverly taking his cue.

'That tall, blonde girl with the large blue eyes.'

'The one in the pink bathing suit?'

'That's right. With the freckle in the small of her back.'

'A freckle? A mole, I always understood.'

'No, it was a freckle, eye-witnesses tell me. Just over the base of the spinal cord. Well, anyway, what was her name?'

'Now what was it? Eulalie something? Clarice something? No, it's gone. But I'll find out for you when we get home. I know her intimately.'

Here they pause, but not for long. There is a sound of quick, emotional breathing. The author is standing beside them, a rapt expression on his face.

'Pardon me, gentlemen,' he says, 'for interrupting a private conversation, but I chanced to overhear you saying that you were intimately acquainted with a tall, blonde girl with large blue eyes, in the habit of wearing bathing suits of just the type I like best. It is for a girl of that description that I have been scouring the country for years. Where may she be found?'

'In God's Back Garden – Hollywood,' says Mr Zukor.

'Pity you can't meet her,' says Mr Mayer. 'You're just her type.'

'If you were by any chance an author,' says Mr Zukor, 'we could take you back with us tomorrow. Too bad you're not.'

'Prepare yourself for a surprise, gentlemen,' says the victim. 'I *am* an author. George Montague Breamworthy. "Powerfully devised situations" – *New York Times*. "Sheer, stark realism" – *New York Herald-Tribune*. "Whoops!" – *Women's Wear*.'

'In that case,' says Mr Mayer, producing a contract, 'sign here.'

'Where my thumb is,' says Mr Zukor.

The trap has snapped.

That was how they got me, and it was, I understand, the usual method of approach. But sometimes this plan failed, and then sterner methods were employed. The demand for authors in those early talkie days was so great that it led to the revival of the old press gang. Nobody was safe even if he merely looked like an author.

While having a Malted Milk Greta Garbo with some of the old lags in the commissary one morning about half-way through my term of sentence, I was told of one very interesting case. It appeared that there was a man who had gone out West hoping to locate oil. One of those men without a thought in the world outside of oil, the last thing he had ever dreamed of doing was being an author. With the exception of letters and an occasional telegram of greeting to some relative at Christmas, he had never written anything in his life.

But by some curious chance it happened that his appearance was that of one capable of the highest feats in the way of literary expression. He had a domelike head, piercing eyes, and that cynical twist of the upper lip which generally means an epigram on the way. Still, as I say, he was not a writer, and no one could have been more surprised than he when, walking along a street in Los Angeles, thinking of oil, he was suddenly set upon by masked men, chloroformed, and whisked away in a closed car. When he came to himself he was in a cell on the Perfecto-Zizzbaum lot with paper and a sharpened pencil before him, and stern-featured men in felt hats and raincoats were waggling rubber hoses at him and telling him to get busy and turn out something with lots of sex in it, but not too much, because of Will Hays.

The story has a curious sequel. A philosopher at heart, he accepted the situation. He wrenched his mind away from oil and scribbled a few sentences that happened to occur to him. He found, as so many have found, that an author's is the easiest job in existence, and soon he was scratching away as briskly as you could wish. And that is how Noël Coward got his start.

But not every kidnapped author accepted his fate so equably. The majority endeavoured to escape. But it was useless. Even if the rigours of the pitiless California climate did not drive them back to shelter, capture was inevitable. When I was in Hollywood there was much indignation among the better element of the community over the pursuit of an unfortunate woman writer whom the harshness of her supervisor, a man of the name of Legree, had driven to desperation. As I got the story, they chased her across the ice with bloodhounds.

The whole affair was very unpleasant and ·shocked the soft-hearted greatly. So much so that a Mrs Harriet Beecher Stowe told me that if MGM would meet her terms for the movie, she intended to write a book about it which would stir the world.

'Boy,' she said to me, 'it will be a scorcher!'
I don't know if anything ever came of it.

I got away from Hollywood at the end of the year because the gaoler's daughter smuggled me in a file in a meat pie, but I was there long enough to realize what a terribly demoralizing place it is. The whole atmosphere there is one of insidious deceit and subterfuge. Nothing is what it affects to be. What looks like a tree is really a slab of wood backed with barrels. What appears on the screen as the towering palace of Haroun al-Raschid is actually a cardboard model occupying four feet by three of space. The languorous lagoon is simply a smelly tank with a stagehand named Ed wading about it in bathing trunks.

It is surely not difficult to imagine the effect of all this on a sensitive-minded author. Taught at his mother's knee to love the truth, he finds himself surrounded by people making fortunes by what can only be called chicanery. After a month or two in such an environment could you trust that author to count his golf shots correctly or to give his right sales figures?

And then there was – I am speaking of the old days. It is possible that modern enlightened thought has brought improvements – the inevitable sapping of his self-respect. At the time of which I am writing authors in Hollywood were kept in little hutches. In every studio there were rows and rows of these, each containing an author on a long contract at a weekly salary. You could see their anxious little faces peering out through the bars and hear them whining piteously to be taken for a walk. One had to be very callous not to be touched by such a spectacle.

I do not say that these authors were actually badly treated. In the best studios in those early talkie days kindness was the rule. Often you would see some high executive stop and give one of them a lettuce. And it was the same with the humaner type of director. In fact, between the directors and their authors there frequently existed a rather touching friendship. I remember one director telling a story which illustrates this.

One morning, he said, he was on his way to his office, preoccupied, as was his habit when planning out the day's work, when he felt a sudden tug at his coat-tails. He looked down and there was his pet author, Edgar Montrose (Book Society – Recommendation) Delamere. The little fellow had got him in a firm grip and was gazing up at him, in his eyes an almost human expression of warning.

Well, the director, not unnaturally, mistook this at first for mere playfulness, for it was often his kindly habit to romp with his little charges. Then something seemed to whisper to him that he was being withheld from some great peril. He remembered stories he had read as a boy – one of which he was even then directing for Rin-Tin-Tin – where faithful dogs dragged their masters back from the brink of precipices on dark nights, and, scarcely knowing why, he turned and went off to the commissary and had a Strawberry and Vanilla Nut Sundae Mary Pickford.

It was well that he did. In his office, waiting to spring, there was lurking a foreign star with a bad case of temperament, whose bite might have been fatal. You may be sure that Edgar Montrose had a good meal that night.

But that was an isolated case. Not all directors were like this one. Too many of them crushed the spirit of the captives by incessant blue-pencilling of their dialogue, causing them to become listless and lose appetite. Destructive criticism is what kills an author. Cut his material too much, make him feel that he is not a Voice, give him the impression that his big scene is all wet, and you will soon see the sparkle die out of his eyes.

I don't know how conditions are today, but at that time there were authors who had been on salary for years in Hollywood without ever having a line of their work used. All they did was attend story conferences. There were other authors whom nobody had seen for years. It was like the Bastille. They just sat in some hutch away in a corner somewhere and grew white beards and languished. From time to time somebody would renew their contract, and then they were forgotten again.

As I say, it may be different now. After all, I am speaking of twenty-five years ago. But I do think it would be wise if author-fanciers exercised vigilance. You never know. The press gang may still be in our midst.

So when you take your pet for a walk, keep an eye on him. If he goes sniffing after strange men, whistle him back.

And remember that the spring is the dangerous time. Around about the beginning of May, authors get restless and start dreaming about girls in abbreviated bathing suits. It is easy to detect the symptoms. The moment you hear yours muttering about the Golden West and God's Sunshine and Out There Beyond The Stifling City put sulphur in his absinthe and lock him up in the kitchenette.

LAUGHING GAS

1

I had just begun to write this story, when a literary pal of mine
who had had a sticky night out with the P E N Club blew in
to borrow bicarbonate of soda, and I thought it would be as
well to have him vet what I'd done, in case I might have foozled
my tee-shot. Because, except for an occasional anecdote in the
Drones smoking-room about Scotsmen, Irishmen and Jews, and
even then I generally leave out the point, I've never told a story
in my life. And the one thing all the cognoscenti stress is that
you must get started right.

So I said: 'I say, can I read you something?' and he said: 'If
you must,' and I said: 'Right ho.'

'I am trying to get down on paper,' I said, 'a rather rummy
experience that happened to me about a year ago. I haven't got
very far yet. I start with where I met the kid.'

'What kid?'

'The kid I met,' I said, and kicked off as follows:

*The kid was sitting in one armchair. I was sitting in another. His
left cheek was bulging. My left cheek was bulging. He was turning
the pages of the* National Geographic Magazine. *So was I. In
short, there we both were.*

He seemed a bit restless, I thought, as if the National Geographic *wasn't holding him absolutely spellbound. He would put
it down for a minute and take it up for a minute and then
put it down for a minute again, and it was during one of
these putting-it-down-for-a-minute phases that he looked over at
me.*

'Where,' he asked, 'are the rest of the boys?'

At this point, my literary pal opened his eyes, which he had
closed in a suffering sort of way. His manner was that of one
who has had a dead fish thrust under his nose.

'Is this bilge,' he asked, 'to be printed?'

'Privately. It will be placed in the family archives for the benefit of my grandchildren.'

'Well, if you ask me,' he said, 'the little perishers won't be able to make head or tail of it. Where's it all supposed to be happening?'

'In Hollywood.'

'Well, you'll have to explain that. And these armchairs. What about them? What armchairs? Where?'

'Those were in a dentist's waiting-room. That's where the kid and I met.'

'Who is this kid?'

'He turns out to be little Joey Cooley, the child film star, the Idol of American Motherhood.'

'And who are you?'

'Me?' I said, a bit surprised, for we had been at school together. 'Why, you know me, old man. Reggie Havershot.'

'What I mean is, you've got to introduce yourself to the reader. He doesn't know by intuition who you are.'

'You wouldn't let it gradually dawn upon him in the course of the narrative?'

'Certainly not. The first rule in telling a story is to make it thoroughly clear at the outset who's who, when, where and why. You'd better start again from the beginning.'

He then took his bicarbonate and withdrew.

Well, then, harking back and buckling down to it once more, my name, as foreshadowed in the foregoing, is Reggie Havershot. Reginald John Peter Swithin, third Earl of Havershot, if you want to be formal, but Reggie to my pals. I'm about twenty-eight and a bit, and at the time of which I am writing was about twenty-seven and a bit. Height six feet one, eyes brown, hair a sort of carroty colour.

Mark you, when I say I'm the third Earl of Havershot, I don't mean that I was always that. No, indeed. I started at the bottom and worked my way up. For years and years I plugged along as plain R. J. P. Swithin, fully expecting that that would be the name carved on my tombstone when the question of tombstones should arise. As far as my chances of ever copping the title went, I don't suppose I was originally more than about a hundred-to-eight shot, if that. The field was full of seasoned performers who could give me a couple of stone.

But you know how it is. Uncles call it a day. Cousins hand

in their spades and buckets. And little by little and bit by bit, before you know where you are – why, there you are, don't you know.

Well, that's who I am, and apart from that I don't know that there is much of interest to tell you *re* self. I got my boxing Blue at Cambridge, but that's about all. I mean to say, I'm just one of those chaps. So we'll shift on at once to how I happened to be in Hollywood.

One morning, as I was tucking away the eggs and bacon at my London residence, the telephone rang, and it was old Horace Plimsoll asking if I could look in at his office on a matter of some importance. Certainly, I said, certainly, and off I went. Only too pleased.

I liked old Plimsoll. He was the family lawyer, and recently, what with all the business of taking over and all that, we had been seeing a good deal of one another. I pushed round to his office and found him, as usual, up to the thorax in bills of replevin and what not. He brushed these aside and came to the surface and looked at me over his spectacles.

'Good morning, Reginald,' he said.

'Good morning,' I said.

He took off his spectacles, polished them and put them on again. 'Reginald,' he said, giving me the eye once more, 'you are now the head of the family.'

'I know,' I said. 'Isn't it a scream? Have I got to sign something?'

'Not at the moment. What I wished to see you about today has to do with a more personal matter. I wished to point out to you that, as head of the family, certain responsibilities devolve upon you, which I feel sure you will not neglect. You have obligations now, Reginald, and those obligations must be fulfilled, no matter what the cost. *Noblesse oblige.*'

'Oh, ah?' I said, not liking the sound of this much. It began to look to me like a touch. 'What's the bad news? Does one of the collateral branches want to dip into the till?'

'Let me begin at the beginning,' said old Plimsoll. He picked a notice of distraint or something off his coat sleeve. 'I have just been in communication with your Aunt Clara. She is worried.'

'Oh yes?'

'Extremely worried, about your Cousin Egremont.'

Well, of course, I tut-tutted sympathetically, but I can't say I was surprised. Ever since he grew to man's estate, this unfortunate aunt has been chronically worried about the lad under advisement, who is pretty generally recognized as London W1's most prominent souse. For years everybody has been telling Eggy that it's hopeless for him to attempt to drink up all the alcoholic liquor in England, but he keeps on trying. The good old bull-dog spirit, of course, but it worries Aunt Clara.

'You know Egremont's record?'

I had to think a bit.

'Well, one Boat Race night I saw him put away sixteen double whiskies and soda, but whether he has beaten that since or not—'

'For years he has been causing Lady Clara the gravest concern. And now . . .'

I raised a hand.

'Don't tell me. Let me guess. He's been bonneting policemen?'

'No. He—'

'Throwing soft-boiled eggs at the electric fan in the better class of restaurant?'

'No. He—'

'Not murder, surely?'

'No. He has escaped to Hollywood.'

'Escaped to Hollywood?'

'Es-caped to Hollywood,' said old Plimsoll.

I didn't get his drift, and said so. He continued snowing.

'Some little while ago, Lady Clara became alarmed at the state of Egremont's health. His hands were shaky and he complained of spiders on the back of his neck. So, acting on the advice of a Harley Street specialist, she decided to send him on one of these cruises round the world, in the hope that the fresh air and change of scene—'

I spotted the obvious flaw.

'But these boats have bars.'

'The bar-attendants had strict orders not to serve Egremont.'

'He wouldn't like that.'

'He did not like it. His letters home – his almost daily wireless messages also – were full of complaints. Their tone was uniformly querulous. And, when, on the homeward journey, the boat touched at Los Angeles, he abandoned it and went to Hollywood where he now is.'

'Golly! Drinking like the stag at eve, I suppose?'

'Direct evidence on the point is lacking, but I think that one may assume such to be the case. But that is not the worst. That is not what has occasioned Lady Clara this excessive perturbation.'

'No?'

'No. We have reason to believe – from certain passages in his latest communication – that he is contemplating matrimony.'

'Yes?'

'Yes. His words leave no room for doubt. He is either betrothed or on the verge of becoming betrothed to some young woman out there. And you know the sort of young women that abound in Hollywood.'

'Pippins, I have always been given to understand.'

'Physically, no doubt, they are as you describe. But they are by no means suitable mates for your cousin Egremont.'

I couldn't see this. I should have thought, personally, that a bird like Eggy was dashed lucky to get any girl to take him on. However, I didn't say so. Old Plimsoll has a sort of gruesome reverence for the family, and the remark would have hurt him. Instead, I asked what the idea was. Where did I come in? What, I asked, did he imagine that I could do about it?

He looked like a high priest sicking the young chief of the tribe on to noble deeds.

'Why, go to Hollywood, Reginald, and reason with this misguided young man. Put a stop to all this nonsense. Exert your authority as head of the family.'

'What, me?'

'Yes.'

'H'm.'

'Don't say "h'm".'

'Ha!'

'And don't say "ha". Your duty is plain. You cannot shirk it.'

'But Hollywood's such miles away.'

'Nevertheless, I insist that it is incumbent upon you, as head of the family, to go there, and without an instant's delay.'

I chewed the lower lip a bit. I must say I couldn't see why I should go butting in, trying to put a stopper on Eggy's – as far as I could make out – quite praiseworthy amours. Live and let live is my motto. If Eggy wanted to get spliced, let him, was the way I looked at it. Marriage might improve him. It was difficult to think of anything that wouldn't.

'H'm,' I said again.

Old Plimsoll was fiddling with pencil and paper – working out routes and so on, apparently.

'The journey is, as you say, a long one, but perfectly simple. On arriving in New York, you would, I understand, take the train known as the Twentieth Century Limited to Chicago. A very brief wait there—'

I sat up.

'Chicago? You don't go through Chicago, do you?'

'Yes. You change trains at Chicago. And from there to Los Angeles is a mere—'

'But wait a second,' I said. 'This is beginning to look more like a practical proposition. Your mention of Chicago opens up a new line of thought. The fight for the heavyweight championship of the world is coming off in Chicago in a week or so.'

I examined the matter in the light of these new facts. All my life I had wanted to see one of these world's championships, and I had never been able to afford the trip. It now dawned upon me that, having come into the title and trimmings, I could do it on my head. The amazing thing was that I hadn't thought of it before. It always takes you some little time to get used to the idea that you are on Easy Street.

'How far is it from Chicago to Hollywood?'

'Little more than a two days' journey, I believe.'

'Then say no more,' I said. 'It's a go. I don't suppose for a moment that I'll be able to do a thing about old Eggy, but I'll go and see him.'

'Excellent.'

There was a pause. I could see that something else was coming.

'And – er – Reginald.'

'Hullo?'

'You will be careful?'

'Careful?'

He coughed, and fiddled with an application for soccage in fief.

'Where you yourself are concerned, I mean. These Hollywood women are, as you were saying a moment ago, of considerable personal attractions . . .'

I laughed heartily.

'Good Lord!' I said. 'No girl's going to look at me.'

This seemed to jar his reverence for the family. He frowned in a rebuking sort of way.

'You are the Earl of Havershot.'

'I know. But even so—'

'And, if I am not mistaken, girls have looked at you in the past.'

I knew what he meant. A couple of years before, while at Cannes, I had got engaged to a girl named Ann Bannister, an American newspaper girl who was spending her holiday there, and as I was the heir apparent at the time this had caused some stir in the elder branches of the family. There was a considerable sense of relief, I believe, when the thing had been broken off.

'All the Havershots have been highly susceptible and impulsive. Your hearts rule your heads. So . . .'

'Oh, right ho. I'll be careful.'

'Then I will say no more. *Verbum* – ah – *sapienti satis*. And you will start for Hollywood as soon as possible?'

'Immediately,' I said.

There was a boat leaving on the Wednesday. Hastily throwing together a collar and a toothbrush, I caught it. A brief stay in New York, a couple of days in Chicago, and I was on the train to Los Angeles, bowling along through what I believe is called Illinois.

And it was as I sat outside the observation car on the second morning of the journey, smoking a pipe and thinking of this and that, that April June came into my life.

The general effect was rather as if I had swallowed six-pennorth of dynamite and somebody had touched it off inside me.

2

These observation cars, in case you don't know, are where the guard's van is on an English train. You go through a door at the end on to a platform with a couple of chairs on it, and there you sit and observe the countryside. Of which, of course, there is no stint, for, as you are probably aware, there's a lot of America, especially out in the Western districts, and once you get aboard a train for Los Angeles you just go on and on.

Well, as I say, on the second morning of the journey I was sitting on the observation platform, observing, when I was stunned by the door opening.

That's not quite right, of course, and when I fix and revise I must remember to polish up that sentence. Because I don't mean the thing got me on the head or anything like that. What stunned me was not the door opening, but what came through it. Viz., the loveliest girl I had ever seen in my life.

The thing about her that hit the spectator like a bullet first crack out of the box was her sort of sweet, tender, wistful gentleness. Some species of negroid train-attendant had accompanied her through the door, carrying a cushion which he put down in the opposite chair, and she thanked him in a kind of cooing, crooning way that made my toes curl up inside my shoes. And when I tell you that with this wistful gentleness went a pair of large blue eyes, a perfectly modelled chassis, and a soft smile which brought out a dimple on the right cheek, you will readily understand why it was that two seconds after she had slid into the picture I was clutching my pipe till my knuckles stood out white under the strain and breathing through my nose in short, quick pants. With my disengaged hand I straightened my tie and if my moustache had been long enough to twirl there is little question that I would have twirled it.

The coloured brother popped off, no doubt to resume the duties for which he drew his weekly envelope, and she sat down,

rather like a tired flower drooping. I dare say you've seen tired
flowers droop. And there for a few moments the matter rested.
She sniffed the air. I sniffed the air. She watched the countryside winding away. So did I. But for all practical purposes we
might have been on different continents.

And the sadness of this was just beginning to come over me
like a fog, when I suddenly heard her utter a sharp yowl and
saw that she was rubbing her eye. It was plain to the meanest
intelligence that she had gone and got a cinder into it, of which
there were several floating about.

It solved the whole difficult problem of how I was ever going
to break down the barriers, if you know what I mean, and get
acquainted. It so happens that if there is one thing I am good
at, it is taking things out of eyes – cinders, flies, gnats on
picnics, or whatever it may be. To whip out my handkerchief
was with me the work of a moment, and I don't suppose it was
more than a couple of ticks later before she was thanking me
brokenly and I was not-at-all-ing and shoving the handkerchief
up my sleeve again. Yes, less than a minute after I had been
practically despairing of ever starting anything in the nature of
a beautiful friendship, there I was, fixed up solid.

The odd thing was, I couldn't see any cinder, but it must
have been there, because she said she was all right now and, as
I say, started to thank me brokenly. She was all over me. If I
had saved her from Manchurian bandits, she couldn't have been
more grateful.

'Thank you ever, *ever* so much,' she said.

'Not at all,' said I.

'It's so awful when you get a cinder in your eye.'

'Yes. Or a fly.'

'Yes. Or a gnat.'

'Yes. Or a piece of dust.'

'Yes. And I couldn't help rubbing it.'

'I noticed you were rubbing it.'

'And they say you ought not to rub it.'

'No, I believe you ought not to rub it.'

'And I always feel I've got to rub it.'

'Well, that's how it goes.'

'Is my eye red?'

'No. Blue.'

'It feels red.'

'It looks blue,' I assured her, and might have gone on to add that it was the sort of blue you see in summer skies or languorous lagoons, had she not cut in.

'You're Lord Havershot, aren't you?' she said.

I was surprised. The old map is distinctive and individual, but not, I should have said, famous. And any supposition that we had met before and I had forgotten her was absurd.

'Yes,' I said. 'But how——?'

'I saw a photograph of you in one of the New York papers.'

'Oh, ah, yes, of course.' I recalled that there had been blokes fooling about with cameras when the boat arrived at New York. 'You know,' I said, giving her a searching glance, 'your face seems extraordinarily familiar, too.'

'You've probably seen it in pix.'

'No, I've never been there.'

'In the pictures.'

'In the . . . Good Lord!' I said. 'You're not April June, are you?'

'Yes.'

'I've seen dozens of your pictures.'

'Did you like them?'

'I loved them. I say, did you say you'd been in New York?'

'Yes. I was making a personal appearance.'

'I wish I'd known.'

'Well, it wasn't a secret. Why do you wish you had known?'

'Because . . . Well, I mean to say . . . Well, what I mean is, I rather hurried through New York, and if I'd known that you were there I – er – I wouldn't have hurried.'

'I see.' She paused to tuck away a tendril of hair which had got separated from the main body and was blowing about. 'It's rather draughty out here, isn't it?'

'It is a bit.'

'Suppose we go back to my drawing-room and I'll mix you a cocktail. It's nearly lunch-time.'

'Fine.'

'Come along, then.'

I mused to some extent as we toddled along the train. I was thinking of old Plimsoll. It was all very well, I felt, for old Plimsoll to tell me to be careful, but he couldn't possibly have anticipated anything like this.

We reached the drawing-room and she rang the bell. A negroid bloke apeared – not the same negroid bloke who had carried the cushion – another – and she asked for ice in a gentle voice. He buzzed off, and she turned to me again.

'I don't understand English titles,' she said.

'No?' I said.

'No,' she said. 'There's nothing I enjoy more than curling up with a good English book, but the titles always puzzle me. That New York paper called you the Earl of Havershot. Is an Earl the same as a Duke?'

'Not quite. Dukes are a bit higher up.'

'Is it the same as a Viscount?'

'No. Viscounts are a bit lower down. We Earls rather sneer at Viscounts. One is pretty haughty with them, poor devils.'

'What is your wife? A Countess?'

'I haven't got a wife. If I had, she would be a Countess.'

A sort of faraway look came into her eyes.

'The Countess of Havershot,' she murmured.

'That's right. The Countess of Havershot.'

'What is Havershot? The place where you live?'

'No. I don't quite know where the Havershot comes in. The family doss-house is at Biddleford, in Norfolk.'

'Is it a very lovely place?'

'Quite a goodish sort of shack.'

'Battlements?'

'Lots of battlements.'

'And deer?'

'Several deer.'

'I love deer.'

'Me, too. I've met some very decent deer.'

At this point, the ice-bearer entered bearing ice. She dropped the livestock theme, and started to busy herself with the fixings. Presently she was in a position to provide me with a snort.

'I hope it's all right. I'm not very good at making cocktails, I'm afraid.'

'It's fine,' I said. 'Full of personality. Aren't you having one?'

She shook her head, and smiled that soft smile of hers.

'I'm rather old-fashioned. I don't drink or smoke.'

'Good Lord! Don't you?'

'No. I'm afraid I'm very quiet and domestic and dull.'

'No, I say, dash it. Not dull.'

'Oh, but I am. It may seem odd to you, considering that I'm in pix, but I'm really at heart just a simple little home body. I am never happier than among my books and flowers. And I love cooking.'

'Not really?'

'Yes, really. It's quite a joke among my friends. They come to take me out to some party, and they find me in my kitchen in a gingham wrapper, fixing a Welsh rarebit. I am never happier than in my kitchen.'

I sipped my snootful reverently. Every word that she uttered made me more convinced that I was in the presence of an angel in human shape.

'So you live all alone at – what was the name of the place you said?'

'Biddleford? Well, not exactly. I mean, I haven't really checked in yet. I only took over a short while ago. But I suppose I shall in due season settle down there. Old Plimsoll would have a fit if I didn't. He's our family lawyer, you know, and has views on these things. The head of the family has always hung out at the castle.'

'Castle? Is it a castle?'

'Oh, rather.'

'A real castle?'

'Oh, quite.'

'Is it very old?'

'Definitely moth-eaten. One of the ruins that Cromwell knocked about a bit, don't you know.'

That faraway look came into her eyes again. She sighed.

'How wonderful it must be, having a lovely old home like that. Hollywood is so new and . . . garish. One gets so tired of its garishness. It's all so—'

'Garish?'

'Yes, garish.'

'And you don't like it? I mean, you find it too garish?'

'No, I don't like it. It jars upon me terribly. But what can I do? My work lies there. One has to sacrifice everything to one's work.'

She sighed again, and I felt that I had had a glimpse of some great human tragedy.

Then she smiled bravely.

'But let's not talk about me,' she said. 'Tell me about yourself. Is this your first visit to America?'

'Yes.'

'And why are you going to Hollywood? You are going to

Hollywood, I suppose? Not getting off somewhere before Los Angeles?'

'Oh, no, I'm bound for Hollywood all right. On business, as you might say, more or less. You see, a splash of family trouble has arisen. There's a cousin of mine making rather an ass of himself in those parts. You haven't run into him, by any chance, have you? Tall, butter-coloured-haired chap named Egremont Mannering?'

'No.'

'Well, he's in Hollywood and, from all accounts, planning to get married. And what we feel, knowing Eggy, is that the bride-to-be is probably some frightful red-hot mamma. In which event, it is imperative that a spanner be bunged into the works. And I was told off to come along and do it.'

She nodded.

'I see. Yes, I don't wonder you are anxious. Most of the girls in Hollywood are terrible. That is one of the things that make the place so uncongenial to me. That is why I have so few real friends. I know people think me prudish, but what is one to do?'

'I see what you mean. Bit of a problem.'

'Rather than mix with uncongenial people who think about nothing but wild parties, I prefer to be lonely. Though, after all, can one ever be lonely if one has one's books?'

'True.'

'And flowers.'

'Quite.'

'And one's kitchen, of course.'

'Absolutely.'

'But here we are, talking about me again! Go on telling me about yourself. Was it just to find your cousin that you came to America?'

'Not altogether. I rather saw my way of killing two birds with one stone, as it were. There was this heavyweight championship fight on in Chicago, and I particularly wanted to see it.'

'You really enjoy watching fights?'

'I know what you mean,' I said. 'Nine times out of ten they're absolute washouts, of course. But this one was a corker. It was worth coming four thousand miles just to see that fifth round.' The recollection of it stirred me deeply, and I had to rise in order to illustrate. 'It had been pretty good even before that, but in the fifth everything just boiled over. The champion managed to work his man into a neutral corner and copped him squarely on the nose. The challenger came back with a beauty to the eye. They clinched. The referee broke them. Champion to chin, challenger to lower ribs. Another clinch. Break. In-fighting all over the ring. Challenger landed lightly, champ to nose again, then right on the smush. Blood flowing in quarts, and the air thick with teeth and ears and things. And then, just before the bell went, the champ brought one up from the floor . . .'

I broke off here, because she had fainted. I had thought at first, when she closed her eyes, that she had done so merely in order to listen better, but this was apparently not the case. She slid sideways along the seat and quietly passed out.

I was gravely concerned. In the enthusiasm of the moment I had forgotten the effect my narrative might have on this sensitive plant, and I was not quite certain what was the next move. The best way, of course, of bringing round a swooned subject is to bite the ear, but I couldn't very well bite this divine girl's ear. Apart from anything else, I felt I didn't know her well enough.

Fortunately, before I was called upon to take any steps, her eyelids fluttered and she gave a little sigh. Her eyes opened.

'Where am I?' she murmured.

I looked out of the window.

'Well, I'm a stranger in these parts myself,' I said, 'but I think somewhere in New Mexico.'

She sat up.

'Oh, I feel so mortified!'

'Eh?'

'You must think me so silly, fainting like that.'

'My fault entirely. I oughtn't to have dished the dreadful details.'

'It wasn't your fault. Most girls would have enjoyed it. Though I think there is something terribly unfeminine . . . Go on, Lord Havershot, what happened after that?'

'No, no. I wouldn't dream of telling you.'

'Do. Please.'

'Oh, well, putting the thing in a nutshell, he soaked him on the button, don't you know, and his day's work was done.'

'Could you get me a glass of water?'

I leaped to the bottle. She sipped in a fluttering sort of way.

'Thank you,' she said. 'I feel better now. I'm sorry I was so silly.'

'You weren't silly.'

'Oh, but I was. Terribly silly.'

'You weren't silly at all. The whole episode reflects great credit on your womanly nature.'

And I was about to add that I had never in my puff beheld anything that had stirred me more deeply than the way she had turned her toes up, when the negroid bloke poked his nose in at the door and announced that lunch was served.

'You go along,' she said. 'I'm sure you must be starving.'

'Aren't you coming?'

'I think I'll just lie here and rest. I still feel . . . No, you go along.'

'I should like to kick myself.'

'Why?'

'For being such a chump. Sullying your ears like that.'

'Please! Do go and get your lunch.'

'But will you be all right?'

'Oh, yes.'

'You're sure?'

'Oh, yes, really. I shall just lie here and think of flowers. I often do that – just lie around and think of flowers. Roses, chiefly. It seems to make everything beautiful and fragrant again.'

So I pushed off. And as I sat eating my steak and fried, I put in some pretty intensive thinking between the mouthfuls.

Of course I saw what had happened. These volcanic symptoms were unmistakable. A chap's heart does not go pit-a-pat, as mine was doing, for nothing. This was the real thing, and what I had taken for a strong man's passion when I had got engaged to Ann Bannister two years ago had been merely Class B stuff. Yes, there was no getting away from it. At long last Love had wound its silken fetters about Reginald Havershot.

I had suspected this from the first. The very moment I had set eyes on this girl, I had received the distinct impression that she was my soul-mate, and everything that had passed between us had made me more certain on the point. It was that sweet, tender, gentle wistfulness of hers that had got in amongst me to such a marked extent. I suppose this is always the way with beefy birds like me. Something draws us instinctively to the fragile flowerets.

It was in a sober, thoughtful spirit that I polished off the steak and put in a bid for deep-dish apple pie with a bit of cheese on the side.

3

And I'll tell you why I was sober and thoughtful. It was because I recognized that this, as they say in the stories, was not an end but a beginning. I mean to say, it was all very well to have fallen in love at first sight, but that didn't take me very far. Where, I was asking myself, did I go from there? What of the future? In other words, what steps was I to take in order to bring about the happy finish? The fact had to be faced that if banns were ever to be put up and clergymen were ever to say 'Wilt thou, Reginald?' some pretty heavy work lay ahead of me. In no sense could the thing be looked upon as a walkover.

You see, I have kept it from you till now, but there are certain defects in my personal appearance which prevent me being everybody's money where the opposite sex is concerned. I am no flier in the way of looks. Externally, I take after the pater, and if you had ever seen the pater you would realize what that means. He was a gallant soldier and played a hot game of polo, but he had a face like a gorilla – much more so, indeed, than most gorillas have – and was, so I am informed, affectionately known to his little circle of cronies as Consul, the Almost Human. And I am his living image.

These things weigh with girls. They shrink from linking their lot with a fellow whose appearance gives the impression that at any moment he may shin up trees and start throwing coconuts.

However, it was too late to do anything about that now. I could only hope that April June would prove to be one of those rare spirits who can pierce the outer husk, as it were, and penetrate to the soul beneath. Because I haven't got such a bad soul, as souls go. I don't say it's the sort of soul you would write to the papers about, but it's well up to the average.

And I'm bound to say that, as the days went along, I found myself perking up a bit. I seemed to be making progress. No one could have been matier than April during my first week in Hollywood. We motored together, bathed together, and had long talks together in the scented dusk. She told me all about her ideals, and I told her all about the old homestead at Biddleford and how Countesses were presented at Court and had the run of the Royal Enclosure at Ascot and a lot of other things she seemed interested in. And there was absolutely nothing in her manner to suggest that she was in any way repelled by the fact that I looked as if I belonged in Whipsnade.

In fact, to cut a long story short, her chummy attitude so encouraged me that by the end of the first week I had decided to chance my arm and have a go at it.

The occasion I selected for pressing the button and setting the machinery in motion was a party she was giving at her house on Linden Drive. She explained that she didn't like parties, as they seemed to her hollow, but that a girl in her position was expected to give one every now and then, particularly if she had been away for awhile.

It was to be one of those jolly Beverly Hills outdoor dinner parties, where you help yourself at the buffet, squash in any-where, and top off the meal by diving into the swimming-pool. The proceedings were to begin somewhere after nine and before ten, so I rolled up at about nine forty-five.

This, as it turned out, was on the early side. A few scattered couples had arrived and were strolling about under the coloured lanterns, but April was still dressing and the orchestra hadn't started to play and altogether it was apparent that there was going to be a bit of a lull before the revelry really got into high.

In these circs, it seemed to me that the best way of passing the time would be to trickle over to the table where the drinks were and brace myself with one or two. In view of what lay before me, I wanted to feel at the top of my form – which I wasn't at the moment, owing to having been kept awake a good deal during the night with a touch of toothache.

As I approached the table, I noticed that my idea of going and doing a bit of stoking up, though good, was not original. It had occurred also to a tall, slender bloke with butter-coloured hair. He was standing there in a rooted sort of way, as if he meant to take a lot of shifting, and he seemed to be putting a good deal of custom in the way of the bar-tenders. And there was something about him, something in his technique as he raised and lowered his glass, which somehow struck me as oddly familiar. Also, I felt I had seen that hair before. And the next moment I had identified him.

'Eggy!' I cried.

He had just emptied his glass as I spoke, which was fortunate, for at the sound of my view-halloo he leaped about six inches in the air. Returning to earth, he leaned towards the chap behind the bar, his bosom heaving a bit.

'I say,' he asked in a low, trembling tone, 'you didn't hear a voice then, by any chance, did you?'

The chap said that he thought he had heard someone say something about eggs.

'Oh, you did hear it?'

'Eggy, you old ass,' I said.

This time he turned, and stood staring at me. His face was drawn and anxious.

'Reggie?' he said, in a doubting sort of way.

He blinked a couple of times, then put a hand out and prodded my chest cautiously. As his finger touched solid shirt-front, a look of relief spread over his features.

'Phew!' he said.

He asked the chap behind the bar for another Scotch, and it was not until he had received and taken a liberal swig of this that he spoke again. When he did, his voice was grave and reproachful.

'If you know me a million years, Reggie, old man,' he said, wiping a bead of persp. from his brow, 'never do a thing like that again. I thought you were thousands of miles away, and when I heard your voice, all ghastly and hollow . . . calling my name . . . like a ruddy banshee . . . It's the one thing I'm scared of, hearing voices,' he said. 'I'm told that till you do that you're all right, but once the voices start coming it's the beginning of the end.'

He shuddered and finished the rest of his drink at a gulp. This appeared to complete the cure, for he became easier in his manner.

'Well, well, well,' he said, 'so you're here, are you, Reggie? Ages since I saw you last. Six months come Sheffield Wednesday, or thereabouts. What on earth are you doing in Hollywood?'

'I came to see you.'

'You did?'

'Yes.'

'Pretty cousinly. Have a spot. I can recommend the Scotch. Bar-bloke, would you be so good as to mix a Scotch and soda for my relative here and the same for me.'

I attempted to dissuade.

'I wouldn't have any more.'

'You haven't had any yet.'

'If I were you, I mean. You're sozzled already.'

'Half sozzled,' he corrected, for he is rather exact in these matters.

'Well, half sozzled, then. And it's only ten o'clock.'

'If a man isn't half sozzled by ten o'clock, he isn't trying. Don't you worry about me, Reggie, old man. You don't understand the wonders of the Californian climate yet. So superbly bracing is it that day by day in every way you can put away all you want to, and not a squawk from the old river. That's what they mean when they speak of California as an earthly Paradise, and that's why train-loads of people are pouring in all the time from the Middle West with their tongues hanging out. I expect that's why you came here, isn't it?'

'I came to see you.'

'Oh, yes. You told me that, didn't you?'

'Yes.'

'And did I say it was cousinly?'

'Yes.'

'And so it is. Most cousinly. Where are you staying?'

'I've got a bungalow at a place called the Garden of the Hesperides.'

'I know it well. Have you a cellar?'

'I've got a bottle of whisky, if that's what you mean.'

'It's precisely what I mean. I shall make a point of looking you up. A fellow can't have too many oases. Meanwhile, drink hearty and have another.'

Something about all this had been puzzling me, and now I discovered what it was. On the train, I remembered, I had spoken of Eggy to April, and she had specifically stated that she didn't know him. Yet here he was, at her house, throwing his weight about like a reveller in a comic opera.

'What are you doing here?' I asked, resolved to probe this mystery.

'Having a dashed good time,' he responded heartily, 'and all the better for the sight of your honest face. Delightful, seeing you again, Reggie. Later on, you must tell me what brought you to California.'

'You don't know April June.'

'April who?'

'June.'

'What about her?'

'I was saying, you don't know her.'

'No, but I'd love to. Any friend of yours. If she is a friend of yours.'

'This is her party.'

'It does her credit.'

'You weren't invited.'

His face cleared.

'Now I understand. Now I see what you're driving at. Good heavens, laddie, you don't have to be invited to go to people's parties in Hollywood. You just saunter along till you see coloured lanterns, and walk in. Many of my happiest evenings have been spent as the guest of people who didn't know me from Adam and hadn't a notion I was there. But, by an odd chance, I'm not gate-crashing tonight. I was brought here. What did you say that name was? April—?'

'June.'

'That's right. It all comes back to me. My fiancée is April June's press agent, and she brought me here.'

I felt that this was a good opportunity of tackling this fiancée business. I had been wondering how to bring it up.

'I wanted to talk to you about that.'

'About what?'

'About this engagement of yours.'

I spoke pretty crisply, with a goodish amount of head-of-the-family-ness, for the old conscience was prodding me a bit. I felt I had been letting Horace Plimsoll and my Aunt Clara down rather badly. I mean to say, they had sent me out here to find this bird and reason with him, and I had been out here a week without giving him a single thought. Since I had got off the train at Los Angeles he had absolutely passed from my mind. It just shows what love can do to you.

He weighed the remark carefully.

'Engagement?'

'Yes.'

'My engagement?'

'Yes.'

'What about it?'

'Well, what about it?'

'Happiest man in the world.'

'Aunt Clara isn't.'

'This Aunt Clara being who?'

'Your mother.'

'Oh, the mater? Yes, I know her. Should we drink to the mater?'

'No.'

'Just as you say. Though it seems a bit uncivil. Well, what's wrong with the mater? Why isn't she the happiest man in the world?'

'Because she's worrying herself pallid about you.'

'Good Lord, why? I'm all right.'

'What the devil do you mean, you're all right? You ought to be ashamed of yourself. You go sneaking off to Hollywood, and I find you here, mopping up the stuff like a vacuum cleaner . . .'

'Aren't you being a bit pompous, old man?'

The point was well taken. I was, of course. But it seemed to me that pomposity was of the essence. I mean to say, you can't tick a bloke off properly unless you come over a bit mid-Victorian.

'I don't care if I am. You make me sick.'

A look of pain came into his face.

'Is this Reginald Havershot speaking?' he said reproachfully. 'My cousin Reginald, who on New Year's Eve two years ago, in the company of myself and old Stinker Pomeroy, broke twenty-three glasses at the Café de l'Europe and was thrown out kicking and screaming—'

I checked him with a cold gesture. My great love had purified me so intensely that it was loathsome to me to listen to these reminiscences of what had happened to my baser self two years ago.

'Never mind that,' I said. 'I want to know about this business of yours. How long have you been engaged?'

'Oh, a certain time.'

'And you are going to get married?'

'My dear chap, that's the whole idea.'

It was a little difficult to know what to say. Old Plimsoll had told me to exercise my authority, but I didn't see how it was to be done. Eggy had plenty of money of his own. If I had threatened to cut him off with a shilling, he would simply have asked to be shown the shilling, pocketed it, thanked me, and carried on according to plan.

'Well, if you're going to get married,' I said, 'you'd better stop drinking.'

He shook his head.

'You don't understand, old man. I can't stop drinking. I have a shrewd idea that this girl got engaged to me in order to reform me, and pretty silly she would feel if I went and reformed on my own. You can see how it would discourage her. Probably she would lose interest and chuck me. You've got to think of these things, you know. The way I look at it, the safe, sane and sound policy is to keep reasonably pie-eyed till after the ceremony and then sober up by degrees during the honeymoon.'

It was a theory, of course, but I hadn't time to go into it then.

'Who is this girl you're engaged to?'

'Her name is . . .' He paused, and his brow wrinkled. 'Her name . . . Now, if you had asked me that an hour ago – nay, even half an hour ago . . . Ah!' he said, perking up. 'Here she comes in person. She'll be able to tell us.'

He waved cordially at someone behind me. I turned. A slimmish sort of girl was coming towards us across the lawn. I couldn't see if she was pretty or not, because her face was in the shadow. She waved back at him.

'Hello, Eggy. There you are. I thought you would be.'

Something in her voice caused me to start and gaze narrowly at her as she came into the light. And at the same moment something in the cut of my jib caused her to start and gaze narrowly at me. And in half a tick we were gazing narrowly at each other – she at me, I at her. And in half a tick after that our last doubts were dispelled.

Reading from left to right, we were myself and Ann Bannister.

4

'Ann—!' I cried.

'—Bannister!' cried Eggy, slapping his forehead. 'I knew it would come back. It was on the tip of my tongue all along. Hullo, Ann. This is my cousin, Reggie.'

'We have met.'

'You mean before this moment?'

'A long time before this moment. We're old friends.'

'Old friends?'

'Very old friends.'

'Then, obviously, a small drink is indicated. Bar-bloke—'

'No,' said Ann. 'You get right away from that bar.'

'But aren't we going to celebrate?'

'No.'

'You go and take a walk round the block, Egremont Mannering, and don't come back till your brain is like a razor.'

'My brain is like a razor.'

'Two razors, then. Off you go.'

There had always been something compelling about Ann. I had noticed it myself in the old days. She was one of those small, brisk, energetic girls, abundantly supplied with buck and ginger, who have a way of making the populace step around a bit. Eggy trotted off like a lamb in a his-not-to-reason-why manner, and we were alone together.

We stood in silence for a moment. I was brooding on the past, and I suppose she was, too.

Just to keep the record straight, I'd better tell you about this past that we were brooding on. This Ann Bannister, as I said, was a newspaper girl, and I had met her when she was taking a holiday at Cannes. We became chummy. I asked her to marry me. She right-hoed. So far, so good.

And then, quite unexpectedly, the engagement went and busted itself up. One moment, it was buzzing along like a two-year-old, and all was gas and gaiters. The next, it had come a stinker.

What happened was this. One night, we were sitting side by side on the terrace of the Palm Beach Casino, watching the silver moon flood the rippling Mediterranean, and she squeezed my hand, and I leaned towards her tenderly, and she leaned towards me, waiting for the loving observation which she had every reason to suppose would emerge, and I said:

'Gosh! My feet hurt!'

Well, they did, I mean to say. Even as I leaned towards her, they had given me a sudden twinge of acute agony. I was trying out a new pair of dress shoes that night, and you know what new patent leather can do to the extremities. But, undoubtedly, I should have chosen another moment for introducing the topic. She took it rather hard. She seemed upset. In fact, she turned away, and petulantly, at that. So, thinking to heal the breach, I bent forward to plant a gentle kiss on the back of her neck.

Well, that was all right, of course – I mean to say, as an idea. The trouble was that I forgot that I had a lighted cigar in my mouth, and when the fact was drawn to my attention, it was too late. Leaping like a scalded kitten, she began calling me a soulless plug-ugly and breaking off the engagement. And next day, when I called at her hotel with flowers to take the matter up again, I found that she had left. Yes, she had gone out of my life.

And here she was, two years later, back again.

I'm bound to say I was a bit embarrassed at finding myself *vis-à-vis* with this chunk of the days that were no more. It's always embarrassing to run unexpectedly into a girl you used to be engaged to. I mean, you don't quite know how to comport yourself. If you look chirpy, that's not much of a compliment to her. Whereas, if you look mouldy, you feel that she's patting herself on the back and saying: 'Aha! I thought losing me would make the poor clam think a bit!' and that offends a fellow's pride. I suppose the wheeze really is to have one of those cold, inscrutable faces you read about in books.

She, on her side, women having the gift more than men, had already pulled herself together.

'Well!' she said.

A pleased smile had come into her face, and she was looking at me as if I had been just some fairly mere acquaintance who meant nothing much in the scheme of things, but whom she was quite glad to see.

'Well, fancy meeting you here, Reggie!'

I saw that this was the right attitude. After all, the dead past is the dead past. I mean to say, the heavy stuff was over between us. At the time when she had severed relations, the thing had, of course, stuck the gaff into me to quite a goodish extent. I won't say that I had not been able to sleep or touch food, because I've always slept like a log and taken my three square a day, and not even this tragedy could break the habit of a lifetime, but I certainly had felt a bit caught in the machinery. Sombre, if you know what I mean, and unsettled, and rather inclined to read Portuguese Love Sonnets and smoke too much. But I had got over all that ages ago, and we could now meet on a calm, friendly footing.

So I spoke, as she had done, with an easy cordiality.

'Me too,' I said. 'Fancy meeting you here.'

'How are you?'

'Oh, I'm fine.'

'The feet quite all right?'

'Oh, quite.'

'Good.'

'You're looking well.'

She was, too. Ann is one of those girls who always look as if they had just stepped out of a cold bath after doing their daily dozen.

'Thanks. Yes, I'm all right. What has brought you to Hollywood, Reggie?'

'Oh, this and that.'

There was a slightish pause. I felt a bit embarrassed again.

'So,' I said, 'you're affianced to old Eggy?'

'Yes. I do seem to run in the family, don't I?'

'You do a bit.'

'Do you approve?'

I considered this.

'Well, if you ask me,' I said, 'I think it is a far, far better thing that Eggy is doing than he has ever done. But where do you get off? Doesn't this open up a pretty bleak future for you?'

'Why? Don't you like Eggy?'

'I love him like a brother. One of my oldest pals. But I should have thought that for domestic purposes someone who was occasionally sober would have suited you better.'

'Eggy's all right.'

'Oh, he's all *right*. He enjoys it.'

'There's lots of good stuff in Eggy.'

'Quite. And more going in every minute.'

'His trouble is that he has always had too much money and too much spare time. What he needs is a job. I've got him one.'

'And he's accepted office?'

'You bet he's accepted office.'

I was rather overcome.

'Ann,' I said, 'you're a marvel!'

'How so, Mister Bones?'

'Why, making Eggy work. It's never been done before.'

'Well, it's going to be done now. He starts to work tomorrow.'

'That's splendid. One feels a certain pang of pity for whoever it is he's starting to work for; but that's splendid. The family were worried about him.'

'I don't wonder. I can't imagine anybody more capable of worrying a family than Eggy. Just suppose if Job had had him as well as boils!'

The garden was beginning to fill up now, and several thirsty souls had come prowling up to the table like lions to the drinking hole. We moved away.

'Tell me about yourself, Ann,' I said. 'You're working hard all the time, of course?'

'Oh, yes. Always on the job – such as it is.'

'How do you mean, such as it is? Don't you like it?'

'Not very much.'

'But I should have thought it would just have suited you, being a press agent.'

'A what?'

'Eggy told me you were April June's press agent.'

'He was a little premature. That's what I'm hoping to be, if all goes well, but nothing's settled yet. It all depends on whether something comes off or not.'

'What's that?'

'Oh, just an idea I've got. If it works out as I'm hoping she says she will sign on the dotted line. I shan't know for a couple of days. In the meantime, I'm a sort of governess-companion-nursemaid.'

'A what?'

'Well, I don't know how else you would describe the job. Have you ever heard of Joey Cooley?'

'One of these child stars, isn't he? I have an idea. April June told me something about him being in her last picture.'

'That's right. Well, I look after him. Tend him and guard him and all that.'

'But what about your newspaper work? I thought you worked on newspapers and things.'

'I did a short while ago. I was on a Los Angeles paper. But the depression has upset everything. They let me go. I tried other papers. No room. I tried freelancing, but there's nothing in freelancing nowadays. So, having to eat, I took what I could. That's how I come to be governess-companion-nursemaid to Joey.'

I must say I felt a pang. I knew how keen she had been on her work.

'I say, I'm frightfully sorry.'

'Thanks, Reggie. You always had a kind heart.'

'Oh, I don't know.'

'Yes, you did. Pure gold and in the right place. It was your poor feet that let you down.'

'Oh, dash it, I wish you wouldn't harp on that.'

'Was I harping?'

'Certainly you were harping. That's the second time you've dug my feet up. If you knew what gyp those shoes were giving me that night . . . I thought they were going to burst every moment like shrapnel . . . However, that is neither here nor there. I'm awfully sorry you're having such a rotten time.'

'Oh, it's not really so bad. I don't want to pose as a martyr. I'm quite happy. I love young Joseph. He's a scream.'

'All the same, it must be pretty foul for you. I mean, I know you must want to be out and about, nosing after stories and getting scoops or whatever you call them.'

'It's sweet of you to be sympathetic, Reggie, but I think I'm going to be all right. I'm practically sure this thing I was speaking of will come off – I don't see how there can be a hitch – and when it does I shall rise on stepping-stones of my dead self to higher things.'

'Good.'

'Though, mind you, there's a darker side. It won't be all jam being April June's press agent.'

'What! Why not?'

'She's a cat.'

I shuddered from stem to stern, as stout barks do when buffeted by the waves.

'A *what*?'

'A cat. There's another word that would describe her even better, but "cat" meets the case.'

I mastered my emotion with an effort.

'April June,' I said, 'is the sweetest, noblest, divinest girl in existence. The loveliest creature you could shake a stick at in a month of Sundays, and as good as she is beautiful. She's wonderful. She's marvellous. She's super. She's the top.'

She looked at me sharply.

'Hullo! What's all this?'

I saw no reason to conceal my passion.

'I love her,' I said.

'What!'

'Definitely.'

'It can't be true.'

'It is true. I worship the ground she treads on.'

'Well, for crying in the soup!'

'I don't know what that expression means, but I still stick to my story. I worship the ground she treads on.'

She went into the silence for a moment. Then she spoke in a relieved sort of voice.

'Well, thank goodness, there isn't a chance that she'll look at you.'

'Why not?'

'It's all over Hollywood that she's got her hooks on some fool of an Englishman. A man called Lord Havershot. That's the fellow she's going to marry.'

A powerful convulsion shook me from base to apex.

'What!'

'Yes.'

'Is that official?'

'Quite, I believe.'

I drew a deep breath. The coloured lanterns seemed to be dancing buck and wing steps around me.

'Good egg!' I said. 'Because I'm him.'

'What!'

'Yes. Since we ... er ... last met, there has been a good deal of mortality in the family and I've copped the title.'

She was staring at me, wide-eyed.

'Oh, hell!' she said.

'Why "oh, hell"?'

'This is awful.'

'It is nothing of the kind. I like it.'

She clutched my coat.

'Reggie, you mustn't do this. Don't make a fool of yourself.'

'A fool of myself, eh?'

'Yes. She'll make you miserable. I may be going to depend on her for my bread and butter, but that shan't stop me doing my best to open your eyes. You're such a sweet, simple old ass that you can't see what everybody else sees. The woman's poison. She's frightful. Everybody knows it. Vain, affected, utterly selfish, and as hard as nails.'

I had to laugh at that.

'As hard as nails, eh?'

'Harder.'

I laughed again. Whole thing so dashed absurd.

'You think so, do you?' I said. 'Funny you should say that. Extremely funny. Because the one thing she is is gentle and sensitive and highly strung and so forth. Let me tell you of a little episode that occurred on the train. I was describing round five of the recent heavyweight championship contest to her, and when I came to the bit about blood her eyeballs rolled upwards and she swooned away.'

'She did, did she?'

'Passed right out. I never saw anything so womanly in my life.'

'And it didn't occur to you, I suppose, that she was just putting on an act?'

'An act?'

'Yes. And it worked, apparently. Because now I hear that you follow her everywhere she goes, bleating.'

'I do not bleat.'

'The story going the round of the clubs is that you do bleat. People say they can hear you for miles on a clear day. My poor Reggie, she was just fooling you. The woman goes to all the fights in Los Angeles and revels in them.'

'I don't believe it.'

'She does, I tell you. Can't you see that she was simply making a play for you because you're Lord Havershot? That's all she's after – the title. For heaven's sake, Reggie, lay off while there's still time.'

I eyed her coldly and detached my coat from her grasp.

'Let us talk of something else,' I said.

'There's nothing else I want to talk about.'

'Then don't let's talk at all. I don't know if you realize it, but what we're doing is perilously near to speaking lightly of a woman's name – the sort of thing chaps get kicked out of clubs for.'

'Reggie, will you listen to me?'

'No. I jolly well won't.'

'Reggie!'

'No. Let us drop the subj.'

She gave a little sigh.

'Oh, very well,' she said. 'I might have known it would be no use trying to drive sense into a fat head like yours . . . April June!'

'Why do you say "April June" like that?'

'Because it's the only way to say it.'

'Well, let me tell you I resent your saying "April June" as if you were mentioning the name of some particularly unpleasant disease.'

'That is the way I shall go on saying "April June".'

I bowed stiffly.

'Oh, right oh,' I said. 'Please yourself. After all, your methods of voice production are your own affair. And now, as I observe my hostess approaching, I will beetle along and pay my respects. This will leave you at liberty to go off into a corner by yourself and say "April June", if you so desire, till the party is over and they lock up the house and put the cat out.'

'They don't put her out. She lives here.'

I made no reply to this vulgar crack. I felt that it was beneath me. Besides, I couldn't think of anything. I moved away in silence. I could feel Ann's eyes on the back of my neck, like Eggy's spiders, but I did not look round. I pushed off to where April was greeting a covey of guests and barged in, hoping ere long to be able to detach her from the throng and have a private word with her on a tender and sentimental subject.

Well, of course, it wasn't easy, because a hostess has much to occupy her, but eventually she seemed satisfied that she had got things moving and could leave people to entertain them-selves, so I collared a table for two in a corner of the lawn and dumped her down there. And we had steak and kidney pie and the usual fixings, and presently we started wading into vanilla ice-cream.

And all the while my determination to slap my heart down before her was growing. Ann's derogatory remarks hadn't weak-ened me in the slightest. All rot, they seemed to me. As I watched this lovely girl shovelling down the stuff, I refused to believe that she wasn't everything that was perfect. I braced myself for the kick-off. At any moment now, I felt, it might occur. It was simply a question of watching out for the psychological moment and leaping on it like a ton of bricks the second it shoved its nose up.

The conversation had turned to her work. She had said something about her chances of doing a quiet sneak to bed at a fairly early hour, because she was supposed to be on the set, made up, at six on the following a.m. for some retakes; and the mere idea of being out of the hay at a time like that made me quiver with tender compassion.

'Six o'clock!' I said. 'Gosh!'

'Yes, it's not an easy life. I often wonder if one's public ever realize how hard it is.'

'It must be frightful.'

'One does get a little tired sometimes.'

'Still,' I said, doing a spot of silver-lining-pointing, 'there's money in it, what?'

'Money!'

'And fame.'

She smiled a faint, saintly sort of smile and champed a spoonful of ice-cream.

'Money and fame mean nothing to me, Lord Havershot.'

'No?'

'Oh, no. My reward is the feeling that I'm spreading happiness, that I am doing my little best to cheer up this tired world, that I am giving the toiling masses a glimpse of something bigger and better and more beautiful.'

'What ho,' I said reverently.

'You don't think it silly of me to feel like that?'

'I think it's terrific.'

'I'm so glad. You see, it's a sort of religion with me. I feel like a kind of priestess. I think of all those millions of drab lives, and I say to myself what does all the hard work and the distasteful publicity matter if I can bring a little sunshine into their drab round. You're laughing at me?'

'No, no. Absolutely not.'

'Take Pittsburgh, for instance. They eat me in Pittsburgh. My last picture but one grossed twenty-two thousand there on the week. And that makes me very happy, because I think of all those drab lives in Pittsburgh being brightened up like that.

And Cincinnati. I was a riot in Cincinnati. People's lives are very drab in Cincinnati, too.'

'It's wonderful!'

She sighed.

'I suppose it is. Yes, of course it is. All those drab lives, I mean. And yet is it enough? That is what one asks oneself sometimes. One is lonely now and then. One feels one wishes one could get away from it all and be just an ordinary happy wife and mother. Sometimes one dreams of the patter of little feet . . .'

I waited no longer. If this wasn't the psychological moment, I didn't know a psychological moment when I saw one. I leaned forward. 'Darling,' I was just about to say, 'stop me if you've heard this before, but will you be my wife?' when something suddenly went off like a bomb inside my head, causing me to drop the subject absolutely.

It happened in a flash. One moment, I was all fire and romance, without a thought for anything except that the girl who was sitting beside me was the girl I loved, and that I was jolly well going to put her in touch with the facts: the next, I was hopping round in circles with my hand pressed to my cheek, suffering the tortures of the damned.

Whether by pure spontaneous combustion, or because I had inadvertently taken aboard too large a segment of ice-cream, the old Havershot wisdom tooth had begun to assert its personality.

I had had my eye on this tooth for some time, and I suppose I ought to have taken a firm line with it before. But you know how it is when you're travelling. You shrink from entrusting the snappers to a strange dentist. You say to yourself 'Stick it out, old cock, till you get back to London and can toddle round to the maestro who's been looking after you since you were so high.' And then, of course, you cop it unexpectedly, as I had done.

Well, there it was. A fellow can't pour out his soul under those conditions. In fact, I don't mind admitting that at that juncture all thoughts of love and marriage and little feet and what not had passed for the nonce completely out of my mind. With a hasty word of farewell, I left her sitting and proceeded to the chemist's shop by the Beverly-Wilshire Hotel in quest of temporary relief. And next day I was in the dentist's waiting-room, about to keep my tryst with I. J. Zizzbaum, the man behind the forceps.

So here we are again at the point where, if you remember, I originally wanted to start the story, only my literary pal headed me off. There I was, as I told you, sitting in an armchair, and across the room in another armchair, turning the pages of the *National Geographic Magazine*, was a kid of the Little Lord Fauntleroy type. His left cheek, like mine, was bulging, and I deduced that we were both awaiting the awful summons.

He was, I observed, a kid of singular personal beauty. Not even the bulge in his cheek could conceal that. He had large, expressive eyes and golden ringlets. Long lashes hid these eyes as he gazed down at his *National Geographic Magazine*.

I never know what's the correct course to pursue on occasions like this. Should one try to help things along with a friendly word or two, if only about the weather? Or is silence best? I was just debating this question in my mind, when he opened the conversation himself.

He lowered his *National Geographic Magazine* and looked across at me.

'Where,' he asked, 'are the rest of the boys?'

5

His meaning eluded me. I didn't get him. A cryptic kid. One of those kids who, as the expression is, speak in riddles. He was staring at me enquiringly, and I stared back at him, also enquiringly.

Then I said, going straight to the point and evading all side issues:

'What boys?'

'The newspaper boys.'

'The newspaper boys?'

An idea seemed to strike him.

'Aren't you a reporter?'

'No, not a reporter.'

'Then what are you doing here?'

'I've come to have a tooth out.'

This appeared to surprise and displease him. He said, with marked acerbity:

'You can't have come to have a tooth out.'

'Yes, I have.'

'But I've come to have a tooth out.'

I spotted a possible solution.

'Perhaps,' I said, throwing out the suggestion for what it was worth, 'we've both come to have a tooth out, what? I mean to say, you one and me another. Tooth A and Tooth B, as it were.'

He still seemed ruffled. He eyed me searchingly.

'When's your appointment?'

'Three-thirty.'

'It can't be. Mine is.'

'So is mine. I. J. Zizzbaum was most definite about that. We arranged it over the phone, and his words left no loophole for misunderstanding. "Three-thirty," said I. J. Zizzbaum, as plain as I see you now.'

The kid became calmer. His alabaster brow lost its frown,

and he ceased to regard me as if I were some hijacker or bandit. It was as if a great light had shone upon him.

'Oh, I. J. Zizzbaum?' he said. 'B. K. Burwash is doing mine.'

And, looking about me, I now perceived that on either side of the apartment in which we sat was a door.

On one of these doors was imprinted the legend:

I. J. ZIZZBAUM.

And on the other:

B. K. BURWASH.

The mystery was solved. Possibly because they were old dental college chums, or possibly from motives of economy, these two fang-wrenchers shared a common waiting-room.

Convinced now that no attempt was being made to jump his claim, the kid had become affability itself. Seeing in me no rival for first whack at the operating-chair, but merely a fellow human being up against the facts of life just as he was, he changed his tone to one of kindly interest.

'Does your tooth hurt?'

'Like the dickens.'

'So does mine. Coo!'

'Coo here, too.'

'Where does it seem to catch you most?'

'Pretty well all the way down to the toenails.'

'Me, too. This tooth of mine is certainly fierce. Yessir!'

'So is mine.'

'I'll bet mine's worse than yours.'

'It couldn't be.'

He made what he evidently considered a telling point.

'I'm having gas.'

I came right back at him.

'So am I.'

'I'll bet I need more gas than you.'

'I'll bet you don't.'

'I'll bet you a trillion dollars I do.'

It seemed to me that rancour was beginning to creep into the conversation once more, and that pretty soon we would be descending to a common wrangle. So, rather than allow the harmony of the proceedings to be marred by a jarring note, I dropped the theme and switched off to an aspect of the matter which had been puzzling me from the first. You will remember that I had thought this kid to have spoken in riddles, and I still wanted an explanation of those rather mystic opening words of his.

'You're probably right,' I said pacifically. 'But, be that as it may, what made you think I was a reporter?'

'I'm expecting a flock of them here.'

'You are?'

'Sure. There'll be camera men, too, and human interest writers.'

'What, to see you have a tooth out?'

'Sure. When I have a tooth out, that's news.'

'What!'

'Sure. This is going to make the front page of every paper in the country.'

'What, your tooth?'

'Yay, my tooth. Listen, when I had my tonsils extracted last year, it rocked civilization. I'm some shucks, I want to tell you.'

'Somebody special, you mean?'

'I'll say that's what I mean. I'm Joey Cooley.'

Owing to the fact that one of my unswerving rules in life is never to go to a picture if I am informed by my spies that there is a child in it, I had never actually set eyes on this stripling. But of course I knew the name. Ann, if you remember, had spoken of him. So had April June.

'Oh, ah,' I said. 'Joey Cooley, eh?'

'Joey Cooley is correct.'

'Yes, I've heard of you.'

'So I should think.'

'I know your nurse.'

'My what?'

'Well, your female attendant or whatever she is. Ann Bannister.'

'Oh, Ann? She's an all-right guy, Ann is.'

'Quite.'

'A corker, and don't let anyone tell you different.'

'I won't.'

'Ann's a peach. Yessir, that's what Ann is.'

'And April June was talking about you the other day.'

'Oh, yeah? And what did she have to say?'

'She told me you were in her last picture.'

'She did, did she?' He snorted with not a little violence, and his brow darkened. It was plain that he was piqued. Meaning nothing but to pass along a casual item of information, I appeared to have touched some exposed nerve. 'The crust of that dame! In *her* last picture, eh? Let me tell you that *she* was in *my* last picture!'

He snorted a bit more. He had taken up the *National Geographic Magazine* again, and I noted that it quivered in his hands, as if he were wrestling with some powerful emotion. Presently the spasm passed, and he was himself again.

'So you've met that pill, have you?' he said.

It was my turn to quiver, and I did so like a jelly.

'That what?'

'That pill.'

'Did you say "pill"?'

' "Pill" was what I said. Slice her where you like, she's still boloney.'

I drew myself up.

'You are speaking,' I said, 'of the woman I love.'

He started to say something, but I raised my hand coldly and said 'Please,' and silence supervened. He read his *National Geographic Magazine*. I read mine. And for some minutes matters proceeded along these lines. Then I thought to myself: 'Oh, well, dash it,' and decided to extend the olive branch. Too damn silly, I mean, a couple of fellows on the brink of having teeth out simply sitting reading the *National Geographic Magazine* at one another instead of trying to forget by means of pleasant chit-chat the ordeal which lay before them.

'So you're Joey Cooley?' I said.

He accepted the overture in the spirit in which it was intended.

'You never spoke a truer word,' he replied agreeably. 'That's about who I am, if you come right down to it. Joey Cooley, the Idol of American Motherhood. Who are you?'

'Havershot's my name.'

'English, aren't you?'

'That's right.'

'Been in Hollywood long?'

'About a week.'

'Where are you staying?'

'I've a bungalow at the Garden of the Hesperides.'

'Do you like Hollywood?'

'Oh, rather. Topping spot.'

'You ought to see Chillicothe, Ohio.'

'Why?'

'That's where I come from. And that's where I'd like to be now. Yessir, right back there in little old Chillicothe.'

'You're homesick, what?'

'You betcher.'

'Still, I suppose you have a pretty good time here?'

His face clouded. Once more, it appeared, I had said the wrong thing.

'Who, me? I do not.'

'Why not?'

'I'll tell you why not. Because I'm practically a member of a chain gang. I couldn't have it much tougher if this was Devil's Island or the Foreign Legion or sump'n'. Do you know what?'

'What?'

'Do you know what old Brinkmeyer did when the contract was being drawn up?'

'No, what?'

'Slipped in a clause that I had to live at his house, so that I could be under his personal eye.'

'Who is this Brinkmeyer?'

'The boss of the corporation I work for.'

'And you don't like his personal eye?'

'I don't mind him. He's a pretty good sort of old stiff. It's his sister Beulah. She was the one who put him up to it. She's the heavy in the sequence. As tough as they come. Ever hear of Simon Legree?'

'Yes.'

'Beulah Brinkmeyer. Know what a serf is?'

'What you swim in, you mean.'

'No, I don't mean what you swim in. I mean what's down-trodden and oppressed and gets the dirty end of the stick all the time. That's me. Gosh, what a life! Shall I tell you something?'

'Do.'

'I'm not allowed to play games, because I might get hurt. I'm not allowed to keep a dog, because it might bite me. I'm not allowed in the swimming-pool, because I might get drowned. And, listen, get this one. No candy, because I might put on weight.'

'You don't mean that?'

'I do mean that. It's in my contract. "The party of the second part, hereinafter to be called the artist, shall abstain from all ice-creams, chocolate-creams, nut sundaes, fudge and all-day suckers, hereinafter to be called candy, this is to be understood to comprise doughnuts, marshmallows, pies in their season, all starchy foods and twice of chicken." Can you imagine my lawyer letting them slip that over!'

I must say I was a bit appalled. We Havershots have always been good trenchermen, and it never fails to give me a grey feeling when I hear of somebody being on a diet. I know how I should have felt at his age if some strong hand had kept me from the sock-shop.

'I wonder you don't chuck it.'

'I can't.'

'You love your Art too much?'

'No, I don't.'

'You like bringing sunshine into drab lives in Pittsburgh and Cincinnati?'

'I don't care if Pittsburgh chokes. And that goes for Cincinnati, too.'

'Then perhaps you feel that all the money and fame make up for these what you might call hideous privations?'

He snorted. He seemed to have as low an opinion of money and fame as April June.

'What's the good of money and fame? I can't eat them, can I? There's nothing I'd like better than to tie a can to the whole outfit and go back to where hearts are pure and men are men in Chillicothe, Ohio. I'd like to be home with mother right now. You should taste her fried chicken, southern style. And she'd be tickled pink to have me, too. But I can't get away. I've a five years' contract, and you can bet they're going to hold me to it.'

'I see.'

'Oh, yes, I'm Uncle Tom, all right. But listen, shall I tell you something? I'm biding my time. I'm waiting. Some day I'll grow up. And when I do, oh, baby!'

'Oh, what?'

'I said "Oh, baby!" I'm going to poke Beulah Brinkmeyer right in the snoot.'

'What! Would you strike a woman?'

'You betcher I'd strike a woman. Yessir, she'll get hers. And there's about six directors I'm going to poke in the snoot, and a whole raft of supervisors and production experts. And that press agent of mine. I'm going to poke him in the snoot, all right. Yessir! Matter of fact,' he said, summing up, 'you'd have a tough time finding somebody I'm not going to poke in the snoot, once I'm big enough. I've got all their names in a little notebook.'

He relapsed into a moody silence, and I didn't quite know what to say. No words of mine, I felt, could cheer this stricken child. The iron had plainly entered a dashed sight too deep into his soul for a mere 'Buck up, old bird!' to do any good.

However, as it turned out, I would have had no time to deliver anything in the nature of a pep talk, for at this moment the door opened and in poured a susurration of blighters, some male, some female, some with cameras, some without, and the air became so thick with interviewing and picture-taking that it would have been impossible to get a word in. I just sat reading my *National Geographic Magazine*. And presently a white-robed attendant appeared and announced that B. K. Burwash was straining at the forceps, and the gang passed through into his room, interviewing to the last.

And not long after that another white-robed attendant came and said that I. J. Zizzbaum would be glad if I would look in, so I commended my soul to God, and followed her into the operating theatre.

6

I. J. Zizzbaum proved to be rather a gloomy cove. He looked like a dentist with a secret sorrow. In reply to my 'Good afternoon,' he merely motioned me to the chair with a sombre wave of the hand. One of those strong, silent dentists.

I, on the other hand, was at my chattiest. I am always that way when closeted with a molar-mangler. I dare say it's the same with you. I suppose one's idea is that if one can only keep the conversation going, the blighter may get so interested that he will shelve the dirty work altogether in favour of a cosy talk. I started in right away.

'Hullo, hullo, hullo. Here I am. Good afternoon, good afternoon. What a lovely day, what? Shall I sit here? Right ho. Shall I lean my head back? Right ho. Shall I open my mouth? Right ho.'

'Wider please,' said I. J. Zizzbaum sadly.

'Right ho. Everything set for the administration of the old laughing gas? Good. You know,' I said, sitting up, 'it's years since I had gas. I can't have been more than twelve. I know I was quite a kid, because it happened when I was at a private school, and of course one leaves one's private school at a very tender age. And, talking of kids, who do you think I met in the waiting-room? None other than little Joey Cooley. And it's an odd coincidence, but he's having gas, too. Shows what a small world it is, what?'

I broke off, abashed. It did not need the quick wince of pain on I. J. Zizzbaum's mobile face to tell me that I had made a bloomer and said the tactless thing. I could have kicked myself.

Because it had suddenly flashed upon me what the trouble was and why he was not this afternoon the sunny I. J. Zizzbaum whose merry laugh and gay quips made him, no doubt, the life and soul of the annual dentists' convention. He was brooding on the fact that the big prize in the dentistry world, the extraction of little Joey Cooley's bicuspid, had gone to his trade rival, B. K. Burwash.

No doubt he had been listening in on all that interviewing and camera-clicking, and the shrill cries of the human interest writers as they went about their business must have made very bitter hearing – rubbing it in, I mean to say, that old Pop Burwash was going to get his name on the front page of all the public news-sheets and become more or less the World's Sweetheart, while all he, Zizzbaum, could expect was my modest fee.

It was enough to depress the most effervescent dentist, and my heart bled for the poor bloke. I hunted in my mind for some soothing speech that would bring the roses back to his cheeks, but all I could think of was a statement to the effect that recent discoveries in the Congo basin had thrown a new light on something or other. I had this on the authority of the *National Geographic Magazine*.

It didn't seem to cheer him up to any marked extent. Not interested in the Congo basin, probably. Many people aren't. He simply sighed rather heavily, levered my jaws a bit farther apart, peered into the abyss, sighed again as if he didn't think highly of the contents, and motioned to his ADC to cluster round with the gas-bag.

And presently, after a brief interlude during which I felt as if I was being slowly smothered where I sat, I was off.

I don't know if you are familiar with this taking-gas business. If you are, you will recall that it has certain drawbacks apart from the sensation of being cut off in your prime by stoppage of the windpipes. It is apt to give you unpleasant dreams and visions. The last time I had had it, on the occasion which I had mentioned in my introductory remarks, I remember that I had thought somebody was shoving me down into the sea, and I had a distinct illusion of being pried asunder by sharks.

This time, the proceedings were still rummy, but not quite so bad as that. The sharks were not on the bill. The stellar role was played by little Joey Cooley.

It seemed to me that he and I were in a room rather like the waiting-room, only larger, and as in the real waiting-room, there were two doors, one on each side.

The first was labelled:

I. J. ZIZZBAUM.

The other:

B. K. BURWASH.

And the Cooley kid and I were jostling one another, trying to get through the Zizzbaum door.

Well, any chump would have seen that that wasn't right. I tried to reason with the misguided little blighter. I kept saying: 'Stop shoving, old sport; you're trying to get into the wrong room,' but it wasn't any use – he simply shoved the more. And presently he shoved me into an armchair and told me to sit there and read the *National Geographic Magazine*, and then he opened the door and went through.

After that, things got blurred for a while. When they clarified somewhat, I was still sitting in a chair, but it was a dentist's chair, and I realized that I had come out from under the influence.

The first thing I saw was I. J. Zizzbaum in his white coat. He was regarding me with a kindly smile.

'Well, my little man,' he said, in a fatherly sort of way. 'Feeling all right?'

And I was just about to ask him what the dickens he meant by calling me his little man – for the Havershots, though matey, have their sense of dignity – when I suddenly perceived that we were not alone. The room was absolutely crammed.

Ann Bannister was there, standing on the other side of me, but I didn't object to that. If she had somehow got wind of this operation of mine and something of the old love and affection still lingered in her bosom, causing her to want to be with me in my hour of trial, well, that was all right. Dashed decent of her, I felt. But I strongly resented the presence of all these other birds. I mean to say, perfect strangers have no right to come flocking round a chap when he's having a tooth out. Then, if ever, he is surely entitled to a spot of privacy.

There was a whole mob of them, and I had a sort of vague feeling I'd seen them before somewhere. Some were male, some female. Some had cameras, some hadn't. I sat up, feeling a bit huffy. I was surprised at I. J. Zizzbaum allowing them on the premises, and I was just going to tell him so – and I didn't intend to mince my words – when I made a rather odd discovery – to wit, that the chap in the white coat wasn't I. J. Zizzbaum. Somebody different altogether.

And I was about to enquire into this, when I discovered

something else. Something that made me draw in my breath quickly with a startled 'What ho!'

When I had entered the waiting-room, I must mention, I had been clad in a quiet grey suit with powder-blue socks matching the neat tie and melting, as it were, into the tasteful suede shoes. And now, by Jove, I'm blowed if I wasn't wearing knickerbockers and stockings. And then suddenly I caught sight of my face in the mirror and saw that it was of singular beauty, topped off with golden ringlets. And the eyes staring into mine were large and expressive and had long lashes.

'Hell!' I cried.

Well, I mean to say, who wouldn't have? I saw right away what had happened. Someone, as the poet says, had blundered. Joey Cooley and I must have gone under gas at exactly the same moment and, owing presumably to some bad staffwork during the period when we were simultaneously sauntering about in the fourth dimension, or whatever they call it, there had been an unforeseen switch. The impetuous young cuckoo had gone and barged into my body, and I, having nowhere else to go, had toddled off and got into his.

His fault, of course, the silly ass. I had told him to stop shoving.

7

I sat staring at myself in the mirror, and was still in full goggle when the bird in the white coat who had called me his little man – B. K. Burwash, I took him to be – stepped forward.

'You'll want this, eh?' he said, still speaking in that fatherly manner, and I saw that he was holding out a little cardboard box.

I continued to goggle. I hadn't any time for cardboard boxes. I was still trying to adjust myself to this new twist in the scenario.

A bit breath-taking, the whole affair, you will agree. Of course, I had read stories where much the same sort of thing had happened, but I had never supposed that a chap had got to budget for such an eventuality as a possible feature of the programme in real life. I know they say you ought to be prepared for anything, but, I mean, dash it!

Besides, it all seemed so sudden. In the stories there had always been a sinister scientist who had messed about with test-tubes, or an Egyptian sorcerer who had cast spells, and the thing had taken weeks, if not months. If quick service was desired, you had to have a magic ring or something. In either case, you didn't get results casually like this – out of a blue sky, as it were.

'The tooth,' explained B. K. Burwash. 'You'll want to keep it.'

I trousered the box absently, a proceeding which brought a howl of protest from the mob. The simple action seemed to get them all worked up.

There was a babble of voices.

'Hey!'

'Don't put that away.'

'We want to get a shot of you looking at it.'

'Sort of musing over it.'

'Hold it up and kind of smile at it.'

'Like as if you were saying to yourself: "Well, well!" '

'Have you a statement for the Press?'

'What do you think of the political situation?'

'Has the President your confidence?'

'What is the future of the screen?'

'Give us a message for the people of America. Something snappy with a heart-throb in it.'

'Yay. And how about your favourite breakfast food?'

I had always known Ann Bannister as a girl of character and decision, and I must say my heart warmed to her at this juncture. She took the situation in hand right away, and started hustling them out as if she had been a bouncer in a waterfront pub who had just taken office and was resolved to make good.

'Give the poor child a chance, can't you?' she cried. 'What's the idea of worrying him at a time like this? How would you like it?'

The fellow who had asked for a message to the people of America said that it was as much as his job was worth to go back to the office without one.

Ann remained firm.

'I'll give you all the messages you want,' she said. 'I'll give you anything you like, only get out of here.'

And she went on hustling them out, and presently, by sheer personal magnetism, had cleared the room, and B. K. Burwash and I were alone.

'Quite a lot of excitement,' said B. K. Burwash. 'Ah, well, the penalties of Fame!'

He smiled as he spoke – the jolly, beaming smile of a dentist who, in addition to pouching a nice fee, knows that he has just had about a thousand dollars' worth of free advertisement.

I was not able to share his merry mood. The dazed feeling passed off, leaving me all of a twitter. I could see now that I had gone and got myself into a very nasty jam.

I mean to say, life's difficult enough as it is. You don't want to aggravate the general complexity of things by getting changed into a kid with knickerbockers and golden curls. A nice thing it was going to be if this state of affairs proved to be permanent. Bim, obviously, would go any chance I might have had of leading April June to the altar. A girl in her position wasn't going to walk up the aisle with a kid in knickerbockers.

What, too, would the fellows at the Drones say if I were to saunter in with golden curls all over me? They wouldn't have it at any price. The Drones is what I would call a pretty broad-minded club, but they simply wouldn't have it. 'You can't do that there 'ere' about summed up what the attitude of the committee would be.

Little wonder, then, that I was in no frame of mind to frisk and frolic with this debonair dentist.

'Never mind about the penalties of Fame, B. K. Burwash,' I said urgently. 'We can discuss all that later. What I wish to do now is issue a statement. A frightful thing has happened, and unless prompt steps are taken through the proper channels, there is going to be a nasty stink kicked up. I may say I happen to know the ringleaders.'

'Just lean back and relax.'

'I won't lean back and relax. I want to issue a statement.'

And I was about to do so, when the door opened and a woman came in. She seemed a bit shirty. She was pshawing and tchahing as she entered.

'All this fuss!' she said. 'I've no patience with them. As if the child wasn't conceited enough already.'

She was a tall, rangy light-heavyweight, severe of aspect. She looked as if she might be an important official on the staff of some well-known female convict establishment. That this was not so was proved by the fact that B. K. Burwash addressed her as Miss Brinkmeyer, and I divined that this must be the woman the kid Cooley had said he disliked.

'I think the little man is feeling all right now, Miss Brinkmeyer,' said B. K. Burwash.

She greeted these kindly words with a snorting sniff indicative of disgust and contempt. I could see why the kid Cooley didn't like this woman. I didn't like her myself. She lacked that indefinable something which we know as charm.

'Of course he's feeling all right. Why wouldn't he be?'

B. K. Burwash said that he always felt a certain anxiety after giving gas. This seemed to stir her up further.

'Pah! Stuff and nonsense! Gas, indeed. When I was a child nobody ever gave me gas. When I was a child, my father used to tie a string to me and fasten it to the barn door and slam it. And it didn't get into the papers, either. All this fuss about a tiny little tooth, which wouldn't ever have started aching if he hadn't been eating candy on the sly, though knowing perfectly well what Clause B (2) in his contract says. I intend to get to the bottom of this candy business. Somebody is bootlegging it to him, and I mean to find out who it is. He's as artful as a barrel-load of monkeys—'

I was conscious of a growing annoyance. I had fallen into a reverie and was once more endeavouring to grapple with the problems confronting me, and her voice interrupted my meditations. It was a harsh, rasping voice, in its timbre not unlike a sawmill.

I shushed her down with a gesture.

'Don't talk so much,' I said curtly.

'What did you say?'

'I said "Don't talk so much." How can I think with all this gabble going on? For heaven's sake, woman, put a sock in it and let me concentrate.'

This got a fair snicker out of B. K. Burwash, though I hadn't intended to strike the humorous note. It caused Miss Brinkmeyer to pinken and breathe heavily.

'I'd like to put you across my knee and give you a good spanking.'

I raised a hand.

'No horse-play, if you please,' I said distantly.

And then something occurred to me, and the whole situation seemed to brighten. I had just remembered what the kid Cooley had said when sketching out his plans for what he was going to do when he was big enough.

Well, goodness knew he was big enough for anything now. My branch of the family has always run to beef a bit, myself not least. When I boxed for Cambridge, I weighed fourteen stone in the nude.

I gave a hearty chuckle, the first I had felt like emitting for some considerable time.

'Woman,' I said, 'you would do better, instead of threatening violence to others, to look out for yourself. You don't know it, but you are in a very sticky spot. The avenger is on your track. When the blow will fall, we cannot say, but some day, in some place, you are going to get a poke in the snoot. This is official.'

B. K. Burwash became graver. He seemed troubled.

'I hope I did not overdo that gas,' he mused. 'I don't like this. It sounds like delirium. The little fellow's manner has been strange ever since he came to.'

La Brinkmeyer scouted this theory.

'Stuff and nonsense! He isn't delirious. He's talking that way just to be aggravating.'

'You think so?'

'Of course. Have you ever had to look after a sassy, swollen-headed, wisecracking child star who thinks he's everybody just because a lot of fool women crowd to see him on the screen and say doesn't he look cute and sweet and innocent?'

B. K. Burwash said no, he had not had this experience.

'Well, I've been doing it for a year, and I know his ways.'

This seemed to reassure the dubious dentist.

'You feel, then, that there is no cause for anxiety?'

'Of course there isn't.'

'You relieve me. I was afraid he was not quite himself.'

'He's himself, worse luck.'

'Ha!' I exclaimed, smiling a bit, for this struck me as quaint. Ironical, you might say. 'Funny you should say that. Because myself, in a nutshell, is precisely what I'm bally well not.'

It seemed an admirable opportunity to issue that statement. The topic could not have been more neatly introduced.

'Madam,' I began, 'and you, B. K. Burwash, prepare yourselves for a bit of a surprise. Unless I am very much mistaken, this is going to make you sit up a trifle.'

'Oh, be quiet.'

'The poet Shakespeare has well said that there are more things in heaven and earth than are dreamed of in our philosophy. One of these has just broken loose in this very room. You will doubtless be interested to learn that owing to an unforeseen crossing of the wires in the fourth dimension—'

'Stop this nonsense and come along.'

'But I wish to issue a statement. Briefly, then, owing, as I say, to funny work in the fourth dimension . . . mark you, I call it the fourth, but it may quite easily be the fifth . . . I'm a bit shaky on dimensions—'

'You'll be shaky if I start shaking you, as I shall in a minute, I know I shall. I've no patience with you. Will you come *along*!'

I came along. And if you feel that this was weak of me, I can only say that the Albert Memorial would have come along in precisely the same manner, had Miss Beulah Brinkmeyer attached herself to its wrist and pulled. I left the chair like a cork emerging from a bottle under the ministrations of a sinewy butler.

'Oh, all right,' I said, resigning myself to the inev. 'Pip-pip, Burwash.'

As a matter of fact, I was not sorry I had been interrupted

in the issuing of my statement, for Reason had suddenly returned to her throne and I perceived that I had been on the point of making an ass of myself.

I mean to say, the one lesson one learns from these stories about coves getting switched into other coves' bodies is that on such occasions statements are no good. No use whatever. Just a waste of breath. The chaps in the stories always try to make them, and nobody ever believes a word. I resolved that from now on I would be cold and taciturn and refrain from all attempts to put myself right with the public. However irksome it might be to remain silent on a topic concerning which I had so much to say, a complete reserve was, I saw, the wiser policy.

Contenting myself, accordingly, with a word of warning to the effect that if she shook me I should be sick, I accompanied Miss Brinkmeyer to the door. My demeanour as I did so was not jaunty, for I was, I must confess, apprehensive and ill at ease. I was asking myself how I was going to render supportable a life spent in the society of this decidedly frightful old geezer. In comparing her to Simon Legree, the Cooley child had shown himself an astute judge of character. She seemed also to possess many of the less agreeable qualities of the late Captain Bligh of the *Bounty*.

In the street a sumptuous automobile awaited us, and presently we were rolling along, she sniffing at intervals as if my company gave her the pip, and self leaning back against the cushions with a meditative frown. And after a while the car turned in at a drive gate and pulled up in front of a large white house.

8

Chez Brinkmeyer – at which I gathered that we had now arrived
– was evidently one of the stately homes of Hollywood. The
eye detected spacious lawns, tennis courts, swimming-pools,
pergolas, bougainvillaea, three gardeners, an iron deer, a ping-
pong porch, and other indications of wealth. If further proof
was required that its proprietor had got the stuff in sackfuls, it
was supplied by the fact that the butler, who had opened the
door in response to the chauffeur's tooting, was an English
butler. You don't run to an English butler in Hollywood unless
you are a pretty prominent nib. The small fry have to rub along
with Japanese and Filipinos.

The sight of this one did much to put new heart into me.
He was like a breath from home, a large, moonfaced, goose-
berry-eyed man of the fine old family butler brand and, drinking
him in, I lost some of that feeling I had had of having fallen
among savages. With him around, I felt, the agony of associating
with Miss Brinkmeyer would be greatly diminished.

However, I wasn't allowed much opportunity of feasting the
eyes upon him at the moment, because my companion – or
keeper or jailer or whatever she was – got hold of my hand
again and whisked me in at a brisk pace, eventually fetching up
in a long, low-ceilinged sort of drawing-room with French
windows opening on a patio.

Its only occupant was a stout, billowy bloke with horn-
rimmed spectacles. From the fact that he was wallowing on a
sofa as if the place belonged to him, I took it that it did belong
to him – that he was, in a word, my host, the Mr Brinkmeyer
under whose personal eye I was now to reside.

Once more, the kid Cooley had shown himself a shrewd judge.
He had told me this man was a pretty good sort of old stiff,
and it was apparent from a glance that this was the case. I liked
Mr Brinkmeyer's looks. Of course, after having been with his
sister all this time, I was in no frame of mind to be fussy about

other people's looks – practically anything would have seemed good to me just then, I mean – but he appeared to me kindly.

Of this kindliness he gave evidence with his opening words.

'Ah, here you are,' he said. 'Everything go off all right? Is he feeling quite well?'

Miss Brinkmeyer clicked her tongue.

'Now, for goodness' sake, don't you start. Of course he's feeling quite well. The way everybody talks, you'd think the child had been having a leg amputated or something. I've no patience with all this fuss.'

'Did he make a fuss?'

'I'm talking about the newspaper men. And all those fool women. Pah! Like a lot of hens.'

'They fussed over him?'

'Yes. In the most disgusting way.'

'Great publicity,' suggested Mr Brinkmeyer, in a deferential sort of way.

Miss Brinkmeyer sniffed.

'Very bad for him.'

'But good for the box-office.'

'I don't care. It makes me sick. Simply encouraging him. As if his head wasn't swollen enough already.'

Mr Brinkmeyer was examining me through his horn-rimmed glasses like a benevolent owl.

'It's not so swollen as it was.'

'Eh?'

'I say the swelling seems to have gone.'

'Yes, thank goodness.'

Hoping to establish an atmosphere of bonhomie and good-will, I said it was kind of her to be pleased. She told me to be quiet.

'No, he doesn't look like he's gotten the mumps any more,' she continued. 'He'll be back to normalcy, I guess, in time for unveiling that statue.'

'Yes,' said Mr Brinkmeyer. It seemed to me that he spoke rather gloomily. 'Yes, I guess he will.'

Pursuing my policy of trying to put everybody at their ease, I asked what statue. She told me to be quiet.

'And we won't have to cancel those Michigan Mothers.'

'What Michigan Mothers?'

For the third time she told me to be quiet. Not an easy woman to keep up a conversation with.

'If he'd been looking like a hubbard squash, we'd have had to put them off, and goodness knows what they'd have said, after coming all this way. But the swelling's practically gone already, and he's sure to be all right tomorrow.' She mused a bit, and added: 'As right as he ever is, the little toad.'

I could not pass this.

'I consider that highly offensive,' I said.

For the fourth time she told me to be quiet. Then, attaching herself to my wrist in the old familiar way, she lugged me out and up the stairs to a bedroom on the first floor. Pushing me in, she told me to lie down and go to sleep.

I could scarcely believe that I had heard her aright.

'Sleep?'

'You've got to have your afternoon sleep, haven't you?'

'But, dash it—'

'Oh, be quiet,' she said – making five in all. She then buzzed off, locking the door behind her.

I must say I laughed a shade mirthlessly. Sleep! That struck me as pretty good. Sleep, I mean to say, what? As if I had time for any rot like that. The immediate task confronting me, as I saw it, was to examine the situation and, if possible, ascertain what the hell was to be done about it. Because something would have to be done, and that with the minimum of delay. Avenues would have to be explored and stones not left unturned. What I had got to do was not sleep, but ponder.

I sat down on the bed and started in.

I don't know how long I pondered, but it was a fairish time, and I might have stuck at it indefinitely without getting a bite had I not in the course of my pondering risen from the bed and walked over to the window. The moment I got to the window, things suddenly clarified. I saw now what I ought to have seen at once, that my first move, before taking any other steps, must be to establish contact with the kid Cooley and call a conference.

I didn't suppose that he would be able to suggest any practical solution of our little difficulty – not being an Egyptian sorcerer, I mean – but at least he could give me a few pointers which might be of use to me in this new life of mine. And the best chance I had of getting together with him, it seemed to me, was to go to my bungalow at the Garden of the Hesperides, and see if he had turned up there. I had told him that that was where I lived, and if he remembered my words he would presumably repair thither sooner or later.

We Havershots are men of action, even when we have been turned into kids with golden curls smelling, I now perceived, of a rather offensive brand of brilliantine. There came over me a yearning to be out and about. I felt cramped and confined in this bedroom. Stifled is the word. A couple of feet below the window there was the roof of a sort of outhouse, and from this roof to the ground was a simple drop. Thirty seconds later I was down in the garden, and thirty seconds after that out of it and speeding for the old home.

I don't know if I had actually expected to find the kid at the bungalow. At any rate, he wasn't there. The place was empty. Wherever Joey Cooley was, he was not thinking things over quietly in an armchair at the Garden of the Hesperides.

This being so, there seemed nothing to do but to wait. So I sat down in the armchair myself and began to brood again.

Now, with all the wealth of material for brooding with which these recent disturbing happenings had provided me, it should, one would have thought, have been easy enough for me to keep my mind from straying from the main issue. But no. It strayed like the dickens. Before I had been sitting two minutes, I had switched right off from the items on the agenda paper and was meditating with a sort of hideous tenseness on ice-cream, doughnuts, pumpkin pie, custard pie, layer cake, chocolate cake, fudge, peanut clusters and all-day suckers. I couldn't seem to get away from them. With a terrific effort I would wrench my mind away from ice-cream, and – bingo! – in a flash I would be thinking of doughnuts. And no sooner had I thrust the vision of doughnuts from me than along would come the pumpkin pie and the all-day suckers.

It was a totally new experience for me. I hadn't thought – in an emotional way – of this type of food-stuff for years and years. But now fudge and chocolate cake seemed to be dancing sarabands before my eyes, and I felt that I would have given anything for a good whack at them. Not since the distant days of my first private school had I been conscious of such a devastating hunger. Peckish is not the word. I felt like a homeless tapeworm.

It came over me in a wave what a perfect ass I had been in my previous existence as Reginald, Lord Havershot, not to have laid in a stock of these things against some possible emergency like this. I ought to have told myself, I reflected, that you never know when you may not be going to be turned into a kid of twelve, and that, such an occurrence being always on the cards, it is simply loony not to have a little something handy in the ice-box.

I was, in fact, beginning to feel pretty censorious about my former self, for I can't stand those woollen-headed, thriftless fellows who never think of the morrow, when I was brought up short by the sound of footsteps approaching the front door.

'Reggie,' someone called.

I recognized the voice. It was that of my Cousin Egremont. I remembered that he had said he was coming to pay me a visit in order to sample my cellar, and I might have known he would not let the grass grow under his feet.

'Reggie, old bird. Are you in, Reggie?'

Well, you know how it is. There are moments when you don't want to meet people. You just don't feel in the mood. I was, as I had told Ann Bannister, extremely fond of old Eggy, and in the past – as, for example, on the occasion of that New Year's Eve party of which he had spoken – I had often been glad of his company; but now I found myself shrinking from it. I felt that he would be surprised at finding a golden-haired child where he had expected to find a carroty-haired cousin, and there would be all sorts of tedious questionings and probings, and I simply wasn't equal to it.

So, to avoid the distasteful encounter, I just slid noiselessly from the chair and ducked down behind it, hoping that when he came in and saw nobody in the room he would go away again.

A fat chance, of course. I should have known his psychology better. Eggy isn't the sort of chap who goes away from rooms in which there is Scotch whisky just because they are empty. Let the fixings be there, and he does not worry about missing hosts. He came right in and made for the sideboard like a homing pigeon. I couldn't see him, but I heard a musical plashing, then a gollup, then another musical plashing, then another gollup, then a third musical plashing, and I could read his actions like a book. He had had a couple quick, and was now preparing to have another at his leisure.

Over this one he seemed disposed to linger a bit. The first fierce thirst was slaked, and he could now dally, so to speak, and, as it were, roll the stuff round his tongue. I heard him wander across the room, and the crackle of a match and a wisp of smoke rising to the ceiling showed that he had found my cigars. A moment later, there happened what I might have known would happen. He came over to the armchair and sank into it with a luxurious whoof. It was the only comfortable chair in the room, so naturally he had made a bee-line for it.

So there we were – he plainly all set for a cosy afternoon, and I crouching up against the wall, a bally prisoner. If I had been the Naval Treaty in a safe-deposit box at the Admiralty, I couldn't have been more securely tucked away.

It was one of those situations which make a chap wrinkle the brow and wonder how to act for the best, and I was engaged in doing this when there was a knocking at the front door.

Apparently someone stood without.

9

'Come in,' called Eggy.

I couldn't see, of course, who it was who entered in response to this invitation, but from the fact that he now rose I gathered that the new arrival must be a girl of sorts. You don't get old Eggy hoisting himself out of armchairs just to greet the male sex. The voice that spoke told me I was right. It was a crisp, authoritative voice, but definitely female.

'Good afternoon,' it said.

'Good afternoon,' said Eggy.

'Are you the owner of this bungalow?'

'Oh, no.'

'You seem to be making yourself at home.'

'Oh, that's all right. It belongs to a chap called Havershot, and I'm his flesh and blood. Havershot's. He's my cousin.'

'I see.'

'And on his behalf – I feel sure he would spring to the task, if he were here – may I offer you a spot?'

'A what?'

'A snifter. I can recommend the Scotch.'

'Are you suggesting that I should drink liquor?'

'That's the idea.'

'Well, let me tell you, Mr Man—'

'—ering.'

'Pardon?'

'The name is Mannering.'

'Oh? Well, let me tell you, Mr Mannering, that I don't drink liquor. I have come here collecting subscriptions for the Temple of the New Dawn.'

'The – what was that again?'

'Haven't you ever heard of the Temple of the New Dawn?'

'Not that I remember.'

'Haven't you ever heard of Sister Lora Luella Stott?'

'No. Who is she?'

'She is the woman who is leading California out of the swamp of alcohol.'

'Good God!' I could tell by Eggy's voice that he was interested. 'Is there a swamp of alcohol in these parts? What an amazing country America is. Talk about every modern convenience. Do you mean you can simply go there and *lap*?'

'I was speaking figuratively.'

'I knew there was a catch,' said Eggy, disappointed.

'Sister Lora Luella is converting California to true temperance.'

'How perfectly frightful.'

There was a silence. From her next words, I fancied that the female must have been examining Eggy with a certain intentness, for she said:

'My! You look terrible.'

Eggy said there was no need to be personal. She said yes, there was.

'You're all twitchy, and your eyes are like a fish's. And your skin!'

'It's the best I've got,' said Eggy, a bit stiffly, it seemed to me.

'Yes, and it's the best you'll always have, so long as you go on steeping yourself in that foul stuff. Do you know what that is you're drinking?'

'White Thistle.'

'Black ruin. Shall I tell you what Sister Lora Luella Stott would do if she were here?'

'What?'

'She would dash the glass from your hand.'

'Oh?' said Eggy, and I'm not sure it wasn't 'Ho?' 'She would, would she?'

'That's what she'd do. And she would be right. Even a poor human wreck like you is worth saving.'

'Poor human wreck?'

'That was what I said.'

'Ho?' said Eggy, quite distinctly this time.

There was another silence.

'Tell me,' said Eggy at length, and there was hauteur in his voice. 'Just tell me this, Miss—'

'Prescott.'

'Just tell me this, Miss Prescott. Are you by any chance under the impression – have you allowed yourself to run away with the foolish notion – are you really such a poor judge of form as to imagine that I am stinko?'

'If by "stinko" you mean—'

'I mean stinko. Listen,' said Eggy, with a certain quiet pride. 'British Constitution. Truly rural. The Leith police dismisseth us. She stood at the door of Burgess's fish-sauce shop in Ethelbertha Street, Oswaldtwistle, welcoming him in. Now what?'

I must say I couldn't have found an answer to that, but the female did.

'Pshaw! Very educational for the kiddies, no doubt, but that doesn't mean a thing. All those silly shibboleths.'

'I can say that, too. Silly shibboleths. There. Ethelbertha Oswaldtwistle stood at the door of Burgess's fish-sauce shop, dismissing the Leith police with silly shibboleths. You hear? As clear as a bell. And you cast innuendoes on my sobriety.'

'Pshaw!' said the female, continuing. 'The mere fact that you can say all that makes it all the worse. It means that you have passed the stage where your tongue goes back on you and are headed straight for the danger-line. I know what I'm talking about. My father used to drink till he saw the light, and he prided himself on being able to say anything at any time of the day or night, no matter how swacked he might be, without tripping over a syllable. I always remember what the doctor said to him. "That's only a wayside station," the doc. said. "You're an express and you don't stop at the wayside stations. But, oh boy! Wait till you hit that terminus." '

'Terminus?'

'He meant when he would begin to see things—'

'Don't talk about seeing things!'

'—and hear voices . . .'

'And don't,' said Eggy, 'talk about hearing voices!'

'That's just what I am going to talk about. Somebody's got to do something to snap you out of it. I'm being your best friend, really. You ought to be thanking me on your knees for warning you. Yes, sir, unless you pull up mighty quick, you're slated to get yours. I know the symptoms. What made Pop see the light was meeting a pink rabbit that asked him for a match, and something like that's going to happen to you if you don't take a brace on yourself. So think it over. Well, I mustn't stay here all afternoon, talking to you. I've my subscriptions to collect. How do you feel about a small donation to the cause?'

'Pshaw!' said Eggy, rather cleverly coming back at her with her own stuff.

'Well, I wasn't counting on it,' said the female. 'But you just remember what I've told you.'

She apparently popped off at this point, for the armchair gave a scrunch as Eggy dropped into it again. I could hear him breathing heavily.

Now, during this conversation, though I had been listening attentively to every word, I suppose what they call my subconscious mind must have been putting in a lot of solid work without my knowing it. Because when I turned to my personal affairs once more, I found that my whole mental outlook had changed. I had switched completely round from my former view of things and now saw that in avoiding Eggy I had been making a strategic error.

That frightful hunger for doughnuts and the rest of the outfit was still gnawing me, and I now perceived that something constructive might be done about it. Eggy, instead of being a pest, might prove a life-saver. He wasn't a millionaire, of course, but he had a comfortable income and would surely, I felt, be good for the price of an all-day sucker, if properly approached. I rose, accordingly, with the intention of making a touch.

Mark you, I can see now, looking back, that the moment was ill-chosen. But this didn't occur to me at the time. All I was thinking about was getting the needful. And so, as I say, I rose.

The prospect whom I was planning to contact, as they call it in America, was leaning back in the armchair, still breathing in that rather stertorous manner, and my head came up just behind his. I was thus nicely placed for addressing my remarks to his left ear.

'Eggy,' I said.

I remember once, when a kid – from what motive I cannot recall, but no doubt just in a spirit of clean fun – hiding in a sort of alcove on the main staircase at Biddleford Castle and saying 'Boo!' to a butler who was coming up with a tray containing a decanter, a syphon and glasses. Biddleford is popularly supposed to be haunted by a Wailing Lady, and the first time the butler touched ground was when he came up against a tiger-skin rug in the hall two flights down. And I had always looked on this as the high spot in emotional expression until, as I have related, I rose quietly from behind the armchair and said: 'Eggy.'

The old boy's reaction wasn't quite so immediate as the butler's had been. The latter had got off the mark instantly, as if he had had the wings of a dove, but Eggy for perhaps six seconds just sat in a frozen kind of way, staring straight in front of him without moving a muscle. Then his head came slowly round, and our eyes met.

This was the point at which he really buckled down to it. It was now that after a leisurely start he showed a genuine flash of speed. One piercing scream escaped his lips, and it was still ringing in the air when I found myself alone. Despite the fact that he had been lying back in an armchair when the idea of moving occurred to him, Egremont Mannering was through the front door in – I should say – considerably under a second and a quarter. He was just a blur and a whizzing noise.

I hurried to the window and peered cautiously out. I was curious to see where the dear old chap had landed. At the rate at which he had been travelling, it seemed incredible that he could still be in California, but to my surprise there he was, only a few yards away. I suppose he must have braked very quickly.

With him was a girl in beige, and when she spoke I knew that this must be our recent caller. Presumably she had been starting to walk away, when that fearful yell had brought her back to get the news bulletin. Eggy was clutching at her arm, like a drowning man at a straw.

I must say the girl's appearance surprised me a bit. From the tone of her voice and the general trend of her conversation I had somehow got the impression of somebody of the Beulah Brinkmeyer type but she was quite pretty in, I admit, a rather austere kind of way. She looked like a vicar's daughter who plays hockey and ticks off the villagers when they want to marry their deceased wives' sisters.

'Now what?' she said.

Eggy continued to clutch at her arm.

'Woof!' he said. 'In there!'

'What's in there?'

'A ghastly imp's in there. It poked its head over the back of my chair – absolutely cheek by jowl – and said: "Eggy, old top, I've come for you, Eggy!" '

'It did.'

'You bet it did. "I've come for you, Eggy, old top," it said. Dashed familiar. I'd never met the little bounder in my life.'

'You're sure it wasn't a pink rabbit?'

'No, no, no. It was an imp. Do you think I don't know an imp when I see one?'

'What sort of imp?'

'The very worst type. I disliked it at first sight.'

The girl pursed her lips.

'Well, I warned you.'

'Yes, but how was I to know it was going to happen to me right away like that? It was the awful suddenness of the thing that jarred me. This cad of an imp just appeared. Without a word of warning.'

'What did you expect it to do? Forward a letter of introduction?'

' "I've come for you, Eggy," it said. In a sort of hideous, leering way. "Yoo-hoo, Eggy," it said. "I've come for you, old sport." What ought I to do, do you think?'

'Shall I tell you what you ought to do?'

'That's what I want to know. It said: "Pip-pip, Eggy . . ." '

'There's only one thing to do. Come with me and put yourself in Sister Lora Luella Stott's hands.'

'Is she good about imps?'

'Imps are what she's best at.'

'And has she a cellar?'

'A what?'

'Well, naturally I need a bracer. And I need it quick. It's no use my going to this Stott if she isn't likely to set 'em up.'

The girl was staring at him incredulously.

'You don't mean you're thinking of drinking liquor after what has happened?'

'I never needed a snifter more in my life. Drink liquor? Of course I'm going to drink liquor. I'm going to suck it up in a bucket.'

'You aren't going to swear off?'

It was Eggy's turn to stare incredulously. The girl had spoken as if she couldn't believe her ears, and now he spoke as if he couldn't believe his.

'Swear *off*? At a moment like this? When every nerve in my body has been wrenched from its moorings and tied in knots? What a perfectly fantastic idea! I can't understand an intelligent girl like you entertaining it. Have you overlooked the fact that all this has left me very, very shaken? My ganglions are vibrating like a jelly in a high wind. I don't believe you realize the sheer horror of the thing. "Eggy," it said, just like that, "here I am, Eggy, old bird . . ." '

She gave a sort of despairing gesture, like a vicar's daughter who has discovered Erastianism in the village.

'Well, go your own way. Act just as you please. It's your funeral.'

'I do hate that expression.'

'But when you want it – and you're going to want it pretty soon and mighty bad – remember that there is always a warm welcome waiting for you at the Temple of the New Dawn. No human flotsam and jetsam is so degraded that it cannot find a haven there.'

She walked off, leaving Eggy flat. He, after looking at the bungalow in a hesitating sort of way, as if wondering if it would be safe to go back there and have another go at the Scotch, decided that it wasn't, and tottered off over the horizon to get his bracer elsewhere. And I, having given the Cooley kid another quarter of an hour to turn up, pushed off myself. And presently, after an easy climb on to the outhouse roof, I was back in the bedroom once more feeling hollower than ever.

Only just in time, as it turned out, for scarcely had I sat down on the bed when a key turned in the lock and there was Miss Brinkmeyer.

'Have you had your sleep?' she asked.

The way this woman harped on sleep annoyed me.

'No,' I said. 'I haven't.'

'Why not?'

'I was too hungry.'

'Well, my goodness, if you were hungry, why didn't you ring the bell? I'll send you up your supper.'

She withdrew, and after a bit a footman of sorts appeared – a Filipino, apparently, by the look of him. And conceive my emotion when I observed that on the tray which he carried there was nothing but a few dry biscuits, a glass of milk, and a saucerful of foul prunes.

Well, I tried to reason with the man, pointing out the merits of chump chops and steak puddings, but all he would say was 'Excuse, yes,' and 'Very good, hullo,' and 'No, perhaps, also,' and a lot of rot like that, so eventually I dismissed him with a weary gesture. I then cleaned up the contents of the tray and sank into a reverie.

The shades of evening fell. And after they had been falling for some little while I heard footsteps coming along the corridor. A moment later the door opened and Ann Bannister came in.

10

Ann was looking marvellous. The sight of her cheerful face, to one who when the door began to open had been expecting to see the Brinkmeyer, was like manna in the wilderness. It warmed the cockles of the heart, and I don't mind telling you that they were in need of a spot of warming. Those prunes had tested me sorely.

She smiled at me like one old pal at another.

'Well, Joseph,' she said. 'How are you feeling?'

'Extremely hollow,' I replied.

'But otherwise all right?'

'Oh, quite.'

'No pain where the little toofy-peg used to be?'

'Not a bit, thanks.'

'That's good. Well, sir, you had a great send-off.'

'Eh?'

'All those newspaper boys and girls.'

'Oh, yes.'

'By the way, I gave them the stuff they wanted. It was your press agent's job, really, but he was down fussing over those Michigan Mothers, so I took it upon myself to step into the breach before they tore you asunder. I told them they might quote you as saying that the President had your full support. Was that right?'

'Oh, quite.'

'Good. I wasn't sure how you stood politically. And then they wanted to know what your views were on the future of the screen, and I said you wished to go on record as stating that in your opinion the future of the screen was safe in the hands of men like T. P. Brinkmeyer. It struck me that it wouldn't hurt giving old B. a boost. You like him, and it will please Miss Brinkmeyer – who, if you recall, has not been any too friendly since you put the Mexican horned toad in her bed.'

'What!'

'How do you mean – what?'

'I didn't put a Mexican horned toad in Miss Brinkmeyer's bed, did I?'

'Surely you haven't forgotten that? Of course you did, and very amusing it all was, though Miss Brinkmeyer, perhaps, did not laugh as heartily as some.'

I chewed the lip quite a bit. You wouldn't be far out in saying that I was appalled. I could see that in assuming the identity of this blasted child, I had walked into quite a spot. If ever there was a child with a past, he was it, and I didn't wonder that he was a shade unpopular in certain quarters. The thing that astonished me was how he had managed to escape unscathed all this time.

I had had no notion that this apparently peaceful home was, in reality, such a maelstrom of warring passions. The bally kid was plainly a regular Public Enemy, and I was not surprised that when Miss Brinkmeyer grabbed my wrist and pulled she did it with the air of one who wished it was my neck. I don't say I felt exactly in sympathy with La B., for she was not a woman who invited sympathy, but I did see her point of view. I could follow her mental processes.

'I thought it might soften her a little if you gave the old boy a build-up. You approve?'

'Oh, absolutely,' I replied. I was all for anything that would help to ease the situation in that quarter.

'Well, then they asked for a message to the people of America, and I said something about keeping up courage because Prosperity was just around the corner. Not good, but the best I could do on the spur of the moment. And "Prosperity Just Around Corner, Says Joey Cooley" won't look too bad in the headlines.'

'Far from it.'

'And then I called up the head office of the Perfecto Prune Corporation and told them that you attributed the wonderful way you had come through to the fact that you ate Perfecto Prunes at every meal.'

This hit me very hard.

'*Every* meal?'

'Well, don't you?'

'Do I?' I said, still shaken.

She raised an eyebrow.

'I can't make you out tonight, Joseph. Your manner is strange.

You seem all woozy. First you forget about putting the horned toad in Miss Brinkmeyer's bed, which was certainly last week's high spot, and now you show a shaky grip of the prune situation. I don't believe you've ever really come properly out from under that gas. The effects still linger. What you need is a good rest. You'd better hurry into bed.'

'Bed? At this time of day?'

'It's your regular time. Don't tell me you've forgotten that, too. Come along. I'll give you your bath.'

You might have expected that, after all I had gone through, I would have been hardened to shocks by this time, but such was not the case. At these frightful words the room seemed to swim about me and I gaped at her as through a mist. Although she had told me that she was Joey Cooley's governess-companion-nursemaid, it had never occurred to me that their relations were of this peculiar intimacy. My essential modesty rose in passionate revolt.

'No!' I cried.

'Don't be silly.'

'No! Never!'

'You've got to have a bath.'

'Not in your presence.'

She seemed a bit nonplussed. No doubt a situation of this tenseness had not arisen before.

'You can have your toy duck in the water.'

I waved the suggestion aside.

'It is useless to tempt me with bribes,' I said firmly. 'I will not be tubbed by you.'

'Oh, come along.'

'No, no, a thousand times no!'

Matters appeared to have reached a deadlock. She gazed at me imploringly. I met her gaze with undiminished determination. The door opened. Miss Brinkmeyer entered.

'It's time you had—'

'Now, don't you begin.'

'—your bath,' she concluded.

'That's what I've been telling him,' said Ann.

'Then why isn't he having it?'

Ann hesitated. I could see that she did not wish to make trouble for me with the big white chieftainess, and I honoured her for the kindly thought. I helped her out.

'I don't want to,' I said.

'Want to?' The Brinkmeyer came through with one of her well-known snorts. 'It isn't a question of what you want, it's a question—'

'Of modesty,' I thundered, cutting her short. 'The whole matter is one of principle. One has one's code. To a bath, *qua* bath,' I said, borrowing some of old Horace Plimsoll's stuff, 'I have no objection whatever. In fact, I should enjoy one. But when I am asked to countenance turning the thing into a sort of Babylonian orgy . . .'

The Brinkmeyer looked at Ann.

'What is he talking about?'

'I don't understand. He's funny tonight.'

'He doesn't amuse *me*.'

'Strange, I mean.'

'Nothing strange about it,' snorted the Brinkmeyer. 'That's what that fool of a dentist said. Tried to make me believe it was delirium. I told him the child was just being a pest, the way he always is. And that's what he's being now.'

I delivered my ultimatum. I was civil but adamant.

'I will take my bath, but I cross that bathroom threshold alone.'

'Yes, and splash your hand around in the water and come out pretending you've had it.'

I treated the slur with the silent contempt it deserved. I grabbed my pyjamas and nipped into the bathroom, locking the door behind me. Swift, decisive action while they're still gabbling – that's the only way to handle women. They are helpless in face of the *fait accompli*.

I fancy that the Brinkmeyer shouted a good many things, all probably in derogatory vein, through the door, but the rush of the water mercifully drowned her voice. I drew a piping-hot tub and sank into it luxuriantly. I could now hear what the Brinkmeyer was saying – something about scrubbing behind the ears – but I ignored her. One does not discuss these things with women. I found the toy duck, and it surprised me what pleasure I derived from sporting with it. And what with that and what with the soothing effects of a good long soak, I came out some twenty minutes later with my nervous system much restored. My feeling of *bien-être* was completed by the discovery that the Brinkmeyer was no longer with us. Worsted by my superior generalship, she had withdrawn, no doubt in discomfiture. Only Ann remained to tuck me up.

This she did in a motherly manner which, I confess, occasioned me some surprise. I had always been fond of Ann – indeed, as we have seen, there had been a time when I had loved her – but in my dealings with her I had been conscious right along of – I won't say a hardness exactly but a sort of bright, cocksure, stand-no-nonsense bossiness, such as so many self-supporting American girls have, and this I had always considered a defect. She had lacked that sweet, soft, tender gentleness which had so drawn me to April June. But now she might have stepped straight into that poem about 'A ministering angel, thou', and no questions asked. As I say, it surprised me.

She assembled the blankets about my person, rallying me affably as she did so.

'You are a nut, young Joseph. What's the matter with you tonight?'

'I'm all right.'

'Just one of your humorous efforts, I suppose. You're a funny old bird, aren't you? One of these days, though, if you go on joshing Miss Brinkmeyer, she'll haul off and paste you one. I'm surprised she didn't do it just now.'

These words had rather a sobering effect. I recognized their truth. Now that I looked back on the recent scene, I recalled that I had noticed her hand quiver once or twice, as if itching for the slosh.

'H'm,' I said.

'Yes, I'd be careful, if I were you. Restrain that love of fun of yours. The trouble with you, my Joseph, is that your sense of comedy is too keen. Anything for a laugh is your motto. Well, good night, old cut-up.'

'Good night.'

'Comfy?'

'Fine, thanks.'

'Better get to sleep as quick as you can. You've a busy day tomorrow.' She gave me what seemed to me a significant glance – why, I didn't know. 'Very busy, eh?'

'Oh, rather,' I said, not wishing to betray it.

'It's all fixed for tomorrow evening.'

'Oh, yes?'

'Yes. Well, good night.'

She kissed me on top of the head and pushed off, leaving me to lie there in thoughtful mood. One of the major catches of having been changed into little Joey Cooley, I perceived, was that, until I began to get the hang of things, I wasn't going to be able to understand what people were talking about half the time. A dashed nuisance, of course, but one that had to be faced.

I lay there, gazing pensively at the open window, which had turned into a dark blue oblong with a couple of stars in it. And, as I gazed, these stars suddenly disappeared. Some substantial body had inserted itself between them and me, and I could hear the slither of a leg coming over the sill.

I switched on the light. A figure was standing in the room. It was the figure of a beefy bird in a quiet grey suit, its lower limbs finished off with powder-blue socks matching the neat tie and melting, as it were, into tasteful suede shoes. In fact, to cut a long story short, the third Earl of Havershot in person.

' 'Attaboy!' said this figure in a satisfied tone of voice. 'Here we are at last.'

11

The first thing I noticed about this new and revised edition of little Joey Cooley was that he didn't appear to be at all disturbed by what had occurred. The recent switch seemed to have made little or no impression on him. He was absolutely calm and quite collected. Insouciant would about describe his demeanour. He strolled across to the bed and sat down on it as if he hadn't a care in the world.

I suppose the fact of the matter is that in Hollywood you get to learn to take the rough with the smooth, and after you've lived there for a time nothing rattles you – not even waking up and finding yourself in someone else's body. You simply say: 'Ah, someone else's body, eh? Well, well!' and carry on. His opening remarks did not deal with the switch, but with my supper menu.

'Prunes!' he said, eyeing the stones with a slight shudder. 'It would be prunes. I don't suppose there's a kid alive that's eaten more prunes than I. Well, buddy, you're welcome to them.'

And adding something in a low voice about spinach, he produced from his breast pocket a rather tired-looking ice-cream cone and flicked a bit of dust off it.

The spectacle affected me profoundly. Every fibre in my being seemed to call out for that cone.

'Hi! Give me a lick!' I cried, in a voice vibrant with emotion.

He passed it over without hesitation. If he had been Sir Philip Sidney with the wounded soldier, he couldn't have been nippier.

'Sure,' he said agreeably. 'You can have it all. It's a funny thing, but I don't seem to like ice-cream cones so much as I used to. I could eat my weight in them once, but now they don't kind of have any fascination for me. And it's the same with chocolate cake and fudge and pumpkin pie and doughnuts and—'

I cut him short with a passionate cry.

'Stop it!'

'Eh?'

'Don't mention those things. Do you think I am made of marble?'

'Oh, sorry.'

There was a silence. I finished the cone.

'Gee! You look a scream,' he said.

'So do you look a scream,' I retorted.

'I guess we both look screams,' he went on amiably. 'How do you suppose all this happened? Quite a surprise to me, it was. I woke up in the wrong room with a strange dentist pushing a glass at me and telling me to rinse, and then I found that I was somebody else, and I looked in the mirror and saw that it was you. Handed me a big laugh, that did.'

'I don't see anything funny about it.'

'Maybe you're right. But it tickled me at the time. Hello, I says to myself, there's a mistake somewhere. Have you any idea how the thing was worked?'

I advanced my theory that there had been a mix-up in the fourth dimension. He seemed to think well of it.

'Yessir, that's just about what it must have been, I guess. You never know what's going to happen to you next under this Administration, do you?'

'Well, it doesn't matter how it happened. The point is that it is all most irregular and I want to know what the dickens we're going to do about it?'

'Don't seem to me there's anything we can do about it.'

'We could issue statements.'

'What, tell people you're me and I'm you. Sure we could, if you don't mind being put in the booby-hatch.'

'You think that would be the upshot?'

'Well, wouldn't it?

'I suppose it would,' I said, having mused. 'Yes, I see what you mean.'

There was no question about it that he was right. A clear, shrewd thinker, this kid. The loony-bin is inevitably the portion of those who go about the place telling that kind of story. I saw now that it would not, as I had at one time supposed, be merely a matter of incredulity and let it go at that on the part of one's audience. Strait waistcoats would be called for and padded cells dusted off.

'Besides,' he said, 'I've no kick coming. I call this a good break for me. I like it.'

In spite of the fact that I was in his debt for that ice-cream cone, I found his manner jarring upon me not a little. A dashed sight too smug, was my verdict.

'You do, do you?'

'Sure. I've always wanted to be big, and I am big. Swell! The way I look at it, everything's jakesey-jooksey.'

My annoyance increased. His airy nonchalance gave me the pip. The young blighter appeared to have no thought except for self.

'Jakesey-jooksey, eh?'

'Jakesey-jooksey is right.'

'For you, yes.'

'Well, it's me I'm thinking about.'

'Then think about me for a bit.'

'You?'

'Yes, me. If you want to know my views, I'm extremely sick about the whole bally business. I have a very definite feeling that I have been handed the sticky end of the deal. There I was, buzzing along perfectly happily as a member of the British peerage, eating well, sleeping well, nice income from rents and so on, and just got my golf handicap down to single figures. And what ensues? All of a sudden, without being consulted, I'm changed into a child who has to look slippy in order not to be bathed by females and whose social position seems to be that of some malefactor doing a five-year stretch at Dartmoor or somewhere. Ordered hither, ordered thither . . . lugged into cars, lugged out of them . . . hauled upstairs, bunged into bed-rooms . . .'

He gave me an enquiring look.

'I see you've met the old girl.'

'I have.'

'Did she get hold of your wrist and pull?'

'She did.'

'She used to get hold of my wrist and pull. Full of energy, that dame. I think she eats a lot of yeast.'

'It isn't just energy. There was animus behind it.'

'Eh?'

'I say her actions were inspired by animus. It is patent that she hates your gizzard.'

'Well, yes, we've never been really buddies.'

'And why not?'

'I don't know.'

'I do. Because you didn't conciliate her. Because you never

bothered to exercise tact and suavity. A little more geniality on
your part, a little more of the pull-together spirit, and she might
have been a second mother to you. To take a simple instance,
did you ever bring her a red apple?'

'No.'

'You see!'

'What would I do that for?'

'To conciliate her. It's a well-known method. Ask any of the
nibs at the nearest kindergarten. It would have been the easiest
of tasks to bring her a red apple. You could have done it on
your head. Instead of which,' I said bitterly, 'you go about the
place putting Mexican horned toads in her bed.'

He blushed a little.

'Why, yes.'

'There you are.'

'But that's nothing. What's a Mexican horned toad or so
among friends?'

'Tchah!'

'I'm sorry.'

'Too late to be sorry now. You've soured her nature.'

'Well, she soured mine. All those prunes and spinach.'

'Tchah!' I said again. I was pretty shirty.

We fell into another silence. He shuffled his feet. I stared
bleakly before me.

'Well, there it is,' he said, at length. He looked at my
wrist-watch. 'Say, I guess I'll have to be moving along in a
minute. Before I go, let's get one or two things straightened
out. Havershot you said your name was, didn't you?'

'Yes.'

'How do you spell it?'

'You will find a card-case in that coat.'

He fetched out the card-case.

'Gee!' he said. 'Are you one of those English Oils?'

'I am. Or, rather, I was.'

'I always thought they were string-bean sort of guys without
any chins. That's the way they are in the pictures.'

'I used to go in for games, sports and pastimes to a goodish
extent, thus developing the thews and sinews.'

'Kind of an athlete, eh?'

'Precisely. And that's what makes me so particularly sick
about all this. Look at that arm,' I said, exhibiting it.

'What's wrong with it?'

'What's wrong with it! What future have I got with an arm like that? As far as boxing and football are concerned, it rules me out completely. While as for cricket, can I ever become a fast bowler again? I doubt if an arm like this will be capable of even slow, leg-theory stuff. It is the arm of one of Nature's long-stops. Its limit is a place somewhere down among the dregs of a house second eleven.'

'I don't know what you are talking about.'

'I'm talking about what's going to happen to me in a few years, when I go to school. Do you think I like the prospect of being a frightful little weed who will probably sing alto in the choir and for the privilege of kicking whose trouser seat the better element will fight like wolves?'

'Well, say, listen,' he rejoined hotly, 'do you think I like the prospect of going about for the rest of my life with a face like this?'

'We will not discuss my face.'

'No. Better hush it up, I guess. Golly, what a map!'

'Please!'

'Well, you started it.'

There was a rather stiff silence. We were both piqued. He looked at the watch again.

'I got to be going,' he said. 'I've a call to make down at Malibu. Got to see my press agent.'

'What for?'

'Oh, just to say hello.'

'You can't say hello to press agents looking like that.'

'Oh, yes, that's all right. He'll understand. Say, there's another thing I just thought of. Where do I go nights?'

'I beg your pardon?'

'Well, I've got to sleep somewhere, haven't I? Where were you living?'

'I told you. I have a bungalow at the Garden of the Hesperides.'

'That's all right, then. Well, anything you want to know?'

I thought for a moment. There were, of course, a hundred questions I wanted to ask, but I couldn't think of them. Then something occurred to me.

'What's all this about unveiling a statue?'

'Oh, that's just a statue of old Brinkmeyer.'

'I see.'

So they were shoving up a statue to the old boy, were they? Well, I had no objection. No doubt a thoroughly well-deserved honour. Whether a man who looked like a captive balloon was wise to allow statues of himself to be exhibited was, of course, a question to be decided by himself alone.

'Do I unveil it?'

'Of course you don't. Anything else?'

'They were saying something about some Michigan Mothers.'

'That's a deputation that's come over from Detroit. You receive them.'

'Admirers, are they?'

'That's right. The Michigan branch of the Joey Cooley Faithful Fan Club.'

'They come to pay their respects, as it were?'

'That's the idea. And you receive them.'

'Oh, well, I don't suppose I shall mind that.'

He seized the opening. It was his desire to cheer and encourage.

'Sure you won't. You aren't going to mind anything. You mustn't believe all that stuff I was telling you in the waiting-room. I was feeling kind of down, on account that tooth of mine was giving me the devil. You'll find this a pretty soft racket you've dropped into. You've got about the biggest following of anyone in pictures. Wait till you see the fan mail. And it's sort of fun acting up in front of the camera. Yessir, I think you're going to like it. Well, I must be scramming. Pleased to have met you.'

He moved to the window and shoved a leg over the sill.

'Oh, say, look,' he said, pausing. 'About Ma Brinkmeyer. I almost forgot to tell you. If you ever want another horned toad, you get it from the gardener with the squint and the wart on his nose. He's always around the place. Just tell him it's for putting in Miss Brinkmeyer's bed, and he won't charge you anything.'

He disappeared, to pop up again a moment later.

'Oh, say, look,' he said, 'there's something I ought to warn you about. I'll give you a ring tomorrow.'

I sat up, a-quiver. 'Warn me about?'

'Yay. I haven't time to tell you now, but there's something you've got to watch out for. I'll phone you in the morning.'

He disappeared once more, and I lay back, still a-quiver. I hadn't liked those last words. A sinister ring they had seemed to me to have.

However, I wasn't able to brood on them long. Nature took its toll of the tired frame. Before I knew where I was, my eyes were closing, and I was asleep. My first day as Joey Cooley had ended.

12

I suppose everybody's had the experience at one time or another of waking up after a nightmare in which they were chased by leopards or chewed by cannibals or some such thing and drawing a deep breath and saying to themselves: 'Phew! Good egg! It was a dream, after all.' A dashed agreeable sensation it is, too.

That's how it was with me next morning when, opening my eyes to another day, I reviewed the recent events. It was as if a great weight had rolled off me. For about five seconds, the relief was amazing. 'Well, well,' I felt, 'how very droll, to be sure. Positively bizarre.' And then suddenly it all went phut.

It was catching sight of the sleeve of my pyjama jacket that first made me think a bit. It so happens that in the matter of pyjamas I've always been a trifle on the choosy side. I'm not one of those fellows who just charge into a hosier's and grab anything. They have to be silk for me, and a nice lively pattern, too. And this sleeve, it would have been plain to the most vapid and irreflective observer, was constructed of some foul patent health-conserving wool. It was, moreover, a light, bilious green in colour, like my cousin Egremont at breakfast-time.

'Hullo!' I said to myself. 'What, what?'

And then I saw a beastly little hand protruding from the end of the sleeve, and the truth came home to me. I didn't have to hop out of bed and look in the glass. That half-portion of a hand told its own story. It informed me absolutely officially that what I had been kidding myself was a dream had been no dream at all. I really had become this blasted Cooley child, complete to the last button, and what I had once more to ask myself was: What would the harvest be?

The shock was so severe that I just lay there on my back, staring at the ceiling. It was as if I had walked into a right swing while boxing with the village blacksmith.

However, I was not allowed much time for chewing the bitter

cud. The kid Cooley's day apparently started early. I don't suppose I had been groaning in spirit more than about ten minutes or so when some kind of a secretary hove alongside with a fountain-pen and about a gross of photographs for me to sign. She was followed by a masseur. Then a facial rubber blew in to tune up my features. And after him a hairdresser, who attended to my curls.

And I was lying there, a bit used up, wondering whether the next item on the programme would be a chiropodist or somebody to put me through a course of rhythmical breathing, when the door opened and the butler manifested himself.

'Good morning, sir,' he said.

'Good morning,' I replied. I was glad to see him. As on the previous day, I found him consoling. The sight of that smooth, round face and spreading waistcoat had a restorative effect. 'Come in and take a seat,' I said hospitably, for I had long since become reconciled to the fact of my bedroom being a sort of meeting-place of the nations. 'Or are you just passing through?'

'I have brought your breakfast, sir.'

This had the effect of bucking me up still more, for breakfast in bed is always breakfast in bed, until he went out and reappeared with the tray, and I perceived that all it contained was milk, some stuff that looked like sawdust, and a further consignment of those blighted prunes. A nice bit of news to have to break to a stomach which had been thinking in terms of scrambled eggs and kidneys.

'Hey!' I cried.

'Sir?'

'What's all this?'

'It is your customary breakfast, sir.'

'Hell!' I said, with feeling. 'Well, all right. Better than nothing, I suppose.'

He regarded me with kindly sympathy as I dug into the sawdust.

'It's hard, sir, isn't it?'

'Pretty foul.'

'They tell me it's to keep your weight down.'

'Oh, I suppose they've got some sort of story.'

'It is what is called a balanced diet. But it is not pleasant to be compelled to abet this, if I may so describe it, Spartan regimen. I know what young gentlemen's appetites are.'

'Me, too.'

'I know just how you must feel, sir. You may be a highly important figure in the world of motion pictures, but you are only a small boy, after all, aren't you?'

'And not likely to get larger on this muck.'

'If I had my way, I'd let you eat what you wanted. You're only young once.'

'Twice.'

'Sir?'

'Nothing.'

'What you would enjoy, I dare say, would be a nice plate of sausages.'

'Please!'

'They're having them downstairs. Sausages and buckwheat cakes.'

'Would you torture me, butler?'

'No, sir, it's only that I was thinking that if you could pay me some small honorarium to compensate me for the risk of losing my place, I might contrive to smuggle some up.'

The prunes turned to ashes in my mouth. Not that it altered the taste of them much.

'I haven't any money.'

'None at all, sir?'

'Not a penny.'

He sighed.

'Well, there you are, you see. That's how it goes.'

I finished the prunes in silence, and dipped into the milk. I was musing on this matter of money. There, I saw, lay the nub of my troubles. No cash.

'Could you lend me a bit?'

'No, sir.'

I swigged milk morosely. He sighed again.

'There is a great deal of sorrow in the world, sir.'

'Quite.'

'Look at me.'

I did, pretty sharply. His words astounded me.

'Why, there's nothing wrong with you, dash it. You're all right.'

'Far from it, sir.'

'Don't talk drip, butler. I expect you breakfasted till your eyes bulged.'

'I made a hearty breakfast, yes, sir. But is breakfast everything?'

'I see what you mean. There's lunch, too. And dinner.'

'There's the heartache of the exile, sir. There's the yearning to be away from it all. There's the dull despair of living the shallow, glittering life of this tinsel town where tragedy lies hid behind a thousand false smiles.'

'Oh, is there?' I said aloofly.

I was in no mood to listen to other people's hard-luck stories. I declined to allow this butler to sob on my shoulder. He appeared to be looking to me to hold his hand and be the little mother, and I wasn't going to do it.

'I dare say you are wondering how I come to be here, sir.'

'No, I'm not.'

'It's a long story.'

'Save it for the winter evenings.'

'Very good, sir. Ah, Hollywood, Hollywood,' said the butler, who seemed not to like the place. 'Bright city of sorrows, where fame deceives and temptation lurks, where souls are shrivelled in the furnace of desire, whose streets are bathed with the shamed tears of betrayed maidens.'

'Keep it clean.'

'Hollywood! Home of mean glories and spangled wretchedness, where the deathless fire burns for the outspread wings of the guileless moth and beauty is broken on sin's cruel wheel. If you have finished with the tray, sir, I will take it.'

He popped off sombrely. And as there didn't seem to be any more callers coming – one of those slack periods which occur, no doubt, in the busiest lives – I got out of bed and donned the frilly shirt and knickerbockers and went downstairs to see how things were coming along with the Brinkmeyer family.

They had apparently been breakfasting out in the patio, for there was a white-clothed table in the middle by the goldfish pond. It bore the remains of a meal, and it was with a rush of emotion that I perceived that on a dish in the centre there was lying a derelict sausage. Sated with pleasure, these gorgers hadn't been able quite to make the grade. They had left of their abundance this admirable sausage.

The goldfish were looking up expectantly, obviously hoping for their cut, but my need was greater than theirs. I ate the unclaimed. The goldfish made faces like Leslie Henson and withdrew. And I picked up the morning paper which was lying on the table. I had a not unnatural curiosity to see what it said of yesterday's doings. As I had taken over little Joey Cooley as a going concern with all the goodwill and fixtures, his notices were my notices.

If this journal was a reliable indication of the trend of critical thought, I had had a good press. In spite of the heaviness of my heart and the emptiness of my stomach, I could not but feel gratified to see that I had practically ousted the rest of the world's news from the front page. There was the usual announcement that the President – that old Good Time Charley, bless his heart – was planning to spend another billion dollars of other people's money on something or other, but except for that the only non-Cooley item was a paragraph tucked away in the south-east corner to the effect that the unveiling of the statue of T. P. Brinkmeyer, head of the Brinkmeyer-Magnifico Motion Picture Corporation, would take place today at six p.m. on the Brinkmeyer-Magnifico lot.

I had just begun to turn the pages to see if there was further material inside, hunting absently the while among the dishes in case there might be another sausage somewhere, when Mr Brinkmeyer in person came drifting through the French windows, clad in a dressing-gown and looking more like a captive balloon than ever.

His manner, it seemed to me, was that of a captive balloon with something on its mind. His eyes had a sort of haunted look. He wandered about the patio, followed by the cord of his dressing-gown, rubbing his hands nervously.

' 'Morning,' he said.

'Good morning.'

'Nice weather.'

'Beautiful.'

He gave a sort of giggling groan.

'Well, young man, today's the day.'

'Yes,' I said. I took it that he was alluding to this statue business. 'Quite a binge it will be, no doubt.'

'And I wish it was over!'

He gave another of those groans, and I thought a word of encouragement might help. I could see that he was one of those men who shrink from public functions and beanos.

'Tails up, Brinkmeyer,' I said.

'What's that?'

'I said: "Tails up, Brinkmeyer." You mustn't be nervous.'

'But I am. You know what?'

'What?'

'She says I've got to wear my cutaway coat and a stiff collar.'

'You'll be the belle of the ball.'

'And a gardenia, she says. And spats. I shall feel like a sissy.'

He took another turn about the patio.

'Spats!' he said, looking at me piteously.

I was beginning to be a bit fed up with this business of every bally person I met wanting me to kiss the place and make it well. I liked this old buster, but I had troubles of my own.

'You could scarcely expect to turn up in sneakers and a sweater, my good fellow,' I said – rather unkindly, perhaps, but, as I say, I was annoyed.

'Yay, I know. But spats!'

'Better men than you have worn spats.'

He continued to circulate.

'You know what? Half the trouble in this world comes of people getting ambitious. They don't know when they're well off.'

'Shrewdly put, Brinkmeyer.'

This observation seemed to arrest him. He paused in his patio-prowling and gave me one of his owl-like looks.

'What's that?'

'I said: "Shrewdly put, Brinkmeyer." There is much in what you say.'

'You're talking kind of funny this morning,' he said. Then his mind seemed to skid back to what was on it. 'Listen. I got too ambitious.'

'Yes?'

'There I was, perfectly happy in the cloak and suit business, and I ought to have stuck to it. But no. Nothing would do but I had to go into the pictures. And look at me now. President of the organization, worth every cent of twenty million dollars . . .'

An idea struck me.

'You couldn't lend me a bit, could you?'

' . . . And what does it all amount to? Here I am, got to stand up there in spats, with everybody staring at me, looking like a comic valentine. I might have known it would happen. It's always the way. You get on just the least little bit in this world, and first thing you know they're putting up statues to you. The moment your back's turned. I ought to have stuck to the cloak and suit business.'

I forgot my own troubles. All this was moving me. It occurred to me how little the outside world knew of the discontent that seethed in practically every bosom you met in Hollywood. The casual observer saw these bosoms going about the place and envied them, assuming that, being well provided with the stuff, they must be happy. And all the time discontent seethed. In my own little circle, April June wanted to be a wife and mother. Joey Cooley wanted to be back in Chillicothe, Ohio, eating fried chicken, southern style. The butler wasn't any too pleased with things. And this Brinkmeyer sighed for the cloak and suit business. A bit poignant.

'Those were the days! All friends together like a lot of kids . . . Matching fabrics, joshing the buyers . . .'

I think he would have spoken further on the matter, for his manner seemed to indicate that there was much on his chest, but at this moment Miss Brinkmeyer came out of the house, and he bit back the words that were rising to his lips. He looked sheepish. I, too, as always in the presence of this female, was conscious of a certain embarrassment. We stood there shuffling our feet. It was as if we had been a couple of lads at the dear old school surprised by the headmaster while enjoying a quiet smoke in a corner of the cricket field.

'Ah, my dear,' said old Brinkmeyer, 'I was just having a chat with little Cooley here.'

'Oh?' said Miss Brinkmeyer.

She seemed to be feeling that there was no accounting for tastes. The look she gave me was austere. That horned toad evidently still rankled in all its pristine freshness. It was plain that she saw no reason to revise her opinion that I was just an off-scouring of the underworld.

'About that statue.'

'What about it?'

'Oh, we were just talking about it. Exchanging views.'

'Well, I hope he quite understands what he has to do. We don't want him muddling everything up.'

I started visibly.

'Good Lord!' I said. 'I'm not mixed up in this statue jamboree, am I?'

I was much exercised. Ever since I had ceased to be Reginald, Lord Havershot, people seemed to have been springing something new on me all the time. I wondered if any child had ever led a fuller life than this kid Cooley. Never an idle moment, I mean to say. If not doing so-and-so, busily occupied with such-and-such.

Miss Brinkmeyer threw her hands heavenwards. One noted the touch of fever.

'Well, of all the . . . Don't tell me you've forgotten, after the way you've been rehearsed in every word and move . . .'

I saw that suavity was the note.

'Oh, no, rather not. I'm pretty sure I've got the idea. But you know how it is. So many things on one's mind, don't you know. Just barely possible I may have forgotten a spot or two of the procedure. I'll tell you what. Run over the main points on the programme, and I'll see if I'm clear.'

She swallowed once or twice. Still a bit overwrought, she struck me as.

'The ceremony begins at six sharp.'

'Yes. I know that.'

'While the speeches are going on—'

'Do I make a speech?'

'No, you do *not*, and don't let me catch you trying to. While the speeches are going on, you stand at the back.'

'I can do that all right. Well within my scope.'

'After the speeches comes the unveiling. The moment Mr Hays has unveiled the statue, you run forward with the nosegay and give it to Mr Brinkmeyer.'

I frowned a quick frown.

'Did you say nosegay?'

'Nosegay was what I said.'

'Gosh!'

'For goodness' sake, it's quite simple, isn't it?'

Simple, yes. But what I was feeling was what a priceless pair of asses we should look. I mean, nosegays! And I could see that old Brinkmeyer saw eye to eye with me in this manner. He didn't like the cutaway coat. He didn't like the gardenia. He didn't like the spats. Add a golden-haired child leaping at him with nosegays, and you had something that might well make a man of retiring disposition wish he was back in the cloak and suit business.

I shot him a sympathetic glance, which seemed to be appreciated.

'And as you hand him the nosegay, you say: "Pitty f'owers for 'oo, Mithter B'inkmeyer." '

Well, that didn't seem so bad. Not a frightfully attractive layout, of course, but might have been considerably worse. I might have had to address the multitude at length. Unaccustomed though I was to public speaking, I felt pretty sure I shouldn't blow up in a short, snappy gag like that.

I nodded intelligently.

'I see. Yes, I get that. "Pretty flowers for you, Mr Brinkmeyer." '

She did the bending and stretching exercises once more. She seemed to be registering despair. Her whole demeanour was that of one unable to cope.

'For goodness gracious sake! Are you really dumb, or are you just trying to be aggravating? Haven't I told you a hundred times? Not "pretty" – "pitty". Not "flowers" – "f'owers". Not "you" – " 'oo". And not "Mr Brinkmeyer" – "Mithter B'inkmeyer". Will you please get the line right! We've had conference after conference . . . all the highest-paid authors in the organization working on the thing . . . and you go and mess it up. You say "Pitty f'owers for 'oo, Mithter B'inkmeyer." And, remember, not a syllable more. No wisecracks.'

'Right ho.'

'About my spats, for instance,' said Mr Brinkmeyer.

'Right ho.'

'And don't giggle. Smile, but not giggle.'

'Right ho.'

'And then hold it.'

'The nosegay?'

'The picture.'

This puzzled me.

'What picture? You didn't mention any picture.'

She wandered off on to a side-issue.

'Do you want a good box on the ear?'

'No.'

'Then don't try to be funny. After business with nosegay, speak the line and hold the picture.'

'She means "Don't cut",' explained Mr Brinkmeyer.

'Exactly. Hold it. Wait for the kiss.'

I shook from ringlets to toenails.

'Kiss?'

'That's where I kiss you,' said Mr Brinkmeyer, in an odd, strangled voice, like one speaking from the tomb. Behind their glasses his eyes looked hunted and haggard.

I was still quivering.

'You kiss me?'

'Of course he kisses you. Haven't you been told that over and over and over? Can't you understand plain English? He – kisses – you. It will make a very pretty and appealing picture.'

I was just seeking for words in which to make plain how little it appealed to me, when the footman who had brought me my supper on the previous evening appeared.

'Excuse yes possibly,' he said.

'Well, what is it?'

'Chap at door,' said the footman, becoming clearer.

Miss Brinkmeyer nodded.

'It must be your new elocution teacher,' she said, starting to move towards the exit. 'I think you and the child had better have a run through, Theodore. He's such a lunkhead that he probably hasn't got it even now. You can use the coffee-pot as a nosegay.'

'No need to do the kiss?' said Mr Brinkmeyer, rather pleadingly. 'Just walk the kiss, eh?'

'Certainly. I don't suppose you want to kiss the little insect more than is absolutely necessary,' said Miss Brinkmeyer, and with these offensive words took her departure. I waited till she had disappeared, then fixed Mr Brinkmeyer with a steely eye.

'Brinkmeyer,' I said, in a low, hard voice, 'was this your idea?'

He disclaimed the charge vehemently.

'Sweet suffering soup-spoons, no! Given a free hand, I wouldn't touch you with a pair of tongs.'

It was exactly how I felt.

'Same here,' I said. 'I wouldn't touch *you* with a pair of tongs.'

We gazed at each other with something like affection. Twin souls.

'How would it be if we just shook hands?' I suggested. 'Or you could pat me on the back.'

'No. I've got to kiss you. She says I must. Well, it'll all be over this time tomorrow. There's that. But I wish I'd stuck to the cloak and suit business.'

I was still much moved. I felt that the responsibility should be fixed.

'If it wasn't your idea, whose was it?'

He scowled.

'It was that press agent guy of yours – that Booch – who thought it up. He said it would mean publicity of the right sort, darn him. And Beulah said it was a great notion. Gee! I'm glad that fellow got poked in the snoot. A mystery, they call it. The mystery to me is why nobody ever thought of doing it before.'

I started. The words had touched a chord in my mind.

'Poked in the snoot? Did somebody do that to him?'

'Did they! Haven't you read the paper?'

'Not that bit.'

'Lookut!' said Mr Brinkmeyer, diving for the periodical and opening it at the middle page. His face had lost its drawn look. He had become virtually gay and practically bobbish.

I took the paper, and headlines met my eye.

As follows:

STRANGE OCCURRENCE AT MALIBU
MYSTERY FIEND SMITES TWO
'POKED US IN SNOOT,' SAY VICTIMS

The report beneath these headlines ran thus:

It will be no use Love sending a gift of roses to Cosmo Booch, noted press agent, or Dikran Marsupial, ace director, for some little time to come, because they won't be able to smell 'em. Both are home at this writing with swollen noses, the result of an encounter with what appears to have been a first-class fiend.

As Faust once remarked, there are moments when a fellow needs a fiend, but neither Cosmo Booch, ace press agent, nor Dikran Marsupial, noted director, needed this one when he descended on the former's cosy little cottage beside the sad sea waves of Malibu. They were playing checkers and did not require a third.

An Eye-witness

As to what it was all about, your correspondent has to confess himself a trifle fogged. Cosmo, questioned over the telephone at a late hour last night, was incoherent. So was Dikran. Each made odd spluttering noises, but contributed little or nothing to ye corr.'s enlightenment. Fortunately, there turns out to have been an eye-witness in the shape – if you can call it a shape – he would do well to knock off starchy foods – of George G. Frampton, well-known and popular member of the Hollywood Writers' Club.

Fiend Gives George Elbow

George G. Frampton, as all the world knows, is attached to the commercial side of the *Screen Beautiful* (ace motion-picture magazine), and it was in the course of one of his whirlwind drives for subscriptions, advertisements, or what have you that he found himself at Malibu. He was, indeed, on the point of calling upon Mr Booch to take up the matter of a half-page in the Special Number, when he was interested to find himself thrust to one side by a fiend.

Leaped Fence

George knows very few fiends, and this one, he says, was a complete stranger to him. He described him as of powerful physique and gorilla-esque features, and states that he was dressed in a quiet grey suit with suede shoes, as worn by the better class of fiend. He leaped the low fence which separates the Booch domain from the waterfront and proceeded to the porch.

In a Flash

It all happened, says George, who can turn a phrase as well as the next man, in a flash. The fiend leaped on to the porch and immediately dispelled any notion that might have been lurking in the minds of the checker players that here was a mere kibitzer who had come to breathe down the backs of their necks and offer advice, by pasting Cosmo Booch squarely on the schnozzle. And while Cosmo was calling on the Supreme Court to have this declared unconstitutional, he did precisely the same to Mr Marsupial. He then left by the front or carriage entrance.

Mentally Unbalanced?

The whole affair is wrapped in mystery. All your correspondent could get from the two victims was the statement: 'He poked us in the snoot.' They were unable to offer any explanation. They had never seen their assailant before, nor – this is our guess – do they want to see him again. All they want is something to reduce the swelling. Another facet of the mystery is – Why, if he was going to punch anybody, did not the fiend punch George G. Frampton? The fact that, being in a position to poke George in the snoot, he did not do so opens up a disquieting line of thought. Is the locality haunted by a mentally unbalanced fiend?

We are watching developments closely.

Mr Brinkmeyer, who had been reading over my shoulder, seemed a bit querulous.

'I can't see what they want to call him a fiend for,' he said. 'Why fiend? Sounds kind of a good scout to me. Stepped right up and let him have it. I'd like to meet that fellow.'

'So would I,' I said, and I meant it. I wished to get in touch with little Joey Cooley without delay, and reason with him.

For I had read this excerpt, as you may suppose, with mixed feelings. While the broad, basic fact that the man responsible for me getting kissed by the President of the Brinkmeyer-Magnifico Motion Picture Corporation had got it on the nose was far from displeasing, I could not disguise it from myself that the thing cut both ways.

However much your soul may have gone into someone else's body, you see, you can't help feeling a sort of responsibility for the body that used to be yours before someone else's soul went into it. You don't want the new tenant damaging its prestige and lowering it socially.

If this sort of thing was to continue, it seemed to me a mere question of time before the escutcheon of the Havershots would be blotted by the circumstance of the head of the family getting bunged into a dungeon cell for thirty days without the option.

I felt very strongly that this child Cooley must be talked to like a father. Some older and wiser head must buttonhole him and counsel prudence and restraint.

As I reached this conclusion, the footman entered.

'Telephone perhaps possibly,' he said.

'For me?' said Mr Brinkmeyer.

'No, thank you, please. For the young juvenile.'

'That's right,' I said. 'I was expecting a call. Lead me to the instrument.'

13

The telephone was in a sort of booth place along the hall. I closed the door carefully to ensure privacy, and flung myself on it, making eager hunting noises.

'Hullo,' I said. 'Hullo. Hullo.'

It was plain the moment he gave tongue that the child was in the pink. There was a merry ring in his voice.

'Hello? Is that you?'

'Yes.'

'This is the hundred and fiftieth Duke of Havershot.'

'Not Duke. Earl. And third, you ass.'

'Well, how's everything? Have you had breakfast?'

'Yes.'

'How were the prunes?'

'Damn the prunes!'

He chuckled fruitily.

'You'll have to learn to love them, buddy. Guess what I had for breakfast?'

'I decline to guess what you had for breakfast.'

'Well, believe me, it was good. Say, listen, have you seen the paper?'

'Yes.'

'Read about the Malibu Horror?'

'Yes.'

'Rather a good notice, I thought. Say, listen, did you ever do any boxing?'

'Yes.'

'I thought you must have. My timing was nice.'

'It was, was it?'

'Yessir. I seemed to be getting a lot of steam behind the punch. Well, I'm obliged. I got those two bozoes a couple of beauts! You'd ought to have seen it. Bam! ... Wham! ... and down they went. I near died laughing.'

It seemed to me that it was time to squelch this kid. Too

bally exuberant altogether. He appeared to be under the impression that this was the maddest, merriest day of all the glad new year – a view in which he was vastly mistaken.

I spoke with considerable acerbity.

'Well, you've gone and landed yourself in a nice posish. A dashed nice posish, I don't think.'

'Says which?'

'What the hell do you mean, says which?'

'I mean, why?'

'Do you realize that you are a fugitive from justice?'

'What of it?'

'You won't be so dashed airy when the hands of the gendarmes fall upon your shoulder and they shove you in chokey for assault on the person.'

He laughed jovially. Getting more exuberant all the time.

'Oh, that's all right.'

'You think so, do you?'

'Sure. Those two ginks had never seen me before. You never met them, did you?'

'No.'

'Well, then.'

'But suppose you run into them again.'

'They won't recognize me.'

'Of course they will.'

'No, they won't. Not after I've shaved off this moustache.'

I uttered a quavering cry.

'You aren't going to shave off my moustache?'

I spoke with feeling, for I loved the little thing. It had been my constant companion for years. I had tended it in sickness and in health, raising it with unremitting care from a sort of half-baked or Hitler smudge to its present robust and dapper condition. More like a son than a moustache it had always been to me.

He appeared to be not without decent instincts, for there was a marked touch of remorse in his voice as he replied.

'Got to,' he said regretfully. 'It's going to make all the difference.'

'It took me years to grow it.'

'I know, I know. It's a shame. Say, listen, I'll tell you what I'll do to meet you. You can cut off my curls.'

'Oh, right ho. Thanks.'

'Don't mention it.'

This gentleman's agreement concluded, he dismissed the subject and turned to one which he evidently considered of greater import.

'Well, that's that. Now I want to talk about this statue thing.'

His words brought back the bleak future that lay before me.

'Yes, by Jove. You never told me I'd got to be kissed by old Brinkmeyer.'

This seemed to amuse him. I heard him snicker.

'That's what you're worrying about, is it?'

'Of course it is.' A sudden tremor seized me. 'You don't mean there's anything else, do you?'

He snickered again. A sinister snicker.

'You betcher. You don't know the half of it. If being kissed by old Brinkmeyer was all the trouble that was ahead of you, you could go singing about the house. It's the statue.'

'Eh?'

'Yessir. That's what you want to watch out for. That statue.'

'Watch out for it?'

'Yay.'

'What do you mean?'

I put the question a bit acidly, for he seemed to me to be talking drivel, and it annoyed me. I mean, how the dickens do you watch out for a statue?

'You've got to take steps.'

'What steps?'

'Immedjut steps. You got to act promptly. What you want to do is hustle round to the studio right away . . . No, you can't go right away, because you've an elocution lesson . . . I guess you won't be able to fit it in this morning . . . But first thing this afternoon . . .'

'What on earth are you talking about?'

'I was just wondering . . . No, this afternoon's no good, either. There's those Michigan Mothers. Gee! I guess you'll just have to let it go. Too bad.'

I was conscious of a sudden qualm about those Michigan Mothers. I don't know why. Probably because the way things were being sprung on me in this new life of mine had made me suspicious of dirty work on all sides.

'Listen,' I said. 'When you say I've got to receive these bally Mothers, what do I have to do?'

'Oh, nothing. They just kiss you.'

'What!'

'That's all. But, of course, it's going to cut into your time. I don't see when you're going to be able to get at that statue, quite.'

I ignored this babble of statues. My mind was wrestling with this frightful thing.

'They *kiss* me?'

'That's right. They form a line and march past, kissing you.'

'How many of them?'

'Oh, just a handful. This is only a branch lodge. I wouldn't say there'd be more than five hundred.'

'Five hundred!'

'Six at the outside. But, as I was saying, it'll take time. I don't see how you'll be able to attend to that statue.'

'But, look here, do you mean to say I've got to be kissed by Mr Brinkmeyer *and* six hundred Michigan Mothers?'

'It's a shame, because a couple of minutes with a sponge and some carbolic or sump'n' would prob'ly fix it. Well, I guess your best plan is stout denial. After all, they can't *know* it was you. Yes, take it by and large, seems to me that's the best thing. Just good little old stout denial. I've known it to work.'

It came to me as through a mist that he was saying something.

'What's that?'

'I'm telling you. You won't have time to sponge it off, so I say – stick to stout denial.'

'Sponge what off?'

'I'm telling you. I say they can't *know* it was you.'

'Know it was me what?'

'They may suspect, but they can't be certain.'

'Certain of what?'

'It might have been anyone. Just put that to them. Get tough. Say "Why me, huh? How do you know it was me? It might have been anyone." Ask 'em to prove it.'

'Prove what?'

'I'm telling you. About this statue.'

'What about it?'

'Day before yesterday,' said this ghastly kid, at last getting down to the stark facts, 'I went and painted a red nose on it.'

You can't reel much in a small telephone-booth, but I reeled as far as the conditions would permit.

'You painted a red nose on it?'

'Yessir.'

'Why?'

'It seemed a good idea at the time.'

'But, good Lord . . .'

'Well, darn it, if there's a statue going to be unveiled and you suddenly find a pot of paint lying around on one of the sets, you don't want to waste it,' said the kid – reasoning, I had to admit, not unsoundly.

But though I could follow the psychology, it didn't make things any better for me. I was still shaken to the core.

'But what will happen when they see it?'

'Ah!'

'Hell's foundations will quiver.'

'There'll be a fuss,' he conceded. 'Yessir, there'll be a fuss, right enough. They'll start running around in circles yelling their heads off. But if you stick to stout denial you'll have 'em baffled.'

'I shall not have 'em baffled. They won't be baffled for a single ruddy instant. What's the use of stout denial? Do you think I haven't been you long enough to know that your name in this vicinity is mud? Miss Brinkmeyer will leap to the truth. She will immediately see all. A fat lot of good it will be denying it to her, stoutly or not stoutly.'

'Well, I don't see what else you can do.'

'You don't, eh?'

'No, sir, not now you haven't time to hustle along with a sponge of carbolic or sump'n'. Nothing to be done about it.'

I resented this supine attitude.

'There's a dashed lot to be done about it.'

'Such as—?'

Well, there, of course, he rather had me. Then a great idea struck me. I saw daylight.

'I'm going to get out of this.'

'What, away from it all?'

'Yes.'

'Where to?'

I felt better. The whole scheme was beginning to shape itself.

'Well, look here, you will be going back to England shortly.'

'Why?'

'Of course you will. You live there.'

'I never thought of that.'

'You've got to look after the estate.'

'Gosh! Have I got an estate?'

'Of course you've got an estate. And a social position and so on. Not to mention tenantry and what not. You'll have to be there to attend to things.'

'I couldn't do it!'

'What!'

'No, sir. I couldn't do it in a thousand years. Look after an estate, what I mean, and maybe get the Bronx cheer from all that tenantry. I shan't go near England.'

'You will. And you'll be all right, because I shall be at your side, to advise and counsel. I shall sneak away from here and join you on the boat. You'll have to adopt me or something – old Plimsoll can tell us the procedure – and then I can live with you at Biddleford and in due season go to Eton and after that to Cambridge, and run the estate for you, and eventually be the prop of your declining years. You won't have to do a thing except just loll back and watch your arteries harden.'

'That's the idea, is it?'

'And a jolly good idea.'

'I see.'

'And, of course, in order to get away, I shall require money. You must, therefore, send round immediately by bearer in a plain sealed envelope a few hundred dollars, enough to pay my fare to— Hullo! Hullo! Are you there?'

He wasn't. At the first mention of parting with the stuff he had hung up.

I came out of the booth – I might say distraught. Yes, I will say distraught, because distraught was just what I was. I could see no happy ending. Actions speak louder than words, and from the fact that this foul child had bunged the receiver back on its hook the moment we started to go into committee of supply, it was clear that he had definitely declared himself out of the financial end. He was resolved to stick to his cash like glue and not let me have a penny of it.

And cash from some source I must secure with the minimum of delay. The storm clouds were gathering. Ere long the lightning must strike. After what the kid had told me about the statue, it did not need a razorlike intelligence to show me that things were hotting up, and that flight was the only course.

To remain here would mean not only being subjected to a deluge of kisses from Mr Brinkmeyer and the Michigan Mothers – this I might, by biting the bullet and summoning up all my iron fortitude, have endured – but shame and exposure in the matter of the statue's red nose. That was the rub. For following swiftly on that shame and exposure would come the reckoning with Miss Brinkmeyer – a woman who already had been restrained from clipping me on the earhole only by the exercise of will-power beyond the ordinary. No amount of will-power could prevent her taking action now. I could not but feel that on an occasion like this it would probably run to a Grade A spanking with the back of a hair-brush.

Yes, unquestionably I had got to get the stuff.

But, equally unquestionably, there didn't appear to be a single damned source from which I could do so.

There was Eggy, of course. He, no doubt, if informed of the position of affairs, and made to understand that only a temporary loan from him stood between a fondly loved cousin and the back of Miss Brinkmeyer's hair-brush, would let me have a bit. But how was I to establish contact with him? I hadn't a notion where he was living. And my movements were so restricted that I was not in a position to go wandering from party to party till I hit on one where he was gate-crashing.

Besides, I had to have money now, immediately. In another few hours it would be too late.

It was hopeless. There was nothing to be done. It was an unpleasant conclusion to be forced to come to, but there was no getting away from it, I was stymied. I would have to stay where I was and accept what the future might bring, merely trusting that when the worst happened a telephone directory or a stout bath towel placed in the interior of my knickerbockers would do something to ease the strain.

Musing thus, I came abreast of the drawing-room. This drawing-room hadn't a door, just an archway with curtains across it. And suddenly, as I was about to pass by, from the other side of these curtains there proceeded a voice.

'Oh, yes,' it said. 'Oh, quite.'

I halted, spellbound. The speaker was Eggy.

14

I thought for a second that I must have imagined it. I mean, it seemed too good to be true that the one chap I wanted to see should have popped up out of a trap like this so exactly at the psychological moment. I couldn't have been more surprised if I had been Aladdin just after rubbing the lamp.

To make sure, I crept to the curtains and peeped through.

It was Eggy all right. He was sitting on the edge of a chair, sucking the knob of his stick. Opposite him sat Miss Brinkmeyer. Her back was towards me, but I could see Eggy's face clear enough. It was, as always at this time of day, greenish, though not unpleasantly so. He is one of those fellows with clean-cut, patrician features whom green rather suits.

Miss Brinkmeyer was speaking.

'I'm glad you agree with me,' she said, and there was an unwonted chumminess in her manner, as if she were getting together with a kindred soul. 'As a teacher of elocution, you should know.'

The mystery was solved. Putting two and two together, I was enabled to follow the run of the scenario. I remembered that Ann had told me that she had got Eggy a job. The kid Cooley had mentioned that I had an elocution lesson this morning. And when the footman had announced his arrival just now, Miss Brinkmeyer had said: 'What ho, the elocution teacher,' or words to that effect.

All quite simple, of course, and I wasn't a bit surprised to find Eggy operating in this capacity. Since the talkies came in, you can't heave a brick in Hollywood without beaning an English elocution teacher. The place is full of Britons on the make, and if they can't get jobs on the screen, they work the elocution-teaching racket. References and qualifications are not asked for. So long as you're English, you are welcomed into the home. I am told that there are English elocution teachers making good money in Hollywood who haven't even got roofs to their mouths.

'Nothing,' said Miss Brinkmeyer, continuing, 'is more important in talking pictures than a good accent. Looks, acting, personality . . . they don't mean a thing if you've got a voice like a bad dream.'

'True.'

'Like this child has. Have you ever seen him on the screen?'

'Well, no. What with one thing and another—'

'There you are. And you come from England.'

'Yes.'

'London?'

'Yes.'

'Lived there right along, I guess?'

'Oh, rather.'

'And you've never seen a Cooley picture. That's what I mean. Mr Brinkmeyer will have it that the little boll-weevil's voice is all right, because look what he grossed last time in Kansas City or wherever it may be, and all stuff like that. But what I tell Mr Brinkmeyer is that America isn't everything.'

'Quite.'

'You can't afford to neglect Great Britain and the Dominions. Look how he flops in London, I tell Mr Brinkmeyer. And now you bear me out by saying you've never so much as seen him.'

'Ah.'

'I guess pretty nearly nobody has over there, judging by the returns. And why? Because he's got an Ohio accent you could turn handsprings on.'

'Tut.'

'And what I tell Mr Brinkmeyer is that it's got to be sandpapered around the edges as soon as ever it can be, or we'll be losing out on him.'

'Quite.'

'Of course, naturally we don't want him to have one of those regular English accents. But there's a sort of in-between way of talking that goes everywhere. Like Ronald Colman and people.'

'Ah.'

'And that's what I want you to teach him.'

'Quite.'

'Of course, I don't know what your methods are. Miss Bannister just said you were the most celebrated teacher of elocution in London and had trained all the announcers of the British Broadcasting Corporation . . .'

This seemed to startle old Eggy a bit. He didn't quite swallow his stick, but very nearly.

'Did she?' he said, having drawn it to the surface again.

'Sure. She said you were particularly good at ironing out their Lancashire accents. That's what gave me the idea that you might be able to cope with this Ohio affliction this child has got.'

'Oh, quite. We must see what we can do . . . Er . . . Miss Bannister all right this morning?'

It was the first thing he had said that hadn't gone well. Miss Brinkmeyer drew herself up with a good spot of chill on. I couldn't think what she had got against Ann, but it was plain she didn't like her.

'I haven't seen Miss Bannister this morning.'

'No?'

'When I do, I shall have something to say to her.'

'Why, is anything up?'

'I would prefer not to discuss it.'

'Oh, quite.'

A bit of a lull followed. The jarring note had been struck, and it had knocked the conversation temporarily endways. Miss Brinkmeyer sat with folded arms. Eggy sucked his stick.

Miss Brinkmeyer was the first to come out of the silence.

'Well, as I was saying, I don't know what your methods are. I haven't a notion how you experts start on this kind of proposition—'

Eggy perked up.

'I'll tell you,' he said. 'Methods differ. There are various schools of thought. Some have one system, some another. I, personally, like to begin by taking a good stiff Scotch and soda—'

'What!'

'Or, better, two Scotch and sodas. This keys up the brain and puts one in the vein to instruct. So if you have Scotch in the house . . .'

'We have not.'

'Then make it rye,' said Eggy, full of resource.

Miss Brinkmeyer eyed him coldly.

'We have no liquor of any description.'

'None?'

'None.'

'Oh?' said Eggy, and I suppose that was about all a chap who had had such a setback to his dreams and visions could have been expected to say.

'Mr Brinkmeyer and I are regular attendants at the Temple of the New Dawn.'

'Oh?' said Eggy. He took another suck at his stick, as if trying to extract what poor refreshment he could from that.

'Yes. I had some little difficulty in persuading Mr Brinkmeyer to become a disciple, but eventually I succeeded, and he now sits under Sister Stott.'

Eggy removed the stick from his mouth, squared his shoulders, cleared his throat, and spoke in a firm, resonant voice.

'He sits under Sister Stott.'

'That's what I said – he sits under Sister Stott.'

'I mean, I can say it.'

'I don't understand you.'

'Pretty good, don't you think?'

'What is good?'

'Being able to say it.'

It seemed to seep through into Eggy's mind that an explanation would be in order.

'I was only thinking of something that happened yesterday. I met a girl who talked the most subversive rot. I had been rattling off things like "British constitution" and "The Leith police dismisseth us" without an effort, and she tried to make me believe that being able to say things didn't affect the issue. She scared me a bit, I confess, but today I can see through her specious arguments. Perfectly absurd, I mean, to pretend that a fellow is not absolutely all right if he can say things like "British constitution" and "The Leith police dismisseth us," not to mention such a complex and intricate sentence as "He sits under Stister Stott" . . . or, rather, he stits . . . Wait,' said Eggy, marshalling his forces. 'We mustn't allow ourselves to become confused. This is a perfectly straight, clean-cut issue. Putting the thing in a nutshell, then, he stots . . .'

He paused. A rather worried look came into his face. And then just as he was starting to have another go at it, his voice died away in a sort of whistling sigh. The stick, slipping from his nerveless grasp, clattered to the floor. He sat rigid in his chair, his Adam's apple going up and down very slowly. He had caught sight of me peering through the curtains.

I couldn't see Miss Brinkmeyer's face, but I imagine it wore an enquiring look. One of those odd looks. Her voice sounded odd.

'Is something the matter, Mr Mannering?'

The green of Eggy's face had shaded away to a delicate white. I had come through the curtains and was standing there giving him an encouraging smile. I wanted to put the old chap at his ease.

'No,' he said. 'Oh, no. No, thanks.'

'You seem unwell.'

Eggy swallowed once or twice.

'No, not a bit, thanks. Never better.'

He removed his eyes from mine with a powerful effort.

'If only it wouldn't grin!'

'Grin?'

'I can't see why it has to grin.'

'I beg your pardon?'

'Nothing,' said Eggy. 'Nothing. Only there's something so sort of ghastly and gloating about it. Pink rabbits, now, must be quite different.'

It seemed to be beginning to dawn on Miss Brinkmeyer that she had run up against something rather hot.

'Would you like a glass of water?'

'Eh? No. No, thanks.'

There was a silence.

'I say,' said Eggy, 'tell me about this Temple, will you. It attracts me. This girl I was speaking of mentioned it yesterday, and I liked the sound of it. One of these Cure establishments, is it? I mean, take the case of a fellow – let's call him A – who's been hitting it up a bit. Do you take him in and make him over?'

'That is just what they do.'

'Even if he is a bit far gone?'

'No wreck is too far gone for Sister Stott to save.'

'I have an idea I'll join up. I'm practically a teetotaller already, of course, but I've been having a bit of imp trouble lately. Nothing serious, but annoying. Where do I find this Temple?'

'It's out at Culver City.'

'Do you have to be proposed and seconded and all that?'

'You just walk in. All are welcome.'

'That's good.'

'But we haven't time to talk about that now.'

'No, no. Quite.'

'I want to warn you about this child. Be firm with him.'

'Oh, rather.'

'Stand no nonsense from him. He'll try to put something over on you if he thinks he can.'

'A tough egg, what?'

'As tough as they come. I should describe him as a kind of human hydrophobia skunk.'

I wasn't going to stand this sort of thing. Constructive criticism, yes. Vulgar abuse, no.

I stepped forward.

'I heard that remark,' I said coldly.

Miss Brinkmeyer turned.

'Oh, you're there, are you?'

'Good God!' said Eggy. 'Can you see it, too?'

'I beg your pardon?'

'Can you see an imp standing over there?'

'Imp is right. This is the Cooley child.'

'It is?'

'Certainly.'

'Phew!' said Eggy, sinking back in his chair and beginning to mop his brow.

Miss Brinkmeyer gave me one of her unpleasant looks.

'Your hair's all out of curl. Why can't you keep it tidy? This is Mr Mannering, who is going to grapple with that accent of yours. Say "How do you do, Mr Mannering." '

I was perfectly willing to meet her over so small a point.

'How do you do, Mr Mannering?' I said.

'How do you do?' said Eggy. 'I think I've met your astral body.'

'Well, you've heard him speak now,' said Miss Brinkmeyer, rising. 'I'll leave you to it. I have to see the cook. Do what you can about that voice of his. Get that Ohio twang out of it, if you have to use an axe.'

For some moments after she had gone, Eggy sat plying the handkerchief and heaving like a troubled ocean. Presently he put the handkerchief away.

'Golly, what a relief!' he said. 'You gave me a nice shock, my lad, I can tell you. You ought to do something about that astral body of yours – keep it on the chain or something. You may not know it, but yesterday it got loose somehow and came and breathed in my left ear, not only causing me alarm and despondency but putting me on an entirely wrong track and leading me to take a completely mistaken view of the state of affairs. Of course, it's all right now. I see that the whole thing . . .'

I stood wrapped in thought. Now that I had succeeded in getting him alone, I was wondering how best to approach the rather delicate matter in hand.

'I see now that the whole thing was a perfectly natural psychic phenomenon. A perfectly natural psychic phenomenon,' he repeated, as if the words did him good. 'I don't say I understand it – probably our minds are not meant to understand these things – but I expect it's happening all over the place all the time. And that girl tried to kid me that I was breaking up! It just shows how you ought never to listen to people. They mean well, but they talk rot. Do you realize that if we hadn't met like this, so that I was able to see that the whole thing was a perfectly natural psychic phenomenon, I should by this time have been a bally teetotaller? I assure you. My mind was made up. I was fully resolved to go to that Temple of whatever it is and sign on for the duration.'

I continued to muse. My position, I could see, would require careful explanation. It would be necessary, of course, to issue a statement, and this would have to be done in just the right way.

I had little doubt that in the end I would be able to get the salient data across to him. Eggy, though jumpy, is not at all a sceptical chap. To take but one instance, he believes everything the racing experts in the morning papers write. He would, I fancied, make a receptive audience.

But, of course, the preliminary *pourparlers* would have to be done just so.

His voice took on a peevish note.

'What an ass that girl was. Suppose her father did see a pink rabbit. Suppose it did ask him for a match. What of it? These things are entirely a matter of the individual. What will cause one man to see pink rabbits will have no effect whatsoever on another who is made of sterner stuff. It's a question of constitution and, I fancy, of glands. I've got a magnificent constitution and my glands are top-hole, so I have nothing to worry about. But I mustn't go gassing on like this all the morning. Probably boring you stiff. Besides, I'm supposed to teach you elocution.

'Well, I've heard your voice, laddie, and I agree with the old girl that something's got to be done about it. It wants massage or amputation or something along those lines. It's that "*ow*" that seems to be the main snag. The way you said "How do you do?" sounded like a banjo with stomach trouble. Suppose we start by treating that. Repeat this after me. "How now, brown cow ..." '

I came to a decision. It was no good beating about the bush. I must lay my cards on the table. Explanations might be necessary later, but first of all I must get straight down to what old Plimsoll calls the *res*.

'Listen,' I said, 'I've got something to say to you.'

'Exactly. "How now, brown cow." Come on, laddie, all together now. Repeat after me: "How now, brown cow, do not frown beneath the bough." '

I refused to be diverted from my purpose in order to humour him with any such drivel.

'I must begin by mentioning,' I said, 'that I am your cousin Reggie Havershot.'

Eggy had been repeating 'How now, brown cow' in an inviting and encouraging manner, but this stopped him like a bullet. He blinked several times.

'Did you say something then?' he asked, in a low, rather hollow voice.

'I said that I was your cousin Reggie Havershot. It's quite simple,' I went on reassuringly. 'My soul got into the wrong body.'

There was silence for a moment. He seemed to be drinking it in. Then, just as I thought he had begun to grasp the gist, he heaved a long, shuddering sort of sigh and with a gesture of sad resignation stooped and picked up his hat and stick.

'This is the end,' he said. 'I give up. If anyone asks for me, I shall be at the Temple of the New Dawn. Address letters care of Sister Stott.'

He passed through the curtains with bowed head.

'Hi! Wait a minute!' I cried and, legging it after him, collided with some solid body. For an instant everything went black, and it was not long before I discovered the reason for this. I was standing with my face embedded in a human stomach.

I backed a bit, and looked up. It was the butler in whose midriff I had been parking myself.

15

'Oof!' he said, massaging the wound.

'Woof!'

Had I been my usual courteous self, I should no doubt have paused to apologize and condole, for there was no question that I had caught the man a stinker. His face was a vivid mauve and his gooseberry eyes were watering freely. But I had no time now for doing the civil thing to butlers. I wanted to overtake Eggy and go on with my statement.

With this end in view, I hared for the front door, only to find he was nowhere in sight. He had gone, leaving not a rack behind.

It was in sombre mood that I returned to the hall. The butler was still there, looking somewhat restored. The purple flush had left his face, and he had ceased to knead his waistcoat. He was leaning against the wall, puffing gently. Nature and a robust constitution had apparently pulled him through.

I gave him a bleak look. I found it hard to forgive him for his untimely intrusion. But for encountering him in the fairway, I should have been able to resume my chat with Eggy, amplifying the statement I had made with corroborative detail, as old Plimsoll would say. And owing to being delayed, I had lost him. He had vanished beyond recall, like the dew off a rose. Blast all butting-in butlers was the way I felt about it.

'Sir,' said this one, as I floated by.

I gave him another bleak look. His conversation was the last thing I desired. I wanted to brood.

'Might I have a word with you, sir?'

I went on floating by.

'I have had an idea, sir. With reference to the matter we were speaking of over your breakfast-tray.'

I continued to pass along.

'This matter of money, sir.'

This checked me. No other word in the language would have done it. I stopped, looked, and listened.

'You mean you've thought of a way by which I can collect a bit of capital?'

'Yes, sir. I fancy I have found the solution to our problem.'

I goggled. He did not look a remarkably intelligent man. And yet, if credence was to be given to his words, he had succeeded where many a fine thinker would have failed.

'You have?'

'Yes, sir.'

'You mean that on reflection you can advance me a trifle?'

'No, sir.'

'Then what *do* you mean?'

He became a bit conspiratorial. He looked this way, and he looked that. He peeped into the drawing-room and he peered up the stairs.

'It came to me as I was cleaning the silver, sir.'

'What did?'

'This idea, sir. I have often found that my brain is at its nimblest when I am cleaning the silver. It is as though the regular rhythmical motion assisted thought. His lordship frequently used to say—'

'Never mind about his lordship. What's your idea?'

He repeated the Secret Society stuff. 'Are we alone and unobserved?' his manner seemed to say. He lowered his voice to a whisper.

'The tooth, sir!'

I did not follow him. 'What's the truth?'

'Not truth, sir – tooth, sir.'

'Tooth?'

'Yes, sir. What crossed my mind, as I cleaned the silver, was the tooth. It came to me all of a sudden.'

I could make nothing of this. His words were the words of a plastered butler. But surely no butler could be plastered at so early an hour as this. Even Eggy hardly ever was.

'Whose tooth?'

'Yours, sir.' A look of anxiety came into his face. 'You have the tooth, sir?'

I continued to grope. 'I had a tooth out yesterday.'

'Yes, sir. That's the one I mean. Did the dentist give it to you, sir?'

'How do you mean, give it to me? He took it from me.'

'Yes, sir, but when I was a small lad and had a tooth extracted the dentist would always give it to me to keep among my knick-knacks. And I was hoping—'

I shook my head.

'No. Nothing of that sort oc—' I paused. A sudden recollection had come to me. 'Yes, he did, by Jove. I've got it here in a cardboard box.'

I felt in my pocket, and pulled the thing out. The butler uttered an ecstatic 'Ha!'

'Then all is well, sir,' he said in a relieved voice, like a butler who has had a weight taken off his mind.

I still didn't get it. 'Why?'

He became the Black Hander once more. He looked this way and he looked that. He peeped hither and peered thither. Then he lowered his voice to such a whisper that I couldn't hear a damn' word.

'Speak up,' I said sharply.

He stooped and placed his lips to my ear.

'There's gold in that thar tooth!'

'Gold? Filling, do you mean?'

'Money, sir.'

'What!'

'Yes, sir. That was what suddenly came to me as I was cleaning the silver. One moment, my mind was a blank, as you might say. The next, I'd got it. I was polishing the cup Mr Brinkmeyer won in the Motion Picture Magnates' Annual Golf Tournament at the time, and it just fell from my hands. "Puncture my vitals!" I said . . .'

'Eh?'

' "Puncture my vitals", sir. It was a favourite expression of his lordship's in moments of excitement. "Puncture my vitals!" I said. "The tooth!" '

'Meaning what?'

'Think sir, think! Reflect what a position you hold in the public esteem, sir. You are the Idol of American Motherhood. And the fans are inordinately desirous of obtaining souvenirs of their favourites, I can assure you. I have known large sums to change hands for one of Mr Fred Astaire's trouser buttons, very large sums indeed. And the human appeal of a trouser button cannot be compared with that of a tooth.'

I quivered. I had got his meaning at last.

'You think this tooth could be sold?'

'Over the counter, sir, over the counter.'

I quivered again. The man was beginning to inflame me.

'Who would buy it?'

'Anybody, sir. Any of the big collectors. But that would take time. My idea would be to approach one of these motion-picture magazines. The *Screen Beautiful* suggests itself. I should be vastly surprised if they didn't give two thousand dollars for it!'

'What!'

'Yes, sir, and they'd get their money back a dozen times over.'

'They would?'

'Certainly they would, sir. What would happen is, they'd run a competition for their readers. A dollar to enter the contest and the Cooley tooth to go to whoever did whatever it was – like it might be naming the twelve most popular stars in their correct order, or something like that.'

My head was buzzing. I felt as if I had backed an outsider in the Grand National and seen it skip over the last fence three lengths in front of the field.

'Two thousand dollars?'

'More, sir. Five, if you had a good agent.'

'Do you know a good agent?'

'What I would suggest, sir, is that you employed me to handle the deal for you.'

'Would you?'

'I should be proud and happy to do so, sir. For the customary agent's commission.'

'What would that be?'

'Fifty per cent, sir.'

'Fifty? I know an author whose agent sells his stuff for ten.'

'Literary productions, yes, sir, but not teeth. Teeth come higher.'

'Fifty's much too much. Dash it, it's my tooth.'

'But you are not in a position to trade.'

'I know, but—'

'You need somebody who knows how to talk terms.'

'Do you know how to talk terms?'

He laughed indulgently.

'You would not ask that, sir, if you had ever seen me negotiating for my commission with the local tradesmen.'

I stood musing. The conversation might have reached a deadlock, had he not made a gesture.

'Well, well, sir, we will not haggle. Shall we say twenty?'

This seemed more reasonable.

'Right ho.'

'Though twenty per cent on the transaction will not make me a rich man. However, it shall be as you say. Might I have the box, sir, and perhaps a line in your handwriting, guaranteeing authenticity. These magazine editors have become very suspicious of late, ever since *Film Fancies* was took in by a Clark Gable undervest which proved to be spurious. I have a fountain-pen, sir. Perhaps you would just write a few words on the box.'

'Something like "Authorized tooth of J. Cooley. None other is genuine"?'

'That would do admirably, sir. Thank you, sir. Thank you, sir. I will take it to the magazine office directly luncheon is concluded. Until then I fear that my official duties will confine me to the premises.'

Some hours later, I was pacing beside the swimming-pool, humming a gay air. Luncheon was over. So were my troubles. The future, once so dark, seemed bathed in a golden glow.

The smooth, efficient way in which this excellent butler had taken charge was enough to show me that I could have placed my affairs in no better hands. He might have been selling teeth on commission all his life. He had rung up the *Screen Beautiful*, arranged for an interview, settled that the money, when a figure had been arrived at, was to be paid in small bills, and had gone off to the office to close the deal.

I had had a rotten lunch, at which the spinach *motif* had been almost farcically stressed, but despite the aching void within me I felt a new child. I was all buoyancy and optimism. Even if this butler proved to be less of a spell-binder than I took him to be and only managed to get a couple of thousand, that would be ample for my purpose. And something in his calm, purposeful face and quiet, confident manner seemed to tell me that he would extract the top price.

And so, as I say, I hummed a gay air, and would no doubt have continued to hum it for some little time, had not my attention been attracted by an intermittent low whistling which appeared to proceed from a clump of bushes across the lawn. I supposed, at first, that it was merely some local bird doing its stuff, but a few moments later a female voice spoke.

'Hey! Joseph!'

Ann's voice. I went across to see what she wanted.

16

The bushes were so thick that I couldn't see her at first. Then her face came into view and I noted that she, like the recent butler, had gone all conspiratorial. One of her eyes was closed in a significant wink, and attached to her lips was a finger. She was also wiggling her nose warningly, and when she spoke, it was in a croupy whisper.

'S'h!' she said.

'Eh?'

'Secrecy and silence!'

'How do you mean?'

'Where's Miss Brinkmeyer?'

'I don't know. Why?'

'There is dark work afoot, young Joseph. Speak low, for the very walls have ears. I've got a pork pie for you.'

'What!'

I don't know when I've been so profoundly moved. At that moment, my devotion to April June very nearly transferred itself to this girl before me. It was as if I were getting on to her hidden depths for the first time. I spoke in a trembling voice.

'You've got it on you?'

'It's in the house.'

'What size pork pie?'

'A big one.'

'Gosh!'

'Not so loud. Are you sure Miss Brinkmeyer's nowhere around?'

'I haven't seen her.'

'I'll bet she pops up . . . There!'

From the direction of the house there had come a rasping voice, and, turning, I perceived the neighbourhood curse hanging out of an upstairs window. She was regarding me in a nosey and offensive manner.

'What are you doing there?' she asked, plainly of the opinion that whatever it might be it was something I ought not to be doing. Even at this distance one sensed the lack of trust and simple faith.

It was a moment for swift and constructive thought.

'I am watching a beetle,' I said.

'A what?'

'There is a beetle here. I am watching it.'

'You are not to bring beetles into the house.'

I raised my eyebrows. Wasted on her at that range, of course.

'It is not my intention to bring it into the house. I am merely observing its habits.'

'Oh? Well, don't get yourself all mussed up.'

She disappeared, and Ann bobbed up once more like a wood-nymph.

'You see. Your every movement is watched. Conveying pork pies to you, young Joseph, is like carrying despatches through the enemy's lines. I was going to tell you to slip in here and await my return, but it isn't safe. I forgot she could see us from her bedroom window. I'll tell you what. Stroll casually along and nip into the bathing-hut. I'll join you there!'

It was, as may be supposed, with no little chagrin that I walked off. Every minute that separated me from that pie was like an hour. I made for the bathing-hut, chafing.

There was a gardener inside, cleaning it out with a mop.

'Good afternoon, sir,' he said.

The purity of his enunciation surprised me a bit, for he looked Japanese and I should have expected something that sounded more like a buffalo pulling its foot out of a swamp. However, I was not at leisure to go into this, for I wanted to get him out of here with the greatest possible despatch.

'Are you going to be long?' I said.

'You wish to sit in this hut, sir?'

'Yes.'

'I have just finished. There, I think that will do.'

He did a couple of dabs with his mop and came out. As he passed me, I saw that he had a squint and a wart on his nose, and I divined that this must be the man of whom Joey Cooley had spoken. I felt very much inclined to take up the matter of horned toads with him. The window from which Miss Brinkmeyer had spoken was next but one to my bedroom, numbering off from the right, so that I now knew where to go in order to deposit horned toads where they would do most good. And after the way she had butted in just now, upsetting my schemes, she needed a sharp lesson.

However, I resisted the urge, and went into the hut. And presently Ann appeared.

I sprang to my feet eagerly, but my dreams were not yet to come true. All she was carrying was what Miss Brinkmeyer would have called a nosegay of roses. I stared at it dully.

'I'm sorry,' said Ann, noting my perturbation and reading its cause aright. 'You'll have to wait a little longer. I was just coming out of the hall, when Miss Brinkmeyer came downstairs. I had to cache the stuff hurriedly in an Oriental vase. I'll get it as soon as the coast's clear, so don't look so shattered.'

I tried not to look shattered, but the disappointment had been severe and it was difficult to wear the mask.

'And, anyway, here's something that will make you laugh,' said Ann. 'You see these roses. Who do you think sent them?'

I shrugged my shoulders moodily. It did not seem to me to matter who had sent them. Roses as a substitute for pork pie left me very tepid.

'Who?'

'April June.'

My lethargy slipped from me like a garment.

'What!'

'Yes. I thought that would hand you a giggle.'

It hadn't handed me a giggle at all. She had got the wrong angle entirely. I was profoundly touched. The thought of April June finding time in the midst of her busy life to send flowers to a sick – or tolerably sick – child made me glow all over. It even made me forget the hunger that gnawed me.

There seemed to me something so beautifully characteristic about the kindly act. That gentle heart, I felt, had functioned so absolutely in accordance with the form book. All the old devotion came sweeping back over me.

'Yes, she has sent you roses. Conscience, I suppose.'

'Conscience?' I said coldly, for she had spoken in a nasty dry way which I didn't at all like. I found myself eyeing her askance. The warmth of emotion which her offer of a pork pie had aroused in me was fading. I began to feel that I had been wrong about her hidden depths. A shallow girl, I now considered. 'Conscience?' I said. 'What do you mean?'

'I suppose she felt she owed you something, after horning in on your big scene like that and trying to steal your publicity the way she did. I'm sure I don't know what that girl needs a press agent for. There isn't one in the business who can teach her anything about sneaking the spotlight.'

'I don't understand you.'

She laughed.

'Hasn't anyone told you about that? Yesterday, when you were under the gas, the door suddenly burst open and April June rushed in. "Where is my little pal?" she cried, clasping her hands and acting all over the lot. "I want my little pal" – directing, as she spoke, a meaning glance at the newspaper boys, who snapped her in six positions – including bending over you and kissing your unconscious brow. Somebody then led her gently away, shaking with sobs. Oh, horse-feathers!'

I gave her another cold look. The expression which she had used was new to me, but one could gather its trend. Her ribald and offensive tone jarred upon me indescribably.

'I consider her behaviour little short of angelic,' I said.

'What!'

'Certainly. There is no other word for it. How many girls in her position would have bothered to take time off in order to come and kiss brows?'

She stared. 'Are you trying to kid me?'

'I am not.'

'You mean you really don't think April June is a pill?'

The first time I had heard this monstrous word applied to the woman I loved – by Joey Cooley over the *National Geographic Magazine* – I had, it will be remembered, choked down my indignation and extended the olive branch. But now I was in no mood to overlook the slur.

'That is quite enough,' I said. 'Either cease to speak derogatorily of that divine woman, or leave my presence.'

She was plainly piqued. A sudden flush mantled her cheek. I could see that she burned, not with shame and remorse, but with resentment.

'Oh?' she said. 'Well, if that's the way you feel about it . . . all right, then. Goodbye.'

'Goodbye.'

'And not a bit of that pork pie do you get. No, sir, not a sniff of it.'

I confess that I wavered. The thrust was a keen one. But I was strong. I waved a hand nonchalantly – or as nonchalantly as I could.

'That is entirely your affair,' I said in a reserved manner.

She paused at the door. Her bearing betrayed irresolution. Her better self, it appeared, was not wholly dead.

'You'd like that pie.'

I vouchsafed no answer.

'And you know you think her a pill. You've told me so yourself.'

'I would prefer not to discuss the matter.'

'Oh, very well.'

She was gone. I sat there, brooding.

My thoughts were very bitter. Now that I was at leisure to devote myself to concentrating on it exclusively once more, I realized all that that pork pie had meant to me. My whole policy was wrapped up in it. And the reflection that April June would never know what I had given up for her sake stung like a serpent's tooth.

Presently I rose and wandered out into the sunshine, tightening my belt in the hope of dulling the ache within me. I walked at random, too *distrait* to care where I was going, until an unwonted softness in the terrain caused me to look down, and I saw that I had strayed off the path on to a border, beyond which was the low wall which encircled the Brinkmeyer estate. And I was about to put myself into reverse, for I had little doubt that one got hell in this establishment for trampling on the flower-beds, when I was arrested by the sight of a head. It shot up over the wall and said 'Yah!' The apparition was so unexpected that I halted in my tracks and stood staring.

It was a red head, whose roundness and outstanding ears gave it a resemblance to one of those antique vases with handles on each side, and it belonged to a tough-looking boy with green eyes and spots on his face. He was eyeing me in a manner unmistakably hostile.

'Yah!' he said.

The lad was a complete stranger to me. But then, so was almost everybody else I met in this new world of mine. To Joey Cooley, I presumed, he would have been well known. From his aspect and tone of voice I deduced that this must be someone whom my predecessor had at one time or another offended by word or act.

My silence seemed to spur him on to further flights.

'Yah!' he said. 'Little Lord Fauntleroy!'

I was conscious of a rising resentment. At the outset, I had no views about this young blister one way or the other, but now there was beginning to burgeon within me a very definite feeling that what he wanted was a good sock on the jaw. That epithet 'Little Lord Fauntleroy' had pierced the armour and struck home. Ever since my awakening in the chair of B. K. Burwash, those golden ringlets had been my hidden shame. And I have no doubt, so stirred was I, that I should have leaped the wall and attacked him with tooth and claw, had not I been brought up short by the sight of that miserably inadequate hand which had so depressed me earlier in the day. To try to sock anybody on the jaw with a hand like that would have been just labour chucked away. With a sigh, I realized that a pitched battle was out of the question.

I was obliged to fall back on words.

'Yah!' I said, feeling that there was no copyright in that very effective ejaculation. It wasn't too bright, of course, but it was something.

'Yah!' he replied.

'Yah!' I came back, as quick as a flash.

'Yah!' he riposted. 'Sissy! Pansy! Cake-eater!'

I began to fear that he was getting the better of the exchanges.

'Curly-top! You look like a girl.'

A happy recollection came to me of something which Barmy Fotheringay-Phipps of the Drones had once said to Oofy Prosser in my presence, on the occasion of Oofy declining to lend him ten bob till next Wednesday. It had made Oofy, I recalled, as shirty as dammit.

'You look like a spotted dog,' I said.

It was the right note. He winced and turned vermilion. I suppose a profusely spotted chap dislikes having it drawn to his attention what a profusely spotted chap he is.

'Come on out here,' he cried. 'I dare you.'

I did not reply. I was feeling my arm, to see if, after all, something could not be done about this. But the forearm was like a match-stick and the biceps like a pimple. Hopeless.

'I dare you! I double dare you!'

Suddenly, out of a clear sky, the solution came to me. I have said that I was standing on a flower-bed. This flower-bed, I now perceived, was adorned by a small tree, on which the genial California sun had brought out a great profusion of hard, nobbly oranges. It altered the whole aspect of affairs. Say it with oranges! The very thing.

To pluck one and let fly was with me the work of an instant. And conceive my gratification on discovering that Joey Cooley, whatever his shortcomings in the matter of physique, was an extraordinarily fine shot with an orange. David, having his unpleasantness with Goliath, could not have made better target practice. My missile took the lad squarely on the tip of the nose and before he could recover from his natural surprise and consternation I had copped him again no less than thrice – one on the left eye, one on the right eye, and one on the chin, in the order named. I then plucked more fruit and resumed the barrage.

The thing was a walkover. It was the old story. Brains tell. The untutored savage jumps about howling threats and calling for dirty work at close quarters, and the canny scion of a more enlightened race just stays away and lets him have it at long range with his artillery, causing him to look a bit of an ass.

This red-headed stripling looked more than a bit of an ass. He stuck it out for another half-dozen oranges, and then decided to yield to my superior generalship. He legged it, and I got him on the back of the neck with a final effort.

Final, because as I poised myself for another pop my arm was gripped by an iron hand, and I found myself whirling in the air like a trout fly.

'For goodness gracious sake!' said Miss Brinkmeyer, seeming not a little moved. 'Can't I take my eye off you for a single minute without your being up to some fool game? You've ruined my orange tree.'

I had not much breath with which to make a reasoned defence, and I think she did not hear what I said about military necessity. She lugged me to the house.

'You get off to your room this instant,' she said, among a number of other remarks of a deleterious nature, 'and don't you dare to leave it till it's time to go to the studio.'

I could not but feel that it was a poorish sort of homecoming for one who had conducted himself with such notable resource in a difficult situation and achieved so signal a victory, but there was nothing to be accomplished by arguing the point. It was evident that she would not be a good listener. I permitted her, therefore, to escort me to my room, and she went off, banging the door. I lay down on the bed and gave myself up to thought.

I speculated as to the identity of the spotted lad, and wondered what was the source of his obvious distaste for Joey Cooley. Knowing Joey Cooley, I imagined that this measles case probably had a good deal of right on his side, but all the same I was glad that I had put it across him. My pride was involved. There are some remarks which one does not forgive, and if you have been forced to assume the identity of a kid with golden ringlets, 'Little Lord Fauntleroy' is one of them.

But it was only for a brief space that I was able to relive the recent scene and glory in my prowess. Abruptly, as if a button had been pressed, that agonizing desire for food began to assert itself once more.

I was still wrestling with it, when I heard footsteps outside the door and Ann came in.

'Here you are, you little mutt,' she said. 'I hadn't the heart to hold out on you.'

She thrust something into my hand. It was a large, succulent pork pie.

I had nothing to say. In these supreme moments one hasn't. I just raised the thing to my lips and dug my teeth into it.

And, as I did so, the door burst open, and there was Miss Brinkmeyer, looking like Lady Macbeth at her worst.

'Just as I suspected!' she cried. 'I knew someone was bootlegging the stuff to him, and I had an idea it was you all the time. Miss Bannister, you're fired!'

I stood at the crossroads. Two alternatives presented themselves before me. I could stop eating and plead for Ann with all the eloquence at my disposal, or I could keep on pitching in, so as to wolf as much as possible before the pie was wrested from my grasp.

I chose the nobler course. I pleaded.

Not a damn' bit of use, of course. I might just as well have remained silent and devoted my energies to getting mine while the going was good. The verdict was in, and there was no appeal. Acting from the kindliest motives, my benefactor had got the boot.

I was told to be quiet. I was shaken. I was de-pied. Ann popped off. The Brinkmeyer popped off. I was alone.

With a moody oath, I began to pace the floor. This took me near the window. Being near the window, I glanced out of it. And there, snipping a bush that stood beside the outhouse, was the gardener with the squint and the wart on his nose.

I paused. The sight of him had opened up a new line of thought.

A moment later, I was on the outhouse roof, attracting his attention with a guarded 'Hoy!'

17

The line of thought which the sight of this squint-cum-warted gardener had opened up was, briefly, as follows. I had Joey Cooley's assurance that the honest fellow had Mexican horned toads in his possession, and was prepared to supply them gratis with no cover charge, provided that their destination was Miss Brinkmeyer's bed. And what had suddenly occurred to me, as these ideas do, was that there was no reason now why I should not avail myself of his services.

There could be no question that La Brinkmeyer badly needed a horned toad in her bed. If ever a woman had asked for one, she was that woman. And it now struck me that the only objection to allotting her one – the fear of an aftermath or bitter reckoning – had been removed. That whole aspect of the matter could be dismissed, because when the storm burst I shouldn't be there. As soon as the butler returned with the cash and put me in funds, I proposed to absent myself. Establishing contact with the reptile, therefore, and grabbing her hair-brush and hastening to get in touch with me, Miss Brinkmeyer would find that my room was empty and my bed had not been slept in.

So I nipped on to the outhouse roof and called 'Hoy!' and the gardener came civilly up to ascertain my wishes.

I found that by lying on my stomach and shoving my head out I was able to conduct the conversation in a cautious undertone.

I came to the point at once. It was no time for beating about the bush.

'I say,' I said. 'I want a horned toad.'

He seemed interested.

'For the usual purpose?'

'Yes.'

'You desire quick delivery?'

'Immediate.'

He sighed.

'I am sorry to say I am all out of horned toads at the moment.'

'Oh, dash it.'

'I could do you frogs,' he said, on a more hopeful note.

I considered this.

'Yes, frogs will be all right. If slithery.'

'The ones I have are very slithery. If you will wait, I will fetch them at once.'

He went off, to return a few minutes later with a covered basket, which he handed up to me, saying that he would be glad if I would let him have it back when I had finished with it, as it was the one in which one of his colleagues kept his lunch. I reassured him on this point, and sped off to do the necessary.

The discovery of Miss Brinkmeyer's gala costume laid out on the bed in her room, ready to be assumed for the evening's binge, caused me to make some slight alteration in my plans. I placed a frog in each boot and distributed the remainder among the various objects of lingerie. It seemed to me that the moral effect of this would be greater than if I inserted them between the sheets.

The gardener was waiting below when I reached the roof again. He said he hoped that all had gone well, and once more I was struck by the purity of his diction, so out of keeping with his Japanese exterior.

'You speak extraordinarily good English,' I said.

He seemed gratified by the tribute.

'Very kind of you to say so, I'm sure,' he replied with the suggestion of a simper. 'I fancy, however, that you are labouring under a slight misapprehension. You have probably been led by my make-up into supposing that I am of foreign extraction. This is not the case.'

'Aren't you a Jap?'

'Externally only. I came here in this rude disguise in the hope of attracting Mr Brinkmeyer's notice. Once on the spot, you see, there is always the possibility of being able to catch the boss's eye. B-M have a Japanese picture scheduled for production, and I am hoping for a small role.'

'Oh, I see.' I had been in Hollywood long enough to know that very few things there are what they appear to be. 'You're an actor?'

'I play character parts. And I am hoping that an occasion may arise which will enable me to run off some little scena which will impress Mr Brinkmeyer. But I realize now that I would have done better to join the indoor staff. They are in so much closer contact with Mr Brinkmeyer. I particularly envy Chaffinch.'

'Chaffinch?'

'The butler. He is very fortunately situated.'

'But he's not an actor?'

'Oh, yes, indeed. Virtually all the domestic staffs of the big motion-picture magnates are composed of character actors. It is the only way we can get at them. It is perfectly useless going to these casting offices. They just take your name, and there is an end of it. That's the trouble with Hollywood. The system is wrong.'

I was amazed.

'Well, I'm blowed! He took me in.'

'I expect so.'

'I could have sworn he was genuine. That stomach. Those bulging eyes.'

'Yes, he is quite the type.'

'And he talked about serving with his lordship and all that.'

'Atmosphere. He is a most conscientious artist.'

'Well, I'm— Golly!' I said, breaking off abruptly. A sudden frightful thought had come to me. 'Here, take this basket. I've got to make a phone call.'

I buzzed off and dashed down to the telephone-booth in the hall. It was no moment for speculating as to what I should say if Miss Brinkmeyer caught me at the instrument. I was a-twitter with apprehension, and I'll tell you why.

In entrusting to this Chaffinch the negotiations in the matter of the tooth, my whole policy had been based on the belief that he was the butler he pretended to be. The honesty of butlers is a byword. There is no class of the community more trustworthy. A real butler would perish rather than stoop to anything which might even remotely be described as funny business.

My acquaintance with actors of the minor type, on the other hand, had left me with a rooted conviction that they are hot. I may be prejudiced, allowing my outlook to be coloured by the fact that during my University days a member of the cast of *His Forgotten Bride*, playing the small towns, once took five quid off me in a pub at Newmarket at a game which he called Persian Monarchs, but that is how I feel. Ever since that occasion, I have said to myself: 'Reginald, avoid actors. They are mustard.'

And so, as I searched through the telephone directory for the number of the *Screen Beautiful*, nameless fears surged in my bosom. For the first time, it had struck me like a blow from a stuffed eel-skin that if this bally *Screen Beautiful* was housed within anything like a reasonable distance, Chaffinch should long since have returned from his mission. I had seen him start off directly after lunch, and it was now well past four o'clock.

And it wasn't as if he had walked. With my own eyes I had beheld him get into a taxi.

I found the number, and the awed manner in which my name was received at the office switchboard might have gratified me, had the circumstances been other than what they were. But this, unfortunately, they were jolly well not. Respect was no good to me. I wanted reassurance.

But I didn't get it. Two minutes later, the blow had fallen and I knew the worst. I was informed by the editor in person that five thousand dollars in small bills had been handed to my agent more than an hour and a half ago. And when, endeavouring to control my voice, which showed a disposition to wobble all over the scale, I asked how long it would take to do the point-to-point trip in a fleet taxi, I was told ten minutes. It was then, cutting short some rot at the other end about illustrated interviews and personal messages, that I hung up the receiver.

There was no possibility of mistake. The facts were plain. My innocence had been taken advantage of. Trusting blindly to this blighted Chaffinch, I had been done down, double-crossed and horn-swoggled. No doubt this fiend in butler's shape was even now on his way east with the stuff in his jeans, gone beyond recall.

I had certainly not had good luck with this telephone-booth. Twice only had I entered it, and on both occasions I had come out distraught. I had writhed in agony the first time, and I writhed in agony now. The thought that there was no cash coming to me and that I must abandon my dreams of escape into a wider, freer world made me stagger like Eggy on his birthday.

And then, creeping softly into my mind, there came another thought. Madly confident of being able to make a speedy getaway from the danger zone, I had filled Miss Brinkmeyer's bedroom with frogs.

I wasted no more time in fruitless regret. I had come down those stairs pretty quick. I went up them even quicker. Unless

these frogs were gathered and removed with all possible despatch, the imagination boggled at the thought of what would
ensue. The issue was clearly defined. I had got to get them out
before Miss Brinkmeyer discovered them, or I should be properly
parked up against a fire-plug.

I don't know if you have ever tried to gather frogs. It is one
of the most difficult forms of gathering there is. Rosebuds –
easy. Nuts in May – simple. But to collect and assemble a
platoon of lively young frogs against time is a task that calls for
all that a man has of skill and address.

The situation was further complicated by the fact that I could
not at the moment recall how many of the creatures I had
strewn. The gardener had given me of his plenty, and I had just
scattered them carelessly, like a sower going forth sowing. I had
not bothered to count. At the time, anything in the nature of
a census would have seemed immaterial. It was only now, as I
stood stroking my chin reflectively, and trying to remember
whether the six I had in my pocket completed the muster-roll,
that I appreciated the folly of being casual in matters of this
kind.

I stood pondering with bent brows, and might have gone on
pondering indefinitely, had not my meditations been interrupted
by the dickens of an uproar in the garden below. Stirring things
seemed to be in progress. Alarums, as the expression is, and
excursions. What impressed itself chiefly on the ear was a shrill
feminine squeaking.

Well, if the hour had been two in the morning, I should, of
course, being in Hollywood, have taken no notice, merely
assuming that one of the neighbours was giving a party. But as
early as this it couldn't be a party. And, if not a party, I asked
myself, what?

It took me but an instant to slide to the window and look
out. I found myself gazing upon the spacious grounds and part
of the marble swimming-pool but unfortunately my view was a
good bit obstructed by a pergola covered with vines. The squeals
were proceeding from some point outside my range of vision.
For the time being, therefore, this female squealer was to me
simply a voice and nothing more. Cross-examined regarding her,
all I could have said at this juncture was that she had good
lungs.

The next moment, however, further data were supplied.
Round the corner of the swimming-pool, moving well, came

Miss Brinkmeyer, and close on her heels a figure dressed in a quiet grey suit. And as its lower limbs twinkled in the evening light, I saw that they were finished off with powder-blue socks and suede shoes.

I don't suppose it is given to many fellows to stand looking out of a first-floor window, watching themselves chivvy a middle-aged lady round a swimming-pool. The experience, I can state authoritatively, is rummy.

It takes the breath a bit. And yet, mind you, distinctly diverting. My relations with Miss Brinkmeyer being what they were – she, I mean to say, since my arrival in this joint having shown me so consistently her darker, less lovable side – I found myself enjoying the spectacle whole-heartedly. So much so that my annoyance when the runners passed out of sight was considerable.

And when, a moment later, there came to my ears the squishy slosh of a heavy body falling into water, I cursed pretty freely. I had that sickening feeling of having missed something good which is always so rotten.

But on top of this came other thoughts, notably the reflection that if Miss Brinkmeyer had fallen into the pool, it would not be long before she was seeking her bedroom in order to change her clothes. I was still uncertain about those frogs, but it was plain that I could not remain and conduct further researches. I might have secured the full quota or I might not, but even if I hadn't, I must depart while the strategic railways in my rear were still open.

It had taken me some minutes to arrive at this conclusion, but once it had been arrived at I did not delay. My bedroom, as I have said, was next door but one. I nipped into it like a homegoing rabbit.

It was only after I had reached it that my efforts to solve the frog problem were rewarded with success. I remembered now. There had been eight frogs originally. Six I had on my person. The other two I had placed in my hostess's boots, where they still remained.

18

The effect of this discovery was to put a bit of a crimp in the wholesome enjoyment I had been feeling at the thought of Miss Brinkmeyer falling into the swimming-pool. I could see that a difficult and complex situation had arisen. It was too late now to go back and collect these frogs: yet to do nothing and just let Nature take its course must infallibly lead to unpleasantness on a rather major scale. For this was not one of those occasions when mere formal apologies would serve.

It was, in short, not easy to see what to do for the best, and I was still wrinkling the brow and endeavouring to frame a practical policy, when the Filipino footman entered.

'Excuse yes, you come no, please undoubtedly,' he said.

Although, as I have indicated, I was in something of a doodah, curiosity for the moment overcame mental agitation.

'Tell me,' I said, 'do you talk like that because it's the only way you can, or are you another of these character actors who appear to be such common objects of the wayside in this house?'

He dropped the mask.

'Sure,' he said, in faultless American. 'You got me right, brother. I do comedy bits and homely pathos. One of these days, if I can catch the old buzzard alone and he can't duck, I'm going to uncork a rapid-fire dialect monologue with the tear behind the smile that'll make Mr Brinkmeyer sign on the dotted line quicker'n a chorus girl can eat caviare. We're most of us in the profesh downstairs.'

'So I am told. I say,' I said, for I was still hoping against hope, 'you haven't seen Chaffinch about anywhere, have you?'

'He's gone.'

'I know he's gone. I thought he might have come back.'

'No, he's quit. He phoned me from the station an hour ago and said he'd had an unexpected legacy from his rich uncle in Australia and was leaving for New York right away. Lucky stiff.'

I don't suppose I had really hoped much against hope, but I now ceased to hope against hope at all. In the light of this first-hand information, it would have been a fat lot of good trying to be optimistic. My intuition had not deceived me. The hound, as I had divined, had done a bunk with the syndicate's cash-box and was now far away. I uttered a soft moan and ran a fevered hand through my ringlets.

However, one of the advantages of being Joey Cooley was that you were never able to worry about anything long, because just as you started buckling down to it, something even worse was sure to happen and you had to switch off and begin worrying about that.

'Well, come on, kid,' said this footman. 'Snap into it.'

'I beg your pardon?'

'The old girl told me to fetch you along.'

This was the point where I stopped worrying about Chaffinch. My jaw dropped a couple of notches.

'She wants to see me?'

'That's the idea.'

'Did she say what about?'

'No.'

'The word "frogs" was not mentioned, by any chance?'

'Not that I know of.'

A faint hope began to stir that this might not be the hand of doom falling, after all. I proceeded to Miss Brinkmeyer's room, and found that she had taken to her bed, beside which Mr Brinkmeyer was standing. The clothes which had been lying on the bed had been put away, and so had the boots with their sinister contents. Where they had been put, I did not know, but it seemed pretty evident that the worst had not yet happened, and this so bucked me up that I became rather breezy.

'Well, well, well,' I said, tripping in, rubbing my hands and smiling a sympathetic smile. 'And how are we, how are we, ha, ha?'

Something squashy hit me in the face. The patient had thrown a hot-water bottle at me. I saw what had happened. I had been too breezy. There is always this danger.

'Will you stop grinning and giggling!' she cried.

Old Brinkmeyer, in his kindly way, tried to pour oil on the troubled waters.

'She's nervous,' he said apologetically. 'She's had a bad shock.'

'I'll bet she has,' I agreed, switching off the smile, as it didn't seem to have gone with a bang, but plugging away at the sympathy. 'Bound to tickle up the nervous system, getting bunged into swimming-pools. I said to myself when I saw what was happening—'

Miss Brinkmeyer, who after launching the bottle had sunk listlessly back against the pillows, sat up.

'Did you see it?'

'Oh, rather.'

'Would you be able to identify the scoundrel?'

'Fiend,' corrected Mr Brinkmeyer, who liked to get these things right. 'Must have been that fiend we've been reading about in the papers.'

'Would you be able to identify this fiend?'

'Oh, absolutely. Short, slight chap with delicate, handsome features.'

Miss Brinkmeyer snorted.

'He was nothing of the kind. He was enormous and looked like a gorilla.'

'I don't think so.'

'Tchah!' said Miss Brinkmeyer, with that warmth which she so often displayed in my society. 'The child's an idiot.'

Mr Brinkmeyer again essayed a spot of oil-pouring.

'Here's an idea,' he said. 'Could he have *been* a gorilla?'

'You're an idiot,' said Miss Brinkmeyer. 'Worse than the child is.'

'I was only thinking that they're doing a Darkest Africa picture down at MGM—'

'Oh, go into your dance,' said Miss Brinkmeyer wearily.

'Well, one of the gorillas might have got loose,' urged Mr Brinkmeyer deferentially. 'Anyway, the cops'll be here soon. Maybe they'll find a clue.'

'Maybe they won't,' said Miss Brinkmeyer, who seemed to have little faith in the official force. 'Still, never mind that now. What I wanted to see you about was this: I've put those Michigan Mothers off.'

'What!' I cried. This was great news. 'Told them to buzz back to Michigan, eh? Splendid. You couldn't have done better.'

'Don't talk like an imbecile. Of course I have not told them to go back to Michigan. I've postponed the reception till tomorrow. I'm much too unstrung to meet them today.'

'And she can't come to the unveiling of the statue,' said Mr Brinkmeyer. 'Too bad, too bad.'

'I certainly can't. And I can only hope that you and the child between you will not mess the whole affair up. Well, that's all. Take him away,' she said to Mr Brinkmeyer, closing her eyes after a short, shuddering look at me and sinking wearily back on the pillows again. 'The sight of him seems to make me worse. It's that fatheaded stare of his, I think, principally. Take him back to his room and keep him there on ice till it's time to go to the studio.'

'Yes, my dear,' said Mr Brinkmeyer. 'Very good, my dear. And you try to get a nice, long sleep.'

He led me out. His manner, until the door had closed behind us, was the quiet, sober manner which one likes to see in a brother who tiptoes from a sister's sick-bed. Nothing could have been more correct. But out in the passage it relaxed a trifle, and when we had entered my room he beamed like the rising sun and slapped me on the back.

'Whoopee!' he said.

The slap had been so hearty that it had sent me reeling across the floor. I fetched up against a chest of drawers and turned enquiringly.

'I beg your pardon?'

'She's not coming to the statue.'

'So I gathered.'

'You know what this means?' said Mr Brinkmeyer, trying to slap me on the back again but missing by several inches owing to my adroit footwork. 'It means I'm not going to wear my cutaway coat and stiff collar.'

'Oh?'

'And I'm not going to wear a gardenia.'

'Oh?'

'And I'm not going to wear spats.'

I found his enthusiasm infectious.

'And the kiss,' I cried. 'We'll cut the kiss?'

'Sure.'

'Just exchange a couple of civil nods, eh?'

'That's right.'

'In fact, why not eliminate the whole unpleasant nosegay business altogether?'

But he was not, it appeared, prepared to follow me quite so far as that. He shook his head.

'No. I guess we'll have to keep the nosegay sequence. It's one of the things the sob-sisters are sure to write up, and if she doesn't see anything about it in the papers tomorrow, she'll ask questions.'

I saw that he was right. These presidents of important motion-picture corporations are no fools.

'Yes,' I conceded. 'That's true.'

'But no kiss.'

'No kiss.'

'And no stiff collar, no gardenia, and no spats. Whoopee!' said Mr Brinkmeyer once more, and on this cheerful note withdrew.

For some moments after he had left, I paced the floor in a state of no little exhilaration. The future, true, had not entirely lost its grim aspect. Those Michigan Mothers had merely been postponed, not cancelled: the statue's nose remained as red as ever: and two of my frogs were still at large. But I had been sufficiently schooled by adversity by this time to be thankful for anything in the shape of a bit of luck, and the thought that I was not going to be kissed in public by T. P. Brinkmeyer was enough to make me curvet about the room like one walking on air.

And I was still doing so when I was brought to a halt by the sight of a cupboard door opening cautiously. A moment later, a face appeared. A face which, despite the fact that its upper lip had recently been shaved, I had no difficulty in recognizing.

'Hello,' said the Cooley child, emerging. 'How's tricks?'

A wave of indignation passed through me. I had not forgotten his behaviour on the telephone.

'Never mind about tricks,' I said frostily. 'What the devil did you ring off for like that when I was talking to you on the phone? What about that money?'

'Money?'

'I told you I had to have money in order to get away.'

'Oh, you want money, do you?'

'Of course I want money. I explained the whole situation in the most limpid manner. If I don't get some in the next couple of hours, ruin stares me in the face.'

'I see. Well, I haven't any on me, but I'll go and send you some.'

I felt that I had misjudged this lad.

'You will?'

'Sure. Don't give the thing another thought. Say, did you hear all that out in the garden? Nice little bit of luck, finding her like that. I never expected I'd get such quick action. Matter of fact, I wasn't gunning for her at all, really. I came to get that notebook.' He broke off. 'Hello! Listen. That'll be the constabules.'

Voices had become audible below. One was Mr Brinkmeyer's and mingling with it came the deep notes that always proceed from the throats of the gendarmerie. Once you've heard a traffic cop asking for your driving licence, you cannot fail to spot the timbre.

'You'd better leg it,' I advised.

He betrayed no alarm. His air was that of one who has the situation well in hand.

'No, sir,' he said. 'I'm safe enough here. This is the last place they'd think of looking. They probably imagine I'm a mile away by now. All they'll do is fuss around for a while, and then go and spread a drag-net and comb the city. Well, buddy, I'm sitting on top of the world. I'm having one swell time. Yessir! Those two guys yesterday, a couple of supervisors this morning, and now Ma Brinkmeyer. I'd call that a pretty good batting average. How's everything coming out at your end?'

It was pleasant to be able to pour out my troubles into an attentive ear. I told him about Chaffinch, and he was becomingly sympathetic. I told him about the frogs, and he said whatever might happen, I should have the consolation of knowing that I had done the fine, square thing. When I told him about Ann's dismissal, he dismissed the affair with a wave of the hand.

'She's all right. She's going to get some press-agent job. Say, I ought to put you wise about that, by the way.'

'She told me.'

'Oh, she did? Okay, then. Well, I hope she lands it, because she's one of the best, Ann is. She didn't say who she was going to be press agent for, but one of the big stars, I guess. So she'll be all right.'

I might have informed him that Ann's prospective employer was April June, but I thought it wiser to refrain. Experience had taught me that any mention of April June was likely to draw some distasteful crack from him, which could not fail to cast a blight on our newly formed intimacy. I did not wish to have to tick him off for some ill-judged speech, when it was so imperative that he be conciliated and given no excuse for changing his mind about that money. So I merely said: 'Oh, ah,' in a guarded manner, and turned to a subject which had a good deal of interest for me, viz., the mystery of the spotted boy.

'I say,' I said, 'I was out in the garden just now, and a boy with spots on his face popped up over the wall and said "Yah!" Who would he be? He seemed to know you.'

He considered.

'Spots?'

'Yes.'

'What sort of spots?'

'The ordinary kind. Spotty spots. And he had red hair.'

His face lightened.

'I guess I know who you mean. It must have been Orlando Flower.'

'Who's he?'

'Just one of these ham actors that's jealous of a fellow's screen genius. Pay no attention to him. He don't rate. We were in a picture together once, and he thinks I squared the cutting-room to snip out his best scenes. Did he say anything besides "Yah"?'

'He called me Little Lord Fauntleroy.'

'That was Orlando Flower all right. He always called me Little Lord Fauntleroy. You don't have to worry about him. I just used to sling oranges at the poor sap.'

'What an extraordinary coincidence! I slung oranges at him.'

'You couldn't have made a better move. Keep right on along those lines. It's what he needs.' He paused, and moved to the window, scanning the terrain below with a keen eye. 'Well, those cops seem to have beaten it. I guess I'll be scramming, too. But give me that notebook first.'

'Notebook?'

'Sure. I told you that's what I came for.'

'What notebook?'

'I told you about that, too. You remember? When we were in that waiting-room. The notebook where I used to write down folk's names that I was planning to give a poke in the snoot to.'

I viewed him with concern. My old fears about lowering the Havershot prestige had become active again. Whatever his antecedents may have been, he was now the head of the family, and any shoving in prison cells that might happen to him would reflect upon the proud Havershot name. On his own showing, he had already rendered himself liable to the processes of the Law by aggravated assault on the persons of a press agent, a director, two supervisors and Miss Brinkmeyer, and here he was, contemplating fresh excesses.

'You don't want to go poking any more people in the snoot,' I urged.

'I do, too, want to go poking lots more people in the snoot,' he rejoined with some warmth. 'Where's the sense in having this lovely wallop of yours if I don't use it? There's a raft of guys down on that list, but I can't seem to remember them without the prompt copy. So come across.'

'But I don't know where your dashed notebook is.'

'It's in your hip pocket.'

'What, this hip pocket?'

'That's right. Reach for it, buddy.'

I reached, as desired, and found the thing. It was a rather dressy little brochure, tastefully bound in limp mauve leather with silver doves on it. He took it with marked gratification.

'Attaboy, Junior,' he said. 'Louella Parsons gave me that for a Christmas present,' he added, fondling it lovingly. 'She told me to write beautiful thoughts in it. And did I what! It's full of beautiful thoughts. Thanks,' he said. 'Goodbye.'

He made for the window.

'And you'll send that money by messenger right away?' I said. I didn't want any mistake about that.

He paused with one leg over the sill.

'Money?'

'That money you're going to let me have.'

He laughed heartily. In fact, he laughed like a ruddy hyena.

'Say, listen,' he said. 'I was only kidding you when I told you I was going to give you that money.'

I reeled.

'What!'

'Sure. It was just a bit of phonus-bolonus. I was stringing you along so's I could get hold of that notebook. I'd be a fine sap giving you money. I want it all myself.' He paused. He had been turning the pages of the notebook, and now a sudden pleased smile came into his face. 'Well, for sobbing in the beer!' he said. 'If I'm not the goof! Fancy me forgetting her! Believe it or not, it had absolutely slipped my mind that the one person I've always wanted to poke in the snoot was April June.'

I reeled again. The child, the notebook and the room seemed to swim about me. It was as if this frightful speech had been a fist that had smitten me on the third waistcoat button.

Until he spoke those dreadful words, my whole mind had been absorbed by the horror of his treachery in the matter of that money. It had not occurred to me that there might be still darker depths of infamy to which he could descend. Now, all thoughts of money left me. I uttered a strangled cry.

He was clicking his tongue in gentle self-reproach.

'Here I've been, wasting my time on all this small stuff, when I ought to have been giving her hers right away. Well, I'll be off and attend to it now.'

I found speech.

'No, no!'

'Eh?'

'You wouldn't do that?'

'I certainly would.'

'Are you a fiend?'

'You betcher I'm a fiend. See daily press.'

He trousered the notebook, shoved the other leg over the sill and was gone.

A moment later, his head reappeared.

'Say, I knew there was something I wanted to tell you,' he said. 'Watch out for Tommy Murphy.'

He vanished again. There was a scrabbling noise and a thud. He had dropped to the ground and was off upon his hideous errand.

19

I stood aghast. Then tottering to bed, I sat aghast. What the little perisher had meant to convey by those parting words I had no idea, nor did I devote any time to trying to fathom their mystic significance. My mind was wholly occupied with the thought of the fearful predicament of the woman I loved. Contemplating the ghastly outrage which this young bounder was planning, I found everything swimming about me once more. My blood froze and my soul recoiled in horror.

And talking of souls, what beat me was how the dickens he came to have one like the one he'd got. In our first conversation, if you recollect, he had mentioned a mother who lived in Chillicothe, Ohio. Surely this mother must have taught him the difference between right and wrong and instilled into his infant bosom at least the rudiments of chivalry. The merest ABC of mothercraft, that, I should have supposed. I know, if I was a mother, the very first thing I would do would be to put the offspring straight about the homage and deference which the male owes to the more delicate sex and give him the low-down on the iniquity of pulling this James Cagney stuff.

But I soon abandoned this train of thought. It was no time for sitting weakly on beds and speculating about mothers. April, I saw, must be warned, and that without delay. She must be approached immediately and informed that if the Lord Haver-shot, for whom she had begun to entertain feelings deeper and warmer than those of ordinary friendship, called at her home and showed signs of trying to get within arm's reach, it was imperative that she cover up and sidestep. If possible, she must be given a few elementary lessons in the art of ducking and rolling away from the punch. Only thus could the shapeliest nose in Hollywood be saved from a brutal assault which might leave it slanting permanently sideways.

Two minutes later, I was in the telephone-booth, hunting feverishly through the J's in the directory.

Her name was not there. The numbers of famous stars, I should have remembered, are seldom recorded. It would be necessary for me, I perceived, to repair to her house in person. I left the booth with that end in view, and ran into Mr Brinkmeyer in the hall.

The president of the Brinkmeyer-Magnifico Motion Picture Corporation had unmistakably gone about his task of scrapping the cutaway-coat-and-stiff-collar programme in a big way. He was loosely and comfortably dressed in a tweed suit which might have been built by Omar the Tent Maker, and his neck was draped in roomy flannel. No spats appeared above his violin-case shoes, nor was there a flower in his buttonhole.

There were, however, flowers in his hand, and these he now offered to me.

'Hello,' he said affably. 'I thought you were in your room. We'll have to be starting in a minute. I was just coming to give you this.'

I looked at it dully. Preoccupied.

'The nosegay,' he explained.

I took it in an absent manner, and he laughed merrily. I had never seen a sunnier motion-picture president.

'Gosh!' he said. 'You're all dolled up like a gangster's corpse, aren't you? You look like a dude waiting at a stage door. Gee! It kind of brings back the old days. When I was in the cloak and suit business, I used to wait at stage doors with bouquets. I remember once—'

I checked him with a gesture.

'The story of your life later, Brinkmeyer, if you don't mind,' I said. 'I can't stop now.'

'Eh?'

'Most important appointment. Matter of life and death.'

He stared. It was plain that he was fogged. His air was that of a man who would appreciate a fuller explanation.

'Eh?' he said again.

I confess that I danced like a cat on hot bricks. I wouldn't have minded him staring and saying 'Eh?' but the trouble was that while doing so he remained rooted to the spot, and his physique was such that he blocked up the entire passage. There wasn't room to edge past him, and he was not one of those men you can brush aside. And unless I could speed without delay on my mission of mercy, April June's nose was not worth a moment's purchase.

What the upshot would have been, had the deadlock continued, I cannot say. But fortunately there now proceeded from upstairs, rending the air and causing the welkin to ring like billy-o, a female scream. I recognized it immediately for what it was – the heart cry of a woman who has just found a frog in her bedroom.

'Gosh!' said Mr Brinkmeyer, quivering all over as if he had heard the Last Trump.

He turned and began to mount the stairs. It would not be correct to say that he leaped up them, for I suppose a full thirty years must have passed since he had been able to leap up anything: but he got off the mark with a swiftness most commendable in a man of his waistline. And the obstacle between me and the front door having been removed, I nipped ahead pretty smartly myself, and before you could say, 'Service and Co-operation' was out on the steps.

The car was waiting there, with the chauffeur sitting woodenly at the wheel. I tapped him on the arm.

'Take me immediately to Miss April June's house,' I said.

The chauffeur was a square, stocky man with a face like a suet pudding. It was a face that did not mislead the observer. Looking at it, you felt that there sat a slow-thinking man, and he was a slow-thinking man. He eyed me bulbously.

'How's that?'

'Take me at once to Miss April June's house.'

'Whose house?'

'Miss April June's.'

'You want to go to Miss April June's house?'

'Yes. At once.'

He sucked in his lips thoughtfully.

'You're going to the studio.'

'Yes. But—'

'The studio – that's where you're going.'

'Yes. But—'

'I was told to bring the car round to take you and Mr Brinkmeyer to the studio.'

'Yes, yes. But—'

'And you can't go to the studio till Mr Brinkmeyer's ready. But I'll tell you what I'll do, while we're waiting,' he said, stepping down from his seat. 'I'll recite you "Gunga Din". See? Then you go to the old man and you say: "That's a very remarkable chauffeur you've got, Mr Brinkmeyer. Seems to me like he's wasted, driving a car. You'd ought to use him in a picture." Lookut,' said the chauffeur. ' "Gunga Din", by the late Rudyard Kipling.'

I uttered a wordless protest, but you cannot stop 'Gunga Din' addicts with wordless protests. He drew a deep breath and raised one arm stiffly. The other he kept across his stomach, no doubt for purposes of self-defence. He looked more like a suet pudding than ever.

' "You may talk o' gin and beer—" '

' I don't want to talk o' gin and beer.'

' "When you're quartered safe out 'ere—" '

'I want to go—'

' "An' you're sent to penny-fights an' Aldershot it." '

'Look here—'

' "But when it comes to water you will do your work on slaughter" – other way round, I mean to say – "an' you'll lick the bloomin' boots of 'im that's got it." '

He removed the arm that lay across his stomach and raised it – first, however, warily lowering the other and putting that across his stomach. I suppose all reciters learn to take these precautions.

' "Now in Injia's sunny clime . . ." ' Here he apparently noticed that I was a restless audience who was going to be difficult to hold, for he added: 'And so on and so forth,' as if feeling that it would be necessary to condense the thing a bit. ' "Was our regimental *bhisti*, Gunga Din",' he concluded hurriedly.

He paused for breath here, and I seized the opportunity to offer him ten dollars if he would take me to April June's.

You wouldn't have thought a gleam could have come into those eyes, but one did.

'Got it on you?'

'No.'

'I thought you hadn't. It was "Din! Din! Din! You limpin' lump o' brick-dust, Gunga Din! Hi! Slippy *hitherao*! Water, get it! *Panee lao* . . ." '

I abandoned the fruitless task. It was a long, long trail to April June's bijou residence on Linden Drive, and I had hoped not to be compelled to undertake it on foot, but I saw that there was no alternative. Leaving him babbling about 'squidgy-nosed old idols', I sped out into the great open spaces.

And I hadn't gone more than a couple of hundred yards, by Jove, when I was arrested by a 'Hey!' in my rear, and turned to see a figure in a grey suit and powder-blue socks, the whole terminating in tasteful suede shoes.

For one moment as I beheld him, I had the idea that the voice of conscience must have been whispering in this changeling's ear, causing him to abandon his foul project. Such, however, was not the case. His first words told me that his hat was still in the ring.

'Suddenly remembered,' he said, 'that I don't know April June's address. You can tell me, I guess. Where do I find this beasel, buddy?'

I eyed him with all the cold loathing at my disposal. I was revolted to the core. That he should expect me, who had told him that I loved this girl, to sit in with him on his loathsome programme of giving her a poke in the snoot struck me as being about as near the outer rim as you could get.

'You tell me,' he said, 'and I'll slip you that money you wanted.'

'No,' I said firmly. I did not waver for an instant. To my mind, the man who sells the woman he loves for gold is a bit of a tick, and I know other fellows who think the same. 'No, certainly not.'

'Ah, come on.'

'No. My lips are sealed.'

His brow darkened. I had never realized before what an ugly brute I looked when peeved. He so closely resembled a gorilla at this juncture that I should not have been surprised if he had suddenly started beating his chest, as I believe gorillas do when things aren't going too well. The spectacle was an intimidating one, but my chief emotion, oddly enough, was not alarm but a marked increase in the fervour of my love for April June. I felt that a girl who could contemplate matrimony with a chap with a face like that must be a girl in a million.

He clenched a fist and advanced a step.

'You'd best come clean.'

'I will do no such dashed thing.'

'Suppose I poke *you* in the snoot?'

'I defy you.'

'Tough, eh? What could you do if I did?'

'I could call for assistance,' I said quietly. I pointed down the road. 'You will observe that we are not alone. You see that boy standing over there by the lamp-post? One slosh from you, one yell from me, and off, no doubt, like the wind he will be bounding to fetch the police force.'

My words appeared to baffle him less than I had hoped and expected. About now, it seemed to me, he ought to be looking fairly thwarted, but he wasn't. He didn't look thwarted a dashed bit. In fact, I noted that he was smiling in a nasty way, as I have seen fellows smile at the bridge table when producing the unexpected trump.

'Friend of yours?'

'No. I have never seen him before. But I have little doubt that he has enough civic spirit to rally round in the event of any sloshing, even though not personally acquainted with the victim.'

'Husky-looking guy.'

I had not examined the boy closely up to this point, but I now did so, and I agreed with him. He appeared to be a lad, for his years, of considerable muscular development. Not that I could see what that had to do with it. I had never suggested that I expected physical aid from him.

'Yes,' I said. 'He seems robust.'

'I'll say he is. Listen, shall I tell you something?'

'Do.'

He smiled unpleasantly.

'I will,' he said. 'Before Joey Cooley became the Idol of American Motherhood, a kid named Tommy Murphy had the job. His pictures used to gross big. And then I came along, and he dropped right into the discard. Nobody needed him any more, and he didn't get his contract renewed, and it made him pretty sore. Yessir, good and sore it made him. Ever since then he's been going around saying he wants my blood and claiming he's going to get it. Well, sir, if that boy has tried to catch me once, he's tried a dozen times and, believe me, it's taken some mighty shifty foot work to hold him off.'

A cold hand seemed to clutch my vitals. I began to get the drift.

'That's Tommy Murphy over there by that lamp-post. He puts in most of his time waiting outside the house, hoping for the best. I guess he saw you come out and followed you.'

The cold hand tightened its clutch. It was plain that in assuming the outer envelope of this gifted child I had stepped straight into a bally jungle, full of sinister creatures that might pounce at any moment. I had had no idea, till I became one, that the life of a child star in Hollywood was one of such incessant peril. I was not surprised that my companion had dreamed so wistfully of getting away from it all and going back to Chillicothe, Ohio. Miss Brinkmeyer alone was enough to take the gilt off the gingerbread. Add Tommy Murphy and you had something which might fairly be called a bit above the odds.

'Now, if you'd have been nice and told me where April June lives, I'd have stuck around and seen you home. But now I won't. I'll just walk off and leave you to it. Unless you change your mind and slip me that address.'

Well, it was a pretty frightful posish for a lover to be placed in, you'll admit. I shot a swift glance at this Murphy. It merely served to confirm my former opinion. I had said he looked robust, and he was robust. He was one of those chunky, square sort of striplings. He might have been the son of that chauffeur. And now that I examined him more closely, it was easy to note the hostility in his eye. It would not be too much to say that he was glaring at me like a tiger at the day's steak.

The landscape seemed to flicker, and I flickered a bit myself. What with the peril in which I stood and the peril in which April June stood, I don't mind admitting that I was all of a dither.

But Love triumphed over Self.

'No,' I said. 'Positively no.'

'You mean that?'

'Definitely.'

He shrugged my shoulders.

'Okay. Have it your own way. Well, sir, I wouldn't be in your shoes for something. No, sir! Because it isn't only Tommy Murphy. As I was coming along, I saw Orlando Flower lurking around. I guess I'd call him kind of tougher than Tommy, really. Though I don't know. It's a close thing. So I wouldn't be in your shoes for something. Still, have it your own way.'

With another of those bally sneers of his, he pushed off, and I was left alone in the world.

Alone, that is to say, except for the blister Murphy, who now came heading in my direction at the rate of knots. His eyes were gleaming with a nasty light – glittering, in fact – or you might say glinting – and he was licking his lips.

He looked like a boy whose dreams have come true, and who has found the bluebird.

20

Eyeing this Murphy, as he halted before me and stood measuring his distance, I found it extraordinarily difficult to believe that he could ever have been the idol of American Motherhood. American Motherhood, I felt, must be an ass. The boy did not appear to me to possess a single lovable quality. He looked like something out of a gangster film. Not at all the sort of chap you would take to your club.

I backed a step. In fact, I backed several steps. And after I had finished backing about the eighth, the ground became more yielding under my feet, and I found that I was standing on grass. There is a regulation in Beverly Hills, you may or may not know, which compels the householder to shove his residence a certain distance away from the road and put a neat lawn in front of it, and at this crisis in my affairs I was dashed glad that this was so. It seemed only too evident that in the near future I was going to be called upon to do a good bit of falling, and anything that might tend to make this falling softer was so much gained.

Up to this point, I should mention, the proceedings had been conducted in silence, broken only by stertorous and menacing breathing on the part of the thug Murphy and a faint chattering of teeth from me. It now occurred to me that a little chitchat might serve to ease the tension. This frequently happens. Get a conversation going, I mean to say, and before you know where you are you have discovered mutual tastes and are fraternizing.

Barmy Fotheringay-Phipps told me once that he was confronted on a certain occasion by a steely eyed bloke who wanted two pounds six and eleven for goods supplied, and he managed to get him on to the subject of runners and betting for that afternoon's meeting at Hurst Park, and ten minutes later he, the bloke, was standing him, Barmy, a pint of mild and bitter at a nearby hostelry, and he, Barmy, was touching him, the bloke, for five bob to be repaid without fail on the following Wednesday.

Well, I wasn't expecting quite such a happy issue as that, of course, for I'm not the silver-tongued orator Barmy is and never have been, but I thought it possible that some good might come of opening a conversation, so I backed another step and managed to dig up a kindly smile.

'Well, my little man,' I said, modelling my style on that of B. K. Burwash. 'What is it, my little man?'

I detected no softening in his demeanour. He continued to breathe heavily. There ensued a bit of a conversational vacuum.

'I can't stop long,' I said, breaking a silence which threatened to become embarrassing. 'I have an engagement. Nice, meeting you.'

And, so saying, I endeavoured to edge round him. But he proved to be just as difficult a chap to edge round as Mr Brinkmeyer. Dissimilar in physique, they both had that quality of seeming to block every avenue. When I edged to the right, he shifted to the left, and when I shifted to the left, he edged to the right, and there we were aziz again.

I tried once more.

'Are you fond of flowers? Would you like a nosegay?'

Apparently no. As I extended the nosegay, he knocked it out of my hand, and the sickening violence with which he did so added to my qualms. I stooped and picked it up, and had another shot.

'Do you want my autograph, my little man?' I said.

The moment the words were out of my mouth, I realized that I had said the wrong thing. The last topic, of course, that I should have brought up was that of autographs. Altogether too painful and suggestive. There had been a time, no doubt, when this lad before me had had to write them for the fans till he got corns on the fingers, and since the advent on the silver screen of little Joey Cooley, the demand had been nil. In mentioning autographs, therefore, I was simply awakening sad memories of vanished glory – in a word, dropping salt into the exposed wound.

If I had not spotted this for myself, his reaction would have told me I had made a floater.

'Autograph!' he said, in an unpleasant, low, growling voice that seemed to proceed from the left corner of his mouth. His eyes glinted tigerishly, and once more I sought in vain for an explanation of how he had ever come to be regarded with esteem by the mothers of America.

He began to speak. He spoke well and fluently – as it turned out, much too fluently, for it was the fact that he postponed direct action in favour of this harangue that dished his plans and aims.

You've probably noticed how often the same thing happens in detective stories. There's always a bit, I mean to say, where the villain has got the hero tied up in a chair or lashed to a bed and is about to slip it across him with the blunt instrument. But instead of smacking into it, the poor ass will persist in talking. You feel like saying: 'Act, man, act! Don't waste valuable time taunting the chap,' because you know that, if he does, somebody is sure to come along and break up the twosome. But he always does it, and it always lays him a stymie.

It was so on the present occasion. A cooler head than Tommy Murphy's would have seen that the right thing to do was to get down to fundamentals straight away. But no, he chose to stand there with his chin out, telling me what he proposed to accomplish when once he was ready to begin.

He said, still in that hoarse, unpleasant voice that seemed to suggest that he had ingrowing tonsils: 'Autograph, huh?'

He said: 'Autograph, huh?'

He said: 'Don't you worry about autographs.'

He said:

'That'll be all about autographs from you. Do you know what I'm going to do to you? I'm going to soak you good, in case anyone should ask you. Do you know what I'm going to do to you? I'm going to knock the stuffing clean out of you. I'm going to lay you out like a pickerel on ice. I'm going to fix you so's there ain't nobody's going to sit and say "Oh, isn't he cute?" because you won't have any face left to be cute with. Do you know what I'm going to do to you? I'm going—'

Here he broke off – not because he had finished, for he had evidently plenty more to say, but because the ground on which we were standing suddenly sort of exploded.

Concealed here and there about these Beverly Hills lawns, you see, are little metal thingummies with holes in them, by means of which they are watered. One twiddle of a tap and the whole thing becomes a fountain. And this was what had happened now. Unseen by us, some hidden Japanese hand had turned on the juice, and there we were, right in the thick of it.

Well, it wasn't so bad for me. Owing to my policy of steadily backing, I had reached a spot which, for the nonce, was comparatively dry. But the excrescence Murphy chanced to be standing immediately over one of the thingummies, with the result that he copped it right in the eyeball. Ironically enough, after what he had been saying, it soaked him good.

His attention was diverted. Nobody could fail to let his thoughts wander a bit if he suddenly received about a pint and a half of water in the face, and for an instant Tommy Murphy's thoughts wandered. He leaped like the high hills, and I became pretty brisk and strategic. While he was still in mid-air, I was off and away, legging it down the road. I recalled that it was by this method that the child Cooley had been enabled to save himself embarrassment on other occasions.

Until this moment, except for a little casual orange-bunging, I had had no opportunity of trying out this new body of mine and seeing what it was good for. My mirror had told me it was ornamental, and I had already divined that it was not any too muscular. With a gush of thankful emotion, I now discovered that it could run like blazes. As a sprinter over the flat, I was in the highest class.

I headed down the street at a capital pace. Uncouth noises in my rear told me that the hunt was up, but I had little fear that I would be unable to shake off my pursuer's challenge. These solid, chunky kids are only selling platers, at the best.

My judgement of form had not misled me. Class told. I entered Linden Drive a leader by several lengths, and was drawing so far ahead that I should have been able to come home on a loose rein, when somebody barged into me and I went base over apex into a bush.

And when I had extricated myself from this bush and come right side up again, I found myself gazing into the bountifully spotted face of Orlando Flower.

My position, in short, was precisely that of an African explorer who, breezing away from a charging rhinoceros, discovers, just as he has begun to think that everything is jakesey-jukesey, that he is *vis-à-vis* with a man-eating puma.

Orlando Flower, like Tommy Murphy, proved to be in conversational mood. He stood over me, clenching and unclenching his fists, but he, too, postponed action in favour of talk.

'Yah!' he said.

At our previous meeting, it will be recalled, I had countered his 'Yah!' with an equally vigorous 'Yah!' of my own. But on that occasion there had been a stout wall between us, and with this obstacle removed I felt singularly little in the vein for back-chat. At this close range, there was something hideously disconcerting in the spectacle of those green eyes set close together among their encircling spots. Joey Cooley had confessed himself unable to decide whether this boy or Tommy Murphy was the tougher egg, and I experienced the same difficulty in arriving at a verdict. But of one thing I was certain. I was not equal to saying 'Yah!' to him.

I maintained an uneasy silence, accordingly, and he said 'Yah!' again. And as he did so, there was a hoarse cry from down the road, and Tommy Murphy approached at a lumbering gallop. He came up and stood puffing, having evidently found the going a bit gruelling. It was some moments before he was able to speak. When he did so, he said 'Hey!'

The boy Flower seemed displeased at the interruption.

'Well?' he said, with some acidity.

'You lay off of him,' said Tommy Murphy.

'Who, me?' said Orlando Flower.

'Yay, you,' said Tommy Murphy.

Orlando Flower gave him an unpleasant look.

'Huh?' he said.

'Huh,' said Tommy Murphy.

'Huh?' said Orlando Flower.

'Huh,' said Tommy Murphy.

There was a pause.

'I saw him first,' said Tommy Murphy.

It was a good legal point, of course, but Orlando Flower had his answer.

'Oh, yeah?'

'Yeah.'

'I caught him, didn't I?'

'I saw him first, didn't I?'

'I caught him, didn't I?'

'I'm telling you I saw him first.'

'I'm telling you I caught him.'

'You lay off of him.'

'Who, me?'

'Yay, you.'

'Huh?'

'Huh.'

'Huh?'

'Huh.'

And having thus got back to where they had started, they paused again and stood sticking out their chins at one another, while I remained in the offing, holding the nosegay and experiencing mixed emotions.

Chief among these, of course, was a rather vivid apprehension. It was far from agreeable to have to stand and listen to this brace of thugs arguing and disputing as to which should have the privilege of dotting me. But mingled with this alarm were pique and wounded pride. The whole situation was extremely humiliating for an old Boxing Blue.

Presently the huh-ing broke out again.

'Huh,' said Orlando Flower.

'Huh,' said Tommy Murphy.

'Huh,' said Orlando Flower.

There was a moment's silence. Then Tommy Murphy spoke.

'Huh,' he said, like one who has just thought of a new and original repartee.

The psychology of these two young pustules was a sealed book to me. I could not follow their mental processes. There appeared to me to be absolutely nothing about this last 'Huh' that made it in any way different from the 'Huhs' which had preceded it. But there must have been, because its effect on the boy Flower was immediate. Flushing beneath his spots, he flung himself on Tommy Murphy, and they came to the ground together in a clawing mass.

Well, I don't say I'm a particularly intelligent chap, but even an ass like that chauffeur who had recited 'Gunga Din' would have known what to do in a situation like this. Pausing only to kick them in the stomach, I picked up my feet and passed lightly on my way.

As I reached April's door and pressed the bell, I looked over my shoulder. The two combatants had separated and risen and were staring at me helplessly, baffled by my adroitness and resource. I don't suppose two growing boys ever looked so silly.

I waved my hand derisively at them.

'Yah!' I said. 'I wasn't speaking to you,' I added to the butler who had opened the door and was regarding me with some surprise. 'Just chatting with a couple of acquaintances down the road.'

21

The butler, when I asked to see April June, seemed a bit doubtful about the advisability of ushering me in. April, he explained, was expecting a visitor and had told him to tell callers that she was not at home. Fortunately, he appeared to come to the conclusion that a half-portion like myself could hardly be counted as a caller, and presently I was seated in a chair in the living-room, endeavouring to catch up with my breath.

As I sat there, a wave of not unmanly sentiment poured over me. It was in this room that I had so often talked with April, bending an attentive ear as she spoke of her ideals and coming back with something informative about the English order of precedence and the right of Countesses to squash into dinner ahead of the wives of Viscounts. The whole atmosphere was redolent of her gentle presence, and I am not ashamed to say I sighed. In fact, when I reflected how hopeless now my love was, I came within a toucher of shedding tears.

My wistful melancholy was accentuated by the sight of my photograph standing in the place of honour on her writing-table. There were other photographs about the room, some female with 'Fondest love from Mae' and that sort of thing on them, others male and bearing legends like 'All the best from Basil', but the only one on the writing-table was mine, and I thrilled at the sight of it.

And when I say thrilled, I mean partly with gratification, of course, but quite a bit, in addition, with an icy horror at the thought of how easily, if she had reached the stage where she kept his photograph on her desk, the current Lord Havershot would have been able to get within punching distance of this girl. Had I not come to warn her to keep on her toes and watch his left hook, the worst must inevitably have occurred. I could see her, unapprised of his low designs, starting up with a pretty cry of delight as he entered the room and hurrying forward with her guard down to greet him. And then, as she stood there with the love-light shining in her eyes . . . socko!

A gruesome picture, and one well calculated to make a chap shudder. I should probably have shuddered even more than I did, had there not begun to steal into my consciousness at this juncture a rummy sensation which I could not at first analyse. Then I got on to it. It was suddenly borne in upon me that I was dying of thirst. What with the warmth of the day and the fact that I had so recently been taking vigorous outdoor exercise, the epiglottis seemed to have become composed of sandpaper. Already I was gasping painfully like a stranded fish, and it seemed to me that if I didn't climb outside something moist in about half a jiffy, I should expire in dreadful agonies.

And this thought had scarcely flitted into my mind when I noticed that all the materials for a modest binge were hospitably laid out on a table in the corner. There was the good old decanter, the jolly old syphon, the merry bucket of ice, and, in brief, the whole bag of tricks. They seemed to be beckoning to me, and I tottered across like a camel making for an oasis and started mixing.

Of course, I ought to have realized that, while this urge to have a couple of quick ones was Lord Havershot's, the capacity for absorbing the stuff would be little Joey Cooley's; but at the moment, I confess, it didn't occur to me. I filled a flagon and drained it at a gulp.

It didn't seem to taste as good as I had expected, so I had another to see if I really liked it. Then, refilling my glass and lighting a cigarette from the box on the table, I returned to my chair. And I had scarcely seated myself when I became aware of an odd sort of buzzing in the head, accompanied by an extraordinarily urgent desire to burst into song. It puzzled me a bit, for, except in my bath, I'm not much of a singer as a rule.

I was pleased to find that I was in exceptionally good voice. No doubt I was not in a mood to be critical, but I must say my performance delighted me. The number which I had selected for rendition was that old and tried favourite, the 'Eton Boating Song', and it came out as smooth as silk, except that I noted a tendency on the part of the words to run into each other a little. In fact, after a while, I found that I got on better by substituting 'umpty-tumpty-tiddles' and 'tiddly-umpty-tums' for the existing libretto, and I was giving these out with a will, waving my glass and cigarette rhythmically as I sang, when a voice, speaking from behind me, said 'Good evening.'

I switched off in the middle of an 'umpty', and turned. I found that I had been joined by an elderly female.

'Oh, hullo,' I said.

'Good evening,' she said again. She seemed a kindly, amiable old soul, and I warmed to her immediately. What attracted me about her particularly was the fact that she had a face exactly like that of a horse of mine at home, of which I was extremely fond. It made me feel that I was among friends.

The instinct of the Havershots, on beholding the opposite sex enter a room in which they are seated, is, of course, to shoot up like a rocket. It occasioned me, therefore, no little embarrassment now to find that I was unable to do this. I had a couple of shots, but each time was compelled to sag back again. The old *preux chevalier* spirit was functioning on all six cylinders, but the legs seemed to have worked loose at the joints.

'I say, I'm awfully sorry,' I said, 'but I don't seem able to get up.'

'Please don't trouble.'

'Touch of sciatica, I expect.'

'No doubt.'

'Or lumbago.'

'Very likely,' she neighed graciously. 'My name is Pomona Wycherley.'

'How do you do? Mine is—'

'Oh, I don't need to be told your name, Mr Cooley. I'm one of your fans. Have you come to see Miss June?'

'Yes. I want to see her on a matter of—'

'And you have brought her those lovely flowers,' she said, eyeing the nosegay, which was lying by my chair looking a bit shopsoiled after its recent vicissitudes. 'How sweet!'

The idea of shoving the nosegay off on to April as a mark of my personal esteem had not occurred to me before, but I saw now that this would be an excellent scheme.

'You think she'll like them?'

'She's sure to. You seem very warm, Mr Cooley. Did you hurry here?'

'You bet I hurried. The fact is, I was rather beset by scoundrels. There was a boy named Tommy Murphy—'

'Oh, was Tommy Murphy chasing you?'

'You know about Tommy Murphy?'

'Oh, yes. It's all over Hollywood. I believe they have bets in some of the studios on whether or not he will catch you.'

'Extremely dubious taste.'

'He didn't catch you, I hope?'

'Temporarily only. I eluded him. I also eluded a kid named Orlando Flower. In fact, I eluded both of them. It took a bit of earnest sprinting, of course, and, as you say, it has left me warm.'

'So you mixed yourself a little drink?'

I blushed. Her words had brought home to me how remiss I was being.

'I say,' I said. 'Can I offer you a spot?'

'No, thank you.'

'Ah, come on.'

'No, thank you, really.'

'You're sure?'

'Quite, thanks. It's so early in the evening, isn't it?'

'Is it?' I said, surprised. 'The usual hour for a snort, surely?'

'You seem to speak as an expert. Do you often take what you call a snort at this time?'

'Oh, rather.'

'Fancy that. Whisky?'

'Whisky invariably.'

'And I see you smoke as well.'

'Oh, yes. In fact, rather better.'

'Always cigarettes?'

'Sometimes cigarettes. I prefer a pipe.'

'Well, well! At your age?'

I couldn't follow this – possibly because the buzzing sensation in my head had now become more pronounced. The keen edge of my mind seemed a bit blunted.

'My age?' I said. 'Why, dash it, I'm twenty-seven.'

'What!'

'Absolutely. Twenty-eight next March.'

'Well, well, well! I should never have thought it.'

'You wouldn't?'

'No.'

'You wouldn't have thought it?'

'I certainly would not.'

Why this should have struck me as so droll, I don't know, but it amused me enormously, and I burst into a hearty guffaw. I had just finished this guffaw and was taking aboard breath with which to start another, when the door opened and in came April, looking extraordinarily ultra in some filmy stuff. *Mousseline de soie*, I shouldn't wonder, or something along those lines. Anyway, it was filmy and suited her fragile loveliness like the dickens.

When I say she came in, she didn't right away. She stood framed in the doorway, gazing wistfully before her as if in some beautiful reverie. At this point, however, I unleashed the second guffaw, and it seemed to hit her like a bullet. She started as if she had stepped on a tin-tack.

'You!' she said, in an odd, explosive sort of way. 'What are you doing here?'

I took a sip of whisky and soda.

'I wanted to see you on a matter of vital importance,' I said gravely, and was annoyed to find that the sentence had come out as one word. 'I want to see you up-on a mat-ter of vit-al import-ance,' I added, spacing it out a bit this time.

'He has brought you a lovely bouquet,' said Miss Wycherley.

The nosegay didn't seem to go very big. I was not feeling strong enough to pick it up, but I shoved it forward with my foot and April looked at it in – it seemed to me – a rather distant manner. She appeared not too pleased about something. She swallowed once or twice, as if trying to overcome some powerful emotion.

'Well, you can't stay here,' she said at length, speaking with something of an effort. 'Miss Wycherley has come to interview me.'

This interested me.

'Are you an interviewer, old horse?' I said.

'Yes, I'm from the *Los Angeles Chronicle*. I wonder if I could take a photograph of you?'

'Charge ahead.'

'No, don't put your glass down. Just as you are. The cigarette in your mouth, I think. Yes, that's splendid.'

April drew a deep breath.

'Perhaps,' she said, 'you would prefer that I left you together?'

'Oh, don't go,' I urged hospitably.

'No, no,' said Miss Wycherley. 'I would like to interview you both. Such a wonderful chance, finding you both here like this.'

'Exactly,' I agreed. 'Two stones with one bird. Dashed good idea. Carry on,' I said, closing my eyes so that I could listen better.

The next thing I remember is opening my eyes and feeling considerably clearer in the bean. That strange, blurred sensation had passed. I take it that I must have dozed off for a moment or two. As I came to the surface, April was speaking.

'No,' she was saying in a low sweet voice, 'I have never been one of those girls who think only of themselves and their career. To me the picture is everything. I work solely for its success, with no thought of personal advantage. In this last picture of mine, as you say, many girls might have objected to the way the director kept pushing little Joey Cooley here forward and giving him all the best shots.' Here she paused and flashed an affectionate glance in my direction. 'Oh, you're awake, are you? Yes, I'm talking about you, you cute little picture-stealer,' she said with a roguish smile that nearly made me fall at her feet then and there. 'He is a dreadful, dreadful little picture-stealer, isn't he?' she said.

'He certainly ran away with that one,' assented the horse-faced female.

'Don't I know it!' said April, with a silvery little laugh. 'I could see from the start what the director was trying to do, of course, but I said to myself: "Mr Bulwinkle is a very experienced man. He knows best. If Mr Bulwinkle wishes me to efface myself for the good of the picture," I said to myself, "I am only too pleased." I felt that the success of the picture was the only thing that mattered. I don't know if you see what I mean?'

Miss Wycherley said she saw just what she meant, adding that it did her credit.

'Oh, no,' said April. 'It is just that I am an artist. If you are an artist, you cease to exist as an individual. You become just part of the picture.'

That about concluded her portion of the entertainment, for at this point Miss Wycherley, perceiving that the mists of sleep had rolled away, turned to me and wanted to know what I thought about things. And as it happens that I hold strong views on the films, I rather collared the conversation from now on. I told her what I thought was wrong with the pictures, threw out a few personal criticisms of the leading stars – mordant perhaps, but justified – and, in a word, generally hauled up my slacks. I welcomed this opportunity of voicing my views, because in the past, whenever I had tried to do it at the Drones, there had always been rather a disposition on the part of my audience to tell me to put a sock in it.

So for about ten minutes I delivered a closely reasoned address, and then Miss Wycherley got up and said it had all been most interesting and she was sure she had got some excellent material for tomorrow's paper, and that she must be getting back to the office to write it up. April conducted her to the front door and saw her off, while I, observing that one of my shoelaces had worked loose in the recent race for life, got out of my chair and started to tie it up.

And I was still in the stooping posture necessitated by this task, when I heard a soft footstep behind me. April had returned.

'Half a jiffy,' I said. 'I'm just—'

The words died in my throat. For even as I spoke them a jarring agony shot through my entire system and I whizzed forward and came up against the chesterfield. For an instant I had an idea that one of those earthquakes which are such a common feature of life in California must have broken loose. Then the hideous truth came home to me.

The woman I loved had kicked me in the pants.

22

I rose to my feet with some of the emotions of a man who has just taken the Cornish Express in the small of the back. She was standing looking at me with her hands on her hips, grinding her teeth quietly, and I gazed back with reproach and amazement, like Julius Caesar at Brutus.

'I say!' I said.

To describe myself as astounded at what had occurred would be to paint but a feeble picture of the turmoil going on beneath my frilly shirt. I had lost my grip entirely. I found the situation one in which it was not easy to maintain a patrician calm.

To the idea that there was practically nothing that couldn't happen to the unfortunate bird who had been rash enough to take on the identity of little Joey Cooley I had become by this time, of course, pretty well accustomed. That T. Murphies and O. Flowers should be going about seeking to commit mayhem on my person I was able to accept as in the natural order of things. If it had been Miss Brinkmeyer who had thus booted me, I could have understood. I might even have sympathized. But this particular spot of bother had come as a complete surprise. When it came to April June catching me fruity ones on the seat of the bags, I was frankly unable to follow the run of what Mr Brinkmeyer would have called the sequence.

'I say, what?' I said.

In addition to being shaken to my foundations spiritually, I was in none too good shape physically. The wound was throbbing painfully, and I had to feel the top of my head to make sure that the spine had not come through. Not since early boyhood, a time when a certain exuberance in my manner had, I believe, rather invited this sort of thing, could I recall having stopped such a hot one.

'I say, dash it!' I said.

Yet even now my love was so deep that had she expressed anything in the nature of contrition or apology – pleaded that her foot had slipped, or something like that – I think I would have been willing to forgive and forget and make a fresh start.

But she didn't express anything of the dashed kind. She seemed to glory in her questionable conduct. There was unmistakable triumph and satisfaction in her demeanour.

'There!' she said. 'How did you like that? Laugh that off!'

But nothing was farther from my thoughts than merriment. I couldn't have laughed at that moment to please a dying aunt.

For I saw now what must have happened. The exacting conditions of life in Hollywood, with its ceaseless strain and gruelling work, had proved too much for this girl's frail strength. Brainstorms had ensued. Nervous breakdowns had bobbed up. In a word, crushed by the machine, she had gone temporarily off her onion.

My heart bled for her. I forgot my aching base.

'There, there,' I said, and was about to suggest a cup of hot tea and a good lie-down, when she continued:

'Maybe that will teach you not to go crawling to directors so that they will let you hog the camera!'

The scales fell from my eyes. I saw that my diagnosis had been wrong. The shocking truth hit me like a wet towel. This was no nervous breakdown caused by overwork. Incredible though it might seem after all she had been saying about the artist not caring a hoot for personal glory so long as the picture came out well, it was straight professional jealousy. It was the old Murphy-Flower stuff all over again, only a dashed sight more serious. Because in adjusting my little difficulties with Thomas and Orlando I had had plenty of room to manoeuvre in. Now, I was cooped up within four walls, and who could predict the upshot?

I have made it pretty clear, I think, in the course of this narrative, that what had so drawn me to April June had been her wistful gentleness. In her, as I have repeatedly suggested, I could have put my shirt on it that I had found a great white soul.

There was nothing wistful and gentle about her now. The soft blue eyes I had admired so much were hard and had begun to shoot out sparks. The skin I would have loved to touch was flushed, the mouth set in a rigid line, the fingers twitching. She seemed to me, in brief, to be exhibiting all the earmarks of one of those hammer murderesses you read about in the papers who biff husbands over the coconut and place the remains in a trunk; and with all possible swiftness I removed myself to the other side of the chesterfield and stood staring at her dumbly. And, as I did so, I realized for the first time how a hen must look to a worm.

She went on speaking in tones that bore no resemblance whatever to those which had so fascinated me at our first meeting. The stuff came out in a high, vibrating soprano that went through me like a bradawl.

'And maybe you'll know enough after this to keep away when I'm receiving the Press. I like your gall, coming butting in when a special representative of a leading daily paper is approaching me for my views on Art and the trend of public taste! You and your bouquets!' Here, baring her teeth unpleasantly, she kicked the nosegay. 'I've a good mind to make you eat it.'

I sidled a little farther behind the chesterfield. Less and less did I like the turn the conversation was taking.

'I did think I would be safe from you in my own home. But no. In you come oozing like oil.'

I would have explained here, if she had given me the opportunity, that I had had an excellent motive in so oozing, for I had come solely in order to save her from a fate which, if not exactly worse than death, would have been distinctly unpleasant. But she did not give me the opportunity.

'Trying to attract all the attention to yourself, as usual. Well, if you think you can get away with that, think again. You can just throw hay on that idea. You expect me, do you, not only to act as a stooge for you in front of the camera, but to sit smiling in the background while you horn in and swipe my interview?'

Again I endeavoured to assure her that she was totally mistaken in her view of the situation, and once more she nipped in ahead of me.

'Of all the nerve! Of all the crust! Of all the— But what,' she cried, breaking off, 'is the sense of standing here talking about it?'

I felt the same myself. It seemed to me that nothing was to be gained by continuing the conference.

'Quite,' I said. 'Right ho. Then I'll be pushing, what?'

'You stay where you are.'

'But I thought you said—'

'Let me get at you!'

I could not accede to her request, which even she must have seen was unreasonable. With a swift movement of the hand she had possessed herself of a large, flat, heavy paper-knife, and the last thing I was prepared to do was to let her get at me.

'Now, listen,' I began.

I got no farther, because, as I spoke, she suddenly came bounding round the side of the chesterfield, and I saw that it was no time for words. Acting swiftly, I did a backwards leap of about five feet six. It was the manoeuvre which is known in America as beating the gun. With equal promptitude she did a forwards leap of perhaps four feet seven. And I, hearing that paper-knife whistle past my knickerbockers, put in a sideways leap of possibly three feet eight. This saved me for the nonce, but I could not but note that my strategic position had now changed considerably for the worse. She had driven me from my line of prepared fortifications, and I was right out in the open with both flanks exposed.

The moment seemed ripe for another attempt at conciliation.

'All this is most unpleasant,' I urged.

'It'll get worse,' she assured me.

I begged her not to do anything she would be sorry for later. She thanked me for the thought, but protested that I was the one who was going to be sorry. She then began to advance again, stealthily this time, like a leopard of the jungle; and, as I backed warily, I found myself reflecting how completely a few minutes can alter one's whole mental outlook. Of the love for this girl which so short a while before had animated my bosom there remained not a trace. That paper-knife of hers had properly put a stopper on the tender passion. When I remembered that I had once yearned to walk up the aisle by her side, with the organ playing 'The Voice That Breathed O'er Eden', and the clergyman waiting to do his stuff, I marvelled at my fatheadedness.

But she didn't give me time for anything lengthy in the way of musing. She leaped forward, and things began to brisk up again. And it was not long before I saw that this was going to be quite a vigorous evening.

To describe these great emotional experiences in detail is always pretty difficult. One is not in the frame of mind, while they are in progress, to note and observe and store away the sequence of events in the memory. One's recollections tend to be blurred.

I can recall setting a cracking pace, but twice the paper-knife caught me on the spot best adapted for its receipt, once when I had become entangled in the standard lamp by the fireplace, and again when I tripped over a small chair, and both were biffs of unparalleled juiciness. Their effect was to bring out all that was best in me both as a flat racer and as a performer over the sticks, and I nipped away and took almost in my stride the piano on which in happier circumstances she had once played me old folk-songs. I found myself behind the chesterfield again.

And such was the lissomeness which peril had given me that I think that I might now have managed to reach the door and win my way to safety, had not an imperfect knowledge of local conditions caused me to make a fatal bloomer. She was coming up smartly on my right and, like an ass, I thought that it would be quicker to go under the chesterfield instead of round it.

I have said that I had sat many a time in this room and knew it well, but when I did so I was referring to that part of it which met the eye. I had no acquaintance with the bits you couldn't see. And it was this that undid me. Thinking, as I say, to take a short cut by wriggling under the chesterfield and coming out on the other side – a manoeuvre, mind you, which would have been Napoleonic if it had come off, because it would have put me within nice easy distance of the door – I dropped to the ground. Only to discover, as I started to wriggle, that the bottom of the bally thing was not a foot from the floor. I got my head in, and then I stuck.

And before I could rise and make for more suitable cover, she was busy with the paper-knife.

It seemed to speak to my very soul. I remember, even in that supreme moment, wondering how the dickens a female of her slight build and apparently fragile physique could possibly get that wristy follow-through into her shots. I had always looked upon the headmaster of my first school as a very fine performer with the baton, but he was not in it with this slim, blue-eyed girl. I suppose it is all largely a matter of timing.

'There,' she said, at length.

I had got round the chesterfield now, and we stood regarding each other across it. The brisk exercise had brought a flush to her cheek and a sparkle to her eyes, and she had never looked more beautiful. Nevertheless, the ashes of my dead love showed no signs whatever of bursting into flame again. I rubbed the spot and eyed her sombrely. It gave me a certain moody satisfaction to think that she was not going to be warned of

what awaited her when Reginald, Lord Havershot, at last found
his way to her door.

'There,' she said again. 'That'll teach you. Now scram.'

Even had the word been unfamiliar to me, I would have
gathered from the gesture which accompanied it that I was being
dismissed from her presence, and I was all for it. The quickest
way out was the way for me. I made for the door forthwith.

And then, in spite of everything, my better self asserted itself.

'Listen,' I said. 'There's something—'

She waved the paper-knife imperiously.

'Go on. Get out of here.'

'Yes, but listen . . .'

'Scram,' she said haughtily. 'This means you.'

I sighed resignedly. I shrugged my shoulders. I think, though
I am not sure, that I said: 'So be it.' Anyway, I started to move
for the door again. And then something over by the window
caught the corner of my eye, and I stopped.

There, with their noses pressed against the glass, were
Tommy Murphy and Orlando Flower.

I stood congealed. I saw what had happened. From the fact of
their standing side by side in apparent amity, it was evident that
the state of friction which had existed between them existed no
more. They must have talked things over after my departure and
decided that the best results were to be obtained by calling a halt
on cut-throat competition and pooling their resources. They had
formed an alliance. A merger is, I believe, the technical term.

The faces disappeared. I knew what this meant. These two
young blots had gone off to take up a commanding position
outside the front door.

April June advanced a step.

'I told you to scram,' she said.

I still hesitated.

'But, I say,' I quavered, 'Tommy Murphy and Orlando Flower
are out there.'

'What of it?'

'We're not on very chummy terms. In point of fact, they want
to knock the stuffing out of me.'

'I hope they do.'

She hounded me to the front door, opened it, placed a firm
hand on the small of my back, and shoved. Out into the night
I shot, and as the door slammed behind me there was a whoop
and a rush of feet, and with a sickening sense of doom I realized

that I was for it. Only fleetness of foot could save me now, and I was no longer fleet of foot. Nothing slows up a runner like the sort of thing I had been going through. The limbs were stiff and in no sort of shape for sprinting.

The next moment eager hands had clutched at me, and with a stifled 'Play the game, you cads!' I was down.

And then, just as I was trying to bite the nearest ankle in the hope of accomplishing something, however trivial, before the sticky finish came, a miracle happened. A voice cried: 'Stop that, you little beasts!', I heard the musical ring of two well-smacked heads, followed by two anguished yelps, and my assailants had melted away into the dusk.

A hand seized my wrist and helped me to my feet, and I found myself gazing into the sympathetic eyes of Ann Bannister.

23

A snort of generous indignation told me that Ann's fine nature was deeply stirred. And even in the gathering darkness I could see her eyes flashing.

'The little brutes,' she said. 'Did they hurt you, Joey dear?'

'Not a bit, thanks.'

'Sure?'

'Quite. They hadn't time. Owing,' I said, with genuine feeling in my voice, 'to your prompt action. You were magnificent.'

'I did move pretty quick. I thought they were going to massacre you. Who were they?'

'Tommy Murphy and Orlando Flower.'

'I'd like to boil them in oil.'

I, too, felt that a touch of boiling in oil would do the young hell-hounds good, and regretted that it was not within the sphere of practical politics. However, I pointed out the bright side.

'You must have made them sit up a bit with those buffets of yours,' I said. 'They sounded good ones.'

'They were. I nearly sprained my wrist. I don't know whether it's Tommy or Orlando, but one of them's got a head like concrete, darn him. Still, all's well that ends well. Hullo! I thought you told me they didn't hurt you?'

'No.'

'Then why are you limping?'

It was an embarrassing question. After the stand I had taken in our conversation that afternoon, championing April June's sweetness and gentleness against all counter-argument, it would have made me feel a bit of a chump to reveal what I might call the paper-knife side of her character. I feared the horse-laugh and the scornful 'I told you so'. The best of women cannot refrain from these.

'I'm a bit stiff,' I said. 'I've been sitting.'

'And sitting makes you stiff, does it? You octogenarians! It's always your joints that go back on you. What were you doing there, anyway? Had you been calling on April June?'

'I did look in for a moment.'

'Knowing that Tommy Murphy and that Flower boy were just lurking and waiting for their chance! Really, young Joseph, you ought to scrap that head of yours. It isn't worth the upkeep. What did you want to see April June about?'

Here, too, I was unable to reveal the true facts.

'I went to give her a nosegay.'

'A *what*?'

'Flowers, you know. A bouquet.'

She seemed bewildered. 'You didn't?'

'Yes, I did.'

'Well, this beats me. I simply can't understand you, Joseph. One of these strange, inscrutable personalities, if ever there was one. I've heard you say a hundred times that you think April June a pill. In my presence, you have many a time and oft alluded to her as a piece of cheese. And yet you brave fearful perils to bring her gifts of flowers. And when I ventured on a few criticisms of her this afternoon, you drew yourself up to your full height and bit my head off.'

Remorse gripped me. 'I'm sorry about that.'

'Oh, don't apologize. All I'm saying is that it's puzzling. By the way, how much of that pork pie did you manage to get away with? I left early, if you remember.'

'Not much. I'm frightfully sorry about that, too.'

'I bet you are.'

'I mean that you lost your job because of your kindly act.'

'Oh, that's all right. I wasn't looking on it as my life work, anyway. Don't give it a thought, Joey. By this time tomorrow I expect to be your late hostess's press agent. I was coming to see her, to talk things over, and that's how I happened to be on the spot just now. I suppose I ought to go back, but I don't like to leave you alone. I shouldn't be surprised if Tommy and his little friend weren't still lurking in the shadows somewhere. They're like the hosts of Midian. They prowl and prowl around.'

Precisely the same thought had occurred to me. I begged her with a good deal of earnestness on no account to leave me alone.

'Yes, I think you need my stout right arm.' She mused for a moment. 'I'll tell you what let's do. Could you manage a soda?'

'I certainly could.'

'All right. Then if you don't mind me taking you a little out of your way, we'll go to the Beverly-Wilshire drug store and I'll buy you one. I can phone her from there.'

I assured her that I did not mind how much out of my way she took me, and in another jiffy we were breezing along – she talking idly of this and that; I silent, for my soul was a mere hash of seething emotions.

And if you want to know why my soul was a mere hash of seething emotions, I'll tell you. It was because in the brief space of time which had elapsed since she had caught Tommy Murphy and Orlando Flower those two snorters on their respective ear-holes, love had been reborn within me. Yes, all the love which I had lavished on this girl two years ago and which I had supposed her crisp remarks at Cannes had put the bee on for good was working away at the old stand once more, as vigorously as ever.

Many things, no doubt, had contributed to this. Reaction from the meretricious spell of April June, for one. Her gallant behaviour in the late turn-up, for another. But chiefly, I think it was her gay, warm-hearted sympathy, her easy kindness, her wholesome, genial camaraderie. And, of course, that pork pie. Anyway, be that as it may, I loved her, I loved her, I loved her.

And a lot of use it was loving her, I felt bitterly, as I champed a moody nut sundae at the drug store while she did her telephoning. Of all the sad words of what-d'you-call-it and thingummy, the saddest are these – It might have been. If only I'd had the sense to realize right away that there could never be any other girl in the world for me, I wouldn't have fooled about eating ice-cream at that party of April June's, and I wouldn't have started the old tooth off, and I wouldn't have gone to I. J. Zizzbaum at the same time that little Joey Cooley was going to B. K. Burwash, and, in short, none of this business would have happened.

As it was, where did I get off? She was betrothed to my cousin Eggy, and, even if she hadn't been, I was in no possible shape to ask her to share my lot. All the old obstacles which I had recognized as standing between myself and April June stood just as formidably between myself and her. In what spirit, even if she had been free, would she receive a proposal of marriage from Joey Cooley?

Heigh-ho, about summed it up, and I was murmuring it to myself in a broken sort of way, when she came out of the telephone-booth and joined me in a second nut sundae.

'I've talked to her,' she said. 'Everything's set.'

I didn't know what she meant by this, but I said 'Oh, yes?'

and plugged away at my sundae, finishing it as she began hers. She asked me if I would like another. I said I would, and she ordered it. A princely hostess.

'Well,' she said, resuming conversation, 'you've had a busy afternoon, haven't you?'

I laughed a trifle mirthlessly. 'I have, indeed.'

'How did everything go off?'

'I beg your pardon?'

'Mr Brinkmeyer's statue. The unveiling.'

I started as if she had bitten me in the leg. A lump of nut sundae fell from my nerveless spoon. Believe it or not, what with the pressure of other matters, I had clean forgotten all about that statue.

'Gosh!' I exclaimed.

'What's the matter?'

It was some moments before I could speak. Then, frankly and without evasion, I told her all. She listened with flattering attention, pursing the lips a bit when I came to the frog *motif*.

'You think Miss Brinkmeyer has found those frogs?' she said.

'If I can read the female voice aright,' I replied, 'I am dashed certain she has found them. And by this time she will have learned that I gave the unveiling a miss, and it will have been reported to her that the statue, when unveiled, had a red nose. In short, if ever a bloke was in a hell of a jam, I am that bloke.'

'You mustn't say "Hell", Joey.'

'There are times,' I replied firmly, 'when one has jolly well got to say "Hell". And this is one of them.'

She seemed to see my point. 'Yes, you're certainly in a swivet.'

The word, I took it, was American for 'soup'. I nodded gloomily.

'Still, there's one thing. They'll have forgotten all about it tomorrow.'

'You think so?'

'Well, of course.'

Her optimism infected me. 'That's fine,' I said.

She rose. 'The best plan is for me to take you home now,' she said. 'Come along. Everything's going to be all right.'

I allowed her to escort me to the Brinkmeyer residence. And it was only after she had left me at the gate that I saw the flaw in her specious reasoning. True, when one took into consideration the speed with which life in Hollywood moved, it might quite well happen, as she predicted, that the morrow would bring oblivion. But what she had omitted to take into her calculations was what the dickens was going to happen tonight.

I found my thoughts straying in the direction of Miss Brinkmeyer. After all that had occurred, it seemed too much to hope that I should find her in sunny mood. In fact, the nearer I got to my destination, the more firmly convinced did I become that that hair-brush of hers must be regarded as a moral certainty.

It was, accordingly, in pensive mood that I shinned up on to the outhouse roof. And I hadn't set foot on it before I began to suspect the worst. There was a light in my bedroom, and I found the circumstance sinister.

Moving softly I crossed the roof, and peered in. It was as I had feared. That light indicated trouble. The blind had not been drawn, and I was enabled to get a clear view of the interior.

My inspection revealed Miss Brinkmeyer sitting bolt-upright in a chair. Her face was stony, and yet one noted on it a certain wistful, yearning look, as if she were waiting for something. She wore a pink dressing-gown, and in her hand, tightly grasped, was a hair-brush.

That look was explained. That something for which she was waiting was me.

I tiptoed back across the roof and noiselessly descended into the garden. I could see that what the situation demanded was clear, hard, intensive thinking. And I was burning up the brain cells pretty earnestly, when all of a sudden I became aware of a bloke standing beside me.

'Hey,' he said.

'Hullo?' I said.

'Are you the Cooley kid?' he said.

'Yes,' I said.

'Pleased to meet you,' he said. A civil cove.

'Pleased to meet you,' I replied, not outdone in courtesies.

'Right,' he said.

Something wet and sploshy came slapping over my face, and I smelt the smell of chloroform. And it was suddenly borne in upon me that, on top of everything else I had been through that day, I was now being kidnapped. It seemed to me to put the tin hat on things.

'Well, this is a nice bit of box-fruit!' I remember saying to myself as I passed out.

And I meant it.

24

Chloroform is a thing I don't happen to be frightfully well up on – all I know is what I read in the thrillers – but in ordinary circs, I imagine, it doesn't take the bloke on the receiving end very long to come out from under it. And had all this occurred in the afternoon's earlier stages, I have no doubt that I should have been up and about in no time, as good as new.

But it will be recalled that I had had rather a full day, of a nature to tax the constitution and sap the vitality and all that, and that I hadn't been any too robust to start with. The result was that, having gone off like a lamb, I stayed off like a lamb, taking no interest in the proceedings for a very considerable time. I have a sort of dim recollection of going along in a car and fetching up at a house and being carried in; but the first thing I really remember is waking up in bed and finding that it was next morning. Bright sunlight was streaming in at the window, one or two birds were doing a spot of community singing, and the distant sound of churchbells told that it was Sunday.

There's nothing like a good sleep for putting one in form. Tired Nature's sweet restorer, somebody calls it, and he's not so far wrong. I was delighted to find that, except for a little stiffness about the curves, natural after that paper-knife episode, I felt myself again. I rose and went to the window and looked out.

The house stood at the bottom of a lane, at the end of which was a main road of sorts. The Ventura Boulevard I discovered that it was later. This was a part of the country I had not seen before, and I was examining it with interest, when I suddenly became aware of a scent of sausages and coffee so powerful and inviting that I sprang for my clothes and started making my simple toilet without further delay. A moment before, I had been speculating as to the chances of these birds who had kidnapped me cutting fingers and things off me and slipping them in the parcel post in order to encourage the Christmas spirit in whoever was supposed to kick in with my ransom; but it didn't seem to matter so much now. I mean to say, if they let me get at those sausages first, I wasn't disposed to be fussy about what they did afterwards.

I was nearly ready for the dash downstairs, when there was a bang on the door and a voice spoke.

'Hello, there,' it said.

'What ho,' I replied.

'How's it coming?'

'How's what coming?'

'How do you feel?'

'Hungry.'

'Okay. There's sausages and pancakes.'

'Pancakes?' I said, my voice trembling.

'Sure,' replied this unseen bloke. A matey desperado. 'You just slip on something loose and come and join the party.'

Two minutes later, I was in the living-room, taking my first look at the gang. They were seated round a table, on which was a dish of sausages so vast that the sight of it thrilled me like a bugle. It was plain that there was going to be no stint.

As these were the first kidnappers I had met, I drank them in with a natural curiosity. There were three of them, all wearing full-size beards which made them look like a group photograph of Victorian celebrities. I can't say that all this foliage made for *chic*, but I suppose fellows in their line of business are obliged to think more of the practical side of things than of appearances. In any case, things were not as bad as they might have been. The beards were false ones. I could see the elastic going over their ears. In other words, I had fallen among a band of criminals who were not wilful beavers, but had merely assumed the fungus for purposes of disguise.

It may be that this discovery prejudiced me in their favour, but I must say they seemed very decent coves. There appeared to be a distinct disposition to set the young guest at his ease. They introduced themselves as, respectively, George, Eddie and Fred, hoped I had slept well, and invited me to seat myself at the table. George helped me to sausages, Eddie said that the pancakes would be along in a minute and that if the sausages were not fixed as I liked them I had only to say the word, and Fred made a civil apology about the chloroform.

'I'm sorry about that, kid,' he said. 'You're feeling all right after it, eh?'

'Never better,' I assured him. 'Never better.'

'Swell. You see, George and Eddie been giving me the razz on account me slipping the sponge on you that way . . .'

'You shouldn't have did it,' said George, shaking his head.

' 'Tisn't as if he'd of been likely to of squawked,' said Eddie.

'Yay, I know,' said Fred, 'but there's a right way and a wrong way of doing everything. A fellow's got his technique, hasn't he? The artist in a fellow's got to have expression, hasn't it?'

'That's enough,' said George, who appeared to be something in the nature of president of this organization, speaking with a frigid note of rebuke. 'You go and look after those pancakes.'

'Oh, shoot,' mumbled Fred – evidently dashed, poor chap. 'I don't see where a fellow's technique's got to be stifled.'

He shuffled off into the kitchen, and George seemed to think it necessary to make an apology for him.

'No hard feelings, I hope?' he said. 'Fred thinks too much about technique. It's his temperament. You gotta excuse it.'

I begged him not to give the matter another thought.

'Anyway,' said Eddie, 'I'll say this for him – he cooks a pancake that has to be tasted to be believed.'

And shortly afterwards Fred returned with a smoking platter, and I tested the statement and found it correct. I am not ashamed to confess that I pitched in till my insides creaked. It was only some little time later that I found myself in a position to listen to the breakfast-table conversation.

Like all other breakfast-table conversations taking place at that moment in the Hollywood zone, it dealt with the motion pictures. George, who was reading the Sunday paper while he stirred his coffee absently with the muzzle of his automatic, said he saw where this new Purity Drive seemed to be gaining ground. He read out a paragraph about there being a rumour that Mae West's next picture was going to be *Alice in Wonderland*.

Fred and Eddie said they were glad to hear it. Eddie said it was certainly time somebody came along and threw water on the flames of the tidal wave of licence which had been poisoning the public mind, and Fred said Yay, that was about the way he had always felt.

'This is going to be a break for you, kid,' said George. 'Your stuff's clean.'

'Ah,' said Fred.

'You'll find yourself on top of the heap.'

'Sure,' agreed Eddie. 'He'll reap his reward.'

'If,' said George, striking a warning note, 'they give him the right sorta story. Clean or not clean, you gotta have a strong, human, compelling story. These guys that do your stuff, kid, they don't seem to have good story sense.'

'Ah,' said Fred.

'You gotta watch out for that kid,' said Eddie.

'It's the system that's wrong,' said George. 'I blame the studio heads.'

'The Moguls,' said Eddie.

'The Mandarins,' said Fred.

'The Hitlers and Mussolinis of the picture world,' said George. 'What do they do? They ship these assortments of New York playwrights and English novelists out here and leave it all to them. Outside talent don't get a chance.'

'Ah,' said Fred.

'Well, lookut,' said George. 'Some guy from outside grabs him a swell idea for a picture, and what happens? The more he submits it to the Script Department, the more they don't read it. I've got a whale of an idea at this very moment for a story for you, kid, but what's the use? They wouldn't so much as look at it.'

'Was that the one you were telling us about Tuesday?' asked Eddie.

'The one about Public Enemy Number Thirteen?' asked Fred.

'Sure, that's the one,' said George, 'and it's a pippin.'

'You bet it's a pippin,' said Eddie.

'That's just about what it is,' said Fred.

I finished my pancake. 'It's good, is it?' I said.

'I'll say it's good,' said George.

'I'll say it's good,' said Eddie.

'*I'll* say it's good,' said Fred.

'I expect it's good,' I said.

'Listen!' said George, in a sort of ecstasy. 'Listen, kid. Get a load of this, and see if it's not like mother makes. There's this gangster that's been made Public Enemy Number Thirteen – see – and he's superstitious – see – and he feels he won't never have any luck just so long as he's got this Thirteen hoodoo – see – so what does he do?'

'Get this, kid,' said Eddie.

'Get this, kid,' said Fred.

They were leaning forward, beards twitching with excitement.

'He's too kind-hearted to go shooting up one of the Public

Enemies that's higher on the list, though he knows that if he does that'll make him Public Enemy Number Twelve. . . .'

'I see it as a Lionel Barrymore part,' said Eddie.

'Warner Baxter,' said Fred.

'Bill Powell,' said George curtly, putting them both in their places. 'So he gets an idea for pulling a play that'll put the Government wise to how good he is, so's maybe they might even promote him to Number One or Two, and here's the idea. Him and his gang get on a liner that's carrying a lot of gold across to the other side, and they hold up the captain and the officers and take charge of the ship and steer for the coast of South America, and when they're there they're going to blow the boat up and escape into the interior with the gold. See?'

I didn't want to damp the chap, but I had to point out a flaw. I mean, after all, that's what these story conferences are for.

'I don't think you need be discouraged,' I said. 'I can see you've got an idea. But you haven't worked it out.'

George bridled.

'How do you mean? What's wrong with that ship sequence?'

'You get your comedy there,' said Eddie. 'You'd make the captain a comedy type. I see Charles Butterworth.'

'Joe Cawthorne,' said Fred.

'Edward Everett Horton,' said George.

'Where's your love interest?' I asked quietly.

The question plainly rattled them. George scratched his chin, Eddie and Fred their left cheek and head respectively.

'Love interest?' said George. He brightened. 'Well, how does this strike you? Coast of South America, girl swimming out to the anchored ship. The air is heavy with the exotic perfume of the tropics . . .'

'Flamingoes,' suggested Eddie deferentially.

'Sure,' said George. 'Flamingoes. The air is heavy with the exotic scent of the tropics and a cloud of pink flamingoes drifts lazily across the sky, and there's this here now prac'lly naked girl swimming out to—'

I shook my head.

'Too late,' I said. 'By the time you get to South America, you're in your fourth reel.'

George banged the table.

'Well, hell,' he said, 'never mind about the love interest . . .'

'You've got to have the heart-throb,' I insisted.

'No, you haven't, not if your story's strong enough. Look at *All Quiet on the Western Front.*'

'Yeah,' said Eddie. 'And *Skippy.*'

'Yeah,' said Fred. 'And *The Lost Patrol.* How much do you think that one grossed?'

'I still maintain that you must have a love interest.'

'Don't you worry about love interest,' said George. 'Let's get on to where you blow in. These gangsters scuttle the ship – see – and they get off in the boat – see – same as in *Mutiny on the Bounty* – see – and, well, sir—'

'Well, sir—' said Eddie.

'Well, sir,' said George, 'supposing that in this boat there's a little bit of a golden-haired boy – cute . . .'

'Ah,' said Fred.

'Get the idea?' said George, rising. 'Is that good, or is it good? Hey, Fred, Eddie, come on over here. Squat down on this rug. Lookut, kid. The rug's the boat, and there's nobody in it but just the gangsters and you. See? And they fall for you.'

'They *love* you,' said Eddie.

'Ah,' said Fred.

'That's what they do,' said George. 'They love you. And there's only just so much food and water, so the gangsters push each other overboard so's you will have enough . . .'

'Until—' said Eddie.

'There's only—' said Fred.

'Until,' said George, 'there's only you and Public Enemy Number Thirteen left.'

'And get this, kid,' said Eddie. 'Who—'

'Yes, get this, kid,' said Fred. 'Who do you think—'

'Yes, tilt up your ears for the big smash, kid,' said George. 'Who do you think Public Enemy Number Thirteen turns out to be? Just your long-lost father. That's all. Nothing but that. Maybe that ain't a smacko? There's a locket you're wearing round your neck – see—'

'And this bozo takes a slant at it while you're asleep – see—'

'And,' said George, 'it's yessir sure enough the picture of the dead wife he loved . . .'

At this point I interrupted the story conference.

'Hands up!' I cried, pointing the pistol which George, the silly juggins, had left lying by his cup. 'Hands up, you frightful bounders!'

25

I don't know when I've seen three bearded blokes so thoroughly taken aback. And I wasn't surprised. I don't know much about kidnappers, but I imagine it can't be often that they have their victim turning round on them and putting them on the spot like this. To George, Eddie and Fred, you could see that this had come as a totally new experience. They scrambled to their feet and stood gaping.

Fred was the first to speak.

'Hey!' he cried. 'Be careful what you're doing with the gat!'

'Didn't your mother teach you it's dangerous to point guns at people?' asked Eddie, a bit severely.

And George wanted to know if this was any way to act. Was that, he demanded, a system?

All this shook me a good deal, of course. I found it hard to meet their reproachful eyes. A minute before, I mean to say, we had been all pals together, and I could not deny that I was bursting with their pancakes. In a way, it was a bit as if the guest of honour at a civic banquet had risen in his place and started throwing plates. One felt the same sense of social strain.

But I crushed down the momentary weakness and was firm again.

'I don't care,' I said. 'You shouldn't have kidnapped me. It's a dashed low trick, kidnapping people. Ask anybody.'

They seemed stunned. George particularly.

'But wasn't you told?' he said.

'Told what?'

'Wised up, George means,' explained Eddie. 'Wised up that this was all sim'ly a publicity stunt.'

'What!'

'One of those press gags,' said George. 'The lady came to us—'

'What lady?'

'We never got her name, but she says: "I'm representing this big star – see—" '

'What big star?'

'We never got her name, either. But it seems where the lady that come to us is the press agent for some big star and she wants us to snatch you – see – and hide you away somewheres – see – and then just as all the mothers in America is running around in circles and saying: "Oh, Hell! Can no one save our darling boy?" this big star's going to come along and rescue you – see – and that'll put her on the front page.'

I smiled a cynical smile. I wasn't going to swallow bilge like that. I may be an ass, but I'm not a silly ass.

'Ha!' I said. 'A likely story!'

'It's true,' insisted Eddie. 'See that's wet, see that's dry . . .'

I smiled again.

'Perfect rot, my dear chap.'

'But—'

'If this was just a press stunt, why didn't you simply ask me in a quiet and civil manner to come along with you instead of soaking me to the gills in your beastly chloroform?'

George looked at Fred reproachfully.

'There! You see!'

Eddie looked at Fred reproachfully, too.

'You see! There!'

'I knew that chloroform of yours would get us into trouble,' said George.

Fred's beard drooped. You could see he felt his position acutely. He muttered something about technique.

'I don't believe a single dashed word,' I said. 'You talk about this press agent and you don't know her name, and you talk about this star and you don't know her name either. I never heard anything so bally thin in my life. No,' I said, summing up, 'what the thing boils down to is this – you're simply a lot of low twerps who kidnapped me in order to cash in, and you can jolly well march out of this room into the cellar, if you've got a cellar, after which I shall telephone to the constabulary and lodge a complaint.'

This got in amongst them. It isn't easy to be sure, when fellows are bearded to the eyebrows, but I rather think they blenched.

'No, say, don't do that,' urged George.

'You wouldn't do that,' pleaded Eddie.

'Yes, I would,' I said. 'And I'm dashed well going to.'

'What, after all those pancakes?' said George.

'Pancakes have nothing to do with it,' I snapped testily, for I knew that I was on thin ice there. I could see that, in a sense, I was outraging the sacred laws of hospitality, which, as everyone knows, is a rotten sort of thing to do, and, if persisted in, gets one cut by the County. I changed my mind about telephoning the police. I preserved unimpaired the austerity of my demeanour, but inwardly I decided that after I had shut them up in the cellar I would just go off and call it a day.

Not being able to read my thoughts, however, these blighters continued to be in a twitter.

'Gee!' said Eddie.

'Gosh!' said Fred.

'If he does phone the cops,' said George, 'you know what will happen?'

'Gosh!' said Fred.

'Gee!' said Eddie.

'I'll tell you what'll happen,' said George. 'We'll be left to take the rap. The dame that hired us – see – is going to swear she never did no such thing – see – and then where'll we be? In the cooler, facing a kidnapping charge.'

'Gee!' said Fred.

'Gosh!' said Eddie.

They paused a while in thought.

'Seems to me,' said George, 'one of us had best rush him and get that gun away.'

'That's right,' said Fred. 'You rush him, Eddie.'

'You rush him, George,' said Eddie.

'You rush him, Fred,' said George. 'Or, listen, we'll do it perfectly fair, so's there won't be any complaints. We'll count out. Eeny, meeny, miney, mo, catch a nigger by the toe, tiddly-iddly-umpty-whatever-it-is . . . You're it, Fred.'

'Snap into it, Fred,' said Eddie.

'Yes, no sense in wasting time,' said George. 'Make one of those quick springs of yours.'

'Like a leopard,' said Eddie.

'Yes, say, I know, but listen,' said Fred.

At this tense moment a voice spoke.

'What is all this?'

April June was standing in the doorway.

26

It was a nasty shock. I think if I hadn't been so full of pancakes, I should have tottered. I decided to take a firm line from the start.

'Stand back, woman,' I cried. 'I am armed!'

Her agitation seemed to equal mine.

'You little bonehead,' she said feverishly, 'what do you think you're doing? Haven't you any sense? At any moment my press agent will be here with the reporters and camera men, and what sort of a rescue party is it going to be if they find you carrying on in this way? And haven't you any sense?' she proceeded, turning to George and Eddie and Fred with gleaming eyes. 'My press agent tells me that she explained most carefully exactly what you were to do, and here you are, simply fooling about. The reporters aren't supposed to find you romping with the child. He ought to be tied to a chair and you ought to be menacing him with threats. The first thing the camera men will want is a shot of him tied up and you menacing him with threats and me standing there with the gun!'

'But lady,' said George. 'Pardon me, lady, are you the lady the lady said was the lady she was press agent for? The big star?'

'Of course I am, you poor fish.'

'Pleased to meet you, lady.'

'Never mind about being pleased to meet me—'

'Say, it's April June!' said Eddie.

'That's right,' said Fred.

'Of course I'm April June.'

'Listen, George,' said Eddie. 'What was that story we were doping out couple days ago – the one you said would be a natural for Miss June?'

'You remember, George,' said Fred. 'The one about—'

'Why, sure,' said George. 'Listen, lady, if you've a minute to spare, I'd like to approach you on a little scenario me and the boys have sort of thrown roughly together. It's where this big business man has a beautiful secretary—'

April June stamped what, if I hadn't felt it on my trouser seat, I would have called a dainty foot.

'I don't want to hear any stories. I want to know why you haven't tied him up.'

George waggled his beard apologetically.

'We hadn't the heart, lady.'

'Not,' added Eddie, 'while he was eating pancakes.'

'We was aiming to get around to it later,' said Fred.

'And then,' explained George, 'we got to mulling over a story sequence . . .'

April stamped again.

'And now you've probably ruined the whole thing. Tie him up, quick. Hurry. Even now it may be too late.'

'But, lady, that Roscoe he's got is loaded.'

'What on earth did you want with a loaded gun?'

'That's Fred,' said Eddie, directing another reproachful glance at him. 'He's so thorough.'

'He likes doing things right,' said George.

'I'm an artist,' said Fred defiantly. 'I saw that gun as loaded. That's how I felt it – felt it *here*,' he said, slapping his chest.

'The fact of the whole matter is,' said George, 'Fred's never been the same man since he was an extra in *Lepers of Broadway*.'

April June turned on me with a look which in its way was almost as bad as a paper-knife.

'Give me that gun!'

I hesitated. I wanted to be very sure of my facts before I did anything drastic.

'Is it true,' I asked, 'what these birds were saying? This is simply a publicity stunt?'

'Of course it is. Haven't you had it explained to you over and over again? Miss Bannister told me she had thoroughly coached you and that you understood.'

'By Jove, yes, of course,' I said. I saw the whole thing now. This was the meaning of all those occasional observations which I had found cryptic. You remember. When Ann had said about my having a busy day tomorrow and all that, and when the kid Cooley had mentioned something about putting me wise.

'All the papers were notified last night that you had been kidnapped . . .'

Of course, yes. That was why Ann had been so sure that all

my crimes in the matter of frogs and statues would be forgotten next day.

' . . . And this morning I am to find you and rescue you. Give me that gun and get yourself tied up, quick. I hear the car.'

And yet, in spite of everything, I still hesitated. It was all very well for her to tell me to get myself tied up, but how was I to be certain that this was not a ruse? I knew what a formidable adversary this woman was, even when one had full possession of one's limbs and was in a position to dodge. To expose myself to her fury in a tied-up condition might quite easily be simply asking for it. I didn't want another of those unilateral infractions of hers.

This tense meditation caused me to relax my vigilance. I lowered the weapon, and the next moment the squad of beavers were on me. I was assisted to a chair, and ropes were coiled around me. Footsteps sounded outside. April secured the gun. The beavers raised their hands and registered alarm.

'Move a step and I shoot, you scoundrels!' cried April. And so saying, she cocked an expectant eye at the door. But it was not a gaggle of reporters and camera men who entered. Simply Ann Bannister by herself.

A bit of an anticlimax, what? I thought so, and I could see that April June thought so, too. I mean to say, rather like somebody in a comic opera saying 'Hurrah, girls, here comes the royal bodyguard!' and one drummer-boy entering left.

April stood there with her eyes swivelling round in their sockets.

'Where are the reporters?' she cried.

'I haven't brought them,' said Ann shortly.

'And the camera men?'

'I haven't brought them.'

'Not brought them?' I don't say April was foaming at the mouth, but it was a near thing. 'What do you mean, you haven't brought them? Great heavens!' she cried, registering about six mixed emotions. 'Don't I get *any* co-operation?'

The beavers looked at one another.

'No reporters, lady?' said George, pursing his lips.

'No camera men, lady?' said Fred and Eddie, raising their eyebrows.

'No,' said Ann. 'Not one. And if you will give me a moment to explain, I will tell you why not. It's no use going on with this thing. It's cold.'

'Cold?'

'Cold,' said Ann. 'There's not a cent's worth of publicity in rescuing Joey Cooley now. The poor kid's name is mud and his screen career finished.'

'What!'

'Yes. You have a Sunday paper there. Haven't you seen? On the front page?'

'We've only read the movie section and the funnies,' said George.

'Oh? Well, take a look at it now. You are an old chump, Joseph,' said Ann, eyeing me commiseratingly. 'Why on earth did you want to go and be funny with a female interviewer? I told you your sense of comedy would get you in trouble some day. You didn't expect her to know you were kidding, did you? And do you think the fans will believe you said it just for a laugh? I'm afraid you'll never be able to live this down. There is a photograph on the front page of the *Los Angeles Chronicle*,' she said, turning to April, 'showing Joey Cooley smoking a cigarette with a highball in his hand. In the accompanying letterpress he states that he is twenty-seven years old and prefers a pipe.'

April snatched up the paper and began to read. George looked at Eddie. Eddie looked at Fred.

'Seems to me, boys,' said George, 'the deal's off.'

'Ah,' said Fred.

Eddie nodded briefly.

'No sale,' he said.

'Nothing to keep us here now,' said George. 'If we hurry, we'll just be in time for church.'

'Ah,' said Fred.

'Ah,' said Eddie.

They shook their heads at me reproachfully, removed their beards, put them away in a cupboard, and taking prayer-books from this cupboard, withdrew in what I thought rather a marked manner.

Ann turned to me, angelically sympathetic.

'Poor old Joseph!' she said. 'It's your old weakness – anything for a laugh. And it must have been funny, too. But I'm afraid you've done for yourself. American Motherhood will never forgive this. As a matter of fact, when I left, there were six hundred Michigan Mothers gathered outside Mr Brinkmeyer's house, calling on him to bring you out so they could tar and feather you, and demanding that he pay their expenses to and from Detroit. So I'm afraid—'

There was a sort of low, whistling sound, like an east wind blowing through the crannies of a haunted house. It was April June drawing in her breath.

'Not a word about me in the whole interview from beginning to end,' she said, in a strange, hard quiet voice that suggested the first whisper of a tornado or cyclone. 'Not – one – word! Not so much as a single, solitary, blanked, by-golly syllable. *My* interview!' she proceeded, her voice gathering volume. '*My* private and personal interview. *My* individual and exclusive interview, and this little bohunkus wriggles in and hogs the whole shooting-match! Let me get at him!'

A sort of shiver passed through her frame and she began to slide across the room, clenching and unclenching her hands. Her teeth were set, her eyes large and luminous, and it seemed to me that Reginald was for it.

And then with a quick movement Ann stepped between us.

'What are you going to do?'

'Plenty.'

'You won't touch this child,' said Ann.

I couldn't see April now, for Ann was in the way, but I heard her do that drawing-in-breath business again, and most disagreeable it sounded. I thought she was going to say 'Huh?' but she didn't. She said 'No?'

'No?' she said.

'No,' said Ann.

There was a silence. I remember once, years ago in the old silent days, seeing a picture where the heroine, captured by savages, lay bound on an altar, and all that stood between her and the high priest's knife was the hero, who was telling the high priest to unhand her. I knew now how that heroine must have felt.

'Get out of my way,' said April.

'I won't,' said Ann.

April whistled a bar or two.

'You're fired,' she said.

'Very well,' said Ann.

'And I'll see that nobody else engages you as a press agent.'

'Very well,' said Ann.

April June stalked to the door. She paused for an instant on the threshold, glared at Ann, glared at me, and stalked out.

An unpleasant girl. I can't think why I ever liked her.

Ann cut my bonds, and I left my seat. I turned to her and opened my mouth, then shut it again. It had been my intention to thank her with all the eloquence I could scoop up for her splendid conduct in thus for a second time saving me from the powers of darkness, but the sight of her face stopped me.

She was not bathed in tears, for she was not the sort of girl who weeps to any great extent, but she looked licked to a splinter, and I realized what it must be meaning to her, losing like this the job for which she had worked so hard and on which she had been counting so much. Whole thing unquestionably a pretty nasty jar.

And she had dished her aims and dreams purely in order to save me from the fury of A. June. My admiration for her courage and unselfishness, seething on top of all the pancakes I had eaten, threatened to choke me.

'I say,' I said, foozling the words a bit, 'I'm frightfully sorry.'

'It doesn't matter.'

'But I am.'

'That's all right, Joseph.'

'I – I don't know what to say.'

'It's quite all right, Joey dear. You don't suppose I was going to stand by and let her—'

'But you've lost your job.'

'I'll get another.'

'But she said—'

'Perhaps not as a press agent – I suppose she has enough influence to queer me in that way – and, anyhow, press agent jobs don't come along all the time – but something.'

An idea struck me, enabling me to look on the bright side. If you could call it the bright side.

'But, of course, you don't really need a job. You're going to get married,' I said, wincing a bit as I spoke the words, for the idea of her getting married was dashed unpleasant – in fact more or less like a spear-thrust through the vitals.

She looked at me in surprise.

'How do you know that?'

I had to think quick.

'Oh – er – Eggy told me.'

'Oh, yes. He came to give you an elocution lesson yesterday, didn't he? How did you get on?'

'Oh, fine.'

'You must have done, if you call him "Eggy" already.'

'He's got quite a bit of money.'

'So I believe. But it won't be any use to me, because the engagement is off.'

'What!'

'Broken. Last night. So I shall have to be looking out for a job, you see. I have an idea that I shall end up as a dentist's assistant. The girl who helps Mr Burwash told me she was leaving. I might get her place.'

I was unable to speak. The thought of Eggy's foul treachery in tying a can to this noble girl, and the thought of Ann – my wonderful Ann – wasting her splendid gifts abetting B. K. Burwash in his molar-jerking, combined to tangle up the vocal cords.

'But we won't waste valuable time talking about that now,' said Ann. 'What we've got to think of is what is to become of you.'

'Me?'

'Why, yes, my poor lamb. We shall have to dispose of you somehow. You can't go back to Mr Brinkmeyer.'

I saw that she was right. Contemplating her swivet, I had rather given a miss to the fact that I was in no slight swivet myself. And the mental anguish of sitting tied up in a chair with April June bearing down on me had helped to take my mind off it. When an angry woman is spitting on her hands and poising herself to give you one on the submaxillary, you find yourself concentrating on the immediate rather than the more distant future. Into this I was now at liberty to peep.

'Gosh!' I said.

'It's a problem, isn't it? Have you any views?'

'I had thought of going to England.'

'England?'

'If, of course, I could collect the necessary cash.'

'But why England?'

Not, in the circs, easy to answer, that.

'Oh, I just thought of it.'

'Well, think of something else, my poor child. You certainly get the craziest ideas, Joseph. Apart from the fact that you would have nowhere to go when you got there, you couldn't so much as begin to get there. Where's your passport? Do you think a shipping office would sell transportation to anyone of your age? You would be detained for enquiries and then mailed back to Miss Brinkmeyer.'

I hadn't thought of that. In conceiving the plan of going to England and settling down at Biddleford, I had, I am free to admit, merely sketched out the broad, general outlines of the thing, leaving the details to be filled in later.

'There's only one thing. You must go home to your mother at Chillicothe, Ohio. So listen. I can't drive you there myself, because my car's only borrowed, but I'll go to the nearest garage and hire something to take you home. Your mother can pay when you arrive. I will explain to them. All right, then, I'll be going. Goodbye.'

'Goodbye.'

'I'll be back to see you off. Cheer up, Joseph. Things will dry straight one of these days.'

She pushed off. There was a pancake left on the dish. I ate it moodily. Then, feeling stifled indoors, I wandered out of the house and started to walk up the lane, kicking stones.

She had told me to cheer up, but I was dashed if I could do it. She had said that things would dry straight one of these days, but I was blowed if I could see when. The more I contemplated the general outlook, the ballier it seemed.

I mean to say, leaving Ann's swivet out of it and concentrating on my own, what was the position of affairs? Hopeless love gnawed at my heart, and would doubtless continue so to gnaw. But, even apart from that, how about it?

The future seemed to me to look about as black as it could stick. I hadn't been any too keen on being a child star, when all my tastes and habits lay in the direction of being a third earl, but it would have been a dashed sight better than being an ex-child star, as I was now.

There might have been some faint satisfaction to be gained from feeling that one was the Idol of American Motherhood. Of this I was now deprived. Taking a line through the attitude of those Michigan specimens, it was only too plain that the sole emotion American Motherhood would feel towards me from now on would be a strong desire to bounce a brick off my head.

Presumably I would have to settle down to a life of retired obscurity with Joey Cooley's parent in Chillicothe, Ohio. And while he had told me that this parent cooked an excellent fried chicken, southern style, I can't say I found myself relishing the prospect much. You know how it is, getting to know a strange woman. It takes you a long time to feel at your ease. Difficult at the outset to discover mutual tastes and congenial subjects of conversation.

With all this on my mind it is not surprising that as I turned into the main road I was in a pretty profound reverie. What jerked me out of it was the sound of a motor bicycle coming along at the dickens of a speed. And, looking round, I found the bally thing right on top of me.

I had just time to note that the occupant of the saddle was clad in a quiet grey suit and that his socks, which were of powder blue, melted into tasteful suede shoes, when there was a yell and a toot, one of the handlebars biffed me on the head, and I turned three somersaults and knew no more.

27

When I came to, I was lying by the side of the road with my eyes shut and a nasty lumpy feeling in the skull. A voice was speaking.

'Hey!' it said.

My first idea was that I was in Heaven and that this was an angel trying to get acquainted, but I was too occupied with skull to take a look and ascertain. I just lay there.

'Hey,' said the voice again. 'Are you dead?'

A moment before, I should have replied 'Yes' without hesitation, but now doubts were beginning to creep in. The bean was clearing. I thought it over a bit longer and was convinced.

'No,' I said.

And by way of producing evidence to back up the statement, I opened my eyes. They fell upon something which brought me up with a round turn.

For an instant, I thought that I was having those things chaps have that begin with 'h'. Then the bean cleared still further and I saw that this was not so.

Standing before me was little Joey Cooley in person. There was no possibility of error. There were the knickerbockers, there were the golden curls. And at the same moment I caught sight of my legs, stretching out towards the horizon. They were long and beefy and clad in quiet grey trousers, terminating at the ankles in powder-blue socks that melted, as it were, into tasteful suede shoes.

I suppose some fellows would have been nonplussed. Possibly a day or so earlier I might have been nonplussed myself. But the vivid life which I had been living of late had sharpened my faculties, and I was on to what had happened in a flash.

We were back again as before.

I could see quite easily how the thing had been worked. It was that smash that had done the trick. At the precise moment when it had laid me out cold, it must have laid the kid Cooley out cold, and while we were both laid out cold we had done another of our switches. I had no recollection of the incident, but no doubt we had got together in the fourth dimension, talked the thing over briefly, and decided that now was an admirable opportunity of getting back to what I believe, though I wouldn't swear to it, is called the *status quo*.

'What ho!' I exclaimed.

After what had passed between this young shrimp and myself at our last meeting, I would have been well within my rights, no doubt, in being a bit stand-offish. We had parted, I mean to say, if you remember, on distant terms, he having shrugged my shoulders and sneered at me and gone off and left me alone with the ravening Murphy. But I was feeling much too bucked to be sniffy. I fairly beamed at the little Gawd-help-us.

'What ho, what ho!' I said. 'I say, do you notice anything?'

'Notice what?'

'Why, the old *status quo*, if that's the expression I want. Have you observed that we're back again?'

'Oh, yes. I got that. How do you suppose it happened?'

I hadn't had time to think it all out, of course, but I gave my view for what it was worth. He nodded understandingly.

'I see. Same old routine. It wasn't my fault,' he went on, with a touch of sullen defensiveness in his voice. 'I blew my horn.'

'Oh, quite.'

'What were you doing, wandering around on the road that way?'

'Just musing.'

'And how do you come to be here at all?'

'This is where George and Eddie and Fred brought me.'

'Who are George and Eddie and Fred?'

'Rather decent coves. Kidnappers.'

His face cleared.

'Oh, that kidnapping stunt came off all right, did it?'

'Not a hitch.'

'And this is their hide-out? That house down the lane there?'

'That's right.'

'What happened?'

'Well, it's a long story. We started off with some breakfast—'

He uttered an exclamation.

'Breakfast! So that was it? The moment I got back into this body of mine, I thought you must have been doing something to it since I had it last. It seemed fuller. It had kind of lost that hollow feeling. Breakfast, eh? What did you have?'

'Sausages, followed by pancakes.'

His eyes lit up.

'Any left?'

'You can't want any more already.'

'I do too.'

'There may be some in the kitchen. Can you cook sausages?'

'I'm not sure. But I can try. And maybe there'd be some bacon, as well. And eggs. And bread. If I've got to go back to Ma Brinkmeyer, with Clause B of my contract operating, I'll need to stoke up.'

The time had come, I saw, to break the news to him.

'I wouldn't go back to the Brinkmeyers, if I were you.'

'Talk sense. My contract's got three years to run.'

'Not now.'

'Eh?'

'Haven't you seen the Sunday paper?'

'No. Why?'

'Well, I'm sorry to say,' I said, 'that inadvertently, if you know what the word means, I've rather let you in a bit.'

And in a few simple words I informed him of the state of affairs.

I needn't have worried. I've never seen a child so profoundly braced. In supposing that he would be all broken up at the news that his professional career had been ruined, I had been right off the mark. Nowhere near it.

'Well, sir,' he said, regarding me affectionately, 'I'll say you've done me a good turn all right. You couldn't have done me a better turn if you'd sat up nights studying how to. No, sir!'

I was astounded.

'You're pleased and gratified?' I said, quite unable to grasp.

'You bet I'm pleased and gratified. This lets me out nicely. Now I can go straight back to Chillicothe.' He broke off, his exuberance waning a bit. 'Or can I?'

'Why not?'

'How am I to get there?'

I waved a hand lightly. And the relief of being able to wave my own hand was simply terrific.

'Oh, that's all arranged.'

'It is?'

'Oh, rather. There will be a car here shortly to take you.'

'Well, that's swell. Whose idea was that?'

'Ann Bannister's.'

'It would be. What a girl!'

'Ah!'

'There's a girl that's got a head on her shoulders.'

'And what a head!'

'I love Ann.'

'Me, too.'

He seemed surprised.

'You?'

'Certainly.'

'Do you love two of them, then?'

'I beg your pardon?'

'You told me you were that way about April June.'

I shuddered.

'Do me a favour,' I said. 'Don't mention that name to me. How right you were, young Cooley! How unerring was your judgement of character. When you called her a pill.'

'She's a pill, all right.'

'Definitely a pill.'

'A whale of a pill.'

'A frightful pill.'

'Yessir!'

'Yessir!'

We seemed to be pretty straight on that point. I turned to another.

'Rummy,' I said, 'that you hadn't seen the Sunday paper. Don't you read it as a rule?'

It seemed to me that a slight shadow passed over his brow again. He appeared a trifle embarrassed, I thought.

'Why, yes,' he said, 'I do. Only today I was stopped – sort of.'

'Stopped – sort of?'

'Yes, interrupted – kind of – before I could get down to it.'

'Who interrupted you?'

'This cop.'

'Which cop?'

His embarrassment increased.

'Say, listen,' he said, 'there's something I ought to tell you. I was meaning to let you have it before this, but we got to talking of other things. It was this way. I'd just bought the paper this morning, and I was starting to read it on the street outside the Garden of the Hesperides, when up comes a cop on a motor bicycle and asks me am I Lord Havershot?'

'To which you replied—?'

'Yessir. He then ups and pinches me for assaulting Ma Brinkmeyer. It's an open-and-shut case, he says, because it seems where when I was chasing her around that pool I dropped your card-case.'

'Great Scott!'

'Sure. But wait. You ain't heard nothin' yet. You know that lovely wallop of yours, the one that travels about eight inches, with a sort of corkscrew twist on it?'

I tottered.

'You didn't—'

'Yessir. Plumb on the snoot. Down he went, and I swiped his motor bike and lit out. I was heading for Mexico. And let me tell you sump'n'. If I was you, if that motor bike is still working, why, I'd keep right on heading for Mexico. If I was you. Yessir. And now I think I'll be going along and snaring myself a sausage. These pancakes of yours seem to be kind of wearing off a little.'

He disappeared down the lane, and I made a beeline for the motor bike to look it over. If this body of mine, for whose rash acts I must now once more take the responsibility, had been going about hitting policemen, I could see that his advice about getting over the border into Mexico was sound.

It was a dashed sight more than the bike was. The thing was a mere *macédoine*. I concluded my post-mortem and turned away. Not by means of this majestic ruin could I win to safety.

It seemed to me that the best thing I could do would be to wait till the hired car came to fetch the kid and get him to give me a lift to this Chillicothe place of his, which would at least take me into another State, and I went to the house to ask him if this would be all right. I found him in the kitchen, preparing to get busy with a large frying-pan, and he said it would be quite all right. Glad of my company, he was decent enough to say.

'And you'll be sitting pretty, once you're over the State line,' he said. 'They can't get at you there.'

'You are sure of that?'

'Sure I'm sure. They'd have to extradicate you, or whatever it's called.'

A horn tooted without.

'Hello,' he said. 'Somebody at the door. If it's for me, tell 'em I'm not ready yet.'

I was struck by a disquieting thought.

'Suppose it's somebody for me?'

'The cops, you mean? Couldn't be.'

'It might.'

'Well, if it is, poke 'em in the snoot.'

It was with a good deal of uneasiness that I made my way to the front door and opened it. I had not this child's simple faith in snoot-poking as a panacea for all ills. Outside, a car was standing, and my relief was substantial on perceiving that it was not a police car, but just one of those diseased old two-seaters which are so common in Hollywood.

Somebody was getting out of it. Somebody who seemed strangely familiar.

'Golly!' I exclaimed.

I had recognized our caller. It was my cousin Eggy.

28

This human suction-pump being absolutely the last chap I was expecting to see, I just stood there and gaped at him as he wriggled out. It took him a moment or two to get clear, for this was a pint-size two-seater and he is one of those long, thin, straggly fellows, built rather on the lines of a caterpillar or a hose-pipe. However, he managed it at last and came forward with a cheery 'What ho!' Or, rather, with a cheery 'What!' and a sort of gargling gurgle. For before he could add the 'ho!' he saw me standing at the doorway and the spectacle seemed to wipe speech from his lips. He shot back as if he had collided with something red-hot, and for perhaps a quarter of a minute stood blinking and making a low rattling noise in the recesses of his throat.

Then he smiled a sickly smile.

'Hullo,' he said.

'Hullo.'

'Good morning, George.'

'George?'

'I mean, Good morning, Eddie.'

'Eddie?'

'That is to say, Good morning, Fred.'

I snatched at what appeared to me the only possible explanation, though even at his best I had never seen the old boy like this.

'You're blotto,' I said.

'Nothing of the kind.'

'You must be. If you can't see that I'm Reggie. What's all this rot about George and Eddie and Fred?'

He blinked again.

'You mean you really *are* Reggie?'

'Of course.'

He stood for a moment mopping his forehead, then spoke in an injured voice.

'I wish you wouldn't do this sort of thing, Reggie. I've had to speak to you about it before.'

'What sort of thing?'

'Why, suddenly popping up in places where no one would ever dream you could possibly be and confronting a chap who's expecting to see somebody totally different. A most unpleasant shock it gave me, seeing you standing there, when I had expected to see George or Fred or Eddie. Naturally I thought that you must be George or Fred or Eddie and that my eyes had gone back on me again. You ought to have more consideration. Put yourself in the other fellow's place. Think how you would feel in his position.'

I was astonished.

'Do you know George and Fred and Eddie?'

'Of course I do. Splendid chaps.'

'Are you aware that they are kidnappers?'

'They may be kidnappers in their spare time. I met them at the Temple of the New Dawn. They're churchwardens there, and pretty highly thought of by the flock. Eddie lent me his hymn-book at evensong yesterday, and we had a lemonade after the service, and they asked me to look in this morning for lunch and a round of golf. Nice fellows. No side about them. Do you know the Temple of the New Dawn, Reggie?'

'I've heard of it.'

'You ought to join us. Wonderful place. A girl called Mabel Prescott put me on to it. It's a sort of combination of a revival meeting and a Keeley Cure Institute. I signed on yesterday.'

'About time, I should think.'

'The nick of time. I was pretty far gone.'

'You've been pretty far gone for years.'

'Yes, but in these last two days things have come to a head, if you know what I mean. It's really been most extraordinary. I was going along just the same as usual, without a care in the world, mopping it up here, sopping it up there, when all of a sudden I had a sort of collapse. I went right to pieces.'

'Yes?'

'I assure you. It was like Mabel was saying. I didn't stop at wayside stations: I went right on and hit the terminus. The first thing I knew, my eyesight had gone phut. The symptoms were rather odd. I started seeing astral bodies. Have you ever been annoyed by astral bodies, Reggie? Most unpleasant. They poke their heads up from behind chairs.'

'What do they do that for?'

'I can't imagine. A whim, no doubt.'

'May be just a hobby?'

'Call it a hobby if you like. Anyway, they do. Mine did. It was the astral body of a child star named Joey Cooley. I happened to be out at your bungalow at the Garden of the Hesperides, and there he was, right behind the chair. When I say "he", I mean, of course, his wraith or phantasm.'

'I see.'

'So did I, and it gave me a hell of a jolt. But I think I should have carried on, considering it a mere passing weakness, had it not been for what occurred the very next day. I'm going to tell you something now that you will find very hard to believe, Reggie, old man. Yesterday morning I had to go and give an elocution lesson to this same Joey Cooley, and after the natural embarrassment of seeing in the flesh one whom I had met only the day before a phantasm or wraith, we got down to it. I said to him: "What you want to do, laddie, is watch your '*ow's*'. They're rotten. Say: 'How now, brown cow, why do you frown beneath the bough?' " and do you know what I could have sworn I heard him reply?'

'What?'

'That he was you! Just imagine! "It may interest you to know," he said, "that I am your cousin Reggie Haver-shot." '

'He did?'

'Positively. "I might mention in passing," he said, "that I am your cousin Reggie Havershot." '

'Well, well.'

'Exactly. I saw at once what it meant. In addition to my eyes handing in their portfolio, my ears had gone west also. Well, I know when I'm licked. I tooled straight round to the Temple of the New Dawn and asked for an entrance form. And, as I say, that's how I came to know George and Fred and Eddie. Where are they, by the way?'

'They said something about going to church.'

'Ah? They meant the Temple. Matins start at eleven. I'd better go and join them there. And now tell me, Reggie, how on earth do you come to be—' He broke off, and started to sniff. 'I say, do you smell something burning?'

I sniffed, too.

'Yes, I do seem to— What's the matter?' I asked, for he had

given a sudden jump and was now stepping slowly back, his eyes a bit enlarged and his tongue moving over his lips.

He seemed to brace himself.

'It's nothing,' he said, 'nothing. Just a trifling relapse. A slight return of the old trouble. I suppose I must expect this sort of thing for a little while. You remember we were speaking of Joey Cooley's astral body? Well, it's in again. Just behind you. Don't encourage it. Pretend not to notice it.'

I turned. The Cooley kid was standing in the doorway, holding a smoking frying-pan from which proceeded a hideous niff of burned sausages.

'Say,' he said.

'Voices,' said Eggy, wincing. 'It spoke.'

'Say, I don't seem to be fixing these sausages just right,' said the kid. 'They sort of curl up and turn black on me. Hello, who's this?'

I gave him a warning glance.

'You haven't forgotten your elocution teacher?' I said meaningly.

'Eh?'

'Yesterday morning. Your elocution teacher. Chap who came to teach you elocution.'

'Oh, sure. Sure. Yes, my elocution teacher. I remember. How are you, elocution teacher? How's tricks?'

Eggy came forward cautiously.

'Are you real?' he asked.

'I guess so.'

'Do you mind if I prod you?'

'Go ahead.'

Eggy did so, and heaved a relieved sigh.

'Ah! It wasn't that I doubted your word. It was only— It's all most confusing,' he said, a little petulantly. 'I mean, sometimes you're real and sometimes you're not. There seems to be no fixed rule. Well, I still don't see what you're doing here.'

'I'm trying to cook me some sausages, but I don't seem to do it so good. Can you cook sausages?'

'Oh, rather. At school, I was an adept. I could fry a sausage on the end of a pen. Would you like me to come and help you?'

'Will you?'

'Certainly.'

He started off, and I leaped forward and detained him by grabbing at his coat. Until this moment, what with talking of other things, I had forgotten that this was the man who had let Ann down with a thud by callously breaking off their engagement.

'Wait!' I said. 'Before you go, Egremont Mannering, I want a full explanation.'

'What of?'

'Your scurvy behaviour.'

He seemed surprised.

'What do you mean? I haven't been scurvy.'

'Ha!' I said, laughing a hard laugh. 'Your engagement is broken, isn't it? You've oiled out of marrying Ann, haven't you? If you don't call it scurvy, winning a girl's love and then saying: "April fool, it's all off!" there are some who do. I appeal to you, young Cooley.'

'Sounds pretty scurvy to me.'

'As it would to any fine-minded child,' I said.

Eggy seemed all taken aback.

'But, dash it, all that has nothing to do with me.'

'Ha! You hear that, Cooley?'

'I mean, it wasn't I who broke off the engagement. It was Ann.'

I was stunned.

'What!'

'Certainly.'

'She broke off the engagement?'

'Exactly. Last night. I looked in to tell her about my joining the Temple, and she gave me the push. Very sweetly and in the kindliest spirit, but she gave me the push. And if you want to know what I think was the reason, throw your mind back to what I was telling you a couple of nights ago at that party. You were urging me to swear off, and I said that if I did Ann would chuck me, because it was only to reform me that she had taken me on at all. You follow the psychology, Cooley?'

'Sure.'

'If a girl gets engaged to a chap to reform him and he goes and reforms on his own, it makes her feel silly.'

'Sure. It's what happened in *Pickled Lovers*.'

'That's what it must have been, you see. Come on, young Cooley. Sausages ho!'

I grabbed his coat again.

'No, wait!' I said. 'Wait! Don't go yet, Eggy. You don't appreciate the nub.'

'How do you mean, the nub?'

'I mean the poignancy of the situation. When Ann gave you the push last night, she was self-supporting. She had a good job in prospect. Today, she is on the rocks. The job has fallen through. I happen to know that she is more or less broke. So somebody's got to look after her. Otherwise, all that stands between her and the bread-line is the chance of getting taken on as a dentist's assistant.'

'Not really?'

'Absolutely. She would have to wear a white dress and say: "Mr Burwash will see you now." '

'She wouldn't like that.'

'She would hate it.'

'It would make her feel like a bird in a gilded cage.'

'Exactly like a bird in a gilded cage. So there's only one thing to be done. You must go to her and ask her to take you on again.'

'Oh, but I can't do that.'

'Of course you can.'

'I can't. There are technical difficulties in the way. The fact is, old man, immediately after Ann had given me the air last night, I toddled round to Mabel Prescott and I'm now engaged to her.'

'What!'

'Yes. And she isn't the sort of girl you can go to the day after you've become betrothed to her and tell her you've changed your mind. She's – well, I would call her rather a touchy girl. A queen of her sex, mind you, and I love her madly, but touchy.'

'Oh, dash it!'

'The best I could expect if I went and told her there was a change in the programme would be to have my neck wrung and my remains trampled on. But listen,' said Eggy. 'Ann's all right. Why can't she just go on being nursemaid to this young sausage merchant here?'

'She was fired yesterday.'

'By Jove, she does keep getting fired, doesn't she? It's what I always say. What's the use of getting jobs? You only lose them.'

The Cooley child, who had been standing frowning thoughtfully and scratching his chin with the handle of the frying-pan, now spoke.

'Here's a suggestion, boys. May be nothing in it, but we're all working for the good of the show. Why don't *you* marry Ann?'

I quivered.

'Who, me?'

'Yay. You told me you loved her.'

'Does he? Well, that's fine,' said Eggy.

'Swell,' said the child. 'Couldn't be better.'

At this point, they appeared to notice that I was ha-ha-ing hollowly.

'What's the matter?' asked Eggy.

'Ann wouldn't look at me.'

'Of course she would.'

'Sure she would,' said the child. 'He's an Oil,' he added to Eggy.

'I know he's an Oil. And the type of Oil of which England is justly proud.'

'Any dame would like to marry an Oil.'

'I cannot conceive anything more calculated to buck the average dame up like a week at Skegness,' assented Eggy heartily.

They seemed to have got it all reasoned out between them, but still I shook my head.

'She wouldn't look at me,' I repeated. 'I'm the very last chap in the world she would dream of marrying.'

The Cooley half-portion addressed Eggy in what I imagine he intended to be a confidential whisper. It sounded like somebody calling coals.

'He's thinking of his face.'

'Oh?' said Eggy. 'Oh, ah, yes, of course. Yes, to be sure.' He coughed. 'I wouldn't worry about your face, Reggie,' he said. 'I can assure you that from certain angles – in certain lights – what I mean is, there's a sort of rugged honesty . . .'

'What does a fellow's face matter, anyway?' said Joey Cooley.

'Exactly.'

'Looks don't mean a thing. Didn't Frankenstein get married?'

'Did he?' said Eggy. 'I don't know. I never met him. Harrow man, I expect.'

'It's the strong, passionate stuff that counts,' said the Cooley child. 'All you got to do is get tough. Walk straight up to her and grab her by the wrist and glare into her eyes and make your chest heave.'

'Exactly.'

'And snarl.'

'And, of course, snarl,' said Eggy. 'Though when you say "snarl" you mean, I take it, not just make a noise like a Pekingese surprised while eating cake, but add some appropriate remark?'

'Sure. Like "Sa-a-ay, listen, baby!" If he does that, she'll fall.'

'Then we'll leave you to it, Reggie. The only thing that remains is to find her. Does anybody know where she would be at this hour?'

'She'll be right back any moment now.'

'Then all is well,' said Eggy. 'You just potter about and brush up your snarling, old man, while I repair to the kitchen with young Goldilocks here and show him how to cook a sausage which his astral body will appreciate. Are you with me, kid?'

'I'm in front of you, buddy. Let's go.'

They moved off in the direction of the kitchen, and I wandered up the lane again and stood staring dumbly down the road. And presently I saw a car coming along, with Ann at the wheel.

I stepped out into the road, and she shoved the brakes on with a startled yip.

29

'Reggie!' she cried.

Surprised to see me, of course. I don't blame her. Probably the last fellow she had anticipated barging into.

'*Reggie!*'

'Hullo, Ann,' I said.

She got slowly down and gave me the astonished eye. Her face had gone a bit pink, and then it had gone a bit pale, and now it had started going pink again. What mine was doing over this period, I can't say. No doubt looking perfectly foul.

There was a long silence. Then she said:

'You've shaved your moustache.'

'Yes.'

There was another long silence. I gazed at her in the sort of agonized, hopeless way young Joey Cooley would have gazed at a sausage if there had been an insurmountable barrier between him and it. Because I knew I hadn't a chance. All those things she had said to me at Cannes two years ago, when severing our relations, came back to me. No girl was going to take on a chap who answered to the description she had given of me in those few tense moments immediately following the impact of my lighted cigar on the back of her neck.

She started speaking again.

'Whatever . . .' she began, and I think she was going to add 'are you doing here?' but she stopped. A chilliness came into her manner. 'If you have come bleating after April June, she left long ago. You will probably find her at her home.'

I was definitely incensed.

'I did not come bleating after April June.'

'Really?'

'It is not my practice to bleat after the lady you mention.'

'Oh, but surely? The story going the round of the clubs—'

'Curse the clubs and blast the story that's going round them.' I laughed another of my hard ones. 'April June!' I said.

'Why do you say "April June" like that?'

'Because it's the only way to say it. April June is a pill.'

'What!'

'Slice her where you like, she's still boloney.'

She raised a couple of eyebrows.

'Reggie! The woman you love?'

'I don't love her.'

'But I thought—'

'I dare say you did. But I don't. Whole story much exaggerated.'

I was pretty shirty. Enough to make a chap fly off the handle a bit, all this rot about my loving April June. There was only one girl I loved – or, as I could see now, ever had loved. The above Ann, to wit.

For the first time since this spot of conversation had started, she smiled.

'Well, your words are music to my ears, Reggie, but you can't blame me for being a little surprised. After the way you were raving about her two days ago—'

'Much can happen in two days.'

'Don't I know it! What did happen?'

'Never mind.'

'I merely asked. Well, thank goodness you've seen through her. That's off my mind.'

I shook a trifle, and my voice became a bit throaty.

'Were you worried about me, Ann?'

'Of course I was worried about you.'

'Ann!'

'I would have been worried about anybody who was thinking of getting married to April June.'

'Oh?' I said, a bit damped, and silence fell again.

She looked down the road.

'I'm expecting a car,' she said.

I nodded. 'I know.'

'Clairvoyant?'

'No. I've been talking to the Cooley kid.'

'What! But you don't know Joey Cooley?'

I nearly laughed when she said that.

'Yes, I've met him.'

'When? Where?'

'We were having mutual teeth out that day, and we fraternized in the Zizzbaum-Burwash waiting-room.'

'Oh, I see. And you've been talking to him now? Reggie, you haven't explained yet. How on earth do you happen to be here like this? I took it for granted that you had come after April June, but you say—'

I had to do a bit of quick thinking.

'I just chanced to be out for a ride on my motor bicycle and saw him and stopped to pass the time of day.'

'You mean he was out here in the road?'

'Yes.'

She looked anxious.

'I hope he's not roaming about all over the countryside. He ought to have stayed in the house till I got back.'

'He is in the house now. He's in the kitchen with Eggy.'

'Eggy! Eggy's not here?'

'Yes. He came to spend the day with some pals of his who own the house.'

'I see. It sounded like a miracle at first. Have you been talking to him?'

'Yes.'

She looked down and slid her foot about on the concrete road. Her air was that of one who would have kicked a stone, if there had been a stone to kick.

'Did he tell you . . .?'

'Yes.'

'Oh, so you know about that, too?' She laughed, though not too bobbishly. 'Well, you were right just now when you said that much can happen in two days, Reggie. Since I saw you at that party, I've broken my engagement and lost a couple of jobs.'

'So I hear.' I hesitated. 'You're a bit up against it, Ann, aren't you?'

'Yes, a little.'

'Any money?'

'Not much.'

'And no job in prospect?'

'Not a very dazzling one, anyway.'

'What are you going to do?'

'Oh, I'll be all right.'

I passed a finger round the inside of my collar. Something told me it was no good, but I had a pop at it.

'You wouldn't consider marrying me, would you?'

'No.'

'I thought not.'

'Why?'

'Oh, I just thought you wouldn't.'

'Well, you were right. I don't like charity.'

'What do you mean, charity?'

'I mean what you are offering me. "Cophetua swore a royal oath – 'This beggar maid shall be my queen.' " If I'd been her I'd have said: "Oh, yeah?" '

'I don't know what you're talking about.'

'Oh, yes, you do, Reggie. You haven't changed. I told you you had a heart of gold, and you're just the same sweet old thing you always were. You're sorry for me.'

'Nothing of the kind.'

'Oh, yes. And don't think I don't appreciate it. It's dear of you, and just like you. But the pride of the Bannisters is something frightful. No, I won't marry you, Reggie – bless you all the same and thanks for asking me.'

She gave herself a little shake, like a dog coming out of a pond. It was as if she were chucking off her all this rot of marrying me. 'Well, that's that!' the shake seemed to say.

She turned to other topics.

'Did you say Joey was in the kitchen?'

'He was heading that way when I saw him last.'

'I'd better go and tell him there will be some delay before his car arrives, or he may be worrying. Not that I can imagine anything capable of worrying young Joseph. I wouldn't call him a neurotic child. I'm hiring a car to take him back to his Ohio home, you see, because he has got to get out of these parts quick. Did you read the paper this morning? That interview?'

'Oh, yes.'

'It will finish him on the screen, poor mite.'

'He doesn't seem to mind that much.'

'I'm glad.'

'In fact, he's thoroughly bucked. He wants to get back to his mother. She cooks fried chicken, southern style.'

'I know. He's often told me about it. Well, he can start as soon as the car comes. The garage people are tuning it up.' She gave a little sigh. 'I shall miss old Joseph. It's a nuisance when people go out of your life, isn't it?'

'And when they come back, what?'

She gave me a queer look.

'Well, it's . . . upsetting sometimes. Funny our meeting again like this, Reggie.'

'Dashed droll.'

'I didn't mean quite that— Well, goodbye.'

She broke off rather abruptly and shoved her hand out. And here, of course, if I had wanted to, was an admirable opportunity of grabbing her wrist and glaring into her eyes and making my chest heave, as the Cooley kid had advised. But I let it go. Quite possibly he was right in claiming that this procedure would bring home the bacon – nobody could say he was not an intelligent child – but I gave it a miss. A ghastly, dull, grey, hopeless sort of feeling had come over me.

'Goodbye,' I said.

She uttered a little choking cry. 'Reggie!'

She was staring at me, her breath coming jerkily. I couldn't imagine why. I squinted down at my waistcoat. It seemed all right. I took a look at my legs. The trousers seemed all right. So did the socks. And the shoes.

'Reggie! What is that on your head?'

Well, it wasn't my hat, because I hadn't got one on. I put up my hand and felt.

'Why, hullo!' I said. 'Blood, by Jove!'

She was pointing at the ditch. A bit on the distraught side it seemed to me.

'What is that?'

I took a dekko.

'Oh, that? That's what's left of a motor bicycle.'

'Yours?'

'Well, I was riding on it.'

'You – you had an accident?'

'A bit of a spill, yes.'

A sort of greenish pallor had spread over her map. Her eyes were goggling, and she was having trouble with the vocal cords. She clucked like a hen and came groping at me with her hands out in a blind sort of way.

'Oh, Reggie, darling! You might have been killed, Reggie darling! You might have been killed! You might have been killed!'

And here she buried her face in her hands and broke into what I believe are called uncontrollable sobs.

I was stunned – (a) by her words, (b) by her behaviour. Neither seemed, as it were, to check up with her recent attitude.

'Did you say "darling"?' I said, groping.

She raised her face. It was still greenish, but her eyes were shining like . . . more like twin stars than anything I can think of.

'Of course I said "darling".'

I continued to grope.

'But you don't love me, do you, by any chance?'

'Of course I love you, you silly ass.'

'But at Cannes you said—'

'Never mind about Cannes.'

'And just now—'

'And never mind about just now.'

I got right down to it. 'But do you mean – I just want to check up my facts – do you mean you *will* marry me, after all?'

'Of course I'll marry you.'

'Good egg!'

'Do you think I'm going to let you run around loose after this? I don't care if you are just marrying me out of pity and – charity.'

I said something about pity and charity so crisp and incisive and so wholly unfitted for the delicate ears of woman that even in the midst of her emotion she gave a little startled jump. Then I began to speak.

You've probably had the experience of taking the cork out of a bottle of champagne and seeing the liquid come frothing out. Well, at this juncture it was as if I had been the said bot. and someone had uncorked me. I opened my mouth, and out it all came. I'm not much of a flier at molten eloquence, as a rule, but I managed it now. I cut loose with everything I had. I never paused for a word. I said this and that and so on and so forth, at the same time kissing her a good deal.

And then, right plumb spang in the midst of my ecstasy, if that's the word – at the very moment, in fact, when I was kissing her for the forty-fifth time – a chilling thought intruded – viz., that, now that we had got everything fixed up on this solid basis, she would, of course, expect me to return to Hollywood with her, there to put in train the preparations for the forthcoming nuptials.

Hollywood, mind you, where the police, I presumed, were even now spreading a drag-net and combing the city for me.

How the dickens was I to explain that I must now leave her and push on to Chillicothe, Ohio?

I mean to say, what reason could I give? How could I make plausible this sudden passionate desire to go to Chillicothe,

Ohio? It would mean issuing a statement, after all. In which event, she would most certainly think I was looney and break off the match in case it was catching.

And then I saw the way. I must say that I didn't like the idea of a kid of Joey Cooley's tender years going all that way alone. It would sound thin, of course, but . . .

I became aware that she was speaking.

'Eh?' I said.

A slight whiffle of impatience escaped her. The old Ann.

'Haven't you been listening?'

'Awfully sorry. My attention wandered a bit.'

'Well, do listen, my precious imbecile fathead, because it's important. It's about young Joseph.'

'Oh, yes?'

'Something has just occurred to me. He's such a child. I don't really think he ought to make that long journey all alone. So . . .'

My heart gave a leap like a salmon in spawning time.

'You want me to go with him?'

'Would you?'

'Rather!'

The air seemed full of pealing bells. I was saved. No tedious explanations . . . No issuing of statements . . . No breaking off of the match on account of lunacy of one of the contracting parties . . .

I kissed her a good deal more.

'You're an angel, Reggie,' she said. 'I don't know many men who would be so unselfish and put themselves out like this.'

'Not at all,' I said. 'Not at all.'

'I think you ought to get away as soon as possible.'

So did I. I kissed her again.

'And then you could come back to Hollywood—'

'No,' I said. 'I'll meet you in New York.'

'Why?'

'I'd rather.'

'Perhaps it would be better.'

'Much better.'

I kissed her again, bringing the total, I should say, about up to the level hundred. Then, hand in hand, we walked down the lane, guided by the scent of frying sausages which told me that Eggy had not overestimated his culinary skill and that little Joey Cooley was busy victualling up against the new day.

THE OLD RELIABLE

1

The sunshine which is such an agreeable feature of life in and around Hollywood, when the weather is not unusual, blazed down from a sky of turquoise blue on the spacious grounds of what, though that tempestuous Mexican star had ceased for nearly a year to be its owner and it was now the property of Mrs Adela Shannon Cork, was still known locally as the Carmen Flores place. The month was May, the hour noon.

The Carmen Flores place stood high up in the mountains at the point where Alamo Drive peters out into a mere dirt track fringed with cactus and rattle-snakes, and the rays of the sun illumined its swimming-pool, its rose garden, its orange trees, its lemon trees, its jacaranda trees and its stone-flagged terrace. Sunshine, one might say, was everywhere, excepting only in the heart of the large, stout, elderly gentleman seated on the terrace, who looked like a Roman emperor who had been doing himself too well on starchy foods and forgetting to watch his calories. His name was Smedley Cork, he was the brother of Mrs Adela Cork's late husband, and he was gazing in a sullen, trapped sort of way at an object which had just appeared on the skyline.

This was the butler, an unmistakably English butler, tall, decorous and dignified, who was advancing towards him carrying on a salver a brimming glass that contained a white liquid. Everything in Mrs Cork's domain spoke eloquently of wealth and luxury, but nothing more eloquently than the presence on the premises of this Phipps. In Beverly Hills, as a general thing, the householder employs a 'couple', who prove totally incompetent and leave the following week, to be succeeded by another couple, equally subhuman. A Filipino butler indicates a certain modest degree of stepping out. An English butler means magnificence. Nobody can go higher than that.

'Your yoghurt, sir,' said Phipps, like a benevolent uncle bestowing a gift on a deserving child.

Lost in daydreams, as he so often was when he sat on the terrace in the sunshine, Smedley had forgotten all about the yoghurt which his sister-in-law compelled him to drink at this time of the day in place of the more conventional cocktail. He sniffed at the glass with a shrinking distaste, and gave it as his opinion that it smelled like a motorman's glove.

The butler's manner, respectful and sympathetic, seemed to suggest that he agreed that there existed certain points of resemblance.

'It is, however, excellent for the health, I believe, sir. Bulgarian peasants drink it in large quantities. It makes them rosy.'

'Well, who wants a rosy Bulgarian peasant?'

'There is that, of course, sir.'

'You find a rosy Bulgarian peasant, you can keep him, see?'

'Thank you very much, sir.'

With a powerful effort Smedley forced himself to swallow a portion of the unpleasant stuff. Coming up for breath, he gave the campus of the University of Southern California at Los Angeles, which lay beneath him in the valley, a nasty look.

'What a life!' he said.

'Yes, sir.'

'It shouldn't happen to a dog.'

'The world is full of sadness, sir,' sighed Phipps.

Smedley resented this remark, helpful though he realized it was intended to be.

'A fat lot you know about sadness,' he said hotly. 'You're a carefree butler. If you don't like it here, you can go elsewhere, see what I mean? I can't, see what I mean? You ever been in prison, Phipps?'

The butler started.

'Sir?'

'No, of course you haven't. Then you wouldn't understand.'

Smedley finished the yoghurt and fell into a moody silence. He was thinking of the will of the late Alfred Cork and feeling how strange and tragic it was that different people should so differently interpret a testator's wishes.

That clause which Al had inserted, enjoining his widow to 'support' his brother Smedley. There you had a typical instance of the way confusion and misunderstanding could arise. As Smedley saw it, when you instruct a woman to support somebody, you mean that you expect her to set him up in an apartment on Park Avenue with an income sufficient to enable him to maintain the same and run a car and belong to a few good clubs and take that annual trip to Paris or Rome or Bermuda or wherever it may be, and so on and so forth. Adela, more frugal in her views, had understood the bequest as limiting her obligations to the provision of a bed, three meals a day and the run of the house, and it was on these lines that her brother-in-law's life had proceeded. The unfortunate man ate well and slept well and had all the yoghurt he wanted, but apart from that his lot these last few years had been substantially that of a convict serving a sentence in a penitentiary.

He came out of his reverie with a grunt. There swept over him an urge to take this kindly butler into his confidence, concealing nothing.

'You know what I am, Phipps?'

'Sir?'

'I'm a bird in a gilded cage.'

'Indeed, sir?'

'I'm a worm.'

'You are getting me confused, sir. I understood you to say that you were a bird.'

'A worm, too. A miserable, downtrodden Hey-you of a worm on whose horizon there is no ray of light. What are those things they have in Mexico?'

'Tamales, sir?'

'Peons. I'm just a peon. Ordered hither, ordered thither, ground beneath the iron heel, treated like a dog. And the bitter part is that I used to have a lot of money once. A pot of money. All gone now.'

'Indeed, sir?'

'Yes, all gone. Ran through it. Wasted my substance. What a lesson this should be to all of us, Phipps, not to waste our substance.'

'Yes, sir.'

'A fool's game, wasting your substance. No percentage in it. If you don't have substance, where are you?'

'Precisely, sir.'

'Precisely, sir, is right. Can you lend me a hundred dollars?'

'No, sir.'

Smedley had not really hoped. But the sudden desire which had come to him for just one night out in the brighter spots of Los Angeles and district had been so imperious that he had thought it worth while to bring the subject up. Butlers, he knew, salted their cash away, and he was a great believer in sharing the wealth.

'How about fifty?'

'No, sir.'

'I'd settle for fifty,' said Smedley, who was not an unreasonable man, and knew that there are times when one must make concessions.

'No, sir.'

Smedley gave it up. He saw too late that it had been a mistake to dish out that stuff about wasting one's substance. Simply putting ideas into the fellow's head. He sat for a moment scowling darkly, then suddenly brightened. He had just remembered that good old Bill had arrived in this ghastly house yesterday. It altered the whole aspect of affairs. How he had come to overlook such a promising source of revenue, he could not imagine. Wilhelmina ('Bill') Shannon was Adela's sister and consequently his sister-in-law by marriage, and if there was anything in the theory that blood is thicker than water, she should surely be good for a trifling sum like a hundred dollars. Besides, he had known dear old Bill since he was so high.

'Where's Miss Shannon?' he asked.

'In the Garden Room, sir. I believe she is working on Mrs Cork's *Memoirs*.'

'Right. Thank you, Phipps.'

'Thank you, sir.'

The butler made a stately exit, and Smedley, feeling a little drowsy, decided that later on would be time enough for going into committee of supply with Bill. He closed his eyes, and presently soft snores began to blend with the humming of the local insects and the rustle of the leaves in the tree above him.

The good man was taking his rest.

Phipps, back in his pantry, was restoring his tissues with an iced lemonade. He frowned as he sipped the wholesome beverage, and his air was tense and preoccupied. The household cat brushed itself insinuatingly against his legs, but he remained unresponsive to its overtures. There is a time for tickling cats under the ear and a time for not tickling cats under the ear.

When Smedley Cork, in their conversation on the terrace, had described James Phipps as carefree, he had been misled, as casual observers are so apt to be misled, by the fact that butlers, like oysters, wear the mask and do not show their emotions.

Carefree was the last adjective that could fittingly have been applied to the sombre man as he sat there in his pantry, brooding, brooding. If he had his elbow on his knee and his chin in his hand, he might have been posing for Rodin's *Penseur*.

It was on Wilhelmina Shannon that he was brooding, as he had been doing almost incessantly since he had admitted her at the front door on the previous afternoon. He was cursing the malignant fate that had brought her to this house and asking himself for the hundredth time what, now that she was here, the harvest would be. It was the old, old story. The woman knew too much. His future hung on her silence, and the question that was agitating James Phipps was, were women ever silent? True, the balloon had not yet gone up, which argued his secret was still unrevealed, but could this happy state of things persist?

A bell rang, and he saw that it was that of the Garden Room. Duty, stern daughter of the voice of God, said Phipps to himself, or words to that effect, and left his lemonade and made his way thither.

The Garden Room of the Carmen Flores place was the one next to the library and immediately below the projection room, a cheerful apartment with a large desk beside the French windows that looked on the swimming-pool. It caught the morning sun, and for those who liked it there was a fine view of the oil wells over by the coast. Bill Shannon, seated at the desk with the tube of a dictaphone in her hand, was too busy at the moment to look at oil wells. As Phipps had indicated, she was forcing herself to concentrate on the exacting task of composing her sister Adela's *Memoirs*.

Bill Shannon was a breezy, hearty, genial woman in the early forties, built on generous lines and clad in comfortable slacks. Rugged was a term that might have been applied to her face with its high cheekbones and masterful chin, but large, humorous eyes of a bright blue relieved this ruggedness and rendered her, if not spectacularly beautiful like her sister Adela, definitely attractive. Her disposition was amiable, and as a mixer she was second to none. Everybody liked Bill Shannon, even in Hollywood, where nobody likes anybody.

She raised the mouthpiece of the dictaphone and began to speak into it, if 'speak' is not too weak a word. Her voice was a very powerful contralto, and Joe Davenport, a young friend of hers with whom she had worked on the Superba-Llewellyn lot, had sometimes complained that she was apt to use it as if she were chatting with a slightly deaf acquaintance in China. It was Joe's opinion that, if all other sources of income failed, she could always make a good living calling hogs in one of the Western states.

'Hollywood!' boomed Bill. 'How shall I describe the emotions which filled me on that morning when I first came to Hollywood, an eager wide-eyed girl of sixteen . . . Liar! You were nearly twenty . . . So young, so unsophisticated. Just a—'

The door opened. Phipps appeared. Bill held up a hand.

'—timid little tot,' she concluded. 'Yes, Phipps?'

'You rang, madam.'

Bill nodded.

'Oh, yes. I want to confer with you in your executive capacity, Phipps. What with one thing and another, it has suddenly been borne in upon me that if I don't get a quick restorative, I shall expire. Have you ever written the *Memoirs* of a silent film star?'

'No, madam.'

'It is a task that taxes the physique to the uttermost.'

'No doubt, madam.'

'So will you bring me a fairly strong whisky and soda?'

'Yes, madam.'

'You really ought to go around with a keg of brandy attached to your neck, like Saint Bernard dogs in the Alps. No delay that way. No time lag.'

'No, madam.'

Bill, who had been sitting with her feet on the desk, put them down. She swivelled around in her chair and fixed her bright blue gaze on the butler. This was the first opportunity she had had since her arrival of a private and undisturbed talk with him, and it seemed to her that they had much to discuss.

'You're very curt and monosyllabic, Brother Phipps. Your manner is aloof. It is as though you felt in my presence a certain constraint and embarrassment. Do you?'

'Yes, madam.'

'I'm not surprised. It's your conscience that makes you feel that way. I know your secret, Phipps.'

'Yes, madam.'

'I recognized you the moment I saw you, of course. Yours is a face that impresses itself on the mental retina. And now I suppose you're wondering what I propose to do about it?'

'Yes, madam.'

Bill smiled. She had a delightful smile which lit up her whole face as if some inner lamp had been switched on, and Phipps, seeing it, was conscious for the first time since three o'clock on the previous afternoon of a lessening of the weight that pressed upon his heavy soul.

'Not a thing,' said Bill. 'My lips are sealed. The awful truth is safe with me. So be of good cheer, Phipps, and unleash that merry laugh of yours, of which I hear such good reports.'

Phipps did not laugh, for laughter is not permitted to English butlers by the rules of their Guild, but he allowed his lips to twitch slightly and gazed at this noble woman with something approaching adoration, an emotion which he had never expected to feel for a member of the jury which three years before had sent him up the river for what the Press of New York was unanimous in describing as a well-earned sentence. It was a moment or two before he was able to clothe his feelings in words.

'I am sure I am extremely grateful to you for your kindness, madam. You relieve my apprehensions. I am most anxious not to lose my position here.'

'Why? You could get a job anywhere. Walk into any house in Beverly Hills, and they'll lay down the red carpet for you.'

'Yes, madam, but there are reasons why I do not wish to leave Mrs Cork's service.'

'What reasons?'

'Personal reasons, madam.'

'I see. Well, I won't give you away.'

'Thank you very much, madam.'

'I am only sorry that I have occasioned you alarm and despondency. It must have given you a nasty jolt when you opened that front door yesterday and I walked in.'

'Yes, madam.'

'You must have felt like Macbeth seeing Banquo's ghost.'

'My emotions were somewhat similar, madam.'

Bill lit a cigarette.

'Rather odd that you should have remembered me. But I suppose, in the position you were in when we met, you've nothing much to do except study the faces of the jury.'

'No, madam. It passes the time.'

'Too bad we had to send you up.'

'Yes, madam.'

'But we couldn't go against the evidence.'

'No, madam. But might I beg you to lower your voice, madam. Walls have ears.'

'Walls have what?'

'Ears, madam.'

'Oh, ears! That's right. They have, haven't they? What was it like in Sing-Sing?' whispered Bill.

'Not very agreeable, madam,' whispered Phipps.

'No, I imagine not,' whispered Bill. 'Oh, hello, Smedley.'

Smedley Cork, his siesta concluded, had appeared in the French windows.

Phipps left the room, followed by the austere and disapproving look which impecunious elderly gentlemen give a butler who has refused to lend them a hundred dollars, and Smedley took a seat on the sofa.

'I want to talk to you, Bill,' he said.

'And so you shall, pal. What's on your mind? My God, Smedley,' said Bill with the candour of a friend of twenty-five years standing, 'you've aged terribly since I saw you last. I was shocked when I got here and observed what a museum piece you had become. Your hair's as grey as a badger.'

'I'm thinking of having it touched up.'

'It won't do any good. There's only one real cure for grey hair. It was invented by a Frenchman. He called it the guillotine. I suppose it's living with Adela that's done it. I can't imagine anything more calculated to produce silver threads among the gold than constant association with that sister of mine.'

Her words were music to Smedley's ears. He basked in her sympathy. Good old Bill, he told himself, had always been sympathetic. So much so that once or twice only that instinct for self-preservation which saves Nature's bachelors in their hour of need had prevented him from asking her to marry him. Occasionally, in black moods, he regretted this. Then the black mood would pass. The mere thought of being married appalled Smedley.

'It's a dog's life,' he agreed. 'She oppresses me, Bill. I'd be better off in Alcatraz. At least I wouldn't have to drink yoghurt there.'

'Does Adela make you drink yoghurt?'

'Every day.'

'Inhuman. Of course, it's good for you.'

Smedley held up a protesting hand.

'Just as a favour,' he begged, 'don't mention those Bulgarian peasants.'

'Which Bulgarian peasants would those be?'

'The ones it makes rosy.'

'Does yoghurt make Bulgarian peasants rosy?'

'So Phipps says.'

A deep chuckle escaped Bill Shannon.

'Phipps! If my lips weren't sealed, I could tell you something about Phipps. Ever hear of still waters?'

'What about them?'

'They run deep. That's Phipps. What a man! I suppose you look on him as just the ordinary sort of stage butler. Let me tell you that Brother Phipps has quite another side to him. However, as I say, my lips are sealed, so it's no use you trying to institute a probe.'

Smedley was perplexed.

'How do you know anything about Phipps? You only got here yesterday. Had you met him before?'

'I had, and in curious circumstances. But don't ask questions.'

'I don't want to ask questions. I'm not interested in Phipps. I'm off Phipps for life. He has hurt and disappointed me.'

'You don't say? What was the trouble?'

'I asked him for a small loan just now, and would you believe it,' said Smedley, with honest indignation, 'he refused. Turned me down flat. "No, sir," he said. And the fellow's probably rolling in money. Thank Heaven for people like you, Bill. You wouldn't do that sort of thing. You're bighearted. You're a pal, as true as steel. Good old Bill! Dear old Bill! Could you lend me a hundred dollars, Bill?'

Bill blinked. Well though she knew Smedley, she had not seen it coming.

'A hundred dollars?'

'I need it sorely.'

'Are you planning to go on a toot?'

'Yes,' cried Smedley passionately. 'I am. The toot of a lifetime, if I can raise the necessary funds. Do you realize that I haven't had a night out for five years? It's as much as I can do to get the price of a packet of cigarettes out of Adela. I'm just a worm in a gilded cage. So you will let me have that hundred, won't you, Bill?'

A look of gentle pity had come into Bill's blue eyes. Her heart ached for this tortured soul.

'If I had a hundred dollars, my poor broken blossom,' she said, 'I'd give it you like a shot. I think a toot is just what you need, to bring the roses back to your cheeks. But I'm as fiscally crippled as you are. You don't suppose I'd be here, ghostwriting the story of Adela's unspeakably dull life, if I had cash in the bank, do you?' She patted his shoulder commiseratingly. 'I'm afraid I've spoiled your day. I'm sorry. What a lot of succotash people talk about poverty making you spiritual,' she proceeded, in moralizing vein. 'All it's ever done to me is make me envious of the lucky stiffs who've got the stuff, like that boy who used to work with me on the Superba-Llewellyn lot. Did I tell you about him? Got fired, went back to New York, and the first thing you know he wins one of those big radio jackpots. Twenty-four thousand bucks, they said it was in the papers. Would that sort of thing ever happen to me? No, sir, not in a million years.'

'Nor to me. But . . .'

Smedley paused. He looked cautiously over his shoulder. He looked cautiously over his other shoulder. Then he turned and looked cautiously behind him.

'But what?' said Bill, mystified by these manoeuvres.

Smedley lowered his voice to a conspiratorial whisper.

'I'll tell you something, Bill.'

'Well, tell it louder. I can't hear a word.'

'It isn't a thing you can shout from the house-tops,' said Smedley, still conspiratorial. 'If Adela got to hear of it, phut would go any chance I have of becoming a rich man.'

'You haven't any chance of becoming a rich man.'

'That,' said Smedley, 'is where you're wrong. I have, if things pan out as I hope they will. Bill, do you know who this house used to belong to?'

'Of course I do. It's a landmark. Carmen Flores.'

'Exactly. Adela bought it furnished from her estate. All her belongings are still here, just as they were the day when she was killed in that plane crash. Get that. All her belongings.'

'So what?'

Smedley glanced over his shoulder again. He lowered his voice again. If in repose he had looked like a Roman Emperor, he now looked like a Roman Emperor talking over a prospective murder with his second vice-president in charge of assassinations.

'Carmen Flores kept a diary.'

'Did she?'

'So everyone says. I'm looking for it.'

'Why, are you thinking of writing her biography?'

'And if I find it, I'll be on velvet. Think, Bill. Reflect. You know what she was like. Always having violent affairs with all sorts of important characters – stars, studio bosses and what have you – and no doubt writing it up in her tablets at her leisure. Why, finding that diary would be like finding a deposit of uranium.'

'You mean that some of the men up top would pay highly to suppress the little brochure?'

'Practically all the men up top.'

Bill regarded him tenderly. She had always been devoted to Smedley, though far from blind to the numerous defects in his spiritual make-up. If there was a lazier man in the world than Smedley Cork, she had never met him. If there was one more refreshingly free from principles of any kind, she had still to make his acquaintance. He was selfish, idle and practically everything else that he ought not to be. Nevertheless, she loved him. She had loved him twenty years ago when he was a young man with money and one chin. She loved him now, when he was a portly senior with no money and two chins. Women do these things.

'In other words,' she said, 'you are hoping to cash in on a little blackmail.'

'It isn't blackmail,' said Smedley indignantly. 'It's a perfectly ordinary, straightforward business transaction. They want the diary, I have it.'

'But you haven't.'

'Well, if I had, I mean.'

Bill laughed indulgently. The proposition, as outlined, seemed to her pure Smedley. It did not weaken in the slightest her love for him. If someone had come to her and said: 'Wilhelmina Shannon, you are wasting your affection on a totally unworthy object,' she would have replied, 'Yessir. And I like it.' She was a one-man woman.

'You'll never make your fortune, Smedley, honestly or dishonestly. Now, I shall – I don't know how, but somehow. And when I do, I'm going to marry you.'

Smedley quivered.

'Don't say such things, even in fun.'

'I'm not being funny. I've given the matter a good deal of

thought these last twenty years, and when I got here and saw what was left of you after living with Adela all this time, I made up my mind there was only one thing for me to do, and that was to make a quick couple of dollars and lead you to the altar and spend the rest of my life looking after you. Because if ever a man needed looking after, it's you. And it beats me what you're making such a fuss about. You used to be crazy about me.'

'I was young and foolish.'

'And now you're old and foolish, but all the same you're the only man I've ever wanted. It's odd, that. How does that song go? Fish gotta swim, birds gotta fly, I gotta love one man till I die. Can't help—'

'Now, Bill. Please. Listen.'

'I haven't time to listen. I'm lunching with my literary agent at the Beverly-Wilshire. He's in Hollywood for a couple of days. Who knows but what I might contrive to touch him for a hundred? In which case, I'll come back and lay it at your feet, my king.'

Smedley, a correct and fastidious dresser, who even in captivity affected Palm Beach suits of impeccable cut and crease, cast a disapproving eye at the slacks.

'You aren't going to the Beverly-Wilshire dressed like that?'

'I certainly am. And don't forget what I said about marrying you. Go off into a corner and start practising saying "I will," against the moment when the minister taps you on the chest and says: "Wilt thou, Smedley, take this Wilhelmina?" Because you're for it, my lad.'

She passed through the French windows on her way to the garage where her jalopy was. Her voice came booming back to him.

'Fish gotta swim, birds gotta fly, I gotta love one man till I die. Can't help lovin' that man of mine.'

Smedley Cork leaned limply against the back of the sofa, grateful for its firm support. Warm though the morning was, he shivered, as only a confirmed bachelor gazing into the naked face of matrimony can shiver.

2

Joe Davenport was giving Kay Shannon lunch at the Purple Chicken down Greenwich Village way. He would much have preferred to take her to the Colony or the Pavillon, but Kay held austere views on the subject of young men wasting their substance in riotous living, even if they had recently won radio jackpots. Like her Uncle Smedley, she felt that there was no percentage in it. What Joe's stomach, which had high standards, considered a pretty revolting meal had drawn to its close, and only the last hurdle, the coffee, remained to be surmounted.

The waiter brought the coffee, breathed down the back of Joe's neck and withdrew, and Joe, who had been speaking of the lethal qualities of the management's spaghetti, abandoned the topic and turned to the one always uppermost in his mind on the occasions when he lunched with Kay.

'So much for the spaghetti theme,' he said. 'I will return to it later, if you wish. For the moment, there are weightier matters on the agenda paper. Don't look now,' said Joe, 'but will you marry me?'

Kay was leaning forward, her chin cupped in her hands and her eyes fixed on him with that grave, intent glance which always made him feel as if some hidden hand had introduced an egg whisk into his soul and started rotating it. It was this gravity of hers that had attracted him so strongly from the first. There was, he had begun to feel just before he met her, too much female smiling in this world, particularly in the cheese-cake zone of Hollywood, in which until a short while before, he had had his being. It had sometimes seemed to him that his life, till Kay came into it, had become an inferno of flashing teeth and merry squeals.

'Marry you?'

'That's right.'

'You do get the oddest ideas,' said Kay.

She glanced over her shoulder. The Purple Chicken is one

of those uninhibited Greenwich Village restaurants where the social amenities are not rigorously observed, and in the far corner a man who might have been a neo-Vorticist sculptor and a girl who looked as if she did bead work had begun to quarrel as loudly and cosily as if they had been at home. Turning back, she caught Joe's eye, and he frowned rebukingly.

'Don't pay any attention to those two,' he urged. 'Our marriage wouldn't be like that. They probably aren't married, anyway.'

'He seems to be talking to her like a husband.'

'Ours would be an unbroken round of bliss. Do you read Blondie? Then you will admit that the best husband in America is Dagwood Bumstead. Well, I have much in common with him – a loving heart, a gentle nature, a fondness for dogs and a taste for exotic sandwiches. Marry me, and you will be getting a super-Dagwood. Never a harsh word. Never a cross-eyed look. Your lightest wish would be law. I would bring you breakfast in bed every morning on a tray and sit and smoke to you when you had a headache.'

'It sounds wonderful. Tell me something,' said Kay. 'I notice that, when you give me lunch, you always wait till the coffee comes before proposing to me. Why is that? Just a habit?'

'On the contrary, it is very subtle stuff. Psychology. I reason that a girl full to the brim is more likely to be in softened mood than one in the process of staying the pangs of hunger. And I hate proposing with the waiters listening in and making bets in the background. Well, will you?'

'No.'

'You said that last time.'

'And I say it this time.'

'You're really turning me down again?'

'I am.'

'In spite of the fact that you are bursting with my meat?'

'I had spaghetti.'

'It makes no difference. The moral obligation of a lady bursting with a gentleman's spaghetti to do the square thing by the gentleman is equally strong.'

The sculptor and the bead worker had paid their bill and left. Freed of their distracting influence, Joe felt better able to concentrate on the matter in hand.

'It really is extraordinary,' he said, 'this way you've got of saying no every time I offer you a good man's love. No . . .

No . . . No . . . You might be Molotov. Not that it matters, of course.'

'No?'

'There you go again. I believe you say it in your sleep.'

'Why doesn't it matter, Mr Bones?'

'Because you're bound to marry me eventually, if only for my money.'

'How much have you got?'

'A thousand dollars.'

'Is that all?'

'What do you mean, is that all? I know of many a poor man who would be glad of a thousand dollars. Many a poor woman, too. Your Aunt Bill, for one.'

'I was going to say, Is that all you have left out of that jackpot?'

'Oh, well, money slips away. That has been my constant trouble as a bachelor, just as it has been Bill's constant trouble as a spinster. Have you heard from Bill lately?'

'No.'

'I had a telegram from her this morning.'

'What on earth was she telegraphing about?'

'She has some big scheme on.'

'What scheme?'

'She didn't say. The communication was rather mystic. She just spoke of her big scheme.'

'I'll bet it's crazy.'

'I'll bet it isn't. Bill crazy? The Old Reliable? As shrewd a woman as ever ate Corned Beef Hash Betty Grable at a studio commissary. Bill's a woman with ideas. When we were co-workers on the Superba-Llewellyn lot, there was a traffic cop out on Cahuenga Boulevard who lurked beside his motor cycle in a dark corner and sprang on it and dashed out to pursue motorists and give them tickets. We used to watch him from our windows, and we all burned to do something to the man, but only Bill had the vision and intelligence to go out and tie a chain to his back wheel while he was in the drug store and fasten the other end to a hydrant, so that the next time he sprang on his machine and started off, he was brought up short and shot over the handlebars and looked about as silly as I ever saw a traffic cop look. There you have Wilhelmina Shannon in a nutshell. A woman who gets things done. But to return to what I was saying, as a bachelor I have found it difficult to keep the cash from melting away. It will be different when I am married and settled down.'

'I'm not going to marry you, Joe.'

'Why not? Don't you like me?'

'You're nice to lunch with.'

'Nice is surely a weak adjective.'

The waiter was hovering in a meaning manner, and Joe, reading his thoughts, asked him for the bill. He looked across the table at Kay and felt, not for the first time, that life was very strange. You never knew what it was cooking up for you. When, as he was leaving Hollywood, Bill Shannon had told him to get in touch with her niece Kay in New York, where she was working in a magazine office, he had done so, he remembered, purely to oblige good old Bill. A young man who never lacked for feminine society, he had anticipated small pleasure or profit from adding one more to the list of telephone numbers in his little red book. But Bill had told him to get in touch, so he had got in touch. And from that simple, kindly act, had resulted all these emotional earthquakes which were upsetting him so deplorably.

'Bill ought to have warned me what I was coming up against,' said Joe, pursuing this train of thought. ' "When you hit New York," she said, "go and say Hello to my niece Kay." Like that. Casual. Offhand. Not a suggestion that she was introducing into my life a girl with a heart of stone who would disorganize my whole existence and turn me into a nervous wreck. Talk about La Belle Dame Sans Merci.'

'Keats!' said Kay, surprised. 'A well-read young man, this. I must try to get his autograph. I didn't know you went in for poetry.'

'All the time. Whenever I have a spare half-hour, you will generally find me curled up with Keats's *latest*. "Ah, what can ail thee, wretched wight, alone and palely loitering?" I tell you,' said Joe, 'if that wretched wight were to walk into this restaurant at this moment, beefing about La Belle Dame Sans Merci having him in thrall, I would slap him on the back and tell him I knew just how he felt.'

'Though, of course, he was a lot worse off than you are.'

'How do you make that out?'

'He didn't have a little red book of telephone numbers.'

Joe started and, though most of his friends would have said that such a thing was impossible, blushed.

'What do you know about my little red book?'

'You left it on the table once when you went to speak to someone. I glanced idly through it. Who are they all?'

'Chunks of my dead past.'

'M'm.'

'Don't say M'm. Those girls mean nothing to me. Ghosts, that's what they are. Just so much flotsam and jetsam left stranded by the tide on the beach of memory. Bring any one of them to me on a plate with watercress around her, and I wouldn't so much as touch her hand. Nobody but you exists for me now. Don't you believe me?'

'No.'

'That word again. By the beard of Sam Goldwyn, there are moments when I feel an almost overpowering urge to bean you with a bottle.'

Kay raised her coffee spoon.

'Stand back. I am armed.'

'Oh, it's all right. I'm not going to. I would only get hell from Emily Post.'

The waiter brought the bill, and Joe paid it absently. Kay was looking at him again in that odd, speculative way of hers.

'It isn't the little red book that worries me,' she said. 'If you're a reformed Casanova, that's fine. Shall I tell you the reason why I won't marry you, Joe?'

'I wish you would. Clear up this historic mystery.'

'I'll only be saying what you know already.'

'That's all right. Just so long as you talk about me.'

Kay took a sip of coffee, found that it had become cold and put the cup down. The restaurant had emptied, the waiters retired to some secret lair of their own. She could speak without being overheard.

'Well, then, it's because you're not what the French call an *homme sérieux*. If you know what that means.'

'I don't.'

'I'll try to explain. Let's just run through your case history. I had it from Bill. She said that when you and she were in New York, before you both went to Hollywood, you were doing quite well as a writer.'

'For the pulps.'

'Well, what's wrong with that? Half the best known writers today started on the pulps. But they stuck to it and worked.'

'I don't like the way you said that.'

'Then you got a job with Superba-Llewellyn and went to Hollywood. Then you got fired.'

'It happens to everybody.'

'Yes, but most people when they get fired don't ask for a personal interview with the boss of the studio and in the course of conversation throw a richly bound copy of the *Saturday Evening Post* at his head. What made you do that?'

'It seemed a good idea at the time. He had incurred my displeasure. Did Bill tell you about it?'

'Yes.'

'Bill talks too much.'

'So you got yourself blacklisted. Not very balanced behaviour, do you think?'

Joe patted her hand indulgently.

'Women don't understand these things,' he said. 'There comes a time in the life of every man placed in juxtaposition with Ivor Llewellyn when he is compelled to throw copies of the *Saturday Evening Post* at his head. It's why they publish the *Saturday Evening Post*.'

'Well, all right. I still think it was unbalanced, but if you say so, all right. We now come to the matter of that radio jackpot. When you get a lot of money by a miracle, winning a radio jackpot—'

Joe, though saddened by the turn the conversation had taken, was obliged to chuckle.

'I always get a hearty laugh out of that,' he said. 'I'm sitting in my squalid flat one rainy evening, feeling extremely dubious as to the whereabouts of my next meal, when the telephone tinkles and a hearty character at Station W.J.Z. asks me to listen to a Mysterious Voice on a record and see if I can identify it. And whose mysterious voice is it? None other than that of Mr Ivor Llewellyn, which had been ringing in my ears ever since that episode to which you have alluded. Having identified it, I am informed by the hearty character that I have won the big jackpot and scooped in wealth beyond the dreams of avarice. It just shows that nothing is put into this world without a purpose, not even Ivor Llewellyn. But I interrupt you.'

'You do.'

'I'm sorry. Carry on. You were saying . . .?'

'I was saying that the first thing you do when by a miracle you get a lot of money is to stop writing and just loaf.'

'You wrong me.'

'Have you written a single story since you won that money?'

'No. But I've not been loafing. I've been looking about me, crouching for the spring. The view I take is that there must be something better for me to do than hammer out cowboy stories for the pulp magazines. Now that I have a bit of capital, I can afford to wait and study the market. That's what I'm doing, studying the market.'

'I see. Well,' said Kay, getting up, 'I must be going. And I still stick to it that you're not an *homme sérieux*.'

A feeling of desolation swept over Joe. It had been there in a modified form all the time, but it was only now that he actually seemed to realize that in a few days he would be separated from this girl by three thousand miles of mountain and desert and prairie. And if ever there was a job that called for uninterrupted personal supervision, it was this job of breaking down Kay Shannon's customer's sales resistance.

'Oh, don't go yet,' he said.

'I must. I've a hundred things to do.'

'Heavy day at the office?'

'I'm packing. My vacation starts tomorrow.'

'You never told me that.'

'I suppose it slipped my mind.'

'Where are you going?'

'Hollywood. What's the matter?'

'Nothing's the matter.'

'You barked like a seal.'

'I always bark like a seal at about this hour. So you're going to Hollywood?'

'Well, Beverly Hills. I'm going to stay with my aunt.'

'Bill?'

'No, this is another one. Bill's sister. Much higher in the social scale than Bill. She's one of the old aristocracy of Hollywood. Adela Shannon.'

'What, *the* Adela Shannon? The silent film star?'

'That's the one.'

'I've heard Bill speak of her. Bill didn't seem to like her much.'

'I don't like her much myself.'

'Then why are you going to stay with her?'

'Oh, I don't know. One must go somewhere. She invited me.'

'Where does she live?'

'Up in the mountains at the top of Alamo Drive. What used to be the Carmen Flores place. You probably know it.'

'She owns that palace, does she? She must have plenty of money.'

'She has. She married a millionaire.'

'You'll be doing the same thing yourself, if I find my niche and really get going. Well, expect an early phone call from me.'

'Expect a what?'

Joe laughed. His depression had vanished. The sun had broken through the clouds and all was for the best in this best of all possible worlds.

'Did you think to escape me by running off to Hollywood? Girl, you have been living in a fool's paradise. I'm going there myself in a couple of days.'

'What! But you're blacklisted in Hollywood.'

'Oh, I'm not going to work there. No doubt they will come begging me to, but I shall draw myself up and say: "Not after what has occurred." And I shall say it stiffly. No, I'm going to confer with Bill about this scheme of hers. Rightly or wrongly, she seems to think that my cooperation is needed to make it a success. She was very emphatic that I must drop everything and come running. It's a pity we won't be able to travel together, but there are one or two things I have to do before I can leave the metropolis. However, you will be hearing from me in due season. In fact, you'll be seeing me.'

'You aren't thinking of strolling in on Aunt Adela?'

'I might.'

'I wouldn't.'

'She can't eat me.'

'I don't know so much. She's not a vegetarian.'

'Well, we will see, we will see. And as regards the matter which we have been discussing, we will leave things as they are for the time being. I shall continue to love you, of course.'

'Thanks.'

'Not at all,' said Joe. 'A pleasure. It'll be something to do.'

3

'Hollywood,' said Bill Shannon, 'is not the place it used to
be. Hollywood,' said Bill, 'once a combination of Santa Claus
and Good King Wenceslas, has turned into a Scrooge. The dear
old days are dead and the spirit of cheerful giving a thing of
the past.'

She was sharing a pot of coffee with Joe Davenport in the
main dining-room of the Beverly Hills hotel, and her resonant
voice rang through it like rolling thunder. Listening to her, Joe
felt as if he were a section of the voting public being harangued
by a Senator of more than ordinary lung power.

'Why, look,' said Bill. 'There was a time when only a person
of exceptional ability and determination could keep from getting
signed by a studio. Top level executives used to chase you along
Sunset Boulevard, pleading pitifully with you to accept a contract. "Come and write for us," they begged, and when you told
them you weren't a writer, they said: "Well, come and be a
technical adviser." And when you said you didn't want to be
a technical adviser, they said: "Then come and be a vocal
instructor." So you said: "Oh, all right, I'll be a writer. I shall
want fifteen hundred a week." "Or two thousand?" they said.
"It's a rounder figure. Simplifies book-keeping." And you said:
"Oh, very well, two thousand. But don't expect me to do any
work!" And they said: "Of course not, of course not. What an
idea! We just want to have you around the place." But all that
is over. Now? Ha! Nowadays, if they sign you up at all, it's
just to have the fun of firing you.'

All this was in response to Joe's casual question 'Well,
how's dear old Hollywood?' and he felt like someone who has
thoughtlessly punched a hole in a dam. Overcoming the dazed
sensation of being a twig tossed along on foaming waters, he
found himself able to guess at the cause of his companion's
emotion.

'Don't tell me they've handed you the black spot, Bill.'

'That's what they've done. Driven me out into the snow. And I always thought they looked on me as the Little Mother around the place. A sort of studio mascot.'

'When did this happen?'

'Last week. I dance into my office with my hat on the side of my head, singing "I'm to be Queen of the May, mother, I'm to be Queen of the May," and there on the desk the brusheroo in its little blue envelope. A most unpleasant shock, you can take it from me. I had to go off to the commissary and restore myself with a Malted Milk Bette Davis.'

Joe nodded understandingly.

'It's this economy wave.'

'False economy.'

'I suppose Hollywood's in a pretty bad way these days?'

'Down to its last billion.'

'One might have expected that something like that would happen when they let me go. A suicidal policy. What are you going to do?'

'For the moment, I'm staying with my sister Adela. I'm ghostwriting the story of her life. By the way, Kay clocked in a day or two ago. Did you see anything of her in New York?'

Joe laughed one of those hollow, mirthless laughs.

'Did I see anything of her in New York! The answer to your question, Wilhelmina, is in the affirmative. My misguided old friend, you little knew what you were letting me in for when you told me to go and say Hello to that girl. Lowered morale. Depression and debility. Night sweats and loss of appetite. I love her, Bill.'

'You do?'

'I do.'

'Well, I don't know that I blame you. She's an attractive young squirt.'

'I would prefer that you did not allude to her as a squirt. An angel, if you like. A seraph, if you wish. But not a squirt.'

'Just as you say. And how's it all coming along? Does she respond? Are you her dream man?'

'To use a favourite word of her own, no.'

'She won't marry you?'

'That's her story.'

'Ask her again.'

'I have asked her again. How do you think I fill in the time? I've asked her twelve times. No, sorry, fourteen. I overlooked a couple of small ones. The score would be fifteen if I had been able to get her on the phone just now, but she was out. Bill, who would a Mrs Cork be?'

'My sister Adela. She married a well-to-do millionaire of that name. Why?'

'I was just wondering. We exchanged a word or two over the wire. Well, that's how matters stand. I keep proposing to her, and she steadfastly continues to be a black frost in my garden of dreams. So now you know why I look pale and wan.'

'You look like a particularly healthy tomato. And you're crazy if you pay any attention to a girl when she says no. I'm in love with a man who's been saying no for the last twenty years. But do I despair? Not by a jugful. I keep after him, and I think I'm softening him up. What are you goggling like that for?'

Joe hesitated.

'Well, I'm sort of surprised.'

'Why?'

'I somehow didn't associate you with the tender passion.'

'Why not?'

'Or, rather,' said Joe, catching his companion's eye, which had begun to look menacing, 'it astonished me that anyone could resist you for twenty years.'

'That's better.'

'I think you'll get him. Persevere, Bill.'

'I will. And you persevere, too.'

'Right. Let's all persevere.'

'We'll make it a double wedding.'

'That's the spirit.'

'And now, for heaven's sake, let's change the subject and get down to business. We can't waste the whole day talking about love. You got my telegram?'

'That's why I'm here.'

'And my letter, giving you full details of this scheme of mine?'

'I never got any letter.'

'And I'll tell you why. I've just remembered I forgot to mail it. But I can supply you with all the facts now. My boy, we're on the eve of making a stupendous fortune. We've got a gold mine.'

'Proceed, Bill. You interest me strangely.'

Bill tapped his chest with an impressive finger.

'Has it ever occurred to you, Joe, that all these years you and I have been in this writing game on the wrong end.'

'How do you mean, the wrong end?'

'The loser's end. The sap's end. We've been perfect suckers. Where is it getting us, toiling for the pulps and being wage slaves in Hollywood? Nowhere.'

'So . . .?'

'So we're going to be literary agents.'

'Eh?'

'I should say authors' representatives. It sounds better. We're going to loll back and let the other fellows do the work and take our ten per cent like officers and gentlemen.'

'What has given you that idea?'

'It came to me like a flash the other afternoon when I was lunching with my personal bloodsucker, who has been putting in a few days in Screwball Centre. I had noticed from the first that the man seemed nervous and depressed, and just after I had touched him for a couple of hundred dollars during the smoked salmon course he suddenly buried his face in his hands with a low groan and said that this was the finish. It couldn't go on, he said. He had got to retire, he said. He said he had reached a point where he never wanted to see an author again. He said authors did something to him. He said he supposed Providence had had some sort of idea at the back of its mind when it put authors into the world, but he had never been able to figure out what it was, and he pined for a quiet evening of his life in some remote spot like the Virgin Islands, where he could reasonably hope to be free from them. So, to condense a novelette into a short-short, I arranged with him to give me first refusal of the goodwill and effects, or whatever they're called. But we've got to act like lightning, because a week from now, if we haven't clinched the deal, he will go elsewhere. So now is the time for all good men to come to the aid of the party.'

Joe found himself a good deal infected by her enthusiasm. The thought of becoming an authors' representative had not presented itself to him before, but he could see now that it was just the sort of thing he had been subconsciously looking for when studying the market. Like all writers, he had long held the view that of all the soft snaps in this modern civilization of ours that of the authors' representative was the softest. Given the modest intelligence necessary for putting a typescript in an envelope and licking the gum, a man could scarcely fail in that branch of industry. Whoever went around in patched clothes with holes in his shoes and had to skip a meal from time to time, it was not the authors' representative.

He had begun to weave an opalescent daydream in which Kay, learning that he had become one of that opulent little band who represent authors, flung herself weeping on his chest, remorseful that she had ever wronged him by failing to classify him as what the French call an *homme sérieux*, when Bill continued her remarks.

'He's asking twenty thousand.'

Joe's daydream broke into fragments like a soup-plate coming apart in the hands of a careless scullery maid. He gave a soft gurgle, and when he spoke, spoke in a low, grating voice.

'Twenty thousand?'

'That's all. He started by talking some wild, visionary stuff about thirty, but I soon put a stop to that.'

'You expect to get twenty thousand dollars?'

'Why not?'

'Which bank are you going to burgle?'

Joe shrank back in his chair. Wilhelmina Shannon was raising her voice again.

'What do you mean, which bank am I going to burgle? I'm looking to you to put up the capital. Aren't you putrescent with money?'

'I've a thousand dollars, if you call that putrescent.'

'A thousand? What's become of that radio jackpot?'

'Gone with the wind.'

'You dissolute young rat.'

'High cost of living, taxes and so on. And a thing you're overlooking, Bill, is that these radio jackpots aren't solid cash. Don't be misled by what you read in the papers. Most of mine was tinned soup. Would this man of yours settle for eight thousand tins of mixed soups? Maybe he's fond of soup. I could do him tomato, asparagus, green pea, chicken gumbo . . .'

An old gentleman who was drinking something through a straw at a table at the other end of the room leaped convulsively and nearly swallowed the straw. This was because Bill was raising her voice still higher.

'So one more dream turns blue,' said Bill. 'Can you direct me to a good Old Women's Home?'

Her anguish touched Joe. His was a resilient nature, and already he had begun to recover from the gloom into which he had been plunged.

'Don't be a defeatist, Bill. Why shouldn't we raise the money somewhere?'

'Where?'

'There used to be a place called Perelli's down at Santa Monica where one could engage in games of chance. I presume it still exists. I might take my thousand and look in there tonight.'

'Don't be a fool.'

'Perhaps you're right. Well, why shouldn't we float a loan in some quarter? Hollywood must be full of rich sportsmen who would like a flutter.'

'I've never met them.'

'What about Mrs Cork?'

'Adela? The slowest woman with a dollar west of Dodge City. No, this is the end. Doom, desolation and despair. Well, see you in the breadline,' said Bill, and moved ponderously to the door, a female Napoleon retreating from Moscow.

For some minutes after she had left him, Joe sat musing on the capriciousness of fate, which lures you on with golden promises and then turns round and lets you have it on the base of the skull with the stuffed eelskin. But his, as has been said, was a resilient nature, and it was not long before there began to glimmer through the cloud wrack a small but distinct silver lining. It might be that he would have to postpone becoming a millionaire for a while, but money is not everything and the world, he reminded himself, though admittedly grey in spots, still contained the girl he loved. And by chartering a yellow taxi from the stand outside the Marion Hunter bookshop and going to the top of Alamo Drive, he could feast his eyes on the house where she was in residence. With a little luck, he might even catch a glimpse of her.

Twenty minutes later, seated in a yellow taxi, he was gazing out of the window at a broad gateway and a tree-lined strip of concrete drive which led to a house unfortunately invisible from where he sat. He felt like some pilgrim visiting a shrine, and mingled with his reverence was the earthier feeling that when Mrs Adela Cork had taken a millionaire for a husband, she had picked a good one. The grounds, he could see, were spacious and expensive, and when there suddenly appeared, crossing the drive with a tray of cocktails, what was plainly an imported English butler, any doubt that he might have had as to this being one of the Stately Homes of Hollywood was dispelled.

It was probably the sight of those cocktails that suggested to him that it was about time to be getting back and making arrangements for dinner. The California evening had mellowed to twilight, and his stomach, always inclined to the policy of Do It Now, was sending up peremptory messages to the front office. Reluctantly, for he regretted the necessity of yielding to his lower nature, he was about to notify the charioteer that the homeward journey might commence, when along the drive and out of the gate came toddling a large, stout, elderly gentleman who looked like a Roman Emperor who has been doing himself too well on the starchy foods, and so impressive was his exterior that it immediately occurred to Joe that here, first crack out of the box, he had found the very man of whom he was in search, one of those big shots who feed sums like twenty thousand dollars to the birds.

For to Joe, meeting him here, it was obvious who this was. It could be none other than the plutocrat Cork, the super-tax-paying mate of Kay's Aunt Adela. You had only to cast an eye on the man to see that he had the stuff in sackfuls. It is difficult to explain exactly, but there is something about these very rich men which marks them off from the common herd. They look different. The way they walk is different. They say: 'Hey, taxi!' differently.

This was what the other was now saying and for a moment Joe was puzzled that such a Crœsus should be hailing taxis. Then he saw that the explanation was quite simple. Something – trivial, one hoped – must have gone temporarily wrong with the Lincoln, the Cadillac and the two Rolls-Royces in his garage.

His lightning mind perceived that here was a heaven-sent opportunity of fraternizing with this gilt-edged security and starting a beautiful friendship.

'I am going to Beverly Hills, sir,' he said, poking his head out of the window, full of charm. 'Could I give you a lift, sir?'

'Very kind of you, sir.'

'Not at all, sir.'

'Thank you, sir.'

'Don't give it a thought, sir. Hop in, sir, hop in.'

The taxi rolled off down the mountain-side, and Joe braced himself to be fascinating.

4

The midday sun, pouring into the Garden Room on the following morning, found Bill Shannon seated at the desk, the dictaphone tube in her hand, a peevish frown on her face. One would have said that she was not enjoying working on the *Memoirs* of her sister Adela, and one would have been right. Bill in her time had been many things, crime reporter, sob sister, writer of stories for the pulp magazines, Press agent, minor actress and baby-sitter, but this was the most uncongenial task which she had ever undertaken.

As far as she could ascertain from the voluminous notes which the heroine of the *Memoirs* had placed at her disposal, nothing had ever happened to Adela that was of the remotest interest to anyone except herself. She had apparently never done anything in all her years of silent stardom but eat, sleep, get married, and have her photograph taken. It was not easy to see how the Adela Shannon Story could be stretched to cover three hundred pages of entertaining reading for the American public.

But Bill was conscientious and resolved to give of her best, and it was with splendid determination that she ignored the sunshine that was trying to lure her out into the open spaces.

'It was all so new and strange,' she boomed into the mouthpiece, 'and I was just a timid little tot . . . Oh, dammit, I've used timid little tot before . . . and I was so young, so unsophisticated, so dazzled and bewildered by the glitter and glamour of this world . . . No, we want some adjectives there . . . of this strange, new, magic world into which I had been plunged . . . Oh, blast it, I said new and strange a moment ago . . . of this marvellous, magical, fairyland world into which I had plunged like a diver diving into some rushing, sparkling stream. Who could have dreamed—'

Phipps came shimmering through the door, in his capable hands a whisky and soda on a tray. She welcomed him with a glad cry like that of a diver diving into some rushing, sparkling stream who finds the water warmer than she had expected. No Israelite in the desert, watching manna descending from the skies just when he had been saying to himself how well a spot of manna would go down right now, if only he had it, could have shown a more instantaneous approval and enthusiasm.

'Phipps, you're a mind-reader.'

'I thought you might be in need of refreshment, madam. You have been working all the morning.'

'And no interruptions, thank heaven. Where is everybody?'

'Mrs Cork went to Pasadena, madam, to address a ladies' club on Some Recollections of the Silent Screen. Miss Kay and his lordship are playing golf.'

'And Mr Smedley?'

'I have not seen Mr Smedley, madam.'

'Probably around somewhere.'

'No doubt, madam.'

Bill took a sip and a swallow and composed herself for conversation. She had reached a point in her labours when she was glad of the interruption which would have irked her earlier, and she was particularly glad to be interrupted by Phipps. This butler intrigued her. Since their get-together of the previous day, she had been thinking not a little about his curious case.

'I wish you would explain something that's been puzzling me, Phipps.'

'Certainly, madam, if it is within my power.'

Bill addressed herself to the glass again. Its amber contents were cool and refreshing. She lit a cigarette and blew a puff of smoke at a fly which had wandered in and was circling about her head.

'It's this,' she said, putting the question which she hoped would lead to a solution of the mystery which had been vexing her. 'You remember – how shall I put it, always bearing in mind that walls have ears – you remember that lawsuit of yours?'

'Yes, madam.'

'The one where I was a member of the jury.'

'Yes, madam.'

Bill discouraged the fly with another broadside.

'Well, here's where I can't get the thing straight. It seemed to me that on that occasion, and the rest of the boys and girls felt the same, that the gentleman who was digging up the details of your past and dishing them out to the intelligent twelve, of whom I was one, established rather clearly that you were an expert safeblower.'

'Yes, madam.'

'And it didn't take me long after I'd got here to see that you were certainly an expert butler.'

'Thank you, madam.'

'Well, which came first, the chicken or the egg?'

'Madam?'

Bill saw that she had not made herself clear.

'I mean, are you a safeblower—'

'An ex-safeblower, madam.'

'You're sure you spell it with an ex?'

'Oh, yes, madam.'

'Well, be that as it may, are you a safeblower magically gifted with the art of buttling, or a butler who has somehow picked up the knack of blowing safes?'

'The latter, madam.'

'You aren't really Mike the Mugg or something like that, just posing as a butler for your own subtle ends?'

'Oh, no, madam. I have been in service from a very early age. Domestic service is a tradition in my family. I started my career as what is known as a hall boy in a large establishment in Worcestershire.'

'Where the sauce comes from?'

'I believe the condiment to which you allude is manufactured in that locality, madam.'

Phipps stood silent for a moment, his thoughts apparently back in those happy days when life had been simple and free from problems and complexities. Apart from having to carry logs of wood up stairs and deposit them in bedrooms, hall boys in English houses have it pretty soft.

'In due course,' he proceeded, coming out of his reverie, 'I rose to be an under-footman, then a footman and finally a butler. And it was after I had achieved that position that I entered the employment of an American gentleman and came to this country. I had always had a desire to visit the United States of Northern America. That was some ten years ago.'

'And when did you learn to bust safes?'

'About five years after that, madam.'

'What gave you the idea?'

Phipps looked cautiously over his shoulder. Having done this, he directed a searching glance at Bill, as if he were weighing her in the balance. He seemed to be asking himself whether it would be wise and judicious to confide in a woman who, though of course they knew each other quite well by sight, was after all a stranger. Then the benevolence of his companion's rugged face overcame his doubts. There was that about Bill Shannon which always encouraged people to confide in her.

'It came to me quite unexpectedly one evening when I was reading a volume entitled *Three Dead At Midways Court*, madam. I have always been fond of that type of literature, and in the course of my perusal of these fictional works – known, I believe, as whodunits – I was struck by the frequency with which the butler proved to be the criminal.'

'I know what you mean. It's always the butler. It's an occupational disease.'

'What is termed the Heavy in *Three Dead At Midways Court* turned out to be the butler, and until the final chapter nobody had suspected him for a moment. It started a train of thought. I mused, madam. Butlers, I told myself, never are suspected for a moment, and it occurred to me that a butler in a wealthy household who had acquired the technique of opening safes would be very advantageously placed. There he would be, if you follow me, madam, with the valuables at his elbow, if I may use the expression, and it would be extremely simple for him, by leaving a window open, to invest his operations with the appearance of what is known as an outside job. So to cut a long story short, madam, I made cautious enquiries and eventually found a practitioner in Brooklyn who in return for a fee was willing to impart his skill to me.'

'In twelve easy lessons?'

'Twenty, madam. At first I was not a very apt pupil.'

'But you picked it up all right as you went along?'

'Yes, madam.'

Bill drew a deep breath. She was no rigid moralist, her temperament being one that always inclined her to take a tolerant view of the straying from the straight and narrow path of those with whom she associated, but she had a rudimentary conscience. And though she had never been fond of her sister Adela, she could not but feel that a word of warning should be given that exasperating woman. The generosity of the late Albert Cork, combined with her personal and private fortune, the outcome of years of pulling down a huge salary in the days before there was any income tax to speak of, had left Adela with enough jewellery to equip half the blondes in Hollywood, and it seemed unfair to allow her to go on giving board and lodging to a butler who, as had been established in court, could open safes with a twiddle of his finger tips.

'I ought to tell Mrs Cork,' she said.

'There is no necessity, madam. I have put all that sort of thing behind me.'

'Says you, if I may use a homely phrase indicating doubt and uncertainty.'

'No, madam, I assure you. Apart from the moral aspect of the matter, I would not dream of taking upon myself the risks inseparable from my former activities. My experience of American prison life has left me with no desire to repeat it.'

Bill's face cleared. This was sense.

'I see what you mean. I remember reading an article in the *Yale Review* about the Reformed Criminal. The writer pointed out that there is nobody with such a strong bias toward honesty as the man who has just come out of prison. He said that if someone had been laid up for a year in hospital as the result of going over Niagara Falls in a barrel, the one outdoor sport in which he would be reluctant to indulge on emerging would be going over Niagara Falls in a barrel. Or, putting it another way, the burned child fears the fire.'

'Precisely, madam, though the actual quotation is "A burned child dreadeth the fire." It occurs in Lyly's *Euphues*.'

'Is that a favourite bedside book of yours?'

'I glanced through it, madam, when I was in the service of the Earl of Powick, in Worcestershire. There was very little else to read in his lordship's library, and it rained a good deal.'

'I've come up against that sort of thing myself. I once went to Valparaiso as a stewardess on a fruit boat, and the only book on board was *The Plays of William Shakespeare*, belonging to the chief engineer. By the time the voyage was over, I knew them by heart. I suppose that's why I quote him a good deal.'

'No doubt, madam. A very admirable writer.'

'Yes, he wrote some good stuff. But tell me all about your college days, Phipps. What's it like in Sing . . .?'

'Hist, madam.'

'How do you mean, hist? Oh, I get you.'

Outside the French windows a voice had suddenly made itself heard, singing a gay melody. A moment later, a long, lean young man, who appeared to have giraffe blood in him, came in, carrying a bag of golf clubs. Phipps greeted him with respectful devotion.

'Good morning, m'lord.'

'Good morning, Lord Topham,' said Bill.

'Oh, good morning,' said the young man. Then, as if to clarify his meaning, he added the words 'Good morning, good morning, good morning!' He beamed at Bill and the butler. 'Well, Miss W. Shannon,' he proceeded, 'and you, Phipps, this is the maddest, merriest day of all the glad new year. I say this to you without reserve, Phipps, and you, Miss W. Shannon. Not only the maddest, but also the merriest day of the glad new year. I broke a hundred this morning, a feat which has eluded my every effort since I first took driver in hand at the age of twenty. A whisky and soda would not come amiss, Phippsy. You might take it to my room.'

'Very good, m'lord,' said Phipps. 'I will attend to the matter immediately.'

Lord Topham gazed after him admiringly as he disappeared in the stately manner habitual with him.

'You know, that chap makes me feel homesick. Absolutely. I never expected to find an English butler in Hollywood.'

'All sorts of English oddities turn up in Hollywood,' said Bill. 'Excuse me.' She picked up the mouthpiece of the dictaphone and began speaking into it. 'Who could have dreamed that in a few short years the name of Adela Shannon would have been known to the whole wide world from China to Peru? Who would have supposed that before I made my third picture, I would have become loved, worshipped, idolized by the prince in his palace, the peasant in his cot, the explorer in the jungle and the Eskimo in his frozen igloo? So true it is – so true— Ha!' said Bill. 'So true it is that one touch of nature makes the whole world kin and that courage, patience and perseverance will always find a way. I will now describe my first meeting with Nick Schenk.' She lowered the instrument. 'Sorry,' she said. 'I have to jot these things down when the inspiration comes.'

Lord Topham was impressed, as the layman always is when privileged to observe genius in the throes of composition.

'Oh, absolutely,' he agreed. 'What was that about glue?'

'Igloo. It's a sort of gloo they have up in the Arctic Circle.'

'I see.'

'Stickier than the usual kind.'

'Quite. What are you doing? Working on a picture?'

'Not on a picture, no. I'm ghostwriting the story of my sister Adela's life.'

'How's it coming?'

'Not too smoothly.'

'Pretty much of a somewhat ghastly sweat, I imagine. I couldn't write anything if you paid me, much less talk it into that sewing-machine thing. Mrs Cork was a big pot in the silent films, wasn't she?'

'One of the biggest. They called her the Empress of Stormy Emotion.'

'Must have made a lot of money.'

'Quite a good deal.'

'I mean, you don't get a house like this for nothing.'

'No. But here she is, to give you all the figures, if you want them.'

The door which led to the main portion of the house had opened, and a strikingly handsome woman of about Bill's age was sailing in with that air of confidence and authority which is so noticeable in Empresses of Stormy Emotion, even when the passage of time has made them ex-Empresses. Adela Cork was tall and stately, with large, dark, slumberous eyes which could, and did, light up in a baleful blaze when things were not going exactly as she desired. She had something of the imperious look of those portraits of Louise de Querouaille which make the beholder feel what a man of steely nerve King Charles the Second must have been to associate on terms of intimacy with anything so formidable. Formidable was the word to describe Bill's sister Adela. Each of her three husbands, even the late Alfred Cork, who was as tough a citizen as ever owned an oil well, had curled up before her like carbon paper: and directors who were getting on in years sometimes woke trembling in the night, having dreamed that they were back in the pre-talkie days arguing some technical point with the former Adela Shannon.

At the moment, her mood was reasonably benevolent, though she proposed later on to have a word with Bill about those slacks. Her lecture had been well received, and she was still in the gentle glow of amiability induced by the applause of two hundred intelligent Pasadena matrons.

'Good morning,' she said. 'Good morning, Lord Topham.'

'Good morning, good morning, good morning, good morning.'

'Hello, Adela,' said Bill. 'Lord Topham was just saying how much he admired this house.'

Adela smiled rewardingly on this worthy guest. She was fond and proud of Lord Topham. She had been to great trouble to extract him from the clutches of a prehensile hostess who had seemed at one time to have acquired permanent possession, and her attitude toward him was a little like that of a collector toward a valuable piece of bric-à-brac which he has wrested from a rival connoisseur.

'It is nice, isn't it? I bought it just as it stood from the estate of Carmen Flores, the Mexican star who was killed in that plane crash last year.'

Lord Topham was interested. He was a great reader of *Screen Topics, Screen Secrets* and other organs of that nature.

'Oh, really? Carmen Flores, what? Fancy that.'

'You have heard of Carmen Flores?'

'Absolutely. Well, I mean to say, one would, wouldn't one? She, as it were, lives in legend and song. By way of being what Americans call a red-hot mother, was she not?'

'Absolutely,' said Bill. 'I have often thought that if walls had tongues as well as ears . . . Walls do have ears. Did you know that?'

'No, really?'

'Absolutely,' said Bill. 'I had it from a reliable source. Well, as I was saying, I have often thought that if walls could speak, these walls could say a mouthful. Not that what they said would ever get past the Johnston office.'

'Absolutely not,' said Lord Topham, nodding sagely. 'So this is where she lived, is it? Well, well. Who knows but that on that very sofa . . . I forget what I was going to say.'

'Just in time,' said Bill. 'Quickly changing the subject, tell Adela about your triumphs on the links this morning.'

Lord Topham required no coaxing.

'Oh, ah, yes. I broke a hundred, Mrs Cork. Do you play golf?' he asked, though a glance at his hostess should have told him that it was a foolish question. Women like Adela Cork do not lower themselves to these trivial pastimes. With a stretch of imagination one could picture Mrs Siddons or the mother of the Gracchi playing golf, but not Adela.

'No,' she said. 'I do not.'

'Oh! Well, the idea of the game is to bash the old ball round the course in a minimum of strokes, and anyone who can accomplish the enterprise in under a hundred bashes is entitled to credit and respect. I did it for the first time this morning, and the news will stun my circle of friends across the sea. If you'll excuse me, I'll be going and telling old Twingo about it.'

'Twingo?'

'A pal of mine in London. May I use your telephone? Thanks awfully,' said Lord Topham, and hastened out to shoot the hot news across the Atlantic.

Bill smiled sardonically.

'Pal of mine in London . . . May I use your telephone . . . Just like that.'

Adela bridled. She resented criticism of her favoured guest.

'Very rich men don't bother about these trifles. Lord Topham is one of the richest men in England.'

'I'm not surprised. His personal expenses must be very small.'

'And I do wish, Wilhelmina,' said Adela, changing the subject, 'that you would dress decently when you are in a civilized house. Slopping about in those slacks. You look perfectly revolting. What do you suppose Lord Topham thinks?'

'Does he think?'

'Dungarees!' said Adela, wrinkling her nose with distaste.

Bill was one of the few people whom Adela Cork could not intimidate.

'Never mind about my dungarees,' she said. 'Just tell yourself that they cover a warm heart and let it go at that. How was your lecture? Did you massacre them?'

'It was a great success. Everybody most enthusiastic.'

'You're back early. Couldn't you touch the girls for lunch?'

Adela clicked her tongue.

'My dear Wilhelmina, have you forgotten that I am giving a big luncheon party today? All sorts of important people are coming, including Jacob Glutz.'

'Of Medulla-Oblongata-Glutz? The man who looks like a lobster?'

'He does not look like a lobster.'

'Pardon me, he looks much more like a lobster than most lobsters do.'

'Well, whatever he looks like, I don't want him mistaking you for one of the gardeners. I trust you intend to change into something reasonably respectable before he arrives.'

'Of course. These are just my working clothes.'

'Have you been working on the *Memoirs*?'

'All the morning.'

'Where have you got to?'

'Your first meeting with Nick Schenk.'

'No further than that?'

Bill felt that this sort of thing must be checked at the outset. It was bad enough being compelled by poverty to write those *Memoirs* at all, without having Adela biting at her heels and baying after her like a bloodhound. A pang shot through her as she thought of that literary agency, now gone beyond recall.

'My good woman,' she said, 'be reasonable. The story of your great career will be a very important contribution to American literature. It is not a task that can be hurried. One proceeds slowly. One chisels and polishes. You don't suppose Lytton Strachey raced through his *Life of Queen Victoria* like a Bowery bum charging into a saloon for a quick beer?'

'I see. Yes, I suppose you're right.'

'You bet I'm right. I was saying to Kay yesterday . . . What's the matter?'

Adela had uttered an exclamation. She was looking cautiously over her shoulder. It seemed to Bill that her life these last days had been passed exclusively in the society of people who looked cautiously over their shoulders. She watched her sister, mystified, as she went to the door, opened it quickly and peered out.

'I thought Phipps might be listening,' said Adela, closing the door and coming back into the room. 'Wilhelmina, there is something I want to ask you. About Kay.'

'What about her?'

Adela sank her voice to a stage whisper.

'Has she ever spoken to you of anyone called *Joe*?'

'Joe?'

'I'll tell you why I ask. Yesterday afternoon the telephone rang as I was coming through the hall. I answered it, and a man's voice said "Kay? This is Joe. Stop me if you've heard this before, but will you marry me?"'

Bill clicked her tongue.

'The boy's crazy. That's no way to—'

'I said: "You are speaking to Mrs Cork," and he said "Oops! Sorry!" and rang off. Have you any idea who it could have been?'

Bill was able to supply the information.

'I can tell you who it must certainly have been. A young writer of my acquaintance named Joe Davenport. We were at Superba-Llewellyn together till he got fired. Shipped out to Hollywood at the same time in a crate of twelve. There is nothing surprising in the fact that he should have been asking Kay to marry him. I believe he does it every hour on the hour. He loves her with a fervour you don't often see off the Superba-Llewellyn lot.'

'Great heavens!'

'Why? Don't you approve of young love in springtime?'

'Not between my niece and a Hollywood writer who hasn't even got a job.'

'Joe may be out of a job, but he has a glittering future, if he can find some sporting soul to lend him twenty thousand dollars. If he had the capital, he could buy a lucrative Authors' Representativery. Would you care to lend him twenty thousand dollars?'

'I would not. Is Kay in love with this man?'

'Well, she gives a sort of rippling laugh, a kind of amused tee-hee, whenever I mention his name. Maybe that's a good sign. I must consult Dorothy Dix.'

Adela bristled.

'What do you mean, a good sign? It would be a disaster if she became entangled with a man like that. I am hoping she will marry Lord Topham. That is why I invited her here. He is one of the richest men in England.'

'So you told me.'

'I went to endless trouble to get him away from the Gloria Pirbrights, just so that Kay could meet him. Gloria was sticking to him like flypaper. I shall speak to Kay very seriously. I am not going to have any nonsense.'

'Why don't you get Smedley to speak to her?'

'Smedley!'

'I always think a man can do these things so much more impressively. Women are apt to get shrill. And Smedley is the brother of the husband of the sister of Kay's father. Puts him almost *in loco parentis*, you might say.'

Adela uttered a sound which in a woman of less impressive beauty would have been a snort.

'As if he could do anything. Smedley is a poor sheep who can't say boo to a goose.'

'Well, name three sheep who can.'

'Oh!'

'Yes?'

Adela was looking at Bill accusingly. Her manner was austere. In a hundred silent pictures she had looked just like that at a hundred heavies who had attempted in their uncouth way not to do right by our Nell. It was plain that some thought had floated into her mind which was reducing sisterly love to a minimum.

'Smedley!' she said. 'I knew there was something I wanted to ask you, but talking about Kay put it out of my head. Wilhelmina, have you been giving Smedley money?'

Bill had hoped that secrecy and silence might have been preserved on this point, but apparently it was not to be. She replied with as much nonchalance as she could manage on the spur of the moment.

'Why, yes, I did slip him a hundred dollars.'

'You idiot!'

'I'm sorry. I couldn't resist his pleading eye.'

'Well, you will be interested to hear that he was out all night on what I suppose was a drunken orgy. I went to his room after breakfast, and his bed had not been slept in. He must have sneaked off to Los Angeles with your precious hundred dollars.'

Bill did her best to soothe.

'Well, why agonize? He hasn't had a night out for years. Where's the harm in an occasional bender? Boys will be boys.'

'Smedley is not a boy.'

'What I always say is that as we shall pass this way only once, it surely behoves us – if behoves is the word I want – to do whatever in us lies to increase the sum of human happiness and—'

'Bah! Stuff and nonsense.'

'Yes, I suppose that is one way of looking at it.'

Adela went to the bell and pressed it.

'The only bright side of the thing,' she said, 'is that he will probably not return in time for lunch, and if he does, he will be in no condition to be at the table, to bore Mr Glutz with those interminable stories of his about Broadway in the Thirties.'

'That's right,' said Bill. 'Always look for the silver lining. What are you ringing for?'

'I am expecting my masseuse. Oh, Phipps,' said Adela, as the door opened, 'has the masseuse arrived?'

'Yes, madam.'

'She is in my room?'

'Yes, madam.'

'Thank you,' said Adela coldly. 'Oh, Phipps.'

'Madam?'

Adela's face, which had hardened as she spoke of Smedley, grew harder.

'I wanted to see you, Phipps, to give you a piece of news which I think will be of interest to you.'

'Yes, madam?'

'You're fired!' said Adela, allowing the stormy emotion of which she had been Empress to leap from her eyes and scorch the butler like a jet from a flame thrower.

5

Butlers, as the chronicler has already had occasion to remark in his observations on these fauna, are trained to hide their emotions. Whatever the turmoil in their souls, outwardly they aim at the easy insouciance of the Red Indian at the stake, and it is consequently not often that anyone is privileged to see one of them look aghast. But Phipps was now looking definitely aghast. His jaw had fallen and his eyes were round and horror-stricken.

He cast a tortured glance at Bill. 'Have you betrayed your promise?' the glance said. Bill's eye met his. 'Good heavens, no,' said Bill's eye. 'I haven't said a word. This is something completely new, and nobody more surprised than the undersigned.' Adela, having exploded her bomb, continued to ferment in silence.

'Fired, madam?' faltered Phipps.

'That's what I said.'

'But, madam—'

Bill intervened in her robust way. As Roget would have put it in his *Thesaurus*, she was surprised, astonished, perplexed, bewildered and at a loss, but she was not the woman to accept this sort of thing with meek detachment. She liked Phipps and wished him well, and he had told her that he particularly desired to remain in Adela's employment. Why this should be so, she could not imagine, but if that was how he felt, this totally unexpected thunderbolt must have been devastating. He was probably, she reflected with a pang, experiencing much the same sense of having been hit over the head with a blunt instrument as had come to her the previous afternoon on learning from Joe Davenport that his entire capital consisted of a few dollars and eight thousand tins of mixed soups.

'What do you mean, Adela? You can't fire *Phipps*.'

One would have said a moment before that it would have been impossible for even an Empress of Stormy Emotion to look sterner and haughtier than Adela Cork was looking. But at these words the proud severity of her manner took on a still more repellent coldness.

'Can't I?' she said crisply. 'Watch me.'

Bill became vehement. There were moments – this was one of them – when she had a nostalgic yearning to be back in the days of their mutual nursery, to return to the golden age when, if Adela annoyed her, she had been in a position to put a worm down the back of her neck or to smite her shrewdly with one of those hard objects which lie about nursery floors.

'You're crazy. You're like the base Indian who threw a pearl away richer than all his tribe. I haven't been long in this joint, but I've been here quite long enough to have got Phipps taped as the Butler Supreme.'

'Thank you, madam.'

'He's terrific. He out-Arthurs Treacher. He lends lustre to the whole establishment. That harsh, grating sound you hear from time to time is the envious gnashing of the teeth of all the other Beverly Hills employers who haven't got him. Fire him? Absurd. What on earth put a silly idea like that into your head?'

Adela continued stony.

'Have you quite finished?'

'No. But go on.'

'I am firing Phipps for a very good reason. Wouldn't you fire a butler who spends his whole time sneaking around in your bedroom?'

'Doing *what*?'

'That's what Phipps does. A couple of days ago I found him in my room, routing about in one of the closets. He said he had seen a spider.'

'Madam—'

Adela silenced the wretched man with an imperious gesture. She went on speaking in a voice that rose and vibrated with stormy passion.

'Yesterday he was there again. He said he had seen a mouse. As if there was the slightest possibility that there could be mice and spiders in my bedroom. And if it had been brimming over with mice and spiders, what business was that of his? I told him that if he ever put his ugly nose in my room again, I'd fire him. And this morning, as I was leaving for Pasadena, I went back to get a handkerchief, and there he was, if you please, under the dressing-table, with his fanny sticking up like a mesa in the Mojave desert. You leave at the end of the week, Phipps. I trust,' concluded Adela, her hand on the door-handle, 'that I am a broad-minded woman, but I'm not going to share my bedroom with the butler.'

The sound of a door vigorously slammed died slowly away, leaving silence behind it. Bill was endeavouring to adjust her faculties to these sensational happenings. Phipps was standing rooted to the spot to which he had been rooted since his late employer's opening remarks, still exhibiting all the symptoms of having received a powerful blow in the solar plexus.

'For heaven's sake, Phipps, what's all this?' said Bill.

The butler came slowly to life, like a male Galatea. His face was pale and drawn.

'Would you object if I took a sip of your whisky and soda, madam?' he said in a low voice. 'I do not often indulge, but this has come as a shock.'

'Help yourself.'

'Thank you, madam.'

'And now,' said Bill, 'supply a few footnotes.' There was something of severity in her manner as she eyed the butler. 'Does this mean that you have been going back to your old activities? I thought you told me you had put all that sort of thing behind you.'

'Oh, no, madam, nothing like that.'

'Then what were you doing, routing about in cupboards and crawling under dressing-tables?'

'I . . . er . . . I was looking for something, madam.'

'I gathered that. But what?'

Once again the butler directed that searching glance at her. And, as before, the scrutiny apparently proved satisfactory. After the briefest of pauses, he replied, speaking in the hushed voice of the man who knows that walls have ears.

'The diary of the late Miss Flores, madam.'

'Good God!' said Bill. 'Isn't this where I came in?'

Phipps, having decided to be confidential, was now in the mind to hold nothing back.

'It was a remark of Mr Smedley's that gave me the idea, madam. Mr Smedley chanced to observe one night at dinner that it was highly probable that the late Miss Flores had kept a diary and that, in the event of her having done so, the volume was presumably somewhere on the premises. I was handing the potatoes at the moment, and the dish literally trembled in my grasp, madam. For the thought occurred to me immediately that the sort of diary kept by the sort of lady the late Miss Flores was would be worth a great deal of money to whoever found it.'

Bill eyed him gravely.

'Have you ever had that odd feeling, when somebody tells you something, Phipps, that you've heard it all before somewhere? Like hearing the familiar strains of some grand old anthem to which you have listened in childhood?'

'No, madam.'

'It happens sometimes. Well, go on.'

'Thank you, madam. I was saying that such a diary would be extremely valuable. The late Miss Flores, madam, was hot stuff, if I may venture to use the expression. In one quarter or another there would be a ready market for any diary which she had kept.'

'True. So you looked for it?'

'Yes, madam.'

'But didn't find it?'

'No, madam.'

'Too bad.'

'Yes, madam. Thinking the matter over, I reached the conclusion that, if the late Miss Flores had kept a diary, she would have secreted it somewhere in her sleeping apartment, the room now occupied by Mrs Cork.'

'So you said to yourself, "Yoicks! Tally ho!"?'

'Not precisely that, madam, but I proceeded to institute a diligent search, confident that I would eventually succeed in discovering its whereabouts.'

'That was why you were so anxious not to lose your job here?'

'Precisely, madam. And now I am leaving at the end of the week. It is very bitter, madam,' said Phipps with a sigh that seemed to come up from the soles of his shapely feet.

Bill reflected.

'You've still got a couple of days.'

'But Mrs Cork will be on the alert, madam. I really could not go through the ordeal of being caught by her again.'

'Was she emotional?'

'Yes, madam. It was like being apprehended by a tigress while in the act of abstracting one of its cubs, madam.'

Bill shrugged her shoulders.

'Well, my heart bleeds for you, but I don't know what to advise.'

'No, madam.'

'It's a problem.'

'Yes, madam.'

'You might—'

Bill broke off. She had been about to suggest that the butler might slip into Adela's bedtime Ovaltine what is known as a knockout drop or Mickey Finn. She had one in her possession, the gift of a Third Avenue bartender with whom she was on cordial terms, and would have been delighted to lend it to him. But at this moment Kay came in through the French windows, a bag of golf clubs over her shoulder, and the conference had to be suspended.

'Hi, Bill,' said Kay.

'Good morning, my child.'

'Good morning, Phipps.'

'Good morning, miss.'

Rosy with exercise, tanned by the Californian sun, Kay presented an attractive picture. Bill, looking at her, could follow Joe Davenport's thought processes and understand his habit of proposing to her every hour on the hour.

'You two look very serious,' said Kay. 'What goes on?'

'Phipps and I were discussing the situation in China,' said Bill. 'He has been holding me spellbound.'

'Well, don't let me stop you.'

'Quite all right. Some other time, eh, Phipps?'

'Any time that suits you, madam.'

Kay threw her bag of clubs into a corner.

'Well, Bill. Working away?'

'Like a beaver.'

'On the *Memoirs*?'

'On the *Memoirs*.'

'Are they interesting?'

'Not in the least. I never realized before what dull lives silent screen stars led. It's agony, debasing my God-given talents with such hack-work.'

'It's a shame they let you go from the studio.'

'The loss is theirs. I've just got an idea for the finest B picture ever screened, and Superba-Llewellyn could have had it if they had not madly dispensed with my services. I shall write it up for *Horror Stories*. It's about a sinister scientist who gets hold of a girl and starts trying to turn her into a lobster.'

'A lobster?'

'You know. Those things that look like studio executives. He collected a covey of lobsters and mashed them up and extracted the juice, and he was just going to inject the brew into the gal's spinal column with a hypodermic syringe when her betrothed rushed in and stopped him.'

'Why did he do that?'

'He didn't want the girl he loved to be turned into something that looked like a studio executive. Isn't that good psychology?'

'I mean why did the sinister scientist act that way?'

'Oh, just a whim. You know what these sinister scientists are.'

'Well, it sounds fine. Full of meat.'

'Full of lobsters. Were you ever turned into a lobster, Phipps?'

'No, madam.'

'You're sure? Think back.'

'No, madam. I have not had that experience.'

'Well, go and ask the cook if she ever was.'

'Very good, madam,' said the butler courteously, and left the room. He had resumed his professional mask, and not even Sherlock Holmes, looking at his impassive face, could have guessed what vultures were gnawing at the bosom beneath that form-fitting shirt.

'Why all this research?' asked Kay.

'I'm a conscientious artist. I like to get my stuff right. If I'm doing a gangster story, I get it vetted by a gangster. If it's a hydrogen bomb story, I consult the firm that makes hydrogen bombs. And so on.'

'Yours must be very interesting work, Miss Shannon.'

'Well, it has brought me into contact with a lot of interesting people. I suppose I know more yeggs and thugs and crooks socially than anyone else in the United States. They send me cards at Christmas.'

'You're a disreputable old bird, aren't you, Bill? I wonder Aunt Adela has you in the house.'

'I'm doing those *Memoirs* of hers cheap. She never could resist a bargain. And don't use that expression "old bird". Hoity-toity, what next? However, as a matter of fact, the real reason why I sent Phipps away to chat with the cook was that I wanted to take his mind off his troubles. Adela has just fired him.'

'Fired Phipps? Why?'

'It's a long story, too long to tell now. We'll go into it later. How was your golf game?'

'Weak and sinful. Lord Topham trimmed me. He broke a hundred.'

'Yes, he has just been releasing the story.'

'So you've seen him? Where is he?'

'Still at the telephone, I imagine. He went off to put in a transatlantic call about it at Adela's expense to a friend of his in London called Bingo or Stingo or something. And, while on the subject of telephones, Adela informs me that your young man called up yesterday. She wants to discuss it with you.'

'What young man?'

'Have you a dozen? Joe Davenport. Adela intercepted a proposal of marriage from Joe to you yesterday, and you wouldn't be far out in saying that she is exercised in her mind. She's hoping you'll marry that pleasant but quarter-witted ornament of the British peerage, Lord Topham.'

'Really? I suppose that's why she invited me here.'

'She specifically told me so.'

'Well, of course, it would be wonderful to be the wife of a man who can break a hundred. On the other hand—'

'Exactly. On the other hand. Don't overlook the fact that if you marry Topham, you'll have half a dozen imbecile children saying "Absolutely, what?" all the time in an Oxford accent.'

'Really, Miss Shannon!'

'Just a sneak preview.'

Phipps appeared.

'The cook desires me to say that she has never been turned into a lobster, madam.'

'We must face it like men, Phipps. Stiff upper lip, eh?'

'Yes, madam. I wonder if you could inform me of Mrs Cork's whereabouts, madam?'

'I imagine she's in her room. You know that room of hers. She was going to have a massage, if you remember.'

'Ah, yes, madam.'

'Do you want to see her?'

'Yes, madam.'

'I wouldn't at the moment.'

'No, madam.'

'What was it you wanted to see her about?'

'I wished to notify Mrs Cork that a Mr Davenport has arrived, madam.'

Kay uttered a cry.

'What?'

'Yes, miss. He is in the garage, putting his car away. His suitcases are in the hall.'

'His *suitcases?*'

'Yes, miss. I gathered from the gentleman that he passed the evening with Mr Smedley last night and Mr Smedley invited him to spend a few weeks with us. Thank you, miss.'

Phipps bowed slightly, and withdrew.

Bill was the first to break the silence which followed his departure.

'Well, well,' said Bill.

Kay did not speak. She was feeling a little breathless. Phipps's announcement had given her the curious illusion of being the heroine of one of the silent films popularized by her Aunt Adela, in which the great feature had always been the pursuit of virtue by something pretty tough in the way of male pursuers. She had known that Joe was a pertinacious young man, but she had never suspected that his pertinacity would have carried him to such lengths as this. Even the most licentious of clubmen or the most bearded of desperadoes might well have hesitated to bring himself and suitcases into the home of Mrs Albert Cork on the invitation of her impecunious brother-in-law.

'Well, well,' said Bill. 'The soul of hospitality, Smedley. You would think he was a Southerner.'

'He must be crazy,' said Kay. 'He can't invite people here. This isn't his house.'

'As Adela will no doubt point out to him.'

Another facet of the mystery engaged Kay's attention.

'And what did Phipps mean, he passed the evening with Joe? Uncle Smedley never goes out. He told me so.'

'He did last night. He was on a toot.'

'So that's why he wasn't at dinner. I thought he had a headache.'

'He probably has.'

Kay was agitated. She was very fond of her Uncle Smedley, and the thought of what lay before him as the result of his thoughtless bonhomie touched her gentle heart.

'Do you think Aunt Adela will give him the devil?'

'If you want to bet against it, five will get you ten. But let's not discuss Smedley,' said Bill. 'Let us rather turn to the sacred meeting due to take place in a moment or two. So we are to have your young man with us for a few weeks, are we? Well, well, well.'

Kay had flushed. This may have been because Bill, her motion-picture training having taught her that a scene always goes better to a musical accompaniment, had begun to hum Mendelssohn's 'Wedding March', putting a good deal of feeling into it.

'Don't call him my young man. And it's more likely to be for a few minutes.'

'Do you think Adela will throw him out?'

'Don't you?'

'No. Not after I have pleaded his cause. I shall use all my eloquence on his behalf. We alumni of Superba-Llewellyn must stick together.'

Phipps appeared in the doorway.

'Mr Davenport,' he announced, and Joe came in, bringing, in Bill's opinion, the sunshine with him. Though suffering from the slight headache inevitable on the morning after an evening passed in the society of Smedley Cork when that earnest reveller was making up leeway after five years of abstinence, he was plainly in radiant spirits. He beamed on Bill and Kay, particularly the latter, with an almost Tophamic exuberance.

'Hello, there,' he said, and would no doubt, like Lord Topham, have added that this was the maddest, merriest day of all the glad new year, if he had happened to think of it. 'Hello, Bill.'

'Hello, Joe.'

'And, as I live and breathe, if it isn't my favourite glamour girl, Kay. Hello, Kay.'

'Good morning.'

'Well, here I am. Where's my hostess?'

'Having a massage. Well, Joe, if I'd known you were coming, I'd have baked a cake. You could have knocked me down with a feather when Phipps told us you were to be today's big surprise for my sister Adela.'

'Today's unpleasant surprise,' said Kay.

Joe looked hurt. The wrong note, he seemed to be saying, the wrong note entirely. On this morning of mornings he wanted there to be smiling faces about him. And nobody, not even a reasonably modest young man, likes to be told that his arrival is going to cast a blight on the home.

'Is it my imagination,' he said plaintively, 'or am I getting a rather tepid reception? I haven't got leprosy, you know.'

'You might just as well have,' said Kay.

'You don't think Mrs Cork will be pleased to see me?'

'You'll be lucky if you escape with a few flesh wounds. I warned you, you remember, that day at lunch.'

Bill intervened. She, too, thought the conversation was taking too morbid a tone.

'Nonsense,' she said. 'You may expect a warm Southern Californian welcome from Adela. Wait till I have reasoned with her.'

'Can anyone reason with Aunt Adela?'

'I can. I will play on her as on a stringed instrument. Don't you worry, Joe. I guarantee you will be treated as a ewe lamb. So you ran into our Smedley last night?'

'Yes.'

'An odd coincidence.'

'Not so very. I was outside the gate here in a taxi, and he came along and we fraternized.'

'What were you doing outside the gate in a taxi?'

'Just gazing. I gave him a lift down the hill. And when we found that he was at a loose end and I was at a loose end, it seemed the sensible thing to join forces. We started off with a bite at Mike Romanoff's.'

'And then?'

'We looked in at Mocambo. He began to unbend rather at Mocambo.'

'I can imagine.'

'After that we went on to Ciro's.'

'Where he unbent still further?'

'A good deal further.'

'That was when he invited you to come and stay here?'

'Yes.'

Bill nodded.

'I think I can reconstruct the scene. First, he climbed on the table and took his coat off and announced that he could lick any two men in the room.'

'Any three.'

'Then his mood seemed to soften. He climbed down, put his coat on, cried a little and invited everybody present to come and stay at his mountain home. "Particularly you, my dear fellow," he said to you.'

'You might have been there.'

'A pity I wasn't. What happened after that?'

'Well, all of a sudden I lost him. One moment he was there, the next he wasn't. Did you ever see the Indian Rope Trick?'

'No, but I know what you mean. He vanished?'

'Like a pea from under the shell. I don't know where he went.'

'Probably to one or more of the numerous joints on Ventura Boulevard. I know Smedley on these occasions. Eye-witnesses have informed me of his habits. He likes to get about and see fresh faces. The faces are always nice and fresh along the Ventura Boulevard, and no doubt he felt that he would be able to express and fulfil himself better if he were alone. I think, Kay, it might be as well if you whistled up the bloodhounds and started a search, to see if he got home all right.'

'I think it might.'

'We know that his bed was not slept in.'

'What!'

'So Adela says. She inspected it after breakfast. He was out all night.'

'Why does he do these things?'

Bill could answer that.

'Because he's a fathead. I have watched Smedley Cork burgeon from boyhood to man's estate. As a boy, he was a small fathead. He is now a large fathead. Tell me more,' said Bill, as Kay hurried out. 'Did Smedley do his imitation of Beatrice Lillie?'

'No, I don't remember that.'

'He usually does on these occasions, I'm told. First, his imitation of Beatrice Lillie, then in response to gales of applause, "Gunga Din" by the late Rudyard Kipling. It's terrific, I believe. How did you pass the long hours?'

Joe's face, which had become a little grave as the result of the introduction of the Mrs Cork motif, cleared. He began to beam again.

'Bill,' he said, 'I have tidings of great joy. You remember those characters who brought the good news from Aix to Ghent? Well, they weren't in my class, simply not in my class. I have good news that is good news. This is where you leap about and clap your little hands, my Wilhelmina. You ask me how we passed the long hours. Well, as soon as I thought the time was ripe, I started talking business.'

Bill's eyebrows rose.

'Business? With Smedley?'

'Selling him our authors' representatives scheme. It wasn't easy going, because his attention seemed to wander a good deal. I would put the thing with crystal clarity, and he would just sit back, looking glassy-eyed, like a fish on a slab, and when I said: "Well, how about it?" he was rather apt to spring to his feet and utter what I imagine were college yells of some prehistoric vintage. Putting the question aside, if you know what I mean. Which, of course, rendered it difficult for me to make a convincing sales talk. But I persevered, I kept at it, and you will be relieved to hear, pardner, that all is well. Snatching at a moment when he was having a comparatively lucid interval, I drove the thing home, and he's going to put up that twenty thousand we require as the first step up the ladder of wealth. For heaven's sake, woman,' said Joe, amazed, 'why aren't you leaping about and clapping your little hands? Haven't you been listening? Pop Cork has definitely promised to put up that twenty thousand we need to buy the agency.'

A sad, pitying look had come into Bill's face, the look of a mother forced to notify a loved child that his chances of obtaining candy are but slim, if not non-existent.

'There is a snag,' she said.

'Eh? What snag?'

'The fact that Smedley hasn't a cent in the world.'

'What!'

'Not a cent.'

Joe stared. He could make nothing of this.

'But you told me he was a millionaire.'

'Never.'

'You did. At the hotel yesterday. You said your sister married a millionaire.'

Bill's sad, pitying look deepened.

'Smedley isn't Adela's husband, my poor misled young friend. Adela's husband is no longer with us. Up there,' said Bill, pointing heavenwards. 'The gentleman with the harp. Smedley is merely his brother, and, as I say, he hasn't a cent in the world. For I hardly suppose that after such a majestic bender as he appears to have been on last night, he has anything left of the hundred I slipped him yesterday.'

Joe was rocking on his base.

'You mean that last night he was just kidding me?'

'I don't think intentionally.'

'Purely accidental, eh?'

Bill sighed. She was feeling like a mother who, in addition to having to notify him that there is no candy, has been compelled to strike a loved child on the base of the skull with a stocking full of sand.

'It's like this, Joe. When under the influence, poor Smedley gets delusions of grandeur. He believes he's back in the days when he really did have a lot of money ... before he fooled it all away on musicals which closed on Saturday and repertory companies nobody bought tickets for and Czechoslovak ballets and seasons of grand opera in English. He was at one time Broadway's leading angel. I suppose he backed more flops than any other two men in the business. Whenever there was any-thing more than ordinarily hopeless in the way of a dramatic opus knocking around, the cry immediately went up: "Where's Smedley?" It couldn't last. Five years ago his last few thousands went into a sweet little whimsical comedy adapted from the French which ran from a Friday night till the end of the week, and since then he has been penniless and dependent for his three squares a day on the grudging bounty of my sister Adela.'

She paused, and Joe, who had been clutching at the desk, slowly relaxed his grip.

'I see,' he said.

'I'm afraid this is something of a blow.'

'It is, rather. Yes, quite a disappointment. I believe I'll take a turn in the garden and brood on it a little.'

'I wish I could have broken it more gently.'

'Oh, that's all right,' said Joe dully.

He passed through the French windows with bowed head, and Adela, appearing simultaneously in the doorway, gazed after him in surprise.

'Who is that?' she asked.

'Eh?' said Bill absently. Her thoughts were still occupied with Joe and the collapse of his hopes and dreams.

'That strange young man who just went out.'

Bill braced herself for combat.

'The young man to whom you allude,' she said, 'is not in the least strange. He is a perfectly normal, wholesome young man of the type which has made America what it is. That is Joe Davenport. You remember we were speaking of him not long ago.'

Adela reeled.

'Davenport! That man. What is he doing here? Did you invite him?'

'Not I. Smedley.'

Adela's beautiful eyes were bulging. She looked like Louise de Querouaille on one of her bad mornings. If some former associate of hers, with whom she had worked in the era when films were silent, had chanced to wander in at this moment and catch a glimpse of her face, he would have climbed the nearest jacaranda tree and pulled it up after him. Just so had she been wont to look in the old days when bursting in on a director in his office with the dreaded 'I should like a word with you, Mr Marsupial!' on her lips.

'Are you telling me that Smedley – *Smedley* – has been inviting people to my house?'

'That's right. It appears that they ran into one another last night and hobnobbed, and Smedley insisted on him coming to take pot luck for a week or two. You'll like Joe. One of the best.'

'Ha!'

Bill's manner became firm.

'Now listen, Adela,' she said. 'I had anticipated that you might be a little difficult about this, and I have formed my plans.'

'And I have formed mine. I shall order Phipps to throw this person out.'

'You will do no such thing. You will welcome him in and treat him like a ewe lamb. And when I say ewe lamb, I mean EWE LAMB. Adela, you and I were children together.'

'I have been trying to live it down ever since.'

'And when we were children together,' proceeded Bill, her voice cold and hard, 'I used, if you remember, to put worms down the back of your neck from time to time, when such a corrective to your insufferable behaviour seemed to be indicated. Persist in your refusal to become the genial hostess to my friend Joe Davenport, and I shall resume that practice.'

'We are not amused.'

'No, and you'll be still less amused after lunch when, as you show Jacob Glutz the rose garden, you find me sliding up behind you with a fistful of worms.'

Adela gasped. Forty years of acquaintance with her sister Wilhelmina had left her with the unpleasant feeling that she was not a woman to be trifled with. There might be things which her sister Wilhelmina would hesitate to do, but, she was forced to admit, not many.

'I believe you mean it!'

'Of course I mean it. Not one worm, mark you, but a bevy of worms. Large, fat, sticky worms, Adela. Slithery, writhing, wriggly worms. Cold, clammy—'

Adela capitulated.

'There is no necessity to labour your point,' she said stiffly.

'You see reason?'

'I am prepared to be civil to this friend of yours.'

'Good. Oh, Joe,' called Bill, going to the French windows. 'Come here a minute, will you? Start practising that sunny smile of yours, Adela. I want to see it split your face from side to side. And when you address your guest, let your voice be like that of a turtle dove calling to its mate. Joe, I want you to meet your hostess. My sister, Mrs Cork.'

Joe's head was still bowed. Communing with nature, as represented by the orange trees, the lemon trees, the jacaranda trees and the rattlesnakes, had done little to alleviate the despondency which had him in its grip. Dully he was aware of something large and feminine confronting him, and he bowed in its direction.

'How do you do?' he said.

'How do you do?' said Adela with a visible effort.

'I have just been telling my sister that you are to be her house guest,' said Bill. 'She is overjoyed. Eh, Adela?'

There was a momentary silence.

'Yes,' said Adela.

'She says yes. So you may take up residence with an easy mind. Your status, as I foreshadowed, will be that of a ewe lamb.'

'Well, that's fine.'

'Yes, I think you will enjoy it. Ewe lambs live the life of Reilly. Ah, Lord Topham,' said Bill, as that gentleman entered with a brief What ho. 'Come and shake hands with Joe Davenport.'

'Hullo,' said Lord Topham, doing so.

'Hello,' said Joe.

'Hullo-ullo-ullo.'

'Yes,' said Joe.

There was another momentary silence.

'Perhaps you would show Mr Davenport his room, Lord Topham,' said Adela, seeming to speak with difficulty. 'It is the one next to yours.'

'Right ho,' said Lord Topham, for the task was well within his scope. He led Joe out. Through the open door he could be heard starting to describe to this new friend of his how he had broken a hundred this morning.

Bill sighed the contented sigh of the woman who has got things done.

'Well, Adela,' she said, 'I really must congratulate you. You were superb. Just the right note of warm but ladylike ecstasy. You might have been the Queen of Sheba welcoming King Solomon. But why do you look like that? Is there something on your mind?'

A wistful expression had come into Adela's face.

'I was only thinking,' she said, 'that a dozen times since you have been in this house I could have dropped something heavy on your head from an upper landing – and I didn't do it.'

'Of all sad words of tongue and pen, the saddest are these, It might have been. Well, Kay? What luck?'

Kay had come in, looking worried.

'I can't find him anywhere. Good morning, Aunt Adela. I've been trying to find Uncle Smedley.'

A whistling sound, like escaping steam, came from Adela's nostrils.

'I want to find Smedley myself,' she said grimly. 'I want to ask him what he means by inviting his revolting friends to my house.'

Bill seemed surprised.

'Why, I thought you liked Joe. You were charming to him just now. Perhaps Phipps can help us,' she said, as the butler came in bearing cocktail materials on a tray. 'Phipps, have you seen Mr Smedley?'

'Not since last night, madam.'

'You don't know where he is?' said Kay.

'Oh, yes, miss,' said the butler brightly. 'He is in prison.'

7

It was not immediately that any of those present found themselves able to comment on this front page piece of news. Speech was wiped from their lips, and nothing left to them but the language of the eye, which is always unsatisfactory. Then Kay spoke.

'*Prison?*'

'Yes, miss. Mr Smedley is in the hands of the constabulary. He spoke to me on the telephone from the jail this morning.'

A shuddering cry broke from Adela's lips. Totting up the household expenses week by week and watching him at meals having twice of everything, she had sometimes – for she was a dreamer – aren't we all? – thought how nice it would be if her brother-in-law were a disembodied spirit, his mortal remains safely tucked away in the family vault, but she had never hoped that he would some day go to prison. Prison leads to publicity of the wrong sort, not only for the captive himself but for his relatives by marriage. KIN OF ADELA SHANNON JAILED, INSET-PHOTOGRAPH OF ADELA SHANNON – Adela Shannon was feeling, and the picture thus conjured up gave her an unpleasant, fluttering sensation internally, as if she had been swallowing butterflies.

'Oh, Lord!' she said.

'He suggested that I should come and take the requisite steps through the proper channels,' proceeded Phipps. 'But I was unable to leave my domestic duties.'

'It didn't occur to you to mention this to anyone?' said Bill.

'No, madam. Mr Smedley asked me to respect his confidence.'

Adela was clenching and unclenching her hands, going through the movements as if she were gripping a brother-in-law's throat. The thought may have been passing through her mind that in omitting to throttle Smedley earlier she had been remiss. One keeps putting these things off and is sorry later.

'Did you learn any details?' asked Bill.

'Yes, madam. Mr Smedley supplied me with the facts. While visiting a night club on the Ventura Boulevard last night, he stabbed the master of ceremonies with an oyster fork. The latter, visibly taken aback, summoned the management, who summoned the police, who removed Mr Smedley to the station house. I hope it will not get into the papers, madam.'

'I, too, Phipps. At the thought of what Louella Parsons would do with this the imagination boggles.'

'Yes, madam. It boggles perceptibly.'

'Phipps,' said Adela in a strangled voice, 'you may go.'

'Very good, madam.'

Relieved of the butler's presence, Adela was able to give full expression to the emotions surging within her. For some moments, she proceeded to speak of her brother-in-law in terms which could scarcely have been more severe if he had been a fiend with hatchet who had just slain six. It was almost a perfect character sketch of the absent man, and might have continued indefinitely had she not run out of breath. Bill, listening, was aware of an unwilling respect for a woman she had never liked. Adela, she felt, might have her faults, but you had to admire her vocabulary.

'Take it easy,' she urged.

'Take it easy? Ha! So this is what happens when I stop watching Smedley for a single instant. He's incorrigible.'

'A word I'll bet he couldn't have said last night.'

Phipps appeared.

'I thought you would wish to know, madam,' he said in a discreet, hushed voice, 'that Mr Smedley has just returned. He was entering the front door as I passed through the hall.'

'He's not in prison?' said Kay.

'Apparently not, miss.'

'How was he looking?'

'Not very roguish, miss.'

Adela's eyes flashed fire. Indeed, there was a sort of incandescence about her whole person. A bystander, had one been present, would have felt that if he had slapped her on the back, he would have burned his hand. Not that any bystander, unless exceptionally reckless, would have ventured to slap her on the back.

'Where is he?'

'He has gone to his room, madam, to shave.'

'And have a bath, no doubt,' said Bill.

'He has had a bath, madam. He was washed by the authorities.'

'Phipps,' said Adela, 'you may GO.'

'Very good, madam.'

'You'd better run up and view the body, Kay,' said Bill. 'He'll be wanting someone to hold his hand.'

Kay was looking apprehensively at Adela, who was staring before her with quivering nostrils.

'Bill, do do something. She's working herself up.'

'So I noticed,' said Bill. 'In moments of emotion, Adela always resembles those priests of Baal who gashed themselves with knives. But leave it to me. I'll attend to her.'

'What a comfort you are, Bill.'

'The Old Reliable.'

'Bless you.'

Kay hurried out, and Bill came back to Adela, who was now grinding her teeth.

'Now then, Adela,' she said briskly, 'simmer down. Come off the boil, will you please.'

'Don't talk to me!'

'That's just what I'm going to do. Adela, you make me sick.'

'Well, really!'

Bill, veteran of a hundred sisterly battles stretching back into the misty past of a mutual nursery, allowed her voice to rise. It was on these occasions that she was grateful to Providence for having equipped her with sound, healthy vocal cords. A situation like this could not have been handled adequately by a woman missing on one lung.

'Sick,' she repeated. 'Sitting there licking your lips at the prospect of tearing the stuffing out of poor old Smedley. What an infernal tyrant you are. You love harrying and torturing people. You're like Simon Legree, though you lack Simon Legree's charm of manner. I always maintain that you killed old Al Cork.'

Adela, who had been about to take up the Simon Legree issue, decided to dispose of this charge first.

'My husband was run over by a sightseeing omnibus.'

Bill nodded. There was, of course, something in what she said.

'That may have helped,' she agreed, 'but it was being married to you that really did it. But it's silly having these family fights,' she went on, in milder vein. 'I'm sorry if I was rude.'

'You're always rude.'

'Well, ruder than usual. But I'm fond of Smedley. I was fond of him when he was a boy of fifteen with pimples. I was fond of him in his middle period, when he was scattering his money on Broadway turkeys. And I'm fond of him now. Some sort of mental flaw in me, I guess. Maybe I ought to see a psychiatrist. Still, there it is. So won't you skip the red tape and treat him decently?'

Adela bridled.

'I was under the impression that I had "treated him decently". I have supported him for five years. And a great strain it has been.'

'Strain be damned!'

'Must you curse and swear?'

'Of course I must. What do you expect me to do when you insult my intelligence by trying to put gobbledy-gook like that over on me? Strain, indeed! You could afford to support a dozen Smedleys. Al Cork left you enough money to sink a ship, not to mention specific instructions that you'd *got* to support Smedley. And whatever you spend on the poor devil, you get back in the gratification it affords your sadistic instincts to have him under your fat thumb. Am I being rude again?'

'You are.'

'I thought I was. All right, let's let it go. But don't forget about the quality of mercy. It isn't strained, you know. No, sir! It droppeth as the gentle rain upon the place beneath. So they tell me.'

'Quality of mercy? Stuff and nonsense.'

'You'd better not let Shakespeare hear you saying that.'

'I—'

Adela broke off, and stiffened. Her aspect had become that of a leopardess sighting its prey. Smedley was entering the room, followed by Kay.

'Ah!' she said.

Smedley, normally so dapper, was looking soiled and crumpled, like a Roman Emperor who has sat up too late over the Falernian wine. With the best intentions in the world, police officials, hustling a man out of a night club into the waggon and subsequently thrusting him into a cell, tend to spoil his crease. Smedley's Palm Beach suit looked as if it had been slept in, as indeed it had. But, oddly for a man with a criminal record and the appearance of a tramp cyclist, he was not slinking into the room with a shamefaced slouch, but striding in boldly in quite a dominant manner. His chin was up – both his chins were up – and in his bloodshot eye there gleamed defiance. It was as though from some inner source he had obtained courage and resolution.

Adela flexed her muscles.

'Well, Smedley?' she said.

'Well?' said Smedley.

'You rather had her there,' said Bill.

Smedley blinked. He peered as if he found some difficulty in focusing his gaze.

'Why, hello, Bill.'

'Hello, my old stag at eve.'

'I didn't see you. For some reason my eyes aren't at their best this morning. Floating spots. You look very yellow.'

'It's your imagination. I'm really a pretty pink.'

Adela, who had seated herself at the desk, rapped it imperiously. One felt that she would have preferred to have had a gavel, but, like Phipps when operating on a safe, she could do a lot with her finger tips.

'Never mind how Wilhelmina looks,' she said. 'I am waiting for an explanation.'

Bill raised her eyebrows.

'You feel that a man needs to explain why he stabbed a night club master of ceremonies? Just doin' what comes naturally, I'd say. But I should like to know why you aren't in prison, Smedley. Phipps gave us to understand that you were in a dungeon with dripping walls, being gnawed by rats. What happened? Did the jailer's daughter smuggle you in a file in a meat pie?'

'The judge let me off with a caution.'

'You see,' said Bill triumphantly. 'The quality of mercy *isn't* strained. Perhaps you'll believe me another time.'

Adela uttered a stricken moan, a moan of a good woman calling on heaven to witness her wrongs. Her voice shook and quivered as it would unquestionably have shaken and quivered in the days of her screen triumphs, had not her deeper emotions in that backward age had to be expressed in sub-titles.

'The shame of it!' she cried. 'The brother-in-law of Adela Shannon thrown into prison with all the riff-raff of Los Angeles!'

Kay caught Bill's eye.

'I suppose the society *is* a bit mixed in those prisons,' she said.

'Everything very informal, I believe,' said Bill.

'Does one dress?'

'Just a black tie.'

'PLEASE!!!' said Adela.

She turned to the prisoner again.

'Well, Smedley? I am still waiting for an explanation.'

'Tell her it's a poor heart that never rejoices.'

'Wilhelmina, please!'

'Well, it is,' said Bill. 'Ask anyone.'

'Have you an explanation?'

A curious writhing movement of the upper part of his body seemed to suggest that Smedley was trying to square his shoulders.

'Certainly I have an explanation. A complete and satisfactory explanation. I was celebrating.'

'Celebrating? Celebrating what?'

'The most amazing piece of good fortune that ever happened to a deserving man. I was telling Kay about it upstairs.'

Kay nodded.

'It's a real romance,' she said. 'It would make a good B picture.'

Bill frowned.

'Don't mention B pictures in my presence, girl. Would you twist the knife in the wound?'

'Oh, Bill, forgive me.'

'Quite all right, my child. You did but speak thoughtlessly. Tell us more, Smedley.'

Smedley swelled impressively. It was his moment. He was a man who as a rule found difficulty in getting himself listened to in the home circle. He had a fund of good stories, but Adela had a way of cutting them short in the opening stanzas. This was the first time in something like five years that he had actually been encouraged to hold the floor.

'Well, sir,' he said, 'it's like Kay was saying. It's a real romance. Yesterday evening I was out on the terrace, thinking of this and that, and suddenly my guardian angel whispered in my ear—'

'Oh, go and lie down,' said Adela wearily.

Smedley gave her a haughty look.

'I will not go and lie down.'

'No,' said Kay. 'I think you ought to hear about his guardian angel.'

'I am always glad to hear about guardian angels, always,' said Bill. 'What did yours whisper in your ear?'

'It whispered "Smedley, my boy, try the top of the wardrobe." '

Adela closed her eyes. She may have been praying, but more probably not.

'I really cannot endure this much longer.'

'I, on the other hand,' said Bill, 'could listen for ever. Proceed, Smedley. What wardrobe? Where?'

'The one in Adela's bedroom.'

Adela started convulsively. Nor can she fairly be blamed for doing so. She was wondering if a woman's personal sleeping quarters had ever been so extensively invaded. First Phipps, and now Smedley. Was her bedroom her bedroom, she was asking herself, or was it the Grand Concourse of the New York Central Railroad terminal?

She shot a basilisk glare at the speaker.

'Have you been messing about in my room?'

'I went in there for a moment, yes. There was something I was trying to find.'

Sudden enlightenment came upon Bill.

'Ye gods!' she said. 'The diary?'

'Yup.'

'You were after that?'

'Yup.'

'Was it there?'

'Yup. Yessir, plumb spang on top of the wardrobe.'

'You've got it?'

'In my pocket,' said Smedley, patting it.

Adela was looking from Bill to Smedley, from Smedley to Bill, dangerously, exasperated by the mystic turn the conversation had taken. She disliked people who spoke in riddles in her presence, particularly if one of them was a jail-bird who had brought disgrace on her home and the other a sister whom she wished she had never allowed to come into it. There were probably no two individuals in America who could have occasioned her more irritation by wrapping their meaning up in cryptic speech. Her resemblance to a peevish leopardess became more marked.

'What are you talking about? What diary? Whose diary?'

'Carmen Flores's,' said Kay. 'Uncle Smedley's been trying to find it for weeks.'

Bill sighed. Hers was a feeling heart.

'Alas, poor Phipps,' she said. 'What made you think of the wardrobe, Smedley?'

'If a woman has anything to hide, that's where she puts it. Well-known fact. It's in all the detective stories.'

'Don't you ever read Agatha Christie?' said Kay.

'Who is Agatha Christie?' asked Adela.

'My dear Adela!' said Bill.

Smedley gave a short, unpleasant laugh.

'Just a dumb bunny,' he said.

Adela drew herself up and directed at her brother-in-law a look of the sort which Evil Eye Fleagle of Brooklyn would have described as a full whammy.

'Don't you call me a dumb bunny, you . . . you fugitive from a chain gang!'

Smedley, in his turn, drew himself up.

'And don't you call me a fugitive from a chain gang. The idea!'

'I called you a fugitive from a chain gang because that's what you are. Don't the police want you?'

'No, the police do not want me.'

'How I sympathize with the police,' sighed Adela. 'I know just how they feel.'

Smedley stiffened.

'Adela, I resent that crack.'

'It doesn't matter what you resent.'

'Oh, doesn't it?'

'I think it does, Adela,' said Bill. 'This has put Smedley in a very different position from what he was this time yesterday.'

'I don't know what you mean.'

'It's very simple.'

Joe came in. He had seen his room, heard in pitiless detail the story of how Lord Topham had broken a hundred that morning, and he was now planning to go out into the garden and commune with nature again, not that he expected to derive any solace from doing so. He was still in the depths. Listlessly, he observed that the Garden Room seemed to have become the centre of a conference, but he paid its occupants but slight attention and was making for the French windows, when Bill's powerful voice halted him in his tracks.

'Yesterday, Smedley was not in possession of the diary of the late Carmen Flores. Today he is. There isn't a studio in Hollywood that won't pay through the nose for it.'

Smedley corroborated this.

'I was on the phone to Colossal-Exquisite last night. They say they'll give fifty thousand.'

'Fifty thousand!' gasped Adela.

'Fifty thousand,' said Smedley.

Adela rose slowly to her feet.

'You mean that they . . . You mean fifty thousand *dollars*?'

'Fifty thousand dollars,' said Smedley.

Joe tottered to the sofa, and collapsed on it. His head was spinning. It seemed to him that an unseen orchestra had begun to play soft music in the Garden Room.

'Have you closed with the offer?' asked Bill.

'No. I'm waiting till all the bids are in. I'm expecting big things from Medulla-Oblongata-Glutz.'

'But you can't get less than fifty thousand.'

'That's right,' said Smedley. He took the diary from his pocket, and gazed at it reverently. 'Isn't it astounding that a small book like this should be worth fifty grand!'

'It must be red-hot stuff. Have you read any of it?'

'I can't. It's in Spanish.'

'Too bad.'

'Quite all right,' said Smedley, quick to point out the bright side. 'One of the gardeners at the Lulabelle Mahaffy place down the road is a Mexican. I'm going to take it around to him and have him translate it. We're good friends. He gave me a shot of that Mexican drink once that they call – no, I've forgotten the name, but it lifts the top of your head off.'

On Adela during these exchanges there had descended a curious calm. It was as if she had been thinking and had been rewarded with an idea whose effects had been to still the tumult within her. Her fingers were twitching a little, but her voice, when she spoke, was quiet and unusually amiable.

'I picked up a little Spanish when I made that personal goodwill tour in South America,' she said. 'I might be able to help you. May I look?'

'Sure,' said Smedley cordially. Speak civilly to Smedley Cork and he would speak civilly to you. 'There's an entry for the twenty-first of April that I'd like to have translated. It's got six exclamation marks against it in the margin.'

He gave Adela the book. Her fingers, as she took it, were twitching more noticeably than ever. She started for the door, and Smedley, suddenly filled with a nameless fear, gave tongue.

'Hey! Where are you off to?'

Adela turned.

'A thing as valuable as this ought not to be left lying about. I will put it in the safe in the projection room.'

'You will not. I want it on my person.'

Adela unmasked her batteries.

'Well, you aren't going to have it on your person,' she said crisply. 'For five years, Smedley, you have been living on me, and it is high time you made some contribution to the household expenses. This is it.'

'But – but—'

'This is it,' said Adela. 'Fifty thousand dollars. A very nice first instalment. And, Wilhelmina,' she said, changing the subject, 'will you kindly go and take off those damned dungarees. You look like a rag-picker.'

8

The slam of the closing door was drowned by the cry, resembling in its general features the howl of some bereaved beast of the jungle, which broke from Smedley's lips. Phipps, in his remarks to Bill on the previous day with reference to the attitude of Mrs Adela Cork toward those whom she found exploring her bedroom, had spoken of the emotional behaviour of tigresses when robbed of their cubs. It is to be doubted whether even the most neurotic tigress could have put more naked anguish into what in motion picture circles is called a 'take' than Smedley was now doing. His eyes seemed to protrude from their sockets, and a third chin had been added to his normal two by the limp sagging of his jaw.

Bill, also, appeared a little taken aback by this unforeseen development.

'Hell!' said Bill. 'Hi-jacked!'

Smedley had joined Joe on the sofa.

'In broad daylight!' he moaned incredulously. His bosom swelled with righteous indignation. 'I'll – I'll write to the *Los Angeles Examiner.*'

'No wonder that woman rose to impressive heights on the silent screen.'

'But she can't do this,' cried Joe.

'I know she can't,' said Bill. 'But she has.'

She crossed the room with a firm step and touched the bell. She was a woman of action, not one of your weak, fluttering women who waste precious time in lamentations. It had taken her scarcely a moment to see what Napoleon would have done in a crisis like this. Put Napoleon in a tight corner, and the first thing he did was summon up his reserves and send them into battle.

This was what Bill now proposed to do. The ringing of that bell was the bugle call which would bring Phipps hurrying to the front line, and it was on Phipps that she was relying to snatch victory out of defeat. If something valuable has been wrested from you and deposited in a safe and you have at your call a butler who has taken twenty lessons in the art of opening safes and become good at it, it is mere common sense to avail yourself of his skill.

Smedley was still vibrating. He raised his hands in a passionate gesture.

'I'll write to *Variety*!'

Bill regarded him maternally.

'Pipe down, Smedley.'

'I won't pipe down. I'll write to Walter Winchell.'

'No need to get excited,' said Bill. 'Absolutely not, as Lord Topham would say. Ah, Phipps.'

The butler had manifested himself silently in the doorway.

'You rang, madam?'

'Yes. Come in. Phipps,' said Bill, 'I'm afraid the moment has arrived when we must cease to hide your light beneath a bushel.'

'Madam?'

'Smedley, have you ever served on a jury?'

As far as an English butler can quiver, Phipps quivered. He gave Bill a startled look.

'Madam, please!'

Bill ignored the interruption.

'I was on one some little time ago,' she said. 'The one that sent Phipps here up the river for three years.'

'Madam, you promised—'

'And do you know what he had done to earn that three years sojourn in the coop? Do you know what he got his scholarship at Sing-Sing for? Safe-blowing.'

If she had anticipated a stunned reaction to her words, she was not disappointed. Smedley stopped blowing invisible bubbles and stared dumbly at the butler. Kay gave a sharp squeak and stared dumbly at the butler. Joe said 'What?' He, too, stared dumbly at the butler. Phipps stared dumbly at Bill. Not even Julius Caesar, receiving Brutus's dagger thrust, could have packed more pain and disappointment into a glance. Those reproachful eyes made Bill feel that something in the nature of an apology was in order.

'I'm sorry, Phipps,' she said, 'but this is a military necessity.'

Smedley found speech.

'You mean,' he said, marvelling, 'that Phipps – *Phipps* – was a safeblower?'

'And a darned good one, too. He blew a beautiful safe.'

'Then—'

'Exactly. That is why I brought up the subject. Phipps, we've got a job for you.'

Though far from having recovered completely from one of the worst shocks of his life, the butler was sufficiently himself again to be able to speak.

'Madam?'

'We want you to open Mrs Cork's safe. The one in the projection room.'

'But, madam, I have retired.'

'Then this is where you make a comeback.'

Icy resolution descended upon Phipps. It was those operative words 'Mrs Cork's safe' that steeled him to resist to the uttermost this call upon his services. As Lyly so neatly put it in his *Euphues*, the burned child dreadeth the fire, and a butler who has thrice been caught by Mrs Cork hunting for diaries in her bedroom does not lightly undertake the even more perilous task of burgling safes belonging to a woman of her intimidating personality. Call on James Phipps to make a burglarious entry into Fort Knox and it is possible that he might decide to oblige, but Mrs Cork's safes were immune.

'No, madam,' he said respectfully, but firmly.

'Ah, come on.'

'No, madam.'

'Think well, Phipps. Are you prepared to stand before the bar of world opinion as a man who refused to bust a safe to oblige an old friend?'

'Yes, madam.'

'I should have mentioned at the outset,' said Bill, 'that your cut will be five thousand dollars.'

Phipps started. His iron front began to waver. His eyes, which had been hard and uncompromising, softened, and there came into them the gleam which always comes into the eyes of butlers when they see an opportunity of making quick money. The vision of Adela Cork sneaking up behind him and tapping him on the shoulder as he crouched before her safe began to fade. Every man has his price, and five thousand dollars was about Phipps's.

'That is a lot of money, madam,' he said, impressed.

'It's a hell of a lot of money,' said Smedley, thoroughly concurring.

Bill checked this parsimonious trend of thought with an impatient gesture. How like Smedley, she felt, to haggle at a time like this.

'Customary agent's commission of ten per cent,' she said. 'We mustn't be tightwads. You don't want Phipps to think he's working for Gaspard the Miser. Five thousand of the best, Phipps.'

'Five thousand,' murmured the butler reverently.

'Are you with us?'

'Yes, madam.'

A general sense of relaxation came over those present, such as occurs at a theatrical conference when the man with the money has been induced to sign on the dotted line.

'Good,' said Bill. 'Well, here's the story outline. Last night, Mr Smedley found the diary.'

'Oh, my Gawd!'

Bill patted his shoulder tenderly.

'I know, I know. I know just how you feel. But there it is. Mr Smedley found the diary last night, and this morning Mrs Cork swiped it from him and put it in the safe in the projection room. Will you reswipe it for us?'

That vision of Adela creeping up behind him flashed once more before the butler's eyes. A momentary shudder, and he was strong again.

'For five thousand dollars, yes, madam.'

'Fine. Then we will meet at Philippi – or, rather, here – tonight. Say at one o'clock in the morning.'

'One o'clock in the morning. Very good, madam. Will that be all, madam?'

'That will be all.'

'Thank you, madam.'

'Thank *you*, Phipps.'

'Bill,' cried Smedley, 'you're a marvel. What a brain, what a brain!'

'Wonderful,' said Kay. 'Stupendous.'

'Colossal,' said Joe.

'Super-colossal,' said Smedley.

'You can always trust me, boys,' said Bill. 'The Old Reliable.'

Adela came in. She was wearing the contented look of a woman who has just locked the door of her personal safe on a diary valued at a minimum of fifty thousand dollars. Then her eyes flashed with all their old fire.

'Wilhelmina!' she cried. 'Those dungarees! Are you aware that Mr Glutz's car is coming up the drive?'

'Sorry,' said Bill. 'I was thinking of other things. I will rush up immediately and gown myself in some clinging material which will accentuate rather than hide my graceful outlines.'

'Well, be quick.'

'Forked lightning, my dear Adela, forked lightning.'

9

Smedley Cork, first of the little group of Phipps's admirers and supporters to arrive at the tryst, stood at the open French windows of the Garden Room, staring into the night with unseeing eyes. From somewhere outside the closed door there came the *ping* of a clock striking one, and he heard it with a feeling of amazement. Only one o'clock? He could scarcely believe it. For though in actual fact not more than five minutes had elapsed since he had crept furtively down the stairs and come to the meeting place, it seemed to him that he had been waiting there for weeks. He was faintly surprised that he had not put out tendrils, like a Virginia creeper.

Strained nerves play these tricks on us, and Smedley's nerves were strained at the moment to their uttermost. Reason told him that it was improbable that his sister-in-law, a woman who was fond of her sleep, would take it into her head to roam the house at this hour, but the hideous possibility of such a disaster had not failed to present itself to his shrinking mind, and the native hue of resolution on his face was sicklied o'er with the pale cast of thought. As he stood there waiting for zero hour, his substantial frame twitched and quivered and rippled, as if he had been an Ouled Nail dancer about to go into her muscle dance.

The door opened noiselessly, and Bill came in. She was in her customary excellent spirits. Others might view with concern the shape of things to come, but not Wilhelmina Shannon. She was looking forward with bright enthusiasm to a pleasant and instructive evening.

'Hello, there, Smedley,' she boomed in her breezy, genial way, and Smedley leaped like an Ouled Nail dancer who has trodden on a tin-tack.

'I wish you wouldn't bellow at a fellow suddenly like that, Bill,' he said aggrievedly, having descended to terra firma. He was panting heavily and not feeling at all easy about his blood pressure. 'If anyone had told me that an old friend like you would come and sneak up behind a man at a time like this and yell in his ear without the slightest preliminary warning, I wouldn't have believed it.'

'Sorry, old sport.'

'Too late to be sorry now,' said Smedley moodily. 'You made me bite my tongue off at the roots. Where's Phipps?'

'He'll be here.'

'It's past one.'

'Only just,' said Bill. She joined him at the window and gazed out on the night. 'What were you doing? Admiring the stars? A fine display. Glorious technicolour. Look how the floor of heaven is thick inlaid with patines of bright gold. In such a night as this, when the sweet wind did gently kiss the trees—'

'For God's sake, Bill!'

'Some other time, eh? Not in the mood, no? Just as you say. Still, you can't deny that yonder stars are well worth looking at. Bright, twinkling and extremely neatly arranged. A credit to Southern California. I'll tell you something about those stars, Smedley. There's not the smallest orb which thou beholdest, but in his motion like an angel sings, still quiring to the young-eyed Cherubim. Worth knowing, that. Stop fluttering like a butterfly in a storm. What's the matter with you? Nervous?'

'I'm all of a twitter.'

'Too bad. Ah, Joe,' said Bill, as the door opened again. 'Come in and help me hold Smedley's hand. He's got the heeby-jeebies.'

Joe regarded the sufferer with a sympathetic eye. He, too, was by no means free from that distressing malady. He was conscious of an unpleasant sensation of having been plunged into the middle of a B picture of the more violent type and this was making him gulp a good deal. His had been a sheltered life, and it is disconcerting for a young man who has lived a sheltered life, to find himself involved in happenings of a melodramatic nature. To him, as to Smedley, there had come the thought that they might at any moment be joined by his formidable hostess, and it was not an agreeable reflection. Estimating Mrs Cork's probable reactions to the discovery that her nearest and dearest were planning to burgle her safe, his imagination boggled – as Phipps would have said, perceptibly. He had conceived a wholesome awe of the ex-Empress of

Stormy Emotions. Running over in his mind the women of his acquaintance who could legitimately be classed as dangerous specimens whose bite spelled death, he was inclined to place Adela Shannon Cork at the very top of the list. She had that certain something that the others had not got.

'Where's Phipps?' he asked, having swallowed a little painfully, for something – possibly his heart – seemed to be obstructing his throat.

'He's coming,' said Bill. 'The hour will produce the man.'

Smedley whinnied like a frightened horse.

'But it hasn't produced the man, damn it. Here it is past one and not a sign of him. You keep saying he's coming, but he doesn't come. I'm going up to his room, to see if he's there. I shall probably find him curled up in bed, fast asleep. Curse the fellow. Letting us down like this. If that's the sort of butler England is turning out nowadays, I'm sorry for them.'

He hurried from the room, puffing emotionally, and Bill clicked her tongue disapprovingly, like a Spartan mother who had expected better things of a favourite son.

'Smedley gets so agitated.'

'I don't blame him,' said Joe. 'I'm agitated myself.'

Bill snorted scornfully.

'You men! Just neurotic wrecks, all of you. No sang-froid.'

'All right, I lack sang-froid and I'm a neurotic wreck. But I repeat that I am agitated. That's my story and I stick to it. My feet are chilly, and there's something with long hairy legs running up and down my spine. Suppose this ghastly butler doesn't show up.'

'He'll show up.'

'Well, suppose he can't open the safe?'

To Bill, who with eleven other good men and women true had sat for several days in a jury box while the absent man's capabilities were expatiated on by an eloquent District Attorney, who made a capital story out of it, the question was a laughable one.

'Of course he can open the safe. He's an expert. You should have read what the papers said of him at the time of the trial. He got rave notices.'

Joe became calmer.

'He did?'

'He certainly did.'

'He has your confidence?'

'Implicit.'

Joe expelled a deep breath.

'Bill, you put heart into me.'

'That's good.'

'I suppose it's because one doesn't associate a butler with safeblowing that I was doubtful for a moment. I always thought butlers went about saying "Yes, m'lord," "No, m'lord," "Pardon me, m'lady, Her Grace the Duchess is on the telephone. She desires me to ask if you can spare her a cup of sugar," and all that sort of thing, not blowing safes. But if he carries your guarantee, that's a different matter. I feel now that prosperity is just around the corner.'

'Let's sing to every citizen and for'gner prosperity is just around the corner.'

'Yes, let's. Bill, you know all about women, I take it?'

'I've met a couple.'

'Women like money. Right?'

'Right.'

'And they like a man who does things. A man, I mean, who is what the French call an *om sayrioo*. Correct?'

'Correct.'

'So if Phipps gets that diary and Smedley gives us our twenty thousand and I become a plutocratic partner in a flourishing firm of authors' representatives, it's going to make a whale of a lot of difference, don't you think? With Kay, I mean. She'll feel a new respect for me.'

'She will probably throw herself on your chest and cry "My hero!" '

'Exactly. Something more or less along those lines is what I'm budgeting for. But we need Phipps.'

'We do.'

'Without Phipps we can accomplish nothing constructive.'

'Nothing.'

'Then what it all boils down to is, Where the hell is Phipps? Ah!' said Joe, breaking off and uttering the ejaculation with satisfaction and relief. The door was opening again.

It was, however, not the missing man, but Kay who came in. She was looking charming in pyjamas, mules and a dressing-gown, and at any other time Joe's heart would have leaped up like that of the poet Wordsworth when he, the poet Wordsworth, beheld a rainbow in the sky. Now he merely stared at her bleakly, as if by failing to be a butler with a gift for blowing safes she had disappointed him.

'You!' he said.

'Come aboard, sir,' said Kay. 'Where's Phipps?'

Bill's manner, too, was austere.

'Now don't you begin,' she said, 'I thought I told you to go to bed.'

'Please, sergeant, I got up.'

'Well, you're a naughty girl and will probably come to a bad end, but now you're here, you can make yourself useful. You can be cutting sandwiches.'

'You can't want sandwiches after that enormous dinner.'

'I always want sandwiches,' said Bill. Her momentary annoyance had vanished. She scrutinized Kay critically.

'An attractive little cheesemite, isn't she, Joe? Get those eyes.'

'I've got 'em.'

'Thank you, Bill. I'm glad you think I have nice eyes.'

Joe could not pass this. The first agony of seeing somebody who was not Phipps coming in at the door had abated, and he was able to take in those pyjamas, that dressing-gown and the mules. The wistful thought came to him that, if he and Kay had a little home, this was how she would look in it of an evening.

'Nice!' he said. 'Good God! what an adjective!'

'What Joe means,' explained Bill, 'is that with your limited vocabulary you have failed to spike the *mot juste*. In analysing your appearance, he feels, we must not be satisfied with the first weak word that comes along. We must pull up our socks and dredge the Thesaurus. You probably consider, Joe, that those eyes of hers are more like twin stars than anything?'

'Twin stars is nearer it. You're on the right lines.'

'And her brow? Alabaster?'

'I'll accept alabaster.'

Kay took a seat, kicked off one of the mules and tried unsuccessfully to catch it on her toe. Like her Aunt Wilhelmina, she was in capital spirits and feeling none of the tremors which afflicted the more timorous males.

'If you two have quite finished discussing me—' she said.

'Finished?' said Bill. 'Why, we've scarcely begun. We've barely scratched the surface. I like her bone structure, Joe. She has small, delicate bones.'

Joe endorsed this.

'That was the first thing I noticed about her the day we met, her small, delicate bones. "Gosh!" I said to myself. "This girl's got small, delicate bones." '

'And what happened then?' asked Kay.

'His heart stood still,' said Bill. 'I should have mentioned that when Joe was a boy, he promised his mother he would never marry a girl who didn't have small, delicate bones. Well, Smedley? Did you find him curled up in bed?'

Smedley had come puffing in, more agitated than ever. It was plain that the mystery of the missing butler was preying heavily on what may loosely be called his mind.

'Not a sign of him. He's not in his room. What on earth can have happened to the fellow?' He broke off, leaping in the old familiar way, his eyes protruding from their sockets. 'What's that?'

'What's what?'

'I heard something. Outside there. Footsteps.'

'Be calm, Smedley,' said Bill. 'It's probably Phipps. I'll bet it's Phipps. I think it's Phipps. It *is* Phipps,' she concluded, as a dignified figure detached itself from the darkness outside the French windows. 'Good evening, Phipps.'

'Good evening, madam,' said the butler.

10

With the arrival of the star performer, the spearhead of the movement and, if one may so describe him, the pilot on whom they were counting to weather the storm, a general feeling of relief and relaxation spread itself among the other members of the expeditionary force. Smedley grunted. So did Joe. Kay smiled a welcoming smile. And Bill, as if lost to all sense of what was fitting, went so far as to pat the man on the shoulder. Dressed in what appeared to be his Sunday best, his gaze calm and steady, he seemed so competent, so reliable, so obviously capable of conducting to a successful conclusion any task to which he set the hand holding the bowler hat without which no English butler stirs abroad.

'Well met by moonlight, proud Phipps,' said Bill. 'We thought you were never coming.'

'I am a little late, I fear, madam. I was detained. I am sorry.'

'Not at all. But I admit that we had begun to be somewhat anxious. Mr Smedley in particular had reached a condition where he could have given Mariana at the Moated Grange six bisques and a beating. What detained you?'

'I was in conference with Mr Glutz, madam.'

Smedley's eyes, which had returned to their sockets, popped out again.

'Mr who?'

'Glutz, sir. Of Medulla-Oblongata-Glutz. The gentleman who was with us for luncheon to-day. He sent for me to discuss details of my contract.'

'Your *what*?'

The butler placed his bowler hat on the desk, carefully and a little formally, like Royalty laying a foundation stone.

'My contract, sir. If I might explain. I had withdrawn to my pantry at the conclusion of the midday meal, and Mr Glutz presented himself there and after a few courteous preliminaries opened negotiations with a view to my playing butler roles in his organization.'

'Good God.'

'Yes, sir, I must confess to having experienced a slight feeling of surprise myself when I heard him formulate his proposition. Indeed, I fancied for a moment that this was a mere passing pleasantry on the gentleman's part – what is known in my native country as a bit of spoof and in the United States of Northern America as ribbing. But I soon perceived that he was in earnest. Apparently, he had been greatly impressed by my deportment at the luncheon table.'

'I don't wonder,' said Bill. 'You were right in mid-season form. It was buttling plus.'

'Thank you, madam. One desires to give satisfaction. Mr Glutz expressed much the same opinion. He appeared to feel that if talents like mine – artistry like mine, he was kind enough to say – were transferred to the silver screen, nothing but good could result. He then made me the offer to which I have referred, and I accepted it.'

He ceased, walked to the bowler hat, lovingly flicked a speck of dust off it, and returned to the statuesque pose which he was wont to assume at meal times, looking as if he were about to have his portrait painted by an artist who specialized in butlers. On his audience an awed silence had descended. It is always impressive to be present at the birth of a star.

'Well, well,' said Smedley.

'Fancy!' said Kay.

'So now you're in pix,' said Joe.

'Yes, sir.'

'Extraordinary how everybody in Hollywood wants to get into pix,' said Bill.

'Yes, madam. The aspiration would appear to be universal.'

Bill said it was something in the air, and Phipps said, So one would be disposed to imagine, madam, adding that oddly enough he had occasionally toyed with the idea of embarking on a motion-picture career, but had never seemed to find the time to get around to it: and the conversation might have continued in this purely professional vein, had not Smedley, recovering from his first reactions to the sensational news item, become peevish and fussy again.

'But why on earth had you got to see him at this time of

night?' he demanded, not perhaps unreasonably. 'One o'clock in the morning!'

A well-trained butler's eyebrows never actually rise, but Phipps's flickered as if on the verge of upward movement, and in his voice, as he replied, there was the merest hint of rebuke.

'My domestic duties would not allow me to leave the house before eleven-thirty, sir, and Mr Glutz was insistent that the negotiations be completed without delay. I took the view that his wish was law.'

'Quite right,' said Bill. 'Always keep in with the boss, however much he looks like a lobster. Mr Glutz does look like a lobster, doesn't he?'

'There is perhaps a resemblance to the crustacean you mention, madam.'

'Though what does that matter, provided his heart is in the right place?'

'Precisely, madam.'

'People have told me I look like a German Boxer.'

'A most attractive Boxer, madam.'

'Nice of you to say so, Phipps. Has he given you a good contract?'

'Eminently satisfactory, thank you, madam.'

'Watch those options.'

'Yes, madam.'

'Well, I shall follow your future career with considerable interest.'

'Thank you, madam. I shall endeavour to give satisfaction.'

Smedley, who had a one-track mind, struck the practical note.

'Well, now you're here, let's get to work. We've wasted half the night.'

'It won't take long,' Bill assured him, 'if Phipps is the man he used to be. Eh, Phipps?'

The butler seemed to hesitate. He looked like a butler about to break bad news.

'I am sorry, madam,' he said apologetically, 'but I fear I have a slight disappointment for you.'

'Eh?'

'I have come to inform you – regretfully – that I am unable to undertake the desired task.'

If he had expected to make a sensation, he was not wrong. His words had the effect of a bombshell.

'What?' cried Joe.

'Oh, Phipps!' cried Kay.

'Not undertake it?' bleated Smedley. 'What do you mean?'

It was plain that the spearhead of the movement was embarrassed. He departed from his official impassivity to the extent of shuffling a foot along the carpet and twiddling his fingers. Then his eyes fell on the bowler hat, and he seemed to draw strength from it.

'This unforeseen development has naturally effected a considerable alteration in my plans, sir. As an artist in the employ of Medulla-Oblongata-Glutz, I cannot run the risk of being discovered burgling safes. There is a morality clause in my contract.'

'A *what*?'

'Morality clause, sir. Para Six.'

Smedley exploded. His blood pressure had now reached unprecedented heights. A doctor, scanning his empurpled face, would have clicked his tongue concernedly – or perhaps would have rubbed his hands, scenting business at ten dollars a visit.

'I never heard such infernal nonsense in my life.'

'I am sorry, sir. But I fear I cannot recede from my position.'

'But think of that five thousand.'

'A trivial sum, sir. We motion-picture actors regard five thousand dollars as the merest small change.'

'Don't talk like that,' cried Smedley, shocked to the core. 'It . . . it's blasphemous.'

Phipps turned to Bill, in whom he seemed to see a level-headed ally and supporter.

'I am sure *you* will understand that I cannot jeopardize my contract, madam.'

'Of course not. Your art comes first.'

'Precisely, madam.'

'You've signed on the dotted line, and you must stay signed.'

'Exactly, madam.'

'But, damn it—'

'Hush, Smedley. Be calm.'

'Calm!'

'What you need,' said Bill, 'is a drink. Could you bring us a few fluid ounces of the blushful Hippocrene, Phipps?'

'Certainly, madam. What would you desire?'

Smedley sank into a chair.

'Bring every darned bottle you can lay your hands on!'

'Very good, sir,' said Phipps.

He retrieved the bowler hat from the desk, seemed for an instant about to place it on his head, recollected himself in time and left the room on his errand of mercy.

Silence reigned for some moments after his departure. Smedley in his chair was looking like a man who for two pins would have buried his face in his hands. Joe had gone to the French windows and was staring up at the stars with a lack-lustre eye. Kay had crossed to where Smedley sat and was stroking his head in a rather feverish manner. Only Bill was unmoved.

'Well,' said Smedley, from the depths, 'this is a nice thing to happen.'

'Just Hollywood,' said Bill.

'If a man's a butler, why can't he *be* a butler, instead of gallivanting around getting contracts from studios? And all this nonsense about morality clauses.'

'Cheer up, Smedley. All is not lost. I have the situation well in hand,' said Bill. And such was the magnetism of her personality, that a faint hope stirred in Smedley's bosom. It might be, he felt, that even the present impasse would yield to treatment from one whom, though he did not want to marry her, he had always recognized as a woman of impressive gifts, well worthy of the title of The Old Reliable. He raised a haggard face.

'What are you going to do?'

'I am going to have a drink.'

Joe, at the window, barked bitterly like the seal to which Kay had once compared him.

'Fine,' he said. 'Splendid. You're going to have a drink, are you? That has taken a great weight off my mind. I was worrying myself sick, wondering if you were going to have a drink.'

'And having had it,' proceeded Bill equably, 'I shall press one on Phipps. When he comes back, I propose to ply him with strong liquor and – after his calm judgement has been sufficiently unbalanced – taunt him.'

'Taunt him?'

'What do you mean, taunt him?' asked Smedley, puzzled but still hopeful.

'Sting his professional pride with a few well-judged sneers. Scoff and mock at him for having lost his grip. It ought to work. Phipps, you must remember, till he saw the light, was a very eminent safeblower, and you can't be an eminent safeblower without being a sensitive artist, proud of your skill and resentful of criticism. Imagine how Shakespeare would have felt if, after he had retired to Stratford, somebody had come along and congratulated him on having got out of the theatre game just in time, because it was obvious to everyone that he had been slipping.'

The door opened, and Phipps came in, swaying slightly under the weight of an enormous tray filled with bottles and glasses. He placed it on the desk.

'I have made a wide selection, madam,' he said.

'You certainly have,' said Bill. 'Start pouring, Joe.'

'Right,' said Joe, becoming busy. 'Champagne, Bill?'

'Just a drop, perhaps. I often say that there's nothing like a little something at this time of night to pick you up. Thank you, Joe. But you haven't got yours, Phipps.'

'Nothing for me, thank you, madam.'

'Oh come. We must drink success to your new venture. You are embarking on a career which is going to make you loved, worshipped, idolized by the prince in his palace, the peasant in his cot, the explorer in the jungle and the Eskimo in his frozen igloo, and your launching must be celebrated with fitting rites. Properly speaking, we ought to break a bottle over your head.'

'Well, a very mild one, madam. I have always been somewhat susceptible to the effects of alcohol. It was that that led to me being on trial on the occasion when you were a member of the jury, madam.'

'Really?'

'Yes, madam. The constables would never have apprehended me if I had not been under the influence.'

'Of course, yes, I remember. It came out in the evidence, didn't it? Your employer heard noises in the night, tracked them down to the library, where his safe was, and there you were, lying back in a chair with your feet on the table and a bottle in your hand, singing "Sweet Adeline".'

'Precisely, madam. It rendered me conspicuous.'

During these exchanges, Bill, her massive form interposed between the butler and the desk, had been selecting with almost loving care one bottle after another and blending their contents in a large tumbler. It was liquid dynamite that she was concocting, but her words, as she handed him the mixture, were reassuring.

'Try this for size,' said Bill. 'I think you'll like it. I call it the Wilhelmina Shannon Special. Mild – practically a soft drink – but refreshing.'

'Thank you, madam,' said Phipps, accepting the glass and raising it to his lips with a respectful 'Happy days, madam.' He sipped tentatively, then more deeply, finally drained the bumper with evident relish.

'How was it?' asked Bill.

'Extremely good, madam.'

'Will you have another one?'

'I believe I will, madam.'

Bill took the glass from him and put a second Wilhelmina Shannon Special in preparation.

'Tell me about yourself, Phipps,' she said, chatting as she mixed. 'Our paths parted after that trial. I, so to speak, took the high road, and you took the low road. Let us pick up the threads. What happened after you graduated from Sing-Sing?'

'I secured a position as a butler once more. Thank you, madam,' said Phipps, taking the glass.

'No difficulty about getting signed up?'

'Oh, no, madam. I had a number of excellent references from employers in England, and I came to California, affecting to be a newly arrived immigrant. Ladies and gentlemen in California rarely read the New York papers, I have found. And, after all, three years had passed since my unpleasant experience. I suffered no inconvenience whatsoever.'

'And how about the old life work?'

'Madam?'

'Did you continue to pass the potatoes with one hand and blow safes with the other?'

'Oh, no, madam.'

'Just buttled?'

'Precisely, madam.'

'So it's about four years since you did a job?'

'Yes, madam.'

'Then no wonder you've lost your nerve,' said Bill.

The butler started. A dull flush spread itself over his face, deepening the colour already implanted there by the Wilhelmina Shannon Specials.

'Madam?' he said.

Bill was friendly, but frank.

'Oh, you can't fool us, Phipps. That was a good story of yours about your morality clause, but we see through it.' She turned to Joe. 'Right?'

'Right,' said Joe.

'It's perfectly plain that after your long lay-off, you realized that you were no longer the man you had been. You had lost your grip, and you knew it.' She turned to Kay. 'Right?'

'Right,' said Kay.

'Listen,' said Phipps.

He spoke harshly and in a manner quite lacking in his customary smooth deference. His voice had taken on a novel roughness. His head, as he had said, had never been strong, and there had been that in the beverage assembled by his hostess which might have roughened the voice of a seasoned toper. It was as though the butler in him had fallen from him like a garment, revealing the natural man beneath. That his *amour-propre* had been deeply wounded was plainly to be seen.

'Oh, don't think we're blaming you,' said Bill. 'Some people might say you were a spineless poltroon—'

'*What?*'

'—but that's all nonsense. You aren't a poltroon, you're just prudent. You know when a thing is beyond your powers and you decline to take it on. We respect you for it. We applaud your good sense. We admire you enormously. Right?'

'Right,' said Joe.

Phipps scowled darkly. His eyes were hard and hostile.

'You think I'm scared to bust that pete upstairs?'

'It seems the reasonable explanation. And I don't wonder. It's a tough job.'

'Tough? A lousy little country-house pete? Listen, I've busted banks.'

'You mean piggy banks?'

'No, I don't mean piggy banks. I'll show you,' said Phipps, and started for the door. 'I'll show you,' he repeated, his hand on the handle.

'But where are your tools?' bleated Smedley.

'He doesn't need tools,' said Bill. 'He does it all with his finger tips, like Jimmy Valentine. He is a most gifted artist – or, rather, was.'

'*Was?*' cried Phipps. He wrenched the door open. 'Come on. Let's go.'

'I'll come with you,' said Smedley, entranced.

'So will I,' said Joe. 'And in case you feel faint . . .'

He took up the tray and added himself to the procession. Bill closed the door behind them and came back to Kay, who was regarding her with the light of admiration and respect in her eyes. It was a light that often came into the eyes of those privileged to observe The Old Reliable when at her best.

'So that's that,' said Bill. 'Amazing what you can do with a little tact. And now that we are alone, my girl, sit down and listen to me, because I've a bone to pick with you. What's all this I hear about you and Joe?'

11

Kay laughed.

'Oh, Joe!' she said.

An austere frown darkened Bill's brow. She disapproved of this spirit of levity. Ever a staunch friend, she had been much touched by Joe's story of his romance, with its modern avoidance of the happy ending. Feeling as she did about Smedley, she could understand and sympathize.

'Don't giggle in that obscene way,' she said sternly. 'He's a very fine young fellow, Joe Davenport, and he loves you.'

'So he keeps telling me.'

' "Bill," he said to me only the day before yesterday, and if there weren't tears in his eyes as he spoke, I don't know a tear in the eye when I see one, "Bill, old sport, I love that girl." And then a lot of stuff about depression and debility and night sweats and loss of appetite. And in addition to the tear in his eye, there was a choking sob in his voice, and he writhed like a dynamo. He worships you, that boy. He adores you. He would die for one little rose from your hair. And does he get one? Not so much as a blasted petal. Instead of thanking heaven, fasting, for a good man's love, you reply to his pleadings with the horse's laugh and slip him the brusheroo. Nice goings-on, I must say.'

Kay stooped over and kissed the top of Bill's head. She had had a feeling that this was going to be good, and she saw that she had not been mistaken.

'You're very eloquent, Bill.'

'Of course I'm eloquent. I'm speaking from a full heart on top of three glasses of champagne. Why are you pulling this hard-to-get stuff on Joe? What's wrong with the poor fish?'

'He knows. I told him exactly why I wouldn't marry him, when we had lunch together the day before I left New York.'

'Aren't you going to marry him?'

'No.'

'You're crazy.'

'He's crazy.'

'About you.'

'About everything.'

'Why do you say that?'

'Well, isn't he?'

'Not in the least. A man I respect and admire. Don't you like him?'

'Yes. Very much. He's fun.'

'I'm glad you didn't say "He's a good sort." '

'Why, is that bad?'

'Fatal. It would have meant that there was no hope for him. It's what the boys used to say of me twenty years ago. "Oh, Bill," they'd say. "Dear old Bill. I like Bill. She's a good sort." And then they'd leave me flat on my keister and go off and buy candy and orchids for the other girls, blister their insides.'

'Is that why you're a solitary chip drifting down the river of life?'

'That's why. Often a bridesmaid but never a bride.'

'You poor old ruin.'

'Don't call me a poor old ruin. Does respect for an aunt mean nothing to you? And don't try to steer me off the subject of Joe. Fourteen times you've refused him, he tells me.'

'Fifteen. He proposed again in the rose garden this afternoon.'

Bill snorted indignantly. She rose and walked with measured step to the desk, intending to restore her composure with more champagne, found that the tray of drinks was no longer there, snorted again, this time with disappointment, sighed heavily and returned to her seat.

'Well, I don't understand you,' she said. 'I simply don't understand you. The workings of your mind are a sealed book to me. If I were a girl and Joe Davenport came along and wanted to marry me, I'd grapple him to my soul with hoops of steel. Gosh, when one looks around and sees what a jerk the average young man is, the idea of a girl with any sense in her head turning down a fellow like Joe is incredible.'

'He seems to have made a great impression on you.'

'He has. I regard him as a son.'

'Grandson.'

'I said *son*. Yes, I regard him as a son, and you know how I've always felt about you. You're as fresh as an April breeze, you get off impertinent cracks about grandsons, you mock at my grey hairs and will probably sooner or later bring them in sorrow to the grave, but I love you.'

'Mutual, Bill.'

'Don't interrupt. I say I love you. And I have your best interests at heart. I consider that this J. Davenport is the right man for you, and it is my dearest wish to park myself in a ringside pew and bellow "The Voice That Breathed O'er Eden" while you and he go centre-aisle-ing. It beats me why you aren't thinking along the same lines. It isn't as if you had anything against the poor simp. You admit you like him.'

'Of course I like him. How could anyone help liking Joe?'

'Then what's the trouble?'

Kay was silent for a moment. There had come into her face that grave, intent look which attracted Joe so much. With the toe of one of her mules, she traced an arabesque on the carpet.

'Shall I take my hair down, Bill?'

'Certainly. Tell me all.'

'Well, then, I could fall in love with Joe in a minute – like *that* – if I'd let myself.'

'And why don't you?'

Kay went to the French windows and looked up at the stars. 'I'm – wary.'

'How do you mean, wary?'

'Well . . . Bill, how do you look on marriage? I mean, is it a solemn, sacred what-d'you-call-it that's going to last the rest of your life – or a sort of comic week-end like some of these Hollywood things? I think it's pretty solemn and sacred, and that's where Joe and I seem to differ. No, don't interrupt, or I shall never be able to explain. What I'm really trying to say is that I can't bring myself to trust Joe. I can't believe he's sincere.'

With a powerful effort, Bill had managed to restrain herself from breaking in on what she considered the most absurd speech to which she had ever listened, and she was a woman who had sat in on a hundred studio conferences, but she could maintain silence no longer.

'Sincere? Joe? For heaven's sake! How often do you want him to ask you to marry him before it filters through into your fat little head that he's fond of you?'

'It isn't how often he asks me, it's how he asks me. He does it as if the whole thing were a tremendous joke. And I don't regard love as a joke. I'm stuffy and sentimental and take it seriously. I want someone who takes it as seriously as I do, not someone who can't make love to a girl without making her feel as if she were the stooge in a vaudeville act. How does he expect me to feel,' said Kay, becoming vehement, for the grievance was one that had long been festering within her, 'when his idea of romantic wooing is to grin like a Cheshire cat and say "Don't look now, but will you marry me?" When a girl's with the man she loves, she doesn't want to feel as if she had been wrecked on a desert island with Groucho Marx.'

There was silence for a moment.

'Then – just between us girls – you do love Joe?'

'Of course I do,' said Kay. 'I've loved him right from the start. But I don't trust him.'

Silence fell again. Bill began to see that this was going to be difficult.

'I know what you mean,' she said at length. 'Joe *is* apt to clown. The light comedy manner. The kidding approach. But don't forget that clowning is often just a defensive armour against shyness.'

'You aren't trying to tell me that Joe's shy?'

'Of course he's shy – with you. Every man's shy when he's really in love. That's why he acts like that. He's like a small boy trying to ease the embarrassment of wooing the belle of the kindergarten by standing on his head. Don't you be deceived by the surface manner, my girl. Look past it to the palpitating heart within.'

'You think Joe has a palpitating heart?'

'You betcher.'

'So do I. I think it palpitates for every girl he meets who isn't an absolute gargoyle. I've seen his little red book.'

'His what?'

'Telephone numbers, Bill. Telephone numbers of blondes, brunettes, redheads and subsidiary blondes. Don't you understand the facts of life, my child? Joe is a butterfly, flitting from flower to flower and making love to every girl he meets.'

'Is that what butterflies do?'

'You can't stop 'em. He's another Dick Mills.'

'Another who?'

'A man I was once engaged to. We broke it off.'

'Was he a butterfly?'

'Yes, Bill, he was.'

'And you feel that Joe is like him?'

'The same type.'

'You're all wrong.'

'I don't think so.'

Bill swelled belligerently. Her blue eyes flashed fire. Though of a more equable temperament than her sister Adela and not so ready as that formidable woman to decline on all occasions to Stand Nonsense, she could be pushed just so far. Like Mr Churchill, there were things up with which she would not put.

'It doesn't matter what you think, my girl. Let me tell you something for your files. It is my unshakeable opinion that you and Joe were made for one another. I have studied you both with loving care, I am convinced that you would hit it off like ham and eggs, and I shall omit no word or act to promote the merger. I intend to bring you together, if it's the last thing I do. And you know me. The Old Reliable. And now go and cut those sandwiches. All this talking has made me hungry.'

As Kay started for the door, it opened and Smedley came in, startling both of them. In the pressure of other matters, they had quite forgotten Smedley.

Smedley was looking agitated.

'Where are you going?' he asked. 'Not up to the projection room?'

'She's going to the kitchen to cut sandwiches,' said Bill. 'I thought we needed a little sustenance, to keep the machine from breaking down.'

'I'm glad,' said Smedley, relieved. 'I wouldn't want you to go up there just now. Those drinks you gave Phipps, Bill, have had a curious effect on him. They seem to have . . . er . . . melted his reserve. He keeps stopping work to tell risky stories.'

'Dear, dear. Off colour?'

'Very. There was one about a strip-tease dancer and a performing flea . . .' He looked at Kay, and paused. 'But it wouldn't interest you.'

'I've heard it,' said Kay, and went off to cut sandwiches.

Smedley mopped his forehead. His morale seemed to have hit a new low. The rush and swirl of the night's events had plainly left him weak. Marcus Aurelius, who held that nothing happens to anybody which he is not fitted by nature to bear, would have had a hard time selling that idea to Smedley Cork.

'I'm worried, Bill,' said Smedley.

'You're always worried.'

'Well, haven't I enough to worry me? When I think of what

it means to me to have Phipps open that safe! And he won't concentrate. He lets his mind wander. He's displaying a frivolous side to his nature which I wouldn't have believed existed. Do you know that just before I left he was proposing to imitate four Hawaiians? The man's blotto.'

Bill nodded.

'I ought to be more careful with those Wilhelmina Shannon Specials,' she said. 'The trouble is, I don't know my own strength.'

'And it isn't only that he refuses to get down to his job. It's the noise he's making. Loud bursts of fiendish laughter. I'm so afraid he'll wake Adela.'

'Her room's on the other side of the house.'

'But even so.'

Bill shook her head.

'You know, looking back,' she said, 'where we made our big mistake was in not giving Adela a Mickey Finn. It would have—' She broke off. 'Good heavens!'

'What's the matter?'

Bill was feeling in the pocket of her slacks. When she brought her hand out, there was a small white pellet in it.

'This is a Mickey Finn,' she said. 'It was given me from his personal stockpile by a bartender on Third Avenue, a dear old friend of mine. He said it would be bound to come in handy one of these days, and how right he was. I had intended to slip it into Adela's bedtime Ovaltine, and I forgot.'

'And now too late.

'And now too late,' said Bill. 'Too late, too . . .'

Her voice trailed away. From just outside the door there had come the sound of a loud and raucous laugh. She looked at Smedley, and he looked at her, with a wild surmise.

'Suffering cats!' said Smedley. 'That's Phipps.'

'Or could it have been a hyena?' said Bill.

It was Phipps. He came in, followed by Joe, laughing heartily like one of the Chorus of Villagers in an old-fashioned comic opera. Tray in hand, he selected a bottle, went to the sofa, seated himself on it and leaned back comfortably against the cushions. It was plain that for the time being, he had shelved all idea of work and was regarding this as a purely social occasion.

12

'Good evening, all,' said Phipps genially, and refreshed himself from the bottle. Whatever prudent concern he might once have felt regarding his constitutional inability to absorb alcoholic stimulants in large quantities without paying the penalty had clearly vanished. Wine is a mocker and strong drink is raging, and he liked it that way. Any time wine wanted to mock him, his whole demeanour suggested, it was all right with James Phipps, and the same went for strong drink when it wished to rage. 'Good evening, all,' he said. 'I will now imitate four Hawaiians.'

His obvious eagerness to spare no effort to make the party go would have touched and delighted some such person as a fun-loving Babylonian monarch of the old school, always on the look-out for sympathetic fellow-revellers to help the Babylonian orgy along, but to Smedley his words seemed to presage doom and disaster. What it was that four Hawaiians did when performing for the public entertainment, he did not know, but instinct told him that it was probably something pretty loud, and he quivered apprehensively. Adela's room might, as Bill had said, be on the other side of the house, but, as he had said to Bill, 'even so'.

'No, no!' he squeaked, like a mouse in pain.

'Then I'll sing "Sweet Adeline",' said Phipps with the air of a man who only strove to please. His repertory was wide, and if the audience did not want the four Hawaiians, 'Sweet Adeline' would do just as well.

This time it was Joe who lodged a protest. Joe was fully as agitated as Smedley. He was familiar with 'Sweet Adeline'. He had sung that popular song himself in clubhouse locker rooms, and none knew better than he that its melody contained certain barbershop chords which, dished out as this sozzled major-domo would dish them out, must inevitably penetrate bricks and mortar like butter, rousing a sleeping hostess from her slumbers

as if the Last Trump had sounded. Once more there rose
before his eyes the vision of Mrs Adela Shannon Cork sailing in through the door in a dressing-gown, and that thing
with the long hairy legs went galloping up and down his spine
again.

'No, please, Phipps,' he urged.

The butler stiffened. He was in genial, pleasure-seeking mood
and all prepared to unbend with the boys, but even at the risk
of spoiling the harmony he felt obliged to insist on the deference
due to his position. Once allow the lower middle classes to
become familiar, and where were you?

'Mister Phipps, if *you* please,' he said coldly.

Bill, always tactful, added her weight to the rebuke.

'Yes, be careful how you speak to Mr Phipps, Joe. You can
see he's fractious. I think he's teething. But I wouldn't sing
"Sweet Adeline", Mr Phipps.'

'Why wouldn't I sing "Sweet Adeline"?'

'You'll wake sweet Adela.'

'You mean Ma Cork?'

'Ma Cork is correct.'

Phipps mused. He took another sip from his bottle.

'Ma Cork,' he said meditatively. 'Now, there's a woman I
never cared for. How would it be to go and give her a jolly
good punch in the nose?'

It was a suggestion which at any other time would have
enchanted Smedley, for if ever there was a woman who from
early childhood had been asking, nay clamouring, for a good
sock on the beezer, that woman in his opinion was his sister-
in-law Adela. But now he shuddered from head to foot and
uttered another of his mouselike squeaks.

'No, no!'

'Not give her a punch in the nose? Just as you say,' said
Phipps agreeably. He could be as reasonable as the next man if
you treated him with proper respect. 'Then let's have a gargle.
Not you, Smedley,' he went on. 'You've had enough. The old
coot's been mopping it up like a vacuum cleaner,' he explained
amusedly. He surveyed the coot with an indulgent eye. 'Old
drunken Smedley!' he said. 'Where were you last night, you old
jail-bird? Hey, Smedley?'

Smedley smiled a wry, preoccupied smile. Phipps, piqued,
raised his voice a little.

'HEY, SMEDLEY!!'

Bill said 'Hush!' Joe said 'Hush!' Smedley leaped as if he had been unexpectedly bitten by a shark.

Phipps's sense of grievance deepened. It seemed to him that these people were deliberately going out of their way to ruffle him. When he said: 'Hey!' they said: 'Hush!', and as for the old lush Smedley, who was patently pie-eyed, he didn't so much as bother to answer when spoken to civilly. One would have to be pretty sharp, felt Phipps, on this sort of thing.

'Well, why doesn't he say Hey when I say Hey? When a gentleman says Hey to another gentleman, he expects the other gentleman to say Hey to him.'

Smedley was prompt to retrieve his social lapse.

'Hey,' he said hastily.

'Hey, what?'

'Hey, Mr Phipps.'

The butler frowned. His mood had now definitely darkened. Gone was that warmth of bonhomie and goodwill which had filled him when he came into the room, making him the little brother of all mankind and more like a walking sunbeam than anything. He found in Smedley's manner a formality and lack of chumminess of which he thoroughly disapproved. It was as though he had started hobnobbing with a Babylonian monarch and the Babylonian monarch had suddenly turned around and snubbed him, as Babylonian monarchs are so apt to do.

'Come, come,' he said. 'None of your standoffishness. Say Hey, Jimmy.'

'Hey, Jimmy.'

Phipps, a perfectionist, was not yet satisfied.

'Say it again, more loving like.'

'Hey, Jimmy.'

Phipps relaxed. Smedley's intonation had not been altogether that of a love bird passing a remark to another love bird, but it had been near enough to mollify him. Genuine feeling in it, it seemed to him.

'That's better. Can't have you sticking on dog just because you're a ruddy Society butterfly.'

'Don't you like ruddy Society butterflies?' asked Bill, interested.

Phipps shook his head austerely.

'No. Don't approve of 'em. Comes the Revolution, they'll be hanging on lamp posts. The whole system's wrong. Ain't I a man? . . . AIN'T I, SMEDLEY?'

Smedley leaped.

'Yes, yes, of course you are, Jimmy.'

'Ain't I a gentleman?'

'Of course, Jimmy, of course.'

'Then fetch me a cushion for me head, you old souse. Come on, now. Hurry. I want a little service around here.'

Smedley brought the cushion and propped it behind his head.

'Comfortable – Jimmy?' he said, between his teeth.

The butler froze him with a glance.

'Who are you calling Jimmy? Address me as Mr Phipps.'

'I'm sorry, Mr Phipps.'

'And so you ought to be. I know your sort, know 'em well. Grinding the face of the poor and taking the bread out of the mouths of the widow and the orphan. Comes the Revolution, blood'll be running in streams down Park Avenue and Sutton Place'll be all cluttered up with corpses.'

Smedley drew Bill aside.

'If this is going to continue,' he muttered, 'I cannot answer for the consequences, Bill. My blood pressure is rising.'

'Comes the Revolution,' Bill reminded him, 'you won't have any blood. It'll be running down Park Avenue.'

'I'm going up to listen at Adela's door. Make sure she's asleep. Anything to get away for a moment from that sozzled son of a . . .' He caught Phipps's eye and broke off. He smiled a difficult smile. 'Hey, Mr Phipps!'

The butler's eye was too glazed for fire to flash from it, but his manner showed that he was offended.

'How many times have I got to tell you to call me Jimmy?'

'I'm sorry, Jimmy.'

'Mister Phipps, if you *don't* mind,' said the butler sternly.

Smedley, plainly unequal to the intellectual pressure of the conversation, gave it up and hurried out. Bill, glad to be relieved of his disturbing presence, struck the business note.

'Well, Mr Phipps,' she said, 'how's it coming? If you are feeling sufficiently rested, you might be having another go at that safe.'

'Yes,' agreed Joe. 'We mustn't waste any more time.'

He had said the wrong thing. The butler stiffened again. For some reason, possibly because of that earlier lapse into familiarity, he seemed to have taken a dislike to Joe. He gave him an unpleasant look.

'What's it got to do with *you*, may I ask?'

'Everything. You see, it's this way – Mr Smedley—'

'You mean old drunken Smedley?'

'That's right. Old drunken Smedley is in with Miss Shannon—'

'You mean old dogfaced Bill here?'

'That's right. Old drunken Smedley is in with old dogfaced Bill here and me on a business deal. He's putting up the money.'

'What money?'

'The money he'll get when he gets that diary.'

'What diary?'

'The diary in the safe.'

'What safe?' asked Phipps keenly, like a prosecuting attorney questioning some rat of the underworld as to where he was on the night of June the fifteenth.

Joe looked at Bill. Like Smedley, he found Phipps's conversational methods a little bewildering.

'The safe you're going to open, Mr Phipps.'

'Who says I'm going to open any safes?'

'I don't,' said Bill, taking charge in her competent way. 'You couldn't do it.'

'Do what?'

'Open that safe.'

Phipps was silent for a space, digesting this.

'You say I couldn't open that safe?'

'No. It's hopeless to think of attempting it. Four years ago you would have been able to, yes, but not now. We're all agreed on that.'

'On what?'

'That you were a good man once, but you've lost your nerve. We went into it all before, if you remember, and we came to the conclusion that you no longer had the stuff. You're finished.'

'Ho!'

'A pity, but there it is. Not your fault, of course, but you're a back number. As a safeblower, you're washed up. You buttle like nobody's business, you have a bright future on the silver screen, but – you – can't – open – the safe.'

Wine when it is red – or, as in the case of Phipps, who was drinking *crème de menthe*, green – stingeth like an adder, and so do adverse criticisms of his skill as an artist. Phipps was thus in the position of a man who is stung by two adders simultaneously, and his flushed face grew darker.

'Ho!' he said. 'Can't open the safe, eh? Can't open the ruddy safe? Well, just for that I *will* open the ruddy safe.'

Joe shot a quick, reverential look at Bill. Leave it to The Old Reliable, he was feeling. The Old Reliable would always see you through.

'Thank you, Phipps,' he said.

'Thank *you*, sir,' said the butler automatically. 'I mean,' he added quickly, correcting himself, 'what you thanking me for?'

'I told you. You say you're going to open the safe. Well, if you open the safe, we'll get our money.'

'Ho? And when you do, I suppose you think you're going to marry that young Kay? What a hope. You haven't a chance, you poor fish. *I* heard her turning you down in the rose garden this afternoon.'

Joe started.

'What?'

'Like a bedspread.'

Joe blushed a pretty pink. He had not supposed that he had been playing to an audience.

'You weren't there?'

'Yes, I was.'

'I didn't see you.'

'Nobody don't ever see me.'

'They call him The Shadow,' said Bill.

'And I'll tell you what struck me about the episode,' proceeded Phipps, having looked once more upon the wine when it was green. 'Your methods are wrong. You're too lighthearted and humorous. You won't win the heart of a sensitive girl by cracking gags. What you want to do is to fold her in your arms and kiss her.'

'He daren't,' said Bill. 'It isn't safe. He once kissed a girl in Paris and she shot clear up to the top of the Eiffel Tower.'

'Ho?'

'Just closed her eyes with a little moan of ecstasy and floated up – and up – and up.'

To illustrate, Bill twiddled her fingers, and the butler stared at them austerely.

'Don't do that!' he said sharply. 'It makes me think of spiders.'

'I'm sorry. You dislike spiders?'

'Yes, I do. Spiders!' said Phipps darkly. 'I could tell you something about spiders. You ask me, if you want to hear all about spiders.'

'Comes the Revolution, spiders will be running down Park Avenue.'

'Ah,' said Phipps, as if conceding this as probably correct. He yawned, and swung his feet up on the sofa. 'Well, I don't know what you two are going to do,' he said. 'I'm going to get a little shut-eye. Good night, all. Time for Bedfordshire.'

His eyes closed. He gurgled a couple of times. Then, still clutching the bottle, he slept.

13

Joe looked at Bill, dismayed. In this world one should be prepared for everything, or where is one, but he had not been prepared for this. It had come on him as a complete surprise.

'Now what?' he said.

The new development appeared to have left Bill unconcerned. She regarded the horizontal butler with something of the tender affection of a mother bending over the cradle of her sleeping child, and adjusted the pillow behind his head, which looked like slipping.

'Probably all for the best,' she said. 'A little folding of the hands in sleep will do him good, and we have the rest of the night to operate in. Did you ever see a blotto butler before?'

'Never.'

'Nor I. In which connection, I would state that I'd rather see than be one. When the cold grey light of the dawn comes stealing in through yonder windows in an hour or so, you and I will be in the pink and as fresh as daisies, but one shudders to think how Jimmy Phipps will be feeling. On the morning after a binge like that, the state of man, as Shakespeare says, suffers the nature of an insurrection. There should be a big run on the bromo-seltzer 'ere long. But let's not wander from the point. Though brilliantly lit and not always too coherent in his remarks, the recent pickled herring said one very sensible and significant thing. About your methods of conducting your wooing. Were you listening?'

'I was.'

'He was right, you know. He touched the spot. Your methods *are* wrong. I've been talking to Kay. That girl loves you, Joe.'

'What?'

'She told me so in so many words. The way she actually phrased it has slipped my memory, but the gist of her remarks was that when in your presence she feels as though there was only a thin sheet of tissue paper between her and heaven. And if that isn't love, what is?'

Joe reeled.

'Bill, if you're kidding me—'

'Of course I'm not kidding you. What on earth would I want to kid you for? She loves you, I tell you. You're the cream in her coffee, you're the salt in her stew. But she's wary . . . cagey . . . She's suspicious of you.'

'Suspicious? Why?'

'Because you clown all the time.'

'I'm shy.'

'I told her that, but she didn't believe me. She looks on you as an insubstantial butterfly, flitting from flower to flower and sipping. Are you a sipper?'

'No, I'm not a sipper.'

'You don't play around with girls?'

'Certainly not.'

'Then how about your little red book of telephone numbers?' said Bill.

If she had slapped a wet towel across Joe's face, the effect could not have been more pronounced. When you slap a wet towel across a man's face, he gasps and totters. The eyes widen. The colour deepens. The mouth falls open like a fish's and stays open. It was so with Joe now.

'Red book?' he stammered.

'Red book.'

'Little red book?'

'Little red book.'

'Little red book of telephone numbers?'

'Little red book of telephone numbers.'

The sensation of having been struck with a wet towel left Joe. He became indignant, like a good man unjustly persecuted.

'Why the dickens does everybody make such a song and dance about my little red book of telephone numbers?' he demanded hotly. 'Every red-blooded man has his little red book of telephone numbers. Children start keeping them in the kindergarten. And Kay knows all about my little red book. I explained carefully and fully to her the last time we lunched together that no importance whatsoever was to be attached to that little red book. I told her that the girls in that little red book were mere vestiges of a past that is dead and gone. I've forgotten half their damned names. They are nothing to me, nothing.'

'Less than the dust beneath your chariot wheels?'

'Considerably less. I wouldn't ring one of them up to please a dying grandmother. They're ghosts, I tell you. Spectres. Wraiths.'

'Just wisps of ectoplasm?'

'Exactly. Just wisps of ectoplasm. Listen, Bill. There isn't a girl that exists for me in the world except Kay. She stands alone. Turn me loose on a street corner and have Helen of Troy, Cleopatra, Mrs Langtry, Hedy Lamarr and La Belle Dame Sans Merci parade past me in one-piece bathing suits, and I wouldn't even bother to whistle at them.'

Bill was touched by his simple eloquence.

'Well, that sounds pretty satisfactory. Summing it up, then, you are as pure as the driven snow?'

'If not purer.'

'Good. Then all you have to do, as I see it, is to change the radio comic approach. You can't run a business that way. Cut the Bob Hope stuff down to a minimum. There are two methods of winning a girl's heart,' said Bill. 'The first is to be the dominant male – the caveman – and take her heart by storm. As an illustration of what I mean, I once wrote for *Passion Magazine* where the hero was no end of a character. He was one of the huntin', ridin' and shootin' set of Old Westbury, Long Island, and he had dark, sullen fits of rage, under the influence of which he would grab his girl by the back hair and drag her about the room with clenched teeth. His teeth were clenched, of course, not hers. Hers just rattled. I throw this out as a suggestion.'

'I'm not going to drag Kay about rooms by her hair.'

'It would be a delicate attention. It might just turn the scale. The girl in my story loved it. "Oh, Gerald, Gerald," she said, "you do something to me." '

'No.'

'All right, then, cut business with hair. But you could seize her by the shoulders and shake her like a rat.'

'No, I couldn't.'

'Why not?'

'Because I couldn't.'

'You're a difficult fellow to help,' said Bill. 'You don't meet one half-way. You seem to have forgotten the old Superba-Llewellyn slogan, Service and Cooperation.'

She took the Mickey Finn from her pocket and joggled it thoughtfully in the palm of her hand.

'What's that?' asked Joe.

'An aspirin. I sleep badly. Well, if you won't be a caveman, we must try the second method and melt her heart instead of storming it. We must build you up for sympathy.'

'How do you mean?'

'It's quite simple . . . Thirsty work, these conferences. How about a refresher?'

'That sounds like a good idea. Champagne?'

'I think so. Stick to the old and tried.'

Bill went to the tray, filled two glasses and adroitly dropped the present from her Third Avenue bartender friend into the one which she handed to Joe.

'Yes,' she said. 'We must build you up for sympathy.'

'But how?'

'It's quite simple.'

'You said that before.'

'And I say it again. You know the old poem, Oh, woman, in our hours of ease . . .'

'Uncertain, coy and hard to please . . . Yes, I used to recite it as a kid.'

'It must have sounded wonderful. Why do I miss these things? Well, you remember, then, that we have it straight from the horse's mouth that it requires only a little pain and anguish wringing the brow to turn a girl into a ministering angel. When pain and anguish wring the brow, a ministering angel, thou. It's all in the book of words.'

'So what?'

'Well, take the case of Kay. I am convinced that if Kay, who is now down in the kitchen cutting wholesome sandwiches, were to come in here and find you lying prone and senseless on the floor, her heart would melt like a nut sundae in the Sahara desert. She would fling herself on your prostrate form and shower kisses on your upturned face. That's what Kay would do, if she came in here and found you lying prone and senseless on the floor.'

'But why would I be lying prone and senseless on the floor?'

Bill nodded. She saw what he meant.

'Yes, that wants thinking out. Well, suppose Phipps in a fit of drunken fury had knocked you cold with that bottle he is nursing as a mother nurses her child?'

'But he hasn't.'

'True. Then suppose I had slipped a Mickey Finn in that drink of yours.'

'But you didn't.'

'True, true. I'm just thinking aloud. Well, here's luck.'

'Luck,' said Joe.

They drained their glasses.

'Mickey Finn,' said Bill pensively, 'I wonder why those things are called that?'

'Wasn't there supposed to have been a bartender named Mickey Finn who invented them?'

'Mencken says not, and he probably knows. Mencken knows everything. Any idea how they work?'

'Yes, oddly enough, I have. It came up in a picture I was doing just before they fired me. Apparently you feel no ill effects at first. Then, if you shake your head – like this . . .'

Bill, quick on her feet, caught him as he started to fall. She lowered him gently to the floor, gave him a look in which commiseration and satisfaction were nicely blended, then crossed to the sofa and shook Phipps by the shoulder.

It is never easy to rouse an intoxicated butler who is in the process of sleeping off two Wilhelmina Shannon Specials and a bottle of *crème de menthe*, and for some time it seemed as though her efforts were to be unrewarded. But presently signs of animation began to appear in the rigid limbs. Phipps grunted. He stirred, he moved, he seemed to feel the rush of life along his keel. Another grunt, and he sat up, blinking.

'Hullo?' he said, speaking in a husky whisper, like a spirit at a séance. 'What goes on?'

14

'I am sorry to disturb your slumbers, Mr Phipps,' said Bill apologetically, 'but I can't seem to bring him to.'

'Eh?'

Bill indicated the remains on the floor.

'Perhaps you could lend a hand?' she said. 'Two heads are better than one.'

Phipps rose unsteadily from the sofa. It appeared to his disordered senses that there was a body on the carpet, as had so often happened in the whodunits which were his favourite reading. In those works it was almost impossible to come into a room without finding bodies on the carpet. The best you could say of this one was that there was not a dagger of Oriental design sticking in its back. He closed his eyes, hoping that this might cause the cadaver to disappear. But when he opened them, it was still there.

'What's the matter with him?' he quavered. 'What's he lying there for?'

Bill raised her eyebrows.

'Surely you recall that, doubtless with the best motives, you socked him on the occiput with your bottle?'

'My – Gawd! Did I?'

'Don't tell me you've forgotten?'

'I can't remember a thing,' said the butler pallidly. 'What happened?'

'Well, it started with you getting into an argument about the Claims to Apostolic Succession of the Church of Abyssinia.'

'About *what*?'

'Don't you remember the Church of Abyssinia?'

'I never heard of the Church of Abyssinia.'

'Well, it's a sort of church they have out Abyssinia way and you and Joe Davenport got arguing about its claims to Apostolic Succession. He took one view, you took another. You said this, he said that. Hot words ensued. Angry passions rose. You gradually bumped him with the bottle. A crash, a cry, and smiling the boy fell dead.'

'He's not *dead*?'

'I was only making a good story of it.'

'Well, I wish you wouldn't,' said Phipps, passing a hand across his ashen forehead. He collapsed into a chair and sat puffing unhappily. He was still doing so when the door opened and Smedley came in, followed by Kay, who was carrying a large plate of sandwiches, at which Bill looked with an approving eye. She was feeling just about ready for a little snack.

'Adela must be asleep,' said Smedley. 'I stood outside her door for quite a time, listening, but I couldn't hear anything. Hello,' he went on, Joe having caught his eye. 'What's this?'

'Stretcher case,' said Bill briefly. 'Phipps hit him with a bottle. We were just chatting about it when you came in.'

Kay's eyes widened. The blood slowly left her face. She stood for an instant, staring, and the plate of sandwiches trembled in her hand. Bill, always doing the right thing, took it gently from her. Kay seemed to come to life. With a cry she flung herself beside Joe's prostrate form.

'Oh, Joe, Joe!' she wailed.

Bill helped herself to a sandwich with a quick, gratified smile. It is always pleasant for a kind-hearted woman who wants to bring the young folks together in springtime to see that she has succeeded in doing so. She finished the sandwich and took another. Sardine, she was glad to note. She liked sardine sandwiches.

'Hit him with a bottle?' said Smedley.

'In a moment of heat,' Bill explained. 'The Phippses get very heated at moments.'

'Good God!'

'Yes, a disagreeable thing to have happened. Spoiled the party, as you might say. But there is a bright side. It has had the effect of sobering him.'

'It has? Then listen . . .'

'I believe he's dead,' said Kay, raising a white face.

'Oh, I shouldn't think so,' said Smedley. He dismissed this side issue and returned to the important subject. 'He's sober, is he?'

'Quite. He could say truly rural.'

'Then now's the time for him to get to work. No more fooling about. Phipps!'

'Sir?' said that reveller, now once more his old respectful butlerine self.

'Get busy.'

'Yes, sir.'

'No more nonsense.'

'No, sir.'

'His master's voice,' said Bill, starting on her third sandwich.

Kay, she saw with approval, was now showering burning kisses on Joe's upturned face. This, it will be remembered, was the business she had arranged for her, and it was nice to see it working out so smoothly. She felt like a director whose cast is on its toes and giving of its best.

'Oh, Joe! Joe, darling!' cried Kay. She looked up. 'He's alive.'

'Really?'

'He just moved.'

'Fine,' said Bill. 'This is excellent news. No electric chair for you this time, Phipps.'

'I am relieved, madam.'

'Later on, perhaps.'

'Yes, madam.'

Kay was glaring balefully. Hitherto, she had always liked Phipps, but now it seemed to her that she had never met a beastlier butler.

'You might have killed him,' she said. She spoke bitterly and with clenched teeth, like Bill's huntin', ridin' and shootin' friend from Old Westbury, and would have hissed the words if there had been an 's' in them.

Phipps, still respectful, disputed this point.

'I would not go so far as to say that, miss. Just a simple slosh on the head, such as so often occurs during a religious argument. But if I might be permitted to say so, I would like to express regret and contrition for having taken such a liberty. From the bottom of me heart, miss . . .'

Smedley broke in with his usual impatience. He was in no mood for oratory.

'Now don't stand there making speeches. This isn't the Fourth of July.'

'No, sir.'

'Action, man, action.'

'Yes, sir.'

'Follow me.'

'Yes, sir. Very good, sir.'

The door closed behind them. Bill smiled maternally at Kay and joined her at the sick-bed. She looked down at the invalid, who was now showing definite signs of coming out of his coma.

'He'll be functioning again in a minute,' she said encouragingly. 'Bet you ten cents I know what he'll say when he opens his eyes. "Where am I?" '

Joe opened his eyes.

'Where am I?' he asked.

'Gimme those ten cents,' said Bill.

Joe sat up.

'Oh, gosh!' he said.

'Oh, Joe!' said Kay.

'My head!' said Joe.

'Painful, no doubt,' said Bill. 'What you need is air. We'll get you into the garden. Lend me a hand, Kay.'

'I'll bathe your head, darling,' said Kay tenderly.

Joe blinked.

'Did you say "darling"?'

'Of course I did.'

Joe blinked again.

'And just now . . . Was it just a lovely dream, or did you kiss me?'

'Of course she kissed you,' said Bill. 'Why wouldn't she kiss you? Weren't you listening when I told you she loves you? Can you navigate?'

'I think so.'

'Then we'll take you out and bathe your head in Adela's jewelled swimming-pool.'

Joe blinked for the third time. Even so trivial a muscular effort as blinking affected his head as if some earnest hand were driving red-hot spikes into it, but the agony, though acute, was forgotten in the thrill of ecstasy which shot through him. It seemed to him once again that soft music was playing in the Garden Room. Familiar objects had taken on a new beauty. Even Bill's rugged face, which good judges had compared to that of a German Boxer, now showed itself as something entitling her to get her telephone number into the most discriminating man's little red book.

As for Kay, the thought struck him that if you slapped a pair of wings on her, she could step straight into any gathering of Cherubim and Seraphim and no questions asked. He gazed at her in a stunned way.

'You love me?'

'Certainly she loves you,' said Bill. 'How many times have I to keep telling you? She worships you. She adores you. She would die for one little rose from your hair. But you'll be able to discuss all that while she's ducking your head in the swimming-pool. Come along, and take it easy. I'll bet you're feeling like someone who has annoyed Errol Flynn.'

Supporting the injured man between them, they passed through the French windows. And scarcely had they disappeared when the door opened and Adela came in, followed by a limp and drowsy Lord Topham. Adela was alert and bristling, her escort practically walking in his sleep. He tottered to a chair, sank into it and closed his eyes.

15

The trouble about going up to a sister-in-law's room and listening at her door to make sure she is asleep is that, if your breathing is at all inclined to be stertorous, you are apt to wake her. Although he was not aware of it, Smedley on his recent visit to the exterior of Adela's sleeping apartment had breathed very stertorously. What with the strain of being accessory before the fact to a safeblowing and the emotional disturbance occasioned by hearing Phipps address him as old drunken Smedley, he had puffed and panted like a racehorse at the conclusion of a stiff Grand National.

He had also caused boards to creak and once, overbalancing, had brought his hand sharply against the panel of the door. Indeed, practically the only thing he had not done was to make a noise like an alarm clock, and he had been operating less than a minute and a half when Adela stirred on her pillow, sat up and finally, hearing that bang on the door, got up. With the air of an Amazon donning her armour before going into battle, she put on a dressing-gown and stood listening.

The sounds outside had ceased. A cautious peep a moment later showed that nobody was there. But somebody had been there, and she proposed to look into the matter thoroughly. There was nothing of the poltroon about Adela Shannon Cork. Any one of a dozen silent picture directors could have told you that, and so could each of her three late husbands. As has previously been indicated, she was a woman who stood no nonsense, and under the head of nonsense she classed the presence of unlawful intruders in her house between the hours of one and two in the morning.

But even the most intrepid of women likes on such an occasion as this to have an ally, so after the briefest of delays she proceeded to Lord Topham's room, and with much more difficulty than Smedley had experienced in waking her, roused him to at least a temporary activity.

He appeared now to have turned in again for the night, and she addressed him sharply.

'Lord Topham!'

Gentle breathing was her guest's only reply. Lord Topham was a man who, though resembling Napoleon Bonaparte in no other way, shared with him the ability to drop off the moment his head touched the pillow – or, as in the present case, the back of a chair.

She raised her voice.

'Lord Topham!'

The mists of sleep were not proof against that urgent cry. The visitor from across the seas opened his eyes. Napoleon in similar circumstances would probably have opened his. Adela's voice lacked the booming thunderousness of Bill's, but it was very penetrating when annoyance caused her to raise it.

'Eh?'

'Wake up.'

'Was I asleep?'

'Yes, you were.'

Lord Topham considered the point, remembered that a moment ago he had been dancing the rhumba in Piccadilly Circus, and nodded.

'That's right. I was. I was dreaming of Toots.'

'Of *what?*'

'Girl I know in London. I dreamed that we were treading the measure in Piccadilly Circus. Of all places. Well, I mean to say,' said Lord Topham, smiling a little at the quaint idea, 'would one? In Piccadilly Circus, I mean to say, what?'

Adela was not a psychiatrist, ever ready to listen to people's dreams and interpret them. She made no comment other than an impatient sniff. Then she uttered a sharp exclamation. Her eye, roving about the room, had fallen on the tray of bottles.

'Look!'

Lord Topham sighed sentimentally.

'I'll tell you about Toots. I love her like billy-o, and we had a row just before I sailed for America. She's a sweet girl—'

'Look at those bottles!'

'—but touchy.'

'Who put those bottles there?'

'Very touchy. A queen of her sex, but touchy. Absolutely.'

'Who – put – those – bottles – there? I was right. There are burglars in the house.'

Lord Topham heaved another sigh. This seemed to him about as good a time as any to unbare his soul concerning the tragedy which had been darkening it.

'Takes offence rather readily, if you know what I mean, though an angel in every possible respect. You'll scarcely believe this, but just because I told her her new hat made her look like Boris Karloff, she hauled off and biffed me on the side of the head, observing as she did so that she never wanted to see or speak to me again in this world or the next. Well, a fellow has his pride, what? I admit I drew myself up to my full height—'

'Be quiet. Listen.'

Adela's gaze had shifted to the ceiling. A muffled sound had proceeded from the projection room above. This was because Smedley, becoming conscious of an imperious desire for a restorative and knowing that all the materials were downstairs, had started for the door and tripped over a footstool.

'There is someone in the projection room. Lord Topham! . . . LORD TOPHAM!'

Lord Topham woke, like Abou ben Adhem, from a deep dream of peace. There crossed his mind the passing thought that he was having a rather disturbed night.

'Hullo?'

'Go up.'

'Where?'

'Upstairs.'

'Why?'

'There are burglars in the projection room.'

'Then I'm dashed if I'm going there,' said Lord Topham. 'I was about to tell you, when I dozed off, that I wrote Toots a well-expressed air mail letter the day before yesterday, saying that the fault was mine and pleading for a reconciliation. I'd look a silly ass going and getting bumped off by a bunch of bally burglars before I had time to get an answer. What? Well, I mean to say! I'm expecting a cable any moment.'

Many people would have approved of his attitude. A prudent and sensible young man, they would have said, with his head screwed on the right way. But Adela could not see eye to eye with them. She uttered an indignant snort and prowled restlessly about the room like a caged lioness. It was not long before she discovered the open French window.

'Lord Topham!'

'Now what?'

'The window is open.'

'The window?'

'The window.'

'Open?'

'Yes.'

Lord Topham, though drowsy, could grasp a simple point like this. With a brief 'The window? Oh, ah, the window. You mean the window?' he looked in the direction indicated.

'Yes,' he said. 'Absolutely. Quite. I see exactly what you mean. Open as per esteemed memo. Did you say that there were burglars in the house?'

'Yes.'

'Then mark my words, that's how they got in,' said Lord Topham, and went to sleep.

'And there's someone coming along the corridor!' cried Adela, stiffening from head to foot. 'Lord Topham . . . LORD TOPHAM!!'

'I say, must you? What's the matter now?'

'I can hear someone coming along the corridor.'

'No, really? Well, well.'

Adela snatched a bottle from the table and pressed it into her companion's hand. He peered at it as if, though this was far from being the case, he were seeing a bottle for the first time.

'What's this?'

'You will need a weapon.'

'Who, me?'

'Yes.'

'A weapon?'

'Yes.'

'Why?'

'The moment he appears, strike him with it.'

'Who?'

'The man in the corridor.'

'But I don't want to go striking men in corridors.'

The door opened, revealing a portly form, at the sight of which Adela's pent-up emotions released themselves in an exasperated scream.

'Smedley!' she cried.

'Oof!' cried Smedley.

'Do I strike him?' enquired Lord Topham.

'What on earth,' said Adela, 'are you doing wandering about the house at this time of night, Smedley?'

Smedley stood in the doorway, gulping painfully and endeavouring with little success to adjust himself to the severest of all
the shocks which had tried his morale in the course of this night
of terror. It is not pleasant for a nervous man who comes into
a room expecting a Bourbon highball to find there a sister-in-
law who even under the most favourable conditions has always
made him feel like a toad beneath the harrow.

He continued to gulp. Strange wordless sounds proceeded
from his pallid lips. His resemblance to the sheeted dead who
squeaked and gibbered in the Roman streets a little 'ere the
mightiest Julius fell was extraordinarily close, though to Lord
Topham, who was unfamiliar with the play in which this
powerful image occurs, he suggested more a cat about to have
a fit. In his boyhood Lord Topham had owned a large tortoise-
shell which had distressed himself and family by behaving just
as Smedley was behaving now.

To ease the strain, he repeated his question.

'Do I strike him?'

'No.'

'Not strike him?'

'No.'

'Right ho,' said Lord Topham agreeably. 'I merely asked.'

Adela glared.

'Well, Smedley?'

Smedley at last found speech.

'I – I couldn't sleep. What – what brings you here? Adela?'

'I heard noises outside my room. Footsteps, and someone
breathing. I woke Lord Topham and we came down and saw
those bottles.'

Smedley, still almost too shocked for utterance, contrived
with an effort to keep the conversation going.

'Bottles?'

'Bottles.'

'Oh, yes . . . Bottles. I . . . I think Phipps must have put them
there,' said Smedley, casting an agonized glance at the ceiling.

Adela uttered an impatient 'Tchah!' She had never had a high
opinion of her brother-in-law's intelligence, but tonight he
seemed to have sunk to new depths of idiocy.

'What in the name of goodness would Phipps be doing,
strewing five hundred and fifty-seven bottles about the room?'

'Butlers do put bottles all over the place,' urged Smedley.

Lord Topham endorsed this dictum. His had been a life into

which butlers had entered rather largely, and he knew their habits.

'Absolutely. Quite. He's right. They do, I mean, what? They're noted for it. Bottles, bottles everywhere, in case you want a drink.'

Adela snorted. It was a hard thing to say of anyone, but in her opinion Lord Topham's mentality was about equal to Smedley's.

'And I suppose it's Phipps making those noises in the projection room?' she said witheringly.

Smedley uttered a cry of agony. He was so used to tripping over footstools or his feet or anything that was handy that it had not occurred to him that there had been noises in the projection room. If Adela had heard such noises, it seemed to him that it would be only a matter of moments before she was up and tracing them to their source. And then what?

He stood there, squeaking and gibbering, completely at a loss as to how to deal with the appalling situation. Then relief flooded his soul. Bill was coming in through the French windows, looking so solid, so dependable that, if only faintly, hope stirred in its winding cloths. It might be that matters had reached such a pass as to be beyond the power of human control, but if anyone could take arms against this sea of troubles and by opposing end them, it was good old Bill.

Adela beheld her sister with less pleasure.

'Wilhelmina!'

'Oh, hello, Adela. Hello, Smedley. Pip-pip, Lord Topham.'

'Toodle-oo, Miss Shannon. Do I strike her?' he asked, for it seemed silly to him to have been issued equipment – bottle, one, people striking for use of – and not to employ it in action.

'Oh, be quiet,' snapped Adela. 'What are you doing here, Wilhelmina?'

'Just strolling. I couldn't sleep. What are you?'

'I heard noises.'

'Imagination.'

'It was not imagination. There is someone in the projection room.'

A tenseness came upon Bill. Not so good, this, she was feeling, not so good. She divined, correctly, that Smedley must have been falling over himself and raising enough uproar to wake the whole populace within miles. Phipps, that silent artist, she acquitted of blame.

'Someone in the projection room?'

'I heard the floor creaking.'

'Mice.'

'Mice be damned. It's a burglar.'

'Have you been up there?'

'Of course I haven't. I don't want the top of my head blown off.'

'Precisely how I feel,' said Lord Topham. 'I was explaining to our dear good hostess here that just before I left England I had a row with my girl Toots, and I've written her a well-expressed air mail letter pleading for a reconciliation and am expecting a reply at any moment, so naturally I am reluctant to get the old lemon blown into hash by nocturnal marauders before that reply arrives – a reply, I may say, which I am hoping will be favourable. True, I left the dear sweet creature foaming rather freely at the mouth and tearing my photographs up and stamping on them, but what I always say is that Time, the great healer—'

'Oh, be quiet!'

'Poor Lord Topham,' said Bill. 'You get about as much chance to talk in this house as a parrot living with Tallulah Bankhead. You had a row with your girl, did you?'

'A frightful row. Battle of the century. It was about her new hat, which I described – injudiciously, I see now, as making her look like—'

'Lord Topham!'

'Hullo?'

Adela spoke with a strained calm.

'I do not wish to hear about your friend Toots.'

'But is she my friend? That's the moot point.'

'To hell and damnation with your blasted Toots!' cried Adela, reverting, as she so often did in moments of emotion, to the breezy *argot* of the old silent film days, when a girl had to be able to express herself if she wanted to get anywhere. Her calm had exploded into fragments. She could not have regarded the young peer with more stormy distaste if she had caught him trying to steal a scene from her. 'Will you kindly stop talking about this miserable creature, who has probably got platinum hair and a lisp and is the scum of the underworld. All I am interested in at the moment is that burglar in the projection room.'

Bill shook her head.

'There isn't a burglar in the projection room.'

'I tell you there is.'

'Shall I go and investigate?'

'What good would you be? No, we'll wait for the police.'

Smedley collapsed on the sofa. This was the end.

'Per-per-police?'

'I telephoned them from my bedroom. Why they are not here is more than I can imagine. I suppose they're walking. It would be just like those half-witted imbeciles they call policemen in Beverly Hills to . . . Ah!' said Adela. 'And about time.'

A sergeant and a patrolman were coming through the French windows.

16

The sergeant was a tough, formidable sergeant, who looked as if he had been hewn from the living rock. The patrolman was a tough, formidable patrolman, who gave the same impression. They came in with the measured tread of men conscious of their ability to uphold the Law and make the hardiest criminal say Uncle.

'Good evening, ma'am,' said the sergeant.

Adela was still in difficult mood. Women of her wealth grow to expect their orders to be filled with speed and promptness.

'Good evening,' she said. 'You've taken your time coming. What were you doing? Playing Canasta?'

The sergeant seemed wounded.

'Came as quick as we could, ma'am. You're reporting a burglary?'

Adela gave him a full whammy.

'Don't they tell you *anything* at police headquarters? Yes, as I went to the trouble of explaining carefully over the telephone, there are burglars in the house. They are up in the projection room.'

'Where's that?'

'The room immediately above this one. Smedley, show the officers up to the projection room.'

Smedley quivered like a Roman Emperor hearing the leader of the band of assassins which has just filed into his private apartments say 'Well, here we are, Galba' – or Vitellius or Caligula or whatever the name might be. He cast an imploring glance at Bill, as if pleading with her not to fail him in this dark hour.

Bill, as always, did her best.

'There aren't any burglars in the projection room. Absurd.'

'Absurd, my foot. I heard strange noises.'

Bill caught the sergeant's eye. Her own twinkled.

'She heard strange noises, sergeant. Ha, ha. We women! Poor, timid, fluttering creatures.'

'Listen! Any time *I* flutter . . .'

'Just bundles of nerves, aren't we, sergeant?'

'Yes, ma'am. My wife's like that.'

'My wife's like that,' said the patrolman.

'All women are like that,' said Bill. 'It's something to do with the bone structure of our heads.'

The sergeant said Maybe you're right, ma'am. The patrolman said Yes, she had a point there. His wife, said the patrolman, was a great believer in omens and portents and would you ever catch that woman walking under a ladder, no, ma'am: and the sergeant said his wife always said 'Rabbits, rabbits, rabbits' on the first day of the month, because she held the view that if you said 'Rabbits, rabbits, rabbits' on the first day of the month, you got a present within the next two weeks. Silly, said the sergeant, but there it was.

'Listen,' said Adela, who was showing signs of becoming overwrought.

'Just a moment, Adela,' said Bill. 'Sit down,' she said to the arms of the Law, 'and tell us all about your wives.'

It was a tempting offer, and for a moment the sergeant seemed to waver. But a splendid spirit animates the police force of Beverly Hills, and he was strong again.

'Not just now, ma'am,' he said. 'I guess we'd best take a look at this projection room the lady wants us to take a look at.'

'Waste of time,' said Bill judicially.

'Yes,' agreed Smedley, speaking with a feverish earnestness. 'And you wouldn't like the projection room. Honestly.'

'Besides, there's no hurry,' said Bill. 'Good heavens, the night's yet young. Take a couple of chairs and have a drink.'

A passer-by at this point might have supposed that an ammunition dump had exploded in the near neighbourhood. But it was only Adela.

'Sweet suffering soupspoons!' cried Adela, raising her hands to heaven in a passionate gesture. 'Take a couple of chairs! Have a drink! What *is* this? A college reunion?'

The sergeant shook his head. The bottles on the tray had not escaped his notice, for the police are trained to observe, and his eye had gleamed at the suggestion that he should investigate their contents. It was a pity, he felt, that this admirable woman who looked like a German Boxer was not in charge of the proceedings. Bill, in his opinion, had nice ideas, and it would have been a pleasure to fall in with them. But apparently it was this other dame, whose face seemed oddly familiar for some reason, who was directing operations, and her views were less in keeping with the trend of modern thought.

'No, thank you, ma'am,' he said virtuously. 'Not while we're on duty. Come on, Bill.'

'Is your name Bill?' said Bill.

The patrolman said it was, and Bill said Well, well, well.

'So is mine,' said Bill. 'What an amazing coincidence. Let's curl up on the sofa and have a long talk about it.'

'Later on, ma'am,' said the sergeant. He glanced up at the ceiling, and there came into his face that keen look which policemen wear when constabulary duty is to be done. 'Seems to me I do hear something up there,' he said. 'A kind of creaking noise.'

'All very old houses creak at night,' said Bill. 'This one, I believe, dates back to the early Cecil B. de Mille period.'

'Ask me,' said the patrolman, 'it's more like a sort of scratching sound.'

Bill cocked an ear.

'Ah, yes,' she said. 'I know what that is. That is my sister's poodle. He has a sensitive skin, and he is like the young lady of Natchez, who said: "Where Ah itches, Ah scratches." Are you fond of dogs, sergeant?'

'Yes, ma'am. I've a dog at home—'

'What sort?'

'A Scotty, ma'am.'

'No nicer breed. Very intelligent animals, Scotties.'

'Intelligent? You said it. Say, listen,' said the sergeant.

'Say, listen,' said the patrolman, who wanted to speak of his Boston terrier, Buster.

'Say, listen,' said Adela, who had been fermenting rather freely during these exchanges. 'Listen, you Keystone Kops, are you or are you not going up to that projection room?'

'Sure, lady, sure,' said the sergeant. 'Come on, Bill.'

They started for the door, and Smedley uttered the soft little moan of despair of the man who feels that the doom has come upon him. Tripping over his feet, he fell against the sergeant, who fell against Adela, who asked him what he imagined he was playing at. Football? enquired Adela. Or Postman's Knock?

'Pardon, lady,' said the sergeant courteously. 'The gentleman bumped me.' He paused, staring. 'Say, aren't you Adela Shannon?'

'I am.'

'Well, I'll be a son-of-a,' said the sergeant. 'I seen you in the old silents. You remember Adela Shannon, Bill?'

'Sure,' said the patrolman. 'She used to be the Empress of Stormy Emotion.'

'She still is,' said Bill. 'So you're interested in pictures, are you, sergeant?'

'Yes, ma'am. Are you connected with pix?'

'No longer. I had a job with Superba-Llewellyn, but they fired me.'

'Too bad. Still, that's how it goes.'

'That's how it goes.'

The patrolman laughed a bitter laugh.

'Yes, that's how it goes – in Hollywood,' he said. 'Ha!'

Bill looked at him, interested. She turned to the sergeant.

'He doesn't seem to like Hollywood.'

'No, ma'am.'

Adela clenched her teeth. Her fists were already clenched. She spoke with the strained sweetness of a woman who is holding herself in with all the resolution at her disposal, knowing that if she relaxes for an instant, she will spring into the air, howling like a Banshee. No less than Smedley, who was now a mere jelly, she was finding the proceedings something of a strain. The zealous officers were affecting her like a Viennese director she remembered from the old days, a man at whose head she had once been compelled in the interests of her art to throw one of the swords used by the Roman soldiers in *Hail, Caesar*.

'Might I have your attention for a moment, Mr Louis B. Mayer, and you, Mr Zanuck,' she said. 'Do you intend during the next hour or so to get some action, or is this conference going on for ever? Did you come here to arrest burglars or just to chat about motion pictures? I merely wish to know how matters stand?' said Adela, all charm and consideration.

Bill rebuked her gently.

'You're so impatient, Adela. We have the night before us. Why doesn't your friend like Hollywood?'

The sergeant's brow darkened.

'He tried for a job at Medulla-Oblongata-Glutz last week, and they turned him down on account he wanted to do whimsical comedy and they said he wasn't right for whimsical comedy.'

'You're kidding me.'

'No, ma'am, that's what they said.'

'Astounding. He looks all right for whimsical comedy to *me*.'

'Sure I'm all right for whimsical comedy,' said the patrolman. 'But it's all a closed ring. That's what it is, just a closed ring. If you're new talent, you haven't a chance.'

'It's tough,' said Bill.

'You're right, it's tough,' said the sergeant. 'Say, listen. When I tried to muscle in at Colossal-Superhuman, they had the nerve to say I lacked dramatic intensity.'

'It's incredible.'

A sigh like the wind blowing through the cracks in a broken heart escaped Adela. Her spirit was broken.

'God give me strength!' she moaned. 'I telephone for policemen, and they send me a couple of ham actors. I shall go to bed. Lord Topham . . . LORD TOPHAM!'

Lord Topham sat up, blinking.

'Hullo? Is that Toots?'

Adela was silent for a moment. She seemed to be swallowing something.

'No,' she said at length, speaking with some difficulty. 'It is not Toots. Lord Topham, you have been about as much use up to now as a pain in the neck. Would it be too much to ask you to accompany me to my bedroom?'

'Accompany you to your—?'

'With burglars in every nook and cranny of the house, I don't propose to go up two flights of stairs alone.'

Lord Topham seemed relieved.

'Oh, yes, yes, yes, yes, yes,' he said. 'I thought for a moment . . . Ha, ha, silly of me. Absolutely. Yes, yes, yes, yes, of course. I see what you mean.'

'Bring that bottle.'

'Eh? Oh, the jolly old bottle? Quite, quite.'

'And any time you get through talking about your dramatic intensity,' said Adela, addressing the sergeant, 'you will find the burglars in the projection room. I'll shout through the door and tell them to be sure to wait. Come, Lord Topham.'

'Ladies first,' said Lord Topham gallantly.

'Ladies first, my left eyeball,' said Adela. 'Why, they may be lurking in the corridor.'

Lord Topham went out, followed by Adela. The sergeant, who appeared to have been stung by her parting words, became active.

'Come on, let's go.'

'Oh, not yet,' begged Smedley.

'Yes, sir. We have our duty to do.'

'But I want to hear all about this gentleman's whimsical comedy,' said Bill. 'Do sit down and have a drink.'

'Thank you, no, ma'am.'

'Say when.'

'When,' said the sergeant.

'You?'

'Not for me, ma'am.'

'Say when.'

'When,' said the patrolman.

'That's better,' said Bill. 'Now we're set. Now we're cosy. Why did Medulla-Oblongata-Glutz think you were not right for whimsical comedy?'

'Search me,' said the patrolman, moodily. 'What's Clark Gable got that I haven't got?'

'A moustache, ten million dollars and Lady Sylvia Ashley.'

The sergeant saw that there had been a misunderstanding.

'He is alluding to talent, ma'am.'

'Oh, talent?'

'Yes, talent,' said the patrolman. 'I got talent. I know it. I feel it *here*,' said the patrolman, slapping his chest.

Bill cocked an eye at the sergeant.

'You have talent, too?'

'Sure I got talent,' said the sergeant. 'And who says I lack dramatic intensity? Listen. "Drop that gun, you rat. You know me. Tough Tom Hennessy, the cop that always gets his man. Ah, would you? Bang, bang." That's where I shoot and plug him,' explained the sergeant. 'It's a little thing I threw together with a view to showing myself in a dramatic role. There's more of it, but that'll give you the idea.'

'It's wonderful,' said Bill. 'A poignant and uplifting cameo of life as it is lived today, purifying the emotions with pity and terror.'

The sergeant simpered modestly, one massive foot drawing circles on the carpet.

'Thanks, ma'am.'

'Not at all.'

'Care to look in at the station house some day, I'll show you my stills.'

'I can hardly wait.'

'Yes, ma'am, that's the sort of thing I can do. But they turn me down.'

'That's Hollywood.'

'That's Hollywood.'

'You're right, that's Hollywood,' said the patrolman. 'Lookit, ma'am. Watch. What's this?'

He smiled.

'Joy?' said Bill.

'Joy is right. And this?'

He tightened his lips.

'Grief!'

'Grief is right. And this?'

He raised his eyebrows.

'Horror?'

'You betcher, horror. And I can do hate, too. But it's whimsical comedy I'm best at. Like where the fellow meets the girl and starts kidding her. But could I drive that into their thick skulls at M-O-G? No, ma'am. They turned me down.'

'That's Hollywood,' said Bill.

'That's Hollywood,' said the sergeant.

'You're right, that's Hollywood,' said the patrolman.

'Bright city of sorrows,' said Bill. 'Ah, Phipps.'

The butler had come shimmering through the door. If he felt any surprise or alarm at observing policemen on the premises, he gave no sign of it. He was his usual dignified self.

'I came to see if there was anything more you required, madam.'

'Not a thing, thank you,' said Bill.

'Say, who's this?' said the sergeant.

'My sister's butler. Sergeant—?'

'Ward, ma'am. And Patrolman Morehouse.'

'Thank you. Mr Phipps. Sergeant Ward and Patrolman Morehouse.'

'How do you do?' said Phipps.

'Pleased to meet you,' said the sergeant.

'Hi!' said the patrolman, also indicating pleasure.

Bill showed a womanly concern for the butler's well-being.

'You're up late, Phipps. Couldn't you sleep, either?'

'No, madam. I experienced an annoying wakefulness. Most unusual with me, madam.'

'You should have tried counting sheep.'

'I did, madam, but without avail. So finally, I took the liberty of proceeding to the projection room and running off *Forever Amber*.'

The sergeant uttered an exclamation.

'What's that? Was it you in that projection room?'

'Yes, sir.'

It was plain that the sergeant now saw it all. His trained mind had leaped to the significance of the butler's story.

'Then there you are. There you have the whole mystery explained and the case cleaned up. The lady thought it was burglars.'

'Mrs Cork,' explained Bill. 'She has just left us. She heard noises and became alarmed.'

'I am sorry, madam. I endeavoured to be as silent as possible.'

'I'm sure you did.'

The sergeant wiped his lips, and rose.

'Well, we'll be getting along. Good night, ma'am.'

'Good night. Take care of that dramatic intensity.'

'I will, ma'am.'

'And good luck to your artistic efforts.'

'Thank you, ma'am. But one kind of loses heart. The more you submit yourself to these casting offices, the more they give you the old runaround.'

'That's Hollywood.'

'That's Hollywood.'

'You're right, that's Hollywood,' said the patrolman. 'That tinsel town where tragedy lies hid behind a thousand false smiles, and—'

'Ah, come on,' said the sergeant.

Bill closed the French windows behind them, and Smedley breathed the first carefree breath he had breathed since the dark doings of the night had begun.

'Bill,' he said, 'you're a marvel.'

'Thank you, Smedley. As Phipps would say, I desire to give satisfaction.'

'A marvel,' repeated Smedley. He turned to Phipps. 'Those cops were going up to the projection room, but she kept them talking and headed them off.'

'Indeed, sir? The experience must have occasioned you a great deal of anxiety, madam.'

'Yes, it was a close thing,' said Bill. 'Lucky they were interested in pictures.'

Joe and Kay came in through the French windows.

'Joe's feeling better,' said Kay.

'Good. And you look radiant.'

'Can you wonder?' said Joe. 'She's going to marry *me*.'

'Ah, you fixed it up all right. I thought you would. Kay, an aunt's blessing.'

'Thank you, Bill.'

'In my opinion, nice work. You probably feel the same, Smedley?'

Smedley executed a brief dance step. It might have signified joy, but more probably irritation. Smedley lacked Patrolman Morehouse's skill in registering.

'Yes, yes, yes,' he said, 'but I haven't time to bother about that now. You got it, Phipps?'

'Sir?'

'The diary.'

'Oh, yes, sir. Without any difficulty.'

'Good work, Phipps,' said Joe.

'Thank you, sir.'

'Splendid, Phipps,' said Kay.

'Thank you, miss.'

'Gimme,' said Smedley.

A look of respectful regret came into the butler's face.

'I am sorry, sir, but what you suggest is not feasible, sir.'

Smedley stared.

'What do you mean? You said you had got it.'

'Yes, sir. And I propose to keep it.'

'What?'

'Yes, sir. Would there be anything further, sir? Thank you, sir. Good night.'

He shimmered out, leaving a stunned silence behind him.

'My God!' said Bill, the first to break it. 'Hijacked *again*!' She paused, wrestling with her feelings. 'Go on, Smedley,' she said at length. '*You* say it. I'm a lady.'

17

There are, as everybody knows, many ways of measuring time, and from the earliest ages learned men have argued earnestly in favour of their different systems, with not a little bad blood, one is sorry to say, arising between the representatives of the various schools of thought.

Hipparchus of Rhodes, for instance, who had his own ideas on the way time should be measured, once referred to Marinus of Tyre, who held different opinions, as 'Marinus the flat tyre', which, though extraordinarily witty, was pretty bitter: and when Purbach and Regiomontanus were told the views of Achmed Ibn Abdallah of Baghdad, they laughed themselves crosseyed. Purbach, who was a hard nut, said that Achmed Ibn Abdallah knew about as much about measuring time as his grandmother's cat, a notoriously backward animal, and when kind-hearted Regiomontanus in his tolerant way urged that Ahmed Ibn was just a young fellow trying to get along and one ought not to judge him too harshly, Purbach said 'Oh, yeah?' and Regiomontanus said 'Yeah,' and Purbach said Was that so, and Regiomontanus made him sick. It was their first quarrel.

Tycho Brahe, the eminent Dane, measured time by means of altitudes, quadrants, azimuths, cross-staves, armillary spheres and parallactic rules, and the general opinion in Denmark was that he had got the thing down cold. And then in 1863 along came Dollen with his *Die Zeitbestimmung Vermittelst Des Tragbaren Durchgangsinstruments Im Vertical e Des Polarsterns* – a bestseller in its day, subsequently made into a musical by Rodgers and Hammerstein, who called it *North Atlantic*, a much better marquee title – and proved that Tycho, by mistaking an azimuth for an armillary sphere one night after the annual dinner of the alumni of Copenhagen University, had got his calculations all wrong, throwing the whole thing back into the melting pot.

The truth is that time cannot be measured. To Smedley, slumped in his chair on the terrace on the following morning, it seemed to be standing still. Melancholy had marked him for her own, and each leaden moment that dragged itself by took on the semblance of an hour. To Phipps, on the other hand, chanting a gay air in his pantry, the golden minutes seemed to race. Tra-la, sang Phipps, and Tiddly-om-pom-pom. In all Beverly Hills there was, as of even date, no sunnier butler. Lord Topham had described the previous day as the maddest and merriest of all the glad new year, but it seemed to Phipps that the current one relegated it to second place. God was in his heaven and all was right with the world, he felt. A contract with Medulla-Oblongata-Glutz in one pocket and a fifty thousand dollar diary in the other – what more could a man want?

Well, the way his head was feeling after last night, perhaps a bromo-seltzer. He rose and mixed himself one. And as he drained it, singing between the sips like somebody in a drinking chorus in an opera, his eye fell on the clock. Nearly noon? Time for old Smedley's yoghurt.

Smedley had closed his eyes when the butler arrived on the terrace, and was not aware of his presence till he spoke behind him.

'Good morning, sir,' said Phipps, and Smedley skipped as nearly like the high hills as is within the scope of a seated man.

'Oof!' he said. 'You startled me.'

'That will cure your hiccups, sir.'

'I don't have hiccups.'

'I am sorry, sir. I was not aware of that.'

Smedley, who had been in one of his daydreams, now realized for the first time that the voice which had broken in on his reverie was that of Southern California's most prominent viper. A viper to end all vipers.

'Well, viper,' he said, injecting a wealth of hate and abhorrence into the salutation and with mouth and eyebrows registering scorn, disgust and loathing in a manner which would have extorted the admiration of Patrolman Morehouse, himself no mean specialist in that direction.

'Sir?'

'I said viper.'

'Very good, sir. Your yoghurt, sir.'

'Take that stuff away.'

Joe and Kay came on to the terrace. They had been wandering through the rose garden, discussing ways and means. Kay's view was that love was all and that so long as they had each other, what did anything else matter? It was enough for her, she said, that she was going to marry Joe, because Joe was a woolly baa-lamb. Joe, while conceding that he was a woolly baa-lamb and admitting that love was swell, had rather tended to argue that a bit of the stuff would also come in handy, and from this the conversation turned naturally to Phipps, who in such a dastardly manner had placed that bit of stuff beyond their reach. It would be gratifying, said Joe, to have a word with Phipps. So, coming on to the terrace and seeing him there, he had it.

'Ha!' he said. 'Well, you sneaking, chiselling, two-timing, horn-swoggling highbinder!'

'Good morning, sir.'

Kay, too, was severe.

'I wonder you can look us in the face, Phipps.'

The butler sighed regretfully. His innate chivalry made the thought of having given offence to Youth and Beauty an unpleasant one.

'I am sorry to have been compelled to occasion you inconvenience, miss, but as Miss Shannon so well put it, it was military necessity. One cannot make an omelette without breaking eggs.'

He winced a little. Those overnight potations had left him in a condition where he would have preferred not to think of eggs. His breakfast that morning had consisted of a slice of Melba toast and three pots of black coffee, and even the Melba toast had seemed at the time excessive.

Joe had thought of another one.

'You wolf in butler's clothing!'

'Yes, sir. Precisely, sir,' said Phipps deferentially. He turned to Smedley. 'If you persist in refusing to drink your yoghurt, sir, I shall have no option but to inform Mrs Cork.'

Smedley endeavoured, as usual unsuccessfully, to snap his fingers.

'That for Mrs Cork!'

'Very good, sir.'

'You can go to Mrs Cork and tell her, with my compliments, to boil her head.'

'Very good, sir. I will bear your instructions in mind.'

The butler withdrew, to all appearances oblivious of the fact that six eyes were boring holes in his back, and the emotions of the three on the terrace found expression in words.

'The snake!' said Smedley.

'The hound!' said Joe.

'The reptile!' said Kay.

This made them all feel a little better, but only a little, for it was apparent to the dullest mind that what the crisis which had been precipitated called for was not words, but action. It was Smedley who clothed this thought in speech.

'We've got to do something,' said Smedley.

'But what?' said Joe.

'Yes, what?' said Kay.

There, Smedley admitted, they had him.

'Well, I'll tell you one thing,' he said. 'It's no good trying to formulate a plan of action without Bill. Where is Bill?'

'In the Garden Room,' said Kay. 'I saw her as we passed. I think she's working on Aunt Adela's *Memoirs.*'

'Then come on,' said Smedley.

Left to himself, he would rather not have revisited the Garden Room, with all its sad memories, but if Bill was there, to the Garden Room he must go. It was imperative that the conduct of affairs be handed over to The Old Reliable without delay. The thought crossed his mind that if Bill was capable of concentrating on Adela's ghastly *Memoirs* on the morning after a night like last night, she must be a woman of iron, and it encouraged him. There are certain difficult situations in life where a woman of iron at one's side is just what one most needs.

Bill, as fresh, so far as the eye could discern, as an infant newly risen from its afternoon nap, was seated at the desk, prattling away into the dictaphone as if without a care in the world.

'Ah, Hollywood, Hollywood,' said Bill. 'Bright city of sorrows, where fame deceives and temptation lurks, where souls are shrivelled in the furnace of desire and beauty is broken on sin's cruel wheel.' And if that was not the stuff to give them, she felt, she was vastly mistaken. There was a flat dullness about the story of Adela's life which made the injection of some such purple patch from time to time a necessity. Absolutely, as Lord Topham would have said.

Observing the procession filing in at the French windows, she suspended her activities.

'Hello, boys and girls. Heavens, Smedley, you look like something left over from the Ark,' she said, and marvelled at the mysteries of a woman's heart, which can preserve its love for a man intact even when his appearance is that of flotsam and jetsam. For in describing Smedley as something left over from the Ark, she was really giving him the breaks. Actually, he resembled more closely one of those mildewed pieces of refuse found in dustbins, which are passed over with a disdainful jerk of the head by the discriminating alley cat.

Smedley exhibited pique. None knew better than he that he was not his usual spruce self and, like Regiomontanus, he felt that allowances ought to be made.

'How do you expect me to look?' he protested. 'I haven't been to bed for two nights. Bill, what are we going to do?'

'About Phipps?'

'Of course about Phipps. What else did you think we'd got on our minds?'

Bill nodded sympathetically.

'It's a problem,' she agreed. 'I ought to have reflected, before enlisting Phipps's services, that he is a man of infinite guile.'

'I'll sue him,' cried Smedley. 'I'll fight the case to the Supreme Court.'

'M'm.'

'Yes,' said Smedley, deflated, 'I suppose you're right. Then is there nothing we can do?'

'Can't you force him to give it up?' said Kay.

This pleased Smedley. The right spirit, he considered.

'Good idea. Intimidate the fellow. Stick lighted matches between his toes.'

Bill was obliged to discourage this Utopian dream.

'My dear Smedley, you can't stick lighted matches between the toes of an English butler. He would raise his eyebrows and freeze you with a glance. You'd feel as if he had caught you using the wrong fork. No, the only thing is to try an appeal to his better nature.' She rose, and pressed the bell. 'I guarantee no results. For all we know, Phipps hasn't a better nature.' She regarded Joe solicitously. 'You're looking very gloomy, Joe. Feeling a little low?'

'I could walk under a cockroach.'

'Cheer up. There is still joy in the world, still the happy laughter of children and the singing of bluebirds.'

'That's all right about bluebirds. I want to get married, and I'm down to my last ten dollars.'

Bill stared.

'Last ten dollars? What's become of that thousand you had?'

Joe's manner betrayed a certain embarrassment.

'Well, I'll tell you, Bill. You remember that gambling joint, Perelli's, we were talking about a couple of days ago? After the party broke up last night, I thought I'd go down there and try to make a fast buck.'

'Did you make a fast buck?'

'Unfortunately, no. But there's always a bright side. Perelli did.'

'He cleaned you out?'

'Except for ten dollars.'

'You unbalanced young boll weevil! Kay's right. You're not an *homme sérieux*.'

Kay flared up.

'He is not an unbalanced boll weevil. And what do you mean, saying he's not an *homme sérieux*? I think it was very sensible of him to go to Perelli's. It wasn't his fault he didn't win.'

Bill let it go. This, she felt, was love.

'And anyway, darling,' said Kay, 'I don't know what you are worrying about. Two can live as cheap as one.'

Bill regarded her admiringly.

'You do say some bright things, child. If that's your normal form, Joe won't have a dull moment in your little home.'

'In our little gutter, you mean,' corrected Joe.

'Joe says we shall have to starve in the gutter.'

'You can't,' said Bill. 'There aren't any gutters in Hollywood. Ah, come in, Phipps.'

The butler had manifested himself.

'You rang, madam?'

'Yes. Good morning, Phipps.'

'Good morning, madam.'

'Quite a night last night.'

'Yes, madam.'

'No ill-effects, I trust?'

'I have a slight headache, madam.'

'Well earned. You should keep off the sauce, Phipps.'

'Yes, madam.'

'And now what about things?'

'On what particular point do you desire information, madam?'

Bill did not find his manner promising. Anything less resembling a butler likely to be talked with honeyed words into giving up a diary worth fifty thousand dollars she had never beheld. She persevered, however.

'About the diary. You remember it? It hasn't slipped your mind?'

'No, madam.'

'Having slept on the matter, you still propose to keep it?'

'Yes, madam.'

'And sell it and convert the proceeds to your own use?'

'Yes, madam.'

'Well, I don't want to hurt your feelings,' said Bill, 'but you must have a soul like a stevedore's undervest.'

The butler seemed rather pleased than otherwise. A faint twitch of the upper lip showed that if he had not been an English butler, he might have smiled.

'A very striking image, madam.'

'Has it occurred to you that you will have some exceedingly nasty questions to answer about this on Judgment Day?'

'No doubt, madam.'

'But you don't quail?'

'No, madam.'

Bill gave it up.

'All right, Phipps. You may withdraw.'

'Very good, madam.'

'What do you like at Santa Anita to-day?'

'Betty Hutton, madam, in the fourth race.'

'Thank you, Phipps.'

'Thank *you*, madam.'

18

The door closed. Bill lit a cigarette.

'Well,' she said, 'I did my best. Nobody can do more. When you come up against Battling Phipps, you certainly know you've been in a fight.'

The door reopened.

'Excuse me, madam,' said Phipps. 'I inadvertently omitted to deliver a message entrusted to me by Mrs Cork. Mrs Cork presents her compliments and would be glad if Mr Smedley would join her in the projection room at his earliest convenience.'

Smedley did one of his quick dance steps.

'What? What does she want?'

'Mrs Cork did not honour me with her confidence, sir. But when I left her, she was standing scrutinizing the safe—'

'Oh, gosh!'

'—and heaving gently, sir, like a Welsh rarebit about to come to the height of its fever. Thank you, sir.'

The door closed again.

'Phipps has a very happy gift of phrase,' said Bill.

Smedley was plucking at his collar.

'Bill, she's found out.'

'She was bound to sooner or later.'

'She suspects me. What'll I do?'

'Stick to stout denial.'

'Stout denial?'

'Stout denial. You can't beat it. Get tough. Say "Oh, yeah?" and "Jussa minute, jussa minute," and when speaking, speak out of the side of the mouth.'

'Like Perelli,' said Joe.

'Does Mr Perelli speak out of the side of his mouth?'

'All the time.'

'Then there's your model, Smedley. Imagine that you're the proprietor of a prosperous gambling hell and that Adela is a disappointed client who is trying to sell you the idea that the wheel is crooked.'

Smedley went out, gulping unhappily. Bill wandered to the French windows and looked out on the sunlit garden. Kay came to Joe, who after his brief observation about Mr Perelli had returned to the depths.

'Cheer up, darling,' she said. 'You still have me.'

'And ten dollars.'

'I call ten dollars quite a lot.'

'Yes, but when I leave here, I shall have to tip Phipps with it. Is that a bitter thought? If not,' said Joe, 'how would you describe it?' He looked at Bill, who was waving a friendly hand at someone in the garden. 'What are you waving at?'

Bill turned.

'Come here, Joe.' She pointed. 'What do you see?'

Joe followed her finger with a dull eye.

'Clouds,' he said. 'Black, inky clouds. And murky shadows threatening doom, disaster and despair. Oh, you mean the figure in the foreground?'

'Right. My Lord Topham. He is coming this way, you observe. How have you been getting along with Lord Topham since your arrival?'

'Pretty well. He was telling me about the trouble he has been having with a girl in England called Toots. Apparently she gave him the brusheroo, and he's a bit down about it.'

'You were sympathetic, I hope?'

'Oh, yes.'

'Good. Then he probably looks on you as a bosom friend. A very rich young man, Lord Topham, I understand,' said Bill meditatively. 'One of England's richest, Adela tells me. Something to do with chain stores or provision markets, if I am not mistaken. Anyway, however he gets the stuff, he's got it.'

Joe started. This opened up a new line of thought.

'Good Lord, Bill, you weren't thinking of touching Topham?'

'It is always a sound business principle, when you need twenty thousand dollars, to go to the man who's got twenty thousand dollars.'

'Bill, you're a genius.'

'That's what I kept telling those people at Superba-Llewellyn, but they wouldn't listen to me.'

'Pitch it strong, old friend.'

'I will, Joe, I will.'

The Lord Topham who a moment later dragged his long legs across the threshold of the French windows and added his presence to the little group of thinkers in the Garden Room differed substantially from the exuberant young athlete who had made a similar entrance almost exactly twenty-four hours earlier. Then, it will be remembered, he had had a song on his lips and a gleam in his eye as the result of having broken a hundred on the golf links. For even an anxious lover, awaiting a reply to his well-expressed air mail letter from the girl with whom he has had a falling-out, will temporarily forget the sex angle after doing eighteen holes in ninety-seven strokes for the first time in his life. The Lord Topham of twenty-four hours ago, though the vultures of anxiety had presumably been gnawing at his vitals, had stood before the world as a definitely chirpy man.

Vastly different was the sombre figure that now loomed up behind its eleven-inch cigarette holder. The face was drawn, the eyes haggard, the general appearance that of one who has searched for the leak in life's gaspipe with a lighted candle. Even such a man, so faint, so spiritless, so dead, so dull in look, so woebegone, drew Priam's curtain in the dead of night and would have told him half his Troy was burned. One might have supposed, looking at him, that Lord Topham had been out on the links again and had not been able to do better than a hundred and fifty-seven, taking fourteen at the long dog-leg hole and losing six balls in the lake at the second.

Actually, what was causing his despondency was the fact that shortly after breakfast he had received the cable he had been expecting, and it had been a red-hot one. Miss Gladys ('Toots') Fauntleroy was one of those girls who do not object to letting the sun go down on their wrath, and it is to be doubted whether a more vitriolic ten-bobsworth had crossed the Atlantic Ocean since the days of the late Florenz Ziegfeld. It had caused hope to die and despair to take possession of Lord Topham's soul, and had engendered in him a comprehensive dislike for the whole human race. It was, in short, the worst possible moment anyone could have selected to approach him with the idea of getting into his ribs for twenty thousand dollars.

The newcomer's gloom did not impress itself on those present, so self-centred do we all tend to be in this world. Obsessed with their own personal problems, they merely saw a fabulously rich young man coming in through a French window. They did not pause to ask themselves if his heart was intact or broken, but cluttered joyously about him, giving him a great reception.

'Lord Topham!' cried Kay. 'Do come in, Lord Topham.'

'Yes, do,' cried Joe. 'Just the man we wanted to see.'

'The very person,' said Bill. 'Lord Topham, old boy, could we have a word with you, Lord Topham, old boy?'

She patted his shoulder lovingly and another man in his position might have been pleased and touched by the warmth of her affection. He merely glowered down at her hand as if it had been one of those spiders for which Phipps had so strong a distaste.

'What the dickens are you doing?'

'Just patting your shoulder, Lord Topham, old boy, old boy.'

'Well, bally well don't,' said the old boy morosely.

A chill crept into the hearts of the reception committee. They looked at one another with a growing feeling of uneasiness. Something was wrong, they felt, something was seriously wrong. This was not the effervescent young man they had hoped to see. More like some sort of a changeling. It was with a feeling that little of a constructive nature was likely to result that Joe approached the main item on the agenda paper.

'Listen, Lord Topham. It is within your power to bring joy and happiness into quite a number of human lives.'

'Then I'm dashed if I'm going to do it,' said Lord Topham. 'Would it interest you to know how I feel about the human species? I hope it jolly well chokes. I don't mind telling you that I got a cable from my girl Toots this morning which has definitely turned me into a mis-what's-the-word. I mean one of those blokes who get fed up with their fellow men and go and live in caves and grow beards and subsist on berries from the bush and water from the spring. Don't talk to me about bringing joy into human lives. I have to do without joy, so why shouldn't the ruddy human lives? To blazes with them. Let 'em eat cake.'

'But if you don't help me, I'm ruined.'

'Well, that's fine,' said Lord Topham, brightening a little.

Phipps came softly in, and Bill regarded him with an unfriendly eye.

'You again?' she said. 'The way you keep shimmering in and out, one would think you were the family spectre.'

The butler preserved his equanimity.

'I came to inform his lordship that he was wanted on the telephone, madam. A transatlantic call, m'lord.'

Lord Topham quivered. The cigarette holder, which he had replaced between his lips at the conclusion of his powerful speech, fell to the ground, dashing its cigarette to fragments.

'Eh? What? A transatlantic call? Who is it?'

'A Miss Fauntleroy, m'lord.'

'What! Good Lord! Good heavens! Well, I'm dashed. Well, I'm blowed. Well, I'll be jiggered. Gangway, gangway, gangway!' cried Lord Topham, and was out of the room before one could have said 'What ho.' It seemed incredible that that elongated form, a moment ago so limp, could be capable of such speed on the flat.

Phipps, about to follow, was stopped by Bill.

'Oh, Phipps,' said Bill.

'Madam?'

'One moment, if I may delay your progress. Could you bring us some strengthening cocktails?'

'Certainly, madam.'

'Thank you, but don't go. When we were chatting just now, there was a point I omitted to touch on.'

'Yes, madam?'

'It is this. Had you a mother, Phipps?'

'Yes, madam.'

'Had she a knee?'

'Yes, madam.'

'Then did you not learn at that knee to do the square thing by all and sundry and not to go about steeping yourself in crime?'

'No, madam.'

'H'm. Negligence somewhere. All right, Phipps. Push off. Don't forget those cocktails.'

'I will put them in preparation immediately, madam.'

The door closed.

'Now what would Phipps's mother be like?' mused Bill. 'Something on the lines of Queen Victoria, I imagine.' She turned to Joe. 'Did you say "Oh, hell"?'

'Yes.'

'I thought you did, and it wrung my heart. You take a dim view of the situation?'

'I do.'

'I don't. I have high hopes of Lord Topham.'

'What, after the way he was talking just now?'

'Forget the way he was talking just now. Since then his girl has called him on the transatlantic telephone. Girls don't dig down into their jeans for the price of a transatlantic telephone call unless love has reawakened in their hearts, dispelling like the morning sun the mists of doubt and misunderstanding. I shall be greatly surprised it this does not mean that the second phase has set in – where the female love bird weeps on the male love bird's chest and says can he ever forgive her for speaking those cruel words.'

'Oh, Bill!' cried Kay.

'If such is the case, I don't think I am wrong in assuming that the milk of human kindness will have come surging back into the Topham bosom like a tidal wave, sweetening his outlook and rendering him a good and easy prospect.'

Joe nodded.

'Gosh, I believe you're right.'

'I feel sure of it. We shall see a very different Lord Topham in a moment or two.'

'And then you'll talk to him?'

'And then I'll talk to him.'

Footsteps sounded in the corridor, gay, galloping footsteps. The door was dashed open, and something that might have been a ray of sunshine in form-fitting grey flannel came curvetting over the threshold.

'I say,' cried this new and improved edition of Lord Topham. 'Everything's fine. Everything's all right. Everything's splendid.'

Bill patted his shoulder, this time without provoking a protest.

'Precisely what I was hoping when I heard that your heart-throb was on the telephone. Get them calling up on the telephone, and it's in the bag. She loves you still?'

'Absolutely. She cried buckets, and I said: "There, there!" '

'You could hardly have put it more neatly.'

'She said she had a toothache when she sent that cable.'

'That soured her outlook?'

'Oh, definitely.'

'You mean absolutely, don't you?'

'That's right. Absolutely.'

'Well, well, well, I couldn't be more pleased. I'm delighted. We're all delighted. And now, Lord Topham, could you spare me a moment?'

'Oh, rather.'

'Fine.'

Bill led the young man to the sofa, deposited him there and took a seat at his side.

'Tell me, Lord Topham – or may I call you Topham?'

'Do. Or Toppy. Most of my pals call me Toppy.'

'What is your first name?'

'Lancelot. But I prefer to hush it up.'

'Then shall we settle for Toppy?'

'Absolutely.'

'Right. You notice I am patting your shoulder again, Toppy. Would you like to know why?'

'Very much. I was just wondering.'

'I do it in a congratulatory spirit. Because I am going, Toppy, old boy, to let you in on a big thing.'

'Really?'

'Absolutely. Tell me, my dear Toppy, have you ever seen a man in a fur coat, with three chins, riding in a Rolls-Royce with a blonde on each knee and smoking a five-dollar cigar? Because, if so, you can be pretty sure he was a literary agent.'

'A what?'

'A literary agent.'

'What's that?'

'A literary agent – or authors' representative – is a man who sits in an arm-chair with his feet on a desk, full of caviare and champagne, and gives a couple of minutes to the authors who come crawling in on all fours, begging him to handle their output. Should he consent to do so, he takes ten per cent of the kitty.'

'What kitty would that be?'

'I refer to all emoluments received from these authors' works, which amount to very large sums indeed. Thus, we will suppose that this authors' representative sells a story by some client of his to a prominent editor for – well, taking a figure at random, forty thousand dollars. His cut would be four thousand.'

'It sounds like a jolly good show.'

'It is a jolly good show. Four thousand bucks for telling his secretary to shove a wad of typescript into an envelope and address, stamp and mail it is unquestionably nice sugar. And it's going on all the time.'

'All the time?'

'Practically without cessation. You would be astounded if you knew the amount of money that pours into the coffers of an authors' representative. New clients every hour of the day coming in and pleading to be allowed to give him ten per cent. Well, take an instance. He is sitting in his office one day after a lunch of nightingales' tongues washed down with Imperial Tokay, and in comes someone whom for want of a better name we will call Erle Stanley Gardner. He says: "Good afternoon, my dear authors' representative, would you as a favour to me agree to accept a tenth of my annual earnings? I should mention that I write sixteen books a year, and if only I can get out of the habit of eating, I think I could work it up to twenty. In short, counting in everything, serial, motion picture, radio, television and other rights, I should imagine that your take-home pay on me alone would be at least fifty or sixty thousand dollars per annum. Will you accept me as a client, my dear authors' representative?" And the authors' representative yawns and says he will try to fit him in. "Thank you, thank you," says Erle Stanley Gardner, and goes out. And scarcely has he left than in come Sinclair Lewis and Somerset Maugham. They say: "Good afternoon . . ." and – well, you get the idea. It's a bonanza.'

'A what?'

'A gold mine.'

'Oh, absolutely.'

'I knew you would see it, my dear Toppy. I knew I could rely on your swift intelligence. You have a mind like a razor. Now then, the point is that Joe here and I have the opportunity of buying an old established business of this nature.'

'An authors' representative business?'

'Just that.'

'You'll make a fortune.'

'Exactly. The same thought occurred to me. We shall have to spend the rest of our lives thinking up ways of doing down the income tax authorities. And all we need, to begin operations—'

'You'll have more money than you know what to do with.'

'We shall sprain our wrists, clipping coupons. And all we need—'

'So what I would suggest,' said Lord Topham, 'is that you slip me a hundred dollars as a temporary loan.'

Bill swayed a little.

'Eh?'

'You see,' said Lord Topham, 'owing to circumstances over which I have no control and which give me a headache whenever

I try to understand them, I can't get a penny of my money out of England, not a solitary dashed penny. My pals tell me it's got something to do with there being a Labour Government, composed, as you doubtless know, of the most frightful cads and bounders. Well, this leaves me considerably strapped for the ready, so if you want to earn the undying gratitude of a bloke who is down to a cigarette case and a little small change, now's your chance.'

Bill looked up.

'Joe.'

'Yes?'

'Did you hear what I heard?'

'I did.'

'Then it wasn't just a ghastly dream.'

Lord Topham was going on to explain further.

'What put it into my mind to ask you was what you were saying about your extraordinary wealth. Here, on the one hand, I said to myself, is this dear, sweet creature rolling in the stuff, and here, on the other hand, am I, unable to raise a bean on account of the sinister goings-on of this bally Labour Government who go about seeking whom they may devour. So pretty naturally the thought floated into my mind "Well, dash it!" I mean, a hundred dollars means nothing to you . . .'

A weary look came into Bill's rugged face.

'Have you a hundred dollars, Joe? No, I remember you haven't. Then I suppose . . . Here you are, Toppy.'

'Thanks,' said Lord Topham. 'Thanks most awfully. Yo ho! You know what this means? It means that I can now go to Santa Anita this afternoon with a light heart, ready for any fate. Phipps tells me Betty Hutton is a snip for the fourth and . . . Well, in a nutshell, my dear good preserver, thanks awfully. May heaven bless you, my jolly old multi-millionairess. Yo ho!' said Lord Topham. 'Yo frightfully absolutely ho!'

He passed through the French windows on winged feet.

19

Bill drew a deep breath. Her face was careworn, as if hers was the head upon which all the sorrows of the world had come, and when at length she found speech, she spoke dully.

'So that's that,' she said. 'A disappointment, Joe.'

'Quite.'

'Upsetting.'

'Most.'

'Yes, distinctly upsetting. Until that last awful moment everything seemed to be going so well. It makes me feel as if I had been chasing rainbows and one of them had turned and bitten me in the leg. If only I had remembered to give a thought to existing financial conditions in the British Isles, I would have been spared a painful experience. My last hundred dollars — gone — just like that. And for what? To enable a goofy English peer to back his fancy on the Santa Anita racecourse. Oh, well, I suppose it all tends to make one more spiritual. Ah, Smedley,' she said, as the door opened. 'What news from the throbbing centre of things?'

Smedley was looking warm and glassy-eyed, like a sensitive director of a shaky limited liability company emerging from a stormy meeting of shareholders. It was plain that whatever had passed between him and his sister-in-law in the projection room had not been in the nature of a love feast.

'She's as mad as a wet hen,' he said.

'Too bad,' said Bill. 'One hates to cause Adela distress. What happened?'

'She swears we've got the thing.'

'She little knows. Did you try stout denial?'

'Yes, but it didn't do any good. You can't drive an idea out of Adela's head, once it's in it. You know what she's like.'

'I do, indeed.'

Smedley mopped his forehead. There was a suggestion in his

deportment of Shadrach, Meshach and Abednego coming out of the burning fiery furnace.

'Gosh, I'm a nervous wreck. I wish I had a drink.'

'Phipps will be bringing cocktails in a moment. Ah,' said Bill. 'Here, if I mistake not, is our client now.'

Phipps entered, bearing a loaded tray that tinkled musically. He laid it on the desk with his usual air of being a plenipotentiary to some great court delivering important documents.

'So what was the upshot?' said Bill.

'Eh?' said Smedley, who had been eyeing the cocktails.

'How did it all come out in the end?'

'Adela? Oh, she stuck to it that we had opened the safe, and she seemed to think you were the one who had got the diary. She put on a big act, and finished by saying she had phoned for the police.'

'What?'

A sudden light came into Bill's eye. Her despondency had left her. She was once more The Old Reliable in full command of the situation.

'The police are coming here? Then I think I see daylight. It's better than the arrival of the United States Marines. Phipps!'

'Madam?'

'I greatly fear, Phipps, that you are in a spot. Did you hear what Mr Smedley said?'

'No, madam. My attention was occupied with depositing the cocktails, madam.'

Bill gave him a sympathetic look.

'Stick close to those cocktails, Brother Phipps. You'll be needing one in just a moment. Mr Smedley said that Mrs Cork has sent for the cops.'

'Indeed, madam?'

'I admire your icy coolness. In your place I would be trembling like a leaf.'

'I do not follow your drift, madam.'

'I will continue snowing. The officers of the Law are on their way here, and what will they do when they get here, these officers of the Law? They will spread a dragnet. They will case the joint. They will go through the place with a fine-tooth comb.'

'So I imagine, madam.'

'They will find your hiding-place, the secret nook where you have cached that diary. And then what?'

The butler remained politely puzzled.

'Are you hinting that they might suspect me of the robbery, madam?'

Bill laughed raspingly.

'Well, considering that you have an established place in the hall of fame as an expert safeblower, whom else would they suspect? It begins to look like a sticky week-end for you, Phipps.'

'I disagree with you, madam. It is true that the constables will probably discover the object under advisement, but I have merely to explain that in abstracting it I was operating on Mr Smedley's behalf. My position was that of an agent acting for a principal.'

Bill raised her eyebrows.

'I don't understand you. Are you suggesting that you were *asked* to open the safe? You don't know anything about this, do you, Smedley?'

'Not a thing.'

'You never asked Phipps to open the safe?'

'Certainly not.'

'Did you, Joe?'

'No.'

'Kay?'

'No.'

'Nor did I. The trouble with you, Phipps, is that you will insist on trying to hide your light beneath a bushel. Quite independently and on your own you conceive this brilliant idea of busting the safe and pinching its contents, and you try to give the credit to others. It shows a generous spirit which one cannot help but admire, and in recognition of our admiration we should like to do something for you. Hand the thing over to Mr Smedley, and he will take charge of it. Then you won't have anything to worry about. You follow my reasoning?'

'Yes, madam.'

'I thought you would. Go and get it.'

'I have it on my person, madam.'

Without any visible emotion the butler drew the book from his pocket, placed it on a salver and brought it to Smedley, who took it like a trout jumping at a fly.

'Would there be anything further, madam?'

'No, thank you, Phipps. You will receive your agent's commission, of course.'

Smedley started.

'What, after this?'

'Certainly. We must keep the books straight. And we agents stick together. You will receive your cut in due course, Phipps.'

'Thank you, madam.'

'Sorry you have been troubled.'

'Not at all, madam.'

'After all, you have your Art.'

'Precisely, madam,' said Phipps, and made a decorous withdrawal.

Joe was eyeing Bill devoutly, like a man gazing at some great public monument. His feelings were for a moment too deep for utterance, but eventually he managed to tell Bill she was a marvel.

'She certainly is,' said Kay.

'She ought to have that brain of hers pickled and presented to some national museum,' said Smedley, equally enthusiastic.

'When she's done with it.'

'When she's done with it, of course,' assented Smedley. 'Well, I'm off to see that gardener at the Lulabelle Mahaffys, to get him to translate this thing for me. I shall be in a stronger position to bargain with those fellows at Colossal-Exquisite if I know what's in it.'

'You are going to close with Colossal-Exquisite's offer?' said Bill.

'If it's still firm. Fifty thousand dollars is a nice round sum.'

Bill agreed.

'Very nice. Very round. Yes, I'd take it. Get their cheque, lay aside five thousand for Phipps, slip Joe and me our twenty thousand, and you'll be set.'

Smedley, who had been making for the French windows, briskly like a man to whom time is money, paused. He seemed perplexed.

'Joe and you? Twenty thousand? I don't get this. What are you talking about?'

'For the literary agency.'

'What literary agency?'

'You told me you would put up the money for it,' said Joe.

Smedley stared.

'I said I would put up money for a literary agency? When?'

'The night before last. When we were at Mocambo.'

'This is the first I have heard of this.'

'What! But we were talking about it for hours. Don't you remember?'

Bill was looking grave.

'I was afraid this might happen, Joe. Smedley has a memory like a sieve.'

Smedley bridled.

'I have an excellent memory,' he said stiffly. 'But I certainly have not the slightest recollection of ever having heard a literary agency mentioned. What is this literary agency?'

'The one Bill and I want to buy.'

'And you construed some passing remark of mine into a promise that I would lend you the money?'

'Passing remark be damned. We discussed it for about an hour and a half. You kept patting me on the back and telling me over and over again—'

Smedley shook his head.

'Some mistake. The thing's absurd on the face of it. I wouldn't put up money for a literary agency. Much too risky. I'm going to go back to New York and get into the producing game again. I shall take an office and let it be known that I am prepared to consider scripts. Bless my soul, it will be quite like old times. Well, I can't stand here talking,' said Smedley. 'See you all later.'

He went out, and Joe and Kay, after an instant's stunned silence, came to life and bounded after him. Their voices died away across the garden, and Bill sat down at the dictaphone.

'Ah, Hollywood, Hollywood,' said Bill. 'Home of mean glories and spangled wretchedness, where the deathless fire burns for the outspread wings of the guileless moth, whose streets are bathed in the shamed tears of betrayed maidens.'

She looked up as the door opened.

'Ah, Adela,' she said welcomingly. 'I thought you might be looking in. Yo ho! Yo frightfully absolutely ho!'

20

Adela was looking even more formidable than usual, and her voice when, after fixing Bill for some moments with a baleful stare, she finally spoke, vibrated with stormy emotion.

'So there you are, Wilhelmina.'

It took more than a vibrating voice to lower Bill's morale. She nodded with what seemed to her sister insufferable heartiness.

'Yes, here I am, working away as always. I was just recording your views on Hollywood at the time when Bioscope wouldn't give you a job.'

Adela continued to stare balefully.

'Never mind my views on Hollywood. Wilhelmina, I would like a word with you.'

'A thousand.'

'Five will do. Wilhelmina, where is that diary?'

Bill wrinkled her forehead.

'Diary? Diary?' Her face cleared. 'Oh, you mean the one you were taking care of for Smedley? Isn't it in your safe?'

'You know very well it is not in my safe.'

'I thought you put it there.'

'I did, and it is there no longer. I will give you two minutes to produce it.'

'Me?'

'After that I wash my hands of the matter and the Law can take its course.'

Bill held up a hand.

'Wait. It's coming back. Yes, I thought that line was familiar. It was a sub-title in your *Gilded Sinners*. Do you remember? Where you came in and found your sister burgling the safe?'

'As happened last night.'

'I don't understand you.'

Her pent-up feelings were too much for Adela. She picked up a cocktail glass and flung it emotionally against the opposite wall.

'Sweet artichokes of Jerusalem!' she cried. 'Do you want it in words of one syllable? Then you shall have it. You – stole – that – diary.'

'Diary is three syllables.'

There was a pause. Bill, too, picked up a cocktail glass, but with the intention of making a better use of it than her sister had done. She rattled the shaker with pleasurable anticipation. No other sound broke the silence. Adela was clenching and unclenching her fists, and her eyes were stony. Her late husband, Alfred Cork, encountering her in this mood one morning after he had been out all night playing poker, had taken one look at her and left for Mexico City without stopping to pack. On Bill her demeanour seemed to have made a less pronounced impression. She filled her glass, and drank its amber contents with a satisfied sigh.

'Well?' said Adela. 'Are you going to have the effrontery to deny it?'

Bill seemed amused. She refilled her glass, paying a silent tribute to the absent Phipps. Jimmy Phipps might be about as slippery a customer as ever breathed the pure air of Beverly Hills, with a moral code which would have caused comment in Alcatraz, but he knew how to mix cocktails.

'But, my dear Adela, I can't open safes.'

'You have friends who can. Your friends are well known to be the scum of the earth, thugs who would stick at nothing.'

'The only friend of mine on the premises last night was Joe Davenport, and you can hardly suspect Joe of being a safe-blower. Why, you might just as well suspect Phipps. No,' said Bill, sipping the butler's masterpiece reverently. 'An outside job, if you ask me.'

'An outside job!'

'That's right. Probably the work of an international gang. Damn' clever, these international gangs. Have a cocktail?'

'I will not have a cocktail.'

'You're missing something good. Unlike the international gang.'

Bill's respect for Phipps deepened. The man seemed to have everything. Not only could he mix the perfect martini, but as a word-painter he stood second to none. He had described Adela as looking like a Welsh rarebit about to come to the height of its fever, and it was such a Welsh rarebit at the critical stage of its preparation that she now resembled. In times of crisis,

Smedley was a great shaker in every limb, but he would have had to yield first place to Adela Shannon Cork.

'So you wish me to believe,' said Adela, having struggled with her feelings, 'that it was just a coincidence that my safe was burgled on the one night when it contained that diary?'

'A pure coincidence.'

'A pretty coincidence.'

'And I'm afraid, a most unfortunate coincidence – for you.'

Adela stared.

'What do you mean?'

Bill shrugged her shoulders.

'Surely it's obvious?'

'Not to me.'

Bill's manner became grave. There was concern in it, and sympathy. She hesitated a moment, as if reluctant to break the bad news. One could see she was sorry for Adela.

'Well, consider your position,' she said. 'Smedley had a firm offer of fifty thousand dollars for that diary. He wanted to keep it on his person, but you officiously insisted on taking it from him and putting it in your safe. In other words, you voluntarily assumed full responsibility for it.'

'Nonsense.'

'You won't find it nonsense when Smedley brings a suit against you for fifty thousand dollars.'

'What?'

'Don't forget that he has three witnesses to testify that you took the thing against his expressed wishes. There isn't a jury in America that won't give him your head on a charger.'

'Nonsense.'

'Keep on saying "Nonsense", if it comforts you. I'm merely stating the cold facts. Fifty thousand dollars is what that intelligent jury will award to Smedley, without so much as leaving the jury box. Fortunately you're a millionairess, so it doesn't matter to you. Unless you're one of those women who don't like having to pay out fifty thousand dollars. Some women don't.'

Adela groped her way to the sofa and collapsed on it.

'But . . . but . . .'

'I told you you ought to have a cocktail.'

'But this is absurd.'

'Not absurd. Disastrous. I can't see how the cleverest lawyer could make out any case for you. Smedley will win hands down.'

Adela had taken out her handkerchief and was twisting it agitatedly. Much, if not all, of her stormy emotion had been drained from her. When she spoke, there was quite a fluttering note in her voice.

'But, Wilhelmina—'

'Yes, Adela?'

'But, Wilhelmina, can't you reason with Smedley?'

Bill finished her cocktail and sighed contentedly.

'Now we're getting down to it,' she said with satisfaction. 'Now we're arriving somewhere. I *have* reasoned with Smedley.'

'You have?'

'Yes, he was in here just now, breathing fire and fury. I never saw a man so worked up. Adamant, he was. Insisted on the full amount and not a cent less. You should have seen him striding about the room like a tiger. I doubted at first if I would be able to do anything with him. But I kept after him. I pointed out what a nuisance these lawsuits were and urged him to agree to a settlement. And in the end, you'll be glad to hear, I beat him down to thirty thousand.'

'Thirty thousand!'

'I knew you'd be pleased,' said Bill. She looked at her sister incredulously. 'Do you mean you *aren't* pleased?'

Adela choked.

'It's highway robbery.'

Bill could not follow her.

'I would call it a perfectly ordinary business transaction. Owing to you, Smedley is down fifty thousand dollars. He very decently agrees to accept thirty. Pretty square of him, I should have said. Still, have it your own way. Let him bring his suit, if that's the way you want it. If you would rather pay fifty thousand than thirty thousand, that's your affair. Eccentric, though, it seems to me.'

'But, Wilhelmina—'

Bill pointed out another aspect of the matter.

'Of course, it will mean a lot of unpleasant publicity, I'm afraid. You won't show up well at the trial, you know. The impression the public will get from the evidence is that you're the sort of woman who is not to be trusted alone with anything that isn't nailed down. When your friends see you coming, they will hurriedly store their little valuables in a stout chest and sit on the lid till you are out of sight. Louella Parsons is hardly likely to refrain from comment on the affair, nor is Hedda

Hopper. And I should imagine that the *Hollywood Reporter* would consider you front-page stuff. But as I say,' said Bill, 'have it your own way.'

The picture she had conjured up decided Adela. She rose.

'Oh, very well.' She paused for a moment, to overcome a sudden urge to scream and break the remaining cocktail glasses. 'It's an outrage, but . . . Oh, very well.'

Bill nodded approvingly. One likes to see one's flesh and blood reasonable.

'Good,' she said. 'I'm glad you're taking the sensible view. Trot along to your boudoir and write the cheque. Make it out to me. Smedley has appointed me his agent, to handle the affair.' She accompanied Adela to the door. 'Gosh, how relieved you must be feeling,' she said. 'You would probably like to go into a buck and wing dance.'

Phipps appeared.

'The constables are here, madam.'

'Oh, damn the constables,' said Adela, and sailed past him.

Bill gave the butler a grave look.

'You must excuse Mrs Cork, Phipps, if she is a little brusque. She has just had a bereavement.'

'I am sorry, madam.'

'I, too. Still, these things are sent to us for a purpose. Maybe to make us more spiritual.'

'Quite possibly, madam.'

'You're looking a bit spiritual yourself, Phipps.'

'Thank you, madam.'

'Not at all. Show the officers in.'

'Very good, madam.'

Joe and Kay came through the French windows. They were looking dejected.

'Well?' said Bill.

'No luck,' said Joe.

'He wouldn't listen,' said Kay.

This caused Bill no surprise.

'Smedley is a bad listener. He reminds me of the deaf adder with whom the charmers had so much trouble. But cheer up, Joe. All is well.'

Joe stared.

'All is *what*?'

'Everything's fine.'

'Who says so?'

'I say so.'

'The constables, madam,' announced Phipps.

Sergeant Ward entered, followed by Patrolman Morehouse. Bill greeted them effusively.

'Well, well, well,' she said. 'How delightful seeing you again.'

'Good morning, ma'am.'

'I was thinking only just now how nice it would be if you were to drop in once more. Too often in this world we meet a strange face and say to ourselves: "Have I found a friend? I believe I have found a friend. Yes, by golly, I'm *sure* I've found a friend," and then – *bing* – the face pops off and you never see it again.' She peered at them. 'But you're looking extra-ordinarily cheerful,' she said. 'Has some good fortune come your way?'

The sergeant beamed. The patrolman beamed.

'I'll say it has,' said the patrolman. 'Tell her, sarge.'

'Well, ma'am,' said the sergeant, his granite face wreathed in smiles, 'we've done it.'

'You don't mean—?'

'Yes, ma'am. Got a call this morning from the Medulla-Oblongata-Glutz casting office. We start tomorrow.'

'Well, well. Joy cometh in the morning.'

'Yes, ma'am. Of course, it's only extra work.'

'Only extra work right now,' said Patrolman Morehouse.

'Sure,' said Sergeant Ward. 'Just for the moment. We expect to rise in our profession.'

'Of course you'll rise,' said Bill. 'Like rockets. First, extra work, then bit parts, then big parts, then bigger parts, and finally stardom.'

'Ah!' said the sergeant. 'Hot dog!'

'Hot dog,' said the patrolman.

'You'll be bigger than Gary Cooper.'

'Hell, yes,' said the sergeant. 'What's Gary Cooper ever done?'

Adela came in. She had a slip of paper in her hand, but there was nothing in her demeanour to indicate that she enjoyed carrying it. She came to Bill and gave it to her, reluctantly, like a woman parting with life blood.

'There,' she said.

'Thank you, Adela.'

'And may I remark that I wish you had been strangled at birth.'

The sergeant saluted.

'You sent for us, ma'am?'

'Yes,' said Bill, 'but it was a mistake. My sister thought her safe had been robbed last night. It wasn't.'

'Ah? Well, that's how it goes,' said the sergeant.

'That's how it goes,' said the patrolman.

'Good morning,' said Adela.

'Good morning, ma'am,' said the sergeant.

'Hey!' said the patrolman. 'Excuse me, lady, but may I have your autograph, ma'am?'

Adela paused at the door. She swallowed once or twice before speaking.

'You may not,' she said. 'And one more word out of you on the subject of autographs – or any other subject – and I'll pull your fat head off and make you swallow it. Good MORNING.'

The door slammed. The sergeant looked at the patrolman. The patrolman looked at the sergeant.

'Women!' said the sergeant.

'Women!' said the patrolman.

'Can you beat them!' said the sergeant.

'Why, yes,' said Bill. 'Sometimes. But you need to be a woman yourself and very, very clever – like me. Here, Joe,' she said, and handed him the cheque.

He looked at it listlessly, then staggered.

'Bill! Good heavens, Bill!'

Bill patted her chest.

'The Old Reliable!' she said. 'Which way did Smedley go? I want a word with him.'

21

The home of the Lulabelle Mahaffys, whose gardens were tended by the Mexican gentleman with whom Smedley had gone to confer, stood some two hundred yards down the road from the Carmen Flores place, and it did not take Bill long to cover the distance. She had just arrived in sight of the gate, when she saw Smedley come out and start walking toward her. He was whistling, and there was a jauntiness in his step which bespoke the soul at rest.

'Well?' she said. 'Did you see him?'

'Oh, hello, Bill,' said Smedley. 'No, he wasn't there. It's his day off. But it doesn't matter. I was just coming back to ask you to lend me that jalopy of yours. I want to go down and see those people at Colossal-Exquisite. Bless my soul,' said Smedley, casting an approving glance at the blue sky, 'what a glorious day.'

'For you.'

Smedley was not a man of quick perceptions, but even he could appreciate that this morning, which had brought such happiness to him, had been more sparing with the ecstasy as regarded others. He recalled now what he had neglected to observe at the time of their meeting, that both his niece Kay and that young fellow Davenport had exhibited not a few signs of distress of mind when chatting with him.

'What was all that nonsense young Davenport was talking about a literary agency?' he asked. 'He seemed very excited about it, but I was too busy to listen.'

'Joe and I were thinking of buying one.'

'You? Are you in it too?'

'That's right. As was carefully explained to you. You're like a Wednesday matinée audience, Smedley. You miss the finer points.'

Smedley puffed – remorsefully, it seemed.

'Well, I'm sorry, Bill.'

'Don't give it a thought.'

'But you can understand how I'm placed, a sensible woman like you. I can't afford to go putting up money for literary agencies.'

'You prefer something safer and more conservative, like backing shows on Broadway?'

'That's where the big money is,' said Smedley defensively. 'How much do you think someone would have made if they'd bought in on *Oklahoma*?'

'Or *South Pacific*.'

'Or *Arsenic And Old Lace*.'

'Or *Ladies, I Beg You*,' said Bill, mentioning the little stinker adapted from the French which had cost the other the last thousands of his waning capital.

Smedley blushed. He did not like to be reminded of *Ladies, I Beg You*.

'That was just an unfortunate accident.'

'So that's what you call it?'

'It can't happen again. I shall be bringing to the business now a wealth of experience and a ripened judgement.'

'Ripened judgement, did you say?'

'Ripened judgement.'

'I see. Ripened judgement. God bless you, Smedley,' said Bill, giving him the tender look a mother gives her idiot child. She was feeling, not for the first time, that it was criminal to allow her old friend to run around loose, without a woman's hand to guide him. Somewhere in America, she told herself, there might be a more pronounced fathead than this man she had loved so long, but it would be a weary search, trying to find him.

A klaxon tooted in their rear. If it is possible for a tooter to toot respectfully and deferentially, this tooter did. They turned, and saw approaching a natty little roadster, at whose wheel sat Phipps. It is a very impoverished butler in Beverly Hills who does not own his natty little roadster.

He drew up beside them, and Bill noted suitcases on the seat. It seemed that Phipps was flitting.

'Hello, my bright and bounding Phipps,' she said. 'You off?'

'Yes, madam.'

'Leaving us for good?'

'Yes, madam.'

'Rather sudden?'

'Yes, madam. Strictly speaking my tenure of office should not

have expired until the day after tomorrow, but I chanced to
encounter Mrs Cork not long since, and she expressed a wish
that I should curtail my stay.'

'She told you to get out?'

'That was substantially the purport of her words, madam.
Mrs Cork seemed somewhat stirred.'

'I told you she had had a bereavement.'

'Yes, madam.'

'So this . . . is goodbye?'

'Yes, madam.'

Bill dabbed at her eyes.

'Well, it's been nice seeing you.'

'Thank you, madam.'

'I'll say this for you, Brother Phipps, that when you're
around, there's never a dull moment. We part with no hard
feelings, I trust?'

'Madam?'

'About that diary.'

'Oh, no, madam. None whatever.'

'I'm glad you can take the big, broad view.'

'I find it easier to do so, madam, because the brochure which
I handed to Mr Smedley at the conclusion of our recent
conversation was not the diary of the late Miss Flores.'

Smedley, who had been gazing stiffly into the middle distance, as if resolved not to show himself aware of the presence
of one whom he considered, and always would consider, a viper
of the first water, suddenly ceased to be aloof and detached. He
transferred his gaze to the butler, and his eyes popped, as was
their custom when he was deeply moved.

'What?'

'No, sir.'

'What are you talking about?'

'It was a little thing I borrowed from the cook, sir.'

'But it's in Spanish.'

'I think you will find that it is not, sir, if you will examine
it, sir.'

Smedley whipped the volume from his pocket, gave it a quick
glance and registered triumph.

'Spanish!'

'You are mistaken, sir.'

'Damn it, man, look for yourself.'

Phipps took the book in his deferential way.

'Yes, sir, I was wrong.' He put the book in his pocket. 'You are quite right, sir. Spanish. Good day, sir. Good day, madam.'

He placed a shapely foot on the accelerator.

'Hey!' cried Smedley.

But there was no answer. Phipps had said his say. The car gathered speed. It turned the corner, beyond which lay the broad road leading to Beverly Hills. Like some lovely dream that vanishes at daybreak, James Phipps had gone out of their lives.

That Smedley was reluctant to see him go was manifest in his whole bearing. He did not actually say 'Oh, for the touch of a vanished hand!' but the words were implicit in his actions. Breaking into a clumsy gallop, he started in pursuit. But these natty roadsters are hard to catch, particularly if you are a man of elderly middle age and sedentary habits. If Smedley had been capable of doing the quarter-mile in forty-nine seconds, he might have accomplished something to his advantage, but his distance was the ten-yard dash, and he was not very good even at that.

Presently he came back to Bill, panting and passing a hand-kerchief over a streaming brow, and Bill stared at him with honest amazement.

'If I hadn't seen it with my own eyes,' said Bill, 'I wouldn't have believed it. You *gave* it to him. You handed it to him. If you had served it up to him on an individual skewer smothered in onions, you couldn't have done more.'

Smedley writhed beneath her scorn.

'Well, how could I know he was going to—'

'Of course you couldn't,' said Bill. 'After having exactly the same thing happen yesterday with Adela, how could the thought have entered your mind? And what possible reason could you have to suspect a man like Phipps of anything in the least resembling raw work? All your dealings with him must have established him in your mind as a stainless soul and a paragon of spotless rectitude. Honestly, Smedley, you ought to be in some sort of home.'

'Well, I—'

'Or married,' said Bill.

Smedley quivered as if the two simple words had been a couple of harpoons plunged into his shrinking flesh. He shot an apprehensive look at Bill, and did not like the determined expression on her rugged face.

'Yes,' she said, 'that's what you need – marriage. You want someone to look after you and shield you from the world, and by the greatest good luck I know the very woman to do it. Smedley, I have been potty about you for twenty years – heaven knows why—'

'Bill, please!'

'And, if you didn't suspect it, what probably misled you was the fact that I never told my love, but let concealment like a worm i' the bud feed on my damask cheek. I pined in thought, and with a green and yellow melancholy—'

'No, Bill, really!'

'—sat like Patience on a monument, smiling at grief. But now I have changed my act, and, like Adela, I intend to stand no nonsense. I cannot offer you luxury, Smedley. All I have to lay at your feet is a literary agency which Adela is backing to the tune of thirty thousand dollars.'

Smedley had not supposed that anything would have had the power to divert his mind from the hideous vision of matrimony which her words had brought before his eyes, but this did.

'Adela?' he gasped. 'She's given you thirty thousand dollars?'

'With a merry smile and a jolly pat on the back. And tomorrow Joe and I start for New York and get our noses down to the grindstone. It will be hard work, of course, and it would be nice to have you at our side, doing your bit. For I am convinced that in a literary agency you would find your niche, Smedley. You have the presence which would impress authors. I can just see you giving them five minutes. Editors, too. That Roman Emperor deportment of yours would lay editors out cold. But I can see why you hesitate. You are reluctant to give up your life of luxury under Adela's roof, with yoghurt flowing like water and Adela always on hand for a stimulating chat . . . By the way, I wonder how you stand with Adela just now. She may be the least bit sore with you after all that has occurred, and when Adela is sore with anyone, she shows it in her manner.'

Smedley paled.

'Oh, gosh!'

'Yes, you may not find those chats with her so stimulating, after all. You'd better marry me, Smedley.'

'But, Bill—'

'I am only speaking for your own good.'

'But, Bill . . . Marriage . . .'

'What's wrong with marriage? It's fine. Why, look at the men who liked it so much that, once started, they couldn't stop, and just went on marrying everything in sight. Look at Brigham Young. Look at Henry the Eighth. Look at King Solomon. Those boys knew when they were on a good thing.'

Out of the night that covered him, black as the pit from pole to pole, there shone on Smedley a faint glimmer of light. Something like hope dawned in him. He weighed what she had just said.

Brigham Young – Henry the Eighth – King Solomon – knowledgeable fellows, all of them, men whose judgement you could trust. And they had liked being married, so much so that, as Bill had indicated, they made a regular hobby of it. Might it not quite easily prove, mused Smedley, that marriage was not, as it was generally called, the fate that is worse than death, but something that has its points?

Bill saw his drawn face light up. She linked her arm in his and gave it a squeeze.

'Wilt thou, Smedley,' she said, 'take this Wilhelmina?'

'I will,' said Smedley in a low but firm voice.

Bill kissed him tenderly.

'That's my little man,' she said. 'This afternoon we'll go out in my jalopy and start pricing ministers.'

SHORT STORIES

Monkey Business

A Tankard of Stout had just squashed a wasp as it crawled on the arm of Miss Postlethwaite, our popular barmaid, and the conversation in the bar-parlour of the Anglers' Rest had turned to the subject of physical courage.

The Tankard himself was inclined to make light of the whole affair, urging modestly that his profession, that of a fruit-farmer, gave him perhaps a certain advantage over his fellow-men when it came to dealing with wasps.

'Why, sometimes in the picking season,' said the Tankard, 'I've had as many as six standing on each individual plum, rolling their eyes at me and daring me to come on.'

Mr Mulliner looked up from his hot Scotch and Lemon.

'Suppose they had been gorillas?' he said.

The Tankard considered this. 'There wouldn't be room,' he argued, 'not on an ordinary-sized plum.'

'Gorillas?' said a Small Bass, puzzled.

'And I'm sure if it had been a gorilla Mr Bunyan would have squashed it just same,' said Miss Postlethwaite, and she gazed at the Tankard with whole-hearted admiration in her eyes.

Mr Mulliner smiled gently.

'Strange,' he said, 'how even in these orderly civilized days women still worship heroism in the male. Offer them wealth, brains, looks, amiability, skill at card-tricks or at playing the ukulele . . . unless these are accompanied by physical courage they will turn away in scorn.'

'Why gorillas?' asked the Small Bass, who liked to get these things settled.

'I was thinking of a distant cousin of mine whose life became for a time considerably complicated owing to one of these animals. Indeed, it was the fact that this gorilla's path crossed his that nearly lost Montrose Mulliner the hand of Rosalie Beamish.'

The Small Bass still appeared mystified.

'I shouldn't have thought anybody's path *would* have crossed a gorilla's. I'm forty-five next birthday, and I've never so much as seen a gorilla.'

'Possibly Mr Mulliner's cousin was a big-game hunter,' said a Gin Fizz.

'No,' said Mr Mulliner. 'He was an assistant director in the employment of the Perfecto-Zizzbaum Motion Picture Corporation of Hollywood: and the gorilla of which I speak was one of the cast of the super film *Black Africa*, a celluloid epic of the clashing of elemental passions in a land where might is right and the strong man comes into his own. Its capture in its native jungle was said to have cost the lives of seven half-dozen members of the expedition, and at the time when this story begins it was lodged in a stout cage on the Perfecto-Zizzbaum lot at a salary of seven hundred and fifty dollars a week, with billing guaranteed in letters not smaller than those of Edmund Wigham and Luella Benstead, the stars.'

In ordinary circumstances (said Mr Mulliner) this gorilla would have been to my distant cousin Montrose merely one of a thousand fellow-workers on the lot. If you had asked him, he would have said that he wished the animal every kind of success in its chosen profession, but that, for all the chance there was of them ever, as it were, getting together, they were just ships that pass in the night. It is doubtful, indeed, if he would even have bothered to go down to its cage and look at it, had not Rosalie Beamish asked him to do so. As he put it to himself, if a man's duties brought him into constant personal contact with Mr Schnellenhamer, the President of the Corporation, where was the sense of wasting time looking at gorillas? *Blasé* about sums up his attitude.

But Rosalie was one of the extra girls in *Black Africa* and so had a natural interest in a brother-artist. And as she and Montrose were engaged to be married her word, of course, was law. Montrose had been planning to play draughts that afternoon with his friend, George Pybus, of the Press department, but he good-naturedly cancelled the fixture and accompanied Rosalie to the animal's headquarters.

He was more than ordinarily anxious to oblige her today, because they had recently been having a little tiff. Rosalie had been urging him to go to Mr Schnellenhamer and ask for a rise of salary; and this Montrose, who was excessively timid by nature, was reluctant to do. There was something about being asked to pay out money that always aroused the head of the firm's worst passions.

When he met his betrothed outside the commissary, he was relieved to find her in a more amiable mood than she had been of late. She prattled merrily of this and that as they walked along, and Montrose was congratulating himself that there was not a cloud in the sky when, arriving at the cage, he found Captain Jack Fosdyke there, prodding at the gorilla with a natty cane.

This Captain Jack Fosdyke was a famous explorer who had been engaged to superintend the production of *Black Africa*. And the fact that Rosalie's professional duties necessitated a rather close association with him had caused Montrose a good deal of uneasiness. It was not that he did not trust her, but love makes a man jealous and he knew the fascination of these lean, brown, hard-bitten adventurers of the wilds.

As they came up, the explorer turned, and Montrose did not like the chummy look in the eye which he cocked at the girl. Nor, for the matter of that, did he like the other's bold smile. And he wished that in addressing Rosalie Captain Fosdyke would not preface his remarks with the words 'Ah, there, girlie.'

'Ah, there, girlie,' said the Captain. 'Come to see the monk?'

Rosalie was staring open-mouthed through the bars.

'Doesn't he look fierce!' she cried.

Captain Jack Fosdyke laughed carelessly.

'Tchah!' he said, once more directing the ferrule of his cane at the animal's ribs. 'If you had led the rough, tough, slam-bang, every-man-for-himself life I have, you wouldn't be frightened of gorillas. Bless my soul, I remember once in Equatorial Africa I was strolling along with my elephant gun and my trusty native bearer, 'Mlongi, and a couple of the brutes dropped out of a tree and started throwing their weight about and behaving as if the place belonged to them. I soon put a stop to that, I can tell you. Bang, bang, left and right, and two more skins for my collection. You have to be firm with gorillas. Dining anywhere tonight, girlie?'

'I am dining with Mr Mulliner at the Brown Derby.'

'Mr who?'

'This is Mr Mulliner.'

'Oh, that?' said Captain Fosdyke, scrutinizing Montrose in a supercilious sort of way as if he had just dropped out of a tree before him. 'Well, some other time, eh?'

And, giving the gorilla a final prod, he sauntered away.

Rosalie was silent for a considerable part of the return journey. When at length she spoke it was in a vein that occasioned Montrose the gravest concern.

'Isn't he wonderful!' she breathed. 'Captain Fosdyke, I mean.'

'Yes?' said Montrose coldly.

'I think he's splendid. So strong, so intrepid. Have you asked Mr Schnellenhamer for that raise yet?'

'Er . . . no,' said Montrose. 'I am – how shall I put it? – biding my time.'

There was another silence.

'Captain Fosdyke isn't afraid of Mr Schnellenhamer,' said Rosalie pensively. 'He slaps him on the back.'

'Nor am I afraid of Mr Schnellenhamer,' replied Montrose, stung. 'I would slap him on the back myself if I considered that it would serve any useful end. My delay in asking for that raise is simply due to the fact that in these matters of finance a certain tact and delicacy have to be observed. Mr Schnellenhamer is a busy man, and I have enough consideration not to intrude my personal affairs on him at a time when he is occupied with other matters.'

'I see,' said Rosalie, and there the matter rested. But Montrose remained uneasy. There had been a gleam in her eyes and a rapt expression on her face as she spoke of Captain Fosdyke which he had viewed with concern. Could it be, he asked himself, that she was falling a victim to the man's undeniable magnetism? He decided to consult his friend, George Pybus, of the Press department, on the matter. George was a knowledgeable young fellow and would doubtless have something constructive to suggest.

George Pybus listened to his tale with interest and said it reminded him of a girl he had loved and lost in Des Moines, Iowa.

'She ditched me for a prizefighter,' said George. 'No getting away from it, girls do get fascinated by the strong, tough male.'

Montrose's heart sank.

'You don't really think—?'

'It is difficult to say. One does not know how far this thing has gone. But I certainly feel that we must lose no time in drafting out some scheme whereby you shall acquire a glamour which will counteract the spell of this Fosdyke. I will devote a good deal of thought to the matter.'

And it was on the very next afternoon, as he sat with Rosalie in the commissary sharing with her a Steak Pudding Marlene Dietrich, that Montrose noticed that the girl was in the grip of some strong excitement.

'Monty,' she exclaimed, almost before she had dug out the first kidney, 'do you know what Captain Fosdyke said this morning?'

Montrose choked.

'If that fellow has been insulting you,' he cried, 'I'll . . . Well, I shall be extremely annoyed,' he concluded with a good deal of heat.

'Don't be silly. He wasn't talking to me. He was speaking to Luella Benstead. You know she's getting married again soon . . .'

'Odd how these habits persist.'

'. . . and Captain Fosdyke said why didn't she get married in the gorilla's cage. For the publicity.'

'He did?'

Montrose laughed heartily. A quaint idea, he felt. Bizarre, even.

'She said she wouldn't dream of it. And then Mr Pybus, who happened to be standing by, suddenly got the most wonderful idea. He came up to me and said why shouldn't you and I get married in the gorilla's cage.'

Montrose's laughter died away. 'You and I?'

'Yes.'

'George Pybus suggested that?'

'Yes.'

Montrose groaned in spirit. He was telling himself he might have known something like this would have been the result of urging a member of the Press department to exercise his intellect. The brains of members of the Press departments of motion-picture studios resemble soup at a cheap restaurant. It is wiser not to stir them.

'Think what a sensation it would make! No more extra work for me after that. I'd get parts, and good ones. A girl can't get anywhere in this business without publicity.'

Montrose licked his lips. They had become very dry. He was thinking harshly of George Pybus. It was just loose talking like George Pybus's, he felt, that made half the trouble in this world.

'But don't you feel,' he said, 'that there is something a little undignified about publicity? In my opinion, a true artist ought to be above it. And I think you should not overlook another, extremely vital aspect of the matter. I refer to the deleterious effect which such an exhibition as Pybus suggests would have upon those who read about it in the papers. Speaking for myself,' said Montrose, 'there is nothing I should enjoy more than a quiet wedding in a gorilla's cage. But has one the right to pander to the morbid tastes of a sensation-avid public? I am not a man who often speaks of these deeper things – on the surface, no doubt, I seem careless and happy-go-lucky – but I do hold very serious views on a citizen's duties in this fevered modern age. I consider that each one of us should do all that lies in his power to fight the ever-growing trend of the public mind towards the morbid and the hectic. I have a very real feeling that the body politic can never become healthy while this appetite for sensation persists. If America is not to go the way of Babylon and Rome, we must come back to normalcy and the sane outlook. It is not much that a man in my humble position can do to stem the tide, but at least I can refrain from adding fuel to its flames by getting married in gorillas' cages.'

Rosalie was gazing at him incredulously.

'You don't mean you won't do it?'

'It would not be right.'

'I believe you're scared.'

'Nothing of the kind. It is purely a question of civic conscience.'

'You *are* scared. To think,' said Rosalie vehemently, 'that I should have linked my lot with a man who's afraid of a teentsy-weentsy gorilla.'

Montrose could not let this pass.

'It is not a teentsy-weentsy gorilla. I should describe the animal's muscular development as well above the average.

'And the keeper would be outside the cage with a spiked stick.'

'*Outside* the cage!' said Montrose thoughtfully.

Rosalie sprang to her feet in sudden passion.

'Goodbye!'

'But you haven't finished your steak-pudding.'

'Goodbye,' she repeated. 'I see now what your so-called love is worth. If you are going to start denying me every little thing before we're married, what would you be like after? I'm glad I have discovered your true character. Our engagement is at an end.'

Montrose was pale to the lips, but he tried to reason with her.

'But Rosalie,' he urged, 'surely a girl's wedding-day ought to be something for her to think of all her life – to recall with dreamily smiling lips as she knits the tiny garments or cooks the evening meal for the husband she adores. She ought to be able to look back and live again through the solemn hush in the church, savour once more the sweet scent of the lilies-of-the-valley, hear the rolling swell of the organ and the grave voice of the clergyman reading the service. What memories would you have if you carried out this plan that you suggest? One only – that of a smelly monkey. Have you reflected upon this, Rosalie?'

But she was obdurate.

'Either you marry me in the gorilla's cage, or you don't marry me at all. Mr Pybus says it is certain to make the front page, with photographs and possibly even a short editorial on the right stuff being in the modern girl despite her surface irresponsibility.'

'You will feel differently tonight, when we meet for dinner.'

'We shall not meet for dinner. If you are interested, I may inform you that Captain Fosdyke invited me to dine with him and I intend to do so.'

'Rosalie!'

'There is a man who really is a man. When he meets a gorilla, he laughs in its face.'

'Very rude.'

'A million gorillas couldn't frighten him. Goodbye, Mr Mulliner. I must go and tell him that when I said this morning that I had a previous engagement I was mistaken.'

She swept out, and Montrose went on with his steak-pudding like one in a dream.

It is possible (said Mr Mulliner, taking a grave sip of his hot Scotch and Lemon and surveying the company with a thoughtful eye) that what I have told you may have caused you to form a dubious opinion of my distant cousin Montrose. If so, I am not surprised. In the scene which I have just related, no one is better aware than myself that he has not shown up well. Reviewing his shallow arguments, we see through them, as Rosalie did: and, like Rosalie, we realize that he had feet of clay – and cold ones, to boot.

But I would urge in extenuation of his attitude that Montrose

Mulliner, possibly through some constitutional defect such as an insufficiency of hormones, had been from childhood timorous in the extreme. And his work as an assistant director had served very noticeably to increase this innate pusillanimity.

It is one of the drawbacks to being an assistant director that virtually everything that happens to him is of a nature to create an inferiority-complex – or, if one already exists, to deepen it. He is habitually addressed as 'Hey, you' and alluded to in the third person as 'that fathead'. If anything goes wrong on the set, he gets the blame and is ticked off not only by the producer but also by the director and all the principals involved. Finally, he has to be obsequious to so many people that it is little wonder that he comes in time to resemble one of the more shrinking and respectful breeds of rabbit. Five years of assistant-directing had so sapped Montrose's morale that nowadays he frequently found himself starting up and apologizing in his sleep.

It is proof, then, of the great love which he had for Rosalie Beamish that, encountering Captain Jack Fosdyke a few days later, he should have assailed him with bitter reproaches. Only love could have impelled him to act in a manner so foreign to his temperament.

The fact was, he blamed the Captain for all that had occurred. He considered that he had deliberately unsettled Rosalie and influenced her mind with the set purpose of making her dissatisfied with the man to whom she had plighted her troth.

'If it wasn't for you,' he concluded warmly, 'I feel sure I could have reasoned her out of what is nothing but a passing girlish whim. But you have infatuated her, and now where do I get off?'

The Captain twirled his moustache airily.

'Don't blame me, my boy. All my life I have been cursed by this fatal attraction of mine for the sex. Poor little moths, they will beat their wings against the bright light of my personality. Remind me to tell you some time of an interesting episode which occurred in the harem of the King of the 'Mbongos. There is something about me which is – what shall I say? – hypnotic. It is not my fault that this girl has compared us. It was inevitable that she should compare us. And having compared us what does she see? On the one hand, a man with a soul of chilled steel who can look his gorilla in the eye and make it play ball. On the other – I use the term in the kindliest possible sense – a crawling worm. Well, goodbye, my boy, glad to have seen you and had this little chat,' said Captain Fosdyke. 'I like you young fellows to bring your troubles to me.

For some moments after he had gone, Montrose remained standing motionless, while all the repartees which he might have made surged through his mind in a glittering procession. Then his thoughts turned once more to the topic of gorillas.

It is possible that it was the innuendoes uttered by Captain Fosdyke that now awoke in Montrose something which bore a shadowy resemblance to fortitude. Certainly, until this conversation, he had not intended to revisit the gorilla's cage, one sight of its occupant having been ample for him. Now, stung by the other's slurs, he decided to go and have another look at the brute. It might be that further inspection would make it seem less formidable. He had known this to happen before. The first time he had seen Mr Schnellenhamer, for example, he had had something not unlike a fit of what our grandparents used to call the 'vapours'. Now, he could bear him with at least an assumption of nonchalance.

He made his way to the cage, and was presently exchanging glances with the creature through the bars.

Alas, any hope he may have had that familiarity would breed contempt died as their eyes met. Those well-gnashed teeth, that hideous shagginess (a little reminiscent of a stockbroker motoring to Brighton in a fur coat) filled him with all the old familiar qualms. He tottered back and, with some dim idea of pulling himself together, he took a banana from the bag which he had bought at the commissary to see him through the long afternoon. And, as he did so, there suddenly flashed upon him the recollection of an old saw which he had heard in his infancy – The Gorilla Never Forgets. In other words, Do the square thing by gorillas, and they will do the square thing by you.

His heart leaped within him. He pushed the banana through the bars with a cordial smile, and was rejoiced to find it readily accepted. In rapid succession he passed over the others. A banana a day keeps the gorilla away, he felt jubilantly. By standing treat to this animal regardless of cost, he reasoned, he would so ingratiate himself with it as to render the process of geting married in its cage both harmless and agreeable. And it was only when his guest had finished the last of the fruit that he realized with a sickening sense of despair that he had got his facts wrong and that his whole argument, based on a false premise, fell to the ground and became null and void.

It was the the elephant who never forgot – not the gorilla. It all came back to him now. He was practically sure that gorillas had never been mentioned in connection with the subject of mnemonics. Indeed, for all he knew, these creatures might be famous for the shortness of their memory – with the result that if later on he were to put on pin-striped trousers and a top hat and enter this animal's cage with Rosalie on his arm and the studio band playing the Wedding March, all recollection of those bananas would probably have passed completely from its fat head, and it would totally fail to recognize its benefactor.

Moodily crumpling the bag, Montrose turned away. This, he felt, was the end.

I have a tender heart (said Mr Mulliner), and I dislike to dwell on the spectacle of a human being groaning under the iron heel of Fate. Such morbid gloating, I consider, is better left to the Russians. I will spare you, therefore, a detailed analysis of my distant cousin Montrose's emotions as the long day wore on. Suffice it to say that by a few minutes to five o'clock he had become a mere toad beneath the harrow. He wandered aimlessly to and fro about the lot in the growing dusk, and it seemed to him that the falling shades of evening resembled the cloud that had settled upon his life.

He was roused from these meditations by a collision with some solid body and, coming to himself, discovered that he had been trying to walk through his old friend, George Pybus of the Press department. George was standing beside his car, apparently on the point of leaving for the day.

It is one more proof of Montrose Mulliner's gentle nature that he did not reproach George Pybus for the part he had taken in darkening his outlook. All he did was to gape and say:

'Hullo! You off?'

George Pybus climbed into the car and started the engine.

'Yes,' he said, 'and I'll tell you why. You know that gorilla?'

With a shudder which he could not repress Montrose said he knew the gorilla.

'Well, I'll tell you something,' said George Pybus. 'Its agent has been complaining that we've been throwing all the publicity to Luella Benstead and Edmund Wigham. So the boss sent out a hurry call for quick thinking. I told him that you and Rosalie Beamish were planning to get married in its cage, but I've seen

Rosalie and she tells me you've backed out. Scarcely the spirit I should have expected in you, Montrose.'

Montrose did his best to assume a dignity which he was far from feeling.

'One has one's code,' he said. 'One dislikes to pander to the morbidity of a sensation-avid . . .'

'Well, it doesn't matter, anyway,' said George Pybus, 'because I got another idea, and a better one. This one is a pippin. At five sharp this evening, Standard Pacific time, that gorilla's going to be let out of its cage and will menace hundreds. If that doesn't land him on the front page . . .'

Montrose was appalled.

'But you can't do that!' he gasped. 'Once let that awful brute out of its cage and it may tear people to shreds.'

George Pybus reassured him.

'Nobody of any consequence. The stars have all been notified and are off the lot. So are the directors. Also the executives, all except Mr Schnellenhamer, who is cleaning up some work in his office. He will be quite safe there, of course. Nobody ever got into Mr Schnellenhamer's office without waiting four hours in the ante-room. Well, I must be off,' said George Pybus. 'I've got to dress and get out to Malibu for dinner.'

And, so speaking, he trod on the accelerator and was speedily lost to view in the gathering darkness.

It was a few moments later that Montrose, standing rooted to the spot, became aware of a sudden distant uproar: and, looking at his watch, he found that it was precisely five o'clock.

The spot to which Montrose had been standing rooted was in that distant part of the lot where the outdoor sets are kept permanently erected, so that a director with – let us suppose – a London street scene to shoot is able instantly to lay his hands on a back-alley in Algiers, a medieval castle, or a Parisian boulevard – none of which is any good to him but which make him feel that the studio is trying to be helpful.

As far as Montrose's eye could reach, Spanish patios, thatched cottages, tenement buildings, estaminets, Oriental bazaars, Kaffir kraals and the residences of licentious New York clubmen stood out against the evening sky: and the fact that he selected as his haven of refuge one of the tenement buildings was due to its being both tallest and nearest.

Like all outdoor sets, it consisted of a front just like the real thing and a back composed of steps and platforms. Up these steps he raced, and on the topmost of the platforms he halted and sat down. He was still unable to think very coherently, but in a dim sort of way he was rather proud of his agility and resource. He felt that he had met a grave crisis well. He did not know what the record was for climbing a flight of steps with a gorilla loose in the neighbourhood, but he would have felt surprise if informed that he had not lowered it.

The uproar which had had such a stimulating effect upon him was now increasing in volume; and, oddly, it appeared to have become stationary. He glanced down through the window of his tenement building, and was astonished to observe below him a dense crowd. And what perplexed him most about this crowd was that it was standing still and looking up.

Scarcely, felt Montrose, intelligent behaviour on the part of a crowd with a savage gorilla after it.

There was a good deal of shouting going on, but he found himself unable to distinguish any words. A woman who stood in the forefront of the throng appeared particularly animated. She was waving an umbrella in a rather neurotic manner.

The whole thing, as I say, perplexed Montrose. What these people thought they were doing, he was unable to say. He was still speculating on the matter when a noise came to his ears.

It was the crying of a baby.

Now, with all these mother-love pictures so popular, the presence of a baby on the lot was not in itself a thing to occasion surprise. It is a very unambitious mother in Hollywood who, the moment she finds herself and child doing well, does not dump the little stranger into a perambulator and wheel it round to the casting-office in the hope of cashing in. Ever since he had been with the Perfecto-Zizzbaum, Montrose had seen a constant stream of offspring riding up and trying to break into the game. It was not, accordingly, the fact of a baby being among those present that surprised him. What puzzled him about this particular baby was that it seemed to be so close at hand. Unless the acoustics were playing odd tricks, the infant, he was convinced, was sharing this eyrie of his. And how a mere baby, handicapped probably by swaddling-clothes and a bottle, could have shinned up all those steps bewildered him to such an extent that he moved along the planks to investigate.

And he had not gone three paces when he paused, aghast. With its hairy back towards him, the gorilla was crouching over something that lay on the ground. And another bellow told him that this was the baby in person; and instantly Montrose saw what must have occurred. His reading of magazine stories had taught him once a gorilla gets loose, the first thing it does is to snatch a baby from a perambulator and climb to the nearest high place. It is purely routine.

This, then, was the position in which my distant cousin Montrose found himself at eight minutes past five on this misty evening. A position calculated to test the fortitude of the sternest.

Now, it has been well said that with nervous, highly strung men like Montrose Mulliner, a sudden call upon their manhood is often enough to revolutionize their whole character. Psychologists have frequently commented on this. We are too ready, they say, to dismiss as cowards those who merely require the stimulus of the desperate emergency to bring out all their latent heroism. The crisis comes, and the craven turns magically into the paladin.

With Montrose, however, this was not the case. Ninety-nine out of a hundred of those who knew him would have scoffed at the idea of him interfering with an escaped gorilla to save the life of a child, and they would have been right. To tiptoe backwards, holding his breath, was with Montrose Mulliner the work of a moment. And it was the fact that he did it so quickly that wrecked his plans. Stubbing a heel on a loose board, in his haste, he fell backwards with a crash. And when the stars had ceased to obscure his vision, he found himself gazing up into the hideous face of the gorilla.

On the last occasion when the two had met, there had been iron bars between them: and even with this safeguard Montrose, as I have said, had shrunk from the creature's evil stare. Now, meeting the brute as it were socially, he experienced a thrill of horror such as had never come to him even in nightmares. Closing his eyes, he began to speculate as to which limb, when it started to tear him limb from limb, the animal would start with.

The one thing of which he was sure was that it would begin operations by uttering a fearful snarl: and when the next sound that came to his ears was a deprecating cough he was so astonished that he could keep his eyes closed no longer. Opening them, he found the gorilla looking at him with an odd, apologetic expression on its face.

'Excuse me, sir,' said the gorilla, 'but are you by any chance a family man?'

For an instant, on hearing the question, Montrose's astonishment deepened. Then he realized what must have happened. He must have been torn limb from limb without knowing it, and now he was in heaven. Though even this did not altogether satisfy him as an explanation, for he had never expected to find gorillas in heaven.

The animal now gave a sudden start.

'Why, it's you! I didn't recognize you at first. Before going any further, I should like to thank you for those bananas. They were delicious. A little something round about the middle of the afternoon picks one up quite a bit, doesn't it.'

Montrose blinked. He could still hear the noise of the crowd below. His bewilderment increased.

'You speak very good English for a gorilla,' was all he could find to say. And, indeed, the animal's diction had been remarkable for its purity.

The gorilla waved the compliment aside modestly.

'Oh, well, Balliol, you know. Dear old Balliol. One never quite forgets the lessons one learned at Alma Mater, don't you think? You are not an Oxford man, by any chance?'

'No.'

'I came down in '26. Since then I have been knocking around a good deal, and a friend of mine in the circus business suggested to me that the gorilla field was not overcrowded. Plenty of room at the top, was his expression. And I must say,' said the gorilla, 'I've done pretty well at it. The initial expenditure comes high, of course . . . you don't get a skin like this for nothing . . . but there's virtually no overhead. Of course, to become a co-star in a big feature film, as I have done, you need a good agent. Mine, I am glad to say, is a capital man of business. Stands no nonsense from these motion-picture magnates.'

Montrose was not a quick thinker, but he was gradually adjusting his mind to the facts.

'Then you're not a real gorilla?'

'No, no. Synthetic, merely.'

'You wouldn't tear anyone limb from limb?'

'My dear chap! My idea of a nice time is a curl up with a good book. I am happiest among my books.'

Montrose's last doubts were resolved. He extended his hand cordially.

'Pleased to meet you, Mr. . . .'

'Waddesley-Davenport. Cyril Waddesley-Davenport. And I am extremely happy to meet you, Mr. . . .'

'Mulliner. Montrose Mulliner.'

They shook hands warmly. From down below came the hoarse uproar of the crowd. The gorilla started.

'The reason I asked you if you were a family man,' it said, 'was that I hoped you might be able to tell me what is the best method of procedure to adopt with a crying baby. I don't seem able to stop the child. And all my own silly fault, too. I see now I should never have snatched it from its perambulator. If you want to know what is the matter with me, I am too much the artist. I simply had to snatch that baby. It was how I saw the scene. I *felt* it . . . felt it *here*,' said the gorilla, thumping the left side of his chest. 'And now what?'

Montrose reflected. 'Why don't you take it back?'

'To its mother?'

'Certainly.'

'But . . .' The gorilla pulled doubtfully at its lower lip. 'You have seen that crowd. Did you happen to observe a woman standing in the front row waving an umbrella?'

'The mother?'

'Precisely. Well, you know as well as I do, Mulliner, what an angry woman can do with an umbrella.'

Montrose thought again. 'It's all right,' he said. 'I have it. Why don't you sneak down the back steps? Nobody will see you. The crowd's in front, and it's almost dark.'

The gorilla's eyes lit up. It slapped Montrose gratefully on the shoulder.

'My dear chap! The very thing. But as regards the baby . . .'

'I will restore it.'

'Capital! I don't know how to thank you, dear fellow,' said the gorilla. 'By Jove, this is going to be a lesson to me in future not to give way to the artist in me. You don't how I've been feeling about that umbrella. Well, then, in case we don't meet again, always remember that the Lotos Club finds me when I am in New York. Drop in any time you happen to be in that neighbourhood and we'll have a bite to eat and a good talk.'

And what of Rosalie, meanwhile? Rosalie was standing beside the bereaved mother, using all her powers of cajolery to try to persuade Captain Jack Fosdyke to go to the rescue: and the Captain was pleading technical difficulties that stood in the way.

'Dash my buttons,' he said, 'if only I had my elephant gun and my trusty native bearer, 'Mlongi, here, I'd pretty soon know what to do about it. As it is, I'm handicapped.'

'But you told me yesterday that you had often strangled gorillas with your bare hands.'

'Not *gor*-illas, dear lady – *por*-illas. A species of South American wombat, and very good eating they make, too.'

'You're afraid!'

'Afraid? Jack Fosdyke afraid? How they would laugh on the Lower Zambesi if they could hear you say that.'

'You are! You, who advised me to have nothing to do with the man I love because he was of a mild and diffident nature.'

Captain Jack Fosdyke twirled his moustache.

'Well, I don't notice,' he sneered, 'that he . . .' He broke off, and his jaw slowly fell. Round the corner of the building was walking Montrose Mulliner. His bearing was erect, even jaunty, and he carried the baby in his arms. Pausing for an instant to allow the busily clicking cameras to focus him, he advanced towards the stupefied mother and thrust the child into her arms.

'That's that,' he said carelessly, dusting his fingers. 'No, no, please,' he went on. 'A mere nothing.'

For the mother was kneeling before him, endeavouring to kiss his hand. It was not only maternal love that prompted the action. That morning she had signed up her child at seventy-five dollars a week for the forthcoming picture *Tiny Fingers*, and all through these long, anxious minutes it had seemed as though the contract must be a total loss.

Rosalie was in Montrose's arms, sobbing.

'Oh, Monty!'

'There, there!'

'How I misjudged you!'

'We all make mistakes.'

'I made a bad one when I listened to that man there,' said Rosalie, darting a scornful look at Captain Jack Fosdyke. 'Do you realize that, for all his boasting, he would not move a step to save that poor child?'

'Not a step?'

'Not a single step.'

'Bad, Fosdyke,' said Montrose. 'Rather bad. Not quite the straight bat, eh?'

'Tchah!' said the baffled man; he turned on his heel and strode away. He was still twirling his moustache, but a lot that got him.

Rosalie was clinging to Montrose.

'You aren't hurt? Was it a fearful struggle?'

'Struggle?' Montrose laughed. 'Oh, dear no. There was no struggle. I very soon showed the animal that I was going to stand no nonsense. I generally find with gorillas that all one needs is the power of the human eye. By the way, I've been thinking it over and I realize that I may have been a little unreasonable about that idea of yours. I still would prefer to get married in some nice, quiet church, but if you feel you want the ceremony to take place in that animal's cage, I shall be delighted.'

She shivered. 'I couldn't do it. I'd be scared.'

Montrose smiled understandingly.

'Ah, well,' he said, 'it is perhaps not unnatural that a delicately nurtured woman should be of less tough stuff than the more rugged male. Shall we be strolling along? I want to look in on Mr Schnellenhamer, and arrange about that raise of mine. You won't mind waiting while I pop in at his office?'

'My hero!' whispered Rosalie.

The Nodder

The presentation of the super film, *Baby Boy*, at the Bijou Dream in the High Street, had led to an animated discussion in the bar-parlour of the Anglers' Rest. Several of our prominent first-nighters had dropped in there for much-needed restorative after the performance, and the conversation had turned to the subject of child stars in the motion-pictures.

'I understand they're all midgets, really,' said a Rum and Milk.

'That's what I heard, too,' said a Whisky and Splash. 'Somebody told me that at every studio in Hollywood they have a special man who does nothing but go round the country, combing the circuses, and when he finds a good midget he signs him up.'

Almost automatically we looked at Mr Mulliner, as if seeking from that unfailing fount of wisdom an authoritative pronouncement on this difficult point. The Sage of the bar-parlour sipped his hot Scotch and Lemon for a moment in thoughtful silence.

'The question you have raised,' he said at length, 'is one that has occupied the minds of thinking men ever since these little excrescences first became popular on the screen. Some argue that mere children would scarcely be so loathsome. Others maintain that a right-minded midget would hardly stoop to some of the things these child stars do. But, then, arising from that, we have to ask ourselves: Are midgets right-minded? The whole thing is very moot.'

'Well, this kid we saw tonight,' said the Rum and Milk. 'This Johnny Bingley. Nobody's going to tell me he's only eight years old.'

'In the case of Johnny Bingley,' assented Mr Mulliner, 'your intuition has not led you astray. I believe he is in the early forties. I happen to know all about him because it was he who played so important a part in the affairs of my distant connection, Wilmot.'

'Was your distant connection Wilmot a midget?'

'No. He was a Nodder.'

'A what?'

Mr Mulliner smiled.

'It is not easy to explain to the lay mind the extremely intricate ramifications of the personnel of a Hollywood motion-picture organization. Putting it as briefly as possible, a Nodder is something like a Yes-Man, only lower in the social scale. A Yes-Man's duty is to attend conferences and say "Yes". A Nodder's, as the name implies, is to nod. The chief executive throws out some statement of opinion, and looks about him expectantly. This is the cue for the senior Yes-Man to say yes. He is followed, in order of precedence, by the second Yes-Man – or Vice-Yesser, as he is sometimes called – and the junior Yes-Man. Only when all the Yes-Men have yessed, do the Nodders begin to function. They nod.'

A Pint of Half-and-Half said it didn't sound much of a job.

Not very exalted (agreed Mr Mulliner). It is a position which you might say, roughly, lies socially somewhere in between that of the man who works the wind machine and that of a writer of additional dialogue. There is also a class of Untouchables who are known as Nodders' assistants, but this is a technicality with which I need not trouble you. At the time when my story begins, my distant connection Wilmot was a full Nodder. Yet, even so, there is no doubt that he was aiming a little high when he ventured to aspire to the hand of Mabel Potter, the private secretary of Mr Schnellenhamer, the head of the Perfecto-Zizzbaum Corporation.

Indeed, between a girl so placed and a man in my distant connection's position there could in ordinary circumstances scarcely have been anything in the nature of friendly inter-course. Wilmot owed his entry to her good graces to a combination of two facts – the first, that in his youth he had been brought up on a farm and so was familiar with the customs and habits of birds; the second, that before coming to Hollywood, Miss Potter had been a bird-imitator in vaudeville.

Too little has been written of vaudeville bird-imitators and their passionate devotion to their art: but everybody knows the saying, Once a Bird-Imitator, Always a Bird-Imitator. The Mabel Potter of today might be a mere lovely machine for taking notes and tapping out her employer's correspondence, but within her there still burned the steady flame of those high ideals which always animate a girl who has once been accustomed to render to packed houses the liquid notes of the cuckoo, the whip-poor-will, and other songsters who are familiar to you all.

That this was so was revealed to Wilmot one morning when, wandering past an outlying set, he heard raised voices within and, recognizing the silver tones of his adored one, paused to listen. Mabel Potter seemed to be having some kind of an argument with a director.

'Considering,' she was saying, 'that I only did it to oblige and that it is in no sense a part of my regular duties for which I draw my salary, I must say . . .'

'All right, all right,' said the director.

'. . . that you have a nerve calling me down on the subject of cuckoos. Let me tell you, Mr Murgatroyd, that I have made a life-long study of cuckoos and know them from soup to nuts. I have imitated cuckoos in every theatre on every circuit in the land. Not to mention urgent offers from England, Australia and . . .'

'I know, I know,' said the director.

'. . . South Africa, which I was compelled to turn down because my dear mother, then living, disliked ocean travel. My cuckoo is world-famous. Give me time to go home and fetch it and I'll show you the clipping from the *St Louis Post-Democrat* which says . . .'

'I know, I know, I know,' said the director, 'but, all the same, I think I'll have somebody do it who'll do it my way.'

The next moment Mabel Potter had swept out, and Wilmot addressed her with respectful tenderness.

'Is something the matter, Miss Potter? Is there anything I can do?'

Mabel Potter was shaking with dry sobs. Her self-esteem had been rudely bruised.

'Well, look,' she said. 'They ask me as a special favour to come and imitate the call of the cuckoo for this new picture, and when I do it Mr Murgatroyd says I've done it wrong.'

'The hound,' breathed Wilmot.

'He says a cuckoo goes Cuckoo, Cuckoo, when everybody who has studied the question knows that what it really goes is Wuckoo, Wuckoo.'

'Of course. Not a doubt about it. A distinct "W" sound.'

'As if it had got something wrong with the roof of its mouth.'

'Or had omitted to have its adenoids treated.'

'Wuckoo, Wuckoo . . . Like that.'

'Exactly like that,' said Wilmot.

The girl gazed at him with a new friendliness.

'I'll bet you've heard rafts of cuckoos.'

'Millions. I was brought up on a farm.'

'These know-it-all directors make me tired.'

'Me, too,' said Wilmot. Then, putting his fate to the touch, to win or lose it all, 'I wonder, Miss Potter, if you would care to step round to the commissary and join me in a small coffee?'

She accepted gratefully, and from that moment their intimacy may be said to have begun. Day after day, in the weeks that followed, at such times as their duties would permit, you would see them sitting together either in the commissary or on the steps of some Oriental palace on the outskirts of the lot; he gazing silently up into her face; she, an artist's enthusiasm in her beautiful eyes, filling the air with the liquid note of the Baltimore oriole or possibly the more strident cry of the African buzzard. While ever and anon, by special request, she would hitch up the muscles of the larynx and go 'Wuckoo, Wuckoo'.

But when at length Wilmot, emboldened, asked her to be his wife, she shook her head.

'No,' she said. 'I like you, Wilmot. Sometimes I even think that I love you. But I can never marry a mere serf.'

'A what was that?'

'A serf. A peon. A man who earns his living by nodding his head at Mr Schnellenhamer. A Yes-Man would be bad enough, but a Nodder!'

She paused, and Wilmot, from sheer force of habit, nodded.

'I am ambitious,' proceeded Mabel. 'The man I marry must be a king among men . . . well, what I mean, at least a supervisor. Rather than wed a Nodder, I would starve in the gutter.'

The objection to this as a practical policy was, of course, that, owing to the weather being so uniformly fine all the year round, there are no gutters in Hollywood. But Wilmot was too distressed to point this out. He uttered a heart-stricken cry not unlike the mating-call of the Alaskan wild duck and began to plead with her. But she was not to be moved.

'We will always be friends,' she said, 'but marry a Nodder, no.'

And with a brief 'Wuckoo' she turned away.

There is not much scope or variety of action open to a man whose heart has been shattered and whose romance has proved an empty dream. Practically speaking, only two courses lie before him. He can go out West and begin a new life, or he can drown his sorrow in drink. In Wilmot's case, the former of these alternatives was rendered impossible by the fact that he was out West already. Little wonder, then, that as he sat in his lonely lodging that night his thoughts turned ever more and more insistently to the second.

Like all the Mulliners, my distant connection Wilmot had always been a scrupulously temperate man. Had his love-life but run smoothly, he would have been amply contented with a nut sundae or a malted milk after the day's work. But now, with desolation staring him in the face, he felt a fierce urge toward something with a bit more kick in it.

About half-way down Hollywood Boulevard, he knew, there was a place where, if you knocked twice and whistled 'My Country, 'tis of thee', a grille opened and a whiskered face appeared. The Face said 'Well?' and you said 'Service and Co-operation', and then the door was unbarred and you saw before you the primrose path that led to perdition. And as this was precisely what, in his present mood, Wilmot most desired to locate, you will readily understand how it came about that, some hour and a half later, he was seated at a table in this establishment, feeling a good deal better.

How long it was before he realized that his table had another occupant he could not have said. But came a moment when, raising his glass, he found himself looking into the eyes of a small child in a Lord Fauntleroy costume, in whom he recognized none other than Little Johnny Bingley, the Idol of American Motherhood – the star of this picture, *Baby Boy*, which you, gentlemen, have just been witnessing at the Bijou Dream in the High Street.

To say that Wilmot was astonished at seeing this infant in such surroundings would be to overstate the case. After half an hour at this home-from-home the customer is seldom in a condition to be astonished at anything – not even a gamboge elephant in golfing costume. He was, however, sufficiently interested to say 'Hullo.'

'Hullo,' replied the child. 'Listen,' he went on, placing a cube of ice in his tumbler, 'don't tell old Schnellenhamer you saw me here. There's a morality clause in my contract.'

'Tell who?' said Wilmot.

'Schnellenhamer.'

'How do you spell it?'

'I don't know.'

'Nor do I,' said Wilmot. 'Nevertheless, be that as it may,' he continued, holding out his hand impulsively, 'he shall never learn from me.'

'Who won't?' said the child.

'He won't,' said Wilmot.

'Won't what?' asked the child.

'Learn from me,' said Wilmot.

'Learn what?' enquired the child.

'I've forgotten,' said Wilmot.

They sat for a space in silence, each busy with his own thoughts.

'You're Johnny Bingley, aren't you?' said Wilmot.

'Who is?' said the child.

'You are.'

'I'm what?'

'Listen,' said Wilmot. 'My name's Mulliner. That's what it is. Mulliner. And let them make the most of it.'

'Who?'

'I don't know,' said Wilmot.

He gazed at his companion affectionately. It was a little difficult to focus him, because he kept flickering, but Wilmot could take the big, broad view about that. If the heart is in the right place, he reasoned, what does it matter if the body flickers?

'You're a good chap, Bingley.'

'So are you, Mulliner.'

'Both good chaps?'

'Both good chaps.'

'Making two in all?' asked Wilmot, anxious to get this straight.

'That's how I work it out.'

'Yes, two,' agreed Wilmot, ceasing to twiddle his fingers. 'In fact, you might say both gentlemen.'

'Both gentlemen is correct.'

'Then let us see what we have got. Yes,' said Wilmot, as he laid down the pencil with which he had been writing figures on the tablecloth. 'Here are the final returns, as I get them. Two good chaps, two gentlemen. And yet,' he said, frowning in a puzzled way, 'that seems to make four, and there are only two of us. However,' he went on, 'let that go. Immaterial. Not germane to the issue. The fact we have to face, Bingley, is that my heart is heavy.'

'You don't say!'

'I do say. Heavy, Hearty. My bing is heavy.'

'What's the trouble?'

Wilmot decided to confide in this singularly sympathetic infant. He felt he had never met a child he liked better.

'Well, it's like this.'

'What is?'

'This is.'

'Like what?'

'I'm telling you. The girl I love won't marry me.'

'She won't?'

'So she says.'

'Well, well,' said the child star commiseratingly. 'That's too bad. Spurned your love, did she?'

'You're dern tooting she spurned my love,' said Wilmot. 'Spurned it good and hard. Some spurning!'

'Well, that's how it goes,' said the child star. 'What a world!'

'You're right, what a world.'

'I shouldn't wonder if it didn't make your heart heavy.'

'You bet it makes my heart heavy,' said Wilmot, crying softly. He dried his eyes on the edge of the tablecloth. 'How can I shake off this awful depression?' he asked.

The child star reflected.

'Well, I'll tell you,' he said. 'I know a better place than this one. It's out Venice way. We might give it a try.'

'We certainly might,' said Wilmot.

'And then there's another one down at Santa Monica.'

'We'll go there, too,' said Wilmot. 'The great thing is to keep moving about and seeing new scenes and fresh faces.'

'The faces are always nice and fresh down at Venice.'

'Then let's go,' said Wilmot.

It was eleven o'clock on the following morning that Mr Schnellenhamer burst in upon his fellow-executive, Mr Levitsky, with agitation written on every feature of his expressive face. The cigar trembled between his lips.

'Listen!' he said. 'Do you know what?'

'Listen!' said Mr Levitsky. 'What?'

'Johnny Bingley has just been in to see me.'

'If he wants a raise of salary, talk about the Depression.'

'Raise of salary? What's worrying me is how long is he going to be worth the salary he's getting.'

'Worth it?' Mr Levitsky stared. 'Johnny Bingley? The Child With The Tear Behind The Smile? The Idol Of American Motherhood?'

'Yes, and how long is he going to be the idol of American Motherhood after American Motherhood finds out he's a midget from Connolly's Circus, and an elderly, hardboiled midget, at that?'

'Well, nobody knows that but you and me.'

'Is that so?' said Mr Schnellenhamer. 'Well, let me tell you, he was out on a toot last night with one of my Nodders, and he comes to me this morning and says he couldn't actually swear he told this guy he was a midget, but, on the other hand, he rather thinks he must have done. He says that between the time they were thrown out of Mike's Place and the time he stabbed the waiter with the pickle-fork there's a sort of gap in his memory, a kind of blur, and he thinks it may have been then, because by that time they had got pretty confidential and he doesn't think he would have had any secrets from him.'

All Mr Levitsky's nonchalance had vanished.

'But if this fellow – what's his name?'

'Mulliner.'

'If this fellow Mulliner sells this story to the Press, Johnny Bingley won't be worth a nickel to us. And his contract calls for two more pictures at two hundred and fifty thousand each.'

'That's right.'

'But what are we to do?'

'You tell me.'

Mr Levitsky pondered.

'Well, first of all,' he said, 'we'll have to find out if this Mulliner really knows.'

'We can't ask him.'

'No, but we'll be able to tell by his manner. A fellow with a stranglehold on the Corporation like that isn't going to be able to go on acting same as he's always done. What sort of fellow is he?'

'The ideal Nodder,' said Mr Schnellenhamer regretfully. 'I don't know when I've had a better. Always on his cues. Never tries to alibi himself by saying he had a stiff neck. Quiet . . . Respectful . . . What's that word that begins with a "d"?'

'Damn?'

'Deferential. And what's the word beginning with an "o"?'

'Oyster?'

'Obsequious. That's what he is. Quiet, respectful, deferential and obsequious – that's Mulliner.'

'Well, then it'll be easy to see. If we find him suddenly not being all what you said . . . if he suddenly ups and starts to throw his weight about, understand what I mean . . . why, then we'll know that he knows that Little Johnny Bingley is a midget.'

'And then?'

'Why, then we'll have to square him. And do it right, too. No half-measures.'

Mr Schnellenhamer tore at his hair. He seemed disappointed that he had no straws to stick in it.

'Yes,' he agreed, the brief spasm over, 'I suppose it's the only way. Well, it won't be long before we know. There's a story-conference in my office at noon, and he'll be there to nod.'

'We must watch him like a lynx.'

'Like a what?'

'Lynx. Sort of wild-cat. It watches things.'

'Ah,' said Mr Schnellenhamer, 'I get you now. What confused me at first was that I thought you meant golf-links.'

The fears of two magnates, had they but known it, were quite without foundation. If Wilmot Mulliner had ever learned the fatal secret, he had certainly not remembered it next morning. He had woken that day with a confused sense of having passed through some soul-testing experience, but as regarded details his mind was a blank. His only thought as he entered Mr Schnellenhamer's office for the conference was a rooted conviction that, unless he kept very still, his head would come apart in the middle.

Nevertheless, Mr Schnellenhamer, alert for significant and sinister signs, plucked anxiously at Mr Levitsky's sleeve.

'Look!'

'Eh?'

'Did you see that?'

'See what?'

'That fellow Mulliner. He sort of quivered when he caught my eye, as if with unholy glee.'

'He did?'

'It seemed to me he did.'

As a matter of fact, what had happened was that Wilmot, suddenly sighting his employer, had been unable to restrain a quick shudder of agony. It seemed to him that somebody had been painting Mr Schnellenhamer yellow. Even at the best of times, the President of the Perfecto-Zizzbaum, considered as an object for the eye, was not everybody's money. Flickering at the rims and a dull orange in colour, as he appeared to be now, he had smitten Wilmot like a blow, causing him to wince like a salted snail.

Mr Levitsky was regarding the young man thoughtfully.

'I don't like his looks,' he said.

'Nor do I,' said Mr Schnellenhamer.

'There's a kind of horrid gloating in his manner.'

'I noticed it, too.'

'See how he's just buried his head in his hands, as if he were thinking out dreadful plots?'

'I believe he knows everything.'

'I shouldn't wonder if you weren't right. Well, let's start the conference and see what he does when the time comes for him to nod. That's when he'll break out, if he's going to.'

As a rule, these story-conferences were the part of his work which Wilmot most enjoyed. His own share in them was not exacting, and, as he often said, you met such interesting people.

Today, however, though there were eleven of the studio's weirdest authors present, each well worth more than a cursory inspection, he found himself unable to overcome the dull listlessness which had been gripping him since he had first gone to the refrigerator that morning to put ice on his temples. As the poet Keats put it in his 'Ode to a Nightingale', his head ached and a drowsy numbness pained his sense. And the sight of Mabel Potter, recalling to him those dreams of happiness which he had once dared to dream and which now could never come to fulfilment, plunged him still deeper into the despondency. If he had been a character in a Russian novel, he would have gone and hanged himself in the barn. As it was, he merely sat staring before him and keeping perfectly rigid.

Most people, eyeing him, would have been reminded of a corpse which had been several days in the water: but Mr Schnellenhamer thought he looked like a leopard about to spring, and he mentioned this to Mr Levitsky in an undertone.

'Bend down. I want to whisper.'

'What's the matter?'

'He looks to me just like a crouching leopard.'

'I beg your pardon,' said Mabel Potter, who, her duty being to take notes of the proceedings, was seated at her employer's side. 'Did you say "crouching leopard" or "grouchy shepherd"?'

Mr Schnellenhamer started. He had forgotten the risk of being overheard. He felt that he had been incautious.

'Don't put that down,' he said. 'It wasn't part of the conference. Well, now, come on, come on,' he proceeded, with a pitiful attempt at the bluffness which he used at conferences, 'let's get at it. Where did we leave off yesterday, Miss Potter?'

Mabel consulted her notes.

'Cabot Delancy, a scion of an old Boston family, has gone to try to reach the North Pole in a submarine, and he's on an iceberg, and the scenes of his youth are passing before his eyes.'

'What scenes?'

'You didn't get to what scenes.'

'Then that's where we begin,' said Mr Schnellenhamer. 'What scenes pass before this fellow's eyes?'

One of the authors, a weedy young man in spectacles, who had come to Hollywood to start a Gyffte Shoppe and had been scooped up in the studio's drag-net and forced into the writing-staff much against his will, said why not a scene where Cabot Delancy sees himself dressing his window with kewpie-dolls and fancy notepaper.

'Why kewpie-dolls?' asked Mr Schnellenhamer testily.

The author said they were a good selling line.

'Listen!' said Mr Schnellenhamer brusquely. 'This Delancy never sold anything in his life. He's a millionaire. What we want is something romantic.'

A diffident old gentleman suggested a polo-game.

'No good,' said Mr Schnellenhamer. 'Who cares anything about polo? When you're working on a picture you've got to bear in mind the small-town population of the Middle West. Aren't I right?'

'Yes,' said the senior Yes-Man.

'Yes,' said the Vice-Yesser.

'Yes,' said the junior Yes-Man.

And all the Nodders nodded. Wilmot, waking with a start to the realization that duty called, hurriedly inclined his throbbing head. The movement made him feel as if a red-hot spike had been thrust through it, and he winced. Mr Levitsky plucked at Mr Schnellenhamer's sleeve.

'He scowled!'

'I thought he scowled, too.'

'As it might be with sullen hate.'

'That's the way it struck me. Keep watching him.'

The conference proceeded. Each of the authors put forward a suggestion, but it was left for Mr Schnellenhamer to solve what had begun to seem an insoluble problem.

'I've got it,' said Mr Schnellenhamer. 'He sits on this iceberg and he seems to see himself – he's always been an athlete, you understand – he seems to see himself scoring the winning goal in one of these polo-games. Everybody's interested in polo nowadays. Aren't I right?'

'Yes,' said the senior Yes-Man.

'Yes,' said the Vice-Yesser.

'Yes,' said the junior Yes-Man.

Wilmot was quicker off the mark this time. A conscientious employee, he did not intend mere physical pain to cause him to fall short in his duty. He nodded quickly, and returned to the 'ready' a little surprised that his head was still attached to its moorings. He had felt so certain it was going to come off that time.

The effect of this quiet, respectful, deferential and obsequious nod on Mr Schnellenhamer was stupendous. The anxious look had passed from his eyes. He was convinced now that Wilmot knew nothing. The magnate's confidence mounted high. He proceeded briskly. There was a new strength in his voice.

'Well,' he said, 'that's set for one of the visions. We want two, and the other's got to be something that'll pull in the women. Something touching and sweet and tender.'

The young author in spectacles thought it would be kind of touching and sweet and tender if Cabot Delancy remembered the time he was in his Gyffte Shoppe and a beautiful girl came in and their eyes met as he wrapped up her order of Indian beadwork.

Mr Schnellenhamer banged the desk.

'What is all this about Gyffte Shoppes and Indian beadwork? Don't I tell you this guy is a prominent clubman? Where would he get a Gyffte Shoppe? Bring a girl into it, yes – so far you're talking sense. And let him gaze into her eyes – certainly he can gaze into her eyes. But not in any Gyffte Shoppe. It's got to be a lovely, peaceful, old-world exterior set, with bees humming and doves cooing and trees waving in the breeze. Listen!' said

Mr Schnellenhamer. 'It's spring, see, and all around is the beauty of Nature in the first shy sun-glow. The grass that waves. The buds that . . . what's the word?'

'Bud?' suggested Mr Levitsky.

'No, it's two syllables,' said Mr Schnellenhamer, speaking a little self-consciously, for he was modestly proud of knowing words of two syllables.

'Burgeon?' hazarded an author who looked like a trained seal.

'I beg your pardon,' said Mabel Potter. 'A burgeon's a sort of fish.'

'You're thinking of sturgeon,' said the author.

'Excuse it, please,' murmured Mabel. 'I'm not strong on fishes. Birds are what I'm best at.'

'We'll have birds, too,' said Mr Schnellenhamer jovially. 'All the birds you want. Especially the cuckoo. And I'll tell you why. It gives us a nice little comedy touch. This fellow's with this girl in this old-world garden where everything's burgeoning . . . and when I say burgeoning I mean burgeoning. That burgeoning's got to be done *right*, or somebody'll get fired . . . and they're locked in a close embrace. Hold as long as the Philadelphia censors'll let you, and then comes your nice comedy touch. Just as these two young folks are kissing each other without a thought of anything else in the world, suddenly a cuckoo close by goes 'Cuckoo! Cuckoo!' Meaning how goofy they are. That's good for a laugh, isn't it?'

'Yes,' said the senior Yes-Man.

'Yes,' said the Vice-Yesser.

'Yes,' said the junior Yes-Man.

And then, while the Nodders' heads – Wilmot's among them – were trembling on their stalks preparatory to the downward swoop, there spoke abruptly a clear female voice. It was the voice of Mabel Potter, and those nearest her were able to see that her face was flushed and her eyes gleaming with an almost fanatic light. All the bird-imitator in her had sprung to sudden life.

'I beg your pardon, Mr Schnellenhamer, that's wrong.'

A deadly stillness had fallen on the room. Eleven authors sat transfixed in their chairs, as if wondering if they could believe their twenty-two ears. Mr Schnellenhamer uttered a little gasp. Nothing like this had ever happened to him before in his long experience.

'What did you say?' he asked incredulously. 'Did you say that I . . . *I* . . . was wrong?'

Mabel met his gaze steadily. So might Joan of Arc have faced her inquisitors.

'The cuckoo,' she said, 'does not go "Cuckoo, Cuckoo" . . . it goes "Wuckoo, Wuckoo". A distinct "W" sound.'

A gasp at the girl's temerity ran through the room. In the eyes of several of those present there was something that was not far from a tear. She seemed so young, so fragile.

Mr Schnellenhamer's joviality had vanished. He breathed loudly through his nose. He was plainly mastering himself with a strong effort.

'So I don't know the low-down on cuckoos?'

'Wuckoos,' corrected Mabel.

'Cuckoos!'

'Wuckoos!'

'You're fired,' said Mr Schnellenhamer.

Mabel flushed to the roots of her hair.

'It's unfair and unjust,' she cried. 'I'm right, and anybody who's studied cuckoos will tell you I'm right. When it was a matter of burgeons, I was mistaken, and I admitted that I was mistaken, and apologized. But when it comes to cuckoos, let me tell you you're talking to somebody who has imitated the call of the cuckoo from the Palace, Portland, Oregon, to the Hippodrome, Sumquamset, Maine, and taken three bows after every performance. Yes, sir, I know my cuckoos! And if you don't believe me I'll put it up to Mr Mulliner there, who was born and bred on a farm and has heard more cuckoos in his time than a month of Sundays. Mr Mulliner, how about it? Does the cuckoo go "Cuckoo"?'

Wilmot Mulliner was on his feet, and his eyes met hers with the love-light in them. The spectacle of the girl he loved in distress and appealing to him for aid had brought my distant connection's better self to the surface as if it had been jerked up on the end of a pin. For one brief instant he had been about to seek safety in a cowardly cringing to the side of those in power. He loved Mabel Potter madly, desperately, he had told himself in that short, sickening moment of poltroonery, but Mr Schnellenhamer was the man who signed the cheques; and the thought of risking his displeasure and being summarily dismissed had appalled him. For there is no spiritual anguish like that of the man who, grown accustomed to opening the crackling envelope each Saturday morning, reaches out for it one day and finds that it is not there. The thought of the Perfecto-Zizzbaum cashier ceasing to be a fount of gold and becoming just a man with a walrus moustache had turned Wilmot's spine to Jell-o. And for an instant, as I say, he had been on the point of betraying this sweet girl's trust.

But now, gazing into her eyes, he was strong again. Come what might, he would stand by her to the end.

'No!' he thundered, and his voice rang through the room like a trumpet blast. 'No, it does not go "Cuckoo". You have fallen into a popular error, Mr Schnellenhamer. The bird wooks, and, by heaven, I shall never cease to maintain that it wooks, no matter what offence I give to powerful vested interests. I endorse Miss Potter's view wholeheartedly and without compromise. I say the cuckoo does not cook. It wooks, so make the most of it!'

There was a sudden whirring noise. It was Mabel Potter shooting through the air into his arms.

'Oh, Wilmot!' she cried.

He glared over her back-hair at the magnate.

'Wuckoo, Wuckoo!' he shouted, almost savagely.

He was surprised to observe that Mr Schnellenhamer and Mr Levitsky were hurriedly clearing the room. Authors had begun to stream through the door in a foaming torrent. Presently, he and Mabel were alone with the two directors of the destinies of the Perfecto-Zizzbaum Corporation, and Mr Levitsky was carefully closing the door, while Mr Schnellenhamer came towards him, a winning, if nervous, smile upon his face.

'There, there, Mulliner,' he said.

And Mr Levitsky said 'There, there,' too.

'I can understand your warmth, Mulliner,' said Mr Schnellenhamer. 'Nothing is more annoying to the man who knows than to have people making these silly mistakes. I consider the firm stand you have taken as striking evidence of loyalty to the Corporation.'

'Me, too,' said Mr Levitsky. 'I was admiring it myself.'

'For you are loyal to the Corporation, Mulliner, I know. You would never do anything to prejudice its interests, would you?'

'Sure he wouldn't,' said Mr Levitsky.

'You would not reveal the Corporation's little secrets, thereby causing it alarm and despondency, would you, Mulliner?'

'Certainly he wouldn't,' said Mr Levitsky. 'Especially now that we're going to make him an executive.'

'An executive?' said Mr Schnellenhamer, starting.

'An executive,' repeated Mr Levitsky firmly. 'With brevet rank as a brother-in-law.'

Mr Schnellenhamer was silent for a moment. He seemed to be having a little trouble in adjusting his mind to this extremely drastic step. But he was a man of sterling sense, who realized that there are times when only the big gesture will suffice.

'That's right,' he said. 'I'll notify the legal department and have the contract drawn up right away.'

'That will be agreeable to you, Mulliner?' enquired Mr Levitsky anxiously. 'You will consent to become an executive?'

Wilmot Mulliner drew himself up. It was his moment. His head was still aching, and he would have been the last person to claim that he knew what all this was about: but this he did know – that Mabel was nestling in his arms and that his future was secure.

'I . . .'

Then words failed him, and he nodded.

The Juice of an Orange

A sudden cat shot in through the door of the bar-parlour of the Anglers' Rest, wearing the unmistakable air of a cat which has just been kicked by a powerful foot. At the same moment there came from without sounds indicative of a strong man's wrath: and recognizing the voice of Ernest Biggs, the inn's popular landlord, we stared at one another in amazement. For Ernest had always been celebrated for the kindliness of his disposition. The last man, one would have thought, to raise a number eleven shoe against a faithful friend and good mouser.

It was a well-informed Rum and Milk who threw light on the mystery.

'He's on a diet,' said the Rum and Milk. 'On account of gout.'

Mr Mulliner sighed.

'A pity,' he said, 'that dieting, so excellent from a purely physical standpoint, should have this unfortunate effect on the temper. It seems to sap the self-control of the stoutest.'

'Quite,' said the Rum and Milk. 'My stout Uncle Henry . . .'

'And yet,' proceeded Mr Mulliner, 'I have known great happiness result from dieting. Take, for example, the case of my distant connection, Wilmot.'

'Is that the Wilmot you were telling us about the other night?'

'Was I telling you about my distant connection Wilmot the other night?'

'The fellow I mean was a Nodder at Hollywood, and he found out that the company's child star, Little Johnny Bingley, was a midget, so to keep his mouth shut they made him an executive, and he married a girl named Mabel Potter.'

'Yes, that was Wilmot. You are mistaken, however, in supposing that he married Mabel Potter at the conclusion of that story.'

'But you distinctly said she fell into his arms.'

'Many a girl has fallen into a man's arms,' said Mr Mulliner gravely, 'only to wriggle out of them at a later date.'

*

We left Wilmot, as you very rightly say (said Mr Mulliner), in an extremely satisfactory position, both amatory and financial. The only cloud there had been ever between himself and Mabel Potter had been due, if you recollect, to the fact that she considered his attitude towards Mr Schnellenhamer, the head of the Corporation, too obsequious and deferential. She resented his being a Nodder. Then he was promoted to the rank of executive, so there he was, reconciled to the girl he loved and in receipt of a most satisfactory salary. Little wonder that he felt that the happy ending had arrived.

One effect of his new-found happiness on my distant connection Wilmot was to fill him with the utmost benevolence and goodwill towards all humanity. His sunny smile was the talk of the studio, and even got a couple of lines in Louella Parsons's column in the *Los Angeles Examiner*. Love, I believe, often has this effect on a young man. He went about the place positively seeking for ways of doing his fellow human beings good turns. And when one morning Mr Schnellenhamer summoned him to his office Wilmot's chief thought was that he hoped that the magnate was going to ask some little favour of him, because it would be a real pleasure to him to oblige.

He found the head of the Perfecto-Zizzbaum Corporation looking grave.

'Times are hard, Mulliner,' said Mr Schnellenhamer.

'And yet,' replied Wilmot cheerily, 'there is still joy in the world; still the happy laughter of children and the singing of bluebirds.'

'That's all right about bluebirds,' said Mr Schnellenhamer, 'but we've got to cut down expenses. We'll have to do some salary-slicing.'

Wilmot was concerned. This seemed to him morbid.

'Don't dream of cutting your salary, Chief,' he urged. 'You're worth every cent of it. Besides, reflect. If you reduce your salary, it will cause alarm. People will go about saying that things must be in a bad way. It is your duty to the community to be a man and bite the bullet and, no matter how much it may irk you, to stick to your eight hundred thousand dollars a year like glue.'

'I wasn't thinking of cutting my salary so much,' said Mr Schnellenhamer. 'Yours, more, if you see what I mean.'

'Oh, mine?' cried Wilmot buoyantly. 'Ah, that's different. That's another thing altogether. Yes, that's certainly an idea. If you think it will be of assistance and help to ease matters for all these dear chaps on the P-Z lot, by all means cut my salary. About how much were you thinking of?'

'Well, you're getting fifteen hundred a week.'

'I know, I know,' said Wilmot. 'It's a lot of money.'

'I thought if we said seven hundred and fifty from now on . . .'

'It's an awkward sort of sum,' said Wilmot dubiously. 'Not round, if you follow me. I would suggest five hundred.'

'Or four?'

'Four, if you prefer it.'

'Very well,' said Mr Schnellenhamer. 'Then from now on we'll put you on the books as three. It's a more convenient sum than four,' he explained. 'Makes less book-keeping.'

'Of course,' said Wilmot. 'Of course. What a perfectly lovely day it is, is it not? I was thinking as I came along here that I had never seen the sun shining more brightly. One just wanted to be out and about, doing lots of good on every side. Well, I'm delighted if I have been able to do anything in my humble way to make things easier for you, Chief. It has been a real pleasure.'

And with a merry 'Tra-la' he left the room and made his way to the commissary, where he had arranged to give Mabel Potter lunch.

She was a few minutes late in arriving, and he presumed that she had been detained on some matter by Mr Schnellenhamer, whose private secretary, if you remember, she was. When she arrived, he was distressed to see that her lovely face was overcast, and he was about to say something about bluebirds when she spoke abruptly.

'What is all this I hear from Mr Schnellenhamer?'

'I don't quite understand,' said Wilmot.

'About your taking a salary cut.'

'Oh, that. I see. I suppose he drafted out a new agreement for you to take to the legal department. Yes,' said Wilmot, 'Mr Schnellenhamer sent for me this morning, and I found him very worried, poor chap. There is a world-wide money shortage at the moment, you see, and industry is in a throttled state and so on. He was very upset about it. However, we talked things over, and fortunately we found a way out. I've reduced my salary. It has eased things all round.'

Mabel's face was stony.

'Has it?' she said bitterly. 'Well, let me tell you that, as far as I'm concerned, it has done nothing of the sort. You have failed me, Wilmot. You have forfeited my respect. You have proved to me that you are still the same cold-asparagus-backboned worm who used to cringe to Mr Schnellenhamer. I thought, when you became an executive, that you would have the soul of an executive. I find that at heart you are still a Nodder. The man I used to think you – the strong, dominant man of my dreams – would have told Mr Schnellenhamer to take a running jump up an alley at the mere hint of a cut in the weekly envelope. Ah, yes, how woefully I have been deceived in you. I think that we had better consider our engagement at an end.'

Wilmot tottered.

'You are not taking up my option?' he gasped.

'No. You are at liberty to make arrangements elsewhere. I can never marry a poltroon.'

'But, Mabel . . .'

'No. I mean it. Of course,' she went on more gently, 'if one day you should prove yourself worthy of my love, that is another matter. Give me evidence that you are a man among men, and then I'm not saying. But, meanwhile, the scenario reads as I have outlined.'

And with a cold, averted face she passed on into the commissary alone.

The effect of this thunderbolt on Wilmot Mulliner may readily be imagined. It had never occurred to him that Mabel might take this attitude towards what seemed to him an action of the purest altruism. Had he done wrong? he asked himself. Surely, to bring the light of happiness into the eyes of a motion-picture magnate was not a culpable thing. And yet Mabel thought otherwise, and, so thinking, had given him the air. Life, felt Wilmot, was very difficult.

For some moments he debated within himself the possibility of going back to his employer and telling him he had changed his mind. But no, he couldn't do that. It would be like taking chocolate from an already chocolated child. There seemed to Wilmot Mulliner nothing that he could do. It was just one of those things. He went into the commissary, and, taking a solitary table at some distance from the one where the haughty girl sat, ordered Hungarian goulash, salad, two kinds of pie, ice-cream, cheese and coffee. For he had always been a good trencherman, and sorrow seemed to sharpen his appetite.

And this was so during the days that followed. He found himself eating a good deal more than usual, because food seemed to dull the pain at his heart. Unfortunately, in doing so, it substituted another in his stomach.

The advice all good doctors give to those who have been disappointed in love is to eat lightly. Fail to do this, and the result is as inevitable as the climax of a Greek tragedy. No man, however gifted his gastric juices, can go on indefinitely brooding over a lost love and sailing into the starchy foods simultaneously. It was not long before indigestion gripped Wilmot, and for almost the first time in his life he was compelled to consult a physician. And the one he selected was a man of drastic views.

'On rising,' he told Wilmot, 'take the juice of an orange. For luncheon, the juice of an orange. And for dinner the juice . . .' he paused a moment before springing the big surprise '. . . of an orange. For the rest, I am not an advocate of nourishment between meals, but I am inclined to think that, should you become faint during the day – or possibly the night – there will be no harm in your taking . . . well, yes, I really see no reason why you should not take the juice of – let us say – an orange.'

Wilmot stared. His manner resembled that of a wolf on the steppes of Russia who, expecting a peasant, is fobbed off with a wafer biscuit.

'But aren't you leaving out something?'

'I beg your pardon?'

'How about steaks?'

'Most decidedly no steaks.'

'Chops, then?'

'Absolutely no chops.'

'But the way I figure it out – check my figures in case I'm wrong – you're suggesting that I live solely on orange-juice.'

'On the juice of an orange,' corrected the doctor. 'Precisely. Take your orange. Divide it into two equal parts. Squeeze on a squeezer. Pour into a glass . . . or a cup,' he added, for he was not the man to be finicky about small details, 'and drink.'

Put like that, it sounded a good and even amusing trick, but Wilmot left the consulting-room with his heart bowed down. He was a young man who all his life had been accustomed to take his meals in a proper spirit of seriousness, grabbing everything there was and, if there was no more, filling up with biscuits and butter. The vista which his doctor had opened up struck him as bleak to a degree, and I think that, had not a couple of wild cats at this moment suddenly started a rather ugly fight inside him, he would have abandoned the whole project.

The cats, however, decided him. He stopped at the nearest market and ordered a crate of oranges to be despatched to his address. Then, having purchased a squeezer, he was ready to begin the new life.

It was some four days later that Mr Schnellenhamer, as he sat in conference with his fellow-magnate, Mr Levitsky – for these zealous men, when they had no one else to confer with, would confer with one another – was informed that Mr Eustiss Vanderleigh desired to see him. A playwright, this Vanderleigh, of the Little Theatre school, recently shipped to Hollywood in a crate of twelve.

'What does he want?' asked Mr Schnellenhamer.

'Probably got some grievance of some kind,' said Mr Levitsky. 'These playwrights make me tired. One sometimes wishes the old silent days were back again.'

'Ah,' said Mr Schnellenhamer wistfully. 'Well, send him in.'

Eustiss Vanderleigh was a dignified young man with tortoise-shell-rimmed spectacles and flowing front hair. His voice was high and plaintive.

'Mr Schnellenhamer,' he said. 'I wish to know what rights I have in this studio.'

'Listen . . .' began the magnate truculently.

Eustiss Vanderleigh held up a slender hand.

'I do not allude to my treatment as an artist and a craftsman. With regard to that I have already said my say. Though I have some slight reputation as a maker of plays, I have ceased to complain that my rarest scenes are found unsuitable for the medium of the screen. Nor do I dispute the right, however mistaken, of a director to assert that my subtlest lines are – to adopt his argot – "cheesy". All this I accept as part of the give and take of Hollywood life. But there is a limit, and what I wish to ask you, Mr Schnellenhamer, is this: Am I to be hit over the head with crusty rolls?'

'Who's been hitting you over the head with crusty rolls?'

'One of your executives. A man named Mulliner. The incident to which I allude occurred today at the luncheon hour in the commissary. I was entertaining a friend at the meal, and, as he seemed unable to make up his mind as to the precise nature of the refreshment which he desired, I began to read aloud to him the various items on the bill of fare. I had just mentioned roast pork with boiled potatoes and cabbage and was about to go on to Mutton Stew Joan Clarkson, when I was conscious of a violent blow or buffet on the top of the head. And turning I perceived this man Mulliner with a shattered roll in his hand and on his face the look of a soul in torment. Upon my enquiring into his motives for the assault, he merely uttered something which I understood to be "You and your roast pork!" and went on sipping his orange-juice – a beverage of which he appears to be inordinately fond, for I have seen him before in the commissary and he seems to take nothing else. However, that is neither here nor there. The question to which I desire an answer is this: How long is this going on? Must I expect, whenever I enter the studio's place of refreshment, to undergo furious assaults with crusty rolls, or are you prepared to exert your authority and prevent a repetition of the episode?'

Mr Schnellenhamer stirred uneasily. 'I'll look into it.'

'If you would care to feel the bump or contusion . . .?'

'No, you run along. I'm busy now with Mr Levitsky.'

The playwright withdrew, and Mr Schnellenhamer frowned thoughtfully.

'Something'll have to be done about this Mulliner,' he said. 'I don't like the way he's acting. Did you notice him at the conference yesterday?'

'Not specially. What did he do?'

'Well, listen,' said Mr Schnellenhamer, 'he didn't give me the idea of willing service and selfless cooperation. Every time I said anything, it seemed to me he did something funny with the corner of his mouth. Drew it up in a twisted way that looked kind of . . . what's that word beginning with an "s"?'

'Cynical?'

'No, a snickle is a thing you cut corn with. Ah, I've got it. Sardinic. Every time I spoke he looked sardinic.'

Mr Levitsky was out of his depth.

'Like a sardine, do you mean?'

'No, not like a sardine. Sort of cold and sneering, like Glutz of the Medulla-Oblongata the other day on the golf links when he asked me how many I'd taken in the rough and I said one.'

'Maybe his nose was tickling.'

'Well, I don't pay my staff to have tickling noses in the company's time. If they want tickling noses, they must have them after hours. Besides, it couldn't have been that, or he'd have scratched it. No, the way it looks to me, this Mulliner has got too big for his boots and is seething with rebellion. We've another story-conference this afternoon. You watch him and you'll see what I mean. Kind of tough and ugly he looks, like something out of a gangster film.'

'I get you. Sardinic.'

'That's the very word,' said Mr Schnellenhamer. 'And if it goes on I'll know what to do about it. There's no room in this corporation for fellows who sit around drawing up the corners of their mouths and looking sardinical.'

'Or hitting playwrights with crusty rolls.'

'No, there you go too far,' said Mr Schnellenhamer. 'Playwrights ought to be hit with crusty rolls.'

Meanwhile, unaware that his bread-and-butter – or, as it would be more correct to say, his orange-juice – was in danger, Wilmot Mulliner was sitting in a corner of the commissary, glowering sullenly at the glass which had contained his midday meal. He had fallen into a reverie, and was musing on some of the characters in History whom he most admired . . . Genghis Khan . . . Jack the Ripper . . . Attila the Hun . . .

There was a chap, he was thinking. That Attila. Used to go about taking out people's eyeballs and piling them in neat heaps. The ideal way, felt Wilmot, of getting through the long afternoon. He was sorry Attila was no longer with us. He thought the man would have made a nice friend.

For the significance of the scene which I have just described will not have been lost on you. In the short space of four days, dieting had turned my distant connection Wilmot from a thing of almost excessive sweetness and light to a soured misanthrope.

It has sometimes seemed to me (said Mr Mulliner, thoughtfully sipping his hot Scotch and Lemon) that to the modern craze for dieting may be attributed all the unhappiness which is afflicting the world today. Women, of course, are chiefly responsible. They go in for these slimming systems, their sunny natures become warped, and they work off the resultant venom on their men-folk. These, looking about them for someone they can take it out of, pick on the males of the neighbouring country, who themselves are spoiling for a fight because their own wives are on a diet, and before you know where you are war has broken out with all its attendant horrors.

This is what happened in the case of China and Japan. It is this that lies at the root of all the unpleasantness in the Polish Corridor. And look at India. Why is there unrest in India? Because its inhabitants eat only an occasional handful of rice. The day when Mahatma Gandhi sits down to a good juicy steak and follows it up with roly-poly pudding and a spot of Stilton you will see the end of all this nonsense of Civil Disobedience.

Till then we must expect Trouble, Disorder . . . in a word, Chaos.

However, these are deep waters. Let us return to my distant connection, Wilmot.

In the brief address which he had made when prescribing, the doctor, as was his habit, had enlarged upon the spiritual uplift which might be expected to result from an orange-juice diet. The juice of an orange, according to him, was not only rich in the essential vitamins but contained also mysterious properties which strengthened and enlarged the soul. Indeed, the picture he had drawn of the soul squaring its elbows and throwing out its chest had done quite a good deal at the time to soothe the anguish that had afflicted Wilmot when receiving his sentence.

After all, the young man had felt, unpleasant though it might be to suffer the physical torments of a starving python, it was jolly to think that one was to become a sort of modern St Francis of Assisi.

And now, as we have seen, the exact opposite had proved to be the case. Now that he had been called upon to convert himself into a mere vat or container for orange-juice, Wilmot Mulliner had begun to look on his fellow-man with a sullen loathing. His ready smile had become a tight-lipped sneer. And as for his eye, once so kindly, it could have been grafted on to the head of a man-eating shark and no questions asked.

The advent of a waitress, who came to clear away his glass, and the discovery that he was alone in the deserted commissary, awoke Wilmot to a sense of the passage of time. At two o'clock he was due in Mr Schnellenhamer's office, to assist at the story-conference to which the latter had alluded in his talk with Mr Levitsky. He glanced at his watch and saw that it was time to be moving.

His mood was one of sullen rebellion. He thought of Mr Schnellenhamer with distaste. He was feeling that if Mr Schnellenhamer started to throw his weight about, he, Wilmot Mulliner, would know what to do about it.

In these circumstances, the fact that Mr Schnellenhamer, having missed his lunch that day owing to the numerous calls upon him, had ordered a plateful of sandwiches to be placed upon his desk takes upon itself no little of the dramatic. A scenario-writer, informed of the facts of the case, would undoubtedly have thought of those sandwiches as Sandwiches of Fate.

It was not at once that Wilmot perceived the loathsome objects. For some minutes only the familiar features of a story-conference penetrated to his consciousness. Mr Schnellenhamer was criticizing a point that had arisen in connection with the scenario under advisement.

'This guy, as I see it,' he was saying, alluding to the hero of the story, 'is in a spot. He's seen his wife kissing a fellow and, not knowing it was really her brother, he's gone off to Africa, shooting big game, and here's this lion got him down and is starting to chew the face off him. He gazes into its hideous eyes, he hears its fearful snarls, and he knows the end is near. And where I think you're wrong, Levitsky, is in saying that that's the spot for our big cabaret sequence.'

'A vision,' explained Mr Levitsky.

'That's all right about visions. I don't suppose there's a man in the business stronger for visions than I am. But only in their proper place. What I say is what we need here is for the United States Marines to arrive. Aren't I right?'

He paused and looked about him like a hostess collecting eyes at a dinner-party. The Yessers yessed. The Nodders' heads bent like poplars in a breeze.

'Sure I am,' said Mr Schnellenhamer. 'Make a note, Miss Potter.'

And with a satisfied air he reached out and started eating a sandwich.

Now, the head of the Perfecto-Zizzbaum Motion Picture Corporation was not one of those men who can eat sandwiches aloofly and, as it were, surreptitiously. When he ate a sandwich there was no concealment or evasion. He was patently, for all eyes to see, all ears to hear, a man eating a sandwich. There was a brio, a gusto, about the performance which stripped it of all disguise. His sandwich flew before him like a banner.

The effect on Wilmot Mulliner was stupendous. As I say, he had not been aware that there were sandwiches among those present, and the sudden and unexpected crunching went through him like a knife.

Poets have written feelingly of many a significant and compelling sound . . . the breeze in the trees; the roar of waves breaking on a stern and rockbound coast, the coo of doves in immemorial elms; and the song of the nightingale. But none of these can speak to the very depths of the soul like the steady champing of beef sandwiches when the listener is a man who for four days has been subsisting on the juice of an orange.

In the case of Wilmot Mulliner, it was as if the sound of those sandwiches had touched a spring, releasing all the dark forces within him. A tigerish light had come to his eyes, and he sat up in his chair, bristling.

The next moment those present were startled to observe him leap to his feet, his face working violently.

'Stop that!'

Mr Schnellenhamer quivered. His jaw and sandwich fell. He caught Mr Levitsky's eye. Mr Levitsky's jaw had fallen, too.

'Stop it, I say!' thundered Wilmot. 'Stop eating those sandwiches immediately!'

He paused, panting with emotion. Mr Schnellenhamer had risen and was pointing a menacing finger. A deathly silence held the room.

And then, abruptly, into this silence there cut the shrill, sharp, wailing note of a siren. And the magnate stood spellbound, the words 'You're fired!' frozen on his lips. He knew what that sound meant.

One of the things which have caused the making of motion pictures to be listed among the Dangerous Trades is the fact that it has been found impossible to dispense with the temperamental female star. There is a public demand for her, and the Public's word is law. The consequence is that in every studio you will find at least one gifted artiste, the mere mention of whose name causes the strongest to tremble like aspens. At the Perfecto-Zizzbaum this position was held by Hortensia Burwash, the Empress of Molten Passion.

Temperament is a thing that cuts both ways. It brings in the money, but it also leads to violent outbursts on the part of its possessor similar to those so common among the natives of the

Malay States. Every Hortensia Burwash picture grossed five million, but in the making of them she was extremely apt, if thwarted in some whim, to run amuck, sparing neither age nor sex.

A procedure, accordingly, had been adopted not unlike that in use during air raids in the War. At the first sign that the strain had become too much for Miss Burwash, a siren sounded, warning all workers on the lot to take cover. Later, a bugler, blowing the 'All Clear', would inform those in the danger zone that the star had now kissed the director and resumed work on the set.

It was this siren that had interrupted the tense scene which I have been describing.

For some moments after the last note had died away it seemed as though the splendid discipline on which the Perfecto-Zizzbaum organization prided itself was to triumph. A few eyeballs rolled, and here and there you could hear the sharp intake of breath, but nobody moved. Then from without there came the sound of running footsteps, and the door burst open, revealing a haggard young assistant director with a blood-streaked face.

'Save yourselves!' he cried.

There was an uneasy stir.

'She's heading this way!'

Again that stir. Mr Schnellenhamer rapped the desk sharply.

'Gentlemen! Are you afraid of an unarmed woman?'

The assistant director coughed.

'Not unarmed exactly,' he corrected. 'She's got a sword.'

'A sword?'

'She borrowed it off one of the Roman soldiery in *Hail, Caesar!* Seemed to want it for something. Well, goodbye, all,' said the assistant director.

Panic set in. The stampede was started by a young Nodder, who, in fairness be it said, had got a hat-pin in the fleshy part of the leg that time when Miss Burwash was so worried over *Hearts Aflame*. Reckless of all rules of precedence, he shot silently through the window. He was followed by the rest of those present, and in a few moments the room was empty save for Wilmot, brooding with folded arms; Mabel Potter, crouched on top of the filing cabinet; and Mr Schnellenhamer himself, who, too stout to negotiate the window, was crawling into a convenient cupboard and softly closing the door after him.

To the scene which had just concluded Wilmot Mulliner had

paid but scant attention. His whole mind was occupied with the hunger which was gnawing his vitals and that strange loathing for the human species which had been so much with him of late. He continued to stand where he was, as if in some dark trance.

From this he was aroused by the tempestuous entry of a woman with make-up on her face and a Roman sword in her hand.

'Ah-h-h-h-h!' she cried.

Wilmot was not interested. Briefly raising his eyebrows and baring his lips in an animal snarl, he returned to his meditations.

Hortensia Burwash was not accustomed to a reception like this. For a moment she stood irresolute; then, raising the sword, she brought it down with a powerful follow through on a handsome ink-pot which had been presented to Mr Schnellenhamer by a few admirers and well-wishers on the occasion of the Perfecto-Zizzbaum's foundation.

'Ah-h-h-h-h!' she cried again.

Wilmot had had enough of this foolery. Like all the Mulliners, his attitude towards Woman had until recently been one of reverence and unfailing courtesy. But with four days' orange-juice under his belt, he was dashed if he was going to have females carrying on like this in his presence. A considerable quantity of the ink had got on his trousers, and he now faced Hortensia Burwash, pale with fury.

'What's the idea?' he demanded hotly. 'What's the matter with you? Stop it immediately, and give me that sword.'

The temperamental star emitted another 'Ah-h-h-h-h!' but it was but a half-hearted one. The old pep had gone. She allowed the weapon to be snatched from her grasp. Her eyes met Wilmot's. And suddenly, as she gazed into those steel-hard orbs, the fire faded out of her, leaving her a mere weak woman face to face with what appeared to be the authentic caveman. It seemed to her for an instant, as she looked at him, that she had caught a glimpse of something evil. It was as if this man who stood before her had been a Fiend about to Seize Hatchet and Slay Six.

As a matter of fact, Wilmot's demeanour was simply the normal one of a man who every morning for four days has taken an orange, divided it into two equal parts, squeezed on a squeezer, poured into a glass or cup, and drunk; who has sipped the juice of an orange in the midst of rollicking lunchers doing themselves well among the roasts and hashes; and who, on returning to his modest flat in the evenfall, has got to work with the old squeezer once more. But Hortensia Burwash, eyeing him, trembled. Her spirit was broken.

'Messing about with ink,' grumbled Wilmot, dabbing at his legs with blotting-paper. 'Silly horseplay, I call it.'

The star's lips quivered. She registered Distress.

'You needn't be so cross,' she whimpered.

'Cross!' thundered Wilmot. He pointed wrathfully at his lower limbs. 'The best ten-dollar trousers in Hollywood!'

'Well, I'm sorry.'

'You'd better be. What did you do it for?'

'I don't know. Everything sort of went black.'

'Like my trousers.'

'I'm sorry about your trousers.' She sniffed miserably. 'You wouldn't be so unkind if you knew what it was like.'

'What what was like?'

'This dieting. Fifteen days with nothing but orange-juice.'

The effect of those words on Wilmot Mulliner was stunning. His animosity left him in a flash. He started. The stony look in his eyes melted, and he gazed at her with a tender commiseration, mingled with remorse that he should have treated so harshly a sister in distress.

'You don't mean you're dieting?'

'Yes.'

Wilmot was deeply stirred. It was as if he had become once more the old, kindly, gentle Wilmot, beloved by all.

'You poor little thing! No wonder you rush about smashing ink-pots. Fifteen days of it! My gosh!'

'And I was upset, too, about the picture.'

'What picture?'

'My new picture. I don't like the story.'

'What a shame!'

'It isn't true to life.'

'How rotten! Tell me all about it. Come on, tell Wilmot.'

'Well, it's like this. I'm supposed to be starving in a garret, and they want me with the last remnant of my strength to write a letter to my husband, forgiving him and telling him I love him still. The idea is that I'm purified by hunger. And I say it's all wrong.'

'All wrong?' cried Wilmot. 'You're right, it's all wrong. I never heard anything so silly in my life. A starving woman's heart wouldn't soften. And, as for being purified by hunger, purified by hunger my hat! The only reason which would make a woman in that position take pen in hand and write to her husband would be if she could think of something nasty enough to say to make it worth while.'

'That's just how I feel.'

'As a matter of fact, nobody but a female goof would be thinking of husbands at all at a time like that. She would be thinking of roast pork . . .'

'. . . and steaks . . .'

'. . . and chops . . .'

'. . . and chicken casserole . . .'

'. . . and kidneys *sautés* . . .'

'. . . and mutton curry . . .'

'. . . and doughnuts . . .'

'. . . and layer-cake . . .'

'. . . and peach pie, mince pie, apple pie, custard pie, and pie *à la mode*,' said Wilmot. 'Of everything, in a word, but the juice of an orange. Tell me, who was the halfwit who passed this story, so utterly alien to human psychology?'

'Mr Schnellenhamer. I was coming to see him about it.'

'I'll have a word or two with Mr Schnellenhamer. We'll soon have that story fixed. But what on earth do you want to diet for?'

'I don't want to. There's a weight clause in my contract. It says I mustn't weigh more than a hundred and eight pounds. Mr Schnellenhamer insisted on it.'

A grim look came into Wilmot's face.

'Schnellenhamer again, eh? This shall be attended to.'

He crossed to the cupboard and flung open the door. The magnate came out on all fours. Wilmot curtly directed him to the desk.

'Take paper and ink, Schnellenhamer, and write this lady out a new contract, with no weight clause.'

'But listen . . .'

'Your sword, madam, I believe?' said Wilmot, extending the weapon.

'All right,' said Mr Schnellenhamer hastily. 'All right. All right.'

'And, while you're at it,' said Wilmot, 'I'll take one, too, restoring me to my former salary.'

'What was your former salary?' asked Hortensia Burwash.

'Fifteen hundred.'

'I'll double it. I've been looking for a business manager like you for years. I didn't think they made them nowadays. So firm. So decisive. So brave. So strong. You're the business manager of my dreams.'

Wilmot's gaze, straying about the room, was attracted by a movement on top of the filing cabinet. He looked up, and his eyes met those of Mabel Potter. They yearned worshippingly at him, and in them there was something which he had no difficulty in diagnosing as the love-light. He turned to Hortensia Burwash.

'By the way, my fiancée, Miss Potter.'

'How do you do?' said Hortensia Burwash.

'Pleased to meet you,' said Mabel.

'What did you get up there for?' asked Miss Burwash, puzzled.

'Oh, I thought I would,' said Mabel.

Wilmot, as became a man of affairs, was crisp and business-like.

'Miss Burwash wishes to make a contract with me to act as her manager,' he said. 'Take dictation, Miss Potter.'

'Yes, sir,' said Mabel.

At the desk, Mr Schnellenhamer had paused for a moment in his writing. He was trying to remember if the word he wanted was spelled 'clorse' or 'clorze'.

The Rise of Minna Nordstrom

They had been showing the latest Minna Nordstrom picture at the Bijou Dream in the High Street, and Miss Postlethwaite, our sensitive barmaid, who had attended the première, was still deeply affected. She snuffled audibly as she polished the glasses.

'It's really good, is it?' we asked, for in the bar-parlour of the Anglers' Rest we lean heavily on Miss Postlethwaite's opinion where the silver screen is concerned. Her verdict can make or mar.

' 'Swonderful,' she assured us. 'It lays bare for all to view the soul of a woman who dared everything for love. A poignant and uplifting drama of life as it is lived today, purifying the emotions with pity and terror.'

A Rum and Milk said that if it was as good as all that he didn't know but what he might not risk ninepence on it. A Sherry and Bitters wondered what they paid a woman like Minna Nordstrom. A Port from the Wood, raising the conversation from the rather sordid plane to which it threatened to sink, speculated on how motion-picture stars became stars.

'What I mean,' said the Port from the Wood, 'does a studio deliberately set out to create a star? Or does it suddenly say to itself "Hullo, here's a star. What ho!"?'

One of those cynical Dry Martinis who always know everything said that it was all a question of influence.

'If you looked into it, you would find this Nordstrom girl was married to one of the bosses.'

Mr Mulliner, who had been sipping his hot Scotch and Lemon in a rather *distrait* way, glanced up.

'Did I hear you mention the name Minna Nordstrom?'

'We were arguing about how she became a star. I was saying that she must have had a pull of some kind.'

'In a sense,' said Mr Mulliner, 'you are right. She did have a pull. But it was one due solely to her own initiative and resource. I have relatives and connections in Hollywood, as you know, and I learn much of the inner history of the studio world through these channels. I happen to know that Minna Nordstrom raised herself to her present eminence by sheer enterprise and determination. If Miss Postlethwaite will mix me another hot Scotch and Lemon, this time stressing the Scotch a little more vigorously, I shall be delighted to tell you the whole story.'

When people talk with bated breath in Hollywood – and it is a place where there is always a certain amount of breath-bating going on – you will generally find, said Mr Mulliner, that the subject of their conversation is Jacob Z. Schnellenhamer, the popular president of the Perfecto-Zizzbaum Corporation. For few names are more widely revered there than that of this Napoleonic man.

Ask for an instance of his financial acumen, and his admirers will point to the great merger for which he was responsible – that merger by means of which he combined his own company, the Colossal-Exquisite, with those two other vast concerns, the Perfecto-Fishbein and the Zizzbaum-Celluloid. Demand proof of his artistic genius, his flair for recognizing talent in the raw, and it is given immediately. He was the man who discovered Minna Nordstrom.

Today when interviewers bring up the name of the world-famous star in Mr Schnellenhamer's presence, he smiles quietly.

'I had long had my eye on the little lady,' he says, 'but for one reason and another I did not consider the time ripe for her début. Then I brought about what you are good enough to call the epoch-making merger, and I was enabled to take the decisive step. My colleagues questioned the wisdom of elevating a totally unknown girl to stardom, but I was firm. I saw that it was the only thing to be done.'

'You had vision?'

'I had vision.'

All that Mr Schnellenhamer had, however, on the evening when this story begins was a headache. As he returned from the day's work at the studio and sank wearily into an armchair in the sitting-room of his luxurious home in Beverly Hills, he was feeling that the life of the president of a motion-picture corporation was one that he would hesitate to force on any dog of which he was fond.

A morbid meditation, of course, but not wholly unjustified. The great drawback to being the man in control of a large studio

is that everybody you meet starts acting at you. Hollywood is
entirely populated by those who want to get into the pictures,
and they naturally feel that the best way of accomplishing their
object is to catch the boss's eye and do their stuff.

Since leaving home that morning Mr Schnellenhamer had
been acted at practically incessantly. First, it was the studio
watchman who, having opened the gate to admit his car, proceeded to play a little scene designed to show what he would
do in a heavy role. Then came his secretary, two book agents,
the waitress who brought him his lunch, a life insurance man,
a representative of a film weekly, and a barber. And, on leaving
at the end of the day, he got the watchman again, this time in
whimsical comedy.

Little wonder, then, that by the time he reached home the
magnate was conscious of a throbbing sensation about the
temples and an urgent desire for a restorative.

As a preliminary to obtaining the latter, he rang the bell and
Vera Prebble, his parlourmaid, entered. For a moment he was
surprised not to see his butler. Then he recalled that he had
dismissed him just after breakfast for reciting 'Gunga Din' in
a meaning way while bringing the eggs and bacon.

'You rang, sir?'

'I want a drink.'

'Very good, sir.'

The girl withdrew, to return a few moments later with a
decanter and siphon. The sight caused Mr Schnellenhamer's
gloom to lighten a little. He was proud of his cellar, and he
knew that the decanter contained liquid balm. In a sudden gush
of tenderness he eyed its bearer appreciatively, thinking what a
nice girl she looked.

Until now he had never studied Vera Prebble's appearance to
any great extent or thought about her much in any way. When
she had entered his employment a few days before, he had
noticed, of course, that she had a sort of ethereal beauty; but
then every girl you see in Hollywood has either ethereal beauty
or roguish gaminerie or a dark, slumbrous face that hints at
hidden passion.

'Put it down there on the small table,' said Mr Schnellenhamer, passing his tongue over his lips.

The girl did so. Then, straightening herself, she suddenly
threw her head back and clutched the sides of it in an ecstasy
of hopeless anguish.

'Oh! Oh! Oh!' she cried.

'Eh?' said Mr Schnellenhamer.

'Ah! Ah! Ah!'

'I don't get you at all,' said Mr Schnellenhamer.

She gazed at him with wide, despairing eyes.

'If you knew how sick and tired I am of it all! Tired . . . Tired . . . Tired. The lights . . . the glitter . . . the gaiety . . . It is so hollow, so fruitless. I want to get away from it all, ha-ha-ha-ha-ha!'

Mr Schnellenhamer retreated behind the chesterfield. That laugh had had an unbalanced ring. He had not liked it. He was about to continue his backward progress in the direction of the door, when the girl, who had closed her eyes and was rocking to and fro as if suffering from some internal pain, became calmer.

'Just a little thing I knocked together with a view to showing myself in a dramatic role,' she said. 'Watch! I'm going to register.'

She smiled. 'Joy.'

She closed her mouth. 'Grief.'

She wiggled her ears. 'Horror.'

She raised her eyebrows. 'Hate.'

Then, taking a parcel from the tray:

'Here,' she said, 'if you would care to glance at them, are a few stills of myself. This shows my face in repose. I call it "Reverie". This is me in a bathing suit . . . riding . . . walking . . . happy among my books . . . being kind to the dog. Here is one of which my friends have been good enough to speak in terms of praise – as Cleopatra, the warrior-queen of Egypt, at the Pasadena Gas-Fitters' Ball. It brings out what is generally considered my most effective feature – the nose, seen sideways.'

During the course of these remarks, Mr Schnellenhamer had been standing breathing heavily. For a while the discovery that this parlourmaid, of whom he had just been thinking so benevolently, was simply another snake in the grass had rendered him incapable of speech. Now his aphasia left him.

'Get out!' he said.

'Pardon?' said the girl.

'Get out this minute. You're fired.'

There was a silence. Vera Prebble closed her mouth, wiggled her ears, and raised her eyebrows. It was plain that she was grieved, horror-stricken, and in the grip of a growing hate.

'What,' she demanded passionately at length, 'is the matter with all you movie magnates? Have you no hearts? Have you no compassion? No sympathy? No understanding? Do the ambitions of the struggling mean nothing to you?'

'No,' replied Mr Schnellenhamer in answer to all five questions.

Vera Prebble laughed bitterly.

'No is right!' she said. 'For months I besieged the doors of the casting directors. They refused to cast me. Then I thought that if I could find a way into your homes I might succeed where I had failed before. I secured the post of parlourmaid to Mr Fishbein of the Perfecto-Fishbein. Half-way through Rudyard Kipling's "Boots" he brutally bade me begone. I obtained a similar position with Mr Zizzbaum of the Zizzbaum-Celluloid. The opening lines of "The Wreck of the *Hesperus*" had hardly passed my lips when he was upstairs helping me pack my trunk. And now you crush my hopes. It is cruel ... cruel ... Oh, ha-ha-ha-ha-ha!'

She rocked to and fro in an agony of grief. Then an idea seemed to strike her.

'I wonder if you would care to see me in light comedy? ... No? ... Oh, very well.'

With a quick droop of the eyelids and a twitch of the muscles of the cheeks she registered resignation.

'Just as you please,' she said. Then her nostrils quivered and she bared the left canine tooth to indicate Menace. 'But one last word. Wait!'

'How do you mean, wait?'

'Just wait. That's all.'

For an instant Mr Schnellenhamer was conscious of a twinge of uneasiness. Like all motion-picture magnates, he had about forty-seven guilty secrets, many of them recorded on paper. Was it possible that ...

Then he breathed again. All his private documents were in a safe-deposit box. It was absurd to imagine that this girl could have anything on him.

Relieved, he lay down on the chesterfield and gave himself up to daydreams. And soon, as he remembered that that morning he had put through a deal which would enable him to trim the stuffing out of two hundred and seventy-three exhibitors, his lips curved in a contented smile and Vera Prebble was forgotten.

One of the advantages of life in Hollywood is that the Servant Problem is not a difficult one. Supply more than equals demand. Ten minutes after you have thrown a butler out of the back door his successor is bowling up in his sports-model car. And the same applies to parlourmaids. By the following afternoon all was well once more with the Schnellenhamer domestic machine. A new butler was cleaning the silver: a new parlourmaid was doing whatever parlourmaids do, which is very little. Peace reigned in the home.

But on the second evening, as Mr Schnellenhamer, the day's tasks over, entered his sitting-room with nothing in his mind but bright thoughts of dinner, he was met by what had all the appearance of a human whirlwind. This was Mrs Schnellenhamer. A graduate of the silent films, Mrs Schnellenhamer had been known in her day as the Queen of Stormy Emotion, and she occasionally saw to it that her husband was reminded of this.

'Now see what!' cried Mrs Schnellenhamer.

Mr Schnellenhamer was perturbed.

'Is something wrong?' he asked nervously.

'Why did you fire that girl, Vera Prebble?'

'She went ha-ha-ha-ha-ha at me.'

'Well, do you know what she has done? She has laid information with the police that we are harbouring alcoholic liquor on our premises, contrary to law, and this afternoon they came in a truck and took it all away.

Mr Schnellenhamer reeled. The shock was severe. The good man loves his cellar.

'Not all?' he cried, almost pleadingly.

'All.'

'The Scotch?'

'Every bottle.'

'The gin?'

'Every drop.'

Mr Schnellenhamer supported himself against the chesterfield.

'Not the champagne?' he whispered.

'Every case. And here we are, with a hundred and fifty people coming tonight, including the Duke.'

Her allusion was to the Duke of Wigan, who, as so many British dukes do, was at this time passing slowly through Hollywood.

'And you know how touchy dukes are,' proceeded Mrs Schnellenhamer. 'I'm told that the Lulabelle Mahaffys invited the Duke of Kircudbrightshire for the weekend last year, and after he had been there two months he suddenly left in a huff because there was no brown sherry.'

A motion-picture magnate has to be a quick thinker. Where a lesser man would have wasted time referring to the recent Miss Prebble as a serpent whom he had to all intents and purposes nurtured in his bosom, Mr Schnellenhamer directed the whole force of his great brain on the vital problem of how to undo the evil she had wrought.

'Listen,' he said. 'It's all right. I'll get the bootlegger on the phone, and he'll have us stocked up again in no time.'

But he had overlooked the something in the air of Hollywood which urges its every inhabitant irresistibly into the pictures. When he got his bootlegger's number, it was only to discover that that life-saving tradesman was away from home. They were shooting a scene in *Sundered Hearts* on the Outstanding Screen-Favourites lot, and the bootlegger was hard at work there, playing the role of an Anglican bishop. His secretary said he could not be disturbed, as it got him all upset to be interrupted when he was working.

Mr Schnellenhamer tried another bootlegger, then another. They were out on location.

And it was just as he had begun to despair that he bethought him of his old friend, Isadore Fishbein; and into his darkness there shot a gleam of hope. By the greatest good fortune it so happened that he and the president of the Perfecto-Fishbein were at the moment on excellent terms, neither having slipped anything over on the other for several weeks. Mr Fishbein, moreover, possessed as well-stocked a cellar as any man in California. It would be a simple matter to go round and borrow from him all he needed.

Patting Mrs Schnellenhamer's hand and telling her that there were still bluebirds singing in the sunshine, he ran to his car and leaped into it.

The residence of Isadore Fishbein was only a few hundred yards away, and Mr Schnellenhamer was soon whizzing in through the door. He found his friend beating his head against the wall of the sitting-room and moaning to himself in a quiet undertone.

'Is something the matter?' he asked, surprised.

'There is,' said Mr Fishbein, selecting a fresh spot on the tapestried wall and starting to beat his head against that. 'The police came round this afternoon and took away everything I had.'

'Everything?'

'Well, not Mrs Fishbein,' said the other, with a touch of regret in his voice. 'She's up in the bedroom with eight cubes of ice on her forehead in a linen bag. But they took every drop of everything else. A serpent, that's what she is.'

'Mrs Fishbein?'

'Not Mrs Fishbein. That parlourmaid. That Vera Prebble. Just because I stopped her when she got to "boots, boots, boots, boots, marching over Africa" she ups and informs the police on me. And Mrs Fishbein with a hundred and eighty people coming tonight, including the ex-King of Ruritania!'

And, crossing the room, the speaker began to bang his head against a statue of Genius Inspiring the Motion-Picture Industry.

A good man is always appalled when he is forced to contemplate the depths to which human nature can sink, and Mr Schnellenhamer's initial reaction on hearing of this fresh outrage on the part of his late parlourmaid was a sort of sick horror. Then the brain which had built up the Colossal-Exquisite began to work once more.

'Well, the only thing for us to do,' he said, 'is to go round to Ben Zizzbaum and borrow some of his stock. How do you stand with Ben?'

'I stand fine with Ben,' said Mr Fishbein, cheering up. 'I heard something about him last week which I'll bet he wouldn't care to have known.'

'Where does he live?'

'Camden Drive.'

'Then tally-ho!' said Mr Schnellenhamer, who had once produced a drama in eight reels of two strong men battling for a woman's love in the English hunting district.

They were soon at Mr Zizzbaum's address. Entering the sitting-room, they were shocked to observe a form rolling in circles round the floor with its head between its hands. It was travelling quickly, but not so quickly that they were unable to recognize it as that of the chief executive of the Zizzbaum-Celluloid Corporation. Stopped as he was completing his eleventh lap and pressed for an explanation, Mr Zizzbaum revealed that a recent parlourmaid of his, Vera Prebble by name, piqued at having been dismissed for deliberate and calculated reciting of the works of Mrs Hemans, had informed the police of his stock of wines and spirits and that the latter had gone off with the whole collection not half an hour since.

'And don't speak so loud,' added the stricken man, 'or you'll wake Mrs Zizzbaum. She's in bed with ice on her head.'

'How many cubes?' asked Mr Fishbein.

'Six.'

'Mrs Fishbein needed eight,' said that lady's husband a little proudly.

The situation was one that might well have unmanned the stoutest motion-picture executive and there were few motion-picture executives stouter than Jacob Schnellenhamer. But it was characteristic of this man that the tightest corner was always the one to bring out the full force of his intellect. He thought of Mrs Schnellenhamer waiting for him at home, and it was as if an electric shock of high voltage had passed through him.

'I've got it,' he said. 'We must go to Glutz of the Medulla-Oblongata. He's never been a real friend of mine, but if you loan him Stella Svelte and I loan him Orlando Byng and Fishbein loans him Oscar the Wonder-Poodle on his own terms, I think he'll consent to give us enough to see us through tonight. I'll get him on the phone.'

It was some moments before Mr Schnellenhamer returned from the telephone booth. When he did so, his associates were surprised to observe in his eyes a happy gleam.

'Boys,' he said, 'Glutz is away with his family over the weekend. The butler and the rest of the help are out joy-riding. There's only a parlourmaid in the house. I've been talking to her. So there won't be any need for us to give him those stars, after all. We'll just run across in the car with a few axes and help ourselves. It won't cost us above a hundred dollars to square this girl. She can tell him she was upstairs when the burglars broke in and didn't hear anything. And there we'll be, with all the stuff we need and not a cent to pay outside of overhead connected with the maid.'

There was an awed silence.

'Mrs Fishbein will be pleased.'

'Mrs Zizzbaum will be pleased.'

'And Mrs Schnellenhamer will be pleased,' said the leader of the expedition. 'Where do you keep your axes, Zizzbaum?'

'In the cellar.'

'Fetch 'em!' said Mr Schnellenhamer in the voice a Crusader might have used in giving the signal to start against the Paynim.

In the ornate residence of Sigismund Glutz, meanwhile, Vera Prebble, who had entered the service of the head of the Medulla-Oblongata that morning and was already under sentence of dismissal for having informed him with appropriate gestures that a bunch of the boys were whooping it up in the Malemute saloon, was engaged in writing on a sheet of paper a short list of names, one of which she proposed as a *nom de théâtre* as soon as her screen career should begin.

For this girl was essentially an optimist, and not even all the rebuffs which she had suffered had been sufficient to quench the fire of ambition in her.

Wiggling her tongue as she shaped the letters, she wrote:

Ursuline Delmaine
Theodora Trix
Uvula Gladwyn

None of them seemed to her quite what she wanted. She pondered. Possibly something a little more foreign and exotic . . .

Greta Garbo

No, that had been used . . .

And then suddenly inspiration descended upon her and, trembling a little with emotion, she inscribed on the paper the one name that was absolutely and indubitably right.

Minna Nordstrom

The more she looked at it, the better she liked it. And she was still regarding it proudly when there came the sound of a car stopping at the door and a few moments later in walked Mr Schnellenhamer, Mr Zizzbaum and Mr Fishbein. They all wore Homburg hats and carried axes.

Vera Prebble drew herself up.

'All goods must be delivered in the rear,' she had begun haughtily, when she recognized her former employers and paused, surprised.

The recognition was mutual. Mr Fishbein started. So did Mr Zizzbaum.

'Serpent! said Mr Fishbein.

'Viper!' said Mr Zizzbaum.

Mr Schnellenhamer was more diplomatic. Though as deeply moved as his colleagues by the sight of this traitoress, he realized that this was no time for invective.

'Well, well, well,' he said, with a geniality which he strove to render frank and winning, 'I never dreamed it was you on the phone, my dear. Well, this certainly makes everything nice and smooth – us all being, as you might say, old friends.'

'Friends?' retorted Vera Prebble. 'Let me tell you . . .'

'I know, I know. Quite, quite. But listen. I've got to have some liquor tonight.'

'What do you mean, *you* have?' said Mr Fishbein.

'It's all right, it's all right,' said Mr Schnellenhamer soothingly. 'I was coming to that. I wasn't forgetting you. We're all in this together. The good old spirit of cooperation. You see, my dear,' he went on, 'that little joke you played on us . . . oh, I'm not blaming you. Nobody laughed more heartily than myself . . .'

'Yes, they did,' said Mr Fishbein, alive now to the fact that this girl before him must be conciliated. 'I did.'

'So did I,' said Mr Zizzbaum.

'We all laughed very heartily,' said Mr Schnellenhamer. 'You should have heard us. A girl of spirit, we said to ourselves. Still, the little pleasantry has left us in something of a difficulty, and it will be worth a hundred dollars to you, my dear, to go upstairs and put cotton wool in your ears while we get at Mr Glutz's cellar door with our axes.'

Vera Prebble raised her eyebrows.

'What do you want to break down the cellar door for? I know the combination of the lock.'

'You do?' said Mr Schnellenhamer joyfully.

'I withdraw that expression "Serpent",' said Mr Fishbein.

'When I used the term "Viper",' said Mr Zizzbaum, 'I was speaking thoughtlessly.'

'And I will tell it you,' said Vera Prebble, 'at a price.'

She drew back her head and extended an arm, twiddling the

fingers at the end of it. She was plainly registering something, but they could not discern what it was.

'There is only one condition on which I will tell you the combination of Mr Glutz's cellar, and that is this. One of you has got to give me a starring contract for five years.'

The magnates started.

'Listen,' said Mr Zizzbaum, 'you don't want to star.'

'You wouldn't like it,' said Mr Fishbein.

'Of course you wouldn't,' said Mr Schnellenhamer. 'You would look silly, starring – an inexperienced girl like you. Now, if you had said a nice small part . . .'

'Star.'

'Or featured . . .'

'Star.'

The three men drew back a pace or two and put their heads together.

'She means it,' said Mr Fishbein.

'Her eyes,' said Mr Zizzbaum. 'Like stones.'

'A dozen times I could have dropped something heavy on that girl's head from an upper landing, and I didn't do it,' said Mr Schnellenhamer remorsefully.

Mr Fishbein threw up his hands.

'It's no use. I keep seeing that vision of Mrs Fishbein floating before me with eight cubes of ice on her head. I'm going to star this girl.'

'*You* are?' said Mr Zizzbaum. 'And get the stuff? And leave me to go home and tell Mrs Zizzbaum there won't be anything to drink at her party tonight for a hundred and eleven guests including the Vice-President of Switzerland? No, sir! *I* am going to star her.'

'I'll outbid you.'

'You won't outbid *me*. Not till they bring me word that Mrs Zizzbaum has lost the use of her vocal chords.'

'Listen,' said the other tensely. 'When it comes to using vocal chords, Mrs Fishbein begins where Mrs Zizzbaum leaves off.'

Mr Schnellenhamer, that cool head, saw the peril that loomed.

'Boys,' he said, 'if we once start bidding against one another, there'll be no limit. There's only one thing to be done. We must merge.'

His powerful personality carried the day. It was the President of the newly-formed Perfecto-Zizzbaum Corporation who a few moments later stepped forward and approached the girl.

'We agree.'

And, as he spoke, there came the sound of some heavy vehicle stopping in the road outside. Vera Prebble uttered a stricken exclamation.

'Well, of all the silly girls!' she cried distractedly. 'I've just remembered that an hour ago I telephoned the police, informing them of Mr Glutz's cellar. And here they are!'

Mr Fishbein uttered a cry, and began to look round for something to bang his head against. Mr Zizzbaum gave a short, sharp moan, and started to lower himself to the floor. But Mr Schnellenhamer was made of sterner stuff.

'Pull yourselves together, boys,' he begged them. 'Leave all this to me. Everything is going to be all right. Things have come to a pretty pass,' he said, with a dignity as impressive as it was simple, 'if a free-born American citizen cannot bribe the police of his native country.'

'True,' said Mr Fishbein, arresting his head when within an inch and a quarter of a handsome Oriental vase.

'True, true,' said Mr Zizzbaum, getting up and dusting his knees.

'Just let me handle the whole affair,' said Mr Schnellenhamer. 'Ah, boys!' he went on, genially.

Three policemen had entered the room – a sergeant, a patrolman, and another patrolman. Their faces wore a wooden, hard-boiled look.

'Mr Glutz?' said the sergeant.

'Mr Schnellenhamer,' corrected the great man. 'But Jacob to you, old friend.'

The sergeant seemed in no wise mollified by this amiability.

'Prebble, Vera?' he asked, addressing the girl.

'Nordstrom, Minna,' she replied.

'Got the name wrong, then. Anyway, it was you who phoned us that there was alcoholic liquor on the premises?'

Mr Schnellenhamer laughed amusedly.

'You mustn't believe everything that girl tells you, sergeant. She's a great kidder. Always was. If she said that, it was just one of her little jokes. I know Glutz. I know his views. And many is the time I have heard him say that the laws of his country are good enough for him and that he would scorn not to obey them. You will find nothing here, sergeant.'

'Well, we'll try,' said the other. 'Show us the way to the cellar,' he added, turning to Vera Prebble.

Mr Schnellenhamer smiled a winning smile.

'Now listen,' he said. 'I've just remembered I'm wrong. Silly mistake to make, and I don't know how I made it. There *is* a certain amount of the stuff in the house, but I'm sure you dear chaps don't want to cause any unpleasantness. You're broad-minded. Listen. Your name's Murphy, isn't it?'

'Donahue.'

'I thought so. Well, you'll laugh at this. Only this morning I was saying to Mrs Schnellenhamer that I must really slip down to headquarters and give my old friend Donahue that ten dollars I owed him.'

'What ten dollars?'

'I didn't say ten. I said a hundred. One hundred dollars, Donny, old man, and I'm not saying there mightn't be a little over for these two gentlemen here. How about it?'

The sergeant drew himself up. There was no sign of softening in his glance.

'Jacob Schnellenhamer,' he said coldly, 'you can't square me. When I tried for a job at the Colossal-Exquisite last spring I was turned down on account you said I had no sex appeal.'

The first patrolman, who had hitherto taken no part in the conversation, started.

'Is that so, Chief?'

'Yessir. No sex appeal.'

'Well, can you tie that!' said the first patrolman. 'When I tried to crash the Colossal-Exquisite, they said my voice wasn't right.'

'Me,' said the second patrolman, eyeing Mr Schnellenhamer sourly, 'they had the nerve to beef at my left profile. Lookut, boys,' he said, turning, 'can you see anything wrong with that profile?'

His companions studied him closely. The sergeant raised a hand and peered between his fingers with his head tilted back and his eyes half closed.

'Not a thing,' he said.

'Why, Basil, it's a lovely profile,' said the first patrolman.

'Well, that's how it goes,' said the second patrolman moodily.

The sergeant had returned to his own grievance.

'No sex appeal!' he said with a rasping laugh. 'And me that had specially taken sex appeal in the College of Eastern Iowa course of Motion Picture acting.'

'Who says my voice ain't right?' demanded the first patrol-man. 'Listen. Mi-mi-mi-mi-mi.'

'Swell,' said the sergeant.

'Like a nightingale or something,' said the second patrol-man.

The sergeant flexed his muscles.

'Ready, boys?'

'Kayo, Chief.'

'Wait!' cried Mr Schnellenhamer. 'Wait! Give me one more chance. I'm sure I can find parts for you all.'

The sergeant shook his head.

'No. It's too late. You've got us mad now. You don't appreciate the sensitiveness of the artist. Does he, boys?'

'You're darned right he doesn't,' said the first patrolman.

'I wouldn't work for the Colossal-Exquisite now,' said the second patrolman with a petulant twitch of his shoulder, 'not if they wanted me to play Romeo opposite Jean Harlow.'

'Then let's go,' said the sergeant. 'Come along, lady, you show us where this cellar is.'

For some moments after the officers of the Law, preceded by Vera Prebble, had left, nothing was to be heard in the silent sitting-room but the rhythmic beating of Mr Fishbein's head against the wall and the rustling sound of Mr Zizzbaum rolling round the floor. Mr Schnellenhamer sat brooding with his chin in his hands, merely moving his legs slightly each time Mr Zizzbaum came round. The failure of his diplomatic efforts had stunned him.

A vision rose before his eyes of Mrs Schnellenhamer waiting in their sunlit patio for his return. As clearly as if he had been there now, he could see her, swooning, slipping into the goldfish pond, and blowing bubbles with her head beneath the surface. And he was asking himself whether in such an event it would be better to raise her gently or just leave Nature to take its course. She would, he knew, be extremely full of that stormy emotion of which she had once been queen.

It was as he still debated this difficult point that a light step caught his ear. Vera Prebble was standing in the doorway.

'Mr Schnellenhamer.'

The magnate waved a weary hand.

'Leave me,' he said. 'I am thinking.'

'I thought you would like to know,' said Vera Prebble, 'that I've just locked those cops in the coal cellar.'

As in the final reel of a super-super-film eyes brighten and faces light up at the entry of the United States Marines, so at these words did Mr Schnellenhamer, Mr Fishbein and Mr Zizzbaum perk up as if after a draught of some magic elixir.

'In the coal cellar?' gasped Mr Schnellenhamer.

'In the coal cellar.'

'Then if we work quick . . .'

Vera Prebble coughed.

'One moment,' she said. 'Just one moment. Before you go, I have drawn up a little letter covering our recent agreement. Perhaps you will all three just sign it.'

Mr Schnellenhamer clicked his tongue impatiently.

'No time for that now. Come to my office tomorrow. Where are you going?' he asked, as the girl started to withdraw.

'Just to the coal cellar,' said Vera Prebble. 'I think those fellows may want to come out.'

Mr Schnellenhamer sighed. It had been worth trying, of course, but he had never really had much hope.

'Gimme,' he said resignedly.

The girl watched as the three men attached their signatures. She took the document and folded it carefully.

'Would any of you like to hear me recite "The Bells", by Edgar Allan Poe?' she asked.

'No!' said Mr Fishbein.

'No!' said Mr Zizzbaum.

'No!' said Mr Schnellenhamer. 'We have no desire to hear you recite "The Bells", Miss Prebble.'

The girl's eyes flashed haughtily.

'Miss Nordstrom,' she corrected. 'And just for that you'll get "The Charge of the Light Brigade", and like it.'

The Castaways

Monday night in the bar-parlour of the Anglers' Rest is usually Book Night. This is due to the fact that on Sunday afternoon it is the practice of Miss Postlethwaite, our literature-loving barmaid, to retire to her room with a box of caramels and a novel from the circulating library and, having removed her shoes, to lie down on the bed and indulge in what she calls a good old read. On the following evening she places the results of her researches before us and invites our judgement.

This weekend it was one of those Desert Island stories which had claimed her attention.

'It's where this ship is sailing the Pacific Ocean,' explained Miss Postlethwaite, 'and it strikes a reef and the only survivors are Cyril Trevelyan and Eunice Westleigh, and they float ashore on a plank to this uninhabited island. And gradually they find the solitude and what I might call the loneliness drawing them strangely together, and in Chapter Nineteen, which is as far as I've got, they've just fallen into each other's arms and all around was the murmur of the surf and the cry of wheeling sea birds. And why I don't see how it's all going to come out,' said Miss Postlethwaite, 'is because they don't like each other really and, what's more, Eunice is engaged to be married to a prominent banker in New York and Cyril to the daughter of the Duke of Rotherhithe. Looks like a mix-up to me.'

A Sherry and Bitters shook his head.

'Far-fetched,' he said disapprovingly. 'Not the sort of thing that ever really happens.'

'On the contrary,' said Mr Mulliner. 'It is an almost exact parallel to the case of Genevieve Bootle and my brother Joseph's younger son, Bulstrode.'

'Were they cast ashore on a desert island?'

'Practically,' said Mr Mulliner. 'They were in Hollywood, writing dialogue for the talking pictures.'

Miss Postlethwaite, who prides herself on her encyclopaedic knowledge of English Literature, bent her shapely eyebrows.

'Bulstrode Mulliner? Genevieve Bootle?' she murmured. 'I never read anything by them. What did they write?'

'My nephew,' Mr Mulliner hastened to explain, 'was not an author. Nor was Miss Bootle. Very few of those employed in writing motion-picture dialogue are. The executives of the studios just haul in anyone they meet and make them sign contracts. Most of the mysterious disappearances you read about are due to this cause. Only the other day they found a plumber who had been missing for years. All the time he had been writing dialogue for the Mishkin Brothers. Once having reached Los Angeles, nobody is safe.'

'Rather like the old Press Gang,' said the Sherry and Bitters.

'Just like the old Press Gang,' said Mr Mulliner.

My nephew Bulstrode (said Mr Mulliner), as is the case with so many English younger sons, had left his native land to seek his fortune abroad, and at the time when this story begins was living in New York, where he had recently become betrothed to a charming girl of the name of Mabelle Ridgway.

Although naturally eager to get married, the young couple were prudent. They agreed that before taking so serious a step they ought to have a little capital put by. And, after talking it over, they decided that the best plan would be for Bulstrode to go to California and try to strike oil.

So Bulstrode set out for Los Angeles, all eagerness and enthusiasm, and the first thing that happened to him was that somebody took his new hat, a parting gift from Mabelle, leaving in its place in the club car of the train a Fedora that was a size too small for him.

The train was running into the station when he discovered his loss, and he hurried out to scan his fellow-passengers, and presently there emerged a stout man with a face rather like that of a vulture which has been doing itself too well on the corpses. On this person's head was the missing hat.

And, just as Bulstrode was about to accost this stout man, there came up a mob of camera-men, who photographed him in various attitudes, and before Bulstrode could get a word in he was bowling off in a canary-coloured automobile bearing on its door in crimson letters the legend 'Jacob Z. Schnellenhamer, President Perfecto-Zizzbaum Motion Picture Corp.'

All the Mulliners are men of spirit, and Bulstrode did not

propose to have his hats sneaked, even by the highest in the land, without lodging a protest. Next morning he called at the offices of the Perfecto-Zizzbaum, and after waiting four hours was admitted to the presence of Mr Schnellenhamer.

The motion-picture magnate took a quick look at Bulstrode and thrust a paper and a fountain pen towards him.

'Sign here,' he said.

A receipt for the hat, no doubt, thought Bulstrode. He scribbled his name at the bottom of the document, and Mr Schnellenhamer pressed the bell.

'Miss Stern,' he said, addressing his secretary, 'what vacant offices have we on the lot?'

'There is Room 40 in the Leper Colony.'

'I thought there was a song-writer there.'

'He passed away Tuesday.'

'Has the body been removed?'

'Yes, sir.'

'Then Mr Mulliner will occupy the room, starting from today. He has just signed a contract to write dialogue for us.'

Bulstrode would have spoken, but Mr Schnellenhamer silenced him with a gesture.

'Who are working on *Scented Sinners* now?' he asked.

The secretary consulted a list.

'Mr Doakes, Mr Noakes, Miss Faversham, Miss Wilson, Mr Fotheringay, Mr Mendelsohn, Mr Markey, Mrs Cooper, Mr Lennox and Mr Dabney.'

'That all?'

'There was a missionary who came in Thursday, wanting to convert the extra girls. He started a treatment, but he has escaped to Canada.'

'Tchah!' said Mr Schnellenhamer, annoyed. 'We must have more vigilance, more vigilance. Give Mr Mulliner a script of *Scented Sinners* before he goes.'

The secretary left the room. He returned to Bulstrode.

'Did you ever see *Scented Sinners*?'

Bulstrode said he had not.

'Powerful drama of life as it is lived by the jazz-crazed, gin-crazed Younger Generation whose hollow laughter is but the mask for an aching heart,' said Mr Schnellenhamer. 'It ran for a week in New York and lost a hundred thousand dollars, so we bought it. It has the mucus of a good story. See what you can do with it.'

'But I don't want to write for the pictures,' said Bulstrode.

'You've got to write for the pictures,' said Mr Schnellenhamer. 'You've signed the contract.'

'I want my hat.'

'In the Perfecto-Zizzbaum Motion Picture Corporation,' said Mr Schnellenhamer coldly, 'our slogan is Cooperation, not Hats.'

The Leper Colony, to which Bulstrode had been assigned, proved to be a long, low building with small cells opening on a narrow corridor. It had been erected to take care of the overflow of the studio's writers, the majority of whom were located in what was known as the Ohio State Penitentiary. Bulstrode took possession of Room 40, and settled down to see what he could do with *Scented Sinners*.

He was not unhappy. A good deal has been written about the hardships of life in motion-picture studios, but most of it, I am glad to say, is greatly exaggerated. The truth is that there is little or no actual ill-treatment of the writing staff, and the only thing that irked Bulstrode was the loneliness of the life.

Few who have not experienced it can realize the eerie solitude of a motion-picture studio. Human intercourse is virtually unknown. You are surrounded by writers, each in his or her little hutch, but if you attempt to establish communication with them you will find on every door a card with the words 'Working. Do not disturb.' And if you push open one of these doors you are greeted by a snarl so animal, so menacing, that you retire hastily lest nameless violence befall.

The world seems very far away. Outside, the sun beats down on the concrete, and occasionally you will see a man in shirt-sleeves driving a truck to a distant set, while ever and anon the stillness is broken by the shrill cry of some wheeling supervisor. But for the most part a forlorn silence prevails.

The conditions, in short, are almost precisely those of such a desert island as Miss Postlethwaite was describing to us just now.

In these circumstances the sudden arrival of a companion, especially a companion of the opposite sex, can scarcely fail to have its effect on a gregarious young man. Entering his office one morning and finding a girl in it, Bulstrode Mulliner experienced much the same emotions as did Robinson Crusoe on meeting Friday. It is not too much to say that he was electrified.

She was not a beautiful girl. Tall, freckled and slab-featured, she had a distinct look of a halibut. To Bulstrode, however, she seemed a vision.

'My name is Bootle,' she said. 'Genevieve Bootle.'

'Mine is Mulliner. Bulstrode Mulliner.'

'They told me to come here.'

'To see me about something?'

'To work with you on a thing called *Scented Sinners*. I've just signed a contract to write dialogue for the company.'

'Can you write dialogue?' asked Bulstrode. A foolish question, for, if she could, the Perfecto-Zizzbaum Corporation would scarcely have engaged her.

'No,' said the girl despondently. 'Except for letters to Ed, I've never written anything.'

'Ed?'

'Mr Murgatroyd, my fiancé. He's a bootlegger in Chicago, and I came out here to try to work up his West Coast connection. And I went to see Mr Schnellenhamer to ask if he would like a few cases of guaranteed pre-War Scotch, and I'd hardly begun to speak when he said "Sign here." So I signed, and now I find I can't leave till this *Scented Sinners* thing is finished.'

'I am in exactly the same position,' said Bulstrode. 'We must buckle to and make a quick job of it. You won't mind if I hold your hand from time to time? I fancy it will assist composition.'

'But what would Ed say?'

'Ed won't know.'

'No, there's that,' agreed the girl.

'And when I tell you that I myself am engaged to a lovely girl in New York,' Bulstrode pointed out, 'you will readily understand that what I am suggesting is merely a purely mechanical device for obtaining the best results on this script of ours.'

'Well, of course, if you put it like that . . .'

'I put it just like that,' said Bulstrode, taking her hand in his and patting it.

Against hand-holding as a means of stimulating the creative faculties of the brain there is, of course, nothing to be said. All collaborators do it. The trouble is that it is too often but a first step to other things. Gradually, little by little, as the long days wore on and propinquity and solitude began to exercise their spell, Bulstrode could not disguise it from himself that he was becoming oddly drawn to this girl, Bootle. If she and he had been fishing for turtles on the same mid-Pacific isle, they could not have been in closer communion, and presently the realization smote him like a blow that he loved her – and fervently, at that. For two pence, he told himself, had he not been a Mulliner and a gentleman, he could have crushed her in his arms and covered her face with burning kisses.

And, what was more, he could see by subtle signs that his love was returned. A quick glance from eyes that swiftly fell . . . the timid offer of a banana . . . a tremor in her voice as she asked if she might borrow his pencil-sharpener . . . These were little things, but they spoke volumes. If Genevieve Bootle was not crazy about him, he would eat his hat – or, rather, Mr Schnellenhamer's hat.

He was appalled and horrified. All the Mulliners are the soul of honour, and as he thought of Mabelle Ridgway, waiting for him and trusting him in New York, Bulstrode burned with shame and remorse. In the hope of averting the catastrophe, he plunged with a fresh fury of energy into the picturization of *Scented Sinners*.

It was a fatal move. It simply meant that Genevieve Bootle had to work harder on the thing, too, and *Scented Sinners* was not the sort of production on which a frail girl could concentrate in warm weather without something cracking. Came a day with the thermometer in the nineties when, as he turned to refer to a point in Mr Noakes's treatment, Bulstrode heard a sudden sharp snort at his side and, looking up, saw that Genevieve had begun to pace the room with feverish steps, her fingers entwined in her hair. And, as he stared at her in deep concern, she flung herself in a chair with a choking sob and buried her face in her hands.

And, seeing her weeping there, Bulstrode could restrain himself no longer. Something snapped in him. It was his collar stud. His neck, normally a fifteen and an eighth, had suddenly swelled under the pressure of uncontrollable emotion into a large seventeen. For an instant he stood gurgling wordlessly like a bull-pup choking over a chicken bone; then, darting forward, he clasped her in his arms and began to murmur all those words of love which until now he had kept pent up in his heart.

He spoke well and eloquently and at considerable length, but not at such length as he had planned. For at the end of perhaps two minutes and a quarter there rent the air in his immediate rear a sharp exclamation or cry; and, turning, he perceived in the doorway Mabelle Ridgway, his betrothed. With her was a dark young man with oiled hair and a saturnine expression, who looked like the sort of fellow the police are always spreading a drag-net for in connection with the recent robbery of Schoenstein's Bon Ton Delicatessen Store in Eighth Avenue.

There was a pause. It is never easy to know just what to say on these occasions: and Bulstrode, besides being embarrassed, was completely bewildered. He had supposed Mabelle three thousand miles away.

'Oh – hullo!' he said, untwining himself from Genevieve Bootle.

The dark young man was reaching in his hip-pocket, but Mabelle stopped him with a gesture.

'I can manage, thank you, Mr Murgatroyd. There is no need for sawn-off shot-guns.'

The young man had produced his weapon and was looking at it wistfully.

'I think you're wrong, lady,' he demurred. 'Do you know who that is that this necker is necking?' he asked, pointing an accusing finger at Genevieve Bootle, who was cowering against the ink-pot. 'My girl. No less. In person. Not a picture.'

Mabelle gasped.

'You don't say so?'

'I do say so.'

'Well, it's a small world,' said Mabelle. 'Yes, sir, a small world, and you can't say it isn't. All the same, I think we had better not have any shooting. This is not Chicago. It might cause comment and remark.'

'Maybe you're right,' agreed Ed Murgatroyd. He blew on his gun, polished it moodily with the sleeve of his coat, and restored it to his pocket. 'But I'll give her a piece of my mind,' he said, glowering at Genevieve, who had now retreated to the wall and was holding before her, as if in a piteous effort to shield herself from vengeance, an official communication from the Front Office notifying all writers that the expression 'Polack mug' must no longer be used in dialogue.

'And I will give Mr Mulliner a piece of *my* mind,' said Mabelle. 'You stay here and chat with Miss Bootle, while I interview the Great Lover in the passage.'

Out in the corridor, Mabelle faced Bulstrode, tight-lipped. For a moment there was silence, broken only by the clicking of typewriters from the various hutches and the occasional despairing wail of a writer stuck for an adjective.

'Well, this is a surprise!' said Bulstrode, with a sickly smile. 'How on earth do you come to be here, darling?'

'Miss Ridgway to you!' retorted Mabelle with flashing eyes. 'I will tell you. I should have been in New York still if you had written, as you said you would. But all I've had since you left is one measly picture-postcard of the Grand Canyon.'

Bulstrode was stunned.

'You mean I've only written to you once?'

'Just once. And after waiting for three weeks, I decided to come here and see what was the matter. On the train I met Mr Murgatroyd. We got into conversation, and I learned that he was in the same position as myself. His fiancée had disappeared into the No Man's Land of Hollywood, and she hadn't written at all. It was his idea that we should draw the studios. In the past two days we have visited seven, and today, flushing the Perfecto-Zizzbaum, we saw you coming out of a building . . .'

'The commissary. I had been having a small frosted malted milk. I felt sort of faint.'

'You will feel sort of fainter,' said Mabelle, her voice as frosted as any malted milk in California, 'by the time I've done with you. So this is the kind of man you are, Bulstrode Mulliner! A traitor and a libertine!'

From inside the office came the sound of a girl's hysterics, blending with the deeper note of an upbraiding bootlegger and the rhythmic tapping on the wall of Mr Dabney and Mr Mendelsohn, who were trying to concentrate on *Scented Sinners*. A lifetime in Chicago had given Mr Murgatroyd the power of expressing his thoughts in terse, nervous English, and some of the words he was using, even when filtered through the door, were almost equivalent to pineapple bombs.

'A two-timing daddy and a trailing arbutus!' said Mabelle, piercing Bulstrode with her scornful eyes.

A messenger-boy came up with a communication from the Front Office notifying all writers that they must not smoke in the Exercise Yard. Bulstrode read it absently. The interruption had given him time to marshal his thoughts.

'You don't understand,' he said. 'You don't realize what it is like, being marooned in a motion-picture studio. What you have failed to appreciate is the awful yearning that comes over you for human society. There you sit for weeks and weeks, alone in the great silence, and then suddenly you find a girl in your office, washed up by the tide, and what happens? Instinctively you find yourself turning to her. As an individual, she may be distasteful to you, but she is – how shall I put it? – a symbol of the world without. I admit that I grabbed Miss Bootle. I own that I kissed her. But it meant nothing. It affected no vital issue. It was as if, locked in a dungeon cell, I had shown cordiality towards a pet mouse. You would not have censured me if you had come in and found me playing with a pet mouse. For all the kisses I showered on Miss Bootle, deep down in me I was true to you. It was simply that the awful loneliness . . . the deadly propinquity . . . Well, take the case,' said Bulstrode, 'of a couple on a raft in the Caribbean Sea . . .'

The stoniness of Mabelle's face did not soften.

'Never mind the Caribbean Sea,' she interrupted. 'I have nothing to say about the Caribbean Sea except that I wish somebody would throw you into it with a good, heavy brick round your neck. This is the end, Bulstrode Mulliner. I have done with you. If we meet on the street, don't bother to raise your hat.'

'It is Mr Schnellenhamer's hat.'

'Well, don't bother to raise Mr Schnellenhamer's hat, because I shall ignore you. I shall cut you dead.' She looked past him at Ed Murgatroyd, who was coming out of the office with a satisfied expression on his face. 'Finished, Mr Murgatroyd?'

'All washed up,' said the bootlegger. 'A nice clean job.'

'Then perhaps you will escort me out of this Abode of Love.'

'Oke, lady.'

Mabelle glanced down with cold disdain at Bulstrode, who was clutching her despairingly.

'There is something clinging to my skirt, Mr Murgatroyd,' she said. 'Might I trouble you to brush it off?'

A powerful hand fell on Bulstrode's shoulder. A powerful foot struck him on the trousers-seat. He flew through the open door of the office, tripping over Genevieve Bootle, who was now writhing on the floor.

Disentangling himself, he rose and dashed out. The corridor was empty. Mabelle Ridgway and Edward Murgatroyd had gone.

A good many of my relations, near and distant (proceeded Mr Mulliner after a thoughtful sip at his hot Scotch and Lemon), have found themselves in unpleasant situations in their time, but none, I am inclined to think, in any situation quite so unpleasant as that in which my nephew Bulstrode now found himself. It was as if he had stepped suddenly into one of those psychological modern novels where the hero's soul gets all tied up in knots as early as page 21 and never straightens itself out again.

To lose the girl one worships is bad enough in itself. But when, in addition, a man has got entangled with another girl, for whom he feels simultaneously and in equal proportions an overwhelming passion and a dull dislike – and when in addition to that he is obliged to spend his days working on a story like *Scented Sinners* – well, then he begins to realize how dark and sinister a thing this life of ours can be. Complex was the word that suggested itself to Bulstrode Mulliner.

He ached for Mabelle Ridgway. He also ached for Genevieve Bootle. And yet even while he ached for Genevieve Bootle, some inner voice told him that if ever there was a pill it was she. Sometimes the urge to fold her in his arms and the urge to haul off and slap her over the nose with a piece of blotting paper came so close together that it was a mere flick of the coin which prevailed.

And then one afternoon when he had popped into the commissary for a frosted malted milk he tripped over the feet of a girl who was sitting by herself in a dark corner.

'I beg your pardon,' he said courteously, for a Mulliner, even when his soul is racked, never forgets his manners.

'Don't mention it, Bulstrode,' said the girl.

Bulstrode uttered a stunned cry.

'You!'

He stared at her, speechless. In his eyes there was nothing but amazement, but in those of Mabelle Ridgway there shone a soft and friendly light.

'How are you, Bulstrode?' she asked.

Bulstrode was still wrestling with his astonishment.

'But what are you doing here?' he cried.

'I am working on *Scented Sinners*. Mr Murgatroyd and I are doing a treatment together. It is quite simple,' said Mabelle. 'That day when I left you we started to walk to the studio gate, and it so happened that as we passed, Mr Schnellenhamer was looking out of his window. A few moments later his secretary came running out and said he wished to see us. We went to his office, where he gave us contracts to sign. I think he must have extraordinary personal magnetism,' said Mabelle pensively, 'for we both signed immediately, though nothing was further from our plans than to join the writing staff of the Perfecto-Zizzbaum. I had intended to go back to New York, and Mr Murgatroyd was complaining that his bootlegging must be going all to pieces without him. It seems to be one of those businesses that need the individual touch.' She paused. 'What do you think of Mr Murgatroyd, Bulstrode?'

'I dislike him intensely.'

'You wouldn't say he had a certain strange, weird fascination?'

'No.'

'Well, perhaps you're right,' said Mabelle dubiously. 'You were certainly right about it being lonely in this studio. I'm afraid I was a little cross, Bulstrode, when we last met. I understand now. You really don't think there is a curious, intangible glamour about Mr Murgatroyd?'

'I do not.'

'Well, you may be right, of course. Goodbye, Bulstrode, I must be going. I have already exceeded the seven and a quarter minutes which the Front Office allows female writers for the consumption of nut sundaes. If we do not meet again . . .'

'But surely we're going to meet all the time?'

Mabelle shook her head.

'The Front Office has just sent out a communication to all writers, forbidding inmates of the Ohio State Penitentiary to associate with those in the Leper Colony. They think it unsettles them. So unless we run into one another in the commissary . . . Well, goodbye, Bulstrode.'

She bit her lip in sudden pain, and was gone.

It was some ten days later that the encounter at which Mabelle had hinted took place. The heaviness of a storm-tossed soul had brought Bulstrode to the commissary for a frosted malted milk once more, and there, toying with – respectively – a Surprise Gloria Swanson and a Cheese Sandwich Maurice Chevalier, were Mabelle Ridgway and Ed Murgatroyd. They were looking into each other's eyes with a silent passion in which, an observer would have noted, there was a distinct admixture of dislike and repulsion.

Mabelle glanced up as Bulstrode reached the table.

'Good afternoon,' she said, with a welcoming smile. 'I think you know my fiancé, Mr Murgatroyd?'

Bulstrode reeled.

'Your what did you say?' he exclaimed.

'We're engaged,' said Mr Murgatroyd sombrely.

'Since this morning,' added Mabelle. 'It was at exactly six minutes past eleven that we found ourselves linked in a close embrace.'

Bulstrode endeavoured to conceal his despair.

'I hope you will be very happy,' he said.

'A swell chance!' rejoined Mr Murgatroyd. 'I'm not saying this beasel here doesn't exert a strange fascination over me, but I think it only fair to inform her here and now – before witnesses – that at the same time the mere sight of her makes me sick.'

'It is the same with me,' said Mabelle. 'When in Mr Murgatroyd's presence, I feel like some woman wailing for her demon lover, and all the while I am shuddering at that awful stuff he puts on his hair.'

'The best hair-oil in Chicago,' said Mr Murgatroyd, a little stiffly.

'It is as if I were under some terrible hypnotic influence which urged me against the promptings of my true self to love Mr Murgatroyd,' explained Mabelle.

'Make that double, sister,' said the bootlegger. 'It goes for me, too.'

'Precisely,' cried Bulstrode, 'how I feel towards my fiancée, Miss Bootle.'

'Are you engaged to that broad?' asked Mr Murgatroyd.

'I am.'

Ed Murgatroyd paled and swallowed a mouthful of cheese sandwich. There was silence for a while.

'I see it all,' said Mabelle. 'We have fallen under the hideous spell of this place. It is as you said, Bulstrode, when you wanted me to take the case of a couple on a raft in the Caribbean Sea. There is a miasma in the atmosphere of the Perfecto-Zizzbaum lot which undoes all who come within its sphere of influence. And here I am, pledged to marry a gargoyle like Mr Murgatroyd.'

'And what about me?' demanded the bootlegger. 'Do you think I enjoy being teamed up with a wren that doesn't know the first principles of needling beer? A swell helpmeet you're going to make for a man in my line of business!'

'And where do I get off?' cried Bulstrode passionately. 'My

blood races at the sight of Genevieve Bootle, and yet all the while I know that she is one of Nature's prunes. The mere thought of marrying her appals me. Apart from the fact that I worship you, Mabelle, with every fibre of my being.'

'And I worship you, Bulstrode.'

'And I'm that way about Genevieve,' said Mr Murgatroyd.

There was another silence.

'There is only one way out of this dreadful situation,' said Mabelle. 'We must go to Mr Schnellenhamer and hand in our resignations. Once we are free from this noxious environment, everything will adjust itself nicely. Let us go and see him immediately.'

They did not see Mr Schnellenhamer immediately, for nobody ever did. But after a vigil of two hours in the reception-room, they were finally admitted to his presence, and they filed in and stated their case.

The effect on the President of the Perfecto-Zizzbaum Corporation of their request that they be allowed to resign was stupendous. If they had been Cossacks looking in at the office to start a pogrom, he could not have been more moved. His eyes bulged, and his nose drooped like the trunk of an elephant which has been refused a peanut.

'It can't be done,' he said curtly. He reached in the drawer of his desk, produced a handful of documents and rapped them with an ominous decision. 'Here are the contracts, duly signed by you, in which you engage to remain in the employment of the Perfecto-Zizzbaum Corporation until the completion of the picture entitled *Scented Sinners*. Did you take a look at Para. 6, where it gives the penalties for breach of same? No, don't read them,' he said, as Mabelle stretched out a hand. 'You wouldn't sleep nights. But you can take it from me they're some penalties. We've had this thing before of writers wanting to run out on us, so we took steps to protect ourselves.'

'Would we be taken for a ride?' asked Mr Murgatroyd uneasily.

Mr Schnellenhamer smiled quietly but did not reply. He replaced the contracts in the drawer, and his manner softened and became more appealing. This man knew well when to brandish the iron fist and when to display the velvet glove.

'And, anyway,' he said, speaking now in almost a fatherly manner, 'you wouldn't want to quit till the picture was finished. Of course you wouldn't, not three nice, square-shooting folks

like you. It wouldn't be right. It wouldn't be fair. It wouldn't
be cooperation. You know what *Scented Sinners* means to this
organization. It's the biggest proposition we have. Our whole
programme is built around it. We are relying on it to be our
big smash. It cost us a barrel of money to buy *Scented Sinners*,
and naturally we aim to get it back.'

He rose from his chair, and tears came into his eyes. It was
as if he had been some emotional American football coach
addressing a faint-hearted team.

'Stick to it!' he urged. 'Stick to it, folks! You can do it if
you like. Get back in there and fight. Think of the boys in the
Front Office rooting for you, depending on you. You wouldn't
let them down? No, no, not you. You wouldn't let me down?
Of course you wouldn't. Get back in the game, then, and win
– win – win . . . for dear old Perfecto-Zizzbaum and me.'

He flung himself into his chair, gazing at them with appealing
eyes.

'May I read Para. 6?' asked Mr Murgatroyd after a pause.

'No, don't read Para. 6,' urged Mr Schnellenhamer. 'Far, far
better not read Para. 6.'

Mabelle looked hopelessly at Bulstrode.

'Come,' she said. 'It is useless for us to remain here.'

They left the office with dragging steps. Mr Schnellenhamer,
a grave expression on his face, pressed the bell for his secretary.

'I don't like the look of things, Miss Stern,' he said. 'There
seems to be a spirit of unrest among the *Scented Sinners* gang.
Three of them have just been in wanting to quit. I shouldn't
be surprised if rebellion isn't seething. Say, listen,' he asked
keenly, 'nobody's been ill-treating them, have they?'

'Why, the idea, Mr Schnellenhamer!'

'I thought I heard screams coming from their building yesterday.'

'That was Mr Doakes. He was working on his treatment, and
he had some kind of a fit. Frothed at the mouth and kept
shouting, "No, no! It isn't possible!" If you ask me,' said Miss
Stern, 'it's just the warm weather. We most generally always
lose a few writers this time of year.'

Mr Schnellenhamer shook his head.

'This ain't the ordinary thing of authors going cuckoo. It's
something deeper. It's the spirit of unrest, or rebellion seething,
or something like that. What am I doing at five o'clock?'

'Conferencing with Mr Levitsky.'

'Cancel it. Send round notice to all writers on *Scented Sinners* to meet me on Stage Four. I'll give them a pep-talk.'

At a few minutes before five, accordingly, there debouched from the Leper Colony and from the Ohio State Penitentiary a motley collection of writers. There were young writers, old writers, middle-aged writers; writers with matted beards at which they plucked nervously, writers with horn-rimmed spectacles who muttered to themselves, writers with eyes that stared blankly or blinked in the unaccustomed light. On all of them *Scented Sinners* had set its unmistakable seal. They shuffled listlessly along till they came to Stage Four, where they seated themselves on wooden benches, waiting for Mr Schnellenhamer to arrive.

Bulstrode had found a place next to Mabelle Ridgway. The girl's face was drawn and despondent.

'Edward is breaking in a new quart of hair-oil for the wedding,' she said, after a moment of silence.

Bulstrode shivered.

'Genevieve,' he replied, 'has bought one of those combination eyebrow tweezers and egg-scramblers. The advertisement said that no bride should be without them.'

Mabelle drew her breath in sharply.

'Can nothing be done?' asked Bulstrode.

'Nothing,' said Mabelle dully. 'We cannot leave till *Scented Sinners* is finished, and it never will be finished – never . . . never . . . never.' Her spiritual face was contorted for a moment. 'I hear there are writers who have been working on it for years and years. That grey-bearded gentleman over there, who is sticking straws in his hair,' she said, pointing. 'That is Mr Markey. He has the office next to ours, and comes in occasionally to complain that there are spiders crawling up his wall. He has been doing treatments of *Scented Sinners* since he was a young man.'

In the tense instant during which they stared at each other with mournful, hopeless eyes, Mr Schnellenhamer bustled in and mounted the platform. He surveyed the gathering authoritatively: then, clearing his throat, began to speak.

He spoke of Service and Ideals, of Cooperation and the Spirit That Wins to Success. He had just begun to touch on the glories of the Southern Californian climate, when the scent of a powerful cigar floated over the meeting, and a voice spoke.

'Hey!'

All eyes were turned in the intruder's direction. It was Mr Isadore Levitsky, the chief business operative, who stood there, he with whom Mr Schnellenhamer had had an appointment to conference.

'What's all this?' demanded Mr Levitsky. 'You had a date with me in my office.'

Mr Schnellenhamer hurried down from the platform and drew Mr Levitsky aside.

'I'm sorry, I.G.,' he said. 'I had to break our date. There's all this spirit of unrest broke out among the *Scented Sinners* gang, and I thought I'd better talk to them. You remember that time five years ago when we had to call out the State Militia.'

Mr Levitsky looked puzzled.

'The what gang?'

'The writers who are doing treatments on *Scented Sinners*. You know *Scented Sinners* that we bought.'

'But we didn't,' said Mr Levitsky.

'We didn't?' said Mr Schnellenhamer, surprised.

'Certainly we didn't. Don't you remember the Medulla-Oblongata-Glutz people outbid us?'

Mr Schnellenhamer stood for a moment, musing.

'That's right, too,' he said at length. 'They did, didn't they?'

'Certainly they did.'

'Then the story doesn't belong to us at all?'

'Certainly it doesn't. M-O-G has owned it for the last eleven years.'

Mr Schnellenhamer smote his forehead.

'Of course! It all comes back to me now. I had quite forgotten.'

He mounted the platform once more.

'Ladies and gentlemen,' he said, 'all work on *Scented Sinners* will cease immediately. The studio has discovered that it doesn't own it.'

It was a merry gathering that took place in the commissary of the Perfecto-Zizzbaum studios some half-hour later. Genevieve Bootle had broken her engagement to Bulstrode and was sitting with her hand linked in that of Ed Murgatroyd. Mabelle Ridgway had broken her engagement to Ed Murgatroyd and was stroking Bulstrode's arm. It would have been hard to find four happier people, unless you had stepped outside and searched among the horde of emancipated writers who were dancing the Carmagnole so blithely around the shoe-shining stand.

'And what are you two good folks going to do now?' asked Ed Murgatroyd, surveying Bulstrode and Mabelle with kindly eyes. 'Have you made any plans?'

'I came out here to strike oil,' said Bulstrode. 'I'll do it now.'

He raised a cheery hand and brought it down with an affectionate smack on the bootlegger's gleaming head.

'Ha, ha!' chuckled Bulstrode.

'Ha, ha!' roared Mr Murgatroyd.

'Ha, ha!' tittered Mabelle and Genevieve.

A perfect camaraderie prevailed among these four young people, delightful to see.

'No, but seriously,' said Mr Murgatroyd, wiping the tears from his eyes, 'are you fixed all right? Have you got enough dough to get married on?'

Mabelle looked at Bulstrode. Bulstrode looked at Mabelle. For the first time a shadow seemed to fall over their happiness.

'We haven't,' Bulstrode was forced to admit.

Ed Murgatroyd slapped him on the shoulder.

'Then come and join my little outfit,' he said heartily. 'I've always room for a personal friend. Besides, we're muscling into the North Side beer industry next month, and I shall need willing helpers.'

Bulstrode clasped his hand, deeply moved.

'Ed,' he exclaimed, 'I call that square of you. I'll buy a machine-gun tomorrow.'

With his other hand he sought Mabelle's hand and pressed it. Outside, the laughter of the mob had turned into wild cheering. A bonfire had been started, and Mr Doakes, Mr Noakes, Miss Faversham, Miss Wilson, Mr Fotheringay, Mr Mendelsohn, Mr Markey and the others were feeding it with their scripts of *Scented Sinners*.

In the Front Office, Mr Schnellenhamer and Mr Levitsky, suspending their seven hundred and forty-first conference for an instant, listened to the tumult.

'Makes you feel like Lincoln, doesn't it?' said Mr Levitsky.

'Ah!' said Mr Schnellenhamer.

They smiled indulgently. They were kindly men at heart and they liked the girls and boys to be happy.

George and Alfred

The little group of serious thinkers in the bar-parlour of the Anglers' Rest were talking about twins. A Gin and Tonic had brought the subject up, a cousin of his having recently acquired a couple, and the discussion had not proceeded far when it was seen that Mr Mulliner, the Sage of the bar-parlour, was smiling as if amused by some memory.

'I was thinking of my brother's sons George and Alfred,' he explained. 'They were twins.'

'Identical?' asked a Scotch on the Rocks.

'In every respect.'

'Always getting mistaken for each other, I suppose?'

They would have been, no doubt, if they had moved in the same circles (said Mr Mulliner), but their walks in life kept them widely separated. Alfred was a professional conjuror and spent most of his time in London, while George some years previously had gone to seek his fortune in Hollywood, where after various vicissitudes he had become a writer of additional dialogue on the staff of Jacob Schnellenhamer of the Colossal-Exquisite Corporation.

The lot of a writer of additional dialogue in a Hollywood studio is not an exalted one – he ranks, I believe, just above a script girl and just below the man who works the wind machine – but any pity I might have felt for George for being one of the dregs was mitigated by the fact that I knew his position was only temporary, for on his thirtieth birthday, which would be occurring very shortly, he would be coming into possession of a large fortune left to him in trust by his godmother.

It was on Mr Schnellenhamer's yacht that I met George again after an interval of several years. I had become friendly with Mr Schnellenhamer on one of his previous visits to England, and when I ran into him one day in Piccadilly he told me he was just off to Monte Carlo to discuss some business matters with Sam Glutz of the Perfecto-Wonderful, who was wintering there, and asked me if I would care to come along. I accepted the invitation gratefully, and the first person I saw when I came on board was George.

I found him in excellent spirits, and I was not surprised, for he said he had reached the age of thirty a few days ago and would be collecting his legacy directly we arrived in Monaco.

'Your trustee is meeting you there?'

'He lives there. An old boy of the name of Bassinger.'

'Well, I certainly congratulate you, George. Have you made any plans?'

'Plenty. And the first is to stop being a Yes-Man.'

'I thought you were a writer of additional dialogue.'

'It's the same thing. I've been saying Yes to Schnellenhamer for three years, but no longer. A radical change of policy there's going to be. In the privacy of my chamber I've been practising saying No for days. No, Mr Schnellenhamer!' said George. 'No, no, no! You're wrong, Mr Schnellenhamer. You're quite mistaken, Mr Schnellenhamer. You're talking through your hat, Mr Schnellenhamer. Would it be going too far if I told him he ought to have his head examined?'

'A little, I think.'

'Perhaps you're right.'

'You don't want to hurt his feelings.'

'I don't think he has any. Still, I see what you mean.'

We arrived in Monte Carlo after a pleasant voyage, and as soon as we had anchored in Monaco harbour I went ashore to see the sights and buy the papers, and I was thinking of returning to the yacht, when I saw George coming along, seeming to be in a hurry. I hailed him, and to my astonishment he turned out to be not George but Alfred, the last person I would have expected to find in Monte Carlo. I had always supposed that conjurors never left London except to appear at children's parties in the provinces.

He was delighted to see me. We had always been very close to one other. Many a time as a boy he had borrowed my top hat in order to take rabbits out of it, for even then he was acquiring the rudiments of his art and the skill which had enabled him to bill himself as The Great Alfredo. There was genuine affection in his manner as he now produced a hard-boiled egg from my breast pocket.

'But how in the world do you come to be here, Alfred?' I asked.

His explanation was simple.

'I'm appearing at the Casino. I have a couple of spots in the revue there, and I don't mind telling you that I'm rolling the customers in the aisles nightly,' he said, and I recalled that he had always interspersed his feats with humorous dialogue. 'How do you happen to be in Monte Carlo? Not on a gambling caper, I trust?'

'I am a guest on Mr Schnellenhamer's yacht.'

He started at the mention of the name.

'Schnellenhamer? The movie man? That one who's doing the great Bible epic *Solomon and the Queen of Sheba?*'

'Yes. We are anchored in the harbour.'

'Well, well,' said Alfred. His air was pensive. My words had apparently started a train of thought. Then he looked at his watch and uttered an exclamation. 'Good Lord,' he said, 'I must rush, or I'll be late for rehearsal.'

And before I could tell him that his brother George was also on Mr Schnellenhamer's yacht he had bounded off.

Mr Schnellenhamer was on the deck when I reached the yacht, concluding a conversation with a young man whom I presumed to be a reporter, come to interview him. The young man left, and Mr Schnellenhamer jerked a thumb at his retreating back.

'Listen,' he said. 'Do you know what that fellow's been telling me? You remember I was coming here to meet Sam Glutz? Well, it seems that somebody mugged Sam last night.'

'You don't say!'

'Yessir, laid him out cold. Are those the papers you've got there? Lemme look. It's probably on the front page.'

He was perfectly correct. Even George would have had to say 'Yes, Mr Schnellenhamer.' The story was there under big headlines. On the previous night, it appeared, Mr Glutz had been returning from the Casino to his hotel, when some person unknown had waylaid him and left him lying in the street in a considerably battered condition. He had been found by a passer-by and taken to the hospital to be stitched together.

'And not a hope of catching the fellow,' said Mr Schnellenhamer.

I pointed out that the paper said the police had a clue, and he snorted contemptuously.

'Police!'

'At your service,' said a voice, and turning I saw what I

thought for a moment was General de Gaulle. Then I realized that he was some inches shorter than the General and had a yard or so less nose. But not even General de Gaulle could have looked sterner and more intimidating. 'Sergeant Brichoux of the Monaco police force,' he said. 'I have come to see a Mr Mulliner, who I understand is a member of your entourage.'

This surprised me. I was also surprised that he should be speaking English so fluently, but the explanation soon occurred to me. A sergeant of police in a place like Monte Carlo, constantly having to question international spies, heavily veiled adventuresses and the like, would soon pick it up.

'I am Mr Mulliner,' I said.

'Mr George Mulliner?'

'Oh, George? No, he is my nephew. You want to see him?'

'I do.'

'Why?' asked Mr Schnellenhamer.

'In connection with last night's assault on Mr Glutz. The police have reason to believe that he can assist them in their enquiries.'

'How?'

'They would like him to explain how his wallet came to be lying on the spot where Mr Glutz was attacked. One feels, does one not, that the fact is significant. Can I see him, if you please?' said Sergeant Brichoux, and a sailor was despatched to find George. He returned with the information that he did not appear to be on board.

'Probably gone for a stroll ashore,' said Mr Schnellenhamer.

'Then with your permission,' said the sergeant, looking more sinister than ever, 'I will await his return.'

'And I'll go and look for him,' I said.

It was imperative, I felt, that George be intercepted and warned of what was waiting for him on the yacht. It was, of course, absurd to suppose that he had been associated in any way with last night's outrage, but if his wallet had been discovered on the scene of the crime, it was obvious that he would have a good deal of explaining to do. As I saw it, he was in the position the hero is always getting into in novels of suspense – forced by circumstances, though innocent, into the role of Suspect Number One and having a thoroughly sticky time till everything comes right in the last chapter.

It was on a bench near the harbour that I found him. He was sitting with his head between his hands, probably feeling that if he let go of it, it would come in half, for when I spoke his name and he looked up, it was plain to see that he was in the grip of a severe hangover. I am told by those who know that there are six varieties of hangover – the Broken Compass, the Sewing Machine, the Comet, the Atomic, the Cement Mixer and the Gremlin Boogie, and his aspect suggested that he had got them all.

I was not really surprised. He had told me after dinner on the previous night that he was just off to call on his trustee and collect his inheritance, and it was natural to suppose that after doing so he would celebrate. But when I asked him if this was so, he uttered one of those hollow rasping laughs that are so unpleasant.

'Celebrate!' he said. 'No, I wasn't celebrating. Shall I tell you what happened last night? I went to Bassinger's hotel and gave my name and asked if he was in, and they told me he had checked out a week or two ago and had left a letter for me. I took the letter. I opened it. I read it. And having read it . . . Have you ever been slapped in the eye with a wet fish?'

'Oddly enough, no.'

'I was once when I got into an argument with an angler down at Santa Monica, and the sensation now was very similar. For this letter, this *billet doux* from that offspring of unmarried parents P. P. Bassinger, informed me that he had been gambling for years with the trust money and was deeply sorry to say that there was now no trust. It had gone. So, he added, had he. By the time I read this, he said, he would be in one of those broadminded South American countries where they don't believe in extradition. He apologized profusely, but places the blame on some man he had met in a bar who had given him an infallible system for winning at the tables. And why my godmother gave the trusteeship to someone living in Monte Carlo within easy walking distance of the Casino we shall never know. Just asking for it is the way it looks to me.'

My heart bled for him. By no stretch of optimism could I regard this as his lucky day. All this and Sergeant Brichoux, too. There was a quaver in my voice as I spoke.

'My poor boy!'

'Poor is right.'

'It must have been a terrible shock.'

'It was.'

'What did you do?'

'What would you have done? I went out and got pie-eyed. And here's a funny thing. I had the most extraordinary nightmare. Do you ever have nightmares?'

'Sometimes.'

'Bad ones?'

'Occasionally.'

'I'll bet they aren't as bad as the one I had. I dreamed that I had done a murder. And that dream is still lingering with me. I keep seeing myself engaged in a terrific brawl with someone and laying him out. It's a most unpleasant sensation. Why are you looking at me like a sheep with something on its mind?'

I had to tell him.

'It wasn't a nightmare, George.'

He seemed annoyed.

'Don't be an ass. Do you think I don't know a nightmare when I see one?'

'I repeat, it was no nightmare.'

He looked at me incredulously, his jaw beginning to droop like a badly set soufflé.

'You don't mean it actually happened?'

'I fear so. The papers have featured it.'

'I really slugged somebody?'

'Not just somebody. The president of a motion-picture corporation, which makes your offence virtually *lèse majesté*.'

'Then how very fortunate,' said George, looking on the bright side after a moment of intense thought, 'that nobody can possibly know it was me. That certainly takes a weight off my mind. You're still goggling at me like a careworn sheep. Why is that?'

'I was thinking what a pity it was that you should have dropped your wallet – containing your name and address – on the spot of the crime.'

'Did I do that?'

'You did.'

'Hell's bells!'

'Hell's bells is correct. There's a sergeant of police on board the yacht now, waiting for your return. He has reason to believe that you can assist him in his enquiries.'

'Death and despair!'

'You may well say so. There is only one thing to be done. You must escape while there is yet time. Get over the frontier into Italy.'

'But my passport's on the yacht.'

'I could bring it to you.'

'You'd never find it.'

'Then I don't know what to suggest. Of course, you might—'

'That's no good.'

'Or you could—'

'That's no good, either. No,' said George, 'this is the end. I'm a rat in a trap. I'm for it. Well-meaning, not to be blamed, the victim of the sort of accident that might have happened to anyone when lit up as I was lit, but nevertheless for it. That's Life. You come to Monte Carlo to collect a large fortune, all pepped up with the thought that at last you're going to be able to say No to old Schnellenhamer, and what do you get? No fortune, a headache, and to top it all off the guillotine or whatever they have in these parts. That's Life, I repeat. Just a bowl of cherries. You can't win.'

Twin! I uttered a cry, electrified.

'I have it, George!'

'Well?'

'You want to get on the yacht.'

'Well?'

'To secure your passport.'

'Well?'

'Then go there.'

He gave me a reproachful look.

'If,' he said, 'you think this is the sort of stuff to spring on a man with a morning head who is extremely worried because the bloodhounds of the law are sniffing on his trail and he's liable to be guillotined at any moment, I am afraid I cannot agree with you. On your own showing that yacht is congested with sergeants of police, polishing the handcuffs and waiting eagerly for my return. I'd look pretty silly sauntering in and saying "Well, boys, here I am." Or don't you think so?'

'I omitted to mention that you would say you were Alfred.'

He blinked.

'Alfred?'

'Yes.'

'My brother Alfred?'

'Your twin brother Alfred,' I said, emphasizing the second word in the sentence, and I saw the light of intelligence creep slowly into his haggard face. 'I will go there ahead of you and sow the good seed by telling them that you have a twin brother who is your exact double. Then you make your appearance. Have no fear that your story will not be believed. Alfred is at this moment in Monte Carlo, performing nightly in the revue at the Casino, and is, I imagine, a familiar figure in local circles. He is probably known to the police – not, I need scarcely say, in any derogatory sense but because they have caught his act and may even have been asked by him to take a card – *any* card – and memorize it before returning it to the pack, his aim being to produce it later from the inside of a lemon. There will be no question of the innocent deception failing to succeed. Once on board it will be a simple matter to make some excuse to go below. An urgent need for bicarbonate of soda suggests itself. And once below you can find your passport, say a few graceful words of farewell and leave.'

'But suppose Schnellenhamer asks me to do conjuring tricks?'

'Most unlikely. He is not one of those men who are avid for entertainment. It is his aim in life to avoid it. He has told me that it is the motion-picture magnate's cross that everybody he meets starts acting at him in the hope of getting on the payroll. He says that on a good morning in Hollywood he has sometimes been acted at by a secretary, two book agents, a life insurance man, a masseur, the man with the benzedrine, the studio watchman, a shoe-shine boy and a barber, all before lunch. No need to worry about him wanting you to entertain him.'

'But what would be Alfred's reason for coming aboard?'

'Simple. He has heard that Mr Schnellenhamer has arrived. It would be in the Society Jottings column. He knows that I am with Mr Schnellenhamer—'

'How?'

'I told him so when I met him yesterday. So he has come to see me.'

The light of intelligence had now spread over George's face from ear to ear. He chuckled hoarsely.

'Do you know, I really believe it would work.'

'Of course it will work. It can't fail. I'll go and start paving the way. And as your raiment is somewhat disordered, you had better get a change of clothes, and a shave and a wash and brush-up would not hurt. Here is some money,' I said, and with an encouraging pat on the back I left him.

Brichoux was still at his post when I reached the yacht, inflex-ible determination written on every line of his unattractive face.

Mr Schnellenhamer sat beside him looking as if he were feeling that what the world needed to make it a sweeter and better place was a complete absence of police sergeants. He had never been fond of policemen since one of them, while giving him a parking ticket, had recited Hamlet's 'To be or not to be' speech to give him some idea of what he could do in a dramatic role. I proceeded to my mission without delay.

'Any sign of my nephew?' I asked.

'None,' said the sergeant.

'He has not been back?'

'He has not.'

'Very odd.'

'Very suspicious.'

An idea struck me.

'I wonder if by any chance he has gone to see his brother.'

'Has he a brother?'

'Yes. They are twins. His name is Alfred. You have probably seen him, sergeant. He is playing in the revue at the Casino. Does a conjuring act.'

'The Great Alfredo?'

'That is his stage name. You have witnessed his performance?'

'I have.'

'Amazing the resemblance between him and George. Even I can hardly tell them apart. Same face, same figure, same way of walking, same coloured hair and eyes. When you meet George, you will be astounded at the resemblance.'

'I am looking forward to meeting Mr George Mulliner.'

'Well, Alfred will probably be here this morning to have a chat with me, for he is bound to have read in the paper that I am Mr Schnellenhamer's guest. Ah, here he comes now,' I said, as George appeared on the gangway. 'Ah, Alfred.'

'Hullo, uncle.'

'So you found your way here?'

'That's right.'

'My host, Mr Schnellenhamer.'

'How do you do?'

'And Sergeant Brichoux of the Monaco police.'

'How do *you* do? Good morning, Mr Schnellenhamer, I have been wanting very much to meet you. This is a great pleasure.'

I was proud of George. I had been expecting a show of at least some nervousness on his part, for the task he had undertaken was a stern one, but I could see no trace of it. He seemed completely at his ease, and he continued to address himself to Mr Schnellenhamer without so much as a tremor in his voice.

'I have a proposition I would like to put up to you in connection with your forthcoming Bible epic *Solomon and the Queen of Sheba*. You have probably realized for yourself that the trouble with all these ancient history super-pictures is that they lack comedy. Colossal scenery, battle sequences of ten thousand a side, more semi-nude dancing girls than you could shake a stick at, but where are the belly laughs? Take *Cleopatra*. Was there anything funny in that? Not a thing. And what occurred to me the moment I read your advance publicity was that what *Solomon and the Queen of Sheba* needs, if it is really to gross grosses, is a comedy conjuror, and I decided to offer my services. You can scarcely require to be told how admirably an act like mine would fit into the scheme of things. There is nothing like a conjuror to keep a monarch amused through the long winter evenings, and King Solomon is bound to have had one at his court. So what happens? The Queen of Sheba arrives. The magnificence of her surroundings stuns her. "The half was not told unto me," she says. "You like my little place?" says the King. "Well, it's a home. But wait, you ain't seen nothing yet. Send for the Great Alfredo." And on I come. "Well, folks," I say, "a funny thing happened to me on my way to the throne room," and then I tell a story and then a few gags and then I go into my routine, and I would like just to run through it now. For my first trick . . .'

I was aghast. Long before the half-way mark of this speech the awful truth had flashed upon me. It was not George whom I saw before me – through a flickering mist – but Alfred, and I blamed myself bitterly for having been so mad as to mention Mr Schnellenhamer to him, for I might have known that he would be inflamed by the news that the motion-picture magnate was within his reach and that here was his chance of getting signed up for a lucrative engagement. And George due to appear at any moment! No wonder that I reeled and had to support myself on what I believe is called a bollard.

'For my first trick,' said Alfred, 'I shall require a pound of butter, two bananas and a bowl of goldfish. Excuse me. Won't keep you long.'

He went below, presumably in quest of these necessaries, and as he did so George came up the gangway.

There was none of that breezy self-confidence in George which had so impressed me in Alfred. He was patently suffering from stage fright. His legs wobbled and I could see his adam's apple going up and down as if pulled by an invisible string. He looked like a nervous speaker at a public banquet who on rising to his feet to propose the toast of Our Guests realizes that he has completely forgotten the story of the two Irishmen Pat and Mike, with which he had been hoping to convulse his audience.

Nor did I blame him, for Sergeant Brichoux had taken a pair of handcuffs from his pocket and was breathing on them and polishing them on his sleeve, while Mr Schnellenhamer subjected him to the stony glare which had so often caused employees of his on the Colossal-Exquisite lot to totter off to the commissary to restore themselves with frosted malted milk shakes. There was an ominous calm in the motion-picture magnate's manner such as one finds in volcanoes just before they erupt and make householders in the neighbourhood wish they had settled elsewhere. He was plainly holding himself in with a powerful effort, having decided to toy with my unhappy nephew before unmasking him. For George's opening words had been 'Good morning. I – er – that is to say – I – er – my name is Alfred Mulliner,' and I could see that neither on the part of Mr Schnellenhamer nor of Sergeant Brichoux was there that willing suspension of disbelief which dramatic critics are always writing about.

'Good morning,' said the former. 'Nice weather.'

'Yes, Mr Schnellenhamer.'

'Good for the crops.'

'Yes, Mr Schnellenhamer.'

'Though bad for the umbrella trade.'

'Yes, Mr Schnellenhamer.'

'Come along and join the party. Alfred Mulliner did you say the name was?'

'Yes, Mr Schnellenhamer.'

'You lie!' thundered Mr Schnellenhamer, unmasking his batteries with horrifying abruptness. 'You're no more Alfred Mulliner than I am, which isn't much. You're George Mulliner, and you're facing a murder rap or the next thing to it. Send for the police,' he said to Sergeant Brichoux.

'I *am* the police,' the sergeant reminded him, rather coldly it seemed to me.

'So you are. I was forgetting. Then arrest this man.'

'I will do so immediately.'

Sergeant Brichoux advanced on George, handcuffs in hand, but before he could adjust them to his wrists an interruption occurred.

Intent though I had been on the scene taking place on the deck of the yacht, I had been able during these exchanges to observe out of the corner of my eye that a heavily bandaged man of middle age was approaching us along the quay, and he now mounted the gangway and hailed Mr Schnellenhamer with a feeble 'Hi, Jake.'

So profuse were his bandages that one would hardly have expected his own mother to have recognized him, but Mr Schnellenhamer did.

'Sam Glutz!' he cried. 'Well, I'll be darned. I thought you were in the hospital.'

'They let me out.'

'You look like Tutankhamen's mummy, Sam.'

'So would you if you'd been belted by a hoodlum like I was. Did you read about it in the papers?'

'Sure. You made the front page.'

'Well, that's something. But I wouldn't care to go through an experience like that again. I thought it was the end. My whole past life flashed before me.'

'You can't have liked that.'

'I didn't.'

'Well, you'll be glad to hear, Sam, that we've got the fellow who slugged you.'

'You have? Where is he?'

'Right there. Standing by the gentleman with the handcuffs.'

George's head had been bowed, but now he happened to raise it, and Mr Glutz uttered a cry.

'*You!*'

'That's him. George Mulliner. Used to work for the Colossal-Exquisite, but of course I've fired him. Take him to the cooler, sergeant.'

Every bandage on Mr Glutz's body rippled like wheat beneath a west wind, and his next words showed that what had caused this was horror and indignation at the programme Mr Schnellenhamer had outlined.

'Over my dead body!' he cried. 'Why, that's the splendid young man who saved my life last night.'

'What!'

'Sure. The hood was beating the tar out of me when he came galloping up and knocked him for a loop, and after a terrific struggle the hood called it a day and irised out. Proud and happy to meet you, Mr Mulliner. I think I heard Jake say he'd fired you. Well, come and work for the Perfecto-Wonderful, and I shall be deeply offended if you don't skin me for a salary beyond the dreams of avarice. I'll pencil you in as vice-president with brevet rank as a cousin by marriage.'

I stepped forward. George was still incapable of speech.

'One moment, Mr Glutz,' I said.

'Who are you?'

'George's agent. And there is just one clause in the contract which strikes me as requiring revision. Reflect, Mr Glutz. Surely cousin by marriage is a poor reward for the man who saved your life?'

Mr Glutz was visibly affected. Groping among the bandages, he wiped away a tear.

'You're right,' he said. 'We'll make it brother-in-law. And now let's go and get a bite of lunch. You, too,' he said to me, and I said I would be delighted. We left the boat in single file – first Mr Glutz, then myself, then George, who was still dazed. The last thing I saw was Alfred coming on deck with his pound of butter and his two bananas. I seemed to detect on his face a slight touch of chagrin, caused no doubt by his inability to locate the bowl of goldfish so necessary to his first trick.

NON-FICTION

The following extract from *Bring on the Girls* gives a memorable account of the encounter between P. G. Wodehouse and Guy Bolton, *en route* for Hollywood, and W. C. Fields.

The train to the coast – the famous Chief – was rolling along through the wide open spaces where men are men. It was the second day out from Chicago and Guy and Plum were finishing their lunch in the diner. Ethel was to come on later after they had settled in.

The exodus from the East, which had begun with the coming of sound to the motion pictures, was at its height. Already on the train the two had met a number of authors, composers, directors and other Broadway fauna with whom they had worked in the days before the big crash. Rudolf Friml was there and Vincent Youmans and Arthur Richman and a dozen more. It was like one of those great race movements of the middle ages.

'Well,' said Guy, 'California, here we come! How do you feel?'

'I feel,' said Plum, 'as I should think Alice must have felt when, after mixing with all those weird creatures in Wonderland, she knelt on the mantelpiece preparatory to climbing through the looking-glass.'

'I see what you mean – wondering what kind of freaks she was going to meet this time. Still, maybe it won't be so bad. Hollywood can't have many terrors for two men who have survived Erlanger, Savage, a little Plymouth, junior Breckenridge, the Sisters Duncan – not to mention "Fabulous Felix" and Palmer.'

'Palmer?'

'Hank Savage's private poisoner.'

'Good Lord, I haven't thought of him for years. I wonder what became of him.'

'I hope he perished of his own cooking. I've never forgiven

that bird for the supercilious way he sneered at that really excellent plot of ours about the pawnbroker.'

'I remember dimly something about a pawnbroker—'

'Good heavens, man, it was a superb plot and we might do worse than spring it on W. C. Fields when we get to Hollywood. You can't have forgotten. About a fellow who was the last of a long line of pawnbrokers and his ancestor had loaned the money to Queen Isabella to finance Columbus . . .'

'I remember! The contract turned up, and he found that he owned ten per cent of America. It was a darned good idea.'

'It was a terrific idea, and that hash-slinging sea cook crabbed it with a lot of stuff about thematic archaism.'

At this moment a man in horn-rimmed spectacles paused at their table.

'Oh, there you are,' he said. 'I'll come and have a chat in a minute or two. Can't stop now. See you later.'

He passed on, and they looked after him, puzzled.

'Now who on earth was that?' said Guy. 'He seemed to know us.'

'Probably somebody who was in one of our shows. The train's stiff with actors.'

They dismissed the man from their thoughts and returned to the subject of Hollywood.

'Have you talked to anyone who's been there?' asked Guy.

'Only Bob Benchley, and you know the sort of information you would get from him. He said I mustn't believe the stories I had heard about ill-treatment of inmates at the studios, for there was very little actual brutality. Most of the big executives, he said, were kindly men, and he had often seen Louis B. Mayer stop outside some Nodder's hutch and push a piece of lettuce through the bars.'

'What's a Nodder?'

'Bob explained that. A sort of Yes-Man, only lower in the social scale. When there is a story-conference and the supervisor throws out some suggestion or idea, the Yes-Men all say "Yes". After they have finished saying "Yes", the Nodders nod. Bob said there is also a sub-species known as Nodders' assistants, but he didn't want to get too technical.'

'What else? Is it true that they're all lunatics out in Hollywood?'

'Bob says no. He says he knows fully half a dozen people there who are practically sane – except of course at the time of the full moon . . . Good Lord!'

'What's the matter?'

'I've remembered who that chap was who spoke to us.'

'Who?'

'Palmer.'

'It can't have been.'

'It was. Palmer in person.'

Guy considered.

'I believe you're right. But we shall soon know. He's coming this way.'

It was Palmer – older and with a new and rather horrible briskness about him, but still Palmer. He reached their table and sat down, looking snappy and efficient.

'Well, well,' said Guy.

'Well, well,' said Plum. 'It's a long time since that yacht cruise. How's *Ophelia*?'

Palmer cocked a puzzled eyebrow.

'Ophelia?'

'Your play?'

'Oh, that?' Palmer's face cleared. 'I got tired of waiting for the Colonel to do something about it – he kept changing the subject to corned beef hash whenever I mentioned it – so I threw up my job as cook on the *Dorinda* and came out here. Do you know something?'

'What?'

Palmer's voice was grave.

'I don't want to wrong him, but I've sometimes thought that Colonel Savage may have been stringing me along all the time.'

'Colonel *Savage*?' cried Guy and Plum, horrified.

'I know the idea sounds bizarre, but it has occasionally crossed my mind that he encouraged me to think that he was going to produce my play simply in order to get a free cook on that boat of his. We shall never know, I suppose. Well, as I was saying, after the seventh – or was it the eighth? – trip to Florida I got tired of waiting and came out here. I had a hard time of it for a year or two, but I won through in the end and am now doing extremely well. I'm a cousin by marriage.'

'A . . . what was that?'

'I married the cousin of one of the top executives and from that moment never looked back. Of course, cousins are fairly small fry, but I happen to know that there's a lot of talk going around the Front Office of giving me brevet rank as a brother-in-law before very long.'

'A brother-in-law is good, is it?'

Palmer stared.

'My dear fellow! Practically as high up as a nephew.'

The two authors offered congratulations.

'Well, now we're all going to be in Hollywood together,' said Guy, 'I hope we shall see something of one another.'

'We shall. I'm your supervisor.'

'Eh?'

'On this W. C. Fields picture. If you've finished your lunch, I'll take you along to meet him. What's the time?'

'Two-thirty.'

'Ah, then he may be sober.'

They made their way along the train to the Fields drawing-room, Guy and Plum a little dubious and inclined to shake their heads. They were not at all sure how they were going to like being supervised by a man who thought that in writing a play – and presumably a talking-picture – the scale of values should be at once objective and rational, hence absolute and authentic. And their uneasiness was increased when their overlord said graciously that he hoped they would come to dinner at his Beverly Hills home on the following Saturday, adding that for the sake of old times he would cook the meal himself.

'I'm as good a cook as I ever was,' he said.

Just about, they imagined, and shivered a little.

In the semi-darkness of the drawing-room the first thing the authors heard was a hollow groan and the first thing they saw was a vast something bulging beneath the bedclothes. It stirred as they entered and there rose from the pillow a face rendered impressive by what must have been one of the largest and most incandescent nasal jobs ever issued to a human being. It reminded Plum – who had read his Edward Lear – of the hero of one of that eminent Victorian's best-known poems.

> And all who watch at the midnight hour
> From hall or terrace or lofty tower
> Cry, as they trace the meteor bright
> Moving along through the dreary night
> 'This is the hour when forth he goes,
> The Dong With The Luminous Nose'.

They were to learn later that the comedian was very sensitive about what he considered the only flaw in an otherwise classic countenance and permitted no facetious allusions to it even from his closest friends.

He switched on the light and regarded the visitors with aversion.

'And to what, my merry buzzards, do I owe this intrusion at daybreak?' he asked coldly.

Palmer explained that Mr Bolton and Mr Wodehouse were the two authors to whom had been assigned the task of assembling – under his supervision – the next Fields picture, and the great man softened visibly. He was fond of authors – being, as he often said, an author himself.

'Sit down, my little chickadees,' he said, 'and pass the aspirin. Are you in possession of aspirin?'

Palmer – who no doubt had foreseen this query – produced a small tin box.

'Thank you, thank you. Don't slam the lid. What I need this morning is kindness and understanding, for I am a little nervous. I was up late last night, seeing the new year in. Yes, I am aware,' proceeded Fields, 'that the general consensus of informed opinion in these degenerate days is that the year begins on 1st January – but what reason have we for supposing so? One only . . . that the ancient Romans said it did. But what ancient Romans? Probably a bunch of souses who were well into their fifth bottle of Falernian wine. The Phoenicians held that it began on 21st November. The medieval Christians threw celluloid balls at one another on the night of 15th March. The Greeks were broadminded. Some of them thought New Year's Day came on 20th September, while others voted for 10th June. This was good for the restaurateurs – who could count on two big nights in the year – but confusing for the Income Tax authorities, who couldn't decide when to send in their demands.'

'I never knew that before, Mr Fields,' said Palmer respectfully. There was that about the majestic comedian that made even supervisors respectful.

'Stick around me and you'll learn a lot. Well, you can readily appreciate the result of this confusion of thought, my dream-princes. It makes it difficult for a conscientious man to do the right thing. He starts out simply and straightforwardly by booking a reserved table for the last night in December, and feels that that is that. But mark the sequel. As March approaches, doubts begin to assail him. "Those medieval

Christians were shrewd fellows," he says to himself. "Who knows whether they may not have had the right idea?"

'The only way he can square his conscience is by going out and investing heavily in squeakers and rattles and paper caps on the night of 15th March. And scarcely has the doctor left his bedside next morning, when he starts to brood on the fact that the Phoenicians, who were nobody's fools, were convinced that 21st November was New Year's Eve. Many a young man in the springtime of life has developed cirrhosis of the liver simply by overdoing his researches into New Year's Eve. Last night I was pure Phoenician, and I would appreciate the loan of that aspirin once more.'

He mused in silence for a moment.

'So you're coming out to Dottyville-on-the-Pacific, are you, boys?' he said, changing the subject. 'Poor lads, poor lads! Well, let me give you a word of advice. Don't try to escape. They'll chase you across the ice with bloodhounds. And even if the bloodhounds miss you, the pitiless Californian climate drives you back. The only thing to do is to stick it out. But you'll suffer, my unhappy tenderfeet, you'll suffer. Conditions were appalling enough B S, but they're far worse now.'

'B S?'

'Before Sound – sometimes called the Stereoptician Age, rich in fossils. Pictures first learned to walk. Now they've learned to talk. But the thing they've always managed to do is smell. In this year A S confusion is rife. Not a soul at the studios but is clutching its head and walking around in circles, saying, "Where am I?" And can you blame them? Think how they must have felt at MGM when they found that Jack Gilbert could only talk soprano.

'Yes,' Fields went on, 'confusion is rife. I was out to Pathé in Culver City last month and found the place in an uproar. One of their most popular vice-presidents had just been carted off to the loony-bin, strong men sitting on his head while others rushed off to fetch strait waistcoats and ambulances. It came about thus. As you doubtless know, the Pathé trademark is a handsome white rooster. For years he's been popping up on the screen ahead of their pictures and newsreels, flapping his wings and a-gaping open his beak. And when Sound came in, of course the directors held a meeting and it was duly resolved that from now on he had got to crow right out loud.

'Well, they set to work and brought out all the fancy sound

equipment into the front yard. The countryside had been scoured for the biggest, all-firedest rooster the sovereign state of California could provide. It was a beaut – pure white with a great red comb on him – and they had a swell background fixed up behind him and the sound machines all waiting to catch that mighty cock-a-doodle-do – and – what do you know? – not a yip could they get out of him. He'd strut about, he'd flap his wings, he'd scrabble with his feet, but he wouldn't crow.

'Well, sir, they tried everything. They even went back to the first principle of show business – they brought on the girls. But he wasn't interested, and they began to wonder if it wouldn't be best to send for a psychiatrist. Then one of their top idea men told them that the sure way to make a rooster crow was to get another rooster to crow. He remembered that the second vice-president was pretty good at barnyard imitations, though his crow wasn't his best number. His quack was better and his sow-with-a-litter-of-baby-pigs was his topper. But they thought his crow might get by, so they fetched him out of his office.

' "Crow," they said.

' "Crow?" said he.

' "That's right. Crow."

' "Oh, you mean *crow*?" said the vice-president, getting it. "Like a rooster?"

'And they all said that the more like a rooster he was the better they'd be pleased.

'Well, these vice-presidents don't spare themselves when duty calls. He crowed and crowed and crowed until he rasped his larynx, but not a sign of audience reaction. The rooster just looked at him and went on scrabbling his feet.

' "Now let's all be very calm and rational about this," said the director who had been assigned to shoot the scene. "I'll tell you what's wrong, Adolf. This bird's no fool. He sees you in those yellow slacks and that rainbow shirt and the crimson tie and he's on to it right away that you're no rooster. 'Something wrong here,' he says to himself, and your act don't get over."

' "So here's what you do, Adolf," said the president. "You go out in the street round behind the studio wall where the bird can't see you and start crowing out there. That ought to do it."

'So the vice-president went out on the street and began to crow, and at last the old rooster started to perk up and take notice. He jumped on the perch they had built for him and cleared his throat, and it looked like they were all set to go, when darned if Adolf didn't stop crowing.

' "What's the matter with the fellow?" said the director, and the president yells over the wall:

' "Crow, Adolf, crow!"

'But not a yip out of Adolf, and then someone goes outside to see what's wrong, and there's two cops pushing him into the waggon. They're talking to him kinda soft and soothing.

' "Take it easy," they're saying. "Yes, yes, *sure* we understand why you were crowing. You're a rooster, aren't you? So you come with us, pal, and we'll take you back to the hen-house." '

It was only after they had left the drawing-room that Guy remembered that they had not told the comedian their pawn-broker plot. They had not, of course, had much opportunity, and they consoled themselves with the thought that later on there would no doubt be a formal story-conference where only business would be talked.

The long journey was coming to an end. They breakfasted next morning as the train was pulling out of San Bernadino. There was a strong scent of orange blossoms in the air, turning Guy's mind to thoughts of marriage. He mentioned this to Plum, as they sat in the diner gazing out at the mountains, at snow-capped Old Baldy and the distant shimmering peak of Mt Wilson.

'When are you getting married?' Plum asked.

'As soon as possible, now that we are both out here.'

'You'll probably settle down in Hollywood and spend the rest of your life there.'

Guy shook his head.

'Not if they paid me!'

'Well, they would pay you. Bob Benchley says that's the one redeeming feature of the place – the little man in the cage who hands you out the $100 bills each Thursday.'

'I mean, not if they paid me untold gold. Hollywood may turn out all right for a visit, but—'

'You wouldn't live there if they gave you the place?'

'Exactly. Not even if they made me a brother-in-law, like Palmer. I'm going to get back into the theatre again.'

'Me, too.'

'Venton Freedley said he liked that story of ours about the

fellow who's such a hit with women and the millionaire father who hires him to stop his daughter marrying a titled halfwit.'

'You mean *Anything Goes?*'

'Yes. You still like that title?'

'I think it's great.'

'Vinton says Cole Porter would write the score.'

'Cole does his own lyrics.'

'Yes.'

'That means I'm out. What pests these lyric-writing composers are! Taking the bread out of a man's mouth.'

'You would do the book with me.'

'Do you want me to?'

'Of course I do. You had an idea about a crook escaping on the boat from New York dressed as a clergyman.'

'Public Enemy Number Thirteen.'

'A superstitious crook. Never had any luck when he was Thirteen, so wants to murder one of the top dozen and get promoted to Twelve. We ought to start jotting down some of these ideas before we get all tangled up with Hollywood.'

'Write on the back of the menu.'

Cups and plates were pushed aside. They paid no further attention to the orange groves, the mountains, the advertisements of the secondhand-car dealers, the flaming twenty-four sheets of the picture-houses. They were working.

'I see the whole of the action taking place on a transatlantic liner.'

'Giving the hero six days to disentangle the girl.'

'There'll be another girl – a comic – who's mixed up with the hero. He was out with her on a supper-date when the heroine's father gave him the job, and she follows him aboard. You never saw *Girl Crazy*, did you?'

'No, I was in England.'

'There was a girl called Ethel Merman in it. It was her first job and she made a terrific hit, singing that "I've Got Rhythm" thing of Gershwin's. She puts a song over better than anybody and is great on comedy.'

'She sounds right for this part.'

'Exactly right. We're rolling!'

'Yes, we're rolling.'

But they were also rolling into Pasadena. They had to hurry back to their compartment for their things.

Held on the car platform while suitcases, golf-bags and

typewriters were handed down by the porters, they looked out at the strange new land that was to be their home. Tall eucalyptus . . . blue-flowered jacarandas, feathery pepper trees dotted with red . . . And what looked like a thousand shiny new cars, one of which, they felt, must unquestionably belong to Palmer.

Guy saw all these things without really seeing them. His eyes were on a girl farther down the platform who was searching the faces of the passengers waiting to alight. She turned and saw him . . . smiled and waved.

'Journey's End,' felt Guy.

Palmer came bustling up.

'I wanted to see you two boys,' he said briskly. 'I've had an idea for the Bill Fields picture. Just an outline at present, but something for you to be mulling over. Bill's a pawnbroker, the last of a long line of pawnbrokers. His family have been pawnbrokers for centuries. They started originally in Spain and – get this – it was an ancestor of Bill's who loaned Queen Isabella the money to finance Columbus. She signed a regular contract—'

Guy drew a deep breath. His eyes had glazed a little. So had Plum's.

'—giving this ancestor ten per cent of anything Columbus discovered,' continued Palmer. 'Well, what he discovered – see what I mean – was America. So – this is going to slay you – there's good old Bill with a legal claim to ten per cent of America. Take it from there. Isn't that great?' said Palmer, his horn-rimmed spectacles flashing. 'Isn't that terrific? Isn't that the most colossal idea for a comedian's picture anyone ever heard?'

There was a long silence. The two authors struggled for words. Then they found them.

'Yes, Mr Palmer,' said Guy.

'Oh, *yes*, Mr Palmer,' said Plum.

And they knew they were really in Hollywood.

The following extracts are from letters to W. Townend, reproduced in Wodehouse's *Performing Flea*, his 'Self-Portrait in
Letters'. The notes are by W. Townend.

October 2nd, 1929
. . . So what with this and what with that it seemed to me a
good idea to take a few days off and go to Hollywood. I wanted
to see what the place was like before committing myself to it
for an extended period. I was there three days, but having in
an absent-minded moment forgotten to tell Flo [Ziegfeld] and
Gilbert Miller that this was only a flying visit, I created
something of an upheaval in the bosoms of both. Flo wanted
to have me around as he expected Bill McGuire and Youmans
to come out of their respective trances at any moment, and
rehearsals of my adaptation of *Candlelight* for Gertie Lawrence
were nearing their end and the out-of-town opening coming
along, so Gilbert wanted me around, too. It was a nasty jar,
therefore, when they were told that I had gone to Hollywood,
presumably for good.

It hit Flo hardest, because he loves sending 1000-word telegrams telling people what he thinks of them, and he had no
address where he could reach me. From what Billie Burke (Mrs
Flo) told me later, I gather that he nearly had apoplexy.
However, all was forgotten and forgiven when I returned on
the ninth day. I went to Baltimore, where *Candlelight* was
playing, and got a rather chilly reception from Gertie, but was
eventually taken back into the fold.

Candlelight has since opened in New York and looks like a
hit. We did $18,060 the first week. Gertie is wonderful, as
always. This is the first time she has done a straight show
without music, but she is just as good as she was in *Oh, Kay*.
I don't believe there's anybody on the stage who can do comedy
better.

I liked what little I saw of Hollywood and expect to return there in the summer. I have had three offers of a year's work, but I held out for only five months.

The only person I knew really well out there was Marion Davies, who was in the show *Oh, Boy*, which Guy Bolton, Jerry Kern and I did for the Princess Theatre. She took me out to her house in Santa Monica and worked me into a big lunch at the Metro-Goldwyn which they were giving for Winston Churchill. All very pleasant. Churchill made a speech at the lunch, and when he had finished Louis B. Mayer said, 'That was a very good speech. I think we would all like to hear it again,' and it was played back from an apparatus concealed in the flowers on the table. Churchill seemed rather taken aback.

I wanted to go to Chula Vista, but of course hadn't time. I must do it when I come here again.

I have reluctantly come to the conclusion that I must have one of those meaningless faces which make no impression whatever on the beholder. This was – I think – the seventh time I had been introduced to Churchill, and I could see that I came upon him as a complete surprise once more. Not a trace of that, 'Why, of course I remember you, Mr Addison Simms of Seattle,' stuff.

December 9th, 1929
. . . I have just had a cable from Hollywood. They want me to do a picture for Evelyn Laye. This may mean a long trip out there pretty soon, but I don't expect to stay very long. I shall know more on December 21st when Sam Goldwyn arrives in England.

January 8th, 1930   *17 Norfolk Street*
. . . It looks as if Hollywood was off. I had some sessions with Goldwyn, but he wouldn't meet my price. The poor chump seemed to think he was doing me a favour offering about half what I get for a serial for doing a job which would be the most ghastly sweat. He said, when he sailed today, that he would think things over and let me know, but I'm hoping I have made the price too stiff for him. I don't want to go to Hollywood just now a bit. Later on, in the spring, I should like it. But I feel now I want to be left alone with my novel [*Big Money*].

Four months later Plum set out for Hollywood. Ethel Wodehouse, who had gone to New York at the end of 1929, arranged a contract for him with Metro-Goldwyn-Mayer – six months at $2500 a week with an option for another six months.

June 26th, 1930   *Metro-Goldwyn-Mayer Studios*
I have been meaning to write to you for ages, but I have been in a tremendous whirl of work ever since I arrived in Hollywood. For some obscure reason, after being absolutely dead for months, my brain suddenly started going like a dynamo. I got a new plot for a short story every day for a week. Then I started writing, and in well under a month have done three short stories, an act of a play, and all the dialogue for a picture.

There is something about this place that breeds work. We have a delightful house – Norma Shearer's – with a small but lovely garden and a big swimming-pool, the whole enclosed in patio form. The three wings of the house occupy three sides, a high wall, looking on to a deserted road, the other. So that one feels quite isolated. I have arranged with the studio to work at home, so often I spend three or four days on end without going out of the garden: I get up, swim, breakfast, work till two, swim again, have a lunch-tea, work till seven, swim for the third time, then dinner and the day is over. It is wonderful. I have never had such a frenzy of composition. . . .

California is all right. It's a wonderful relief not having to worry about the weather. Incidentally, it is only in the past few days that it has been really hot and sunny. We had three weeks of dull English weather. Still, it never rained.

I don't see much of the movie world. My studio is five miles from where I live, and I only go there occasionally. If I ever dine out or go to parties, it is with other exiles – New York writers, etc. Most of my New York theatre friends are here.

Odd place this. Miles and miles of one-storey bungalows, mostly Spanish, each with a little lawn in front and a pocket-handkerchief garden at the back, all jammed together in rows. Beverly Hills, where I am, is the rather aristocratic sector. Very pretty. Our house has a garden the size of the garden of any small house at Dulwich, and we pay £200 a month for it.

                                        Metro-Goldwyn Studio,
August 18th, 1930   *Culver City*
. . . I expect to be out here till next spring. I might dash back to England for a week or two before that, but I am not counting

on it, as I expect they will want me to stick on without going away.

As regards ideas I have had another barren spell. Isn't it the devil, how you get these brilliant periods when nothing seems easier than to plot out stories, and then comes the blank? Oddly enough, Hollywood hasn't inspired me in the least. I feel as if everything that could be written about it has already been done.

As a matter of fact, I don't think there is much to be written about this place. What it was like in the early days, I don't know, but nowadays the studio life is all perfectly normal, not a bit crazy. I haven't seen any swooning directors or temperamental stars. They seem just to do their job, and to be quite ordinary people, especially the directors, who are quiet, unemotional men who just work and don't throw any fits. Same with the stars. I don't believe I shall get a single story out of my stay here.

This letter was written about ten months before Plum was to shake the film industry to its foundations and, quite unintentionally, bring about what amounted to a major revolution. His forebodings about not getting a single story out of his stay in Hollywood were quite unjustified. Before he left for home he wrote the funniest skits on film stars and the making of films ever written. The Yes-Men of his stories became portents of the financial storm that was to break with such devastating fury. They can be found among the stories in the book entitled *Blandings Castle* [see pp. 384–479 of this omnibus].

October 28th, 1930   *Metro-Goldwyn Studios*
. . . Well, laddie, it begins to look as if it would be some time before I return to England. The Metro people have taken up my option, and I am with them for another six months and Ethel has just taken a new house for a year. Which means that I shall probably stay that long.

If you came over here and settled down, I think I would spend at least six months in every year here. I like the place. I think California scenery is the most loathsome on earth – a cross between Coney Island and the Riviera – but by sticking in one's garden all the time and shutting one's eyes when one goes out, it is possible to get by.

As life goes on, though, don't you find that all you need is a wife, a few real friends, a regular supply of books, and a Peke? (Make that two Pekes and add a swimming-pool.)

MGM bought that musical comedy *Rosalie* – the thing Guy Bolton, Bill McGuire, George Gershwin, Sigmund Romberg, Ira Gershwin, and I did for Ziegfeld for Marilyn Miller – for Marion Davies. Everyone in the studio had a go at it, and then they told me to try. After I had messed about with it with no success, Irving Thalberg, the big boss (and a most charming fellow incidentally, about the nicest chap I've run into out here – he is Norma Shearer's husband), worked out a story on his own and summoned me to Santa Barbara, where he was spending a few days, to hear it. I drove down there with a stenographer from the studio, and he dictated a complete scenario. When he had finished, he leaned back and mopped his brow, and asked me if I wanted to have it read over to me. I was about to say Yes (just to make the party go), when I suddenly caught the stenographer's eye and was startled to see a look of agonized entreaty in it. I couldn't imagine what was wrong, but I gathered that for some reason she wanted me to say No, so I said No. When we were driving home, she told me that she had had a latish night the night before and had fallen asleep at the outset of the proceedings and slept peacefully throughout, not having heard or taken down a word.

Fortunately, I could remember the high spots of the thing, well enough to start working on it. Unfortunately for some inscrutable reason Thalberg wants me to write it not in picture form but as a novelette, after which I suppose it will be turned into a picture. The prospect of this appals me, and I am hoping that the whole thing will eventually blow over, as things do out here. . . .

February 25th, 1931
Only time for a scribble. The studio has just given me a job which will take up all my time for weeks, though I'll bet when I've finished it, it will be pigeon-holed and never heard of again. . . .

I have been away for a week at Hearst's ranch. He owns 440,000 acres, more than the whole of Long Island! We took Winks [the Wodehouses' Pekingese], who was a great hit.

The ranch is about half-way between Hollywood and San Francisco. It is on the top of a high hill, and just inside the entrance gates is a great pile of stones, which, if you ever put them together, would form an old abbey which Hearst bought in France and shipped over and didn't know what to do with so left lying by the wayside. The next thing you see, having driven past this, is a yak or a buffalo or something in the middle of the road. Hearst collects animals and has a zoo on the premises, and the ones considered reasonably harmless are allowed to roam at large. You're apt to meet a bear or two before you get to the house.

The house is enormous, and there are always at least fifty guests staying there. All the furniture is period, and you probably sleep on a bed originally occupied by Napoleon or somebody. Ethel and I shared the Venetian suite with Sidney Blackmer, who had blown in from one of the studios.

The train that takes guests away leaves after midnight, and the one that brings new guests arrives early in the morning, so you have dinner with one lot of people and come down to breakfast next morning and find an entirely fresh crowd.

Meals are in an enormous room, and are served at a long table, with Hearst sitting in the middle on one side and Marion Davies in the middle on the other. The longer you are there, the further you get from the middle. I sat on Marion's right the first night, then found myself being edged further and further away till I got to the extreme end, when I thought it time to leave. Another day, and I should have been feeding on the floor.

March 14th, 1931   *MGM Studio*

I wish you were here for this weather. It is as warm as summer, and I am bathing regularly. The pool is a nice 62 degrees.

I am doing a picture version of *By Candlelight* now for John Gilbert. This looks as if it really might come to something. Everything else I have done so far has been scrapped. But I doubt if they intend to give me another contract. The enclosed paragraph from *Variety* can only refer to me, and it looks darned sinister. My only hope is that I have made myself so pleasant to all the studio heads that by now I may count as a cousin by marriage or something.

I must stop now, as we have to go out to dinner. Corinne Griffith.

Winks is in great form, and has got quite reconciled to having Johnnie, Maureen O'Sullivan's Peke, as a guest. We are putting Johnnie up while Maureen is in Ireland. Sex female in spite of the name, and age about a year. Very rowdy towards Winks, who disapproves rather. Johnnie is the only ugly Peke I have ever seen. She was run over by a car some months ago and has lost an eye. She looks like one of your tougher sailors.

This was the paragraph from *Variety* to which Plum refers:

'Following *Variety*'s report of the ludicrous writer talent situation, eastern executives interrogated the studios as to instances such as concerned one English playwright and author who has been collecting $2500 a week at one of the major studios for eleven months, without contributing anything really worth while to the screen.'

May 19th, 1931   *Metro-Goldwyn Studio*
Everything is very wobbly and depressed over here these days. We seem to be getting a sort of second instalment of the 1929 crash. The movies are in a bad state, and MGM showed no desire to engage me again when my contract lapsed last week. Meanwhile I am plugging along with *Hot Water* and have done 60,000 words, but it looks like being one of those long ones and I doubt if I shall finish it before mid-August.

Two Hollywood stories, one previous to that interview of mine, the other more recent. The first is supposed to illustrate the Hollywood idea of poverty. A supervisor was giving a writer instructions about the picture he wanted him to work on. He said the outline was that a father has a ne'er-do-well son and gets fed up with his escapades and thinks the only thing to make a man of the young fellow is to force him to battle with the world for himself. So he cuts him off with $500 a week. The other story is quite a recent one, and has to do with the current depression. A man standing in the crowd outside a movie theatre here after a big opening hears the carriage starter calling for 'Mr Warner's automobile', 'Mr Lasky's automobile', 'Mr Louis B. Mayer's automobile', and so on, and he shakes his head. 'At an opening a year from now,' he says, 'there won't be any of this stuff about automobiles. You'll hear them call for Mr Warner's bicycle, Mr Lasky's kiddie car and Mr Louis B. Mayer's roller skates.'

I'm afraid that interview of mine has had a lot to do with the depression in the picture world. Yet I was only saying what everybody has been saying for years. Apparently what caused the explosion was my giving figures and mentioning a definite studio in print. But, damn it all, it never ought to have been in print. It was just a casual remark I happened to drop off the record (though, like an ass, I didn't say that it was off the record). It just shows that with these American reporters you must weigh every word before you speak.

Another story, not a Hollywood one. Wilton Lackaye, the actor, was playing in San Francisco and invited the editor of one of the San Francisco papers to dinner one night. The editor said he was sorry but he couldn't come, because he had a conference. 'A conference?' said Lackaye. 'What's that for?' The editor explained. 'We get together every day for an hour or so and decide what is to be in the next day's paper – matters of policy, emphasis on news and all that sort of thing.' 'Good heavens!' said Lackaye, amazed. 'Do you mean to tell me that you get out that paper *deliberately*?' . . .

Heather Thatcher has turned up to spend a couple of months with us. We gave a big party for her yesterday, which I found rather loathsome, as it seemed to pollute our nice garden. There was a mob milling round in it from four in the afternoon till eleven at night. About twenty people in the pool at one time. The only beauty of having a party in your own home is that you can sneak away. I went upstairs to my room at five and only appeared for dinner, returning to my room at eight sharp. (The perfect host.) I re-read *Cakes and Ale*. What a masterly book it is. . . .

We are toying with a scheme for going round the world in December on the *Empress of Britain*. Sometimes we feel we should like it, and then we ask ourselves if we really want to see the ruddy world. I'm darned if I know. I have never seen any spectacular spot yet that didn't disappoint me. Notably, the Grand Canyon, and also Niagara Falls.

Personally, I've always liked wandering around in the background. I mean, I get much more kick out of a place like Droitwich, which has no real merits, than out of something like the Taj Mahal.

Maureen O'Sullivan's Peke is still with us. She – the Peke, not Maureen – snores like twenty dogs and sleeps under my bed. I'm getting used to it. She is the ugliest and greediest hound I ever met, but full of charm.

The first intimation we had at home that anything had gone wrong was reading in *The Times* a brief report of the interview that was to rock Hollywood.

Although his contract had lapsed the Metro-Goldwyn-Mayer people rang Plum up one day to ask if he would give an interview to a woman reporter for the *Los Angeles Times*. Plum said he would be delighted.

The woman reporter duly arrived and was received by Plum politely and cheerfully. She asked Plum how he liked Hollywood. Plum said amiably that he liked Hollywood and its inhabitants immensely; he said how much he had enjoyed his stay and added, to fill in time and make conversation before the interview proper began, that his one regret was he had been paid such an enormous sum of money without having done anything to earn it.

And that was that.

The interview then got under way and was conducted by both parties on normal question-and-answer lines. The woman reporter withdrew, having got her scoop.

Early the next morning before Plum was out of bed the telephone rang. Someone wanted to speak to Mr P. G. Wodehouse. Plum answered: rather sleepily, I take it. A voice at the other end of the line said it was Reuter's Los Angeles correspondent speaking, and would Mr Wodehouse kindly say if the interview with him in that day's *Los Angeles Times* was authentic. Plum, rather startled at having been aroused at that hour to be asked so trite a question, said that it was. Reuter's correspondent then asked if he might have Mr Wodehouse's permission to cable it across to London and Plum, even more startled, said that he might!

A brief interval elapsed and then the telephone bell rang again. This time an agitated voice demanded if Mr Wodehouse had seen the interview in the *Los Angeles Times*, because if he had . . .

Plum dashed downstairs and grabbed the *Times* and almost the first thing he saw under scare headlines was the interview that was destined to revolutionize the motion-picture industry and put it on a sound basis and cut out the dead wood, the woman reporter having printed every word he had said about his regret at having been paid such an enormous sum of money without having done a thing to earn it!

Before nightfall Plum was the most talked-of man in the United States of America and the bankers went into action.

Some years later I read what the well-known American writer,

Rupert Hughes, had to say about this strange episode in the *Saturday Evening Post*:

'Many authors have been badly treated in Hollywood, but Hollywood has paid high for this idiocy. One of the gentlest and one of the most valuable for Hollywood – P. G. Wodehouse – quietly regretted that he had been paid a hundred thousand dollars for doing next to nothing. This remark was taken up, and it stirred the bankers deeply, as it should have done. But Mr Wodehouse has written no ferocious assaults on those who slighted him.'

September 14th, 1931   *Beverly Hills*

This business of writing to you has taken on a graver aspect, the postal authorities here having raised the ante to 5¢ per letter. I can bear it bravely as far as you are concerned, but I do grudge having to spend 5¢ on a letter to some female in East Grinstead who wants to know if I pronounce my name Wood-house or Wode-house.

My art is not going too well at the moment. I have six more stories to do for the *American* magazine, and ye Ed has put me right out of my stride by asking me to make them about American characters in an American setting, like knowing that if I try to do American stuff, the result is awful. Apparently he doesn't care for Mulliner stories, though I'll swear things like 'Fate' and 'The Fiery Wooing of Mordred' aren't bad, always provided you like my sort of stuff. What puzzles me about it all is that when he commissioned the series he must have known the sort of thing I wrote. It can't have come on him as a stunning shock to find that I was laying my scene in England. What did he expect from me? Thoughtful studies of life in the Arkansas foothills?

I suppose I ought to have taken a strong line and refused haughtily to change my act, but I'm all for strewing a little happiness as I go by, so I told him I would have a pop at some Hollywood stories . . . .

We dined last night with Douglas Fairbanks and Mary Pickford. She is a most intelligent woman, quite unlike the usual movie star. I talked to her all the evening. (Probably bored her stiff.) . . .

Hollywood story. Couple of boxers at the American Legion stadium put on a very mild show, and a spectator, meeting one of them after the fight, reproached him for giving such an inadequate exhibition. The boxer admitted that he had not mixed it up very vigorously, but had a satisfactory explanation. 'Couldn't take no chances of getting mussed up,' he said, 'not with a part in Mae West's new picture coming along.'

A New York actress has just got back to Broadway after a year in Hollywood. She says that she has been so long among the false fronts and papier-mâché mansions on the set that nowadays she finds herself sneaking a look at her husband to see if he goes all the way round or is just a profile.

Non-Hollywood story. Inez Haynes Irwin, wife of Will Irwin, applied for a passport the other day and, assisted by Will Irwin and Wallace Irwin, started to fill up the 'description' form. One of the questions was 'Mouth?' Well, that was all right. She wrote 'Brilliant crimson Cupid's bow with delicious shadowy corners,' but the next question, 'Face?', puzzled her. 'What do I say to that?' she asked. 'Write "Yes",' said Wallace Irwin.

August 24th, 1932   *Domaine de la Fréyère*
. . . Which reminds me of a story I read somewhere – by S. J. Perelman? I can't remember – about a movie magnate who had a wonderful idea for a picture, and he sends to New York for an author, telling him, when he arrives, that every writer on the payroll has been stumped for three months by one detail in the story. Get that one small detail, and the thing will be set.

'We fade in on a street in London,' he says, 'and there's a guy in rags dragging himself along through the fog, a Lon Chaney type guy. He's all twisted and crippled up. He comes to a colossal house in Berkeley Square and lets himself in with a latchkey, and he's in a gorgeous hall full of Chinese rugs and Ming vases, and the minute he's inside he straightens up, takes off his harness and unties his leg, and by golly, he's as normal as you and me, not a cripple at all. Then we truck with him through a door, and he's like in a hospital corridor, and he pulls on rubber gloves and an operating gown and he goes into a room where there's ten, fifteen beautiful dames chained to the wall with practically nothing on. We follow him to a bench that's full of test tubes and scientific stuff, and he grabs a hypodermic needle and he goes around laughing like a hyena and jabbing it into these beautiful dames. And that's where you got to figure out this one thing: *What kind of a business is this guy in?*'

Hôtel Prince de Galles,
June 11th, 1934   *Paris*

I've been meaning to write for ages, but I've been tied up with *The Luck of the Bodkins*. I find that the longer I go on writing, the harder it becomes to get a story right without going over and over it. I have just reached page 180 and I suppose I must have done quite 400 pages! Still, it is in good shape now.

Paris is fine. I don't go out much, as I am working all the time. I have been here for exactly five weeks, except for one day at Le Touquet. I may be going to Le Touquet again for a few days soon, to talk with Guy Bolton about our play for Vinton Freedley *Anything Goes*. But this address will always find me.

I had an offer from Paramount the other day to go to Hollywood, and had to refuse. But rather gratifying after the way Hollywood took a solemn vow three years ago never to mention my name again. Quite the olive branch!

Low Wood,
December 4th, 1934   *Le Touquet*

Lady Dudley (Gertie Millar) lives a few doors off us and when she went to England asked me to exercise her spotted carriage dog occasionally. Well, of course, after I had taken it with me for two days on my walk to get the papers, it proceeded to regard this walk as a fixed ceremony. The day I had to go to Lille, I hear it refused all food and would not be comforted.

I finished *The Luck of the Bodkins* on November 20th, and ever since have been in a sort of coma. Do you get like that after a big bout of work?

As a matter of fact, my present collapse is the result of a strain that has gone on now for almost six months. While in the middle of *The Luck of the Bodkins*, and just beginning to see my way through it, I had to break off and start plotting out that musical comedy, *Anything Goes*, for New York with Howard Lindsay, the director. We toiled all through that blazing weather in Paris, and then we came down here and started all over again with Guy Bolton. In the end we got out a plot, and I wrote a rough version, and sent it off to Guy to rewrite.

Well, I eventually started on *The Luck of the Bodkins* again. Then I got the commission for the novelette [later expanded into the full-length Hollywood novel *Laughing Gas*, see above pp. 15–218] for the *New York Herald-Tribune*, to be done in a hurry. So I started sweating at that and, just as I was in the middle of it, a cable came from America from Vinton Freedley, the manager, saying that the stuff which Guy and I had sent over wouldn't do, and that he was calling in two other people to rewrite it. So there I was, presumably out of that.

I got the novelette finished and sent it over, but was naturally in a panic about it after the débâcle of the musical comedy which, incidentally, had been preceded by the complete failure of the Bolton–Wodehouse comedy in London, because, though it was a commission, I wouldn't have felt able to stand on my rights and demand the money unless the stuff was acceptable. And for weeks I heard nothing.

Meanwhile, *The Luck of the Bodkins* was coming out with great difficulty. Have you had the experience of getting out what looks like a perfect scenario and then finding that it won't write and has to be completely changed?

And then suddenly – or, rather, not suddenly, but in a sort of series of bits of good news – everything came right. My arrangement about *Anything Goes* was that I was to get two per cent of the gross, if I was able to go to New York and attend rehearsals, but if I couldn't I was to give up half of the one per cent to Howard Lindsay. So I was looking on it all the time as a one and a half per cent job (one and a half per cent being the ordinary musical comedy royalty).

You can imagine my relief when I found that the rewriting was not going to affect my royalty very much. Russel Crouse, the rewriter, had consented to do the work for half of one per cent, so I am only down a quarter of one per cent on the normal royalty. Then we heard that the show was a huge success in Boston, and now it has been produced in New York and is the biggest hit for years and years and Cochran has bought it for London.

Meanwhile I had had a cable from the *New York Herald-Tribune*, which said, HAPPY ABOUT LORD HAVERSHOT (that was the name of the hero of the novelette), from which I inferred that it was all right – though don't you hate these ambiguous cables? I mean, the editor might quite easily really have written NOT HAPPY and the French postal officials cut out the word 'not' as not seeming to them important.

Finally, however, a letter arrived with the cheque, just about the time I heard the news of the success of the show.

By that time, I was struggling with the last chapters of *The*

Luck of the Bodkins. Usually when I get to the last fifty pages of a story, it begins to write itself. But this time everything went wrong and I had to grope my way through it all at the rate of two pages a day. I began to get superstitious about it and felt that if I could ever get it finished my luck would be in. On November 29th I was within four pages of the end and suddenly all the lights in the house went out and stayed out.

Still, I finished it next day, and it is pretty good, I think. Frightfully long – 362 pages of typescript – it must be over the 100,000 words.

In October 1936 Plum went to Hollywood for the second time.

1315 Angelo Drive,
Beverly Hills

November 7th, 1936

I am sending this to Watt, because I am not sure if you are still at the flat.

Well, here we are, settled in a house miles away up at the top of a mountain, surrounded by canyons in which I am told rattlesnakes abound, and employing a protection agency to guard the place at nights! We looked at a lot of houses in the valley part of Beverly Hills, where we were before, but couldn't find one we liked, so took this, which is a lovely place with a nice pool, but, as I say, remote. Still, that's an advantage in a way, as we don't get everybody dropping in on us . . . .

Winky has taken on a new lease of life through association with the puppy. (Did I tell you Ethel bought a female puppy just before we sailed?) She ignored her for six weeks, and then suddenly became devoted to her. She races about the garden, chased by the puppy.

The puppy is a comedian. In New York, we had put on Winky's lead and let it trail on the carpet, and we went out, but no Winky followed, though we called to her. When we went back, we found Winks trying hard to get out, but the puppy had seized the lead and was tugging at it.

Everything is very pleasant and placid here, and I am having a good time. But it doesn't seem as interesting as it was last time. I miss Thalberg very much, though I like Sam Katz, for whom I am working. I am collaborating on a musical picture with a man I last saw twenty years ago, when I was sympathizing with him for being chucked out of the cast of one of the Bolton–Wodehouse–Kern musical comedies. He is a wild Irishman named McGowan, who seems to be fighting the heads of the studio all the time. I get on very well with him myself. . . .

I still swim every morning, but the water is beginning to get a bit chilly.

Haven't seen many celebrities yet. We don't see much of anybody except our beloved Maureen O'Sullivan and her husband, John Farrow. He is the man who likes your sea stories so much. I met Clark Gable the other day. Also Fred Astaire. I think Fred is going to do a picture of my *A Damsel in Distress*, with music by George Gershwin. I shall know more about this later.

The puppy Plum mentions in this letter, which was soon to be known as Wonder, became in due course the most travelled, the most celebrated and the longest-lived of all the Wodehouse Pekes, and the only one we never met.

March 7th, 1937   *1315 Angelo Drive*

I meant to send you a lot of clippings about the frosts here, but forgot. Anyway, the gist is that we have had a foul winter and the valley below this house has been wrapped in a dense London fog for weeks, because of the smudge pots which they have been burning to try to save the lemon crops.

Did smudge pots enter into your lemon-life at all when you were out in California? Or was it always warm here then in winter? Lemons have been practically wiped out this year.

I am leading a very quiet life here. Unless I have to go and see my producer, I stay around the house all day except for an hour's walk, and we go up to our rooms at eight-thirty and read and listen to the radio. I enjoy it, though I must say I would like to be nearer home. This place seems very far away sometimes.

Winks is very well. Also the puppy, who now has a new name – Wonder. My day starts when I hear the puppy bark in Ethel's room. I open the door, and the puppy comes leaping out. Winky then pokes her head out of my bed, in which she has been sleeping, and I take them downstairs and let them out. I bring them in when I come down to breakfast, and they then have to be out again in order to bark at the gardener, whose arrival is always a terrific surprise and shock to them, though he has turned up at the same time every morning for four months.

Woman out here has just got a divorce. Stated that her

husband had not worked for months and was a pretty low-down character altogether. 'He was always going to dances,' she said, 'and when he wanted to go to one the other night, he took the only pair of silk stockings I had and cut the tops off so that he could wear them as socks.'

1315 Angelo Drive,
March 24th, 1937   *Beverly Hills*

I finished *Summer Moonshine* yesterday. Young Lorimer, of the *Saturday Evening Post*, called on me about two weeks ago and took away 80,000 words of it, leaving me about another 10,000 to do. I must say the *SEP* are extraordinary. Lorimer left on a Friday, read the thing in the train, arrived Philadelphia Monday night, presumably went to the office Tuesday morning and gave the MS to somebody else, who must have read it Tuesday and given it to Stout, the chief editor, on Wednesday morning and Stout must have read it on Wednesday night, because on Thursday morning I got a telegram saying it had been accepted.

I don't see how they manage to be so quick. They get 75,000 MSS a year, all of which are read.

Price – $40,000.

Against this triumph I have to set the fact that Metro-Goldwyn-Mayer are not taking up my option, which expires in another two weeks. I have had another flop with them. I started gaily in working on a picture with Bill McGuire, and I gradually found myself being edged out. Eventually, they came out into the open and said they had wanted McGuire to write the thing by himself, all along. There seems to be a curse over MGM, so far as I am concerned.

Since then, I have had a number of offers from other studios for one picture apiece. It seems pretty certain that in about two weeks I shall be working on my *Damsel in Distress*, which RKO bought for Fred Astaire. Selznick wants me to do a thing called *The Earl of Chicago* and Walter Wanger asked me to go round, as he had something right in my line. It turned out to be Clarence Budington Kelland's *Stand-In*. I turned it down. I got myself in bad enough last time by criticizing Hollywood, and I didn't want to do a picture which would have been an indictment of the studios.

Raining in buckets today, and snow on the foothills yesterday! The latest gag here is about the New York man who came to Southern California for the winter – and found it!

May 6th, 1937   *1315 Angelo Drive*

Listen. What has become of the old-fashioned California climate? We had a couple of warm days last week, and then went
right back to winter weather again. Today is absolutely freezing.
And it's been the same ever since I got here.

I wish we had taken this house for six months instead of a
year. There seems to be a probability that I shall do a four
weeks' job on the *Damsel in Distress*, but except for that nothing
is stirring. I was told that I was going to do *The Earl of Chicago*,
but I see that Ben Hecht is doing it. The fact is, I'm not worth
the money my agent insists on asking for me. After all, my
record here is eighteen months, with only small bits of pictures
to show for it. I'm no good to these people. Lay off old Pop
Wodehouse, is the advice I would give to any studio that wants
to get on in the world. There is no surer road to success.

May 7th, 1937   *1315 Angelo Drive*

I have been seeing a lot of G. O. Allen, the England cricket
captain, who came home from Australia via Hollywood. He
told me the inside story of the bodyline crisis. He is a bit sick
about the last English team, as everybody failed enthusiastic-
ally on every occasion, and the fast bowlers had to do all the
work.

Our butler got home last night tight as a drum and is still
sleeping it off. Over here, the help take every Thursday off,
and he employed his holiday in getting thoroughly pickled.

I can't fathom the mentality of Pekes. Yesterday Roland
Young came to tea and sat on the sofa with Winks snuggling
up to him on one side and Wonder on the other. The moment
he got up and started to leave, both Pekes sprang down and
attacked his ankles with savage snarls. You would have thought
they had never seen him before, and had spotted him breaking
in through a window.

Interesting that about your visit to the specialist. It's nice to
know that your heart is all right. Isn't it difficult to get accustomed to the idea that one is now at the age when most people
settle down and don't do a thing? I am now exactly the age my
father was when I left Dulwich, and I remember him as
tottering to his armchair and settling in it for the day. That's
one thing about being a writer – it does keep you young. Do
you find you can't walk as far as you used to! I do out here,
but I remember last year in Le Touquet I used to do my seven

miles without feeling it. I think it's mainly the California climate.

Big strike now in the picture industry, which may close all the studios. That'll teach them not to take up my option.

June 24th, 1937   *1315 Angelo Drive*
Life here at present is a bit like being on your *Lancing Island*. We can't go on the mountains because of the rattlesnakes, the butler killed two Black Widow spiders in the garden (deadlier than snakes), and last night and this morning the following episodes occurred. We were taking the dogs for a stroll after dinner, and Wonder didn't follow. We went back and found her playing with a tarantula on the drive! And this morning, when I came out from my swim, I heard her gruffling at something on the steps of the pool, and there was another tarantula, bigger than the first one!

I am sweating away at a picture. The Fred Astaire one, *A Damsel in Distress*, with musical score by George Gershwin. When they bought it, they gave it to one of the RKO writers to adapt, and he turned out a script all about crooks – no resemblance to the novel. Then it struck them that it might be a good thing to stick to the story, so they chucked away the other script and called me in. I think it is going to make a good picture. But what uncongenial work picture-writing is. Somebody's got to do it, I suppose, but this is the last time they'll get me.

September 4th, 1937   *1315 Angelo Drive*
I finished my work on *Damsel in Distress* three weeks ago, and with only one day's interval started on a picture with Eddie Goulding – Englishman whom I used to know in London before the war – now a director here. I am not finding it very pleasant, because he has his own ideas about the thing and rewrites all my stuff, thus inducing a what's-the-use feeling and making it hard not to shove down just anything. Also, I don't like the story.

The money is fine – $10,000 for six weeks and $2000 a week after that – but this blasted Administration has just knocked the bottom out of everything by altering the tax laws, so that instead of paying a flat ten per cent as a non-resident alien I now have to pay ordinary citizen rates, which take away about a third of what one earns.

The taxes are fantastic here and very tough on Hollywood stars because they make so much over a short period and then go into the discard. Nelson Eddy, my neighbour, made $600,000 last year and when all his taxes and expenses were paid found that he had $50,000 left. Well, not bad, even so, one might say. But then the point is that in 1939 his income may be about tuppence! Stars shoot up and die away here before you can breathe.

I'm not enjoying life much just now. I don't like doing pictures. *A Damsel in Distress* was fun, because I was working with the best director here – George Stevens – and on my own story, but as a rule pictures are a bore. And just now I'm pining to get at a new novel, which I have all mapped out. I sneak in a page or two every now and then, but I want to concentrate on it.

October 11th, 1937   *1315 Angelo Drive,*
Just a line to say that we are not staying here for the spring, after all, but are sailing on October 28th, and I shall be back at Le Touquet on November 4th.

                                        1000 Park Avenue,
May 11th, 1952   *New York*
... Listen, Bill. If you want to make a pot of money, come over here and go into domestic service. You can't fail to clean up.

A man and his wife came here from England some years ago and got a job as butler and cook at $200 a month plus their board and lodging. They were able to salt away $150 each pay day. After they had been in this place for a while they accepted an offer from a wealthier family at $300. They had two rooms and bath and everything they wanted in the way of food and wines and were able to put away $250 a month.

About a year later their employer made the mistake of entertaining a Hollywood producer for the weekend, and the producer was so struck by the couple's virtuosity that he lured them away with an offer of $400, to include all expenses plus a car. They now banked $350 a month. And when a rival producer tried to snatch them, the original producer raised their salary to $500, at which figure it remains at moment of going to press. They now own an apartment house in Los Angeles.

We have had a series of blisters – both white and black – in our little home, each more incompetent than the last and each getting into our ribs for $60 a week – which tots up to something over £1000 a year – in spite of the fact that Ethel does all the real work with some slight assistance from me. Ninety per cent of them have been fiends in human shape, our star exhibit being dear old Horace, a coloured gentleman of lethargic disposition who scarcely moved except to pinch our whisky when we were out. We had laid in a stock of Haig and Haig Five Star for guests and an inferior brand for ourselves, and after it had been melting away for a week or two, we confronted Horace. 'Horace,' we said, 'you've been stealing our Haig and Haig and, what's more, you've also been stealing our . . .' He gave us a look of contempt and disgust. 'Me!' he said. 'I wouldn't touch that stuff. I only drink Haig and Haig Five Star.' Well, nice to think that we had something he liked.

I heard of some people here who engaged a maid who had just come over from Finland. She seemed a nice girl and willing, but it turned out that there were chinks in her armour. 'How is your cooking?' they asked. She said she couldn't cook. At home her mother had always done all the cooking. 'How about housework?' No, she couldn't do housework – back in Finland her aunt had attended to all that sort of thing – nor could she look after children, her eldest sister's speciality. 'Well, what *can* you do?' they asked. She thought for a moment. 'I can milk reindeer,' she said brightly.

So if you can milk reindeer, come along. Wealth and fame await you.